Also by Malcolm Bosse

THE JOURNEY OF TAO KIM NAM
THE INCIDENT AT NAHA
THE MAN WHO LOVED ZOOS
THE 79 SQUARES
CAVE BEYOND TIME
GANESH
THE BARRACUDA GANG
THE WARLORD
FIRE IN HEAVEN
CAPTIVES OF TIME

Stranger

SIMON AND SCHUSTER
New York London Toronto Sydney Tokyo

at the Gate

A NOVEL BY

Malcolm Bosse

Simon and Schuster
Simon & Schuster Building
Rockefeller Center
1230 Avenue of the Americas
New York, New York 10020

SIMON AND SCHUSTER and colophon are registered trademarks of Simon & Schuster Inc.

Designed by Sylvia Glickman/Levavi & Levavi
Manufactured in the United States of America

10   9   8   7   6   5   4   3   2   1

Library of Congress Cataloging in Publication data
Bosse, Malcolm J. (Malcolm Joseph)
    Stranger at the gate : a novel / by Malcolm Bosse.
        p.   cm.
    I. Title.
PS3552.077S77   1989
813'.54—dc19   89-5936
                                                          CIP

ISBN 0-671-66785-8

For Jim Ruoff

Something is added to the everlasting earth;
From my mind a space is taken away.

—Jon Silkin: "Death of a Bird"

Love alters not with his brief hours and weeks,
But bears it out even to the edge of doom.

—Shakespeare

Man is a witness to his deeds.

—Quran

Patet Nem
Nine P.M. to Midnight

One

A tiger came out of the jungle and dragged off a little girl who had been playing behind some village huts.

Maggie Gardner found it hard to believe that such things could still happen in the year of 1965, even in Sumatra. But yesterday it had happened fifty kilometers north of Palembang.

As the car pulled up in front of Palembang's teeming market, she had a vision of it happening: the yellow eyes blinking among palm fronds, the low growl, the great jaws opening, the child's shriek of terror as the beast's fangs sank into her neck. Maggie dabbed at her sweaty forehead with a handkerchief and reached for the handle. The driver was out of the car and at her door before she could push it open. Maggie liked to bring some democracy into their relationship by getting out on her own. She rarely succeeded. Her driver preferred to show onlookers how smartly he could swing the door back and salute his passenger, a more attractive foreigner than Dutch women who had come to this market in the colonial days before independence—heavy women bellowing commands, wiping red faces with big squares of batik cloth. Maggie knew what her driver thought of

Dutch women. She also knew that he found her attractive. She knew it every time she got out of the car, sliding carefully across the seat, knees together, to keep him from a better look at her thighs.

Sunlight hit her a muffled blow; she was grateful for the broad-brimmed hat that protected her from the full force of it. Standing beside the car, Maggie, a tall woman among the short Sumatrans, felt clumsy. Without glancing at her driver, who would be studying her buttocks through narrowed eyes, she slouched toward the market. Planking led over a muddy yard to a lattice of iron bars covered by canvas. The canopy formed a dark corridor into the market, like a tunnel into an ant nest. She strolled past a line of old women selling green bananas, big yellow papayas, salak in its scaly brown skin, bright-green limes, and intensely red chilies piled in tall pyramids. Maggie smiled at an ancient woman who sat there, her old skin as dry as bone. Maggie was sweating profusely. Sumatrans never sweated the way she did. The old woman did not smile back.

Halfway down the first line of stalls, Maggie found what she had come for: leather handbags. They were local products, not the splendid bags made by Batak people in the north. She couldn't wait for better, though. She and Vern were leaving this evening for Jakarta and her old bag was badly frayed. She began haggling with a man who leapt down from the tiny space in which he'd been squatting behind the stall. She offered two hundred rupiah; he wanted twelve hundred. They narrowed the difference to nine hundred. Maggie persisted: *"Kalau boleh enam ratus, saya beli, kalau tidak saya cari yang lain."* Offering six hundred, she threatened to go elsewhere.

She felt him appraising her ability to hold out. Then with a shrug, he accepted: *"Baiklah, rugi sedikit, tidak apa."*

Because she'd bargained well for it in a language acquired with difficulty, Maggie knew she would like this bag. Mopping her brow, she went farther into the covered market.

There were cheap sarongs stacked high on wooden counters. There were kerosene burners, bins of nails, trinkets, gunnysacks of rice. Coming out of the market, she squinted through blazing light at the Musi River that had churned through swampland for a hundred and twenty miles before reaching the unpainted shacks of this ugly town. She had lived in Palembang for a number of months, ever since marrying Vern Gardner, a construction engineer who had just finished the flyovers that spanned the main boulevard. Maggie had been a doctoral candidate in anthropology, her field Asian culture. While doing research among the Minangkabau people, she'd contracted malaria. During recuperation at a resort in northern Sumatra, she had met Vern and two weeks later married him—That soon? she still asked herself in wonder—and had come to this dreadful place, where fried dog was served in restaurants and transvestites jeered at passersby in the evening streets.

Pretty girls came up from the riverbank with banana leaves held over their heads for parasols. When they had undulated beyond her sight, Maggie saw in space they'd occupied a one-legged man slouching against a shack, next to a pile of chicken heads for sale. Maggie stared as flies busied themselves along his shrunken calf. Her eyes met his. Six hundred years ago his ancestors had made Palembang one of the great cities of the world. Palembang had built monasteries for thousands of Buddhist monks, sent out to sea the largest ships then known. The one-legged man's arrogant eyes seemed to stare beyond her into the history of empire.

Suddenly she was aware of other eyes watching her. At first she saw someone to the right, to the left. Ahead were half a dozen men, others coming. What she had done was stop on the path. It was a mistake, Maggie knew, to stop anywhere unless you were buying something. Stop to think, and you were surrounded. You had to look purposeful or people closed in.

A man stepped up to say in English, "Hello hello hello. What ke you what?"

Another at his elbow added, "What ke you having bag?"

Maggie said, "Merry Christmas."

"Hello," another man said loudly without a smile. "Buy what?"

A man looking something like him had once pinched her buttocks in the market. When she'd whirled on him, the man had stood his ground until she lowered her raised hand.

"Want what?" he asked harshly.

"Get lost," Maggie told him, searching for boldness, because that alone would get her out of here.

Another man stepped forward. "What do you want?" he asked in Bahasa Indonesia. "What do you want to buy? I will sell it to you," he said confidently.

"I don't want anything," she told him, looking for escape from the circle of smiling men. They wouldn't rape her, but there were stories of foreigners getting knocked around, robbed, humiliated. It was a sport in Palembang. She noticed a shopkeeper leaning out of his warung stall, watching intently, lips parted in anticipation. Maggie glanced at each man deliberately, forcing herself to study each face. "Get lost," she told them evenly. "What I'm saying is drop dead. You don't understand what I'm saying, but I hope I sound confident." She kept talking in a measured continuous way. "So what are you doing, you creeps? Because creeps are what you are; you certainly are creeps, and so I say, gentlemen, drop dead, get lost, you don't scare me." She added with a fierce smile, "Fuck off."

j So much English intimidated the crowd, which parted and let her through. Grad school hadn't taught her how to handle the bored hostile males of Palembang. There should have been a course, Anthropology 2993: Invective and Bravado.

The sun's heat was thrusting deep; she felt her hair getting wet under her straw hat. It would be nice to remove the damn thing and use it for a fan, but Maggie didn't stop walking until the men were left behind, slogging away like drowsy cows. She went through the meat market, a smell of blood and guts ripening the hot air. Feeling momentarily safe, Maggie halted and breathed deeply. Beyond the hat brim she saw a ragged boy sucking his thumb. He stood on the other side of the boardwalk and regarded her with the curious but detached expression of the neglected young. She fanned herself desultorily for a few moments. Then on impulse she walked briskly up to him and thrust a coin into his hand. Staring at it a moment, the boy scampered off. She watched him run for the mudbank shacks beside the Musi. While she was smiling at his jubilant dash for home, two larger boys blocked his way. Between clothing stalls there was scuffling and the child went down. She could see his dark sticklike legs stretched out fatalistically. His attackers vanished in the crowd of shoppers. His legs drew up out of sight. He must have got to his feet and stumbled away.

She should have known better. Giving money to kids could be like wishing them bad luck. She had loved the west coast of Sumatra, the artistic people of Padang, the intricate culture of the Minangkabau. But the east coast and Palembang were another story.

Crossing the street to the edge of a small park, Maggie looked from a discreet distance at a crowd gathered around a shaded area of grass. A man was talking into a microphone; two loudspeakers amplified his voice into a distorted growl. He sat cross-legged behind a box draped with black cloth, a skull and crossbones painted on it. A glass of tea stood on a battered suitcase. The man held up a small red box into which he ostentatiously put a pack of cigarettes. Maggie knew the pack would disappear and later reappear, while he talked up his magical powers and sold concoctions of snake blood and fermented durian to cure every known ailment.

Men gestured for her to join them and watch. She kept her distance, remembering her first encounter with a Palembang medicine man. That one had been selling pieces of marinated alligator. He had called men from the audience to rub their calves with a murky liquid until the veins stood out, swollen and purple. "What family men need!" crowed the hawker, and just as Maggie understood the ultimate goal of his potion, someone deftly cut her shoulder strap and ran off with her bag.

She didn't wait now for the pack of cigarettes to disappear, but turned and headed for the main boulevard, where her driver would have parked the car. Glancing back, she saw another one-legged man; he was hopping along with the aid of a crudely fashioned crutch.

Maggie watched her feet. Running across the sidewalk at erratic intervals were unmarked sewers, only partially covered by lattice. A rank odor drifted up from the blue-gray sludge into humid air that held the stench like a bowl holds water. A cloud obscured the sun. For moments it was cool, as if a breeze had swept across the raised sidewalks—raised because in the wet season everything started to float on the monsoon floods: bottles, cans, banana peels, dead chickens.

Ahead was one of the flyovers Vern had built. The yellow girders bridged the boulevard. Although it had been completed only a few days ago, someone had already painted an advertisement across the metal span: HARI SENAT HARI KECAP CAP IKANMAS (Health Today Goldfish Brand Catsup Today). There were wooden stairs at each end. Vern had wanted them built of metal and the provincial government had paid for metal, but somehow the money for metal had slipped through a bureaucratic crack into the maw of local corruption.

The sun came out again; heat thudded down, enveloping Maggie with renewed intensity. Slick tendrils of brown hair were plastered against her neck. Her blouse stuck to her, so the line of her bra must have been visible. That was part of public life here, though: your physical discomfort was enjoyed by everyone. You blew your nose and they watched, grinning. You swiped at a fly crawling along your neck, and they saw that too and smiled. You sweated and they leaned forward intently to study the wet, clinging blouse. Maggie had developed a look for them, a hard, unblinking regard. She had learned to derive pleasure from staring down their leers. You were tested in Palembang, and you got tougher.

A hawker waved a newspaper at her. The headline in Bahasa Indonesia stated: DEMONSTRATION AGAINST AMERICAN IMPERIALISTS. Over breakfast this morning she had read the article. In Jakarta, rioters had protested the assassination of Malcolm X, a black Muslim who, the article alleged, had been treacherously murdered by the American government.

Since Maggie had first come out to Indonesia, there had been a sharp rise in anti-American sentiment. Postal workers refused to handle traffic for U.S. news agencies. American property had been confiscated, including assets of Caltex and Shell oil companies; Goodyear and U.S. Rubber had lost plantations worth $80 million in Sumatra alone. And after thousands had demonstrated against American air strikes in Vietnam, Sukarno had seized USIS libraries as a testament to his displeasure. And so it went. Maggie no longer called herself an American when people asked her nationality. It was safer to be Belanda or Perancis, Dutch or French.

Ahead was the stairway to one of Vern's flyovers. On her way toward it Maggie was accosted by becak drivers who called out, "Becak! Becak, Nonya!" coaxing her with dirty palms toward their beat-up carriages. The becaks were parked side by side, wheels touching, as close as bees. Drivers were curled up on the passenger seats, drowsy beneath hats, yet with an eye fixed for passersby who might ride. As Maggie walked past them, a few banged hard on the metallic sides of their carriages, each urging on her his own canvas-tented world. A driver swung onto the rag-covered seat of his bike and pedaled slowly behind her, yelling "Becak!" remorselessly.

When Maggie reached the flyover stairway, she was surprised to find beggars had already set up camp there. A young woman and a small girl were huddled at the bottom steps with bundles of rags and a charred pot beside them.

"*Belanda*," the young woman said weakly. She raised a mud-caked hand.

As Maggie fished in her bag for money, she felt the child's gaze. Maggie glanced at the black mop of hair reaching below shoulders so thin that the rest of the girl seemed to hang as from a coat hanger. When Maggie put some coins into the outstretched palm of the mother, she met the child's eyes. There was neither gratitude nor hatred in them, merely her own face reflected from their depths, blurred as in an old mirror. What had this child already suffered? Enough to take light out of her eyes. Maggie turned away from the bleak thought as well as from the girl and collided with a man standing behind her. He grinned from the contact, making sure she knew he liked it. She realized he had been peeking into her open bag.

From the corner of her eye she noticed a jerky movement: another one-legged man making his way by gripping the shoulder of a companion and lurching forward.

Why so many one-legged men? She would ask Vern, who had been out here a long time. Maybe too much knowledge of Asia had made him callous. When she told him about seeing these crippled men, one emotion she knew he wouldn't have was sympathy for them.

With time would she too become callous? She hadn't yet. Watching the man bend and settle himself against the stairway, his stump protruding a few inches below the left leg of his shorts, Maggie was not reconciled to the suffering of these people. In grad school she'd been warned about ineffectual responses to the poverty, sickness, and despair endemic to Southeast Asia, but nothing had actually prepared her for it—the visual onslaught taking her each day deeper into contemplation of misery, until sometimes Maggie Gardner wondered if her delight in so much here could ever compensate for a continuing sense of horror and helplessness. You paid a price to live in such places. But she was willing to pay it.

———————

She looked around for her driver, who would be lounging out of the sunlight, perhaps in the shade of a shop-lined arcade along the boulevard. She saw a young man at work on his transportable warung, pumping up a tire on one of two bikes that formed the housing of his shop. A canopy linked them, and in the tiny space within were two rickety chairs and a table at which he could serve mie goreng and fruit juice squeezed from his own press. At the end of his day he would pack up everything on the bikes and with a helper, probably his wife, pedal into traffic, carrying an entire restaurant between them.

Such enterprise softened her dislike of this ugly, humid city built among mangrove swamps. Maggie asked the young man for a glass of markisa juice. It was too hot for substantial food, but as the warung keeper worked his press vigorously, she thought of her favorite Sumatran dishes: roast buffalo marinated in coconut milk; stringy but pungent dried beef covered with hot chilies; and sardinelike fish with an initial smoky taste, then blinding heat, and an aftermath of fragrant fishiness—improbable favorites for a Midwestern girl raised on mashed potatoes and steak. She'd wash down the fiery food with beer, feeling her mouth go numb, the top of her head sweat, her sinuses clear. Maggie would feel cleansed; it was the way she'd felt in childhood after breaking a stuffy rule.

As she reached for the glass of markisa juice, noise filled the air like a thunderclap. At this instant she saw the young man hurl himself to the ground.

Then she too was on the ground, her cheek pressed to the dusty earth, both the old and new handbags jammed tightly against her chest. There was another explosion, shouting, and yet another explosion—gunshots. Maggie was curled up fetally, gripping the handbags, shockingly aware that death must be close by. And for an instant that seemed to last a long time she slipped into a recollection of her father, swayingly drunk, describing how in Burma he'd leapt into a hole when a bombardment came and found himself clutching a Jap's rotting corpse in the hope it would protect him from shrapnel.

For an instant she remembered.

Then there was a fourth sharp report, a cry of anguish, and silence. Her head still against the ground, she searched across the dust and found the young man, who was timidly raising his head. She raised hers. People along the boulevard were getting to their feet. Some were rushing toward a parked car, the front door of which was flung open, a man hanging headfirst out of it, his forearms resting on the ground.

Maggie found herself in the crowd. Another man was lying faceup near the car with blood oozing from his chest. Flesh protruding through his torn shirt made it look as though he had ruptured internally so that a part of him had blown outward. She hadn't known gunshot wounds did that. Father had never told her.

The man's expression was intent and amazed, in a strange way meditative, giving him the appearance of having come upon a tremendous idea at the moment of death. A fezlike white cap lay nearby. Maggie knew the meaning of the white cap: the dead man was a haji, a Muslim who had made the traditional pilgrimage to Mecca.

She backed away. People stared at the dead man, their expressions rapt, helpless, fearful, as if staring at a river overflowing its banks. Maggie searched the crowd for her driver. A man came up close enough for her to smell cloves on his breath. "What *ke mana* you, ah? *Ke mana* what you *sekarang?*"

Maggie, not understanding, wondered if he was asking her to go somewhere with him. He was looking keenly at her, mouth parted.

"Don't touch me!" she yelled. Her outburst forced him back into the crowd. Then she realized he'd merely asked where she was going.

"Nonya! Nonya!" Running up was her driver, who raised his hand smartly in a military salute.

Moments later she was inside the car. How had she got there? How had her body traveled from place to place? Looking from the car window at people huddling around the corpses, Maggie thought of hunters kneeling beside a kill in a movie.

Her driver was honking at vehicles that had stopped at the sound of gunfire. Finally he maneuvered into traffic that was starting to move again like a beast roused from slumber. Through the front windshield Maggie could see from the backseat one of Vern's flyovers approach and vanish overhead. Looking down at her hands, she tried to control their shaking by clasping them tightly.

"What happened, Pak?" she asked her driver. She heard her voice trembling.

"Someone was shot."

"I know that. Two men were shot. Who were they?"

She watched the driver's shoulders hunch up in an indifferent shrug.

"One was haji," she said. "He wore a white peci."

"Yes, a rich man."

That was true, of course. Only the rich made pilgrimages to Mecca. She persisted, knowing full well that her driver—that any Sumatran witness—would know something about the murders. "What happened, Pak?"

"Haji was out of car. Driver was getting back in car. Man came with pistol, shot them. Missed driver twice. Driver was getting own pistol, but next shot got him, Nonya. Is what I know."

"Why were they killed?"

Shrug again.

"Pak," she said, "why were they killed?"

"Komunis did it."

"The murderer was a Komunis?"

The driver nodded vigorously.

"Did they catch him?"

"No, he run away."

"If he wasn't caught, how do you know he was a Komunis?"

The driver shrugged.

"How do you know, Pak?"

"Komunis," the driver maintained.

It was then Maggie noticed that somehow she had lost the new handbag.

Two

She was still trembling when the car pulled up at the hotel. Two desk clerks smiled as they always did when she appeared in the lobby. This time instead of smiling back, Maggie looked straight ahead. Briskly she traversed the grim little lobby, passing a chaise longue, its cloth faded and torn, a fire extinguisher bolted to the wall, a table piled high with photo albums celebrating the life and times of the hotel owner. She did glance at a framed portrait of Sukarno, who wore a chestful of medals and the boyish grin that had won the hearts of countless women, that had made him, according to Vern, one of the great cocksmen of the century.

Maggie climbed the worn carpet of the curving stairway to the third floor; she paused to get her breath. Since the malaria, her lungs sometimes gave her trouble. Panting and sweating, she looked dully at a Chinese table at the top of the stairs. On it sat a bowlful of cloth-and-wire roses—this in a land of abundant tropical flowers. A cleaning woman was backing out of the "Presidential Suite." Maggie had a glimpse of teak furniture painted a metallic yellow and long crimson drapes appropriate for a Russian winter. To Maggie's knowledge the suite had never been used, yet was cleaned daily.

Getting her breath back, she headed down one of half a dozen corridors. If you chose the wrong corridor, you could end in a cul-de-sac, facing improbable junk: pieces of chair, coils of wire, sandals with broken straps. Rummaging through her handbag, she found an ancient key and unlocked the door to the apartment. Standing just inside were suitcases and next to them a small trunk packed with anthropology books—Mead, Lévi-Strauss, Cassirer, Geertz, Muller, Turnbull—books that had kept her company through the long, hot afternoons of Palembang.

Maggie removed her sweaty clothes and in the bathroom ladled water out of a tiled tub. She poured it slowly from the bamboo scoop over her head and shoulders. Coming in from the heat and ladling cool water over your body was in Southeast Asia almost as good as sex.

Maggie stared in the mirror opposite the tub. Her brown hair, dark from water, framed what men called a pretty face. Her eyes were good; she knew that: wide-set and blue. But her cheekbones were too prominent, her features too large, her mouth too "ample" (the word a boyfriend had once used to describe her mouth—and being literary, he had labeled her full lips "bruised-looking"). In her opinion there was something animalistic about her face. It would have robbed her of a pretense to elegance if she'd had any. Maggie was well aware of the look she actually projected—a rawboned sensual look that sometimes slowed men in their tracks while passing her on the street, here as well as home in Iowa. She liked the idea of appealing to them and smiled easily, but Maggie was no flirt. She wanted to come across rather cool, if not aloof, determined to serve notice that her smile was no more than an expression of civility. Maggie liked to think she judged cautiously what the world had to offer, although Vern accused her of being, in general, too enthusiastic about things. Enthusiasm was not always understood in the Orient, he argued, and she argued back, with a laugh, that he was just trying to keep her in line.

Walking naked to the bedroom, she gripped her left hip appraisingly. Someday she would go to fat like her mother. Too bad she hadn't inherited her father's slimness. But maybe he was slim because nearly all his calories came from whiskey.

Stretching out on the bed, Maggie turned to a gauze curtain fluttering at the window. Beyond it a half-dozen kites hung in the blue air. Sumatran kids loved kites. About all they had to play with were these kites—fiendishly hard to fly. She had tried it herself. Never got the damn thing off the ground, whereas a laughing gang of kids had put up a score of them to dart around like birds. That had been in Padang.

In Padang there were mountains to look at through the window when you lay in bed. Shifting her legs against the warm sheet, Maggie pictured the mountains, their green gorges clotted with mists. It was the sort of image that helped her nap sometimes in the afternoon. She used to have contempt for women who took afternoon naps. Now she did it too. It was the way Indonesians escaped the midday heat—waiting motionlessly, like lizards, for bearable weather.

Right now her husband must be saying good-bye to his construction gang, must be slapping their backs while his mind was on the next destination. That was Vern. Always going somewhere else. Always looking for what he called "another sun."

First thing he ever said to her was about the sun. Said it was too hot to stand under the midday sun. Said anyone with such delicate skin ought to stay in at noon. Said it with a look that made her imagine his hands on her skin. Yet she hadn't been attracted to him. He was about her own height, five ten, with the powerful neck of an aging athlete. They were standing on a promontory overlooking Lake Toba as he kept giving her this line: a girl with fair skin ought to stay out of the noonday sun. Called her a girl, not a woman, in a flat voice unused to subtleties of intonation. Said she must take care of such beautiful skin. Said it while staring boldly at her blouse with two buttons unbuttoned.

That had been in Prapat, the pretty town across from the island of Samosir on Lake Toba in northern Sumatra. She had huffed and puffed her convalescent way up the hill for a better view of the island. She hadn't been there five minutes before he'd come along with this unsolicited advice about her skin, warning her to protect it as if it really were precious, whereas Maggie damn well knew the malaria had left her skin ashen and dry. Even so, Vern later swore it was love at first sight. Had anyone else told her such a thing, Maggie would have laughed. But she believed it of Vern. That was his way: the impulse, the commitment, the determination. She really could imagine him falling in love at first sight. But when they first met she had merely been annoyed. Coldly she thanked him for the advice and turned away. After a long, tense wait, she heard his footsteps crunching gravel on the path, then fade into the distance behind her. She would never have believed that two days later she would cross the lake with this man and shack up with him for a week in a Batak house.

A loud knocking at the door shook her from reverie. Pulling on a robe, she called out, "Who's there?"

"You know who it is," a man's voice replied in a loud whisper. "Where's your husband?"

Rushing to the door, Maggie put her mouth close to it. "He went to a meeting. He'll be gone a couple of hours."

"Doesn't give us much time, sweetheart."

"I know. And I think he's suspicious."

"Then let me in quickly."

Opening the door, Maggie flung herself into her husband's arms.

───────────

She stood in the doorway while Vern took his own bath with the ladle. As he scooped water over his body, the muscles slid beneath his skin as if riding in oil.

He was telling her about his last day with the construction crew. Water flooded down his hairy chest, past his navel, vanishing into dark pubic hair, dripping pearly drops from his balls. She watched the drops form there, glisten, fall.

"And your day?" he asked.

She looked up at his wet tanned face. The features were sketched in, graceless and rugged: thick jaw, broad nose, heavy brow. "I bought a handbag and lost it."

Vern started to towel himself. "You'll find better bags in Jakarta."

"Sweetheart, why are there so many one-legged men in Palembang?"

Lowering the towel, he gave her a puzzled look.

"I saw three today."

Vern started to dry himself again. "I don't know."

"Do you care?"

Vern held the towel to his chest and stared at her. "What is there to care about?"

When she withheld a reply, Vern laughed grimly. "I am not a bleeding heart, Maggie, if that's what you're getting at."

"Neither am I."

"I've never seen any one-legged men in Palembang."

"Neither did I till today." She waited, but Vern kept toweling his thick calves, his brawny thighs. "I saw beggars camping on one of your flyovers," she said. "And there's a big ugly catsup ad plastered to the side of it."

Vern shrugged, drying his groin with short almost finicky strokes. "What they do with the flyovers is none of my business."

"You build them and walk away."

"Of course I build them and walk away. I go to the next thing."

Returning to the bedroom, Maggie lay down. She had the drained feeling of too much exposure to the sun. That was the continuing effect of the malaria, which she called "the bad thing." It never really went away; it hung around just out of sight like a delinquent spirit. Maggie felt rattled, unhappy with Vern. He didn't care about crippled people and he only built something in order to ignore it. Even as she thought such things, she felt ashamed. She knew her high-mindedness was phony, her hostility unjustified, but the nasty mood held on. It would be better if she were alone awhile, until the ill humor worked out of her, but Vern was calling from the bathroom.

"Are you packed?"

She closed her eyes. Maggie hated the mood; it clung to her like sweat.

Then his voice was nearer. "Sweetheart, are you packed?"

Without turning to him, she said, "I saw two men killed today."

"Ah, you were downtown."

Now she turned to stare at him. In jockey shorts Vern was fastening his wristwatch.

"So you know about it." When he shrugged, Maggie said angrily, "Why didn't you tell me you knew?"

"When?"

"When you got home."

"I forgot."

"My God, I saw it happen."

"But I didn't know that, did I?" he asked her with quiet logic. "I'm sorry you had to see it."

23

"I keep wondering who they were."

"An official of Pertamina Oil and his driver." At the bureau Vern sorted through things taken earlier from his pockets: a slide rule, a handkerchief, a wallet. He picked up a gold bracelet and held it high. "This is a present from the gang."

"One of them had a hole in his chest."

Vern sat on the edge of the bed. "Sweetheart, don't let it get to you."

"Of course it gets to me."

"What I mean is, this is the way things are. Sumatrans are hotheaded. Anything's possible."

"This Pertamina official, was he killed for being hotheaded?"

Vern turned the bracelet, examining it. "He was anti-union. Which means anti-Red. He was also a strict Muslim. So the Muslims will say his murder was political and blame it on the Reds. But who knows—maybe he was fooling around with someone's wife."

"Maybe he had a family." Maggie thought of a woman bending over the corpse. What if someday a man knocked on her door and said, "Your husband . . ."

Vern went back to the bathroom. He was moving away. It seemed he always was. In the morning when he left for work, it was like an act of betrayal. Was that what marriage did to you? Maggie wondered. Taught you to begrudge your mate any reasonable freedom? Given her own love of independence, that was ironic. But once she had a new commitment, some kind of job to do again, the idea of liberty— his or hers—wouldn't be a problem because they'd both have it through their work. However, they faced another problem that could be permanent: Vern took jobs anywhere he could get them. He would go anywhere, work on anything. Now they were going to Jakarta, although a job there was uncertain. It was only a possibility. Vern had other possibilities in Delhi, Bombay, Colombo, and she figured for him they were probably interchangeable. So what would happen if she picked up the pieces of her research and embarked on a new project? She would need to dig in, stay put, absorb an environment. And where would Vern be? Rambling off somewhere. Moving out of reach.

At the outset Maggie had convinced herself that Vern's sense of adventure was like her own, that they were both free spirits. But marriage could be proving her wrong. Maybe she needed to sacrifice a part of her freedom for a sense of closeness. It was an idea that surprised her. In the old days her boyfriends had complained of her freewheeling attitude toward relationships. Was her new desire for emotional security a first sign of age?

Vern came back into the bedroom, whistling. Maggie kept staring at the motionless curtain. "Vern," she said, "talk to me."

"What about?"

"About anything."

"Well, we take the seven-o'clock flight—"

"About the murders." To get the conversation going, Maggie asked, "Was it really a Communist plot?"

"It could be. By knocking off a prominent haji the Reds might be warning the santri Muslims to lay off the unions. That's possible. These people commit violence for the symbolism of it."

"I never saw a gunshot wound before." When there was no reply, Maggie turned to him. "I know you saw action. So did my father, but he never got over the killing. It ruined him."

"When we came back, sweetheart, we all reacted differently."

His discreet reply, avoiding criticism of her father, was sweet and thoughtful and turned her mood around for a moment and she smiled at him. But immediately the other mood came back. "Why don't you care about those murdered men? And the one-legged people hobbling around and the beggars?"

"I care."

"I don't think you do."

"Well, maybe I don't." Vern stood with one hand on the bureau. His dark-brown hair was slicked back. The gold bracelet dangled from his thick wrist. "Why should I? I can't change what happens to them."

Maggie turned again to the window. "You don't care."

"Not for what I can't change."

"That seems callous," Maggie said to the curtain, too angry to look at him. "Doesn't it seem callous to you? Am I unreasonable?"

Vern was silent. Still looking at the gauze curtain, she could imagine his face. A lot of women would find him handsome. She tried to think of him that way, but there were no secrets in his face; it withheld nothing, and so already, much against her will, she found him rather stolid-looking.

"My father—" Vern was standing at the foot of the bed; she didn't have to turn to know that or to know his dark eyes were on her. "He once told me the first lesson in life is learning the difference between what you can change and what you can't change. The second is to forget what you can't change. That way you protect your energy. You don't waste what you have."

Now she turned to him. As she expected, the conversation she had forced on him had pinched his features together into a frown.

"I don't commit myself often," he continued thoughtfully. "But when I do I stand by it."

"Sweetheart, I'm the same way. But how can you be so indifferent?"

To avoid more of this, Vern went back to the bathroom.

Maggie turned again to the window. A gob of red wax was on the sill. Last time the electricity had failed, they put a candle there. She thought of Vern quoting his father with reverence, as if quoting Lincoln or Shakespeare. She had never quoted her own father that way. What would Vern think of him if they met? Her husband would think her father was a drunk who had let the memory of war augment a penchant for self-pity. And Vern would be right.

Just now she had treated him shabbily with her self-righteous outburst, accusing him of callousness. The dead haji had unnerved her. Today's killings had left her with a residue of anxiety that still worked in her like a growth, a cancer.

"Sweetheart!" she called from the bed. "I'm sorry."

Vern came to the bathroom door and gave her a bemused smile. "For what?"

"The outburst. Calling you callous. I'm sorry. I was bitchy and unfair, but I'm going to be fine now."

"It's what you saw today, that's all. Asia takes getting used to."

"Maybe I'll never get used to it."

"But you want to. That's half the battle. Anyway, you belong out here."

"Do I?"

"I never saw anyone belong out here more than you do. You're the type."

"Type?"

"You know, restless. Ready to go."

26

"Like you."

"Like me. It's the type that can handle Asia."

Back in Iowa she had been known as a restless type; that was true. But it surprised Maggie to think of herself as someone who would come all the way out here, hoping to dedicate her life to an understanding of Asia, merely because she was restless. Vern hadn't meant to put her down, but in a way he had. She wondered if he had this image of her—flighty, committed to momentary satisfactions. She hoped not. That would make her in his eyes the sort of person she disliked. But somehow she couldn't ask him to explain himself further. They went to bed together wonderfully, but they weren't ready to confess their deepest impressions of each other.

Vern had gone back into the bathroom.

"I think the killings rattled me," she called out. "But I won't think about them anymore."

"That's the way," he said from the bathroom.

"I think I do belong out here." Maggie felt a sudden need to be close to him in the way she knew best. "My husband won't be back for an hour," she said. "If we hurry, we'll have time."

He peered around the bathroom doorway. "Give me a minute."

"Don't be long. You know my husband. When he says an hour he means an hour." Maggie closed her eyes and waited.

Almost from the beginning they had played this game—she the adulterous wife, he the furtive lover. She had rather hoped, for the excitement and fun of it, that they would develop other imagined relationships, but thus far they had explored the potential of only one such idea. In a playful mood they had fixed on it during their week on the island of Samosir.

Maggie often wondered what had possessed her to go with him to the island. That morning when they had met for the second time, she had been sitting on a hillside above the pretty little town of Prapat, staring at the lake below that looked as deep as sin. He came along and sat beside her, not saying a word, not suggesting, as he had done the previous day, that the sun would ruin such delicate skin. It was as if he had given up the idea of seducing her. Later Maggie would tell herself that his decision to remain silent had been Vernon James

Gardner at his best, his cleverest, his most eloquent. Because somehow his unbroken silence had made him belong there beside her—simply part of her life. And when they had finally talked, Maggie agreed to accompany him across the lake to Samosir Island. Accepted the invitation in full knowledge that this rough-hewn fellow would not take her over there just to look around and bring her back untouched to Prapat.

So that was the beginning. They took a launch across the blue stretch of lake to the pine-covered island. Her memory of their week there had long since lost a sequence, a pattern, but returned in disparate bursts of imagery. Embankments along the shore with small tables shaded by umbrellas. Fishermen sculling their dugouts. Smell of charcoal fires mingling with a cool scent of pine. Birds screeching from banyans whose branches hung down in writhing tentacles. Scarred rock. Images without order but as sharply defined in memory as when they had first been experienced.

Dotting the hills were saddle-backed Batak houses, one of which, without consulting her, Vern rented as soon as they reached the island. He didn't have to ask; wordlessly they had pledged themselves to each other, at least for one night, while crossing the lake. How well she remembered the Batak house, its ladder and creaking boards and rice-husk mattress. The toilet was a hole in the floor. This muscular expatriate, who had charmed her through the self-confidence of his silence, took her emphatically in the wood-scented darkness of the Batak house and afterward gasped in descending spirals of breath against her ear like a mindless animal, exciting her to her own orgasm. He had overwhelmed her physically at a time of convalescence when she was most vulnerable, unsure of her sexuality, even of regaining health after such a grave illness.

Two months earlier, when she had contracted malaria, there had been no doctors available, so by the time the Minangkabau got her into Padang for treatment, she was close to death. The experience had shaken Maggie's faith in her body. But in the Batak house, which stood ten feet off the ground on unpainted stanchions with pigs rooting beneath the floor, this stranger, who was a dozen years her senior, had expended on her the casual passion of a longtime lover. He made no concessions to her state of health, did not modulate his desires to accommodate it, but assumed she was ready to be taken with all the vigor at his disposal. Surprised, then delighted, she began to feel her veins pulsing with regained energy, the floodgates of feeling swing open, and she came hard. No curious college boy who wished to discuss orgasms as if they were lab experiments, the man never asked her if it was good but simply took her again sometime in the night when she was half dreaming and again in the morning with roosters crowing and the lake lapping at the hulls of old boats.

They had trekked that next day into the hills, through cool steep forests. Maggie never expected to have the strength for it, yet she did, climbing upward with her hand in his. Together, arms entwined, they looked down at Batak villages and the huge lake, a shimmering light upon its surface as quick and ephemeral as the kisses Vern gave her when they stretched out on the pinecones to make love again.

Her flesh revived under the use he made of it. With her recovery came more images that Maggie would hold until she died. She stood at the window of the Batak house and watched a multitude of birds cannonade into a tree, then swirl out of it, making of its branches a noisy and tumultuous world. There were the mists to remember, pouring in at dawn like swatches of cloth to surround and enmesh them both, clutching their sweaty bodies like fingers, softer than their own fingers that were busy, tireless at each other. Memory of smells too. Acrid smell of sex. Their odors mixing. And the recollection of tastes, his and her fluids sucked into mouths that gave back the pungency in kisses as wet as their skin.

Beyond images and sensations there were other memories. She listened to Vern's stories of years spent in constructing bridges and buildings throughout Asia. His accounts, predictably, were filled with facts, so Maggie imagined the atmosphere—the flat plains of India, the rain forests of Burma—until sometimes she felt they had been to those places together. It was then she developed the idea that they were kindred spirits.

At the week's end Vern invited her to Medan where he was finishing work on a new hotel. She accepted without hesitation, as she had accepted his invitation to cross the lake. There was no use continuing her research among the Minangkabau. They had been suspicious in the first place of a foreign woman living among them. Becoming ill, she had betrayed their trust; they would not want her back. And for Maggie, absorbed by the process of getting well, wherever Vern Gardner was going so would go health and strength. A week after reaching Medan they were married by a Sumatran clergyman. Then they had come to this terrible town of Palembang. And now, thank God, they were leaving it.

She waited for him, eyes closed, an arm flung across her face, sealing her off from everything save the anticipation of his approach. She was waiting for his step: heavy, deliberate, creaking the floorboards. She had first heard this love step of his in the Batak house. Lying awake, satiated with lovemaking, she had heard him get up and go down the ladder. She must have fallen asleep because the next thing she was conscious of was the slow creaking of floorboards when he returned.

"Vern?" she had called into the darkness.

"No, it isn't your husband. He went down to the lake to look at the stars. I'm the guy you met today. Whom you told you wanted to see again."

"What?"

"I said your husband went down to the lake. I've been waiting outside all night just hoping for good luck like this."

This was an odd game, but she decided to go along with it.

"Do you think he'll be gone awhile?"

"He took a walking stick. He's heading down the shore for a long stroll."

"And so you've come for me? To have me? To take me?"

"Isn't it what you want? Didn't you tell me that today?" he asked roughly.

"I did, yes, it's what I want."

"Then quickly—we mustn't get caught. I might have to kill your husband."

She had giggled. That statement seemed too melodramatic even for their scenario. Was he trying to be funny? She hoped so. She hoped this man had a sense of humor. But apparently he hadn't been trying to be funny, because since then she had seen little humor in Vern Gardner. Not that he was stuffy. But he went for the essentials of a situation as a pit bull goes for the jugular, and had little awareness left over for the askew, the slanted, the off-center hilarities of life. His sense of humor was limited to a wry acknowledgment of the human folly that thwarted him in the pursuit of progress.

She was waiting for him, arm across her eyes. At last she heard his ponderous step leaving the bathroom and coming closer. She felt the bed change shape slightly as he knelt on it from the opposite side. There was a long silence, a stillness, and inside this interval of suspended time Maggie knew he was studying with monkish solemnity her breasts, her thighs, her belly, letting the lust build in his loins the way he built a house—steadily, methodically. Then she felt the palm of his hand move gently in a circular motion on her hip. The pressure was astonishingly delicate. He rarely spoke of love except crudely within the terms of their scenario, but he could convey a tenderness through his hands that let her know there was more to Vern Gardner than a hard body, though she liked that too, oh, she did, God, she really did. He was stretching out beside her on the bed. Sometimes, when they stood side by side, Maggie felt taller and clumsier than her husband. But in bed Vern seemed taller and clumsier, and sometimes in her passion Maggie visualized him as a kind of satyr with cloven hooves and a brutal probing sex.

At first this tendency to mythologize her husband didn't worry Maggie. But it seemed after a while that she often transformed him into someone else—not only into the furtive lover but into the cuckolded husband as well and the wild satyr and a mysterious fellow who slept beside her in the early-morning hours, only to leave before sunup, trailing behind him the smell of salt spray or saddle leather or something else romantic. It was all right to share a fantasy with Vern, but this secret indulgence of hers was somehow wrong—corrosive. It depended on thinking of him as someone he was not. And that was negative. She hated negativism, having seen it ruin any chance for happiness her mother might have had. And anyway, there wasn't time for judging the quality of her marriage. Not now. Because Vern was mounting her with wonderful decisiveness.

"We'd better hurry," he gasped. "Your husband might come back."

Beneath him, Maggie gasped too. "Did you hear anything? Was that the door?"

He stopped moving on her for a moment and pretended to listen. "No."

"Then do it." She gripped the hard, smooth knobs of his shoulders.

31

It was like gripping in each hand the slick pommel of a saddle on a bucking horse. For the last time on the island of Sumatra, she let go in her husband's arms. "Oh, for God's sake, sweetheart, do it!" Images, shaken loose by desire, fell away from her mind and escaped her altogether: the dead haji, the one-legged men, the beggars, and the young girl, fifty kilometers northward, who had been dragged off by a tiger in the year 1965.

Three

Dipa Nusantara Aidit, chairman of the Partai Komunis Indonesia, third-largest Communist party in the world, no longer felt safe at PKI headquarters in Jakarta.

He and other members of the Politburo changed their sleeping quarters nightly and conducted business out of different shops daily. They took seriously the persistent rumors that Muslim gangs were planning to torch Communist property and assassinate Red leaders.

This morning Aidit sat at a shadowed table in a small warung where neighborhood people came for their tea, cakes, a quick bowl of noodles. As old men and workers drifted through the warung, Aidit's bodyguard, seated at another table, studied each passing face. A .38 was holstered under his left arm.

Aidit sipped tea from a glass as thick as the spectacles he wore. In his early forties, the chairman had a round, smooth face that gave him a younger look, a look augmented by the smile that came to his lips when he felt uncertain.

Earlier this morning he had often smiled this way during an interview with a political attaché at the Chinese Embassy.

They had discussed, among other things, a shipment of 100,000 small arms from Peking, which had been promised to Sukarno by Chou En-lai. For his own reasons Aidit wanted the deal to go through. So many weapons intended for military volunteers should encourage Sukarno to implement his proposed scheme for a "fifth force" of trained civilians. "Arming the people," as Sukarno put it, would dilute the authority of the army, the Communists' main political foe. Aidit suspected, however, that Sukarno was merely using the idea of a fifth force to keep the army off balance.

Even so, Aidit kept hoping. He believed you must reach for distant goals or never achieve those closer at hand. You must make yourself hope.

He was making himself hope that the arms shipment would go through, notwithstanding the Chinese attaché's cold indifference. That, of course, was the Chinese way. Recently China had praised the Indonesian Communists for their strong anti-imperialist stand, for their rejection of Russia's revisionist scheme to coexist with capitalist systems, and most important, for their growing friendship with Maoist China.

But today the Chinese attaché had stared coolly into space while claiming that "certain problems" had surfaced in regard to the arms shipment. No matter how closely Aidit questioned him, the attaché remained on dead center—there were certain problems, without explaining what they were. Typically Chinese: they offered something, then took it away.

Three men in sarongs and white shirts came into the warung, glancing warily around. Aidit nodded to them. When they sat down at his table, the biggest of them began sniffing the air. It was durian season and the big spiky fruit, piled in a bin, was giving off an odor like ripe cheese. The man turned to look at a huge pyramid of hairy coconuts in the corner. Above his head hung strings of purple mangosteens. Half rising from the bench, he plucked one of the fruit; then his fingers pressed from the purple shell a sweet-sour segment of white meat.

Aidit waited patiently while the big man devoured all of it.

This was Njoto, second deputy chairman of the PKI. Smiling at Aidit, he said, "I didn't eat last night."

"Was she beautiful?" Aidit asked without smiling back. No smile made his question grudging, disapproving.

Njoto rolled his eyes, pleased with himself.

"Have you got the copy?"

Njoto reached into his pocket and pulled out some rolled sheets of paper.

Holding them down with both hands, Aidit read the large childish scrawl. It was a speech that Njoto had written for the chairman to deliver on the twentieth anniversary of independence. It was intended to inspire PKI cadres. Aidit read the first paragraph rapidly.

"Reflect, comrades. Twenty years ago members of the Partai Komunis Indonesia, along with those of other political parties, passively accepted the defeat of the Japanese Fascists. At the war's end they stood by while the Western imperialists returned to take control again of our country. A sobering thought, isn't it: Indonesian men of destiny unwilling to look destiny in the eye! Your comrades in 1945 might have achieved total victory had they taken the vanguard position then. You must learn from their tragic indecision. Comrades, take the vanguard position they refused—with the sun in your faces throwing a shadow across the enemy! Obey the Central Committee!"

Aidit felt it was a good beginning. It moved quickly to the main point, which was strict adherence to instructions from the Central Committee. That was crucial. He took pride in the way he had integrated modern ways of organization into party conduct: standard recruitment practices, promotion by merit, clear identification of roles, a system for appraising procedures.

Njoto, too, understood the importance of discipline. His speech went from warning against complacency to an appeal for fervor to a demand for obedience, linking them in a single paragraph. The method, cumulative from sentence to sentence, had the ultimate effect of dignifying and demanding submission. Njoto might run after women and drink like a Westerner, but he had a Javanese love of words, a feel for Communist theory.

"I'll read the rest later," Aidit said, folding the speech.

Njoto, smiling confidently, didn't bother to ask if it was good. Instead, he called over a warung boy and ordered a bowl of noodles.

Aidit turned to another man, this one wearing a wispy beard. "Any news?"

"A Pertamina Oil official was gunned down in Palembang."

"Our doing?"

The man opened out his hands in an absolving gesture. "He had nothing to do with our people."

"Then we're clear."

"The Muslim press in Sumatra blames us."

Aidit shrugged. "Of course. But we're clear. They can't trace it to us. What really happened?"

"An informant says the oilman wouldn't settle a debt. So the creditor shot him."

"Other news?"

"A dukun from Semarang had a big press conference. He predicts world destruction."

Aidit could understand a soothsayer predicting it for Indonesia—the price of rice had quadrupled in the last three months.

How much suffering will my people endure, Aidit wondered, before turning to communism? He had dedicated his life to the cause, so he couldn't understand others who rejected it. Eighteen years old when the Japanese occupation began, he had felt the despair of the oppressed. During the struggle for independence, he had experienced the confusion of revolutionaries who are uncertain how to govern if they get the chance. He had heard many of his elders call for a return to prewar conditions, and it appalled him to think they would settle for abject peace as their reward for accepting foreign exploitation and racial dishonor again. Aidit had vowed never to live under any but Indonesian rule. By the time independence from Holland was achieved in 1949, the young patriot had decided that communism represented the most advanced and efficient form of nationalism. Marxist Leninism offered a clear blueprint for modernizing the new nation, because in Aidit's view it repudiated compromise with the imperialist West. And so from the early days of independence he had never swerved from his ultimate goal: to save the country through a Communist system uniquely Indonesian, combining in this manner an economic and political philosophy with national pride.

The third man sitting opposite him now spoke. Hartono was only in his mid-twenties, yet had established himself, surely to Aidit's satisfaction, as a party member of formidable talent. Unlike many Communists of Aidit's own generation, young Hartono eschewed doctrine for pragmatism. Aidit envied his detachment, the sort of cold practicality that made Hartono effective.

Chairman Aidit had never learned detachment. It seemed to him that he had always been embattled. In the early days of his own career, he had been perplexed, worried, dejected by the often conflicting demands of theory and action. Instead of emphasizing class struggle, Aidit had created a conservative image for the PKI: opposed to force, attached to parliamentary democracy, sympathetic to Islam, eager to cooperate in the interest of national unity.

Aware that progress for the PKI lay in alliance with Sukarno, he had often swallowed his pride along with his principles. Aidit's private assessment of Sukarno was negative. The swaggering president saw life as a Javanese puppet play, himself as the dalang, or puppeteer, who controlled the drama, created destiny. He liked the idea of revolution because it sustained excitement, not because it led to social change. He envisioned a mythic past coming into harmony with a dynamic present—his own words—both visions, however, were tainted by a perpetual flux of capricious decisions. He professed to be a Marxist while behaving like an uncomplicated populist, whose concept of a social program derived from nostalgia for the sort of primitive cooperation practiced in Javanese villages. Sukarno was ultimately dangerous, Aidit felt, because he was ultimately foolish. How often, during sleepless nights, had Aidit turned around in his mind the irony of beloved Indonesia in the clutches of such a fool—with himself helping that fool because there was no other viable choice.

These were conclusions that Aidit had worked years to arrive at. Hartono came to them effortlessly, one of the new breed who didn't remember the Japanese occupation, much less the Dutch of prewar years. Hartono approached issues with the pristine clarity of someone unencumbered by knowledge of a Western language that made his own seem inferior. He never suffered from a residue of the enforced humility that had been needed to survive the Japanese occupation. He wasn't blinded by the enthusiasm of revolutionaries who weren't prepared to lead a new country through the minefields of foreign and domestic problems. Hartono looked at things for what they were. He made decisions swiftly, almost casually it seemed. It fascinated Aidit, who in two decades had never slept a whole night through. Hartono reported on policy as he might on the weather—as something of persistent but changeable significance, ultimately of doubtful importance.

He did that now, leaning toward Aidit to speak in a soft precise voice. He was reporting on the land-reform program.

Aidit and other senior members of the Politburo had hoped to gain a broad spectrum of political support from this "rural offensive." From the substance of his report Hartono plainly did not agree. There was resistance to land reform from those who would most benefit by it— the peasantry. Cadres were having little success in convincing peasants that through communism they would triumph over the big landowners. Indonesian peasants had lived in bondage too long for them to grasp the idea of justice. Hartono made these observations without emotion. He merely explained the situation as he understood it. For the land-reform program to make any sense to peasants there must be dramatic attempts at radicalization in the countryside: demonstrations everywhere, loud demands for rent reductions and lower interest rates and higher agricultural wages. According to the young Communist, the only thing peasants understood was lots of violent activity.

When Hartono finished his presentation, Aidit studied the impassive face. He figured Hartono was the kind of man who could gather facts and deliver them but never really understand their meaning. There was comfort in that. Aidit said, "Very thorough work, but I wonder why you didn't mention the Muslim reaction to our program."

"I thought it was obvious."

"Nothing is obvious."

"Well, there's no denying that Muslim hostility is our biggest problem."

"I have heard no one denying it," Aidit said with a faint smile.

"Actually, the problem is intensified by a recent upswing in religious feeling."

Aidit continued to smile a tight little smile; the young man might

38

be talking about an upswing in the price of fertilizer. The chairman had long since given up God, but a residue of respect for religious belief still clung to him from a childhood spent in mosques with his father.

"The Council of Religious Scholars is becoming a serious factor," continued Hartono, "in many rural areas."

This somber analysis amused the chairman, who understood from long experience the council's importance in rural life. That was one thing about the old breed, Aidit thought: you had the advantage of memory; you had history helping you make sense of the present. Whereas this clever young man considered the Council of Religious Scholars as a new phenomenon and therefore puzzling. Aidit enjoyed the idea. He sat back, folding his arms.

"The council," Hartono went on, "is encouraging landlords to stop renting land. That way poor farmers work only for wages and can't legally expect a distribution from the harvest."

What Hartono was describing was something as old as the temples dotting the countryside of Java. Aidit nearly said, "Feudalism is like a root that goes down so deeply you can't pull it out." But could Hartono truly understand such a thing? He came from Jakarta where food arrived in trucks at dawn. He didn't know anything about roots; his world was only rice-shoot deep.

Now Hartono was describing other Muslim practices calculated to maintain the status quo. Landlords were leasing lands to Muslim schools but keeping most of the produce grown on that land; in this way the santri landlords took advantage of a legal loophole to hold more property than the law allowed. Religious leaders and gentry conspired to keep the poor in their place. Was this not the reason that a few thinking men in the countryside turned to communism? Aidit wondered if, while collecting data, Hartono had ever asked himself that question.

Finally, the chairman interrupted, having heard enough of the glum report. "Are farmers complaining?" He knew the answer before Hartono gave it: only a few had the courage, much less the imagination, for protest. Aidit searched the young man's face for a sign of the depression he himself felt while contemplating such inertia. Nothing in Hartono's expression conveyed more than self-confidence. Did the new breed really care who took control of government as long as they were part of it?

"I'm hungry," the chairman declared suddenly. "Order some noodles."

Lifting his eyebrows, shocked by what seemed a superficial response to so much bad news, Hartono gave the chairman a long, cold, brilliant stare.

Four

D. N. Aidit left the warung an hour later. He walked rapidly down a side street to a batik shopping district and slipped into a store. In a back room piled high with bolts of cloth, he sat at a small table marked by cigarette burns that had the dirty brown look of motionless roaches.

Soon a heavyset man pulled the room's curtain back and entered. He sat opposite Aidit without a word and wiped his jowly face with an outsized handkerchief.

Studying him, Aidit wondered at the irony of politics. A few years ago Aidit had unleashed public diatribes against this man, had called Subandrio "a traitor to independence" and "a creature of the West," because as foreign minister of Indonesia he had advocated negotiation with Malaya instead of the armed conflict wanted by the PKI. Since then Aidit had supported him against a popular right-wing general for chairmanship of an important state committee. Chairmanship of it had empowered Subandrio to make changes in governmental departments. The PKI had put its propaganda machine at his disposal, allowing him to ease into the second most powerful job in Indonesia.

Now, having wiped his sweaty face dry, Subandrio called out. Instantly a man thrust the curtain aside. "Tea," Subandrio told his bodyguard. To Aidit he said, "You?"

"I've had my quota today."

"So have I, but it's the only way I keep going in such heat. He used to drink more tea than I do, but the doctors won't let him have a drop now."

Aidit understood that by "he" Subandrio meant Sukarno. They never used the president's name in conversation.

"How is he?" Aidit asked.

"Claiming he's healthy. Pounds his chest, shows his muscles like a Dutchman. Now a new Chinese doctor is giving him acupuncture. I wish he'd go back to his Viennese doctors," Subandrio said. "At least they gave him sleeping pills so he could rest. But they made the mistake of telling him he needed a kidney operation. Now he believes only in the Chinese, who don't operate. Remember him decorating that Chinese doctor at Bogor for saving his life?"

"When he had the flu."

"Now he's going to decorate this new one for pricking him with needles."

"What really is his condition?"

"Since the collapse last month, he's been strong enough."

Aidit knew all about the collapse, but wanted Subandrio's version. "Were you there when it happened?"

"Yes. He was speaking against the United Nations as I recall. He yelled 'I am a Marxist!' with a dozen army officers on the rostrum. How they squirmed!"

Aidit laughed; he felt rather easy in the presence of the foreign minister, who had also seen enough of great men to make fun of them.

"He went from the U.N. to his childhood," Subandrio continued. "You know his stories—how he owes everything to a Javanese childhood. Then suddenly he gripped the podium and bent forward. He couldn't get the words out. He had to be helped to a chair. But in a few minutes he waved everyone away and finished the speech. He's been strong since."

"Good."

"Or most of the time. He was a little incoherent at Monday's news conference. The foreign press is talking about it."

Aidit shook his head. "If only he stayed away from women and conserved his strength."

"He will never do that." Subandrio tapped the table with one pudgy hand for emphasis. "Never never never."

"I heard he had a tantrum at the last cabinet meeting."

The foreign minister nodded solemnly.

"These tantrums are more frequent, aren't they?"

"I'm afraid so."

"What do you think?"

"I'm worried." Subandrio leaned forward to cool the surface of his tea.

"If he dies—" Aidit began.

"Oh, I know what happens then. I am out. Or dead. Certainly you are out."

"Or dead."

"And the army has its way." Subandrio lifted the glass, sipped, put the glass down quickly. "Terrible tea. Do find better places for us to meet."

"I understand there's a council."

"You mean the generals? I know the rumor."

"It's only rumor?"

Subandrio shrugged. "Unlike most of them, this one makes sense: seven generals, Yani and Nasution among them, meet frequently at Yani's house. They plot to take over if he dies. Or perhaps before he dies."

"Before? When?"

"I've heard on Armed Forces Day."

A month off. The rumor Aidit had heard had not included a date. "Your assessment?"

"I think it's possible. Yani and Nasution have the necessary power to control the army. They have close friends in the other branches. They have the experience to make a coup work. Yani drinks too much but he's bold. Nasution isn't bold but he has the respect of junior officers. A coup is possible. Such men could succeed."

"And you and I are out or dead." Audit smiled uncertainly. "At last a serious rumor—one for a serious discussion."

43

Subandrio regarded Aidit thoughtfully. "I think you've taken it seriously before now. What's on your mind?"

"I wonder about the army as a whole. About other factors if you consider a coup attempt. For example, loyalty. Many officers are more committed to the president than to the general staff."

"No doubt about it. Especially Javanese officers."

"And officers sympathetic to the Left. Both in the army and air force. Not in the navy."

"I agree. Go on." Subandrio leaned forward.

"All told, they represent a potential counterforce."

"That's a dangerous thought, Aidit."

"If the rumor has truth to it, we're facing more danger than a mere thought."

Subandrio sat back; his shoulders fell as though his worst fear had been confirmed. "You suggest a countercoup?"

"I suggest this: one way to stop a coup is to have another ready."

"Coming from you, that's a surprising suggestion. You're so moderate." Subandrio did not mention those tumultuous days when Aidit had advocated military intervention in Malaya because it would radicalize the country. "Moderate, almost conservative. And here you are planning a coup."

"You know better than that. I merely want to feel out the officer corps, see whom we might count on."

"I agree with feeling them out."

"You agree to give me support?"

"In what way?" Subandrio crossed his arms and sat back stiffly.

"In a slight way." What Aidit really wanted was intelligence reports. Subandrio, as former head of the Central Intelligence Board, could get them—secret dossiers that would be invaluable to the party. There was plenty to gain from Subandrio.

"In a slight way," Subandrio repeated. "Could you be more specific?"

"Give me time. When my people know more, so will you. Our fates are like this—" Aidit wove the fingers of his hands together.

Subandrio gripped the table at its corners for a moment, as if in the act of decision, then rose to his feet. There was sweat on his brow. "Yes," he said, "I agree. If anything happened to him, we'd be out. Or dead."

"And the army in."

"Yes, it's practical to look ahead. We must look at alternatives."

"Then we agree." Aidit got to his feet quickly, extending his hand. After a moment's hesitation, Subandrio extended his own.

When the foreign minister had left, Aidit continued to sit in the hot little room. He asked someone from the shop for an ashtray. After half a dozen butts lay in it, the curtain was pushed aside again. This time a short, very thin man came in.

Aidit did not smile. But the small man smiled. He had lips that never showed teeth even when smiling, eyes with a wary look, ears flat to his head, hair slicked down. Everything about him seemed tucked away, swept back, out of reach.

He was Kamarusaman bin Ahmed Mubaidah—alias Sjam—head of Biro Khusus, the PKI's Special Bureau. It was so special that no one knew of its existence except Aidit and a few other top officials. Sjam's bureau worked to establish secret communication between the party and army officers sympathetic or at least not hostile to communism.

Sjam remained standing until Aidit nodded for him to sit down.

"Forgive me being late," Sjam said in a soft voice. "Today has been difficult. You have no idea about my day." He took out a cigarette and lit it, blowing a slim tube of smoke from pursed lips.

Aidit had no idea about his day, that was true. Aidit had known him for years, yet couldn't imagine how little Sjam spent time that didn't involve Red business.

"I haven't been well lately," Sjam said, then looked sidelong at Aidit, waiting for a response.

Aidit said nothing. He knew that health was a favorite topic of conversation with Sjam. Sjam's own health. When he spoke of it, his quiet voice became animated, then lapsed back into blandness.

"The heat," Sjam continued. "I get sore throats from it and then fever. Doctors never help. What I need is rest and a change of scene."

"Yes," Aidit said coolly. "But now there's work to do."

"I had hoped so." Sjam's tone changed from tremulous self-pity to a kind of jaunty eagerness, as if the idea of work itself was enough to make him feel good.

Aidit described the Council of Generals, not as a rumor but as a *fait accompli,* because if possible he wanted to get a clear reaction from this little man. Sjam was always a potential source of information for the PKI. He had a history of union activity, having been an official of the dockworkers' organization for a number of years. He knew what was coming into and leaving the country illegally. Of more importance was his knowledge of the military. Having been a sort of war hero during the fight for independence, Sjam was able to get close to army officers. His connections with them were labyrinthine, secret, reliable.

Politely he listened to Aidit's description of the Council of Generals. Then vaguely he said, "Yes, I see."

"Have you already heard of the council?"

Sjam shook his head. "This is new to me."

"But the council exists."

"Yes?"

"And I want to know more about it. For example, I want to know how your people react." Aidit referred to Sjam's army contacts as "your people."

"How they react, yes." His habit of repeating phrases had always annoyed Aidit, even though such caution had probably helped Sjam to survive all these years.

"For example," Aidit continued, "I want to know what they would do if the council instigated a coup."

"Yes, I see."

"For example, would the people you know simply accept it or mount a countercoup?"

"I understand what you want. You'd like to know would they do that."

"And if so, how. It would mean a great deal to know if they would strike back at the council." This was not information Aidit expected to get; he merely suggested it to get a further response from Sjam.

"I think it would mean a great deal," the little man said and cleared his throat as if reminding himself of his ill health.

Suddenly the chairman felt certain that Sjam knew a lot about the Council of Generals—more perhaps than Foreign Minister Subandrio knew. But probing further would be a waste of time. Sjam was too experienced at this sort of business to volunteer anything without understanding thoroughly the benefit to himself. "What would be especially valuable," Aidit continued, "is a list of officers who would stand against the coup."

"Yes. Officers sympathetic to our Beloved Leader."

"A list would be valuable. We would know who could be counted on."

"And difficult to get," Sjam said with a grimace. "After all, we're talking about rebellion within the army. If the top generals want something done, it gets done. Disobedience means death. We're talking about a list of traitors to military tradition. We're talking about serious matters, Comrade Aidit."

Whenever Sjam talked about "serious matters," Aidit knew, they had come to the main point of their conversation: money. Without hesitation Aidit reached into his pocket and hauled out a big roll of rupiah. Peeling off a number of them, he paused to regard Sjam, to see if the little man was going to be satisfied. In the early days of their association Aidit had called such payments "consultation fees." But they had worked together too long now for Javanese circumlocutions. He said, "This should take care of your change of scene."

Sjam took the money and counted it carefully. At last he pursed his lips as if blowing out smoke. "It will."

"Officers who would back a countercoup against the Council of Generals."

"Yes, a list."

"And I want a careful day-to-day account of army thinking about the present crisis."

"You'll have it."

"And you'll have enough for more than one change of scene. But work fast. A coup might come as soon as Armed Forces Day."

"A countercoup shouldn't take long to plan. We're talking about professional soldiers."

Aidit smiled at last. One thing about Sjam—he too was professional. He had existed in Jakarta for years on a shady job here, an improbable position there, and while others like him fell by the wayside, ending up in jail or fleeing to another country because of their clandestine activities, Sjam kept going. He lived by retailing information and lived well. Last year Aidit had put a PKI agent on his tail; according to the submitted report, even the agent had been impressed by Sjam's style of living, which included a pleasant house with a garden in a good residential district, a wife and three children, two mistresses, a beach house near Carita. Aidit depended on two things in this matter: Sjam's need to maintain his possessions and the man's long experience as an informant. What he couldn't depend on was Sjam's loyalty or his own knowledge of how the little man went about business.

"One more thing," Aidit said. "There's the question of where you learned about the Council of Generals. Naturally I want the PKI kept out of it."

Sjam shrugged. "Don't worry. I'll say I learned from friends of mine."

"Friends in the army? What friends? Not Communists, I hope."

"Don't you worry."

Aidit had always felt uneasy in the presence of this little man. He had contempt for someone who lived by selling information, but couldn't help admiring Sjam's talent for survival. He never pushed Sjam too far; that was the measure of his own uncertainty. So he said, "I know you'll take care of everything. I'm not worried."

"Of course I'll take care of everything. Well, then—" Sjam started to rise. He seemed like a businessman who having finished one meeting must dash to another. He always looked this way when his pocket held money. As if now he could pay off debts that meant the difference between life and death.

When Sjam had left the room, Aidit sat awhile longer. Uncertainty changed into worry. But then he always worried. He worried about Sjam's reliability—whether he would work at it. Or he might transfer by mistake some critical information about the PKI to the army (by mistake since Sjam wouldn't deliberately impair a source of income). He just might put the PKI in grave danger.

Aidit also worried about Sukarno's health. The greatest structural weakness of the party was its dependence on a sick, unreliable man.

And Aidit worried about the land-reform program. The peasantry had no tradition of political action behind them, no belief in their ability to change things. Rob and cheat them, they merely shuffled away. They didn't know how to fight. Maybe, from the genetic warp of centuries, they could no longer learn. Yet it was on the peasantry that communism in Indonesia depended for ultimate success. Aidit worried too about his wife's cataracts, which were getting worse. He worried about safe houses and the Muslim gangs now roaming the streets.

Finally, he worried about the young party members like Hartono—whether they were capable of carrying on the struggle. Could they find emotional sustenance, as he and members of the older generation had found it, in the goals of independence? He and the old breed understood what it meant to believe, especially when members of other political parties had betrayed the principles of revolution by succumbing to feudal thinking. How could Hartono understand, much less feel, the hope and faith of those brave days? He had been a mere baby when the streets filled with ecstatic cries of victory, and the air stirred with banners proclaiming freedom, and a healthy young Sukarno stood at a microphone to announce the birth of a nation.

Five

As he combed his hair, Vern could see behind him in the mirror his wife in bed, the sheet negligently covering no more than her legs to mid-thigh. Meeting his appreciative gaze, she gave him a smile, though they had just quarreled. He wanted her to stay close to the hotel until they knew how dangerous Jakarta really was. In their first day at the Hotel Indonesia they had heard rumors of youth gangs, both Red and Muslim, roaming the kampongs of Jakarta. Maggie took the rumors seriously, but refused to give in to them: she hadn't come here to stay in a hotel room. She had not studied the language in grad school and worked on it among the Minangkabau simply to prowl through nearby batik shops like a tourist. So they had quarreled.

Vern knew he would lose the argument. There was real passion in her resolve to see Jakarta. It wasn't the little burst of enthusiasm that a tourist feels, hoping to squeeze dry every moment of a two-week holiday. Hers came from a deeper source that he didn't care to locate. Live and let live had always been his motto. This ought to apply especially to someone you loved. And anyway, Maggie wouldn't listen to him; perhaps that's why she belonged in Asia—she created her own agenda. It's what many people did who came out here. They were drawn to alien places where they could start a new life. They were usually people with secret passions, just like Maggie. He only hoped hers wouldn't prove dangerous. He had known a few people out here who had let their driven natures do them in.

Like Rick, a salvage diver he had met in Singapore.

Rick had had Maggie's way of smiling at you suddenly, then turning away as if flashing a message from the depths of consciousness: "I will go all the way when the time comes, only I don't know and surely you don't know either when that will be." Rick's time had come off the coast of Ternate, in the Moluccas, during a salvage operation. A seventeenth-century Portuguese brig, possibly loaded with gold and silver, was down in fifty fathoms of treacherous currents. A diver had already been lost. No one else would dive except Rick, and he went down every day for a week until the currents got him. Vern had heard about it at a bar in Singapore. He could imagine Rick smiling his sudden smile before going over the side, driven by a determination to dive whatever the consequences.

Sometimes when Maggie smiled, Vern had the unsettling impression that he was looking at Rick. In such a reckless but secret smile was a commitment that went beyond anything he himself had ever felt. He feared it in Maggie. He had not married a woman to have her announce suddenly that she wanted to study orangutans for the rest of her life or cross the South China Sea in a rowboat. He hoped marriage would calm his young wife down.

Going over to the bed, he sat on its edge. She did not pull the sheet up, but let his eyes take in her nakedness.

"So you're going to explore Jakarta," he said with a sigh. Glancing at her record player on the table with its adapter plugged into the wall, he added, "Maybe you can find some jazz records."

"I've never found any out here yet."

"You need to try Hong Kong. We'll do that someday. Sweetheart, be careful where you go in this damn place."

After kissing her, Vern left. He knew that within a few minutes the record player would be on, the strains of Bix Beiderbecke's cornet—scratchy now on the overplayed 78—would be following Maggie around the room while she dressed. Vern could take music or leave it, especially early jazz. But it was one of Maggie's passions. She had her heroes and Bix Beiderbecke was perhaps the greatest of them all.

Vernon Gardner loved hotels. He had loved them since childhood, when his father, a traveling salesman, dragged him and his mother from town to town in search of security during the Depression. Until his high-school days he had called places home that were temporary to other people. In Vern's mind it took maybe a day for a hotel to become his permanent residence. His ability to make camp anywhere had enabled him to wander cheerfully through Asia for the last decade.

Coming downstairs this morning in the Hotel Indonesia, Vern was filled with the comforting sense of a new home. He looked forward to eggs and pungent Javanese coffee. Everything was as it should be.

He got an English edition of the Communist daily, *Harian Rakyat,* at the front desk—the only paper available. Over breakfast he picked rapidly through predictable articles. There was lengthy condemnation of "America's provocative aggression and brutal war against the People's Democracy of North Vietnam." D. N. Aidit, chairman of the PKI, had written an editorial called "National Unity Above All," which called for land reform. It contained familiar catch phrases that had followed Vern through the Third World: capitalist bureaucrats, henchmen of Western aggression, running dogs of colonialism. In a long interview a cabinet minister talked about rising inflation (Vern knew the figure was somewhere near 600 percent a month). According to the minister, politicians of the Right sowed dissension by suggesting there was an economic problem: "It is useless to fabricate rumors which encourage everyone to make certain conclusions which could create various consequences." Classic political statement. The newspaper was filled with such wisdom.

Sometimes Vern wondered why he stayed out here to work in countries riddled with corruption. He could take his bride and go back to America. After all, he was at an age when settling down made sense. He could take Maggie to Chicago, for example. But that idea, occurring daily, was daily set aside. The fact was that he liked the confusion and turmoil of Asia, the sense of living at the edge. When Vern got up each day, he anticipated what might happen: the fuckups, the excitement, the challenges.

Right now he wanted to build a hotel on Bali. He had wanted the job ever since hearing of a plan to build hotels there no taller than a palm tree. At present a Japanese company was putting up a huge boxlike pleasure palace on Sanur Beach. But a recent surge of patriotic zeal in the Indonesian parliament had resulted in legislation banning such tall buildings in the future. In a land ignorant of ecology there was, quite suddenly, a flicker of concern for the beauty of Balinese landscape. Buildings no taller than a palm tree.

Such unlikely idealism intrigued Vern Gardner. It stirred in him a memory of his own student idealism: his adoration of the cathedrals of Europe, the Bauhaus, Frank Lloyd Wright—in the days before he surrendered aesthetic dreams to the practical goal of building whatever came along.

It would be fun to design and construct a hotel no taller than a palm tree.

Initially he hadn't had much hope of getting into the project. After all, he was a capitalistic American. But he hadn't been thinking like an Indonesian. By living and working in Sumatra, he'd become family. The nepotism rife in Indonesian business and government, the good ol' boys philosophy, applied to him as well. He had proved himself by learning some of the language, by putting up with heat and petty officialdom. His inquiries about Project Palm Tree (filtered through a local Palembang politician whom he had bribed in order to get the flyovers done) had enabled him to apply. While the flyovers were being completed, Vern had sent his assistant to Jakarta to make initial contacts.

And so here he was, ensconced in a Jakarta hotel, and here came Larry Foard, his assistant, a stocky, rumpled man manuevering among the breakfast tables of the hotel dining room.

They had been a team for years. A boatbuilder from Cornwall, Larry Foard had worked in London shipyards, in Belgian shipyards, in West Africa where he taught boatbuilding and learned to dress his own meat, almost dying of blood poisoning from a diseased calf. Larry Foard was tough, honest, skillful. He was the only Westerner whom Vern had come to trust in Asia, where incompetency was common among expatriates seeking jobs.

Larry shook hands and sat down. With his short legs under the table, he looked like a big man: his shoulders broad, his hands outsized, his head square-jawed, his long, black hair curly and thick. He didn't waste time with amenities; they had worked too long together for that.

Larry said, "Things don't run in a straight line here."

"They didn't in Palembang."

"Straighter than here." The Cornish boatbuilder lit a cigarette and held it between two stubby fingers scarred from carpentry accidents. He told Vern about his two weeks in Jakarta. He had inquired about the conduct of business, especially army business, since Project Palm Tree would be run by the army. There was, for example, the interesting case of a cargo of insecticide that didn't exist. It was sold by a company registered in Liechtenstein. A faked bill of lading was issued by another firm in Singapore. A docking certificate proved that the cargo of insecticide was loaded in Hong Kong on a ship named *The Merdeka*. *The Merdeka* didn't exist either. Yet another company, this one owned by the Republic of Indonesia, paid a half million dollars for the cargo. Who got the money? The Liechtenstein company. Who owned this company? It was registered in the name of a Chinese businessman, a cukong, from Jakarta. Who was this cukong? The financial agent of an army general. Who was this general? The officer in charge of supply at KOSTRAD, the Army Strategic Reserve Command. This supply officer, to pay for the shipment of insecticide that didn't exist, got a letter of credit from Bank Negara Indonesia. Bank Negara Indonesia was controlled by KOSTRAD. Larry guffawed. "So the government paid half a million for something that never was. And the army got richer."

During the next hour, while Vern drank strong Javanese coffee, Larry regaled him with other stories involving fertilizer, parachutes, Bailey bridges, rubber pontoons, converted landing ships, rubber, cinchona, tea.

"These aren't the generals we knew in our war," Larry pointed out grimly. "These fellows control rice mills, auto assembly plants, clothing factories, and other sorts like shoe and umbrella factories, and airlines, rubber processing firms, and chicken farms, and fisheries, and rubber estates. I heard of one enterprising bloke—a lieutenant general—who makes a fortune on foreign film distribution. A group of them do a brisk business in oil. I'm told the main duty of most staff officers is to bring funds into the military treasury—which they share. These chaps are nothing if not bold. They make illegal deposits to

54

private banks in their own names, launder money abroad, deal openly in bribes, kickbacks, smuggling." Larry sat back and speculatively blew a smoke ring. "Of course, in their shoes I'd do the same."

"Why is that?"

"Because their pay is bloody awful. So they create their own income."

"You've done your homework."

"It hasn't been easy. Jakartans are blooming smug. We have an appointment this morning, but they never told me about it until late yesterday. To get the appointment I had to wine and dine one of the OPSUS flunkies, a major in supply. Him and his wife, his mother-in-law, his brother, his brother's very fat wife, and I bought tons of candy for two small nephews. You're laughing, Vern. Think it's a joke? And a Zippo lighter for the major. Plus a dozen cartons of Lucky Strikes."

"Who's the appointment with?"

"A big shot. General Sakirman."

They left the hotel and got into a car that Larry had hired for the day.

"Yes," Larry said with a sigh. "This isn't like Sumatra, old chap. Down here it's strange, it's dodgy, it's a bloody zoo. I'm not keen on it."

Vern turned and looked at the heavyset jaw, the broad weathered face.

"Look over there," Larry said, pointing from the car window as they drove along.

Above the trees of an approaching square Vern saw an obelisk: immense, yet its white-and-gold column looked tawdry and ostentatious.

"National Monument," Larry explained. "They call it Sukarno's Last Erection."

Vern saw a large banner stretching across a side street, stating both in English and in Bahasa Indonesia: BOYCOTT UNITED STATES FILMS.

"About the National Monument," Larry continued, looking back at it. "They say a statue of Sukarno is scheduled to go on top. But he won't let them put it up because his astrologer warned him he'd die a violent death if they did. Bugger!"

Vern nodded silently. Until now he had avoided Jakarta, which from all reports was a rotten town. What he saw from the car windows confirmed it. There were sorry rows of dilapidated huts over which glass-fronted office buildings towered. Streets were buckled from heat that boiled out of the swampland on which Jakarta was built. Every sort of vehicle—bemo, truck, bus, motorcycle, car, becak—lumbered through the hot dust and sent out blasts of exhaust that blackened the stinking canals, old shacks, crumbling walkways. The people of Jakarta looked stricken by sunlight, bathed in its acid whiteness. Their eyes sank back from the glare. They walked with a kind of dragging ponderousness. Yet they managed to keep up a terrific din. Jakarta was like a tin sounding board.

For a moment, searching for peace, he recalled the saddle-backed Batak house he had rented on Samosir Island.

Buffalo horns had been nailed over the entrance to ward off evil spirits. Maggie had loved markisa fruit, sucking out the sweet gelatinous seeds. Because of prevailing winds, the forested hills had the look of animal fur, rubbed one way—Maggie had said that; he wouldn't have thought of it. What he remembered most was the silence. No motors. Not one. Only birds singing and the lake breeze stirring the pines. And the sound of his flesh against hers, slapping against hers in love, and their labored breathing, their whispering.

Vern turned to the Cornish boatbuilder. "You never went to Lake Toba, did you?"

"Not me, mate."

"Go someday."

Six

The car entered a circular drive and stopped at a rambling bungalow with garden, veranda, and tiled roof—more like a stylish villa than an army headquarters. Above the veranda on a white sign in large crimson letters was the acronym OPSUS.

"It stands for Operasi Khusus," Larry explained, "a special operations unit of KOSTRAD, the Army Strategic Reserve Command. What it all really means is the place where business deals are made."

They left the car and stared at the automatic weapons gripped by sentries at the entrance of OPSUS.

As a former serviceman, Vern found the grandiose acronym amusing while appreciating the grim importance it could hold for a military mind. In the foyer three army clerks sat behind the main desk in braid and epaulets. One of them curtly shoved a form at Vern. He filled in not only his passport number and temporary residence but his place of birth and mother's maiden name as well. Then he sat next to Larry on a bench and watched army personnel stride briskly through the foyer, lugging clipboards and satchels, their heels clicking on the marble floor. Anchoring thin walls of plaster with such pretentiously heavy flooring offended his builder's eye.

After a while an adjutant came along and led them through a network of corridors to a door faced with a bronze plaque: LIEU-TENANT GENERAL PRANOT SAKIRMAN, both in English and Bahasa Indonesia. All signs in both languages. No Dutch. Perhaps, Vern thought, the lack of Dutch, which would be the primary foreign language in Jakarta, was meant as a snub of the country's former masters. But why English, with both the British and the Americans on Sukarno's shit list? He guessed the answer was practicality. Wherever you went there was always a touch of it when dollars were at issue, and they sure were here, he thought, as the adjutant led them into an office.

Army clerks behind a long counter were busy at desks piled high with files. A cloud of cigarette smoke drifted through the room, which was chilled by throbbing air conditioners. Vern hated cold rooms in the tropics almost as much as cigarette smoke. Picking up a magazine from the table beside his chair, he put it down again. "Tell me what you know about Sakirman," he said to Larry.

"A chum from my old brigade works at the British Embassy. Tells me Sakirman brings people together for a price."

"What does that mean?"

"By putting people in touch, he sees to it they get the proper licenses."

"Is that what generals do—act as brokers?"

"Like I told you, mate. Their sort of general isn't what we had in our war."

They sat awhile, getting colder. "How was Palembang when you left?" Larry asked finally.

Vern shrugged; then he remembered. "An oilman was murdered on the street our last day there. Maggie saw it happen."

"Who did it?"

"They say the Reds."

"So far Jakarta's calm, except for demonstrations. But the Muslims are restless. Gangs roaming the streets, looking to bash Communist heads."

"Can't Sukarno handle that?"

"They say he's sick. Bad kidneys. And he's got too many women."

"I heard about that in Palembang."

"But Sukarno is still Sukarno," Larry said. "Great Leader of the Revolution and all. I mean, he did defy the Dutch and go to jail for freedom. So the chap can rant and rave and jolly up any bird he can get his hands on and people still love him."

Another adjutant came for them, leading the way deeper into the office. "We must be getting close to Sakirman's lair," whispered Larry as they passed cubicles of clerks.

Finally the adjutant stopped and opened a glass door. A broad-shouldered officer was sitting in a large room at a large desk with a huge portrait of Sukarno behind him.

He rose—not far, being quite short. "I welcome you," General Sakirman said in English. The adjutant placed two chairs in front of the desk. When Vern sat down, he noticed a framed photo of the general and a stout woman and three solemn children. The photo was placed for guests to see.

"Forgive me the wait," said the general. He didn't accompany the apology with a smile. Unusual for an Indonesian, Vern thought. "This is busy today."

Vern smiled in acknowledgment of the perfunctory explanation, noticing on the side wall a large map of Indonesia. It wasn't a military map, because a color legend was coded for TIMBER, RUBBER, PALM OIL, CONSTRUCTION. He was staring at it when the general said in carefully pronounced English, "It is most kind of you to come into here today, Mr. Gardner."

From the way Sakirman angled his chair away from Larry Foard, it was clear to Vern that the general was going to speak solely to him. Sakirman wasn't going to spend time on a subordinate.

He ordered tea from his adjutant who then brought a folder and placed it on the desk, bare save for a phone and the photo. Putting on a pair of horn-rimmed glasses, the general leaned forward and picked up the thin file in both hands, as if clutching something that might get away.

My dossier, Vern thought.

After studying it a few minutes, the general took off his glasses and replaced the folder on his desk. Vern could tell nothing from his broad face. "I forgot to ask you do you, sir, like tea very sugar, Mr. Gardner?"

"I like it Indonesian style."

At last the general smiled, so Vern knew his comment about the tea, both flattering and knowledgeable, had not been wasted.

"Do you speak Bahasa Indonesia, Mr. Gardner?"

"Not as well as you speak English, General."

"No, no. I do not speak good," Sakirman protested with a smile of pride. "I did logistic training three months in States."

"I'm afraid the States has a bad press in Jakarta these days."

"*Jangan kuatir,* Mr. Gardner. To me you are not from States. You are architect from Sumatra. We do business man to man." That sounded as if the dossier had been satisfactory.

"I appreciate that, General."

Sakirman wasn't wearing a single decoration on his khaki shirt, Vern noticed. Most Indonesian officers gloried in medals. It was a good sign that Sakirman had the confidence not to wear them.

Tea came. Vern lifted his cup and nearly gagged on the sweet brew.

"To your taste, Mr. Gardner?"

"To my taste, General."

"Please tell me all of yourself, Mr. Gardner."

"Well, I'm an architect, but most of my life I've worked as a construction engineer." Briefly he described his two years in Malaya, his six in Burma and India. He had worked on anything that came his way: hotels, bridges, roads. Solid, practical stuff. Nothing fancy. Stuff that would hold up in a tropical climate.

"And what are your thinking of Jakarta's future?"

"Well, it has location—right in the middle of the east–west trade route. Of course, a lot depends on what happens to Singapore now that it's independent of Malaysia. The way I see it, there should be a tremendous increase in trade between Singapore and Jakarta because of that. But your country doesn't even need a free Singapore to make good at international trade. You're rich, General: oil, minerals, rubber, coffee, tobacco. What's needed right now, in my opinion, is builders like myself who can put things up so you can use everything that's under your feet."

Sakirman nodded with a smile. Vern felt that the little speech had somehow relaxed the general, who then spoke of Project Palm Tree, adding very little to what Vern already knew about erecting hotels on Bali no higher than a palm tree. Then without a change of tone or emphasis the general offered Vernon Gardner the post of chief architect. Just like that. Obviously the choice had already been made. All that examination of the dossier had merely been Indonesian obfuscation.

Vern wanted the job too much to make a temporary show of resistance. Without a glance at Larry, who always needed money and would take any job anytime, he accepted, contingent, of course, on financial arrangements.

Sakirman leaned forward and frowned. "One issue for clearing up, Mr. Gardner. There is matter of commission."

"Yes," Vern said guardedly. "Commission."

"For OPSUS Fund. I act with your behalf, sir. I have spoken for you."

"Yes, I am certainly grateful. You spoke on my behalf to the— board?"

Sakirman ignored the careful question. "Big project, big money. There is commission."

"I understand that, General. Now about the financial arrangements—"

"Commission for me. Is twenty percent."

Vern felt a smile fixed to his lips. He always felt this way when someone had him in a corner. "Let me understand. You want twenty percent of whatever I make?"

At last the general turned slightly to look at Larry Foard. "What both make."

"But we haven't yet discussed the financial arrangements," Vern persisted. "Or let me put it differently, General. How much does a twenty-percent commission amount to?"

"*Jangan kuatir,* Mr. Gardner," said the general. He then outlined the financial structure of Project Palm Tree; it would take Vern a long time to sort out its complexities. The contracting company for the project was PROPELAD, Proyek Perhotelan Angkatan Darat, the Hotel Project for Ground Forces. At least this made sense, because the actual sponsor was military—the Siliwangi Division of the army, Central Java Area. More than half of PROPELAD's profits, however, went to YADAPOS, Yayasan Dharma Putra Opsus, the Charitable Foundation for the Sons of OPSUS. Everyone from general to private belonged, and their shares were commensurate to their rank. Both

PROPELAD and YADAPOS were subsidiaries of MANTRUST, which confounded the situation, especially because the money supplier was BIN, Bank Industri Negara. This bank was owned by the army.

"*Mengerti?*" Sakirman concluded.

"No, General. I'm afraid I don't quite understand."

"Of no importance, Mr. Gardner. Please you understand this only. More you make, more we make." He swept out both arms to include the entire office complex of OPSUS. "*Jangan kuatir*. We all make. You will do very, very fine," he said patiently, as if speaking to a child.

"Blunt chap, wasn't he?" said Larry when they had left OPSUS and climbed into their car.

"I think he was blunt because he thought we were totally naive," Vern said, narrowing his eyes in the hot glare of late morning. "I'm inclined to believe what he said. When a man tells me he'll get a rake-off of what I make, I figure I'll do pretty good too."

"That's what you hope, chum."

"Don't you think he's been around the block? I do."

Larry withheld agreement.

Vern realized that the Cornish boatbuilder was smarting from Sakirman's contemptuous treatment of him.

As their car inched forward into steamy traffic through a blue exhaust under a flawless sky, Larry said, "The way I spend money is beastly. If I saved it, I could go back to Cornwall."

Vern laughed. He had heard this a hundred times.

"But it's true. I ought to chuck Asia and go home where I belong. I'm knackered by the heat and the hard work. It's bloody hard work, Vern."

Vern turned to him and for a few moments studied the little man's craggy face. "Larry," he said, "am I what you would call callous?"

"Are you what?"

"You heard me. Am I callous?"

"Would you give a damn if I said yes?"

"I'm serious."

"What in hell's wrong? Callous?"

"Tell me straight."

Larry thought about it so long that Vern wondered if he was going to ignore the question.

"Out with it," Vern finally said.

"No, I can't say you're callous. You're—"

Vern turned to the prominent jaw, the seamed forehead. "Well?"

"I think what you are is tough. Tough-minded."

"You had to think that through."

"Fancy I did. Because you could be taken for callous. You don't belong in a drawing room, old chap. Some might take you for callous. Women could."

"Do you think Maggie does?"

"Never implied that. What I mean is you don't care to show a bit of softness even if you feel it. Some women might take that for callous."

"But Maggie understands me." He waited for Larry to respond; the silence grew. "Do you think she does?"

"I think she loves you, old chap. Who knows what a woman understands? I just wonder if she's different from what you think she is."

"Which is what?"

"It may sound like a sod of a thing to say, but I think Maggie wants more than marriage."

"What more?"

Larry shrugged.

"I don't think you like her," Vern said.

"I do, I like her. But she wants more than being a wifey."

"I hope so."

"You say that, chum, but do you actually want a woman who is . . . who is . . ."

"Restless?"

"Yes, I suppose so." Larry added thoughtfully. "Yes. She's someone looking for something, without knowing what it is." He laughed uneasily. "That's a bit thick, isn't it. I mean no harm, old chap. You have to understand the psychology of a short man. It's hard for him to look up to a woman. And your wife is tall. Maggie's a grand old girl, but frankly to me she's a bit daunting."

"She's going out alone today."

"Why shouldn't she? Anyone who could live among those Sumatran people in the hills can take care of herself in Jakarta. You can't be callous and play mother hen at the same time, Vern."

After riding awhile in silence, Larry suggested a peg of gin and bitters. "Jakarta can make a bloke thirsty. What say?"

"We'll try the hotel bar."

"Toast the new job."

"That's it." Easing back on the seat with a sigh, Vern felt in balance again. Hotels on Bali no taller than a palm tree. A new adventure with an old associate. And back at the hotel was the woman he loved. Heat made people touchy, made them say too much, say things they didn't mean. Larry was only being a friend, though he didn't know what he was talking about. Maggie daunting? Larry had never had a permanent relationship with a woman in his life. What did he know?

Vern stared out the window and let Jakarta slip by in a rush of hot air: a city harsh and brilliant, like aluminum glinting in a waste of sand.

Seven

Within a week Maggie Gardner had formed an opinion of Jakarta: she hated its dust, heat, and glare, but loved its waterfront. After visiting the national museum, orchid park, and old town hall, she wandered south wearing a fatigue cap (taken from her father's army duffel bag almost two decades ago—the cap ragged and worn now, but still hers, still precious), its brim turned down. She strolled through the maritime shops that lined the docks; anchors stacked like rusted armor next to kegs of nails and coils of chain. Her jeans and white blouse caught the curious gaze of stevedores crouching in the lee of bulky hulls. On she went to the end of the final pier where Bugis people, renowned seafarers, unloaded timber from their ships. She had read about those famous ships: their teak planking secured only by wooden pegs; their skill at weathering fierce storms in the Java Sea; their ability to compete with modern ships of steel; the reputation of their Bugis masters for committing piracy when cargo consignments were slow.

She recognized from illustrations the square-bowed prahus. They had the look of seagoing birds that seem big-bellied and clumsy until airborne. There were pinisi schooners, smaller bagos, all of them thick, ungainly, until loaded to the gunnels, when their appearance changed and they gave the impression of sleekness and competence. Heading briskly out of harbor under billowy rectangular sails, they left thin, neat wakes. She wanted to be on them. Where she stood, following the progress of those sturdy ships toward the sea-lanes, so had stood pirates and admirals and viceroys and sultans. For centuries travelers had looked from this dock at clouds moving above them like birds in formation. Bird-ships on water, bird-ships in air. From Maggie's vantage point on the sun-swept quay certain things assumed a common identity: birds, ships, clouds, the things that slide toward a horizon of unreachable blue haze.

She was a young woman from Middle America on an Asian waterfront. Ships put out from here for the Spice Islands. She was where exotic words became reality. Tracy had been a girlhood friend who lived on a farm and got to school by truck. Now married to a farmer, she had three kids. "Tracy, remember when we sat in your father's toolshed and swore a pledge to see the world? I have been where ships set out for the Spice Islands." But she would never say this to Tracy. It would only make them sad that they hadn't seen the ships together, that their teenage dream had shot only one of them into the world beyond Iowa.

During those adolescent years, Maggie had nurtured an odd fantasy: someone was outside her room, behind the door, whispering. Although the words were indistinct, she understood the message was trying to tell her where she belonged.

At the moment she belonged on this waterfront in Jakarta, Indonesia, as she had never belonged in Iowa, where her mother had clerked in a store to make ends meet.

Her father used to demand that she listen to his war stories. In spite of drunkenness he had total recall of names, places, dates, and a gift for evoking atmosphere. When his alcoholic repetitions deadened the effect of war on young Maggie, she picked through his slurred words for images of beguiling places. Searching for the reality of such places, Maggie had come to the scene of her father's wartime experiences. It was here that she expected to find where she belonged. This was a conviction and a comfort, like finding Jesus the way some schoolmates had done after failed marriages and careers.

She had come here on a research grant to study the Minangkabau of Sumatra, a close-knit, buffalo-worshiping, matriarchal society.

Maggie had seldom traveled before coming to Asia, so she would never forget crossing Sumatra by air. From her window she looked down on zigzag threads of river conforming to the shape of gullied hills. Sometimes she caught a glint of metal through the massed greenery, suggesting a touch of civilization within tracks of jungle, but most of the miles streamed past without a sign of habitation. Perhaps God had put Sumatra down there and walked away. An odd thought for someone unsure of God's existence. Yet it had been a thought of hers during the plane ride. Puffs of cloud below looked so close to the ground that they seemed attached to it, like spangles sewn on a green gown. Tiny roads like spiderwebbing began to appear in the immense greenness. Would the land be as strange on the ground as it looked from the sky?

The plane landed at the seaside city of Padang. Driving in from the airport she saw a man and a woman pounding rice in a stone mortar with long teak poles. A gray-skinned buffalo was pulling a wagon piled high with huge spiky fruits she would learn were durian—bad-smelling, succulent, and very expensive. Red pompons were fastened to the traces of dokar horses; such gay and frivolous decoration was something she had never expected. The world her father had evoked had been full of mists and jungle and unseen things moving through shadow. Here were orange mailboxes like miniature houses.

At sunset that first day she walked on the beach; waves broke into splinters of yellow light and kids played soccer. Warungs were set along the shore, their benches under umbrellas. Stoves cut from oil drums were fed by gas cylinders; noodles and saté were cooked in immense woks. Islamic music blared on radios, each, it seemed to Maggie, tuned to a different station. She wandered along with squealing kids at her heels, delighted by her light-brown hair. Some of them, reaching up, begged to touch it, until she bent and let their small fingers squirm against her skull to the accompaniment of wild giggling.

Next day she left her hotel for the marketplace. There were hardware shops and clothing bazaars, but what especially fascinated her was the bird market: finches, turtledoves, macaws. That night at the hotel she ordered a Padang-style dinner: curried chicken, goat stomach, small eels. Without hesitation she ate what was put in front of her, although the fiery spices brought tears to her eyes.

Next day, instructions in hand, she contacted a Minangkabau colony in Solok, up in the mountains. She went to live with a widow whose large house testified to a cultural practice of the Minangkabau: husbands emigrated to distant lands, set up businesses, and sent back profits to supply their wives with showy homes. Maggie had a room of her own; all five women in the rambling wooden house did. The kitchen contained four refrigerators, only two of them in actual use. The family of women got along fine. A boy away at school returned for vacation. He was king for a day, but his ultimate destiny was to fulfill the demands of women.

Maggie spent three months in Solok. She met people, eased into their way of seeing things, honed her language skills. Her initial hope of doing valid research became a manageable goal. She had just decided to concentrate on kinship relationships within two clans in Solok and Bukittinggi when it happened: she awoke one morning feeling nauseated and hot, then cold, so cold her teeth clicked violently and her body whipped around. Malaria, the bad thing, had come into her life.

The morning that Vern went to sign his contract at OPSUS for the Balinese project, Maggie left by car for Bogor, a hill town thirty miles south of the swampy heat of Jakarta. Her driver talked incessantly as they ascended into the cool Parahyangan highlands. He was proud of having some English. Fortunately, he had stories to tell and never cared if she understood, much less believed them. The driver claimed that in spite of frequent attempts on his life President Sukarno had never been assassinated because of the magic riding crop he carried. This magic riding crop had been given to him by President Kennedy of the United States of America. As long as he carried it, Bung Karno was safe.

Maggie studied the driver in the rearview mirror. His somber expression could mean he really believed the story. Or he was a good actor.

Kebun Raya in Bogor—largest garden in the world. A guide took her through it. He showed her a tree with an immense root system;

if you cut the trunk, the release of cellular pressure made a whistling sound. There were fifteen thousand species of plant in Kebun Raya, including four hundred kinds of palm tree. She found herself ohing and ahing to please the little guide, who was obviously proud of Kebun Raya; actually, she was impressed by it too. She saw handkerchief trees, Dutch widow trees, almond trees. With him at her side Maggie strolled for two hours, pausing to study rambutan trees with gnarled trunks leaning over ponds, the thin fuzzy branches touching water like old women washing their hair. For a moment she thought of Tracy, of what Tracy might think of rambutan trees. She saw kenaris and sapots and mangoes and chocolate trees and flamboyants.

Returning to the entrance where she paid her guide, Maggie paused for a last look at the tropical greenery.

The guide said in English, "You are happy here, mademoiselle." (He had addressed her in this manner from the beginning, having claimed that his best foreign language was French.) "I see you are happy."

Maggie smiled at him. It was an odd thing for a guide to say, especially after he had been paid. "How do you know I am happy?" she asked.

"I saw it in your face."

Maggie was curious. "Did you see anything else?"

"You want to know about my country. Because you want to stay here."

"That was in my face?"

"It was, mademoiselle."

Well, maybe. Maggie wondered if her ohing and ahing had given him an exaggerated opinion of her enthusiasm. Or did he say these things to please someone who had pleased him? After all, she had tipped him well.

"So you must go to my place—Yogyakarta," he continued. "That is the real Java."

"Yes, I've read it is."

The little man waved his hand dismissively. "Books tell you nothing about Yogya. You must go there; you must see it. You cannot know it quickly. You must live in it. Come back to me before you go and I will give you names. A letter to my family. They will take care of you. And names of others. I know important people. I will give you what you need. Don't worry, mademoiselle, I will take care of it. Come back to me and I will write it down. Shall I do it now?"

Maggie shook her head with a smile.

"Will you come back? I will write everything down."

"You are very generous."

At the compliment he waved again dismissively.

Maggie turned and began walking away. At her back he called out, "You must live there, mademoiselle! Or you will never know!"

Maggie had intended going back to Jakarta, but the guide stimulated in her a desire to see more of Java without delay. She retained an image of him: a face weathered into an old map, eyes in deep folds, a mouth full of stumps. Sudden generosity of spirit—a professor at the university had told her to look for that in Indonesians. They withheld themselves, then without warning offered everything: advice, unlimited time, even possessions. She had just seen this tendency in a tourist guide. She had seen it a couple of times in Sumatra too, the sudden eagerness to share what was good. It was an endearing trait, and encountering it again was something to hope for.

She asked the driver to take her into the tea orchards of Puncak. They climbed steadily through a rugged pass into a land of hot springs, waterfalls, and hillside restaurants at one of which she ate lunch— spicy fish, fried témpé, and rice served on a folded banana leaf. She watched balls of mist slide into hollows and break apart, the white fluff ease into greenery. There was a strange beauty in the process. She wondered if her whole life had been a preparation for these moments in a hilltop restaurant of Puncak. It was as if the whispering voice behind the door had just whispered to her again.

She ordered a beer and was halfway through it, enjoying the sense of isolation that comes with mountain mists, when a tall man approached her table. Behind him was the sun that had broken suddenly through clouds. With sunlight at his back his face was a featureless shadow. Bowing formally, the man introduced himself. He was from Düsseldorf, a textile buyer, by the name of Hauptmann. He apologized for intruding, but there were few opportunities to meet Westerners here, so he had taken the liberty to come over and suggest a chat and naturally would understand if she would rather not.

Maggie hesitated. Impressed by his polite manner, she finally smiled. Hauptmann sat down. His ruddy face, turned now to the sunlight, revealed a man of perhaps fifty. He had a weak chin, a bullish neck, and his sandy hair, slicked down, had a part so keen it might have been made with a razor. They both praised the restaurant and the tea gardens, which Hauptmann tried to visit whenever he was in Jakarta, because, he claimed, they were among the most charming in the world. He called her "madame" and paused, obviously hoping she would identify herself as "mademoiselle." But she understood that he was not someone who would crowd her; in fact, as they talked, he seemed less interested in seduction than in conversation. His English was as precise as the part in his hair.

"So you are now in Jakarta. Not for long, I hope."

"Why is that, Mr. Hauptmann?"

"It is on the edge of explosion."

"We've heard that. But I haven't seen any signs of trouble so far. The waterfront is interesting."

"Jakarta is desperate, unhappy. Jakarta is like"—he paused, searching for an analogy; it made him seem intelligent to her—"a pretty woman who is unhappy. People do not believe her unhappiness because she is pretty."

"I haven't seen that much prettiness in Jakarta."

"You have not seen it with someone who knows." He smiled broadly, and for a moment she thought he might reach across the table for her hand.

So he was in fact trying to seduce her. It was time to straighten him out. "If Jakarta is really that dangerous, then my husband is right. I should be very cautious about what I do."

Hauptmann frowned.

"Do you think my husband is right?"

"Yes," Hauptmann said in a flat, disappointed voice. "He is right."

"But when we go to Bali, where he's going to build a hotel, we'll be out of danger."

"Yes. Out of danger."

In another minute, excusing himself, Hauptmann rose and left, but maintained enough civility to put down money for the beer he had drunk with her.

Maggie was not ready for the return trip to Jakarta. She had her driver go farther into the tea country. At an orchard she resurrected the boldness of her anthropological days by locating the overseer and telling him how interested she was in the operation; he responded by taking her around. He explained that the women pickers were able to collect eleven kilos of leaves in a single day. Maggie watched them in their conical hats bending over the bushes. Strong brown hands were pinching off tender leaves to stuff them into gunnysacks. By sunset these women would earn enough to buy a bowl of rice, some boiled vegetables.

"Why are all the workers women?" Maggie asked.

"Because they are more careful."

"Not because they work for less money?"

"No, no, no."

She wondered if her American bluntness had embarrassed him, because moments later he turned and drifted away.

Maggie stared a moment longer at the women, then went back to the car. On the return trip she felt less confident, less enthusiastic, and the reason was clear: in a foreign land it was easy to convince yourself that you belonged. Almost every moment brought its reward: the new, the strange, the beautiful. Then something could happen— as had happened in the tea garden when she watched the women labor at survival—that pulled you back from a place and you saw it for what it was, a strange country, and what you were in it, an alien.

It was almost dusk when they reentered Jakarta. There was no glare and the lack of it seemed to take an edge off the heat, but drifting up from the angry streets (still choked with traffic) was a terrific stench: garbage, urine, motor exhaust, charcoal smoke, the sludge of canals.

Maggie read the strident messages on banners strung across alleyways: IN THE NAME OF ALLAH ONWARD NO RETREAT. CRUSH IMPERIALISM. CRUSH MALAYSIA. And others in Bahasa: BERDIRI DI ATAS KAI SENDIRI (Stand on Your Own Feet). AMANAT PENDERITAAN RAKYAT (Message of the Suffering of the People). These Communist banners were red on white backgrounds.

A few kerosene lamps were already lit in the bleak depths of dilapidated shops. The sun hovered at the border of tin roofs, ready to sink below swampland on which five million people had spent the day. Jakarta: an unhappy woman. Maggie could still not agree with the German textile merchant that it was also a pretty woman.

At dinner that evening Vern talked at length about progress. In Asia, he claimed, the key to progress was an extended use of hydroelectric power: waterwheels to grind rice or irrigate padis or cut stones. For Jakarta to find itself it must have motorbikes. They were more dependable than buses in a place where a public bus system—where *any* public system—involved corruption the way pregnancy involves sex. Bikes in Jakarta would be a full century ahead of subways. He guessed the Japanese would supply the bikes—they understood marketing. Although Vern had fought against them, he had praised their business sense in hotel bars throughout Asia, enraging colonialists who had spent the war in Japanese prison camps. Of course, he admitted that thousands of bikes would pollute the air, cause traffic jams, and shoot the accident rate sky-high, but nothing could stop them from coming in; they were inevitable.

The drawbacks to progress never troubled Vern; what could trouble her husband, Maggie felt, was any sacrifice of progress to the public good. His faith in going forward no matter what the cost was so complete it often seemed to Maggie simply ruthless. Yet it made him formidable too, and she had always been attracted to disciplined men of strong convictions. One of her college boyfriends had been a finalist in the NCAA mile run; another had majored in ecology; and another has been a nationally known student activist. One thing about Vern: when he discussed progress in an opinionated way it usually led to intense lovemaking.

As it did tonight.

She was lying in bed naked when he came to her, his step ponderous and slow, as if desire made him heavy. She opened her eyes and smiled. Looking down, he told her her sex was beautiful. Maggie laughed. "Sweetheart, every woman's looks the same."

"Not true," he said, putting his hand on her hip. "Believe me." After a pause, he repeated with conviction, "Believe me, it's not true."

Maggie had learned early that most men take any occasion to let a woman know how experienced they are. She had lost her virginity at sixteen in the high-school parking lot and had been sexually active since then. But she let Vern keep his sense of erotic advantage and drew him down to her.

Later she awoke from a nightmare; a large shadowy figure had been chasing her down a narrow corridor of rambutan trees, their limbs reaching out to clutch her. Maggie looked at the window, seeing on its lower edge a faint rim of light blue. It was almost morning. She got up, sweating, and stood at the window. The shadowy figure must have been the German textile merchant. Turning to glance at Vern, she saw him as a large, pale curled-up fetus. It was too early for the record player, but Maggie had a powerful urge to play Bix. Perhaps "Riverboat Shuffle," a showcase for his cottony tone.

Bix.

She had seen a couple of blurred photos of him taken in the twenties, as remote-looking as his playing sometimes sounded. His hair had been parted in the middle; his eyes were set in a gaze that suggested he was looking right out of this world; his ears were pointed like an elf's; his cornetist's mouth seemed oddly small, adolescently pouted, the mouth of a delicate and brooding boy. There were so many legends about him, and Maggie knew them all. He rarely changed his socks, he frequently missed trains, he never got close to anyone, not even to Babe Ruth, who bragged about their friendship. He was a hopeless drunk like her father.

Perhaps at age fifteen she chose Bix for her hero because he too had come from Iowa—and had left it behind. She could think of no one more tragic. His musical training had been shoddy. Self-taught on the cornet, he never learned to use the correct fingering. He never learned to read music well. He never had the technical skills needed to compose large orchestral pieces. Yet he spent hours at the piano in an impossible dream of emulating the work of Debussy. In jazz he was a white innovator at a time when most creative musicians were black and unwilling or unable to share ideas with someone like him.

He died a self-acknowledged failure at the age of twenty-eight from booze and pneumonia. But in his playing Maggie had found a musical analogue to her own search for something beyond the girlhood life she had known in Iowa.

At the window she tried to make out objects in the street, but it was still too dark. Returning to the bed, Maggie sat awhile on its edge. Her eyes were on the broad back of her sleeping husband, but

74

her mind was filled with the memory of a solo from "Jazz Me Blues": the lilting treatment of eighth notes, the legato style, the controlled tone. Someone once said of Bix that he could make a horn sound as if someone were striking a huge bell with a hammer. Perhaps in different circumstances both her father and Bix might have been fulfilled. If they had tried harder? Taken other directions? Set more realistic goals? She felt a sudden urge to pledge herself to a goal, as she and Tracy had done years ago. But pledge herself to what? It was a feckless romantic notion that she got rid of by lying down and closing her eyes and letting the cool sweet air of approaching dawn lull her back to sleep.

Eight

Sjam took a becak to a lower-class kampong in western Jakarta. Shacks huddled against the banks of blue-black canals so choked with garbage that the sluggish water could hardly find a channel through it. Forming a kind of gritty mucus, the garbage stank of fish and urine and decay under glare that exposed everything. The kampong had a stark look, as if an old woman had been caught nude in her bath.

Sjam was sensitive to the appearance of this part of town. As a boy named Kamarusaman bin Ahmed Mubaidah, he had roamed these streets; he still knew them like the back of his hand. At one time or another he had been in most of the little shops along the way with their pyramids of eggs, mounds of spices, trays of dried fish, bins of rice, and twine-wrapped items of hardware dangling from the ceiling. He had stolen from these stores. He could have pointed out the easiest targets: that shop there with boxes of garlic and pepper; that one with bottles of fish sauce and tinned crackers. He had once stolen a red plastic bucket from this one.

His mother had done their laundry and slapped it down to dry on the galvanized tin roofing of a shack just like those he now passed. He hated this neighborhood for its memories of a gnawing stomach, of rats scuttling through the night, of a father hacking up life. Even now, as he walked through these streets in the dry season, Sjam could imagine the damp odor of earthen floors when the canals, swollen by rain, spilled their water into the warrens of western Jakarta, bringing the stench of disease and death. Nothing had changed. The smell of rot that was now only memory would fill his nostrils again once the rains started to fall.

But it was in this neighborhood that Sjam had always found his mistresses. They kept him coming back, those poor girls who were searching for a way out, just as he had once done. Through them he was reminded of the ephemeral nature of success, and each moment spent in their arms constituted for him a kind of warning. He had to keep his wits about him or back he'd come and live the way they did—at the edge, prey to humiliation, subsisting on hope.

Sjam came to a house somewhat neater than most along the dusty lane. A pot of geraniums sat on the windowsill. There wasn't one piece of laundry drying on the roof, which glittered like the sea in sunlight. He was proud of that single spotless roof, because the whole neighborhood knew that he kept the woman who lived here. She had promised to have her laundry done by a local Chinese washerman, to use some of her allowance for that purpose and thereby keep the roof clean. Long ago Sjam had decided that you could judge people by the look of their roof; a roof covered with laundry meant sloppiness below. Only this roof sparkled.

Pleased with that, especially because Endang didn't know he was coming today and therefore could have cheated on the housekeeping allowance by slapping laundry on the roof, Sjam rapped on the door. He heard a dog bark from the backyard in response. He rapped again. The sound he made was very loud for someone his size. He was conscious of being small even for a Javanese. His hatred of the Dutch had been compounded by the contrast between his small skinny body and their big muscular frames.

He continued to wait at the door, feeling uneasy, because eyes from nearby windows were surely watching him. What if she were out, enjoying herself in the stores? Or worse still, with another man? He tried the wooden knob that slid the door back. Secured, it merely rattled. He was acutely aware of sound: hammering, scraping, children crying, women calling, a tinny radio blaring out gamelan music.

Finally the door opened—slowly, in a cautious manner typical of the neighborhood—and her shadowed face appeared, the tip of her nose caught in a shaft of sunlight.

The door opened wide. Turning with a triumphant grin, Sjam glanced at the unseen eyes studying him from shacks across the way. In a ringing voice he admonished her for slowness in coming to the door. And when she apologized, explaining that she had been sweeping the backyard, Sjam made her repeat the explanation loudly enough for spectators to hear.

He had made love to her. That was his first duty. Then he gave her money; that was his second. Then she brewed tea and brought a bowl of noodles to him where he lay propped up in bed, his back against the peeling wall. He had been noting with satisfaction the cleanliness of the room. It was sparsely furnished with a cheap little bureau, a chair, a murky mirror, a calendar tacked on the opposite wall, but it was immaculate. He thought of the buckets of water she had to lug in here, the scrubbing she did on hands and knees, because her floor was wood, not dirt, not like the floor of his own childhood home. She had it better. So all the more reason for her to be scrupulously tidy in a house he paid rent on. Now he regarded her: a small, pallid young woman in a ragged sarong and half-buttoned blouse.

Endang had been a widow for two years. Her husband, a young army officer, had been killed in a guerrilla raid on 12 April 1963 during the initial phase of Confrontation. Thirty Indonesian commandos had unsuccessfully attacked the Malayan police station at Tebedu, in North Borneo. Her husband, treed by a tracking dog, had been shot by a Gurkha rifleman. One of the raiders who escaped had seen the whole thing.

Sjam, veteran of combat against the Dutch during the fight for independence, was somewhat contemptuous of the way Endang's husband had died—treed by a dog. Even so, he never admitted it, because, all things being equal, he rather liked her. Not the best woman in bed, not the worst either. And rather sweet. And above all, dutiful. Sjam judged her humility to be a measure of intelligence. He had had mistresses who thought they had won a kind of victory over him, once they let him take them to bed. That made them arrogant with neighbors, demanding with him. They were stupid. But this one had enough sense to know her place. It endeared her to him in a way. He watched her take the bowl to refill it. There was a prominent curve to her belly that looked suspicious to him. Was she pregnant? He had asked her that a few days ago, but she claimed to have gained a little weight because his generosity allowed her to eat better. That was like a woman. They flattered you whenever you got close to a truth they were keeping secret. She was pregnant, no doubt about it. And with whose child? He would have to get rid of her or let her have the child and pay for it. He didn't know which yet.

After eating a second bowlful of noodles, Sjam sat back and in a relaxed mood bragged about his success in business. He had told this woman that he dealt in foreign trade; the truth was he knew plenty about it, and in a sense he actually dealt in it, because he collected and sold information about illegal shipping transactions. That she rarely understood what he said only added to his pleasure in telling her. He knew his explanation of corruption wouldn't go any farther. He wouldn't have told her anything at all except that sometimes the need for secrecy weighed on his mind like a black viscous mass; he felt an overwhelming desire to tell somebody something. It was physical, like sex.

Casting around for a confidant, however, he had learned early they were hard to come by. He couldn't trust Pono, his assistant, any more than he could trust Communists and army officers, much less the various businessmen for whom he gathered data about shipments and customs procedures.

So now he told her about INKOPAD, the Army Central Cooperative Board, which was controlled by the Central Bank of Indonesia. INKOPAD had recently closed a deal with a Japanese fishing company to operate vessels in the Arafura Sea. Manned by Japanese crews, the ships would be captained by Indonesians. He knew some of the captains. Every one of them was a known smuggler. INKOPAD's joint venture with the Japanese was nothing but a way of smuggling in cameras, watches, and electronics. The first shipment was due next week.

Sjam laughed, while the young woman sewed a patch on a piece of clothing, pursing her lips in the effort to do it well. And that wasn't all, Sjam told her in his soft low voice. INKOPAD was getting an illegal shipment of vegetables and cotton from the country named Texas in the United States of America. It had been arranged by the CIA, according to someone he trusted. Sjam paused, awaiting her reaction, because everyone had heard of the notorious CIA, but she kept sewing as if the name meant nothing to her.

Content that she had no interest in what he told her, Sjam continued to tell her what some people would pay him to tell them. He knew the exact location of a deserted beach where the shipment of Japanese merchandise was going to be unloaded. It would be handled by units of Battalion 237 of the Siliwangi Division. Transport off the beach would be supplied by battalion lorries. The stuff would be stored in a warehouse ten kilometers west of Jakarta.

That's where Sjam came in, although he kept his own part in it safe even from the disinterested ears of his mistress. He had bribed the ship's captain to send him a bill of lading from Hong Kong, the ship's last port. Sjam sold this information to a Chinese agent for MANTRUST, a food supply company headed by Tan Kiong Liep and Sjazrief Margetan. Not many people knew (of course, Sjam did) that they didn't own the company at all, but simply managed it for the Army Logistics and Procurement Command. Now and then MANTRUST liked to deal in a little contraband, especially if the merchandise was expensive. With the bill of lading provided by Sjam, they could work out a price list in advance of negotiating with IN-KOPAD for the entire shipment of merchandise. So one military group was maneuvering to outwit another in a business deal.

Sjam laughed again. Corruption amused him. Whenever he learned of such things from informants, he usually smiled, as if they had just told him a joke. Sjam was shrewd enough to understand that perhaps his success at gathering information had something to do with his attitude—he didn't take things too seriously. He had an easy way about him. People talked to you if you weren't appalled or saddened or angered by what you heard. People liked to unload their secrets on someone who smiled.

Getting up, Sjam gripped the young woman by the shoulders and looked into her eyes. "Don't you do wrong," he warned her.

She shook her head.

The fear that he saw in her face reassured him. On impulse Sjam gave her a few more rupiah as a gift and felt vindicated by his willful generosity when she threw herself down to kiss his feet. He was also gratified at the doorway when she lowered her head in abject submission for all of them in the watchful shacks to see.

He picked up Pono at a cockfighting ring, which at this time of day was deserted. Pono so loved to gamble on the cocks that even when the vicious birds weren't there he spent long hours in the big shed alone, as if summoning up the memory of precious nights when its walls had resonated with the shouting of men like himself who came with fistfuls of rupiah, ready to risk a week's wages on a razor strapped to a bird's spur.

Sjam didn't like Pono, which suited him just fine. It was no good liking whom you worked with. Sometimes it could be fatal. You were lulled into trust; then where were you when trouble came along?

Pono was Sjam's size, and thin too, save for a round paunch that didn't seem to belong to his body. It gave him an unbalanced look, whereas Sjam liked order, even in appearance. Nevertheless, Pono was the right man to run errands and ask routine questions. He did what he was told because he always needed money to cover his gambling debts. For that matter, they both needed money—Sjam to maintain his family in a good neighborhood, to make repairs on his beach house, and to keep Endang (he had given up another mistress last month because of the expense). When two men working together were always in desperate need of money, they had the best chance of success. That was Sjam's philosophy.

"Find Colonel Latief," he told Pono. "You know him?"

"You sent me to him once. Commander of First Infantry Brigade. Heavy man with a mustache. I'd find him at the main garrison."

"Tell him I'll be at the warung at Jalan Jaksa. He knows the place. Tell him urgent. I'll be there waiting. Don't run off. There's more. Then I want you to go down to the docks and find Arief. Ask him when that Pahoka ship is arriving. The one with the bicycles." Sjam roamed through his memory for facts about deep-sea liners, barges, container ships, log carriers, oilers. He needed to know competitors, prices, schedules, and especially illicit cargo consignments. It wasn't easy gathering and supplying information. Often at night, when everything was quiet, he felt unappreciated. Few men had so much of the thick web of Jakarta in their minds as he did in his. He saw countless glittering strands where they saw only a thick rope. Someone who knew as much as he did ought to be paid more.

Looking at Pono, he saw a lack of comprehension in the dark slitty eyes. "The Pahoka ship," he repeated.

"The one with bicycles."

"If it's coming in tomorrow, tell Arief we must talk." Talk about the dope hidden in the rear tires of half the consignment. Dope targeted for West Germany on a ship loaded with cloves and rice, ETD next Tuesday.

"Or at least learn when it's due in."

Pono nodded and turned to leave.

"Wait," Sjam told him. "And go to the Wisma Trading Company and ask for Go Swie Kie."

"I don't know him."

"A Chinese, in accounting. He owes me money. Tell him I have waited long enough. Also tell him I have some information about a shipment from Singapore."

"What kind of shipment?"

"He'll know." It was a shipment of automotive parts with a dubious bill of lading. But Sjam never told Pono any more than was necessary. He was especially careful to exclude his assistant from arrangements made with Chinese cukongs. They were shrewd businessmen with known ability for turning assistants against their superiors. If he told Pono too much, one of these days Pono would be his competitor and a Chinese cukong the beneficiary of their discord.

"Any more?" Pono asked.

"Yes. Come see me at sunset." He meant come to his home and knock at the back door—like a servant. Sjam never gave Pono too many assignments at once. It helped him maintain in his assistant a certain measure of anxiety. As if tomorrow there might not be anything for him to do. "That's all," Sjam said.

Pono's thin shoulders hunched, his narrow face bobbed earnestly, and he was off on his skinny legs, hailing a becak almost before his assignment was fixed securely in a brain teeming with other things: bell-shaped cages with cocks waiting within and the ringside betting and birds tenderly removed and held out on display with feathers closely trimmed so the beaks of opponents couldn't get a quick hold when owners released them and they closed.

Finishing his third cup of tea, Sjam looked up to see a heavyset man with a mustache come into the warung. Colonel Latief was wearing a sarong and white shirt, but he maintained the square-shouldered look of a military man. Sjam had been doing business with him for a year, business in the sense of exchanging information. He never got paid by Latief. He got paid by other men who wanted to know what Latief told him.

Latief had fought in West Irian with a number of comrades who were now big shots on the general staff. Latief, an idealist, had never adjusted to the corruption of Jakarta. He had been overlooked for important assignments because of his ascetic nature. He continued to live by the ideals of the revolution and resented the big cars, fancy women, and high living that had corroded the principles of most officers who had emerged from the jungle into the bright lights of Jakarta. He was obsessed by corruption in the armed forces. He talked gloomily of old combat friends becoming "Jakartanized," using the English term that was fashionable among educated observers of Jakartan antics. He liked to ask questions, throwing them dramatically into the air: Where was pride in tradition? The honor of Java? That sort of thing. Sjam figured he was a little stupid, which of course made him valuable. Latief was a man who could be pumped for information without being given much in return. Latief was anti-Communist. He considered it his military duty to keep tabs on the PKI, and so when they met, Sjam hinted of PKI activities, say, plans for a demonstration here or there. He did it in a way that absolved him of blame in case the demonstration failed to materialize. But he always managed to learn from Latief something of army intentions within the city. This solid information was especially sought by Chairman Aidit, who paid well for it. Talking to Colonel Latief was a pleasure.

When the colonel was seated opposite him, Sjam ordered another tea along with krupuk, tangy misshapen biscuits that he knew Latief liked. Then, leaning forward, in his soft voice he described the Council of Generals and the chance of a coup. Yani and Nasution were apparently heading the council. They wanted to use Sukarno's health as an excuse for taking over the country.

Latief smoothed down his mustache, big fingers patting it anxiously. He wanted to know where Sjam had learned of the council. Sjam told him from Communists. Aidit hadn't wanted that sort of information disclosed, of course. But Latief would believe anything that came from the Red camp; he had implicit faith in Communist ability to ferret out secrets. Evil, in Latief's mind, was always efficient. Sjam had figured that out long ago and used it.

"When will this Council of Generals schedule the coup?" Latief asked.

"Perhaps on Armed Forces Day."

The colonel shook his head sadly. "On the day we should be celebrating independence, not destroying it."

"Yes. I agree." Sjam lit a kretek cigarette and blew clove-scented smoke into the close air of the warung.

"General Yani must be the spirit behind this thing," Latief declared bitterly.

"You think so?"

"He studied in America at Fort Leavenworth. He is an American agent."

"And a spendthrift," Sjam offered, looking out at people passing beyond the shop's zinc overhang. "And a womanizer."

Latief nodded gloomily.

"I was wondering"—Sjam paused until Latief gave him full attention—"would there be officers opposing such a coup?"

"*Would* there be? Of course there would be!"

"Then, perhaps—"

"I know Javanese officers who wouldn't stand for it!"

"For the honor of our country."

"Exactly! Yani and Nasution shoving aside our Beloved Leader of the Revolution? Replacing him with their cars and their whores? I know men who would rather die than let them get away with it. I know I would."

"Praised be Allah."

Latief leaned over his crossed arms to repeat that he would rather die right now, this instant, than let a bunch of corrupt general staffers clean their feet on the ideals of independence. "*You* fought for independence," he told Sjam. "You, of all people, know what I mean. You were there."

Sjam had used that shining part of his personal history to good advantage over the years. What he couldn't understand was the way some men continued to dwell on events long past. He lived in the present. And anyway, he scarcely recognized in today's Indonesia the country that had struggled against the Dutch.

"I know what you mean," he said. "The ideals of independence."

Latief lapsed into a brief period of brooding. Then he spoke of countering these traitors. They had to be stopped by the army itself—soldier against soldier.

Sjam took a drag of his cigarette. It was all going his way.

Latief smoothed down his mustache again. He said the enemy of Indonesia had two heads: one was Communist; the other was the general staff of the army. There must be a reckoning, and it should begin with the army, because everyone knew the Reds were untrustworthy, but the army should be the people's true defense, and so when the army failed, the nation failed too. First attack corruption in the army! Throw out traitors! Cleanse the army, first bastion of the people!

Sjam nodded, puffed, said nothing. He knew when he had opened the floodgates of self-importance in a man.

Latief leaned forward to speak from the heart. He began working through a list of officers who would oppose the Council of Generals.

Sjam smiled blandly. The eager colonel really was stupid.

"I will get Untung. We were in Battalion 328 of the Diponegoro Division. Paracommandos together in West Irian. Untung's a man of honor."

"Yes. Good."

Latief mentioned other names, while Sjam sat back quietly and smoked. Once Latief had unburdened himself of enough patriots to calm his nerves, Sjam suggested that they call a meeting and invite these men to it. He included himself so unobtrusively that Latief accepted his presence as a given in the attempt to plan a countercoup.

"Yani and his bunch will never, never, never succeed," Latief boasted. The idea of opposing the Council of Generals was for him almost as conclusive as carrying out its implications. "There are plenty of Javanese officers we can count on. Line officers recently posted here. A lot of them have been attached to raider battalions. They know the jungle. They have gone in there with shock units. They are army. We can stop Yani and his weaklings."

Sjam found this sort of rhetoric tiresome, but at any rate he learned the names of half a dozen officers who might head up a countercoup. It was something to work on. And he had maneuvered himself into attending the meeting. If anyone objected, he need only bring up his association with Battalion X at Yogya during the fight for independence. That never failed to bring a patriotic gleam to the eyes of veterans. Military men, he felt, were basically stupid. Smugglers were smarter, but they were difficult to handle. He preferred brave men like Latief who were obsessed by their reputations. None were easier to control if you appealed to their sense of honor. Nothing like a sense of honor to cripple a man's judgment.

Nine

They were getting ready for an OPSUS party in celebration of Project Palm Tree. Sitting on the bed, Maggie filed her nails and listened to Bix's "Dardanella." As he shaved, Vern spoke through the open bathroom doorway. "It's hard to see what they're celebrating. The project's not off the ground. I did some preliminary sketches, put them on Sakirman's desk, and two days later they were still untouched."

"Not everyone's gung ho like you, sweetheart."

"But I'm finding new lows of indifference here—or incompetence. It's hard to say which. I haven't even been assigned draftsmen, let alone architects or a single engineer. I've got bookkeepers from Logistics and Budgeting. They spend their time drinking tea in front of fans, telling stories about cockfights. Sweetheart, would you mind lowering the volume on that thing? I can't hear myself think." Except for a few show tunes, music left Vern cold, especially jazz, especially twenties' jazz. What Vern liked best was the nomadic atmosphere of hotel bars, where he could stand with other expatriates and solve the problems of developing nations. Maggie got up and lifted the arm from the record and shut the player off.

"Thanks." Vern smiled at her from the mirror. "Larry's found a girl."

"Naturally." Everywhere Larry Foard went, he found a girl; for him it was like finding a hotel room. Maggie had tried initially to get along with the shipbuilder from Cornwall, but when it was apparent that he viewed Vern's marriage as a betrayal of their mutual trust and the American wife as excess baggage in their wanderings through Asia, she had simply backed off, choosing—wisely, she felt—to avoid Larry rather than spar with him.

Vern came into the room, wiping traces of shaving cream from his square, dimpled chin. His worried expression caused her to stop filing.

He sat on a chair and told her about Larry's girl. She came from East Java and lived in a Muslim neighborhood and yesterday had seen three men murdered. They were Red organizers who had passed by her window with posters. Muslim boys on the corner had attacked them. One boy got a can of kerosene from a nearby warung and poured it over the beaten Reds. Someone lit a match. Then with roofing stanchions pulled from the warung the boys prodded the burning Communists into the street to protect the shops. "Cars drove around the bodies," Vern said. "Of course, sweetheart, you know why I'm telling you."

"The streets of Jakarta are dangerous."

"That's a funny thing about Asia. Life goes on at the same pace day after day and you get lulled into it, and it's not always easy to see everything giving way until all of a sudden—" He snapped his fingers. "I'm disappointed with Sakirman. The project's stalled. I can't see us getting to Bali for a month or two or even three. I'm afraid you're stuck here, sweetheart. In a place you can't take advantage of."

Moved by his concern, Maggie got up and kissed him on the cheek. It was one of those pecks that sometimes carry more feeling than deep kisses. "We'll have fun tonight," Maggie assured him.

———

Vern had told her what to expect: a lot of businessmen in army uniforms selling government licenses for a commission. In the drawing room of the suburban estate where cocktails were served, most of the men wore open-necked uniforms with cascades of service ribbons. Most of their wives wore the formal kain, a wraparound silk skirt, and the kebaya, a long-sleeved blouse of batik with a stole draped over one shoulder. Maggie might have worn a kain too, having been taught by a hotel maid in Medan how to wrap it from right to left (that was in Sumatra; here she noticed it was left to right) and to fit it about the waist and hips so that the inside bottom edge was slightly higher than the outside. Moreover, she had a lovely baju panjang, a long kimonolike blouse, of white organdy from Padang that would have been perfect in this crowd. But afraid to look showy—the wife of a new employee—Maggie had worn a modest Western frock.

Even so, she understood the impression she was making—tallest woman in the room, taller than all but a handful of the men. (Next day General Sakirman would rush into Vern's office and exclaim, "Your wife is very nice woman, very tall," in a voice of awed appreciation.) As Maggie was guided from group to group by one or another of the wives, she tried to stoop a little, holding her hand out awkwardly, feeling round-shouldered, her neck pulled in like a nesting buzzard. For a dismal moment she recalled those school dances back in Iowa: nervous girls lined up so that scared boys could select partners. At fourteen Maggie had slumped in vain, a thin, towering stork, and had lived in agony while the other girls, one by one, were taken to the dance floor. At sixteen, her frame womanly, Maggie had the pleasure of turning down boys finally tall enough to look her in the eye (though they lacked the courage to do it) as they mumbled their invitations to dance.

These Indonesian men were almost as timid. They regarded her with a veiled expression, their interest signaled by sidelong glances, a sudden but slight lifting of eyebrows, a tiny smile. Not until she met General Yani, army chief of staff, did any of them make an impression on Maggie. He was a florid, paunchy man who shouldered his way through the crowd, took her arm, and swung her around to face him. The atmosphere had been so cool and formal that his impulsive familiarity startled her. His eyes level to her throat—and staring below it at her breasts—he introduced himself. Maggie noticed that other people drifted away in deference to him.

"Do you think I am presumptuous?" He pronounced the word perfectly in English, obviously proud of its implications.

"Yes, General, I think you are."

Yani guffawed. "I am glad for you the president is not here tonight." He had not let go of her arm. "If he saw you you'd be in danger."

Slowly but firmly, Maggie pulled free of Yani's grip. "Would he whisk me away in a black car at midnight?"

"Bung Karno is not that way. He does not need guns of American gangsters to get what he wants. He would charm you into his car at noon."

"Charm me?"

"You have seen pictures of him smiling? I am told women cannot resist his smile."

"That's what you're told, General, but do you believe it?"

"I serve my president. So I believe everything about him that is good."

"Is it good to charm married women and whisk them away in your car, even if it's noon?"

Yani giggled, reached out to touch her arm again. But apparently he thought better of it and pulled his hand back. "You will be liked here," he said. When an aide came up and whispered in his ear, Yani said good-bye to Maggie as brusquely as he had gripped her arm.

That exchange with the ebullient general had been the best part of the evening for Maggie, who near midnight found herself alone in the garden and thoroughly bored. From the brightly lit mansion came the sounds of gamelan music and laughter, as the officers got drunk and their wives waited patiently to go home. Maggie had never seen such drinking in Sumatra, where people took Islam seriously. That was one of the best features of Islam in her opinion. Her father had taught her by the example of his own destruction to hate alcohol, although to test herself for signs of self-righteousness Maggie took a drink herself now and then. Since knowing him, she had seen Vern drink a little too much twice—tonight would make the third time. Vern was no alcoholic; Maggie felt she had earned the right to judge such things. But if he drank too much, Maggie would not—could not—make love with him. They had never discussed it, but there was a tacit understanding between them about drinking and sex. Maggie knew that he knew that if he pressed her after drinking, she would push him away. It was a confrontation they had avoided.

The midnight garden was cool as she walked along its scented paths.

In the middle of it, lit by kerosene torches, was a fountain, a tiny stream of water trickling from the mouth of a plaster Cupid: a corny but expensive image of Europe here in Southeast Asia. There was a bench nearby, so Maggie sat down and heard as if from a great distance the gaiety within the house.

A high-pitched voice came through the darkness in heavily accented English, "Do you enjoy this evening?"

Turning, she recognized Mrs. Sakirman, the general's wife whom she had met in the reception line. Mrs. Sakirman, coming into view from another path, was a fat woman with a flat, wide nose, and tightly curled hair worn close to her round head. Her half-moon eyebrows were penciled in, prominent as a clown's makeup in the torchlight.

Maggie answered the question. "I'm enjoying myself very much, thank you."

Mrs. Sakirman's thick glasses were glinting a flickering orange. "When it comes this hour, I like gin rummy or crap but not so much with drinking and dancing." She smiled broadly. "I am not done— is word?—for dancing." Then she asked Maggie a barrage of questions: was the hotel good? was it too noisy? was the heat of Jakarta bearable? was Mrs. Gardner able to eat spicy food? was she from south in States or the north? was she homesick? She tapped Maggie's hand for emphasis. "I must make you like with my country. It is difficult alone in other country. I know. With my husband in your country."

"I already like your country, Mrs. Sakirman."

"Jangan panggil saya Mrs. Sakirman, ya! Panggil saya Susanto."

"Very well, then—Susanto. You must call me Maggie."

They sat quietly for a while, allowing the silence to bind them together against the noise coming from the house. "You have children, Maggie?"

"I haven't yet thought about children. I'm still getting to know my husband."

Again the fat woman tapped her hand. "Waste of time with that," she claimed scornfully and in one phrase settled the issue of her marital life. "Better get children. I have three. Gone away now." She sighed heavily. "So I find things with to do."

"I understand."

"You like Jakarta?"

"I don't yet know it."

"You cannot like Jakarta," the fat woman declared. "You like my Java. All around Yogya."

Maggie recalled her guide at the garden, his pride in that city.

"All secrets are there," Susanto maintained. "You must see Yogya." Again she tapped Maggie's hand. "You and I. We go with Yogya and play gin rummy and I show you secrets."

"I hope someday—" Maggie began.

"Jakarta no good with you. Yogya good. Safe and full of happiness with you, I swear." She belched lightly. "You must go with me and see Yogya. Stay with my house. Listen to gamelan and play cards and eat gudeg and opor ayam and see what taste good. I insist. It is done with us then. End of week!"

Maggie smiled at the fat woman's enthusiasm; perhaps her own had the same outrageous quality: feckless, innocent, wholehearted. They would probably get along.

"Go with car but roads not good so I like train. You like train?"

"I like trains, but—"

"Ride all night, play gin, in morning go with my house in Yogya. It is done, Maggie."

The fat woman got up, adjusted the kain around her wide hips, and without another word ambled toward the house. "Men are boys. All drunk up there. I am host when they leave." Susanto paused to add over her shoulder, "End of week, Maggie."

An hour later they were going home by taxi. Vern took her hand in his and held it tightly against his thigh—a proprietary gesture.

"What was that all about?" His voice was a little slurred.

She thought he was alluding to the general (whatshisname) who had cornered her on the veranda. He had described Communist rallies whose sole purpose was to discredit the Islamic Student Association, of which his son was a proud member. And while lecturing her on the viciousness of the PKI, General Whatshisname had smiled oilily and tossed down two glasses of whiskey and in an abrupt shift from politics had suggested that they have lunch together in a lovely spot outside Jakarta. Leaning toward her, grinning drunkenly, he added what she might have suspected: that the restaurant was part of an inn with rooms; he knew the owner very well, a discreet man. At the time, Maggie had glanced around to see if anyone was watching this character. Perhaps Vern, standing with a group of officers, had taken a quick look at the man hanging over her like drapery. But apparently not. "What was that all about," he repeated, "between you and Sakirman's wife?"

"We had a talk in the garden."

"When we were leaving I heard her say, 'End of week.' "

"She wants me to go to Yogya with her."

"For how long?"

"We never got that far."

"Would you like to go?"

"Of course. Someday."

"Have I told you about her, sweetheart?" He explained that his salary checks were signed by an organization named PROPELAD. The Siliwangi Division of the army owned 60 percent of PROPELAD; Susanto Sakirman owned the rest. Through her family connections, PROPELAD got the loan to finance Project Palm Tree.

"In other words—" Maggie began.

"Our fate is in her hands."

"Well then, in that case I have to go." Maggie meant it as a joke, but no sooner were the words out of her mouth than she began to consider going with Susanto Sakirman to a city where "the secrets" were, where two people had sworn she would find the real Java and happiness.

But Vern diverted her attention from this odd possibility. He had learned tonight that President Sukarno refused to have a large stone removed from his only serviceable kidney because a soothsayer had once predicted his death by a knife. When Maggie laughed at such credulity, she felt Vern squeeze her fingers in mock disapproval. "Now don't you laugh, sweetheart. These army guys don't think it's funny. It doesn't matter if mumbo jumbo or a bad kidney kills Sukarno. If he dies, he's dead. Then the Reds could take over."

"Is there a chance of that?"

"Who knows? Right now he's all the stability this place has got."

"That's a bit scary."

"I hope he hangs on long enough for me to get my hotel built."

"Spoken like the man I married."

When he put his arm around her, Maggie turned to him in the

light flickering past the taxi window. He was grinning like the drunken general who knew a restaurant in an inn with rooms. She could smell the whiskey on Vern's breath. When he leaned forward to kiss her, Maggie moved so that his lips met her cheek. His hand over her shoulder reached down to cup her breast. Her body stiffened and twisted free. After a long, thoughtful silence Vern removed his arm. Then he let go of her hand held against his thigh. She retracted it like a snail going back into its shell.

They rode awhile before Vern said, "Maybe you should go with her. Jakarta is really off-limits to you right now. I was talking about it tonight. No one thinks you can get around safely anymore. Do you want to go?"

"I want to see Yogya, yes."

"Then here's your chance. You can get out of Jakarta and see something worthwhile."

"It's another kind of chance too—for us to be separated. Is that worthwhile?" Maggie glanced at him. Vern was looking straight ahead.

"Are you angry?" she asked.

He kept looking straight ahead. "No. Not really. You don't like boozy men and tonight I'm boozy."

She felt a gulf rising between them in spite of Vern's understanding, and it frightened her. To offset the effect, Maggie leaned toward him and went past his whiskey breath and thrust her tongue into his mouth so forcefully that he stiffened in surprise before meeting her passion with his own.

Ten

On a late afternoon in early September, as a taxi drove Vern and Maggie to Kota Station, he was recalling how Larry Foard had reacted to the news of her trip. "I think she'll be better off out of here, mate," Larry said happily.

"You make it sound as if she were going for a long time."

"It would be better," Larry argued, "if she stayed clear of Jakarta until they make sense of the situation. If you ask me, when there's a muddle out here—I'm talking about any big Asian city—there's an excuse for bad treatment of women, any women, but especially white women."

Vern had agreed. Now he was thinking of the record player that had been packed along with two suitcases. Would Maggie take it along if she were staying only a short time? They hadn't really discussed how long the visit to Yogya would last.

"What are you thinking about?" She took his hand as the taxi lurched through traffic.

"How much I'll miss you."

"I've been thinking we won't be together for our first anniversary."

That was next week. So she had thought of it too.

"I won't be a bride anymore," she added.

Vern turned to study her freckled cheeks, the brown hair dark around her neck where it was sweaty. He loved this woman. She hadn't had an easy time; there was in her the desperate self-reliance of someone who had struggled hard to get free of a grim childhood. In his decade out here he had known other people like Maggie; they had to keep moving; they suffered from the fear that something bad would happen to them if they paused, that the past would catch up to them somehow and grip them by the throat and pull them down into a mire of nasty memories. Maggie had done more than pause; the malaria had brought her to a standstill, and since then she had been idle and perhaps that idleness was working in her veins like a drug. He had seen signs of it: the long moments in front of a hotel window, the constant playing of those scratchy jazz records, the nervous little gestures, the abrupt thoughtful silences. Love had made him sensitive to her moods. Sometimes he felt panicky and humbled by his inability to locate her emotionally. He wanted this trip for her not only because of a smoldering political situation in Jakarta. He wanted her to regain confidence.

Yet he also begrudged her the trip. Vernon Gardner retained the conservative attitude toward marriage that his parents had given him. That residue of upbringing wanted him to say, "You're my wife. You belong here with me." And he was sure there was a part of Maggie that wanted him to say it.

When they got to Kota Station, he said, out of the blue, "Don't worry, sweetheart. Stay as long as you like." Vern saw that the suddenness of his remark, unrelated to anything they had been saying, puzzled her, but he didn't know how to tell her that he was just trying to be magnanimous, that it was a way of letting her know how much he loved her.

As they shouldered through a typical Asian station, filled with travelers clutching possessions of a lifetime in roped containers, Maggie seemed depressed.

Bored in a few weeks, she'd come running back with open arms.

That possibility, tinged with enough doubt to make it probable, finally swung Vern over to complete acceptance of the trip. He felt himself smiling. What the hell. Then as they shoved through crowds to the departure platform, he wondered how long she would be gone. The date of her return was like a sealed envelope neither of them wanted to open.

A man wearing a striped sarong and a white turban came running up to him. "So sorry," he said, breathless. "AC broke down. No AC, no sleepers on train. But Nonya Sakirman say you must go now without stopping, she say."

Vern turned to Maggie. "Afraid you'll cop out."

She cocked her head slightly and studied him. "Should I?"

"Do you want to?"

"Do you want me to?"

"Yes," he said instantly, aware that he wanted her to stay at any cost. "Get another train later." He gripped her arm. "Without AC it'll be terribly hot. Go another time. Go tomorrow."

Maggie slowly pulled free.

He could sense the intensity of her thinking, as if somehow she felt her decision was more important than either of them yet realized. But it was foolish of him to make melodrama out of a simple trip. He said nothing. He would not behave like a possessive fool.

"No," she said. "I'll go now. I said I would. You don't want a clinging woman."

"No, not that," he said, smiling.

"Come, come, please, Nonya," the servant pleaded, reaching for her suitcases. "Nonya Sakirman waiting!"

Hastily kissing her, Vern called at Maggie's tall, receding figure, "When are you coming back?"

Turning, she waved and gave him a little grimace. For an instant she seemed to vanish into an abyss of his mind, retreating from his world into a world of her own making. Vern nearly ran after her. As he watched her climb into the train, turn and wave again, Vern wanted to yell out, "Come back! Don't go!"

Once she had disappeared, however, he felt his anxiety fall away as a sense of heat falls away in the shade. Love did that, he thought. Made you scared of losing what you have.

———

From the train station he went to a late meeting at OPSUS. There were always meetings and at them musyawarah was practiced. Musyawarah meant amiable and constructive discussion, Indonesian style.

What it meant to Vern was delay and obstruction coupled to maneuvers involving graft. He was getting used to a tangle of unresolved expectations and false hopes when any project, his own included, was discussed. Formal plans were drawn up and feted, then laid aside. He watched daily a trail of graph makers and statisticians plod through the corridors: their task was not to map reality but to manufacture optimism by placing any situation in a favorable light. Officers postured among their peers and bragged to their inferiors and dreaded the least criticism from their superiors. They sat in outsized chairs and emulated their erstwhile colonial masters by complicating what was simple.

This meeting was held in a large conference room. Photographers attended, and Jakarta Radio recorded some innocuous speeches. Afterward champagne was served in a private room with gold-painted chairs and red-velvet drapes, while air conditioners rattled and chugged through the conversations. Because the project under discussion had to do with army purchases of rubber (for national security), Vern had been invited merely as a showcase foreigner. He was often invited for this purpose. The idea was to show military tolerance for Western expertise. Technology over politics. On the other hand, General Sakirman kept the press away from him at such meetings. Vern was to be seen, not heard, in this public-relations campaign managed by the army.

General Achmad Yani, the army chief of staff, was at the meeting and to Vern's surprise sought him out and shook his hand. Yani wanted to know everything about Project Palm Tree. His informed questions suggested to Vern more than curiosity—Yani must have a financial share in the hotel.

Abruptly the general took Vern's left forearm in both hands—an Indonesian act of enthusiasm.

"No more business, please. Tell me about your tall wife."

"She's gone to Yogya."

"So you are alone." Yani rolled his eyes in exaggerated longing. "You must miss such a woman."

"I do."

"But she is better there. Until we finish with Red agitators." He pronounced "agitators" in four distinct syllables, as would someone who has had a demanding speech teacher.

So the general, like everyone else, had confirmed Vern's decision to send his wife away. Yogya was safer, and visiting it would give her something to do until the project took them to Bali. But something was wrong.

That's what Vern was thinking while he sat in the hotel dining room. He had drunk champagne at the meeting and then a number of scotches at the hotel bar. He had drunk too much, which is why he leaned forward and talked to an elderly Australian couple sitting two tables away.

He said to them, without prelude, "I see the time coming when Hong Kong and Bangkok and Jakarta will be filled with as many skyscrapers as New York. Coolies will have TV sets. Apotiks will carry drugs as sophisticated as any we can get. They'll have what we have, along with a sunny climate."

The Australian woman said quietly, "And they'll have their glorious past."

"I think," said Vern without hearing the slur in his voice, "they'll give up their past. Except as a tourist attraction."

"Why in the world would they do that?" the old woman asked, shocked.

"To make room for progress. You'll see."

"I surely don't want to see."

"But you will. You can't hold it back. They do what they want in spite of Western ideas of culture. They don't have the leisure to worship a past that didn't do a damn thing for them anyway." He watched the old couple frown grimly. "I sent my wife to Yogya."

They stared at him, assessing the reaction he might want for sharing this news with them.

"I miss her," he added.

The woman nodded with a smile. "Of course you do."

"Have the two of you ever been apart?"

"Never," the man said coldly.

"Only once," the woman corrected her husband with a look at him that could mean the separation had been important.

As if asking for the answer to an unstated question, Vern said, "We were to celebrate our first anniversary in a few days."

"Well, then," said the woman, "you can celebrate it later."

"She took her record player along. That's her prized possession. If she took it along, whether she knew it or not, she meant to stay awhile. Just how long, of course, I can't say. Was it a mistake to let her go?"

"Did you agree to it?" the woman asked with interest.

"I encouraged it. There's nothing for her here in Jakarta."

The woman smiled. "Well, then. You see?" She made an expansive gesture with her hands, as if everything had been explained.

But something was wrong, Vern thought. He got up and wove into the bar for a nightcap. The light was purplish, a sickly glow that poured over bamboo chairs and tables. He sat down at an empty table and ordered scotch from a boy in a Sumatran turban.

"I say, sir, would you mind terribly if I joined you?"

Vern squinted at a little man wearing a Nehru jacket, a pince-nez on his sharp dark nose, a Congress cap. Before Vern could say anything, the small Indian pulled up a chair.

"Name, sir, is Nagarajan. Sorry to be awfully forward, but it seemed rather silly to drink alone."

That was true. Vern introduced himself.

Nagarajan disposed of his personal history with the rapidity that Vern had come to expect of Indians abroad. The man was a spice merchant from Madras who dealt chiefly in cloves. The world's best came from Sulawesi, he claimed. Then he was talking about murder. He had seen Lee Harvey Oswald and Jack Ruby on Singapore television, not when the one took the other's life, not then, although he had heard that particular murder had been captured on film, but he had seen them separately, in handcuffs.

Also in Singapore he had seen *A Hard Day's Night* at the cinema. "Do you enjoy the music of these fellows, the Beatles? I find it flighty."

Vern hadn't yet heard the Beatles. He said, "Yes, flighty."

"I have heard of American discotheques," Nagarajan continued. He was obviously pleased at having his judgment of the Beatles confirmed. "I have heard of the Frug, the Watusi." He was counting them off on his fingers. "The Monkey, the Funky Chicken. Have you seen those dances?"

"I haven't been stateside in a long time."

"Or go-go girls?"

"Sorry."

Nagarajan sighed. He moved on to space flight, praising Edward White's twenty-minute walk outside of Gemini 4. In Nagarajan's opinion this was a product of Western ingenuity in the sciences. Credit must be given.

Vern smiled, acknowledging it had been received.

Martin Luther King had just headed a procession of four thousand demonstrators with a petition in his hand, Nagarajan said. America had learned a good deal from Gandhi, hadn't it? What did Mr. Gardner think of that? And what did Mr. Gardner think of the race riot in Watts, Los Angeles? The fingers went up, the counting began: 35 dead, 4,000 arrested, $40 million in damage. What did Mr. Gardner think of that?

To shift the onus of stating opinions from himself to the Indian, Vern asked about India. How was India doing?

Pressing the pince-nez hard against his nose, Nagarajan leaned forward as if to deliver a statement of exceptional importance.

"I am a member of the Dravida Munnetra Kazhagam," he said. "Allow me to explain, sir. The DMK is devoted to the belief that our Tamil way of life in the south is fundamentally different from that of the Hindi-dominated north. *Fundamentally*. We believe in the purity of our language. What, please tell me, is the purpose of language if not to be spoken with elegance? As it was spoken by that great orator Dr. S. Radhakrishnan, whose faultless command of English was an inspiration to us all!"

"You certainly speak it well yourself," Vern said politely.

Nagarajan beamed. Then his face grew dark as he finished off his drink. "The DMK will uphold the language of the south, sir, no matter how many northern troops are sent down, no matter how many of them come with guns into our very homes! Our bedrooms! We agree to English as the common medium. Indeed we do. We shall not oppose *that*. But we shall never submit to Hindi. We shall never speak it. *Never!* We shall never speak Hindi!"

Nagarajan was breathing hard; Vern truly feared he might have an attack of apoplexy. But the outburst seemed to have cooled Nagarajan off. He lapsed into a brooding silence, so Vern paid for his own drinks and left.

I am drunk, he told himself. It surprised him. He knew how to hold his liquor, but here he was staggering. As he passed the front desk, a clerk motioned to him. "Sir. Mr. Gardner. Can we be sending up to you now?"

"Sending? What?"

The clerk said in a low voice, *"Kupu malam."*

Butterfly? Night butterfly? Vern was still trying to figure that out when the clerk bent closer. "Girl," he said.

"Girl? What made you think I wanted a girl sent up?"

"She is already paid for, Mr. Gardner."

"Paid for? Who could have possibly—"

The clerk handed him a piece of paper. In a large scrawl were the words "Until we finish with Red agitators and the beautiful lady can come back you must do the best you can."

So General Yani had arranged for a night butterfly. It was an act of kindness, Indonesian style. And, of course, from a shareholder in Project Palm Tree.

"Who offered this gift was very generous," Vern said to the clerk, "but unfortunately I am very tired." When the clerk looked confused, Vern added, "Perhaps you can find another accepter of the gift."

This suggestion did not puzzle the clerk. He nodded and smiled.

"Good night," Vern said thickly. Unsteadily climbing the carpeted stairway, he met the elderly Australian couple in the hall. "Hello, there!" he called out gaily. "Good night! Good night! Beastly hot today, wasn't it! Please don't think I hate the glorious past. I just ignore it, and you should too. You know what is *everything*? The future!"

He was ready to stand there swaying and promulgating his theories, but the tall Australian man, eyeing him coldly, brushed past. "Rather warm, yes. Good night."

Vern watched them turn the hallway corner. They were going to their room. They were going to remove their clothes, those two old people who must have spent half a lifetime together. They would climb into bed and maybe sleep with their arms touching. Wasn't it remarkable what people did?

Vern spun into his own room and flung himself on the bed. When he closed his eyes, he felt like a cored apple, reamed out. What did everything mean, the planning and building? He imagined dark-skinned laborers scrambling up bamboo ladders propped against palm trees. Hotel no taller than a palm tree. He felt the bottom drop out of that vision. Why had he drunk so much?

Because of Maggie.

He had lived essentially alone throughout his adult life. There had been women, short-term affairs, nothing like a year with any of them. He missed her already. So he had got himself adolescently drunk.

Love took something out of you. It reamed out whatever it was that made you independent. He was in the middle of another revelation when the light in his head disappeared.

He awakened to a scream of traffic. A fly was busy at his dry lips. A fierce beam of sunlight fell against his eyes. A new day in Jakarta had begun. When he got to his feet, Vernon Gardner squinted at the window and discovered the rest of that revelation. He drank too much because his love for Maggie had unsettled him. He didn't know how to deal with it. And when he drank, she felt for him a definite revulsion. This had not been a grinding daily scene, but between them they didn't need a lot of fighting to know something was wrong. They weren't that way. They could tell with a shrug of the shoulder, a dark glance. Perhaps if he hadn't drunk so much the night of the party, he might never have suggested she go to Yogya with Susanto Sakirman. He had felt Maggie's revulsion for his touch and had reacted to it by telling her to go. Could such a small incident have ongoing significance? Perhaps with them it could. Perhaps somehow they were shaky together.

Going into the bathroom, he stared at a pallid face, bloodshot eyes. Drawing himself up self-consciously, as if to make a declaration, he spoke to the mirror. "Vernon James Gardner, you let your emotions make a damn fool of you. You've taken your last drink." He vowed that from now on when he stood at hotel bars with cronies, he would drink soda water.

Eleven

When Susanto Sakirman claimed they'd play gin rummy on the train ride to Yogyakarta, she meant it.

Before they even reached the suburbs of Jakarta, one of the servants (she had brought three) had whipped out a folding table and set it up in the coach between Maggie and Nonya Sakirman. It looked very modern in the old German-built bogie that must have served this railroad, Maggie estimated, before she had been born, before her parents had been old enough to even think of the act that would bring her into the world. The folding table was covered with green felt. They might have been sitting in a Las Vegas game room instead of a hot, dusty, springless old coach rattling through the Javanese darkness.

Maggie had never been much of a cardplayer. But had she possessed skill, likely as not it wouldn't have been enough to match Susanto Sakirman. This was obvious from the first moment Susanto handled the cards. Her pudgy fingers riffled them with the staccato quickness of a machine gun.

"We keep running score, dear," Susanto explained. "Is one rupiah per point good with you?"

For three hours, while they jiggled into the humid night of Java, Maggie picked up and discarded. She guessed at what the stock held, attempted to build sets, while hearing her companion's brisk "Gin!"

Fortunately there was refreshment. The servants, a man and two girls, kept spiced peanuts coming and iced fruit drinks from thermoses and sugary little cookies. Food could break Susanto's concentration on the cards. "Wait to taste Solo and Yogya things!" she exclaimed while wolfing down a cookie. "Nasi liwet, a salty-sweet rice, dear. And ayam goreng made Yogya way. On sidewalks of Solo they are selling srabi manis. In English—custard? Rice custard on cake and coconut on top." Sweat poured from her face as it did from Maggie's in the stifling heat. Sweating seemed to bring them closer. Susanto could perspire like a Westerner. The dark hands and faces of the servants were as dry as bone.

Cards got tiresome, but Susanto showed no sign of flagging. The more she won the fiercer she became. At the armpits of her blouse were crescent moons of sweat; the batik ridged out along the contours of her pleated flesh. Often her glasses misted up, so she had to rub them dry with a handkerchief. Maggie went to the bathroom a few times. Only the first trip was necessary. The swaying walk to the cramped lavatory freed her a short while from the rat-tat-tat of Susanto riffling the deck.

"Gin!" Susanto was bending over the notepad to record another victory when sluggishly the train braked and shuddered to a halt.

In the ensuing silence Maggie realized how loud the ride had been. Peering through the open window, she saw a nighttime landscape, a slant of moonlight across what seemed to be a field.

Susanto sent her manservant out for news. He returned with a story about a breakdown—or was it sabotage by Communists? His third explanation for the delay involved bandits.

Susanto nodded grimly, closed her eyes, rested her head on the rough seat, and almost instantly began to snore.

Maggie looked at her. Without a word of complaint, Susanto had willed herself to sleep. Maggie noticed other passengers doing the same. In the next row the three servants were turning to get comfy against the hard upright seats. They were like kittens, eyes closed, bodies pliable.

Maggie remembered her mother trying to get comfortable on the couch at home after work. She would throw her neck back against the lace doily; her eyes would stare woefully upward; her stiff skinny body would writhe as if on a bed of live coals. "It was a terrible day today. Ten minutes after they opened the doors, the store was packed full. The linen sale did it. People charged right in and they were everywhere you looked, picking. The way they were, I can't believe I held up for ten hours. Some of them were so nasty if people who knew them had seen them they would be mortified with shame. And they wouldn't buy either. Or they'd go to Nancy. They'd say I wouldn't help them and give me a huffy look and go to her. They'd grin over at me while Nancy took their order, and after all the time I'd wasted on them. Of course, you know Nancy. She loved it. If you knew how my feet felt, and my eyes, the throbbing in them, and a headache going right through the top of my head, you'd appreciate how utterly dead I am. And the worst of it is I can't rest. I'm too exhausted to rest." And she was: with her head thrown back, her eyes staring out of the sunken sockets, her shoeless feet splayed out like those of a corpse on a battlefield.

Maggie found herself listening idly to the hiss of steam outside the window. Maybe it was the thought of her mother that depressed her, as if she had left something important undone without knowing what it was. Or not her mother but Vern—the way they had parted. He had told her, quite coolly, to stay as long as she liked. Once the idea of going to Yogya had taken a firm hold of her imagination, Maggie had wanted to go, but she had wanted to go reluctantly. At the last moment Vern had asked her to stay, but until then he had encouraged her to leave. Was he tired of her? No, she knew he loved her. But perhaps too much closeness had made him nervous. He always said he wasn't used to it. There were people who needed space, and Vern had always lived as though he were one of them. So this separation was probably good for him. And it gave her something to do.

Restless, she got up and went to the vestibule. When her eyes grew accustomed to the darkness, Maggie stepped down. She felt gravel beneath her sandals, a warm breeze on her face. Alongside the train other people were standing or strolling. A few were trying to look across the field.

"Would you want a cigarette?"

Maggie turned to see a man near the carriage. Moonlight cascaded over its roof, hiding his face in a burrow of shadow.

"Tidak, terima kasi," Maggie said.

The orange bead of a burning cigarette zagged from the shadowed side of the carriage. "You are English?"

"Tidak."

"You speak English in coach."

"I'm American," she admitted.

She heard an intake of breath, as if that impressed him.

"You are traveling with the rich fat woman?"

At first Maggie didn't feel like replying. The man's tone was insolent. Yet she said, "We're traveling together."

He stepped from the shadow. Maggie was surprised by his youth and size—younger than herself, perhaps twenty pounds lighter. He came no higher than her shoulder. That relieved her. There had been a hint of menace in the gruff voice coming from the darkness.

"You go to Yogya?" he asked.

"Yes, to Yogya."

"On holiday?"

"Well, in a way."

"Foreigners do not take holiday anymore in Java."

"Did Communists sabotage the train?"

The young man laughed, then drew on his cigarette. The glow illuminated a pair of wide-set eyes, a sharp little nose. He looked clever to Maggie.

"Perhaps they did, perhaps not. What do you think?"

"I think it isn't as dangerous as some people think."

"I think you are correct. Trains from Jakarta to Yogya always breaking down."

"Where did you learn English?"

He waved his cigarette in a grand gesture, insouciant but proud. "Jakarta University."

"I thought maybe abroad."

"You think money for abroad is easy?"

"I meant you speak well enough to have learned abroad. Do you understand?"

"Of course I understand," he said contemptuously.

The long silence between them was filled by the hissing of steam. Maggie wondered if she should go back inside, but it was terribly hot in the train. In spite of his rudeness, the young man interested her, so much so that she stepped closer and gave them each a chance to stare at the other's moonlit face.

"Do you live in Yogya?" she asked him.

"I go there to work."

"What do you do?"

"What do I do?" he said in a mocking tone; his English was skillful enough to bring it off. "I organize."

She waited for an explanation; when none came, she asked him what he organized.

"People. What did you think?"

"Yes. Thank you." Maggie stepped toward the train, determined to go inside and leave his rudeness behind.

"Wait," he said, as she put her foot on the step. "I organize for Partai Komunis Indonesia."

Maggie turned toward him.

"PKI," he said. "Third-large Communist party in world."

"Yes, I know."

"You have lived long in Java?"

"No, but for a year in Sumatra."

"I organize for land reform in villages," he explained with pride. "You understand the land reform?"

"Not as well as I want to."

"Why do you want to?"

"Because it has to do with your country."

"Why do you have interest with my country?"

"Because it has a long history."

He laughed scornfully. "Is that good reason?"

She had tossed off her answer, and he had caught her at it. "And there are other reasons."

"Good reasons?"

Three children, bored by waiting, ran alongside the field, slinging

108

pebbles at one another while two women yelled at them from the train.

Maggie glanced at the irritating young man. The bead of orange in his hand glowed rhythmically when he puffed on the cigarette. Obviously he smoked too much, but of course most Indonesians did.

"I use USIS Library many times," he said abruptly.

"I heard it was a good library when it was open." She needn't tell a Red that Sukarno had closed it because of Communist demonstrations against America.

"I am glad it is closed."

Maggie said nothing. The rice field extended beyond moonlight into a roiling misty distance. No wonder the Javanese believed in ghosts, she thought. They lived in a landscape of fog and moonlight.

"May I ask you?" the young Communist said.

"Ask what you like."

"America has six percent of world population, but use one-half of world resources. I know my facts."

"I see you do."

"Half of world resources. But six percent of world population. Is that fair?"

Maggie said nothing.

"You are wasteful people. You have too much."

"Perhaps so. But we work for what we have."

"Ha!"

Again they lapsed into silence.

"Why have you interest with my country?" he asked after a while, pursuing the unanswered question.

"It's different from my own. I'm curious about what happens here. I've studied it in school. I've lived with people in Sumatra in the hope of understanding them." Maggie paused. "That's the best answer I can give you."

"You have no interest with your own country?"

That was one way of putting it, Maggie thought. She had lost all interest in the farmland of Iowa where her father failed at odd jobs and her mother clerked for peanuts in one grubby store after another. But she couldn't explain that to an Indonesian Communist. "My interest now is in your country."

"Not like you, I never lose interest with my own country."

"Then you are fortunate." Unsure of his understanding, she added, "You are lucky."

"Yes, I am lucky. Indonesia will be great nation under PKI someday. We will make it world power and return to United Nations." He spoke the words as if they were memorized. There was another silence. "Will you kindly please exchange names with me?" he asked next. The sudden formality of his request surprised Maggie. It gave him another dimension, an appeal that his rudeness covered up. Perhaps rudeness gave him confidence to do things. She understood that. In college she had often been rude to hide her uncertainty.

"My name is Maggie."

"Ali here." After a pause, he asked, "Are you Nonya Maggie?"

"Yes, I'm married. But call me Maggie. *Jangan panggil saya nonya. Maggie saja.*"

He giggled at her accent, but complimented her. "Not many *orang asing* speak Bahasa. Why do you learn?"

"I told you. I'm interested in your country."

"Why did America support Belgian in Congo? Why do America support Malaysia? Malaysia is neo-imperial pawns of British."

"You embarrass me by asking things I can't answer."

"You are honest," he observed quietly. Again they were silent.

A man came along from the direction of the locomotive. He was talking to people beside the track. Maggie strained to hear what he was telling them, but it was in Javanese.

When the man reached Ali, they spoke briefly. Then Ali laughed.

"What's happening?" Maggie asked.

"Trouble was broken— I don't know English word. Something break in engine. They fix and will be starting again."

"Do they blame it on the Communists?"

"Not this time, I think."

"Then so much for sabotage. For a dangerous train ride," Maggie said.

"You do not fear my country?"

"I didn't say that. Your country is not too peaceful right now."

"Because Muslim landlords starve the peasant."

"I've heard people say because the army and the Muslims and you Communists are at one another's throats, and because of money and

110

trade and the Third World and the thing happening in Vietnam and world politics."

"Stop! Stop!" He lifted his hands in mock horror.

She could see him smiling even as she was smiling at him.

"May I kindly please really call you Maggie?"

"If I can call you Ali."

"Will we be together again?"

"That's possible. We're both going to Yogya."

"Then I hope so."

"So do I." She climbed aboard. No sooner had Maggie sat down than the train gave a kind of metallic burp and edged forward.

Susanto awakened instantly. Taking the silk hankie from between her big breasts, she dabbed at her sweaty face.

"My deal," she said briskly.

Maggie would not have time to wonder what Vern was doing. Did he miss her? Did he enjoy being alone? But she knew he loved her; that was certain. And out there in the night, flowing past the iron sides of the train, lay a fogbound mysterious country that was drawing her into its darkness like a long, hot tunnel. She hoped to meet Ali again.

"Play!" commanded Susanto.

Maggie turned to the cards.

Twelve

What she didn't know, Ali realized, was that he sat three rows behind her on the right. Where he could observe her. She couldn't know. Otherwise, wouldn't she turn and glance at him? From his vantage point Ali could see her as she bent over the card table. He had a view of her neck, her right ear, her right cheek, her nose. He couldn't see her eyes, but remembered them in the moonlight: set wide apart, large. They must be blue.

He could see a trickle of sweat along that right cheek. She had to have blue eyes.

When he was eight, Dutch soldiers had attacked Yogya. They wore paratrooper boots so large it looked as if they were bringing in huge gouts of mud from the jungle. The troopers had sweaty faces, just like hers, and blue eyes, just as hers must be. Yet they had stared angrily at the people lining their march down Malioboro Street, whereas she had smiled at him in the moonlight. Maggie, Nonya Maggie, had smiled at him.

This tall American woman was honest. Unlike most *orang asing* she hadn't agreed with everything he said from a sense of superiority.

She had talked with him. She had even admitted embarrassment because of her political ignorance. Honesty. Her neck was long, white. The hair above it, looking crumpled now from sweat, was the color of padis after harvest. Small right ear. It seemed too small for such a big woman. She was broad-shouldered and tall. So tall. He had heard men describe the colonial days when Dutch women got out of cars at the Residence. They exposed massive thighs under their cotton frocks. Sweat dripped from their long, fleshy noses. Their bare arms shook like mounds of rice carried in a procession. But Maggie wasn't fat. She wasn't ugly or annoyed or demanding.

Neck, ear, cheek, nose. And when she twisted slightly in contemplation of her cards, Ali had a brief glimpse of her full-lipped mouth. Such big, ample women, did they feel the thrusts of small men like himself when making love? He imagined himself mounting her, of her hand guiding him in. But then her vast fingers losing him altogether, so that she called out in alarm, "Where is it?"

A vile idea. He blinked to rid his mind of such a contemptible image. It left him feeling guilty and dispirited, but then another thought steered him back to a good mood. This was true: he had acquitted himself well when they talked. He had told her what he thought of her country. On Heroes Day, the tenth of November, he should take her to the celebration of Indonesian troops who died in the 1945 Battle of Surabaya. He'd stand with her in the crowd and explain how, at the end of World War Two, the British tried to hold Indonesia for the Dutch. Because that was how colonialists thought. Even if a place didn't belong to you, you held it for someone whose colony it had been. You never considered the idea of giving it back to the people who lived there. And if Maggie looked at him quizzically, he'd add, "Because keeping what isn't his is what the white man calls his burden."

And he would insist on her listening to more, while the festive crowd swirled around them.

Patiently, very patiently and calmly and reasonably, he'd explain the British desire to hold Indonesia until the Dutch could recover sufficiently from the war to resume control. Back would come their imperialistic troops to Javanese shores. Everything would return to normal. The country would be exploited as it had been for three hundred and fifty years. Because wasn't that the Christian way?

She wouldn't argue either, that tall, honest woman. She'd hear him out because that's the way she was.

"Maggie," he'd say—not Nonya Maggie. "I want you, Maggie, to look closely at the crowd gathered here at the Sultan's Palace. They've come to celebrate their freedom. Twenty years ago, people like them nearly annihilated a veteran division of British troops at Surabaya. But they still had to fight four years against the Dutch before getting truly free. They broke through the oppression of three and a half centuries. That's the sort of people we are. That I am. Our men are virile, no matter how small." Would he say that last thing? Well, why not? Satisfied with his imagined boldness, Ali took a nap.

When a trainman came through the bogie shouting "Yogya!" he awoke instantly and looked in her direction. The servants were packing the empty thermoses, folding the table. The fat woman was peering at a notebook, adding up numbers. Maggie never once glanced back, so of course she still didn't know that he was behind her, did she? She was trying to untangle her sweaty hair with a comb.

When the train stopped, Ali decided to wait until she came down the aisle before he left his seat. That way they would see each other as she passed. She'd wonder about how closely he'd been watching her all these hours.

But when the train entered the station, Ali got up with his battered suitcase and raced for the vestibule. While the wheels were still turning, he leapt down and strode rapidly through the murky dawn. Ali hunched his shoulders to make himself less visible to anyone—for example, Nonya Maggie—who might be looking for him.

As he left the station and searched through the waiting crowd for his brother, Ali glanced back fearfully to see if the tall foreigner might be coming out. He didn't want to meet her again, at least not here at the station. After all, there was no need to exchange insipid smiles across a sea of porters, and his brother, Bambang, might be in a surly mood if he were introduced to a Western woman without time to prepare himself for such a surprise.

"Ali!"

He turned to face Achmad, his brother's good friend. Edging forward, Achmad pushed aside becak drivers who were jostling for position in front of the departing passengers.

"Ali!" Achmad was waving. Ali felt relieved that Achmad was wearing civilian clothes. It wouldn't look good for a new organizer for the PKI to be greeted familiarly in a public place by a sergeant of infantry in uniform.

Ali glanced again over his shoulder to make sure Nonya Maggie wasn't coming along. He was so impatient to escape from that possibility that he hardly returned Achmad's greeting. As he moved rapidly through the crowd, he asked the soldier where his brother was and Achmad reported that his brother had a big order at the foundry.

"I was coming into Yogya today, so I said I'd meet you. No, we don't need a becak," Achmad told him when Ali raised his hand to signal a driver. "Look what I have." He had stopped at a motorbike parked near the station entrance. "I bought it last week."

"I thought you army people were complaining about pay and here you buy something like this."

"I saved three years for it."

Soon they were roaring away from the station, with Ali having a glimpse of Maggie at the curb alongside the fat woman and three servants and four porters groaning under a load of luggage. Ali despised the annoyance he felt, but he felt it—Maggie never even looked around for him. She was talking to the fat woman. Ali noticed that she didn't grip her handbag in the fearful way most foreign tourists carried things (vexed, he had watched them in Jakarta). But perhaps she wanted to appear at ease because she knew he might be watching her from a distance.

As Achmad drove down the main thoroughfare of town, Ali imagined the tall attractive woman clutching her handbag *fearfully*. She'd be afraid that these Javanese savages would rob her; his image of colonial superiority so infuriated him that Ali Gitosuwoko resolved never to speak if they met again.

Holding his suitcase with one hand, he circled Achmad's slim waist with the other. Puffs of bluish smoke shot out of motorbike exhausts all along the street. Tinny wails from revved-up bikes had Malioboro Street vibrating like a struck tuning fork. Achmad gripped the handles of his new bike tightly, his elbows tensely angled—the nervous look of ownership. When the immense square around the Sultan's Palace broke them out of traffic, Achmad relaxed and brought his elbows in and half turned to say over his shoulder, "Coming to the village now?"

Ali explained he must first go to his uncle's house.

"Bambang said you were here for vacation."

"No, for work." But Ali withheld any further explanation. It would simply embarrass both of them if he, a Communist, talked about his plans to Achmad, a soldier. Courtesy required him to treat his brother's close friend with deference, although Ali knew that one of these days he might have a confrontation over politics—right in the village—with this sergeant of infantry.

They were driving past the Sultan's Palace, and the stucco of the kraton walls, flaked off in patches, was streaked an ugly gray where monsoon rains had funneled through declivities in the surface. But the palace looked as big and imposing as he had remembered it. The Gitosuwoko family used to spend half the year here in Yogya, half in the outlying village. Whenever the family returned to stay in Yogya, Ali had always run to the Sultan's Palace for a long look at it. This had assumed the importance and sanctity of a secret ritual. Seeing the kraton standing there, its walls high and solid, Ali had been reassured that the world was still in place, that everything was as it should be.

Now he stared at its deteriorating walls and fought down a sense of awe. A new era was in the making, and this palace did not belong to it. Better that its walls cracked, split, fell apart in ruin.

From over his shoulder Achmad said, "I will be in Jakarta next week. The 454th Battalion is going there for Armed Forces Day."

"You'll bivouac in the city?" Ali asked politely, but without much interest in the reply.

"At Halim Air Base. We've been assigned to the Honorary Palace Guard of the Cakrabirawa Regiment."

Ali grunted his approval, although that didn't interest him either.

"Our battalion served under Colonel Untung in the West Irian campaign. Didn't you know that?"

It would be rude to say he had forgotten. "I didn't know."

"Colonel Untung commands the Palace Guard. It's a very great honor."

"Yes," Ali said. "You'll probably see the Presidential Palace," he suggested, trying to show interest.

"Maybe Bapak too. Maybe we'll hear him speak."

Ali didn't tell this country soldier that he had heard Sukarno give many speeches, and that for him it was no longer a stirring experience, because he knew all of the Beloved Leader's rhetorical tricks.

As they drove south of the kraton and its streaked walls, there was even less and slower traffic: fewer bikes and becaks, but more horse-drawn andongs and creaking gerobaks pulled by oxen. They were approaching the Gitosuwoko family kampong, a district well known for batik factories.

In Jakarta Ali lived proudly in a slum. Whenever he had visited Yogya since joining the party, he had been ashamed of the bourgeois character of his family's neighborhood. He felt a growing sense of shame as the district hove into view. The closer the blood tie, the stronger the guilt: that is what old Communists had told him in explanation for their own detachment from family.

Ali told the soldier to stop. "I'll walk from here." When he climbed off the bike, Ali held his hands, palms touching at eye level, in a respectful sembah.

Achmad returned the gesture.

"You have come to work," Achmad said, his eyes narrowing. "For the Communists?"

"Yes."

"Where?"

"In the village."

"In my village?"

"In our village. That's my assignment. To work for land reform."

"We know nothing of land reform," Achmad declared.

"That's why I have come. To help with it."

"I said we know nothing of land reform."

"Then you will learn."

Again, simultaneously, their hands went up in sembahs. Formal. Without enthusiasm.

When Achmad rode off, furiously gunning the motor, Ali watched until the bike faded into a distant swirl of dust. Last time they'd met, nothing so tense had occurred. But of course the situation had changed. The Red Offensive, as Ali and other cadres called it, had begun. Military people like Achmad would either heel under or be destroyed; that's what the militants in the PKI felt, and although Ali

117

hadn't yet accepted all their ideas, he was leaning in their direction.

Turning, he stared down the side road that led homeward. On this very road, so dusty and narrow, he had often bought kueh lapis after school. He did so now, stopping at a warung that also sold jars of petrol. Biting into the sweet rice cake, Ali studied the woven bamboo walls of an old shop and the gate of a brick house beyond it. Behind that gate were fruit trees that he and his friends used to loot years ago. A rich Batak from Sumatra had lived there. When he gave chase during the boys' theft of fruit, they had yelled back at him, "Dog eater!" Many times Ali had hoisted someone or had been hoisted over the brick wall, panting in an ecstasy of lawlessness.

Just now some boys were coming down the lane, eyeing him suspiciously. Sure sign they were up to something. Two carried large objects covered by cloth. Clearly they had fighting cocks in cages and were afraid of being stopped. A campaign in Central Java was afoot to prohibit the sport. The boys slowed their pace, as if that would proclaim their innocence.

Ali smiled. They frowned back. "Fighting cocks?" he asked pleasantly.

The five slid alongside a shop wall, staring balefully at him.

"I used to grow some big roosters," he told them as they edged past. "They got so big because I knew how to feed them. They did best on unhusked rice. Or you powder the husks and mix them with rice. Corn's no good. Forget about that. Their lungs won't develop if you feed them corn. They'll tire out quickly in a fight."

The boys were past. Only one turned to give him a quick glance of disapproval.

Ali chuckled, but somehow their unfriendliness disturbed him. Before Father died, Ali had always felt uneasy when going home. But of course his father had been a famous man, and people compared you to him and whatever you did was never good enough. Father, the greatest dalang of Java, had ignored what people thought. He had smoked with artistic friends, fasted in meditation until the flesh withered on his proud face, turned his back on the practical world, and when the time was ripe had simply and quietly died.

The house was a block away now. Ali turned into a dirt lane. Along the eastern row of shops, away from sunlight, the air was morning cool. From a window came the sound of a gamelan instrument. Some-

118

one was practicing on a gender, the small xylophone strung on resonators. The musician forgot to dampen a metal bar after striking it with a padded hammer, so the sound reverberated wrongly—a rumbling echo instead of a distinct note. Probably a student, a boy. Ali had no musical ability, but he knew when others did. Whoever played that gender had none.

Neither Ali nor his brother, Bambang, had ever shown artistic talent. That was why Father had ignored them and placed all his faith in a younger brother of his, Budi, who was now a great dalang in his own right: Kyahi Dalang Budi Gitosuwoko. It made Ali's blood boil. He couldn't pronounce his uncle's name without feeling his birthright had been stolen from him. People defended Budi, saying he was a man of goodwill, but such protestations only inflamed Ali. He knew the truth! His uncle had robbed him.

Ali came to the end of the lane and turned up another. He stared at an old house with a weedy garden. This house had been here since Ali's childhood, with the same garden, perhaps the same weeds. Behind the house was a grove of bamboo, where it was said a panaspati lived, a fearsome ghost. The panaspati's head was where his genitals should be. He walked on his hands. Fire spurted from his mouth when he tried to spit. He liked to eat young boys. If a boy wished to prove his bravery, he'd run through the grove. Ali had done so, but in great fear and only once. His brother, Bambang, had done it many times—walked slowly through the grove, hands in pockets, whistling. Even then he had been powerfully built. Everyone figured the panaspati was afraid to tangle with him. It earned him the nickname "Bima," after the great warrior of romance who never spoke elevated Javanese to anyone, not even to the gods. The foundry that Bambang worked at was even called Bima's Place by people in the village.

Ahead was the wooden fence, the broken gate of home. Father had never bothered to repair it. As long as Ali could remember, the hinges had creaked, the rusty catch had jiggled loosely. Home was the unchanging past.

_____

Behind the gate stood a big jackfruit, a scraggly group of palms, some flowering bushes. The yard hadn't been swept in a long time; under Ali's feet the leaves crackled. So Uncle Budi was as disdainful of order as Father had been. At least that was the impression made on visitors. People told Ali, "Your uncle doesn't want anything changed. This is to honor your father. To repair and improve it would be wrong. That would be competing with your father. That would be outdoing him. Budi wouldn't think of it." Ali knew better. Uncle was either lazy or miserly. These were the only true explanations for letting things go.

Sunlight struck in the trees, splintering the unswept yard into patterns of blue shadow and clay earth. This was home yet not home, Ali felt. Before reaching the veranda, he made a vow: if Uncle put the dagger between them, he would refuse to kneel and touch it.

Generations had observed this practice whenever someone in the family returned from a long absence. The headman would put his kris on the floor. The returning member would touch the blade with his fingertips. It had been done for as long as Gitosuwokos had had a history.

But today was different. Ali had come home to change things. Tomorrow he'd begin organizing people in the ancestral village. How then could he follow the outdated rituals of a priyayi family? He was committed to the future. He mustn't kiss the heirloom of a family that had lived feudally for centuries. He was a cadre of the PKI. He had come home on the business of a new society.

Satisfied with his resolve, Ali went into the house. The first thing he saw was an old chest. Framed over it was a black-and-white photograph of his mother. A small emaciated woman, she had been dead ten years now. Tuberculosis took her. He could remember her blood-stained handkerchiefs. Now he just stared at the thin figure draped in batik finery, the dangling gold earrings, her long, black hair in double loops festooned with jasmine. Hair that looked too heavy for her. Her face was frozen in an expression of utmost control. Control: the dominating quality of her life was captured in the photo.

Ali padded quietly through the house. He smelled the faint odor of kerosene dumped on last night's coals to reanimate the fire so the cook could boil some breakfast rice. Boil it for Dalang Budi, the present master of the house, a thief of honor. Passing the bedrooms, Ali saw a carpet of light at the open rear door.

Once again he paused, this time to study a leather puppet pinned to the wall.

Like the best dalangs, Father had made his own puppets. Ali had often watched him fashion them from cured buffalo hide. Stripped to a loincloth (he was smaller and thinner than his much younger brother, Budi), Father had worked in the little shop behind the courtyard. First he flayed the hide until it was thin as paper, then cut the silhouette of the puppet with awls and lances. He incised the face, then gashed in the openwork. He painted the figure, covering it with costly gold leaf, because Father, however ascetic and parsimonious, never spared expense in making his puppets.

As a boy, Ali had squatted in the shed entrance to watch Father attach sticks of buffalo horn to the figure. The horn was slick-looking, almost translucent. Father split the main stick down the middle, so that half extended on each side of the puppet. Other sticks controlled the hands. When Father held up the gilded leather by its pearly sticks of horn, Ali had always wanted to shout for joy, but never did. Aside from telling jokes during performances (when called for by scenes with the clowns), Father never smiled, much less laughed or clapped his hands with pleasure. He was called Kyahi Dalang, Venerable Puppeteer.

Now a new dalang occupied the house, a thief.

Standing at the rear doorway, Ali regarded a little pavilion in the inner courtyard. Under its slanted roof of thatch, on unpolished boards, sat the present dalang, his uncle Budi. Cross-legged, he sat in meditation. He wore a dark headdress, a lurik jacket, a cummerbund with kris tucked in the back, and a batik sarong: the ceremonial garb of a priyayi gentleman. He was practicing breath control. Ali could see the broad chest pulsing slightly after long, motionless intervals. Uncle Budi's eyes were fixed at some point beyond the edge of the pendopo.

Ali squatted in the doorway, suddenly awed in spite of himself. The man sitting cross-legged might have just emerged from ancient Java. He seemed to be carved out of stone within a space of the morning air. A few birds strolled along the floor, oblivious to him.

Uncle Budi was not old—perhaps in his early forties—yet, Ali believed, he was an anachronism at a time of social change.

Ali wanted to rush out and yank the man into the year 1965. Instead, he squatted, waited. He couldn't disturb the dalang at meditation.

At last, with a long sigh of resignation, Ali accepted the truth. When the meditation ended, he would walk across the yard to the pendopo. He would slip his sandals off and crawl onto the floor. He would address his uncle in Krama inggil, the most elevated Javanese language, and he would kneel, waiting.

When his uncle reached back and took the kris from its sheath, Ali would crawl farther into the pendopo, eyes lowered.

And when the sinuous acid-etched blade lay on the floor, Ali would lean forward, head pressed against the warm boards. Reaching out, he would touch the cool steel with his fingertips. He, cadre of the Partai Komunis Indonesia, would do this.

And he would hate his surrender.

Thirteen

Maggie Gardner had always thought of herself as adaptable. To get through college she had been a waitress, a census taker, a dog trainer, a file clerk, a floral assistant. At home, from early teen years, she had dealt with a depressed mother, an alcoholic father, a wayward sister who was now God knows where. But nothing in her experience had prepared Maggie for being the houseguest of Susanto Sakirman. She wondered if she was up to it.

The house itself was splendid. It consisted of a sprawling one-story building and half a dozen pavilions set around a large courtyard. Three served as guesthouses, one of which Maggie occupied. Hers faced a garden, rather carelessly but luxuriantly planted in the Indonesian style: hibiscus, bougainvillea, clusters of sunflowers beyond the dappled shade of vine-swathed banyan trees. In the mornings she awoke to the smell of jasmine.

That first morning, still exhausted from the train ride, she had been coaxed up by Susanto, plied with strong coffee, and shoved into a car. She was taken first to the Sultan's Palace. Buildings in the kraton were built low to the ground, Susanto said, because of fréquent earthquakes. There were nine entrances, symbolizing the nine orifices of the human body. She didn't know which orifice was which, Susanto admitted with a smile meant to be wicked. Behind three yellow doors were the private quarters of the sultan, who was now touring Europe. Royal heirlooms were kept inside: manuscripts, jewelry, ceremonial daggers. Gamelan instruments, centuries old, were housed in pavilions. Bronze gongs, xylophones, and drums were sitting there in dusty silence. Susanto bowed to them, as if they were icons. Aged male retainers strolled around the compound in court attire: a sarong, a skullcap of dark batik, a dagger worn at the small of the back. Susanto lowered her bespectacled eyes when they passed.

Back home, after lunch and a short nap, Maggie was summoned to the game room for cards. Susanto had a roulette table in there. Proudly she described its attributes: "Fifteen feet by twenty feet, dear. Correct European size. Wheel is teak." She had a faro table too, and a craps table. It was a veritable casino. Three other Javanese ladies showed up that afternoon, all of them as intense and knowledgeable as Susanto. Maggie lost fifty dollars, U.S., and would have lost more had she not pleaded a headache and gotten the hell out of there, leaving at the roulette table four little women with brocaded seledangs hanging from their shoulders. A male servant spun the wheel, calling out in French, *"Faites vos mises!"*

Next day there were cards in the morning, roulette in the afternoon, and more gambling at night. Maggie developed a real headache. Studying her closely, around two in the morning, when the other players had left, Susanto promised a different kind of day.

After a few hours' sleep, they set out for the batik factories, because Susanto claimed, "Next to kraton is batik most important in Yogya."

As they drove along the dusty lane, Maggie caught sight of a man who looked familiar. He lifted a gate latch, then stepped forward and pulled out a pack of smokes.

Ali.

Though she had seen him only in moonlight, Maggie recognized the young Communist by the way his shoulders hunched when he lit a cigarette. Sticking her head through the open window, she called out "Ali!" and waved, but he just stood there, staring, until the car turned a corner.

Susanto asked who he was.

Maggie explained they had met during the breakdown of the train. She didn't say he was a Communist organizer.

"Be careful to who you talking to," the older woman warned, but added, "He coming from dalang house. Is he of family?"

"I don't know."

"Of family, good. Dalang is famous man. People come from all Java and see him. If boy of family, good. Could not be son, though. Dalang have no boys, girls. Could be boy of brother or someone. If family, good. But please, dear, not wave if you not know." She softened her command with a pat on Maggie's thigh.

When the car pulled up in front of a batik factory, the building looked like the brick houses in the kampongs south of the palace. But inside was a showroom of fabrics: bolts of cambric and silk; finished sarongs and blouses; and piles of machine-printed napkins, place mats, tablecloths.

Susanto moved down the aisles to inspect the goods with the same intensity she gave to cards. She told Maggie it took a long time to make fine batik—six months to a year. The cloth was finely hemmed, washed, soaked in compounds, dried, pounded with mallets; then a design in wax was drawn upon it, dye applied, the wax removed, another dye applied, more wax put on and taken off, and so on. Everything was done laboriously by hand.

Susanto snapped her fingers. "One mistake—all gone." Picking up a piece of linen, she held it up to the light. "Good Yogya batik," she said appraisingly. "Both sides same. See? Print with machine, one side got color stronger. This better, real. Cost plenty." It seemed to please her as much as a straight flush.

They walked into the factory itself where a dozen seated women were drawing designs in wax on cloth. Along the walls were vats of hot water where the waxed cloth was dipped. Looking up and politely sembahing, a woman offered to show Maggie how the work was done.

Maggie watched her create a pattern on cloth with a small copper stylus called a canting, its basin filled with melted wax. The woman explained how the cloth was first dyed with indigo, then with a brown bark substance called ting, and finally with a combination of the two, which resulted in black. These were traditional colors; today other colors, made from chemical dyes, were also used.

Later Susanto whispered that the woman who had explained the process was the wife of an important official. Half these workers were not paid but came to practice the art of aristocrats. Priyayi women liked to do batik "to waste time."

"You mean, spend time," Maggie said with a laugh.

That evening, when Susanto had another group of women in for gambling, Maggie begged off. She went to bed early. Moonlight pooled across her naked thighs as she lay on the warm sheet and listened to Bix at low volume. She had never played a musical instrument. There was no hidden desire in her to emulate creativity. To enjoy and to understand were enough for Maggie. She was the perfect audience: grateful, enthusiastic, tolerant, humble, and committed. She lacked envy of someone who could do what she could not. And yet that voice was always behind the closed door, whispering a message she could not understand, something urgent and provocative and wise and terrible.

———

In the dream she couldn't find him. She ran through the lowland fields into the wooded hills of Samosir Island, then beyond the last saddle-roofed Batak house to a rocky headland where birds alone lived. They circled, black and threatening, while she searched everywhere for him. Then suddenly she noticed his hands clutching the side of the cliff. Vern was hanging by his fingers above a sheer drop into Lake Toba. It was so far below that she couldn't see the water, but she heard the surf breaking. Bending down, she looked at his outsized fingers bulging from tension. She tried to remember something specific about those hands, but couldn't. They were big, as hard as wood, and frightened her. Yet, reaching out, she touched them, and they wriggled softly with a wormlike motion. She wanted to touch them again, but couldn't. Whipping off her sarong—for that's what she wore—she threw one end to him and told him to grab it. Then she tried hauling him to safety by the rope of her sarong. Glancing back, she noticed a crowd had gathered to watch her. People from the hotel: a clerk, a waiter, some others. And she was naked. She kept hauling, frantically. She was naked and they were watching. She was naked and they were watching. Naked and they were watching. When she yelled for help, there was silence.

The dream thrust her suddenly into wakefulness. She lay blinking

126

rapidly at the wall. A lizard darted across it like a green crayon thrown by a child. Her heart hammered.

Exhausted, Maggie dressed slowly and went to the main building. Susanto was having coffee on the veranda.

Maggie sat down beside her and poured a cup of thick kopi tobruk.

"Sleep well?" Susanto asked pleasantly. "We play late last night. I won."

"I slept very well, thank you," Maggie lied. "Susanto, I want to study batik."

Susanto nodded, as if expecting the decision. "I have car taking you. Say I send you. *Jangan kuatir*. Factory take you in."

"Instead of the car taking me, could I bike there? Could I rent one?"

Susanto peered over her glasses. "Servants have bike. Why you bike?"

"I need something like that to do."

"I get you bike. *Jangan kuatir*."

"You're very kind to me."

"Javanese trait," Susanto declared proudly.

Before leaving for the batik factory that morning, Maggie wrote her husband a letter. It was chatty and carefree. She made fun of her decision to study batik: "Will I turn out artsy-craftsy? A big sloppy woman in an apron who's always making something that looks just right for a gift shop?" She told him how much she loved and missed him. But having finished the letter, Maggie read it over and hated it. There was very little in it of her, nothing of him, nothing of them together. She had not found words true enough. There wasn't heart in her this morning to search out what she felt deeply. It was as if she were floating on the surface of a vast ocean, while beneath her lay uncharted zones that she refused to dive to. But Vern should have word from her, so she'd mail the letter. She would do better next time. Because this time she had failed him.

Fourteen

Wobbly on the unfamiliar bike, Maggie pedaled down the lane into the warming air of a sun-filled Javanese morning. A truck, dominating the narrow road, forced her to the side. Otherwise she had nothing to worry about except a few horse-drawn dokars. Suddenly the slim figure of Ali appeared again. He was wearing a sarong and sandals; a blangkon covered his small dark head.

Maggie stopped in his path. "Do you remember me?" she asked.

He stared at her.

"I think you remember me. On the train that broke down."

"Yes."

She put a foot on a pedal. "You don't want to talk to me." She pushed off.

"Wait! Kindly please!"

Maggie stopped and glanced back at him.

"Come with my house. I have coffee." He smiled appealingly. Waving at the lane, he said, "Just there is the house. Kindly please come to have coffee."

Minutes later they sat in a pendopo within the courtyard. Beyond the sloping roof a circle of sunlight seemed to be burning the ground, but within the pavilion the blue air was cool. Maggie loved this feature of Indonesian life: the open-sided pavilion offering shade; the comfort it gave anyone who came from blinding sunshine into its sanctuary.

She watched Ali order coffee from a servant. He then made clear that his uncle lived here, that he was only visiting. The servant waiting on them was not his. He sounded bitter, as if he felt the servant should be his. Maggie would not have expected such possessiveness from a dedicated Communist—at least not in theory.

"I am glad you came," Ali said after a long silence.

"You weren't going to speak to me."

"*Tidak mengerti*. I do not understand, Nonya."

"I'm Maggie. You weren't sure you wanted to talk to me again." Not wishing to embarrass him further, she added, "Have you begun work?"

He had not. Everything went slowly in his country. He must start by visiting the villages daily, paying homage to local officials, having tea. He must not mention land reform until people accepted him again, for though he had been raised here, his years in Jakarta had made him a stranger to these people. But his work was vital for the future of his country. Even though the Land Act of 1960 was in force, peasant exploitation and feudal servitude had made a mockery of Indonesian independence.

He went on to denounce capitalism, the West—specifically America—and local corruption. Maggie watched him sawing the air for emphasis as he recited his speech, which when delivered in Javanese was probably even more rhetorical and impassioned. Perhaps some of the passion was the result of nervousness. Perhaps he still wondered if he should have invited her here.

Coffee came. "What does your uncle think of communism?" she asked.

Raising his cup, Ali blew on the steaming surface. "He is dalang."

"I know that."

"Then you know what he thinks of communism."

"I don't know what a dalang thinks of it."

"Nothing."

129

"I don't understand, Ali."

"Politics has no interest with him. Only wayang is important to Uncle—puppets, theater. And Borobudur."

Maggie knew that Borobudur was an old temple in the vicinity.

"He thinks always of Borobudur," Ali continued. "He fears it will destroy. What is important to Uncle is the world one thousand of years ago."

"It must have been an interesting world."

"Not to me," Ali declared. "Future is nothing to Uncle. He worries for old temple. He controls breath to make mind empty." Ali put down his cup thoughtfully. "You think he can make mind empty?"

"Perhaps some people can."

"Can you, Maggie?"

"I can't."

"I believe none can."

His claim began another long silence, broken intermittently by birdsong. Maggie had finished her coffee and was thinking it was time to leave when suddenly he said, "I want to show you special thing." He regarded her intently. "Things of Java have interest with you?" Rising and giving her a backward glance, he hurried away.

While she waited, Maggie narrowed her eyes until she saw only a slim line of light beyond the edge of the pendopo. Control breath to make the mind empty. She wanted to believe it could happen. She liked the idea of things existing beyond her capacity to experience them.

When Ali returned, he was carrying a board in his arms. Swinging himself onto the pendopo floor, he scuttled forward, holding the board like an offering.

The board was actually a polychromed wooden plaque with two sticklike warriors painted on it. Attached between the figures by a loop of yellow cord was a sheathed dagger.

While loosening and removing the dagger from the board, Ali said, "You know what is this?"

"A kris. I saw them in Sumatra."

"But this is Javanese kris. Understand. There can be none better." He turned the dagger admiringly in his hand. "In Solo is made with different— This." He pointed.

"Hilt."

"Different hilt. Some say more beautiful in Solo. I say not so beautiful as in Yogya." Holding the kris by hilt and tip, Ali offered it to her. "Three hundred years in family. We have two made by two great smiths."

Taking it gingerly from him, Maggie bent forward to study the dagger. There were curves on the blade. Ali said five, each representing a Pandava brother from the great poem of the *Mahabharata*.

The iron in this particular kris, he told her, came from heavenly stone.

"A meteorite?"

"A stone from heaven."

Maggie could not tell from his expression if he was joking or meant it. Nickel in the metal gave the black blade its silvery markings, Ali explained. To make them appear, the blade had been treated with lemon juice and arsenic. "Kris made by Empu Ki Djoko Sukatgo."

"Made three centuries ago, yet you know the smith's name?"

Ali did not conceal his pride. "That is way of my country." He told her how Empu Ki Djoko Sukatgo had pounded and folded two kinds of iron together sixty-four times to make the blade. "In old days a great empu was called magician."

"He surely was. This is beautiful."

When she gave it back to him, Ali shook his head. "You do not understand. A magician makes beauty *and* magic." Carefully he tied the sheathed dagger to the plaque. "Kris filled with magic, they say. They say it is god. Men called pawang—they know these things— they squeeze water from blade of kris. Pawang let you bend it like blade of grass. When he wave hand over blade, hard again like iron."

"Have you seen this?"

"My father once see this."

Maggie did not say what she was thinking: that Ali's father had told him so—hardly proof. But Ali had chosen to accept his father's word publicly, whatever his private judgment of it. She would abide by his choice as an act of friendship. "Your father saw something remarkable."

"Because world of kris is remarkable. Kris has soul," Ali continued. "It talks sometime. It can turn into snake. It swim and flies. Some kris will not go back in—" He pointed to the scabbard.

"Scabbard."

"Without first to draw blood. Some kris hurt a bad owner. Some kris you point at somebody and kill with unseen poison. When danger near, good kris makes noise in scabbard. Good kris bring luck, turn away fire and flood."

"You believe these things, Ali?"

"You ask what I believe? I believe in justice. I believe in communism."

She was getting accustomed to the evasive Javanese mind. "I believe this kris is beautiful. It belongs to your uncle?"

"He hold for family. Everything here"—Ali swept his arm out with a frown—"he hold for family. Not his. Ours. He live here but ours. Gitosuwoko."

Ali's dislike was growing more obvious each time he spoke of his uncle. "So this is a family kris," Maggie said. "Do you have your own?"

"I gave up."

"On principle?"

"Of course, on principle," he said in a voice of annoyance. "Kris is old world. Communism is new."

Again they were silent.

"My brother has kris," said Ali finally. "He makes gongs for gamelan. You like gamelan?"

"I heard some in Medan, in Jakarta."

"Good gamelan is here only."

Maggie saw a man coming into the courtyard. He wore a sarong, a black shirt, a dark blangkon like Ali's, no sandals. He was broad-shouldered and tall for an Indonesian—perhaps her own height.

"My uncle," Ali said in a low voice. "Ki-Dalang Gitosuwoko."

Next to gambling, Susanto had talked more about him than about anything. She was proud of having such a famous dalang in the neighborhood. Only a casino nearby would have mattered more.

In reading about the art of Indonesian puppetry Maggie had learned something about dalangs, the puppeteers: that they sat cross-legged in front of a lit screen and in the course of an evening manipulated half a hundred puppets; impersonated dozens of voices while speaking dialects of Javanese both old and new; sang songs; meowed like a cat or screamed like a murdered man; cued changes in music by tapping signals on the puppet box; improvised action from a complicated scenario; filled the performance with suspense, humor, sadness, so that the audience laughed and cried and cried and laughed—and did all of these things while holding both arms forward at face level from nine at night until six in the morning.

This, then, was a dalang.

She watched him approach, a man in his forties, with a square face, leathery and austere. His cheeks were high and prominent, like those of an Indian, his eyes set wide, his mouth a thin straight line, giving him the economical look of an athlete. He walked softly on the balls of his feet, his thick thighs outlined against a tight sarong.

Ali got up when the dalang reached the pendopo. Got up and raised his hands, palms together respectfully, in front of his face. The effect of this proper greeting was lessened by the obvious reluctance of its execution. Maggie, getting to her feet, saw that. She followed Ali to the edge of the platform, where the dalang stood motionless.

He did not squint in the blazing sunlight, but studied her from flat dark eyes. There was neither approval nor disapproval in them, but their bold stare made her uncomfortable.

After introductions, they sat inside the pendopo. The dalang had learned English during a university stay in Singapore. He spoke it like an English aristocrat, which mildly intimidated Maggie Gardner from Iowa. A servant hurried across the courtyard to take the dalang's order for special tea.

For something to say, Maggie mentioned the family kris.

"My nephew told you kris stories?" the dalang asked with a laugh. "Did you believe them?"

He was blunt for an Indonesian, and he looked at her so steadily that Maggie felt he deserved a blunt reply. "In my country not many people believe in spirits that live in knives."

"I understand. But things do happen beyond the general understanding, Nonya."

"I'm sure they do."

"For example, many of us believe holy men can transport themselves anywhere. Long ago a ruler in Solo visited Mecca every Friday and brought back three green figs as proof. In the palace museum today there are three objects labeled as figs." The dalang stared at her a few moments and sighed.

Maggie wasn't sure if he was sighing at the superstition or at her slowness in deciding how he felt about it. At least she had placed the way he was looking at her; the dalang was studying her the way a man studies a woman. She felt there was nothing spiritual about him, as Susanto claimed. She found herself glancing at his broad feet with square toes, prominent arches, callused heels.

He was saying, "Some people think the tiger is a demon in animal form. They believe there are jungle villages inhabited only by tigers. Thatch for the roof comes from human hair. Rafters are bones of men and walls are skin. People believe such things."

And so they talked on within the blue air of the pavilion. Ali assumed an air of indifference—perhaps defensive, because his uncle rarely turned to him for an opinion. The dalang was looking at her. His eyes didn't blink, and her own seemed to be nailed by an invisible force into a fixed position, so that she saw only his eyes, the dark unwavering circles. He was saying something to her, but in a low voice, whispering instructions she couldn't understand. For an indeterminate length of time (later she would try in vain to assess how long the interval had been) the entire world seemed to drop away. Her mind had opened up and everything had dropped through it like a hole in a sack, leaving her adrift in whiteness.

Then, suddenly, she was back. Turning to Ali, she asked him what he had just said, because she sensed he had said something—perhaps for the first time in minutes.

The young man was staring at her, as if puzzled. "I said I must be honest with you. You sit and hear strange things and not care if we people believe them. You cannot believe them, but you care not if we believe them. You think it good in other people if they have wrong belief. You call it, ah, authentic. Quaint! I know the words. I do not like way you in West thinks of wrong belief for other people. Wrong belief hurt people. If you hear foolish story, you smile and say nothing. Tiger villages, figs of Mecca—you cannot believe, but if we believe, you smile. We must not tell foolish story in my country now. When people believe in foolish story, they never find truth."

While listening to his impassioned plea for honest response from foreigners, Maggie began to feel like herself again. The odd feeling drained away. Perhaps it had been the heat, a mild fainting spell, though never before, not even in the swelter of Palembang, had she felt faint. At any rate, she was compelled to talk away the strange episode. "On some level," Maggie began, "superstitions and foolish stories, as you call them, are true. At least an anthropologist has faith they are." It occurred to her that Ali himself accepted superstition as somehow true when talking about his own father. But of course she kept that idea to herself.

Ali explained to his uncle that Maggie had been a student of anthropology.

The dalang nodded as if the idea didn't interest him.

Tea came.

"This," the dalang said, "is the famous tea called Tiger's Milk."

"Is there a superstition attached to it?" Maggie asked with a smile.

"You can't drink it if you believe in ghosts."

Ali grunted disdainfully and removed the china lid to his cup. Maggie removed the lid to hers and raised the cup, then put it down. She looked at it. Raising it again, she brought the rim close to her mouth, but her hand seemed to reach an invisible barrier less than an inch from her lips. Turning, she caught Ali frowning at her. Again she tried to drink, again failed, and set the cup back on the floor.

"Please drink," the dalang said, gesturing at the cup. "It is Tiger's Milk."

Maggie smiled, feeling sweat break out on her forehead. She picked up the cup again and slowly lifted it, again reaching the invisible barrier. To steady the warm china, she clasped it in both hands.

The dalang leaned forward. "Is anything wrong?"

"I can't seem to drink," she told him sheepishly.

"Because you believe in ghosts."

"Nonsense." She glared at him, but couldn't get the cup any closer, though she clutched it with both hands.

"Ah." The dalang sipped his own tea, then smiled. "I made a mistake. This is *not* Tiger's Milk. This is local tea. Whatever you believe about ghosts, you can drink this. Please. Drink now."

It felt to Maggie as if the air itself had changed weight around her hands. The cup moved easily through it to her lips. She drank, drained the tea. She was surprised by how thirsty she was. A servant dashed forward to refill the cup. She drank that down in a feverish gulp.

"More, Nonya?" the dalang asked.

She couldn't understand what was happening. Three cups later, her thirst still unslaked, Maggie refused the offer of another. Slowly she got to her feet and stared down at the smiling dalang.

"I think I understand," she said, hearing her voice grow thin and high from anger. "You taught me a lesson. Things do happen beyond the general understanding. But an explanation is always possible. Thank you. I'm going." She turned and rushed off the pendopo. Getting her shoes, which lay at the edge, she hurried to the gate, where Ali caught up with her.

"Your uncle," she said, "hypnotized me."

Ali nodded. "I think he did. He could."

"He did." She thought of holding the cup without being able to drink, then of drinking one cup after another. "What did he say before the tea came?"

"He said you would not like Tiger Milk. But you would have thirst."

"Did you know what he'd done, Ali?"

He shook his head. Could she believe him? Perhaps he had known but feared to say anything. Or perhaps the dalang had managed so skillfully that the young Communist hadn't realized what was happening. Or perhaps Ali in his dislike of his uncle had merely switched off during the conversation.

"I am sorry," Ali said, "for what Uncle did with you. He is feudal man. I am man of people, of Communist future."

He seemed so desolate that Maggie almost patted his hand reassuringly.

"I am not like Javanese-born feudal," he continued. "They say one thing, do another because they fear. I am honest Communist. I thought you would not speak with me. So today I would not speak with you. Not first until you spoke. Forgive me."

Maggie realized she was not listening closely to him. She was thinking of the dalang back there. "Nothing to forgive. We are friends."

"I hope we are friends. I hope it."

When she took hold of the bike, Ali stood beside it, shading his eyes from the sun. "I am sorry what he did with you."

Maggie looked at the bike, at Ali's face that seemed hopeful of more forgiveness. Letting the bike go, she turned and started back to the house. Striding briskly across the courtyard, she saw the dalang sitting where she had left him.

Tossing her shoes off and climbing onto the pendopo, Maggie walked across the unpolished wood to stand over him.

"Did you do that to teach me a lesson?"

He looked up, his face impassive. "No, Nonya."

"Then why did you hypnotize me?"

"It was amusing."

She wanted to feel pure anger, but his tone was so relaxed that something unknown to her seemed to be determining his response. She felt curiosity as well as anger. "It was amusing," she repeated sarcastically.

"Yes, amusing."

"Amusing to you perhaps, but not to me."

"You do not see amusement in it?" Now his broad face changed. He began smiling at her.

"In my country," Maggie said, his ironic smile making her furious, "to hypnotize someone without prior agreement is an invasion of privacy."

"Then you live in a country that does not value the unexpected."

"What it values is human rights."

"Did I harm you?"

"You humiliated me."

"To be humiliated must you not have as witness someone who shares your values? My nephew and I do not share your values."

"But you were amused by making a fool of me. You can't deny that." Maggie suddenly felt more of a fool because she was arguing with him.

Again he smiled. This, however, was an open, almost tender smile and caught her off guard. "I admit to an—impulse. Here was a beautiful foreign woman who was going to have tea with me. I was told she was interested in my country, my culture. I had an impulse not to take her seriously. Is that understandable?"

Maggie did not reply.

"When something new and"—he paused, searching for words—"interesting and perhaps significant comes into your life, sometimes you want to make little of it."

"Because you don't know how to deal with it."

"So you understand."

"I think I do. But I would have thought a great dalang would have figured out some other way, less hostile and . . . and more creative, to deal with things new and interesting and perhaps even significant." Maggie liked this little speech; she felt that through it she had paid him back. So without another word she turned and left. Ali was waiting for her at the entrance. As Maggie pedaled away, he shouted at her back, "I believe some people make the mind empty!"

By the time she reached the batik factory, Maggie was convinced that Ki-Dalang Gitosuwoko possessed an outrageous mind: amoral, whimsical, free. He was the most formidable man she had ever met. Better for her that they never meet again.

Fifteen

Sjam wasn't happy. That trouble this morning had shaken him badly. He had been summoned to the Jakarta headquarters of Pertamina. Summoned in the name of Lieutenant General Ibnu Sutowo. On the way there Sjam had felt his hands trembling, though he was not easily frightened.

Sutowo was director of Pertamina, the state authority for distribution of oil and a vast financial complex with a reputation for circumventing the law: it never paid taxes, published no balance sheet, remained beyond rightful control of the National Planning Board, illegally deposited holdings in foreign banks, and masterminded fraudulent deals for the army. Behind this complex maneuvering stood the shadowy figure of General Sutowo, who personally owned (Sjam would know such things) factories and plantations, some fisheries, a rice mill, a travel agency, a hotel, even a restaurant in the country of New York in America. More than once Sjam had seen the general's Rolls-Royce speeding down the streets of Jakarta in the wake of other huge black cars. On the running boards stood bodyguards in their fancy blue uniforms, all of them wearing sunglasses. The small man in the backseat of the Rolls was only a blur, yet his hunched image had remained with Sjam like a bad dream.

And such a man had summoned Sjam to Pertamina.

The gatherer of information thanked Allah that Sutowo didn't want to see him face-to-face; that would have signaled an event of mortal seriousness. Instead, a tall, scowling aide met Sjam in a windowless cubicle somewhere within the immense building.

The trouble was pontoons.

Sjam was told that Pertamina did not welcome his interest in a shipment of rubber pontoons. General Sutowo's name was never mentioned, but Sjam understood whom he had displeased. But why? Yesterday at dockside he had asked about a load of pontoons just arrived from America. They were scheduled for further shipment to southern Sumatra. A stevedore told him they had come from an American army dump. But from the ship's third mate Sjam learned (at some trouble and expense) that on the manifest the pontoons were described as a shipment originating from an American manufacturer. Which meant that the floating bridges, purchased as secondhand merchandise far below cost from the U.S. Army (Sjam understood such deals if anyone did), would be sold here as brand-new. Someone was going to make a nice profit from the disparity.

To Sutowo's aide, however, he said that he had no interest whatsoever in pontoons. He had simply asked about them out of curiosity. He assured the glaring aide that he would never never never ask about them again. Dropping the whole thing was better, wasn't it, than floating one fine morning down a sluggish canal, throat slit from ear to ear? The director of Pertamina had a reputation for asserting his will through blunt action.

Curtly dismissed, Sjam walked into the midday glare wondering why an important man like General Sutowo would bother with the disposal of pontoons. Of course, for someone else the handling of such a shipment could mean a small fortune. But not, surely, for the general. He owned a restaurant in the country of New York and even had his own intelligence service.

Over tea in a shaded warung Sjam cleared up the mystery. Bits of information drifted like flotsam in his head, sometimes for years; then suddenly a piece separated out and proved useful. One of General Sutowo's sons-in-law had purchased a construction business in southern Sumatra; the information had appeared in the newspapers, which Sjam read daily with religious care. So here was the connection between the director of Pertamina Oil and a cargo of secondhand pontoons. Naturally the details of this connection were obscure and would remain so unless someone looked carefully into the matter. The outcome, whatever the specifics, would inevitably mean a large profit for the son-in-law or for the son-in-law's friends or for the friends of the son-in-law's friends. And a tidy sum for anyone who retailed those specifics to parties who might participate in some way too. But uncovering the facts could be dangerous. Sjam had other ways to turn a profit. No sense risking his life for a few rupiah, though the beachhouse roof did need repairing. Safety was everything.

Yet his present association with the PKI was not altogether safe. For that matter, it was dangerous. Sometimes his own audacity amazed Sjam. A cardinal rule that he lived by was to get the most money at the least risk, yet here he was acting on behalf of a political party engaged in mortal combat with the Indonesian Army. The stakes were high enough: control of the nation. In such a game someone like himself was expendable. And surely the pay for his services was not commensurate with the risk. The PKI was stingy compared to businessmen he worked for. So why was he doing it? Sjam knew well enough—because it entertained him. And because a residual love of danger, which had throbbed in his veins during the fight for independence, had remained to haunt him through the years and was now rendering him foolish. Such foolishness, which skirted close to a kind of patriotic commitment, both appalled and fascinated him. Curiosity, which had helped him become successful at collecting information, now made him vulnerable. Foolish, vulnerable—even so, he enjoyed playing Aidit's game.

Even enjoyed it when he had to meet with Njoto, second deputy chairman of the PKI. They didn't get along, yet circumstances were throwing them together. Njoto was coming now into the warung, wearing a sour frown. The Politburo member's hulking frame, more Western than Indonesian in size, made Sjam uncomfortably aware of his own slightness.

Sjam rarely met anyone in the PKI except Chairman Aidit. Through the years, when he did jobs for the party, his isolation enabled him to work stealthily, in a roundabout manner. He thought of himself as a rat sniffing each corner of a dark room. Rats found their way; they could survive better than anything. He liked that in them, and he liked to think he emulated their instincts. When Aidit had created the Special Bureau and hired Sjam to operate it as a mercenary, an important element of the Biro Khusus had been its size—only three operatives. Sjam had laughed then: "Two too many," he said, and Aidit had laughed too. They were men who believed in anonymity, though the chairman couldn't enjoy it himself.

Now, because of the plot against the Council of Generals, Sjam couldn't either. He had to step out of the shadows and act in concert with others. In a decade of working for Aidit, he had met only four other Reds. In recent days he had met a dozen, and today, right now, he had to deal with Deputy Chairman Njoto, whose job was to mobilize selected cadres for an emergency.

When Njoto sat down with no greeting save a quick rude nod, he ordered a beer. Scarcely had it come to the table than he drank it down and ordered another.

Sjam watched in disgust. Vices rarely bothered him; he had seen too much of his fellowmen to care what they did to themselves. But excessive drinking was offensive; he had been brought up by a strict Muslim mother. He understood, of course, why Njoto had comparable dislike of him. Red intellectuals were snobbish. He had seen them recruiting among the poor. An educated fellow like Njoto would get close to people by assuming their traits: the humorlessness, the pettiness, the bitterness that go with grinding poverty. He'd become one of them, never comprehending however that the traits he assumed were precisely those that the poor wished to get rid of. While working with the sniveling unwashed masses, a fellow like Njoto would be as sniveling and unwashed as the worst of them. But after returning to headquarters where men sat at desks and answered telephones, a fellow like Njoto would sneer at sniveling unwashed comrades from the warrens of Jakarta. Sjam figured that an educated fellow like Njoto could smell poverty on someone even if it had been washed off years ago. Sjam feared that his own skin still retained the odor of it. He wondered if Njoto could smell it across the table.

Nothing brought them together over tea and beer, not even the sharing of conspiracy. They conducted their business quickly and left the warung, each in a gloomy mood.

It was in such a mood that Sjam later met his assistant, Pono. They picked up the third member of the bureau, a local organizer named Walujo. He had been assigned to the Special Bureau so the party would have at least one real Communist on its staff. Mercenaries did efficient work, but on principle a party member should be involved too. And act, of course, as a watchdog. This was Aidit's policy.

Walujo was thin, with a sallow face and heavily lidded eyes. Sjam thought of him as someone who stands at the back of the room, making you look uneasily over your shoulder. Walujo gave the impression that if something went wrong, he'd pull out a gun and start shooting.

Meeting Walujo had a beneficial effect on Sjam's mood. He brightened up in the presence of a face that expressed such intense melancholy. Comrade Walujo was someone whom Njoto would smell at a great distance. But you wouldn't need to smell a history of poverty on him; you saw it in the pale cheeks, the sunken eyes.

"How are you, Walujo?" Sjam asked cheerfully.

"Ready, comrade." Walujo called everyone comrade, party member or not. And he was always ready. Work, missions, assignments—that was his life. Walujo was a fanatic whose every breath was Red (that was how Pono, who hated commitment in anyone, described him). Having a fanatic along was a good idea, Sjam argued. When the lines of power were unclear at a meeting, you had an edge if with you was a man who made people uneasy.

So that evening, when Sjam led his two companions into the home of Colonel Latief, he hoped the Red zealot would give them an edge if they needed it.

The other plotters were already there, sitting in Latief's modest living room. The colonel introduced them: Lieutenant Colonel Untung, senior man present, commander of the Palace Guard of the Cakrabirawa Regiment; Major Sujono, commander of Air Defense at Halim Air Base; Major Sigit, the commander of a battalion in

Latief's infantry brigade; and Captain Wahjudi, the commander of an Air Defense battalion in the Jakarta Military Command.

Latief introduced Sjam as "an interested civilian and former freedom fighter." Sjam then introduced his companions as "other interested civilians."

Major Sigit, a square-faced man, leaned forward. "Do you represent the PKI?"

Sjam preferred not to make that association altogether clear until the tone of the meeting had been set. So he replied vaguely. "We are businessmen, but we're progressive. "Progressive" was the Jakartan term for people sympathetic to the Communists.

"We are all progressive here," Sigit said. "Do you represent the PKI?"

"I have access to the Politburo through friends in the party."

"Then you represent the PKI," Sigit declared, sitting back with a triumphant smile.

Sjam glanced at other faces in the room, their features sliding together as if seen underwater. A withered old servant brought in a tray of covered teacups. While pleasantries were exchanged over a first cup of tea, Sjam felt this was quite remarkable: here he sat with a group of men who were going to plan the fate of the nation. Remarkable.

The conversation swirled around him, and Sjam let his real mind enter the brilliant past when he had stalked the streets of Yogya in a firefight with the Dutch. He caught sight of a paratrooper's boot, a big one, and the next moment a square white face appeared around the corner. He pulled the trigger, feeling the chug chug chug of gun against hip. The white face burst into violent bloom. He rammed another clip into place, yelling jubilantly.

From the hot memory of it he almost let a wild cry escape his lips. Sjam looked around. Had anyone noticed a change in him? But as army men do, they were talking among themselves, giving civilians their attention only when necessary.

What a fool I am, Sjam thought. Recalling the past is never profitable. Especially a past in which you risked your life for an idea.

He had got into this conspiracy as the head of a special bureau for a political party, as a mercenary who expected to be paid for specific work. He had been hired to do what he did best—gather information.

Until recently he had turned a profit by telling both army and PKI what they wanted to know. Now he was doing a lot more than that. He had become a conspirator. Somehow the job had squirmed out of shape into a kind of patriotic commitment. He felt young again, filled with the energy of anticipation. Remarkable. Remarkable and foolish.

Sixteen

Untung, as senior officer, made a little speech to the conspirators. He spoke of loyalty to the Great Leader, of principles engendered by Javanese tradition, of their corruption by men who succumbed to greed and licentiousness.

The speech bored Sjam; he fought to suppress a yawn and watched a slim young woman slip past the open doorway, holding an infant in the crook of her arm. Pretty woman. Flowered kebaya and sarong. For an instant his eyes met hers. Latief was a lucky fellow.

Sjam sat back thinking of Endang, not a bad mistress really. He was still thinking of her when a discussion began about arresting the generals.

The conspirators agreed that at the time of the arrests there must be a simultaneous takeover of strategic areas in Jakarta. Loyal troops must secure Radio Republik Indonesia and the telephone exchange in the Telecommunications Building on Merdeka Square. Those objectives were vital. Moreover, they had to take the Defense Ministry, KOSTRAD headquarters, and other nearby military installations. And surround the palace. Bung Karno rarely stayed there these days.

But what if he came in from the Bogor palace at that time? They pondered it. They would have to get him out quickly and rush him to safety or otherwise a force loyal to the generals might kidnap him.

Major Sujono, a deliberate man, spoke up. He had discussed this possibility with Air Vice Marshal Dhani, who suggested that the best place for Bung Karno would be the Halim Air Base. He'd be taken there by helicopter prior to the arrests. If he needed to be removed altogether from the Jakarta area, they'd provide him with a plane.

Everyone agreed that the president should be at Halim when the arrests took place.

So the air marshal was also involved, Sjam noted. That meant power for their side.

"Now," Untung said, clasping his hands, "the arrests." As an experienced paracommando, he led the discussion by suggesting a raid after midnight on the home of each selected general. Rounding them up at that time and place would decrease the chance for accidental violence.

Everyone agreed.

Next came the selection of generals to be arrested. That was done quickly: the army chief of staff, his four assistants, and the inspector of justice. Sjam was surprised that one of the assistants named was Major General S. Parman. Parman was the brother of a high-ranking Red, a member of the Politburo.

Major Sigit turned to Sjam with a smile. "Do you have any objection to Parman?"

"None."

"You were not given orders by the PKI to let him alone?"

"I was not," said Sjam, meeting smile with smile.

Sigit turned away finally with a frown. He had obviously hoped for trouble about Parman: for example, the PKI asking for Parman to be treated with special consideration because of his brother. Sjam didn't know much about either man, but he surely did know that the pursuit of power could estrange close relatives. Perhaps the two brothers envied each other's rise to high rank in his chosen field. Sjam lit a kretek cigarette and sat back, feeling the satisfaction of someone who didn't want power, just its fruits, a few tiny pieces spilled accidentally along the road that men travel on their way to death.

The plotters argued about the inclusion of General Nasution, defense minister. He was difficult to assess. Against the Dutch he'd been a famous guerrilla fighter. During the late fifties he had quelled military uprisings in the outer islands.

Sigit again turned to Sjam with a smile. "Nasution, as you know, is fiercely anti-Red. Should this be held against him?"

Sjam felt a defensive response could ruin the meeting, so he smiled back. Said nothing. Neither did anyone else.

Sigit shrugged, allowing the discussion about Nasution to continue without him. Satisfied with provoking a moment of uneasiness, Sigit didn't seem willing to attack the Communists openly. Sjam figured the man would attack anyone who challenged him on any point, but given a small victory, he would step aside.

In Nasution's favor, during the debate, was his personal hatred of Chief of Staff Yani, the libertine whose corrupt life had influenced a number of junior officers and brought them to ruin (this rhetoric belonged to Untung, who had been overlooked for promotion by Yani, a fact Sjam had obtained recently from Latief).

Also in Nasution's favor was his strict Muslim observance on holy days.

Against him was his power. If not secured, he might serve as a rallying point for the opposition. He was a popular hero too; that counted against him. And finally, he often fought with Bung Karno, who had never trusted his politics and even said so at great length.

This latter claim, urged on the group by Latief, sounded like nothing more than Jakartan rumor to Sjam, but he withheld comment.

They put Nasution on the list. That made seven of the highest-ranking generals in the army.

For a while they sat in silence, absorbing the magnitude of their plot.

Then in his deliberate manner the air force officer, Major Sujono, brought up a final case: General Suharto. As powerful as the other generals, he was chief of KOSTRAD, the Strategic Reserve Command. Should he too be on the list?

He wasn't a member of the council, someone argued.

Not that we know of, someone else said.

Untung was strongly opposed to his inclusion on the list. After all, KOSTRAD was not a fighting unit, but merely an administrative command for moving troops around. They had nothing to fear from

Suharto's headquarters. Moreover, the general had served with distinction in West Irian. He was a quiet family man. Untung stood up to emphasize the next point.

"The great dukun Kyahi Hahfud, whom I have the honor of knowing, has told me personally that he has met and admired General Suharto." Untung glanced around with a smile, as if this were the decisive point. Then he added another for good measure. "General Suharto attended my wedding. He flew in from Surabaya when I was married in Yogya. He stood by me."

They left Suharto off the list.

Lazily puffing on his cigarette, Sjam thought about his fellow plotters. Like most Javanese, they were sentimental. It was a trait he found contemptible. Spitting up blood and gasping for breath, his father had cried tears of gratitude when someone came to visit him on his deathbed. But visitors never brought medicine or food or money. Peering down into the sickroom from branches of a mango tree, where often he sat to view the world, the boy Sjam had hoped, had prayed to Allah, that visitors were bringing something for his dying father, but all they brought were sentimental words. Sitting in the tree, Sjam had felt his belly tighten, his tongue swell. He had hated his father for spilling tears of gratitude while the family starved.

For an instant, while blowing smoke into the close air of Latief's house, Sjam recalled his father's tears seeping down pale sunken cheeks. Then, blowing the image away with the smoke, he attended to the next topic of importance: the composition of participating troops.

Again, as senior line officer present, Untung did most of the talking. Finally they chose seven shock units from the First Honorary Palace Guard Battalion of the Cakrabirawa Regiment; the First Infantry Brigade; the 454th Paratroop Battalion; and the 530th Paratroop Battalion. Except for the Palace Guard, they were all crack troops from the provinces, coming to Jakarta for the Armed Forces Day exercises. These provincial troops had an earned reputation for personal loyalty to their commanders. They were "progressive" as well—many belonged to the Communist party. They resented the high command passionately these days, because their rations had been cut back and the Supply and Logistics Command had stopped the free dispensing of sugar, cooking oil, and rice.

Loyalty and hunger: good criteria, Sjam felt, for selecting troops to undergo a risky mission. Especially hunger. They'd be trucked brooding into Jakarta. They'd be open to suggestion. That's what hunger did to you, put you in the mood to do anything. Sjam knew from experience. He approved of the way these troops were chosen. At last his fellow plotters were using their heads.

Major Sigit turned to him. "What does the PKI offer in support of the movement?"

Because it was an inevitable question, Aidit had supplied Sjam with a ready answer: the PKI volunteers now training at Halim Air Base would be available. Air force personnel were training them for duty as guerrilla fighters in Malaysia. President Sukarno had arranged for the PKI training at Halim despite army protests. Observers saw it as typical Sukarno—a way of dividing army from air force, then playing one against the other.

"You say the PKI volunteers would be available," Major Sigit said. "Available for what?"

"For anything," Sjam said.

"Anything?"

"For whatever you ask of them." Sjam met the skeptical eyes without blinking.

"You are speaking for Chairman Aidit?"

"Yes. I am." It was time to be firm.

"So you are speaking for Chairman Aidit."

"The Gerwani and Pemuda Rakyat youth groups at Halim will be available," Sjam said. Aidit had told him to pledge them irrevocably, if pressed. "What you ask them to do they will do."

Actually, the Reds at Halim were nothing more than kids itching for trouble. Most of them came from PKI goon squads off the streets of Jakarta. They were Communists out of boredom. Sjam knew them all right. They wore Red armbands to add a dash of color to their ragged clothes. They knew who Aidit and Mao were, but not Lenin and Marx. They enjoyed milling around, running here and there, shouldering down anyone who got in their way. They were hungry. A lot of them were sick. All of them were furious at the world. Ready? Of course. Sjam figured the young soldiers at Halim Air Base must be having a grand time with the Gerwani girls, who also always seemed ready. He had watched them carrying banners in support of the

Indonesian Women's Movement, swaying their hips, leering at spectators. They were ready for anything once the banners were tossed aside. Ready for riot, revolution, hashish, quick love in an alley. That's how the Gerwani girls were. And so were their male counterparts in the Pemuda Rakyat, the Popular Youth Front. They were ready. All you had to do was point them in the right direction, like dogs, and tell them to go. Sjam understood them; a long time ago he had been one of them. You took what you could get when you lived like that. You hit out when you could. You made love wherever you could find a place. Sjam knew. He thought suddenly of Endang lying on the bed, one thigh across the other, obscuring the dark patch between her legs.

The plotters had turned to another question. On precisely which date should they move against the generals? Latief, establishing his patriotism, spoke up for Armed Forces Day. The idea appealed to Untung and Sujono. When the others seemed about to agree, Sjam asserted himself for the first time during the meeting. He had been ordered by Chairman Aidit to push for 30 September. "Force it through somehow" were Aidit's words, accompanied by a look of rare passion. So even an Indonesian Communist was a slave to private symbolism. Without knowing why the chairman wanted this particular date, Sjam would try to get it, merely to exercise his talent for persuasion.

He used the argument of prudence. Many people would be involved in the operation, so the chance of accidental disclosure was great. Tactically it was best to act without delay. A careless word, a single careless word—He let the unfinished idea worm into each man's mind, stirring up images of arrest, trial, execution. Then he casually suggested a date earlier than Armed Forces Day. "Why not the thirtieth of September?"

After a brief discussion, they agreed to it.

"I have a name for the operation," said Major Sujono. He had formed an acronym from Gerakan Tigah Puluh September. "GE-TAPS."

They liked that, even Sjam. Although he despised the sentimentality of his people, Sjam shared with them a weakness for acronyms. GE-TAPS put approval on the 30th of September Movement like a king's seal; it gave their plot a new measure of reality.

Their final problem was maintaining political order after the arrests of the generals. People must be assured that Bung Karno, their Beloved Leader, was safe; that until he could resume his duties safely, the government would not collapse.

Colonel Untung led the discussion of such an interim authority. Unknown to the other plotters (except Sjam), he had met with Chairman Aidit about this matter. As a relatively junior officer, Untung had been flattered by Aidit's attention; after all, a man of international fame was consulting him. Together they conceived of a forty-five-member council, drawn primarily from army officers. Until general elections were held sometime in the future, the council would take charge of state affairs in consultation with the president. At Aidit's urging, Untung had agreed to chair the council.

Sjam understood the chairman's generous treatment of a man of little potential. If somehow the plot failed, blame would rest on Untung and other participating officers, not on the Communists. And if it succeeded, who would actually run the council? A man not even on it.

When Untung presented the idea of an interim council to the unsuspecting plotters, there was no immediate response. In order to sidetrack opposition, Sjam said, "Perhaps the colonel might look into this matter of a council, its composition and function, and report back to us."

Tired and sweaty in the little room, the plotters agreed to his suggestion without argument. Save for the actual capture of the generals, the most vital issue of the entire operation was disposed of quickly because of fatigue. Once the coup took place, there would be no time for mulling over the mechanics of such a council. It would simply sweep into power. If all went well, Chairman Aidit would emerge from GETAPS as the most powerful man in the country, with Untung in nominal charge and the Beloved Leader cooling his heels in a palace somewhere, waiting for safe conditions that would never materialize.

Sjam was amused.

The meeting ended quickly. Everyone began filing out. At the door Untung called Sjam aside. They went through the house into the back garden, where they sat down in deck chairs, facing mango trees. Sjam heard a baby crying, then stop. The pretty wife of Latief was surely giving it her breast. Sjam thought about that, tried to imagine the curve and feel of her soft flesh. Lucky fellow, Latief.

"I want your advice," Untung was saying. "The first radio broadcast delivered after the arrests will announce the purge of the army. The second broadcast will explain the Revolutionary Council. Do you think Chairman Aidit will approve?"

"I will ask him, but I think so."

"I want your opinion about a possible third broadcast." Untung took a folded piece of paper from his shirt, adjusted his glasses, and read in a low conspiratorial voice.

"All ranks and equivalent grades in the armed forces of the Republic of Indonesia above that of lieutenant colonel are herewith declared invalid." He peered over his glasses at Sjam. "What do you think?"

The directive would eliminate every rank above Untung's own.

Sjam looked at the man. Shaken by such raw ambition, racked by a moral impulse from his past, Sjam took a deep breath to rid himself of ethical judgment. "Good idea," he finally said, working up the sound of enthusiasm. "Get rid of the general staff. Good, sir."

"Chairman Aidit will approve?"

Approve? Aidit would chortle with glee. If this directive was supported by the nation, Aidit's chief enemies for power would be eliminated.

"I am sure he will," Sjam assured the colonel after a judicious pause.

They rose and walked back through the house. As they did so, Sjam tried to absorb Untung's aspirations. No wonder the colonel hadn't discussed this announcement with his military comrades. They would have been shocked by such a naked thrust for power.

Untung held Sjam's elbow in fraternal guidance as they reached the front door, where host Latief was waiting to say good night. Into the darkness they went, each with a lusty wave.

Beyond earshot of the house, where he was joined by Pono and Walujo, Sjam said bitterly, "Well, tonight we had a chance to see them perform."

"Who perform?" asked Pono.

"Semar, Gareng, Petruk, Bagong."

"Where?" asked Pono in surprise. Sjam had just mentioned four clowns famous for madcap antics in the puppet theater.

"In that room tonight," Sjam told him. "Sitting across from us. They were all there: Semar, Gareng, Petruk, Bagong."

Pono giggled, understanding the sardonic joke. But Walujo plodded on, head down, as if his potential for violence had been wasted tonight.

By the time they had reached a becak station, the gatherer and retailer of information had regained his composure. His strange moral outrage this evening had been amusing, nothing more. He was Sjam again.

Seventeen

At dawn the whores stopped patrolling in front of the Hotel Indonesia and vanished soundlessly, like dew when the sun comes up. But at night they were restless and vocal. Last night, Vern had made the mistake of getting out of General Sakirman's car a few blocks away, just for some fresh air after dinner. Half a dozen women, spotting this lone male, made for him rapidly on spiked heels, yelling their prices and describing their talents in a mixture of English, Dutch, and Bahasa Indonesia. They grabbed his arm, blocked his path, screamed in his face, even pushed him and kept right at him until he reached the hotel entrance. Tough as streetwalkers in Hong Kong, Bangkok, Calcutta, their aggressive tactics seemed out of place in circumspect Indonesia, a typical agrarian society in which civility was the rule. Oh, yeah? His scholarly wife might accept that explanation, but he didn't. A few weeks in the madhouse of Jakarta had shaken his comprehension of this country. For one thing, he just couldn't get a fix on corruption, Jakarta style.

Religion, he felt, was somehow involved. It always was in everything out here. From firsthand experience he knew that corruption in Burma and India had been shaped by religious attitudes. You knew what to expect from Hindus when they wanted to cheat you—a lot of obfuscating noise and random energy: what you found at their religious festivals, an ecstatic movement, a sudden climax. The Burmese Buddhists managed to cheat you more subtly, as they created a pleasant mood for it, a kind of analogy to the tinkling bells that established a mood for prayer. And in Sumatra the righteous link of Islam had encouraged fraternal skulduggery, as Muslim judges defended Muslim swindlers against any claims made by victimized infidels.

Vern didn't claim to understand the mechanism, but somehow the corruption in those places was policed by God. Here in Jakarta it was different. Allah and Shiva and Buddha and all sorts of magicians stirred up a moral stew, an outpouring of homilies savored daily by newspaper and radio. Vern couldn't make heads or tails out of these lectures, except that good was good and bad was bad and you should follow the precepts of the Great Leader of the Revolution: never drink, steal, commit adultery (that was a laugh, coming from Bung Karno), or cheat your fellow citizen. Generalities always. Nothing solid. Only air. The world was really yours for the asking. Just pronounce the Great Leader's name or that of any of the other gods and go to it. A charlatan in Jakarta had no ethical parameters to guide him in working out acceptable deceit and trickery. He did what the moment itself suggested, without fear of divinely coherent punishment. That made him unpredictable, therefore dangerous. Vern was stumped.

He discussed these matters with companions at the hotel bar and discovered they were stumped too. Often the bar was closed on a note of intellectual despair as journalists, exporters, shipping agents, and consulate personnel drank up, shook their heads, and staggered up to their rooms.

Every morning OPSUS sent a car for Vern; it was waiting at the entrance when he came out. And every morning he waved it off. He preferred the fifteen-minute walk to OPSUS headquarters. It wasn't that hot in the morning; sunlight hadn't yet washed the color out of plant life, so he could appreciate the exotic hues. Vern never talked much about it, but he loved flowers, a love inherited from his mother, who had used her knowledge of them to make a financial go of widowhood.

This morning he left the hotel and walked southward into a residential district. It contained splendid villas, often with walls topped by broken glass and barbed wire. A lot of military personnel lived here, along with upper-echelon civil servants, and rich Chinese merchants. There wasn't much traffic. He passed the villa gardens with their flowering trees and clipped lawns, emerging at last into a broad avenue clogged with vehicles and this morning with a long procession of demonstrators wearing Red armbands. They held banners splashed with Communist slogans.

Vern stood on the corner and watched them plod along. They were silent as they marched, eyes fixed on the dusty ground beneath their feet. They looked bored, though it was too early for the march to have come very far. Vern wondered if they needed something to happen before they looked like competent agitators. He started to turn away, but caught a glimpse of sudden movement within the ranks. Demonstrators were peeling out of line, running in his direction. They had nearly reached him before Vern understood that he was what they needed to happen.

He was backing away when about a dozen of them rushed up and circled him. Someone grabbed his arm, but he pulled loose. Someone yelled in English, "What are you do?"

Someone asked the same thing in Dutch, in Bahasa Indonesia.

"*Saya orang Perancis,*" Vern said.

"Go get Wuju," a young man cried out. "He speaks French!"

A boy raced toward the procession. The others stayed where they were, ringing Vern. From over their shoulders he could read the banners across the street: slogans condemning Malaysia, Britain, America, the United Nations, Capitalism, Imperialism, Colonialism, Poverty, and War. The huge red letters wriggled above a solid phalanx of shambling marchers.

Others, trotting up, joined the bunch around Vern. There must have been a score of them already. They had ringed him so closely that he'd backed away from the sidewalk to the edge of some bushes. He felt isolated, as though the Reds had cordoned him off like a building.

In Bahasa he said, "Sorry, but I have to be going. I can't talk now." He didn't try to step past them, however.

"Where did you learn our language?" someone asked so angrily that Vern was afraid to answer.

"He is CIA," someone declared.

The boy who went searching for Wuju returned. "Can't find him," he said breathlessly.

"Anyway, the Frenchman speaks Bahasa," said a young man with a pencil-thin mustache. Reaching only to Vern's shoulder, he asked brusquely, "Are you French or American?"

"Saya orang Perancis. Betul," Vern told the mustachioed boy who seemed to have taken charge.

"Don't believe him," someone yelled. Vern stared at the boy who had yelled. Frail-looking, not more than eighteen, he methodically slapped a chair leg against the palm of his hand. He must have broken the leg off to carry as a club.

"Why were you watching us?" the mustachioed leader asked. He stepped close enough to be within striking range. "You are CIA?"

"I wasn't watching you," Vern said, realizing that's exactly what he had been doing.

"We saw you watching us. You were studying us. You are CIA."

Another boy stepped up alongside the leader. "Are French in the CIA?"

"Yes," someone claimed. "French, British, Americans—all CIA."

The leader ignored this chatter, but kept looking at Vern. "Why do you think we march?" he asked.

"It's none of my business."

The answer seemed to infuriate the leader, who reached out and pushed Vern hard in the chest. "Get him back in there."

The circle closed tighter. Vern realized he was being herded like an animal through a space in the bushes. He glanced back. They were leading him into a vacant lot with a few scraggly trees and a garbage dump. Here he was really isolated. The boys got him under a tree and again surrounded him. He smelled the sweet odor of rotting fruit, but didn't look at the dump. He dared look nowhere but at the long, narrow face of the angry leader.

"We are Pemuda Rakyat," the leader said. "We do not march for you to spy on us."

Vern felt hands on his hips. Someone from behind was going rapidly through his pockets. He felt his wallet lifted, his comb, a pack of Juicy Fruit gum.

"Maybe what we do is none of your business, but our business is justice for mankind," the leader said. "Is that clear?"

"That's clear," Vern said.

"What are you doing in Jakarta?"

"I build things."

"Don't believe him," said the boy with the chair leg.

"Build what?" the leader asked.

Vern glanced around. It was hard to judge how serious a threat these boys were. It could be that he was terribly ignorant about Indonesia. That scared him.

"Build what?" the leader repeated, prodding him in the chest with two fingers.

Vern looked quickly at the boy holding the chair leg; that could be next.

"Build what?" the leader said for the third time.

"Anything needed."

"Don't believe him," a boy said from the circle. "He's a British spy."

"Do you build things for the CIA?" the leader asked.

"I build hotels."

"Capitalist dog," the leader said. "What do you know about Chairman Aidit?"

"He's the leader of your party."

"He's a great man."

"Very well. A great man."

A boy rushing up whispered something to the leader. Then Vern saw an object being passed around the circle from boy to boy. It was a pistol, probably an 8-mm. When it reached the leader, he cocked it and pointed it at Vern's head.

I'll never see her again, Vern thought.

"You build hotels for the CIA?"

"I never—"

"You are CIA. You spied on us. So do you want to see something important?" He pointed with the gun toward a space in the bushes leading out of the vacant lot. "Do you?"

"I'd just rather go about my business."

"Do you want to see something important?" He was waving the pistol back and forth.

"Yes," Vern said. "I suppose so."

"Then see a fight for justice. The enemy is near. You will have something important to tell the CIA. Come along, spy."

Someone hit Vern a sharp blow in the back, almost knocking him over. But then someone else took his arm, as if guiding him, and soon he was trotting along with the whole group of young Reds. They moved rapidly from the lot into a side street, following the mustachioed boy, who often jabbed his pistol in the air, as if a dagger were his natural weapon. As they loped along, Vern noticed other weapons in Red hands: a tire wrench, a length of chain, a knife clamped into a crudely fashioned wooden handle, another pistol of World War Two vintage. All of this stuff came from a gunnysack one of them carried. Vern got the message: these kids had been looking for trouble. The demonstration had been their way of finding it.

They were heading down a street familiar to him from other mornings: the walled villas, the flowering trees, the civil servants trudging to work. Now the neighborhood looked strange. Seeing the gang of young men trotting forward, people began scattering. The street was almost empty save for another group of young men coming from the opposite direction.

They were coming fast, about a score of them. They all wore black pecis and chanted *"La ilaha illa 'llah!"*

As the two groups approached each other, they slowed warily. The Islamic boys kept chanting, but the Communist boys remained silent. A stone's throw apart, both sides halted.

Then without warning the mustachioed Red leader raised his pistol and fired wildly.

The report reverberated among the villas. By instinct and training Vern hurled himself down. From where he lay he could see the initial clash: fists knives clubs flashing in air. There were screams, and for a few moments Vernon Gardner was back on one of the nameless islands of the Pacific, knees up, eyes shut tight, while Jap mortars whistled overhead. But here on a street of Jakarta there was only the occasional pop of small-arms fire. Just to scare people. This is not serious, Vern told himself. He relaxed a little. He watched a bunch of untrained kids flailing at one another.

Then he heard a sound that also came from the past—the deep jumpy rumble of army trucks. From both directions of the street they came. From his Seabee days Vern recognized the old two-tonners: Jap type-97 Isuzus that he'd seen and heard around Finschhafen, New Guinea. Good old 97 Isuzus—abandoned on jungle paths, vined and rusted and stripped by natives who used bits of engine to adorn their frizzy hair. Now he was seeing 97s again, this time with one eye opened while the other was jammed against the warmth of a Jakartan street.

When the trucks came in, the fight ended. Squads of soldiers jumped from the tailgates, rifles at the ready. They wore boots with billowy trousers flared over the tops, grenade belts, berets. Vern raised up on his elbows to watch. Soldiers coming from the Islamic side went right past those boys and joined the troops attacking the Reds. Aside from a few wounded, the Islamic boys ran off, disappearing in seconds.

But the Reds were in for it; Vern saw that coming. And sure enough, at the command Halt! a boy kept running. Coolly taking a secure stance, a trooper let off a burst from his automatic weapon and shredded the boy's back. Another Red had the left side of his face smashed in when one soldier hit him with a rifle butt while two others pinned his arms. Most of the soldiers were using riot clubs. The boy with the chair leg tried to swing it, but was hit from the side. Hit in the leg below his khaki shorts. Hit so hard that Vern could see his leg below the knee shift backwards, as if sliding on an oiled ratchet. The knee partially detached like a mound of heated rubber and hung ball-like against the calf, while the boy screamed screamed screamed into the morning, his whole face pinched inward against his mouth where the scream was pulsing like a heart.

Vern shut his eyes tightly as he'd done to weather a barrage of shelling. And felt a soundless whimper rising in his throat and re-membered, oh, he remembered, how the cold fear of pain and death used to run through his blood like mice.

———

Minutes later, kicked in the side and threatened with more if he didn't rise, Vern got to his feet, headed docilely for the truck, and climbed in. There were a lot of moaning boys inside. The boy who'd lost his kneecap had been shoved against the slats of the canopied truck. His sweaty face was pale, his eyes glassy from shock.

Vern recognized the mustachioed leader who was sprawled nearby, one hand clamped against his ear.

"What in hell happened?" Vern asked in English. "That was nothing but a gang fight."

The leader stared moodily at him. "You are not French. You are American."

"Sure. CIA. A master spy. Who were the other kids? How can I give a good report if you don't tell me?"

"We won," the boy said defensively.

"Of course you won. Who were they?"

"HMI. Muslim students."

"How often do you kids get together?" The leader didn't have enough English for the sarcasm, so Vern rephrased the question. "Do you fight a lot?"

The boy nodded. "HMI hates us. So does army."

That was clear. The fight had been violent but essentially harmless until the troopers arrived. Where was the kid who got shot in the back? The truck was filled with wounded Pemuda Rakyat, some of whom had broken bones, other injuries. And the boy without a knee, propped against the slats like a doll, must be wondering how such pain could come from a desire for something as reasonable as the justice they'd told him would be his if only he fought for it. What every hurt and dying child-warrior through history had been told.

So at last Indonesia was real to Vernon Gardner. He had built some things, had fallen in love at Lake Toba, had put up those flyovers in Palembang, had come here for more work—but rarely had he looked around to see what was happening. Now he was going to pay attention, because people were doing bad things in the name of justice. What he heard was suffering and what he saw was blood. Vern reached down to circle with a hand one of his own knees, wondering what it felt like to lose one when you were eighteen.

Finally the truck halted and the tailgate dropped down. Vern got ready to jump when he was told.

"You." A soldier waved a rifle at him. He jumped.

162

Minutes later an officer behind a desk was questioning him. "Why were you with those Red agitators?"

"They asked me along to watch them fight for justice," Vern said. Instantly he realized his sarcasm was lost on the officer. It had been stupid of him to speak with the arrogance of a foreigner. "I work for OPSUS. What happened was no business of mine."

But the damage had been done. The officer ordered him taken away. Chastened, Vern sat quietly in a windowless little room for hours before being roughly escorted down a number of corridors to another small room. He sat here a long time too. Then he was pushed into a large office with blinds drawn against a searing afternoon sun.

A heavyset major sat behind a desk. Vern stood there until the officer filled a page of notepaper with his scratchy pen. Then he glanced up, face square, eyes cold, mouth set in a skeptical smile.

"Your name is Gardner Vernon?"

"Vernon Gardner."

"I am Major Sigit. I command this battalion." He meant for Vern to be impressed.

Vern said nothing.

"We don't have foreigners mingling with Reds every day."

Vern said nothing.

"Why were you with them?"

"Accidentally I got into their line of march."

"Accidentally?" The smile grew. "You were walking along and accidentally found yourself among them?"

"That's right, Major."

"Strange." The smile widened. "I have heard nothing like it. Well then, after you joined them accidentally, did they hurt or threaten you?"

Vern could have told the truth, but he disliked this man with the nasty smile. He decided to protect the damn fool kids. "Not at all."

"They made no threats?" The major's smile was gone.

"None."

"You saw them attack the Muslim students?"

"I saw the two groups close at the same time."

"You didn't see the Reds attack first?"

"I did not."

The major was frowning. "What are your connections in Jakarta?"

Vern knew what he meant. "I am not American government personnel, I am not CIA. I am an ordinary citizen who builds things. I was walking along and accidentally got caught up in the incident. The kids didn't threaten me. Both groups seemed only too eager to fight, and that's what they did. Please call General Sakirman at OPSUS." He added after a pause, "I think you should contact OPSUS as soon as possible. It would be wise."

Nevertheless, it was twilight before someone from OPSUS was able to free Vernon Gardner from the custody of Major Sigit.

Eighteen

Most evenings Maggie played cards, as a concession to her hostess. After cards she often sat in the garden looking at the large moon of the Indies. On Samosir Island, she had told Vern, "We've been lied to. We've been told there's only one moon. But there must be two. One for the Indies, another for the rest of the world."

Mornings in the batik factory she sat cross-legged alongside the other women and worked, as they did, with a copper canting at linen draped on a small wooden frame. With hot wax she filled in the outline tracing of Parang Rusak, a broken-kris design. Or she tried to fill it in—she was damn clumsy with the canting. When she heated wax in a bowl over a tiny charcoal flame, the result poured out too liquidly and ran all over the cloth. Or not heated sufficiently, the wax failed to penetrate the threads. And in the cross-legged position she felt cramped, to say nothing of awkward, with her long, jean-clad legs thrust into the working space of women on either side. It was hot in the airless room, made doubly so by the charcoal braziers. And from the next room, where men were using copper stamps to mass-produce batik, billows of black smoke emerged that carried the heavy, sweetish stench of molten wax. After a few years of working with so much wax, these men would lack breath for riding bikes or playing badminton.

Maggie learned by trial and error to control the canting. She learned to blow on the spout and clear it of stuck wax. She hoped she was learning patience.

Afterward she liked to stroll nearby through the meticulously swept grounds of the kraton. Sometimes, if court dancers were practicing the serimpi, she would watch them: twenty young girls dancing under the stern eyes of teachers who in their own day had performed for the sultan's court. To the percussive sound of a gamelan orchestra, the girls moved languorously. Most of the movement involved the flicking of a scarf. The footwork was minimal: when toes tapped the floor, such abrupt motion seemed almost violent. Teachers corrected their students by pressing a finger against neck back thigh arm, conforming the body to patterns of perfection invisible to Maggie Gardner from Iowa.

As she sat today on the pavilion's edge and watched, Maggie heard a sharp high-pitched voice behind her. "You are English, Dutch?"

She turned to a little man who must have approached noiselessly through the graveled courtyard. He wore a pair of baggy pants, a rumpled white shirt, and a porkpie hat with a long feather drooping from it.

"French? German? I speak them all. Arabic? I speak that too," he claimed proudly. He smiled from a toothless mouth. There was a huge mole on his left cheek, hairy and ugly. She tried not to stare at it.

"American," she said.

Reaching into the baggy pants, he produced calling cards. Shuffling through them, he found the right one. "My card in English," he said, handing it to her.

MAS SLAMAT
PAINTER SCULPTOR TRANSLATOR GUIDE AUTHOR PHILOSOPHER
AT YOUR SERVICE

"In days of the Dutch," he said, "the use of titles was supervised.

A man must prove his right to use Raden or Mas with his name. About ten years ago the government stopped controlling titles. This was concession to Communists and other radicals. So today people call themselves anything they want. They pretend to greatness. I use Mas because my family earned the right to it many— Decades? Ten years?"

"Yes. Decade: ten years."

"Many decades ago. Do you like serimpi?"

"Very much."

His faint smile suggested to Maggie that he had no faith in her judgment of court dancing. Well, they were even; neither did she. Maggie got to her feet. Standing beside him, she figured he couldn't be much over five feet tall. She felt outsized beside Mas Slamat, who fell into step with her. He swayed like a duck, reminding her of Charlie Chaplin, except this little man was not trying to be funny. Indeed, he was tight-lipped, severe.

"Allow me to accompany you," he said, lifting the porkpie hat off his head in salute. "Where are you going?"

"Home."

"To hotel?"

"No," she said guardedly.

"Where then?"

"To a house where I'm staying."

"Whose house?"

"A friend's house."

"What name?"

Maggie increased her pace, hoping he would go away.

But Mas Slamat waddled along at the pace she set. His sharp little eyes glanced at her sidelong. It gave him a shifty look, which seemed to suit him. He began telling her of the old days in the kraton.

He stopped to point dramatically at an inner courtyard. Animals fought there, he claimed. A square of spearmen cordoned off the area. A tiger was released from its cage to face a buffalo. Nearly always the tiger attacked fiercely but soon tired. The buffalo, however, stood its ground and displayed a secret power that triumphed.

"It allowed the sultan to teach his people a lesson," Mas Slamat said.

They were strolling again. Maggie looked down at him. His eyes were fixed groundward as he swayed along.

"What sort of lesson?" she asked.

He explained that such contests were usually held in honor of Dutch officials. The Dutch didn't know, of course, that the tiger stood for Holland, the buffalo for Java.

"And the buffalo won," Maggie said with a smile. "Yes, that's quite a lesson."

Mas Slamat did not smile back. He had lit a cigarette which dangled from his thin lips. He talked through the smoke. The strangest contest was held in honor of the Dutch governor of Semarang. When the animals were turned loose in the cordoned area, as usual the tiger attacked, but quickly became bored. So they let a second tiger into the square. It did the same. Finally, by prodding them with lit torches, the soldiers got the two tigers to attack each other. Standing motionless nearby, the buffalo watched them fight to the death. Yogya never forgot that battle. Even with reinforcements the white men were bound to lose because they always fought one another. Patient Java would be victorious. Of course, the Dutch governor of Semarang had no idea what had happened; he called the contest entertaining. That was the finest lesson of all: white men did not know when they were made fools of.

"No offense, Nonya," said Mas Slamat. "Come along. I am acquainted with a good place for food." Just beyond the kraton was a makeshift warung on the street. Beneath its canvas awning Mas Slamat ordered two glasses of milk and three sticks of saté. Gulping the milk, wolfing down the saté, he belched loudly. Then to Maggie he said, "Pay the man there, that one seated. Don't let him cheat you. It's two rupiah."

When Maggie walked back to her bike, he accompanied her. She had propped it under a tree on the alun-alun, a parade ground in front of the palace. Watching her unlock the bike and get on, he said, "Where do you go?"

"I told you, Mas Slamat. Home."

"Whose house?"

"I told you." Putting one foot on a pedal, she prepared to push off. She was about to say good-bye when Mas Slamat held the handlebar with a wrinkled hand.

"No need to find other guide," he said. "I am the one. I know everything here. You want to know Yogya, don't you, Nonya?"

Maggie took her foot off the pedal.

"No need to worry. You have found me. I study books and people. I study places. I know it all." Dropping his hand from the handlebar, he wet his lips tensely. "If you work for American consul, I can be your political analyst."

She told him she had no connection with the American government.

His smile was blatantly skeptical. Raising his hand, he touched the hairy mole thoughtfully.

He could be wondering if she was a spy. Maggie said, "I can't help you with the consulate."

"I know everything you need to know."

"Are you looking for work, Mas Slamat?"

That question seemed to catch him off guard. He yanked down the brim of his porkpie hat. "I speak eight languages," he said in a voice of injured pride. "I know people you must meet, things you must see. When you think about my qualifications, you will come looking for me. Then we will talk. I will show you my house." He drew himself up proudly. Doffing the hat again, he swayed off like a duck, a comical but deadly serious figure.

———————

Next day Maggie found him waiting for her when she came out of the batik factory: porkpie hat with droopy feather; tight lips; narrow appraising eyes; outsized hands hanging limp against his baggy pants as if too heavy to lift. Studying her a few moments, he touched the mole—it seemed to help him think.

"How did you know I was here?" Maggie asked.

"I know." He watched her unlock the bike. "I am hungry," he said.

Maggie turned from the bike to look at him.

"Warung nearby," he said.

"Well, a cup of tea would be nice." She began wheeling the bike, allowing him to lead the way.

"Tea doesn't set well on my stomach. I won't have tea. Do you have a cigarette?"

When she gave him one, he didn't thank her, but lit it and puffed vigorously. He pursed his lips in judgment. "American cigarettes are best. Everything American is best." He gave her one of his sly sidelong glances. "I have been thinking about you. I thought all night. I know people you must meet. If you want to be happy in Yogya, you must have help. I will provide that help. Leave everything to me. You are in my hands."

Maggie wheeled the bike on. She didn't know whether to be amused or annoyed. She did know that she would put up with him. She just didn't know why.

"You have met R. Harjanta Prijohoetomo?" he asked after some moments of silence.

"I'm afraid not."

Mas Slamat snorted in trumph. "You have not met R. Harjanta Projohoetomo! Let me handle it. You will meet him today."

"Wait a minute," she said, laughing. "Who is he?"

"Director of World Peace Radiating Center."

"Is he some kind of guru?"

"He is great man. He doesn't work. He sleeps all day, wakes all night. He will teach you meditation and spiritual matters known only to him. Don't worry. I will arrange everything. Here is the place for good cheap food." He added emphatically, "Cheap is always best." Striding into a small dirty warung, he ordered himself chicken with rice. Maggie had tea. He never asked if she was hungry too. Mas Slamat was content to have her wait and pay. Wiping his mouth on his shirtsleeve, Mas Slamat explained the bill to her. Maggie paid, while he stood outside. When she came out of the warung, he questioned her closely. "You paid only four rupiah? Four is enough. *Orang asing* always pay too much. How much did you pay? Five? Six? I told you four. How much?"

She still couldn't understand why she was going along with him. After they set out, she walking the bike, he smoking another bummed cigarette, Maggie asked if he studied with the guru at the World Peace Radiating Center.

"I do not," Mas Slamat told her indignantly. "I am santri Muslim." Once that sank in, he added, "I am haji. I have gone to Mecca."

170

"Where's your white peci?"

"I don't wish to call notice to myself."

Maggie let that go. "What is the guru's name again?"

"R. Harjanta Prijohoetomo. He is great man, holy man."

"But you don't study with him."

"No." Mas Slamat obviously felt this was sufficient explanation. They walked silently in the noon heat.

And then it came to Maggie why she had put up with him. This little fellow who accosted foreigners with calling cards in various languages, who was probably a charlatan, clearly a freeloader, must know a lot about Yogya. He must know about the dalang, who had been in her thoughts ever since that day of the hypnotism.

"Can you tell me about Ki-Dalang Gitosuwoko?" she asked suddenly.

Mas Slamat halted. He stared from under the rim of his porkpie hat. His toothless gums were churning. "I know about it."

"Know about what?"

"He hypnotized you."

"How could you possibly know?"

"I know."

"Did he tell you?"

"Of course not."

"Well, then?"

Short of yanking out his fingernails with hot pincers, Maggie realized she would never know his source of information. That might well be Mas Slamat's single point of honor: protecting informants.

"What is your opinion of the dalang?" she asked on a different tack.

"Great dalang. For Yogya style."

"As opposed to—?"

"I prefer wayang kulit from Surakarta. But for Yogya style"—he puffed vigorously on his cigarette for emphasis—"none better than Ki-Dalang Gitosuwoko. Good singing voice. Handles puppets as well as Ki-Dalang Prawiroharjo used to do. I saw Prawiroharjo many times. I saw him perform *Singangembara*. They say his was the best ever. They say his demons will never be equaled. His Gatutkaca was the best I have seen in that play."

"To get back to Dalang Gitosuwoko."

"Best dalang now. His clowns are very funny."

"How can he dare hypnotize people without their consent?"

Mas Slamat shrugged. "A great man like that, he does what he does."

"He certainly does what he wants."

"You must be Javanese to understand."

"Then help me understand."

"No," he said in a sharp, rude tone.

After walking awhile longer, Maggie got on her bike. Mas Slamat looked surprised. Perhaps he'd been hoping for a big meal somewhere—say, in the Hotel Garuda dining room. Or for new clothes. Or for something else he wanted.

Before pushing off, Maggie said, "Are you telling me you must be born Javanese to understand Javanese things?"

"Is that not usual in countries? You know the world you are born into?"

"Usual but not necessary. You can overcome birth."

"That is true, Nonya. A Frenchman came here years ago. He lived in small house and learned all levels of Javanese language and the old language too. He lived in the small house maybe twenty years and died in it. He understood Javanese things. He would understand the dalang too." Mas Slamat stared a long time at her, his gums working. "You could be like the Frenchman."

"You think so? Why?"

The little man shrugged. "I don't know. People come to Yogya and live awhile and go away. But you could stay here always."

"Why do you think so?" Maggie persisted.

Again he shrugged. "Some can, some can't." For a moment his face pursed up as if he were thinking about the distinction. Then he smiled in the sly sidelong way that gave him a furtive small-animal look. "But don't you worry," he said, treating her again like a rich tourist. "You are in my hands. I will wait for you at the factory tomorrow."

She almost told him not to. But he'd do it anyway. And she felt an appeal coming from Mas Slamat. For money? Solace? Advice? Surely not advice. But the appeal was there, like that of a child who is not sure how to ask for something.

She said, "All right, then. Tomorrow." And she pedaled away. She would write Vern about him. But on second thought she would not;

Vern would think she was running around with charlatans, which of course Mas Slamat most surely was. For a similar reason she would not write about the dalang either. After all, the man had hypnotized her without her consent. What would Vern think of that? The question brought a frown, then a smile to her lips. If Vern knew Yogya, he might think Jakarta in its way was safer.

Nineteen

Maggie sat on the veranda of the main house, sipping tea. She had decided to stay clear of the batik factory. Yesterday it had occurred to her that the other women did batik as a kind of meditation, whereas for her it was merely a craft, something a college girl might try out during a summer vacation. She didn't want to tell her Iowa friends someday, "Look at this, I made it over there." Them and us: I made one just like theirs. She no longer wanted to be on the outside looking in. That had been all right when she worked in anthropology; at least then a perceptible goal had legitimized her interest in things. She hated the idea of being an expatriate traveling from place to place, storing up impressions the way tourists accumulate trinkets that go eventually into closets and drawers.

Maggie had come to a time of decision here in Yogya. For one thing, Susanto was going to Surabaya on business (PROPELAD business), then to Malang for a visit with her husband's family. She did not invite Maggie along. Their companionship, based on mutual curiosity, had become mere tolerance of each other: Maggie wasn't enough of a gambler, and Susanto's attention flagged quickly when turned to anything but poker chips. That they both understood this change in their relationship enabled them now to be frank and considerate—Maggie thanked Susanto for a wonderful time and Susanto insisted that Maggie stay on. After all, there was plenty of room; the servants had nothing else to do; and her husband would be embarrassed if Tuan Gardner's wife moved to a hotel. These were admirably practical arguments, delivered while Susanto devoured a coconut cake.

Maggie asked for a little time to think about it. "Perhaps it would be better if I move to the Hotel Garuda." She was not facing the possibility of returning to Jakarta yet. That was somehow far off; she had turned priorities around in her mind during vague planning for the future, so that Vern would come here rather than she go back to Jakarta.

"No Garuda," Susanto declared, shaking her head. "Hotels no good, dear, for learn a country."

That, Maggie felt from her own experience, was true. She had lived in the hotels of Medan and Palembang like a caged animal. Sometimes she wondered if her bad experiences in Palembang had come from her sense of hotel isolation. Vern had seen most of the Orient, yet sometimes he seemed to lack all understanding of the people, aside from their technological needs, as if they moved in the background while in the foreground he built things. Hotel life was perfect for an expatriate busy with progress, but not for her.

"I accept your offer," Maggie said briskly. "I'll stay here, Susanto. It's very much appreciated. When will you be back?"

Susanto shrugged, and indeed, she always gave the impression of someone huge who could be blown around like a feather. "Use anything in house," she declared. "Use casino too. But word advice." She leaned forward as if they might be overheard. "If you play faro, leave out Nonya Suryadarma. I do not understand, but Utami always win."

Maggie was waiting on the veranda for Ali, who had promised to take her to the gong factory in an outlying village. She waited a long time, but Susanto had explained to her that this was the Javanese way of keeping appointments: *Jam karet disini*—time was rubber here, a stretchable commodity. You could show up later than hell without angering people. So Maggie waited, trying not to show the impatience

175

of a Westerner. Through the midmorning haze she saw Inam approaching, a tiny girl whose mother had served the Sakirman family and who was herself now a housemaid. Maggie liked her. Inam had not yet fully learned the veiled look, the evasive reply, the studied pleasantness that marked the experienced servants. Inam was forthright when she forgot who she was, and this tendency, augmented by humor and intelligence, made her the only person in the Sakirman household whom Maggie tried to reach.

Maggie smiled when the girl came up. "I am staying in the house, Inam."

"Yes, Nonya, we are all glad."

That was probably not true. When did a servant ever want to serve? The staff of eight would obviously prefer the house for themselves. "I won't be much bother," Maggie said. They were talking Bahasa Indonesia.

"We are glad to serve you."

"Inam, I want to learn your language." When the girl smiled as one would smile at a child's grandiose plans, Maggie added, "It's something I really want to do. I mean it." She said, "I know it's difficult."

"Difficult, Nonya. There are three levels of Javanese." She listed them on her fingers. "Ngoko, the low; Madya, the middle; Krama, the high. And another level sometimes. And then there is low and high within the low and high." She raised her eyebrows as if something ironic had occurred to her. "Only the sultan is lucky. He needs to speak only Ngoko, the low level, because everyone else is beneath him."

"If I spoke Javanese with you, what would happen?"

"You would speak Ngoko, the low, to me and I would speak Krama, the high, to you."

"And if I spoke with Nonya Sakirman?"

"Both would speak Krama. But after a while, because you are friends, you would start using words of Madya and both speak Madya." Inam paused thoughtfully. "But she is older, so maybe she would speak Madya to you but you would continue Krama to her."

"And if a stranger came along?"

Inam threw up her hands in merry despair. "You both start with Krama to see who you are, if you are equal or one of you is a higher

176

person. Each of you asks where the other comes from and who your relatives are and your friends. That way you place each other before changing from Krama. If one is higher, you will speak two levels. The one lower speaks Krama and the higher speaks Ngoko. If you are equal, then you can move downward together and speak Madya style. Later, if you like each other, you might slowly put in some Ngoko words and finally speak Ngoko altogether like old friends do and children. But if you go from Krama to Madya and very soon the stranger speaks Ngoko to you, you will be insulted, because it means he has decided you are lower than he is. So you can no longer speak Madya to him and give him such an advantage. What you do then is speak Ngoko too, insulting him back, and get away as fast as you can."

Maggie shook her head. "Javanese isn't a language; it's—forgive me—a frightening way of life."

"That is why some people speak Bahasa Indonesia to each other, because there is only one level and they avoid making mistakes." Inam pursed her lips in the effort to reach a decision. "If a foreigner makes mistake in Javanese and uses the wrong level of speech, it will be forgiven. To learn Javanese, Nonya, is the way to know us and that is what you want."

"Yes, that is what I want." And Maggie did. She swept aside the likelihood that her stay would be too short for her to learn more than a few phrases of Javanese. She was borne upon the crest of a sudden enthusiasm and felt stirring within her an unshakable conviction, though to have put it into words—it encompassed more than language—would have been too much for her. "That's what I want," she repeated. "I hear a Frenchman lived here a long time and spoke like a Javanese."

Inam nodded. "He is remembered."

"Do you know someone who might give me lessons?"

"I do, Nonya. An old guru who speaks English, Dutch. He lives in my kampong."

"What is out there, Inam?"

The girl looked puzzled.

"I mean, there's the kraton and the museum and the theaters, but what else is out there in Yogyakarta?"

"The kampongs."

"Yes, of course. And many things are happening in them I don't understand."

"Many things, Nonya." The girl hesitated, as if preparing to divulge secrets about neighborhood life. Instead, she thrust her hand out and gave Maggie a folded piece of paper. "Left for Nonya. I came to give it to you."

On the paper in precise black letters was printed the following message: "To make amends for our last meeting I wish to take you to see Borobudur. I will send someone tonight for your reply."

Naturally, it wasn't signed. The dalang's arrogance was enough of a signature and that angered her as much as the message itself, which had a condescending tone. Did it or didn't it? Unable to decide, Maggie crumpled the paper and held it in her fist. "I would like to begin lessons as soon as possible."

The girl said nothing. She was expecting something more—a reaction to the note. Obviously she knew who sent it, though it was written in English. Maggie resisted the temptation to ask who had brought it. "Can you arrange for me to meet the language guru tomorrow?"

Since no reaction was forthcoming, the girl turned to leave and said over her shoulder, "I will arrange it, Bu."

"Bu?"

"Javanese for 'Nonya.'"

"So you have given me my first word." When the girl left, crossing the hot courtyard slowly, as if the air had weight to it like water, Maggie sat back and waited. Rubber time began stretching toward noon.

Suddenly with a screech of tires Ali roared into the courtyard on a motorcycle. The large bulbous crash helmet made his thin figure look buglike. He had another helmet for her and instructed her how to put it on. She listened politely. The truth was she'd dated a boy in high school who owned a big Harley-Davidson; she'd learned to ride as well as he did.

"Here we go," Ali said gaily and told her to get behind him and where to put her feet. "You grip me at waist. You must be vigilant."

She had a feeling he had rehearsed the instruction, had looked up the word *"awas"* in his *Kamus Bahasa Inggeris* and found "vigilant." Maggie asked him, "Is this your bike?"

"Bike of village friend. Achmad is sergeant in army."

Odd, she thought: a PKI organizer friendly with an army sergeant. Her surprise must have shown in her face, because Ali explained, as they drove away, that the two families had been close for many years. In the village it didn't matter that he and Achmad were political adversaries. When he asked Achmad for the loan of the bike to come get his guest, the soldier had no choice. Otherwise both families would have been grievously insulted.

He was explaining these ethics while driving at high speed through the streets of Yogya. He was reckless in the manner of an unskilled driver who wishes to look skilled. Maggie held on to his lean body with her clasped hands and hoped for the best.

Beyond the outlying kampongs of Yogya, they came to a swollen river that had only a footbridge fording it. Ali stopped; they both got off the bike and studied the river and bridge. A broad palm leaf came along the brown flood like a puck scooting on a sheet of ice. Maggie pulled at her shirt, wet from perspiration formed between Ali's body and hers. She turned to him. His small, angular face was pinched into a frown.

"You walk," he said. "I ride."

"Ali, that bridge looks pretty narrow." Then she confessed to her knowledge of bikes. She had the experience needed to ride this bike across.

Ali never even glanced at her, but stared at the rapid water. "You walk, I ride."

"Do you swim, Ali?"

He shook his head.

"If you go off the bridge and can't swim, Ali, what will happen? Bad to lose the bike. Worse to lose you. We can do better than that."

He kept looking at the water.

"I really do know bikes, Ali. Give me a chance to show it, will you?"

"I can walk bike," he said.

"But the bridge is too narrow. You can't walk alongside the bike. Please let me ride it across."

Ali knelt and studied the bridge, as if there might be some mathematical solution to the problem. Then, rising, he said emphatically, "You walk. I ride."

Without waiting for a reply, he got on and gunned the motor. He set off, wobbling.

Maggie watched, heart in her mouth, as the front wheel turned violently in wide arcs but started Ali across the shaky footbridge. Under him the slats rattled and dipped in their loose ropework. She followed when he was halfway. She felt the boards ripple and flutter from the motorized power crossing them. One thing she knew now about Ali: he was both reckless and determined, a bad combination for a long life. But she liked the daring in him. For a moment she recalled the square leathery face of his uncle.

So Ali got across. He seemed to have willed it. Then on the other side they were off again, she gripping his lean waist, he tooling down a dirt road that lay between flat expanses of padis. Maggie held on lightly, her eyes peering over his shoulder at great patches of rice shoots and goats that were nibbling at shorn stalks in harvested fields. Women in coolie hats were bending to weed the padis where the rice was still ripening. The air felt cool as it flew past the speeding bike. Peasants trudged the roadside with double baskets of manure strapped to their backs. A brick kiln was smoking next to a field; nearby, under a cluster of sunflowers, some children were squatting along with a dog.

What had Ali said?

The world of rice fields had swallowed her up for a few moments.

He repeated it: "This is real Java."

To which she replied, close to his ear and earnestly, "I believe it."

"I hope you like gong factory."

"Well, I like music."

His helmet turned slightly as though he wished to look at her when he corrected her attitude. "Gong factory better. Gong better than music." He drove farther along the padis before adding, "Soul of music is not in music. Is in gong."

Slatted bamboo fences, broomed lanes, atap roofs. Now she entered another world, this one predominately brown: the earth-hued world of a Javanese village.

Ali drove up to a truck garden and parked the bike. He led Maggie past an old woman weeding in the garden to a group of low wooden buildings from which smoke was rising. In a courtyard some men wearing ragged shorts and undershirts were chiseling at gray lumps of metal.

"Gongs," Ali said. They had been discolored by casting and were now being chased and polished. He pointed to a circle of rice with a banana lying beside it next to a man scraping his chisel across a gong surface. "Banana and rice, they honor gong. No work until prayer."

Leading her to the veranda of the largest building, Ali raised his hands in a respectful sembah to a man squatting in the shade. He squinted from under a battered felt hat, regarding them imperiously from red-rimmed eyes. He began coughing steadily but without discernible inconvenience, as if it were an old habit.

"This," said Ali to Maggie, "is Panji Sepuh. He is prince."

Maggie stared at the coughing man while Ali explained that the foundrymen took their names from an old Muslim tale. Such names enabled them to find the proper spiritual mood for making gongs. Most of the foundrymen had assumed the identity of Prince Panji's half brothers.

Ali took her inside the foundry. Within the dark room were three fires sunk in pits of gray clinkers. Maggie blinked rapidly, adjusting to a gloom punctuated by flares of color in the burning coals. They kept the foundry dark, Ali said, in order to see the metal heating; they judged the metal's thickness by its color. She could see that he liked to explain things. Perhaps his penchant for teaching had led him to communism; it gave him a chance to tell people what they didn't know.

A powerfully built founder came up.

"This is Charangwaspa," Ali said. "First son of younger sister Panji's mother. That is his gong-making name. His other name is Bambang. He is my brother."

Bambang spoke briefly in Javanese, and Ali translated. "Charangwaspa says too bad no big gongs here. Made now in Semarang only. Weigh fifty kilo. Charangwaspa hope you like gong here, but not so big. So good though, I think. The soul is in them."

What would Bix and Louie and Muggsy and Tram think of such

worship of instruments? Maggie wondered. They'd say *we* make the damn music, the horns don't. Bix used to lose his cornets, and more than once he got hold of another in a pawnshop.

Ali's brother now joined two other men who were dressed in black and also wore felt hats. All three were coughing. It reminded her of the batik workers with their bad lungs, except these founders swallowed zinc and copper dust instead of vaporized wax. Every time Maggie breathed, she felt the grit of burned metal sliding down her throat.

Now they were melting copper wire in an iron bowl. Others heated a medium-sized gong at a larger pit. One founder operated a bellows, slapping its side like a pillow being plumped for bed. The bellows' breath stirred a pit of fire into a golden whirlpool. Sparks geysered up around the gong half buried in charcoal. A founder held the heating metal with wood-handled iron tongs.

Hearing a sound like the muffled step of troops, Maggie looked up. Running down to a third pit was a long pipe of iron, cradled in rope loops attached to the atap roof. This pipe ended in a goatskin bellows that was worked, Ali told her, by Doyok, a servant to Prince Panji. Low man was Jangkung, court jester, whose job was to clean the smithy. Maggie began to feel this was as much theater as foundry. Or to think of it another way, men here were living inside a folktale that featured the court of a Muslim ruler.

"Kindly please come out," Ali said, "it is too hot."

Moments later, as she walked with him through the village, away from the screech of chisel on cold bronze, Ali admitted that her presence today would help him in his work. Country people had never lost their awe of Westerners. No matter how much they were told about independence and the threat of interference from colonial powers, villagers still believed the myth of Western superiority. He used the English word "myth."

Abruptly he changed the subject, so abruptly that Maggie wondered how long he had been brooding about it, a question nagging at his consciousness like a tooth beginning to ache. "Where is your husband, Nonya?" For the first time today he used Nonya instead of Maggie.

"In Jakarta. I thought you knew that."

"I know that." He paused as if once again analyzing his knowledge. "You stay here but he stay there."

182

She didn't like the way he said it, a note of disapproval or even of accusation in his voice. So instead of answering him, she asked a question of her own. "Why aren't you married, Ali?"

"How marry? I giving my life to PKI."

They returned to the factory. Founders were lifting a heated gong from fire to anvil. While two men secured it with tongs, others began beating it with large hammers.

"They hit in order," Ali explained.

Bambang (Charangwaspa), senior founder, hit the gong first with the hammer called a palu. The beaklike head of it descended, crashed, rang in the close dark air. Finally they thrust the gong into a big vat of water, the resultant sound like snakes hissing. Hauling the gong out, they let its cooling gray mass fall to the floor.

"Now they heat again," Ali said.

Coughing, they stood in a circle and smoked cigarettes down to their sooty fingertips while waiting for the gong to heat.

It was placed again on the anvil and was again beaten, clanging like the pulse of a huge metallic heart. Ali called Maggie to the foundry door.

Waiting there was a young man about his size and age, wearing a sarong. Ali introduced him as Achmad, sergeant of infantry in the 454th Diponegoro Battalion. With sudden pride, as if he were not a sworn enemy of the army, Ali added that Achmad would soon leave for Jakarta, where his unit would join the Honorary Palace Guard on Armed Forces Day.

The sergeant said nothing, seeming tongue-tied in the presence of a foreigner. She wondered what kind of a soldier he was. Perhaps a good one: unimaginative but dutiful.

"His bike we ride," Ali noted.

"Thank you," Maggie said to the little soldier who stared back lugubriously, as if they shared a private grief.

Ali repeated his name, "Achmad Bachtiar," to emphasize his importance. Sumatra had taught her this too: village loyalties were stronger than national politics. At least until a crisis; that's what Vern often said. "Until they start fighting. All hell breaking loose without notice, sweetheart. Like an avalanche. Then tradition won't mean anything."

So there was tea—Achmad Bachtiar, brother Bambang, Ali, and

herself. Often the men broke into Javanese, but Ali possessed natural courtesy and would guide them back into Bahasa Indonesia for her sake. Maggie had been raised to think of Communists as somber and rude. One of her college classmates had often bragged about being a Communist—and he had been somber and rude. But Ali seemed like an eager boy who was passing through an age of confusion with good grace.

At one point, as they sat with their tea on the veranda of a small whitewashed bungalow—Bambang's house—Ali turned to Maggie and said with a smile that his brother wished to know her opinion of gamelan. Maggie looked at the heavyset founder whose face was that of a bulldog, glowering and sullen. Yet his request came from a courtly desire to be courteous.

So Maggie answered in kind. She was pleased that he wanted to know her opinion of gamelan, even though she had little knowledge of such a great and complex art. (She spoke in English, as if acknowledging that the subject required the best of her linguistic skill. Ali translated, and when his brother heard her graceful statement, he smiled approvingly.) But then she began talking about the music she did understand, Chicago and New Orleans jazz, which depended more on variety of attack and the use of solos than on ensemble work, unlike gamelan. Lapsing into jargon as people do when talking of their obsessions, her talk of "pitch blending and trading eights and fours" did nothing but confirm her own enthusiasm. Ali understood none of the technical words and therefore couldn't translate for his brother, who leaned intently forward, waiting. Aware of her lapse Maggie tried to make amends. "Tell your brother I want to learn everything I can about gamelan. What I know about the music of my country will help me learn."

Ali translated; his brother called out sharply. His wife, a small pretty woman who had served tea, came to the doorway. He spoke harshly— Maggie felt for her benefit—and Bambang's wife left, returning soon with a pencil and paper. During a long silence, unbroken around the table, Bambang scribbled on the paper, after which he gave it to Ali. It was a diagram of a gamelan orchestra, designating the positions of various gongs, drums, and metallophones: sarons, genders, gambangs, bonangs, kenongs, ketuks, and the rest. The diagram, though created rapidly, was exhaustive, and Ali, with Bambang's close and

184

critical supervision, was painstaking in explaining it. Maggie glanced up now and then from the diagram to the square, austere face of Bambang (Charangwaspa) Gitosuwoko, whose dark eyes in their intensity reminded her of the dalang. What a strange family, she thought. All of them, each in his way, formidable.

Later, on the ride back, the rhythmic sound of the motorbike lulled Maggie into fleeting memories of jazz. Through the metallic growl of the motor owned by Sergeant Achmad Bachtiar, she heard the cornet of Bix soar for a few moments into a late Javanese afternoon, above fields growing blue in shadow, above the distant row of palm trees into the top of which a boiling red sun had settled. Bix Beiderbecke spent his last days in the Queens apartment of bassist George Kraslow. Bix had a habit of rising at three or four in the morning to play his cornet. The neighbors, however, didn't complain. They told Kraslow, "Let him play. It's okay with us."

Some people get away with it—*it* being almost anything.

Against Ali's helmeted ear she said, "Your uncle wants to take me to Borobudur."

Ali slowed down as if to think this through. Finally he said, "Uncle know Borobudur."

"Should I go with him?"

Ali's shrug was a refusal to reply.

It had been foolish to ask him. After all, it was none of his business and she knew how he felt about his uncle, and the truth was she had already decided to accept the invitation. She had made up her mind while hearing in imagination the sound of Bix's cornet following the wheels of their bike through a Javanese sunset. The first lyrical notes of his solo in "Singin' the Blues" had filled her memory and then a small voice from within had told her, "What the hell."

They had nearly reached the narrow bridge before speaking again. Ali said, "I do not think he hypnotize next time."

"He better not try. You really don't think he'll try?"

"No. He already have your attention."

Twenty

And so three days later she was sitting beside Kyahi Dalang Budi Gitosuwoko on their way to Borobudur. He picked her up at Susanto's house in a chauffeured car. He wore a batik sarong, black shirt, sandals, a sheathed kris at the small of his back, but no blangkon on his head, which gave the courtly Yogyanese the appearance of being out of uniform. The servants watched intently from doorway and veranda as he accompanied her to the car. As they walked, she felt shorter than he was, though they were about the same height. The dalang had a way of seeming tall.

He sat close to the window, mostly silent during the twenty-five-mile drive to the temple site. Now and then she glanced at his copper-colored face: the thin straight lips, the dark eyes set wide above high cheekbones, like an Apache's, the long-lobed ears, the black cropped hair, and large hands with prominent knuckles that lay rocklike in his lap as if anchoring his emotions.

Maggie was glad of the silence between them as she edged close to her own side of the car. She had no idea what to think of him. She was glad they didn't challenge each other with opinions. She hadn't been this uneasy with a man since college days. It was odd, silly in a way.

She forced herself to concentrate on the landscape. Ahead were blue mountains with skeins of white cloud clinging to their flanks. Otherwise the land was flat, dense with villages. Clove trees, banana trees, dogs, roosters, cows. Rice fields were laid out in long, wavy lines, as if tides of green ocean were cresting and breaking near earthen wall, bamboo fence, the road going by her.

She let the facts of Borobudur work through memory. It was the largest Buddhist stupa in the world, a millennium old. Ten thousand men had worked on it for a century, three hundred years before the great medieval cathedrals of Europe went up. Constructing Borobudur had depleted five generations. No sooner had it been completed, however, than Hindu conquerors overwhelmed the Buddhist kings of Central Java. Into vine-covered neglect the temple fell, much of it buried under volcanic ash until the last century. An apt fate in Maggie's opinion. It had been built in honor of a doctrine that preached the illusion of permanence.

As they approached the site, the dalang suddenly began talking. He explained that a town nearby had been the scene of violence in 1948. In an attempt to win control of the area, some Communists had kidnapped officials and Muslim leaders. They shot these prisoners in a coconut grove within sight of Borobudur. Kidnapping and murder, he told her, within sight of Borobudur. Then the dalang turned again to the window.

She was trying to think of a reply—his sudden words, amounting almost to an outburst on this silent ride, seemed to demand a response—when Borobudur came into view beyond a cluster of palm trees.

Massive, dark, crouching on a hill. It had the look of a fortress, not a temple. She had pictured something taller, less squat. Perhaps she had in mind the silhouette of a Gothic cathedral like Reims or Chartres, the vertical message of a Christian God put into the world long after these Buddhist stones had been placed upon this hill. If Vern were here, she'd discuss with him her first disenchanted impression of Borobudur. An architect might see it differently.

How did the dalang see it? He seemed indifferent, his face toward the window, regarding the rice fields.

Feeling a visitor's need to comment, Maggie said politely, "It's impressive."

"Closer is better," he said without looking at her or at Borobudur either.

The valley was lovely. Maggie wanted to like what she saw, and for this reason, instead of studying the unappealing shape of a squat pyramid, its stones discolored by lichen and pitted by erosion, she turned to look at clumps of palm, at volcanoes hazy blue in the distance, at a lawn coming into view that ascended like a green carpet to the black foot of the temple.

When the car stopped, the driver got out and rushed to the dalang's door, opening it with a bow of respect. Then he walked around and opened Maggie's door without a bow. Borobudur still looked like a huge black toad squatting on a hill. Was closer better? At last the dalang was studying it too. Joining him, Maggie considered how Borobudur had been built. They had simply wrapped unmortared stone around the hillside like a blanket. They had brought a few million cubic feet of volcanic rock from riverbeds and piled it up and carved on it and hauled it up there into position by rope. Thousands of men laboring for one hundred years. What must they have thought, bathed in sweat, straining at ropes, sick from heat and dampness: that the Buddha would lessen their torments in the next life?

These were questions she'd not put to the dalang any more than she'd have put them to Vern. Neither was a man of sentimental imagination. Surely she knew that about Vern. She guessed it about the dalang, who was stepping forward with a glance back at her.

As she came alongside, Maggie remained in step for a few paces, then halted. "Wait," she told him. He stopped. "Before I go up there with you, I want to know what will happen."

"What will happen, Nonya?"

"If what happened the first time will happen again. The Tiger's Milk I couldn't drink because I believed in ghosts."

"That will not happen again."

When they reached the foot of the temple, Dalang Budi suddenly became an attentive guide. It was as if he had hoarded his goodwill for use only when they arrived at the true beginning of Borobudur. Beneath their feet, he explained, lay the lowest of ten levels, with reliefs of daily life carved on the walls. A mantle of stone hid them, symbolizing the removal of earthly desires from the eyes of meditating monks. Circular terraces rising above it represented the spheres of spiritual attainment.

Maggie craned her neck to regard the huge terraces and beyond them dozens of little stupa-houses dotting the upper reaches like beehives. While looking at them she was overcome by a surprising sense of disappointment. This was all interesting, as interesting perhaps as anything she had ever seen, and yet Maggie had expected to learn more. Not about Borobudur, which he so minutely described, but about the dalang. At last she understood the nature of the curiosity that she had come here to satisfy. So as he led her up a stone stairway, Maggie turned to say bluntly, "You are a mystery to me. I'd like to know who you are." And she halted theatrically to force a response.

This otherwise supremely confident man seemed flustered and even at a loss. After his treatment of her at the first meeting, his confusion here delighted Maggie. Perhaps no Javanese woman had ever been bold enough to confront him this way. But then, as they climbed slowly, he searched through the generality of her request for a means of responding. They were bonded for a few moments, she realized, by her own daring and his humility. He stood on the step below (looking up at her in the clear light) and described his childhood: a Muslim school, a love of badminton, and loneliness, the latter unusual for most Javanese boys who were surrounded at home by relatives of all ages. Budi's family had been small, only two sons. His brother had been too old to play with—eighteen years older—and had been in serious training for the profession of dalang throughout Budi's boyhood. In every generation for three centuries the Gitosuwoko family had produced at least one famous puppeteer.

Dalang Budi described his adolescence as they climbed toward a portal in the stairway. He had been targeted for government, especially because his older brother, after fathering three daughters, had produced two sons, either of whom would someday take his place as a dalang. But neither son showed talent, and so Budi had been returned from an international education in Singapore to face the rigors of becoming a puppeteer. He married, but his wife had died without issue five years ago. When his elder brother died the following year, Budi had become head of the Gitosuwoko family. He was forty-three now, with more than a decade of puppeteering behind him.

He had completed this dry account of his life by the time they reached the gateway to the terraces. "We circle clockwise," he told Maggie. "We keep the inner wall always on our right. This is the way of salvation," he said with a smile.

"Do you believe that?"

"The Buddhists believed it a thousand years ago. It is now a matter of respect."

She liked what he said: calm, reasonable, unpretentious. As they began a three-mile walk around four successive terraces, she knew she liked him. She had to admit it. Her liking of him was something already known to her, something familiar, not in dispute, when finally she acknowledged it was possible.

So Maggie allowed herself to like him consciously. She liked his big hands with the prominent knuckles as he moved them through the air during his explanation of bas-reliefs that illustrated the story of Buddha. Halting at mottled stone panels, he talked with the easy authority of an official guide: Queen Maya's dream; Buddha offering a ring to Yasodhara and riding his horse Kanthaka from his comfortable past into a future of hardship and illumination; the Sermon at Benares. Frequently the dalang reached out to touch the stone lovingly, his thick, hard fingers gliding like silk over the pitted surface.

Abruptly Maggie said, "When will I see you perform?"

"When there is a need. We Javanese rather not schedule things too long in advance."

"Whose need?"

"The sultan may want an entertainment. Or there's a special wedding or burial. Or my own need. How long will you be in Yogya?"

"I don't know." On impulse she added, "For some time longer."

"Then you will see me perform."

There was a kind of intimacy to this conversation that unsettled Maggie. She had no wish to make him think she was interested in him (having forgotten her demand for him to tell her who he was). And so she willed herself to find deeper interest in the temple. She encouraged him to play the role of guide.

He explained, as they strolled around the fourth terrace, that foreign commentators believed the builders had had three spheres of spiritual activity in mind when they designed the temple: spheres of desire, form, and formlessness. "This thinking is too rigid for us," the dalang claimed. "Most Javanese believe the temple contains many ideas, not all of them consistent."

He led the way to the squared fifth terrace, which was far more open than the lower ones. There were dagobas set about the terrace—stupas with buddhas inside, seen through holes carved in the covering domes. The dalang reached within a hole. He urged Maggie to do the same, as it was good luck to touch a buddha inside a dagoba.

Maggie reached into a diamond-shaped hole and with her forefinger touched the cool stone arm of a seated buddha. "Do I wish for something specific?"

"If you like."

Maggie thought a moment, but nothing came to her. "Can I wish for good luck in general? For good luck when an accident takes place?"

"I like that very much. I would have preferred your wish to mine."

Once again humility. Yet she did not trust him. He could turn around and do something startling out of an unpredictable impulse that it might amuse him. In a moment of fresh doubt, Maggie wondered if he had orchestrated a show of humility for effect.

But another sensation was overtaking Maggie. Having come from the lower terraces with their inner and outer walls, from those circular passages with their sense of enclosure, out onto the fifth terrace, spacious and open, she felt as though she had been released from prison, both physical and psychological. No longer was she a tourist being guided through facts. She had come upon a place of visual and psychic release. It must have been like this for ancient devotees: by finding limitless space on the broad stonework of the fifth terrace, they had reached enlightenment after a lifetime of the ordinary. But she didn't share this fleeting vision with the dalang. He had strolled to a far corner of the terrace with its view of twin volcanoes among gathering clouds.

There are people, Maggie thought, who don't mind being interrupted at what they're doing. They're sensitive to the demands of others. The dalang was not one of them. There was no conscious generosity in the man, no yielding to the moods of other people, Maggie decided, so she walked over to the bell-shaped central stupa and left him alone. To her surprise he soon joined her; together they stared in silence at the large discolored stupa.

"Some years ago they opened it up and found two things inside," he told her. "A kris was one. No one knows who put it there or why or even how. And an unfinished stone buddha. They took the buddha below and set it on the north wall."

"Why did they do that?"

"To study it in the hope of unlocking a secret. There was something special about this buddha. It had been given a place of honor in the stupa, even though unfinished. There are theories. One is the builders of Borobudur had not yet found enlightenment themselves, so the unfinished statue was a symbol of what they still had to do before reaching Nirvana. Or perhaps to Tantrics of the Left Hand, so mysterious in their rituals, it meant something else. Or the buddha was not finished because it was just not finished."

"And what do you say?"

He glanced past the stupa to the whole vast terrace. "I say this is a place of power and power is a thing in itself. It is fixed in amount. It is gained through absolute concentration, and I think here, in this place, they must have gathered tremendous power. They had to be remarkable people. Sometimes, when power is expressed through people, its outward sign is radiance. It can move from one person to another and to another and to another like stars falling through the night."

"Radiance," she repeated without comprehending, but the dalang had already turned and walked away. His response had gone beyond her question. He had unburdened himself of a deep conviction, something not fully clear to her, on this windswept terrace of release.

As they descended, he stopped to say something. To Maggie it seemed that throughout their visit they had been fascinated by the temple, but often their desire to talk had cut them off from it. When they turned from the centuries-old ruins, they were thinking only of themselves. It reminded her of the self-absorption of lovers, but it wasn't that, it couldn't be that, even though their curiosity about each other resembled the urgency and selfishness of love.

They stood on different stone steps, the dalang below her, while he spoke of jazz.

Ali had told him that she liked jazz. Although the dalang's pronunciation of English was generally excellent, the *j* threw him off sometimes—he said "yazz." He had heard jazz in Singapore on a record player owned by an American student at the university. The names Louis Armstrong, Lester Young, and someone called Monk came back to him. When she asked if he liked their music, he paused. His behavior was somehow familiar, and she located it abruptly: her own speculation about what to say when asked by Ali's brother, Bambang, if she liked gamelan.

The dalang began talking, but with his eyes focused beyond her shoulder, an indication that he was trying to recognize his emotions instead of describing them. He liked jazz, yes, was his polite response. But he talked about gamelan. The parts of melody relied on simultaneous variations: something was always a variation of something else and everything occurred at the same time. Whereas time in jazz was—he spread his hands apart as if pulling invisible taffy—"In one long line. So there is less variety in yazz," he concluded.

"Less variety?" Maggie recalled having told her own audience at the foundry that there was more.

"To my ear less." Said with the odd humility that was beginning to sound real to Maggie. "For gamelan music we Javanese say, *'Ya ngono ning ora gnono*: It is that way, yes, but it is not that way.' "

She didn't understand him any more than her village listeners had understood her when she talked about jazz. She carried with her on their continuing descent the uneasiness of someone wading through a perpetual fog of ambiguities. I'm a fool, Maggie told herself, if I think there is a chance of understanding this man.

Halfway down the stairway, he spoke again of jazz. He wanted to know more about it. Someday would she tell him more? His request, its tone strangely pleading from a man so confident, suggested to Maggie that they both were brooding over a failure of communication.

Reaching the bottom of the stairway, they looked up at the huge mass of stone. "Only one thing is certain about Borobudur," the dalang said.

When he paused as if letting the idea go, Maggie volunteered, "Its mystery?"

"I was thinking of its fate." He told her rain and vegetation were destroying the temple. Its porous volcanic base encouraged the growth of lichen and algae. In the humid atmosphere they eroded the stone.

His hands flared out to illustrate what happened. Watching them imitate the insidious action of tiny plants, Maggie could see it happening: roots splitting the stone, wriggling through it hungrily, eating the ore as if it were the sweet marrow of an animal.

Unless a drainage system was installed, he went on, and unless all the reliefs were cleaned of vegetation, and unless the damage already done was carefully repaired, Borobudur would soon collapse along with the hill it sat on. His hands became the stone bulk rotting in the rain, cracking in the slow inexorable grip of mosses. It was the first time he had given her a hint of his ability to perform. Maggie saw in his hands the motions of a poetry that identified him as an artist.

"Cleaning and repair," she said. "A drainage system. Can't that be done?"

He shrugged, and for an instant she glimpsed the boy he might have been—passionate and thwarted but too proud to show it by more than a shrug. "If there is so much to do," Maggie said, "perhaps the destroyers aren't only rain and vegetation. A third is lack of money." She added with a smile, "You probably think that's an American thing to say."

"It is a true thing to say." The dalang started for the car. Maggie followed at a thoughtful distance. When she reached the car and got in, Dalang Budi was staring from his window.

In a loud voice that got louder Maggie heard herself say, "So it must be restored. I agree with you, I understand you. Borobudur must be restored. Politics and kidnappings and murders and rainwater and lichens and lack of money and everything that holds back progress, all of it, every damn bit of it, all of it has to be put aside, it all has to. Because"—she searched wildly for words to explain her sudden rush of emotion—"because it must be restored, it is great, is a great thing somehow, a great mystery, and it must remain in this place as long as earth has life on it, because it must, because Borobudur must be restored, it must—"

Abruptly she halted, aware that her vision had gone beyond what was communicable and reasonable into the hysteria of a deep, inchoate need. The driver was looking at her, mouth open in reaction to the

194

torrent of incomprehensible words. The dalang was looking at her too. Smiling. He had not smiled quite like this before. To Maggie this smile was like coming upon the fifth terrace—something open, releasing, complete.

"Yes," he said. "We understand each other. Borobudur must be restored."

Twenty-one

Chairman Aidit was still moving daily from safe house to safe house. Yesterday two Muslim boys were chased off the street across from PKI headquarters; they had been carrying bottles stuffed with gasoline-soaked rags, perhaps stimulated to holy anger by their kiyai at pesantren school. Had they not been detected, they might have worked up enough spiritual courage to rush the building with a cry of "*Al Qadir!*" ("Anything He wills can be done!"). And they would have been willing to die then and there, knowing their desires would be fulfilled in heaven.

Aidit feared the Muslims more than he did the army, though to his subordinates he never admitted it: a military force was easier to organize against than a religion. In the old days the Muslim political parties had been marked by spontaneous mass fervor, shouting of slogans, now and then a spasm of unguided violence—typical of organizations lacking leadership and devoted to narrowly defined interests. But last year the principal Islamic party, Nahdatul Ulama, had suddenly become well financed and aggressive. Often lately, the NU

196

seized initiative from the Communists. One of its newspapers, the *Obor Revolusi*, declared in March that it would no longer tolerate slanderous attacks by the Red press; should the attacks continue, the *Obor Revolusi* would ask its admirers to take whatever action they deemed appropriate. That was a direct threat, and that silenced the *Djalan Rakyat*, official PKI organ in East Java, from criticizing the way Muslims reported the news. It had been Aidit's consistent policy, only rarely countermanded by local hotheads, to avoid violence whenever possible.

Now he was close to promoting it. He had never been involved in a riskier enterprise than this plot to subvert the Council of Generals. Though he had strong misgivings, Aidit felt it was a risk he must take. The countercoup had been conceived in haste. There hadn't been time to enlist conspirators in other than a few military units. The PKI itself was not armed in a country whose myths encouraged the belief that good won over evil only by force of arms. And coordinated plans for anti-army demonstrations during the postarrest period were as yet sketchy. Nevertheless, his reading of the political situation convinced him to set aside normal caution. Recent PKI popularity, especially in urban areas, had made the army bases nervous, and nervousness could make them reckless. They had business interests to protect against Red trade unions that were growing more powerful. The economic struggle intensified day by day in factories, oil fields, railroads, shipping companies.

Moreover, Aidit continued to worry about Sukarno's health. If suddenly the Great Leader died, only the PKI and the army were sufficiently organized to take control of the nation. The army would strike first unless something happened that left the high command confused, indecisive. A move against the top-ranking generals would accomplish that.

And finally, tipping the balance in favor of the plot, was Sukarno himself. The Great Leader had given Aidit his private blessing.

It had happened a week ago. In an elaborate palace ceremony Sukarno had bestowed upon Aidit the prestigious medal of Great Son of Indonesia. Afterward they had a talk in the presidential study. Once seated, Aidit regarded the leader closely for signs of illness.

Sukarno looked healthy enough. Tired, but that went with the job.

Paunchy, but that went with middle age. Even so, kidney disease didn't always manifest itself in outward appearance. Aidit had consulted three doctors.

Encouraged by the honor received that morning, he decided to act boldly. As they lit up cigarettes, he mentioned a rumor circulating among informed Jakartans. General staff officers, some of them committed to the CIA of America, were meeting regularly to plan a coup. It was information Aidit knew that Sukarno already had; Subandrio, acting as foreign minister and chief of intelligence, had seen to that. Subandrio had told Aidit that he had told the president and that Sukarno had waved the rumor aside, as he always did threats against his life and power. But Aidit needed to judge Sukarno's reaction himself.

"I hear rumors every day, and I discount them every day," the president said boastfully. "As for this particular rumor, I refuse to believe that patriots, much less army officers, much less general staff officers, would contemplate such a thing. Treason? Not my officers! We are all Indonesians together."

Aidit understood the meaning of this feigned ingenuousness: Sukarno was leaving the door open for hard analysis of a rumor that he probably took seriously but could not yet act upon. The president liked to be convinced of conclusions he was reaching on his own.

"Let's assume," Aidit said, "that a plot exists."

Bung Karno shrugged.

"That a group of generals has been meeting regularly. That they have decided to act against progressive government. That they may even mean to kidnap our Beloved Leader and set up a reactionary state in your place."

Again Bung Karno shrugged.

"In that event," Aidit continued, "a counterplot should be organized by officers loyal to you."

"You take the rumor seriously?"

"I do, Bung Karno."

"If I took rumors seriously, the nation would be on the edge of hysteria every day. We must be judicial."

Aidit waited.

Finally Sukarno said, "What sort of counterplot?" He had removed

198

his peci. He scratched the left side of his head, causing the stiff black hair to stick out childishly.

Aidit noted this. A symptom of kidney disease was itching. The president was now energetically scratching his head.

So engrossed had Aidit become in his observations that he failed to answer Sukarno's question.

Sukarno repeated it, while scratching—changing to the right side of his head. "What sort of counterplot?"

"A counterplot to stop the generals. Arrest them for treason."

Bung Karno stopped scratching; he folded his hands over an ample belly.

"Strike first?"

"Better first than last, under the circumstances."

Sukarno steepled his fingers together; it was a favorite gesture of his, Aidit knew. It meant, "Look, I am thinking, I am involved." Clearing his throat—another theatrical means of establishing the fact of his complete attention—Sukarno said, "Let's assume, for the moment, your counterplotters strike first."

Aidit allowed himself a broad smile. "Not mine, Bung Karno."

"If they strike first, what then?"

"They establish a temporary government. A council."

Sukarno guffawed. "Wonderful. And where am I in all this?"

"Safe. Actually," Aidit said, "controlling things behind the scenes."

"And what is happening on the scenes?"

"The council maintains the revolutionary spirit."

The word "revolutionary" always had a salutary effect on the president. For him, Aidit well knew, revolution meant turmoil and turmoil meant change and change was good for the Javanese soul. "A revolutionary council," Sukarno said with a sigh, as if finishing a good meal.

"A council for keeping order momentarily. That would be the purpose of it."

"Who would be on it?"

Aidit suggested that thirty or forty prominent citizens would be enough.

"To keep order," Sukarno said, his face suddenly hard. "Why?"

"Arresting top generals such as—"

Sukarno raised both hands as if warding off a blow. "Don't tell me their names!"

"The point I am making is this: their arrest might unsettle things."

"What do you mean, things?"

"Throw the operation of government off balance is what I mean. For a few days." Aidit shrugged, as if this were of little importance. "Weeks. Perhaps a month."

"A month is a long time," Sukarno noted sourly.

"But with you still at the helm."

"Behind the scenes."

Again Aidit shrugged and adjusted his thick glasses.

"Behind the scenes," the president said, "is one way people have of saying finished. I am not finished."

"Of course not." Aidit didn't like the direction they were taking. When Sukarno felt threatened, his mind often scattered like a farmyard of nervous chickens. Aidit knew that from experience. He tried to allay Sukarno's fears. "All that matters," he said, "is your safety. And the peace and calm you need to think out the affairs of state, those profound matters that only you can deal with." This sort of flattery would not have worked with himself, Aidit knew, but always in the past it had worked with Sukarno. It did now.

Sukarno sat back, folded his hands contentedly over his paunch, and said, "Continue, please, comrade."

"I simply thought the existence of such a council would help people adjust."

"They have a need to adjust?" Sukarno was frowning.

"If a coup were tried, people would need to think it through—the terrible idea of traitors in the military."

"Yes, it would be a terrible idea."

"Especially the idea of army generals kidnapping you." Aidit let the idea drift above them thickly like the smoke of their cigarettes. "For a short while our people might fear everything could topple down."

"What is everything?" Sukarno often seemed the most simplistic when his mind was clear. The more innocent he behaved the more meretricious he actually was.

Aidit sat a little straighter and felt tension in his jaw. "By everything I mean the entire state. There might very well be absolute panic."

200

"Panic," Sukarno repeated, as if savoring the idea of it.

"People would be terrified if someone plotted to kidnap their beloved Bapak. While you were being protected from further trouble, people would feel a sense of comfort and security if there was a council in place, holding on until you resumed control yourself."

Sukarno sighed, as if only beginning to understand. "So is that it? And you think there really is danger?"

Aidit nodded, after which Sukarno said, "And a council ought to be in place?"

"Such a council would allay the fears of your people, Bung Karno. And maybe even discourage mischief."

Sukarno leaned forward suddenly. "What sort of mischief?"

"Who knows?" Aidit shrugged.

After a long silence, during which Aidit was certain the president had run through a number of ideas and possibilities—an old fox testing the weather before venturing into it—Sukarno thumped his leg decisively with an open hand. "Yes, I see the point. Under such circumstances there could be some disorder."

"Temporary disorder."

"Of course, temporary." He scratched his left hand vigorously with his right. "I wouldn't stand for more. I can see the wisdom of a short-term council."

"When your safety is assured—"

"I never consider personal safety," the president snapped. "You forget there have been seven attempts on my life." Sukarno was proud of escaping assassination attempts. To Aidit's knowledge there had been only four.

The president kept scratching one hand with the other, methodically, continually.

"Let's assume then there might be arrests," Sukarno said, using the measured cadences of someone being logical. "In that case a revolutionary council would be a good idea. Stabilize things, maintain control until I decided to assume it again myself, when I felt my influence would be at peak benefit." He stopped and savored that phrase. "At peak benefit," he repeated. "But of course we must first assume there is a reason for the arrests. Then assume they have been made. But these are only assumptions and should be studied closely."

Aidit had the sinking feeling that Sukarno was drifting off, either lost in this parody of logic or obfuscating the matter for reasons of his own. Aidit took a deep breath. He had come this far, he must go farther or Sukarno might let the entire thing float away like a leaf on a stream.

"President, assuming we have a problem here, I have made up a tentative list of candidates for such a council."

Sukarno raised his thick eyebrows. "You have?"

"A duty someone should perform. I have drawn up the names of patriots."

"Who else knows about this Revolutionary Council?"

"A few patriots."

"Army officers?"

"Officers loyal to Bung Karno, yes."

"I don't wish to know their names."

"I understand."

Aidit watched the president scratch one hand with the other. The sight frightened him and brought on another impulse of boldness. "May I," said Aidit, "tell the others you approve of what I've told you?"

The president stared a few moments, then laughed. "Of course I approve of it. It's a nice exercise in fantasy. A rather clever joke."

Sukarno was approaching the issue of a revolutionary council in a Javanese way. Sukarno approved of it, and by so doing approved of the generals' arrests. But he must keep his approval well within the realm of theory. He'd deny his approval if pressed. Yet it was enough for Aidit. The president of Indonesia was behind the plot.

As Sukarno rose, ending the interview, Aidit had something to add. "You said at a gathering if Indonesia were born again, the best date for it would be the first of October."

"Did I say that?" Sukarno smiled in acknowledgment of a failed memory.

"Because that date would coincide with the anniversary of China's rebirth in 1949."

"I remember."

"That would bring two great nations closer together, merge them in the vital act of birth. China and Indonesia: celebrating their emergence on the same day. I believe you said that."

"Yes, I remember." Sukarno seemed pleased with what, apparently, he had said.

"If patriots moved against treason, their effort should come on a memorable day."

"We both understand the importance of dates."

"Such a movement against treason might, for example, take place on the day prior to October first. So that by the time the traitors were arrested and put in jail it would be October first. Purity of spirit reestablished on that significant date."

"Yes."

"Therefore the countercoup might begin on the night of September thirtieth. It would be remembered forever as the date when enemies of Bung Karno were put to flight. By that I mean the Thirtieth of September Movement. That's a name for it: GETAPS."

Sukarno considered the acronym. A master of creating acronyms, he tested this one, mouthing it silently. Then, as they stood at the door of the study, he gripped Aidit by the shoulder.

Aidit felt the powerful fingers, the famed energy of a man who had bedded legions of women along with six wives.

"I like that," said Sukarno. "GETAPS."

"GETAPS has your blessing?"

"It has my blessing."

"Do I have permission to tell the others?"

Putting his hand on the door handle, the Great Leader smiled broadly. Pockmarked cheeks expanded; dimples appeared alongside his upturned mouth. It was a big smile. It was a smile that Aidit recognized: the Great Leader's smile of dissimulation. And sure enough, Sukarno then said in his public voice, "You know my love of the Communist party. The PKI always has my blessing."

"And GETAPS? Do I have permission—"

"I believe in social justice!" Sukarno boomed out. He opened the door to reveal a uniformed guard on either side of it. Visitors looked up from a bench along the wall. The president's voice maintained its public volume. "Any action enhancing social justice has my blessing. You can quote me on that, Chairman Aidit!"

Going down the marble corridor, Aidit was partially satisfied.

He had hoped for more, for total commitment to GETAPS. Surely the president had more to gain than anyone associated with the plot. Recalcitrant generals would be removed; his old implacable foe, the Indonesian Army, would be too weakened to stand in his way.

There were economic as well as political reasons for Sukarno to back the plot. In recent speeches he had called for a greater commitment to socialism. This plea came on the heels of a visit from the Communist Chinese foreign minister, Marshal Chen Yi. From Aidit's knowledge of Chinese policy, he was certain that the marshal had given Sukarno a warning: move closer to socialism or lose Chinese assistance. What blocked the way to a more radical economy was an army dominated by capitalists. They'd be ruined by a socialist reconstruction of the marketplace. No doubt about it: Sukarno would benefit both politically and economically if the top brass were removed.

Aidit had received a private blessing from the president without Sukarno's going all the way. It was better than nothing. If GETAPS moved toward complete success, the Great Leader would surely get behind it. If anything went wrong, Sukarno would disavow prior knowledge of GETAPS and denounce anyone associated with it. That's how Aidit left his analysis of Bung Karno.

With a step brisk enough to hide uncertainty, he walked out of the palace and into the sunlight, glancing around quickly to spot potential assassins.

He had Sukarno's approval of 30 September. Either the acronym or the historical significance of the date had won over the Great Leader. It was always difficult to tell what went on in the mind of Bung Karno. That made him unpredictable. As a leader should appear, Aidit thought. Sometimes after meeting with the president, Aidit considered him a fool. Other times, uncannily shrewd. And today? Neither or both. Find a consistency in Sukarno, Aidit thought, and you could bring him down. Otherwise go with him. For decades now people had gone with him. Whatever else he was, Sukarno was great.

Now it was 24 September. Aidit was sitting in the small back garden of a local organizer in a Jakartan suburb. Neat by temperament, he let his bulging eyes stare judgmentally at the untidy garden. A space along the north wall was used for a refuse dump, as if there was nothing incongruous about a flower bed laid out near a heap of bottles, a broken bike wheel, half-eaten flyblown fruit. Even so, the host had been kind enough to supply Chairman Aidit with a glass of soda, a plate of rice cakes.

The young aide Hartono came into the garden, carrying a briefcase. His report, as usual, was brisk, confident, meticulous. The rural offensive was going nowhere; that was the gist of it. Letters to regional directors of the party, urging them to intensify their demonstrations against landowners and venal officials, had done little good so far. Hartono read off the statistical proof with a sort of loud metallic relish that hinted of his desire to blame Aidit for everything.

But Aidit believed that no one was to blame for the difficulties of the Communist party in Indonesia. The trouble was built in. Even in the urban areas the shops and factories didn't provide a solid base of mass proletariat, as they had in Russia. In the rural areas the farms didn't supply enough landless peasants, as they had in China. Indonesia was a nation of small landowners not easily susceptible to land-reform policies.

And Hartono knew it, but the young man was looking forward to his own ascent in the party. Aidit was almost sympathetic to Hartono's attitude; after all, he had once been young and ambitious too. Except that he had truly transcended his personal goals in a vision of national brotherhood. If only he felt that was also true of Hartono, he might give the young organizer his full support. Under the circumstances, however, Aidit grew daily more critical of Hartono and denied him guidance.

That meeting ended quickly. For half an hour the chairman read over the reports that Hartono had written. Dispassionate, accurate—superb work. Yet Aidit decided against sending Hartono on a diplomatic visit to Peking, although the young man was surely in line for it. He would send Sumitro, a compliant man in his mid-thirties who had come out of the poorest kampong in Jakarta. It would be the greatest honor of Sumitro's life; he might well live on it for his entire career, having little else to commend him. Aidit felt mean-spirited, yet he could not find it in himself to send the better-qualified Hartono.

He was still struggling with his conscience when a tall man in civilian sarong and white shirt entered the garden. This was Vice Marshal Omar Dhani of the air force. Aidit was startled, having never seen Dhani out of beribboned uniform.

So in the interest of secrecy the flamboyant air marshal had given up a display of rank.

He glanced distastefully at the shabby garden while a chair was provided by their host, who swept it hastily with the back of his hand. Their host was thin, sallow, aging; he had been a Communist for thirty-seven years and bragged of it to anyone who would listen.

Dhani waited until he was gone before sitting down. Then turning to Aidit he stared briefly at the bulging bespectacled eyes. When Dhani spoke, his voice had a curt, disapproving tone, as if trained to sound impatient and unhappy with inferiors. "Well, are you ready?"

"I am. My people are."

Dhani nodded sourly. He was not easily pleased. His hair, brushed carefully back, graying, came to a little tail behind his neck. Dhani was exceedingly vain.

They talked desultorily awhile. The air marshal, known for vehement feeling, denounced Yani and Nasution in a loud voice that rushed into anger. Aidit glanced at the opposite wooden fence, about a foot higher than a man's head. People on the other side could hear the reckless words, but hopefully they'd not understand or they'd think it was one of those crazy Reds who showed up for tea now and then. Clearly the air marshal would stop yelling only when it pleased him. It was foolish, it was dangerous, it was avoidable. It was like a domestic fight of small interest that could suddenly become fatal. Unable to do anything, Aidit sat back, biting his lip.

And Dhani went on. Those two vicious army men had always tried, always, to emasculate the air force; they had lined their pockets (Aidit knew, of course, that that was not true of Nasution), they had seduced every woman in sight (nor that), and they had nothing in their heads but the desire to overthrow Bung Karno and take control of the government.

Dhani spoke not only loudly but with profound bitterness. Evidently the air force officer believed the rumor about a Council of Generals. Aidit no longer did. No fresh evidence had attached it to reality. Perhaps some high-ranking generals met ex officio, but only to keep abreast of events in an anxious time. Logical, predictable, acceptable. But Aidit had decided to treat the rumor as real—to use it. He looked upon it as a chance to forestall later attempts at a coup that might destroy the PKI.

Considering his own stance, he was glad that Dhani really believed in the plot against Sukarno. In a low voice calculated to serve as an example for the air marshal, he said, "GETAPS must go through."

Dhani stared into space, as if considering that possibility. His face relaxed as the idea of GETAPS worked in his mind. Leaning close, he lowered his voice to a conspiratorial whisper. "I invite you to Halim Air Base on the night of the thirtieth."

Aidit had hoped to stay clear of the scene of action. If the plot failed, he wanted the PKI's part in it viewed as minimal. One reason he'd chosen Sjam, an insignificant operator in Jakartan intrigue, to represent him at the conspiratorial meeting was to disassociate himself from it as much as possible. In line with his caution was a decision to send his closest aides out of Jakarta, instead of gathering his lieutenants around him as an experienced general might do before going into battle. He would send his first deputy chairman, Lukman, to Semarang; Njoto, to Sumatra; and Adjitorop, to Singapore. If the plot failed, he'd suffer the consequences alone. That might well be his major contribution to the Communist party of Indonesia, when its history was written. A negative thought. Yet a sensible one. Sighing, he made another decision. Having put himself on this road, he would travel it.

To Dhani he said, "Thank you. I'll come to Halim on the evening of September thirtieth. We'll be together in victory."

Twenty-two

Hearing about the clash between Communist and Muslim youths and his American engineer's part in it, General Sakirman assigned Vernon Gardner a bodyguard.

Hashim was short, muscular, bearded, reputedly brilliant with both knife and pistol. He was a Minangkabau from Sumatra who didn't seem impressed when Vern told him that Nonya Gardner had once lived among his people. Hashim didn't seem impressed by anything. He was simply there, a silent and comforting presence, the ideal bodyguard. Vern had no idea where he lived. Hashim appeared in the morning at the hotel and disappeared when Vern retired for the night. He might have been a genie from a bottle—summoned by the general, set to his task, then put back. All that Vern knew about Hashim was his Minangkabau custom of sending every spare rupiah to his wife in Padang.

Since the street incident, Vern had made it his business to learn more about the Communists of Indonesia. Until World War Two the Dutch had suppressed the party, and it hadn't been strong until the 1950s, when D. N. Aidit gained control. Marxist ideology meant salvation for Aidit and other young intellectuals who had chafed under the Dutch and the Japanese. Yet for all their intense idealism they had fashioned a party of moderation, dedicated more to national unity than to social change. They had become more strident when Sukarno plunged into his passionate if ill-planned scheme to disrupt the creation of Malaysia. For the PKI it had been a way to greater power. They no longer muffled their criticism of fundamentalist Muslims and the power-hungry army. Restraint was a thing of the past. Working in the grim shadow of Sukarno's failing health, the Reds felt compelled to wrest as much power from their enemies as they could while there was still time.

Vern's deepening knowledge of these developments had convinced him he was right to keep Maggie out of Jakarta. General Sakirman agreed that the gadis-gadis (the girls) should be in Central Java, safe from the turmoil here. Vern learned there were other reasons for "gadis" Susanto Sakirman to be stashed somewhere, out of the way.

For one thing there were the trips.

Vern accompanied the general on one of them to Ujung Pandang, capital of South Sulawesi. To Vern's amazement, when they left the plane, General Sakirman said good-bye, and then gave him vague instructions about studying the possibility of building hotels in the area, about returning to the airport tomorrow at 0900 hours. And that was all. Good-bye, good-bye. The general shook his hand, turned, and was off. Standing on the tarmac, Vern watched a big black car drive the general away. Hashim hadn't come on the trip, so Vern couldn't ask him what had just happened—as if Hashim would have given him an explanation. Vern got a becak into town and checked in at the Nusantara Hotel.

There were big garish reliefs of giraffes on the hotel walls and a half-dozen dirty fish tanks in the lobby. From his second-floor room Vern had a view of downtown Ujung Pandang, which didn't seem ready for a big new hotel. It was a port town, ugly in a bland way, filled with swampland heat and exhaust fumes.

A desk clerk told him there were bat caves within becak distance. At a forest reserve he could see butterflies with wingspans as wide as an outstretched hand. Bats and butterflies were the major tourist attractions. So Vern went for a walk. He visited the dark crumbling buildings of Fort Rotterdam, originally the stronghold of a Makassar king. In the museum he learned that Bugis pirates used to terrorize the Indies in ships armed with bronze rammers shaped like the throats of dragons. In the harbor he watched the fleets load and unload.

Soon tired of it, he started back to town, only to be surrounded by a screaming pack of kids, none more than ten years old, who began pinching him. Yelling in a dialect he couldn't understand, they darted around, pinching his legs and buttocks with their tiny fingers. It was like being bitten by nits. And their little faces were screwed up in expressions of frightening hatred and fury. A group of becak drivers, lounging against a godown wall, laughed at the scene. He hailed one and rid himself of the rampaging little gang only when they tired of trotting alongside the becak. Before reaching the hotel, Vern felt the sting of a small rock that had been hurled at him from an alley.

That evening he ate in the hotel dining room, a vast but dimly lit place with white tablecloths and an army of idle waiters dressed in white jackets, tall ornate turbans. As he had done countless times through Asia, Vern sat alone in a room supplied with ceiling fans and underworked waiters.

Fortunately one of them spoke English and seemed eager to practice it by answering his questions.

"Maybe you can tell me," Vern said over dessert, "why I was pinched by children today and had rocks thrown at me."

The waiter, an old wrinkled man, grinned with satisfaction. "Forgive my insulting, tuan. It is not intended. But Bugis people hate you, hate Westerners. In early part of century Dutch soldiers killed here in Celebes. For this mistake, tuan, Bugis people were punished. Called Westerling Massacre, for officer ordered it. People roped together and shot. Thirty thousand shot. The Bugis do not forget."

As Vern was listening to this explanation, he noticed the arrival of two new diners. One was General Sakirman. Holding his arm was a young woman in an apple-green blouse, a sarong. Around her slim neck she wore a filigree gold necklace. Her hair knot was decorated with a large stickpin and some cloth flowers. She was a knockout.

As the couple crossed the dining room, Vern's eyes briefly met those of the general, who displayed no sign of recognition. None. When Vern left the dining room, clerks called him over and once again he was offered a night butterfly; once again he refused. Next day at the airport at 0900 the general drove up in the big black car, boarded the plane, and said good morning.

"Did you find a good site for a hotel?" he asked Vern.

"No, General."

That was the last time they ever mentioned the business trip to Ujung Pandang.

Tonight there was a party that General Sakirman claimed was important to OPSUS. Every party was important to the general, who always invited the American architect to accompany him (no one at OPSUS called Vern what he wished to be called: a builder).

Vern Gardner had more invitations than he could handle, he being one of the few remaining Americans in Jakarta. People gawked at him as if he were a movie star. And so he was dragged to party after party by the general, who showed him off with the crude enthusiasm of a stage mother. Vern didn't mind as long as it maintained his position in Project Palm Tree. He wanted to build that hotel on Bali. Even so, he didn't acquiesce entirely to the general's desires. For example, he rejected proffered girls in the face of Sakirman's obvious displeasure. A display of public lust was the rule not the exception at Jakartan parties. Villas supplied with a plethora of bedrooms and equipped with vast dark gardens were ideal for nightly assignations, for casual encounters after cocktails and buffets and dance bands had set the mood. Here indeed was a world for men who strove mightily to take full advantage of the good life and who watched to see that their comrades did the same. General Sakirman was surprised, then puzzled, and finally contemptuous of the American's restraint. It might have been enough for him to fire such a prude if a replacement had been available.

Tonight's party was held at the Presidential Palace in Bogor. Vern and the general arrived by helicopter on the palace grounds, and when they climbed out, they faced an honor guard of RPKAD paratroopers with their red berets cocked jauntily at identical angles.

Vern had grown accustomed to such parties: the assembly of businessmen, military officers, and politicians; the gamelan orchestra playing in a garden; the abundant champagne; the loud boasting and antics of middle-aged men in the presence of pretty young women supplied for the occasion. There were few wives present; that meant the party would go on for most of the night. Initially at least there was no Sukarno.

Vern wandered from group to group in the grand ballroom, talking briefly to a German exporter, a Chinese cukong, a couple of army officers, one a colonel, a Colonel Latief.

Vern asked him where Sukarno was.

"Sometimes he doesn't come to the parties."

"Even though held in his palace?"

Colonel Latief shrugged. "It is the privilege of the great."

Vern liked that remark, enough to stroll with the colonel through one of the formal gardens.

"A night like this is the best of my country," the colonel said. "The moon, the trees, the scent of flowers." He was a heavy, mustachioed man with a chestful of medals. "It is a pity we are losing the ideals of independence. But we are. We are learning to live with corruption and violence. The army is the people's true defense, yet it is now Jakartanized. Look around you. What do you see? Men of high rank running after whores. Drunkards. Spendthrifts." With that last word the colonel lapsed into brooding silence.

Vern stared at him. Rarely did an Indonesian, much less a military man, criticize the country, especially to a foreigner. It wasn't done. Yet this Colonel Latief, without prompting, had quietly unleashed what would be to the Indonesian mind a treasonable indictment of the nation. This bothered Vern more than casual violence on the street. The loss of control in the upper echelons of a Third World country led to chaos. Vern had seen it in Burma, had seen it begin in India, although control had been returned there and catastrophe had been averted. It scared Vern to see this army officer stroll off in a funk. Absorbed by negative feelings, Colonel Latief had lost sight of what he'd just done: spoken with shameless candor to a foreigner.

But elsewhere things seemed in order—the traditional wine and laughter of a party in Jakarta. General Yani had a group of sycophants ranged around him in a half circle. Seeing Vern, the general called him over.

"You, American," said General Yani with an exaggerated roughness that made his audience titter. "What are you going to build for me?"

212

"Anything you want, General."

"See this pretty lady?" He put his arm around a slim girl. "Build a pleasure palace for her. Can you do that?"

"I can try."

"It must have special features, though," the general said with a smirk; it provoked another chorus of titters, because this went for wit among the general's friends. With a polite nod Vern moved on.

He saw Defense Minister Nasution, ramrod straight in immaculate uniform, talking somberly to another officer. Vern had never met Nasution. On impulse he nearly went up and introduced himself. The Pacific war had given him respect for such officers. He had seen them stand up. He had watched them brave out their fears and lead men. Something about Nasution convinced him that here was one of the hard soldiers, the real stuff.

As Vern took a glass of mango juice from a wandering waiter, there was sudden movement at the entrance to the audience hall, a following sound of applause. Within the milling crowd Vern had a glimpse of Sukarno—tall for an Indonesian, almost Vern's height—well built if paunchy in a midnight-blue Italian silk suit. When the president turned, his profile came into view: slack-jawed, heavily lined—the exhausted face of an aging man. Yet as he moved among well-wishers, Sukarno's gestures were quick, almost boyish. He still possessed the aura of power.

Having had his fill of studying the president, Vern left the hall and went outside to the buffet where he sampled delicacies such as Balinese pelala and bumbu rudjak. He had learned over the years to eat spicy food, but never had he derived the pleasure Maggie did. He missed her. He missed watching her devour the fiery satés and rice dishes. Sitting in a lawn chair on the terrace, he enjoyed the last light in the western sky. When it was gone, the good ol' boys and their girls would be finding little corners of the garden to fuck in. He wanted his wife.

An officer came along and stopped at Vern's chair. "The president wishes to see you, sir."

Vern got up and followed the aide through winding passages that emphasized how really big the palace was. Its size was effectively hidden, the way Frank Lloyd Wright might do with a one-story building: full use of terrain, blend of natural materials, interplay of inside and outside space. Ultimately a house that hunkered down in its setting like a hog in mud.

At a closed door the aide knocked, went inside, and left Vern to wait. He waited a long time, hearing laughter—mostly female—from somewhere down the hall. At last the aide opened the door and briskly gestured Vern in.

Sukarno, blouse unbuttoned to his waist, sat on a large gold embroidered couch between two women. Young and lovely, they leaned toward him, reined in by his arms that enveloped their shoulders. He still wore a peci, but no shoes. Fleetingly Vern wondered if the man slept in that hat.

"Sit down, American," the president ordered in English.

"Thank you, Excellency." Vern sat opposite the couch in a straight chair.

"Call me Bung Karno, the way my people do. Not Excellency. What is this Excellency?" He yanked the girls toward him and smiled at Vern with the ease of someone who smiles often. "You are one of my people now too. I am your brother, Bung, while you work in my country."

Vern smiled faintly.

"Do you speak Jawa? Dutch?"

"I speak a little Bahasa Indonesia."

"Bung Karno."

"Bung Karno."

Bung Karno grinned when Vern did as he was told. "Bahasa Indonesia is just Malay. We fool ourselves thinking it's our own language. I also speak French and German. I have six languages altogether." To emphasize his pride in this accomplishment, Sukarno pulled the girls closer to his chest. "*Gadis-gadis ini sangat mani, betul?*"

"Yes. They're very sweet," Vern replied in English.

"Then you do speak Malay." Sukarno guffawed, as if laughing at himself for being skeptical. "I got my diploma from the Bandung Technical Institute. In architectural engineering. Did you know that?"

"No, Bung Karno."

"So we are truly brothers. I am interested in a builder like you. If politics hadn't interfered, I would have been a builder too. I like such things: town planning, construction. Have you read my speech in

214

which I call Jakarta the lighthouse of the world? My National Monument is a conscious reflection of many styles and very, very symbolic. It has to be for the people. Not many of them know, however, that its dimensions are based upon the numbers seventeen, eight, and forty-five, because they represent the date of the proclamation of independence. It was my idea. And the shape is that of the Hindu lingam, recalling the early history of Java, though some dirty minds have named it Sukarno's Erection. If only that were so! Although there haven't been any complaints today, have there, girls?" He pulled them closer with a guffaw. "What building in the world do you like best?"

"The one I'm working on."

"Did you hear that?" Sukarno was delighted by the answer. He squeezed the two uncomprehending girls to his chest again. His face, pitted by smallpox scars, could blossom into a splendid smile. It encouraged Vern to smile too, this time sincerely.

"French architecture is my favorite," Sukarno said. "I would get down and kiss the feet of Le Corbusier. I say that and people laugh, but I would, I would do it. I would get on my hands and knees and crawl like a worm to him and kiss his feet and ask his blessing like one of your Christians ask the pope. Because Le Corbusier is a genius, a great architect of cities. Critics say I have no taste because of the public buildings I commission. They don't understand the need for symbolism. But for beauty give me the French, especially eighteenth century. I have photographic books about that period. I like things French. As a boy I thought all the time about the French. In my mind I talked to Voltaire, Danton, Jean-Jacques Rousseau. In the silence of my room I saved France single-handedly. You and I can talk because we know French buildings. Not many Americans around for you to talk to."

"No, Bung Karno."

"Are you homesick?"

"No, Bung Karno."

"Do you have friends who work for *Time, Life, Newsweek?*"

"No, Bung Karno."

"Because they are salesmen of hate. They need mental examinations!" Following this outburst, he withdrew his arms from the girls and clasped his hands fretfully. "If reporters from the West would leave me alone, how easy life would be." He looked down at the floor to emphasize this melodramatic self-pity. The girls, sitting erect, glanced nervously at him. With a sigh, he sat back and placed both hands behind his thick neck. Sukarno grinned. "That is not your problem, is it, American? Your problem is building a hotel on Bali. Will you keep me informed of your progress?"

"If you wish, Bung Karno."

"Yes, I wish. I would love to go with you, even for a few days. We could watch the scaffolding go up. We could discuss alterations!" Sukarno laughed. One of the girls, whispering in his ear, got up and left the room. Leaning forward, Sukarno winked at Vern. "Nice girl. I had her three times today already."

The aide came into the room and whispered something too. Sukarno frowned and clapped his knees with his hands. "Well, American, enjoy yourself. Pick a girl. Have you got one yet?"

"Yes," Vern said.

"Good. That's what they're here for. Best of luck on Project Mango Tree."

Rising, Vern didn't correct him about the project's name. When the president waved airily in farewell, Vern bowed slightly and left. Returning to the terrace, he took another glass of mango juice from a tray. From open windows came the unmistakable sounds of sexual activity. Other guests, like Vern, remained on the terrace. General Sakirman was nowhere in sight; Vern figured he better settle in because the general must be up in one of those rooms or somewhere in the garden, unavailable for a long time.

Vern joined two Indonesians in civilian clothes at a lawn table. He asked in English how long the party might last. They studied him critically. At last one replied that it was a palace custom for everyone to remain until the president retired.

When they learned that Vern had just been granted a private audience, their aloofness changed to acceptance. After another drink one of the men—a deputy minister of something—launched into drunken praise of the Great Leader of the Revolution.

"He is wayang hero," the minister slurred, waving his glass around expansively. "In the *Mahabharata* only Bima speaks low Javanese to God. Only Bima alone. Everyone else speaks Krama. Bima's insolence is a mark of absolute fearlessness. And our Bapak, our Bung Karno, he too speaks low Javanese to God."

216

"No," said the other man, an official too. "Bapak is not a character in wayang. He is the dalang who brings the characters to life. He is the dalang of our people. He manipulates us, makes us work. We are his shadow play. There is no life for us except what he dreams is ours."

They continued to outdo each other in praise of Sukarno, while Vern sat back and half listened. It was dawn when apparently the president decided to end the party, because after his air-conditioned Cadillac sped him and his two young companions to a sleeping pavilion in a far corner of the palace grounds, the guests felt that they had permission to leave. Sakirman, weary and rumpled, appeared on the terrace. Vern accompanied him to the front lawn where they boarded a waiting copter. As it left the ground, Vern told himself that Sukarno was still a tough old bird. The Great Leader of the Revolution was still in charge. Let the Reds and the Muslims and the army think about that.

And having a last glimpse of the broad grounds of the palace, its buildings emerging in the dawn like backs of dolphins from the blue sea, he thought of the aging rascal in a sleeping pavilion with the two girls and that thought led inexorably to his wife, to Maggie, who would have liked the spicy dishes of the buffet, who would have held his hand now as the copter churned over the early-morning roofs of Bogor.

Twenty-three

Mornings were best. She left her room and went into the garden, shimmering in the aqueous light of dawn. A breeze ruffled her hair, cooled her cheek. In the tropics, more than elsewhere, it seemed that the time of day governed the breath of life. The sky at daybreak and sunset gave to objects an inner light of vitality, as it did now to the garden. But at high noon this same garden seemed metallic, lifeless, as if the white-hot tornado of the sun had sucked into its blazing whirlpool all the greenery and fragrance below.

This morning, as she sat on a rock wall overlooking the garden, Maggie thought about hands. This was not unusual. Her obsession with hands came from a childhood memory: her father holding her on his lap, one of his big hands covering her knees. She used to lift each finger and inspect it. They were thickset and weathered and moved with the heavy blocklike solidity of wood. She had never felt safer. Of course, later on there had been a different memory of his hands: holding a beer bottle, a shot glass, a tumbler of scotch, a coffee cup filled with cheap gin.

Replacing his, as time went by, had been the exploratory hands of boyfriends and finally the callused experienced hands of Vernon Gardner, but none held her attention the way her father's hands had done in her rapt childhood. None until she saw the hands of fishermen in their boats off the island of Samosir. Hands tireless, ceaselessly in motion, as the fishermen hunched in their dugouts and managed the nets. A paddle in such hands became an extension of the human body. Two fingers governed the paddle, swirling it through tiny arcs of navigation, while the other hand spread the net out, inch by patient inch, into the water. Slow, skillful hands, not a wasted gesture in them. They must be wonderful at love.

Then the dalang's hands expressing his fear of Borobudur's destruction: his fingers working like tentacles into the earthbound heart of the temple, drowning the terraces in rain, trembling and sliding through the air like eviscerated rock collapsing down slopes, his palms closing into the sad wrinkles of exhausted rubble, his knuckles bobbing like raindrops on sunken stone. She had followed the enactment of this tragedy by watching his hands. Maggie would never forget the poetry of their grief as long as she lived. And she hoped someday to see them at their primary task, one she had already witnessed in imagination—holding up the horn rods, moving the shapes across a white screen, with a single motion giving life to a flat leather puppet.

Maggie returned to her room and wrote Vern a letter. He was coming soon to Yogya for a visit and her first few sentences expressed her happiness. Then she told him about her language study with an ancient Javanese guru who bullied her mercilessly. "He won't let me learn the basic language—says I must learn all three speech levels along with two variations right from the start. Says otherwise I won't be able to say anything. Says otherwise I can get another guru. He's an emaciated little fellow whose fingers are the color of teak from a half century of tobacco stains. He is a priyayi and therefore very full of himself. Says I am privileged to learn Javanese in this city, where it is spoken correctly. Says I am fortunate not to be in Surabaya, where they speak a Javanese so corrupt and vile-sounding that it constitutes an insult to any self-respecting person from Yogya or Solo who has to endure hearing it. It is damn hard. Without my Indonesian it would be impossible. Thank God that helps some, because they're both Indic languages. Vern, the verb 'to say' can be *kandha, sanjang, criyos, matur,* and *ngendika,* depending on the status of the person you're talking to. If you talk about someone higher on the social ladder than you are, you must use a higher language. I don't mean talk *to*, I mean talk *about*. Vern, to get the vowels right you have to keep your mouth muscles very tense and clip the sound off so there's no final glide. And the *p*'s and *b*'s are real trouble. If you say the word for 'silver,' which is *'perak,'* the way we would pronounce the *p*, then the Javanese hear it as *'berak,'* which means 'shit.' Why am I telling you all this?" Maggie paused in her writing and asked herself why indeed was she telling him all this? It was bubbling schoolgirl nonsense; at least it would sound that way to Vern. What he wanted to hear was how she felt, felt about him, especially because in a week he would be coming to Yogya. "I guess I'm telling you all this because I'm 'on pins,' as Larry would say, and I miss you and I can't wait to see you, sweetheart, so I'm just rambling on."

When she finally finished the letter, Maggie realized it was as poor as the others she had sent him. The problem was—and she knew it— that love talk had never come easy to her. Not, for God's sake, because of lack of experience. But her mother used to read screen romances and hauled into a grim womanhood the homilies of a more innocent past, so that she had regaled an adolescent daughter with aphorisms about love and happiness. ONLY LOVE MATTERS. HAPPINESS IS CARING FOR OTHERS. That sort of thing, which amazed and mystified Maggie, who had seen little love or happiness in her mother's life. This had made her suspicious of easy beliefs that could be mouthed airily without attachment to the real world of experience. And yet a residue of her mother's convictions, sentimental and mawkish and derived from the trashiest of true-confession magazines, had provided Maggie with some of the psychic baggage that she carried into her own womanhood. At times in the night, sleepless, eyes staring upward, she wondered about love and happiness—those paradisiacal virtues that had eluded her mother—guessed at what they truly were and mulled over the dangerous old axiom that her mother swore by: when you found true love, you knew it as surely as you knew your own name, and only by finding such love could you possibly know the meaning of happiness.

As if to defy her own skepticism, Maggie put on lipstick (she rarely wore it here in Yogya), kissed the letter soulfully, leaving there for

Vern to gape at a corrugated red mouth that looked enormous below her cramped signature, folded the letter, placed it in an envelope, which she then sealed with a drawn-out sigh, said aloud "To hell with it," and headed for the main house.

After her language lesson she came down the narrow dusty path from the little bungalow, which, a few feet away from its door, seemed to be swallowed up by the untended vegetation of its yard; at each step she recited *"Layat lali lilin lagu,"* because the guru had told Maggie, his contempt unbridled, that until she pronounced *l* words higher in her larynx, with the tip of her tongue moving toward the roof of her mouth, no one in Java would have the slightest idea what she was saying. And then the other words had started whirling in her head: *mbuh* in Ngoko and *kilap* in Krama and *duka* in Krama inggil for "I don't know." This was something she had better learn fast. So intent was she on the debris left in her mind by the lesson that Maggie ran into him head-on as he waited for her outside the gate, his hands raised in a sembah of greeting, his umbrella hooked over one scrawny arm.

Mas Slamat was one Javanese who was never late. His wrinkled face was determinedly serious under the porkpie hat squared on scanty white hair.

"You are late," he said, ignoring her apology for crashing into him (she felt his bony chest through his shirt; it was like a washboard).

"Late?" Maggie noticed that he didn't wear a watch. She glanced at her own. "Mas Slamat, by a couple of minutes."

"I didn't think you would ever come out of there." He added with a malicious little smile, "I don't think you will learn from him."

"I hope I will. Are we ready to go?"

"Then you are going?" he asked skeptically.

"Of course. We planned it, didn't we?"

He ran a large thumb across his ugly mole, a gesture of indecision. Probably he couldn't decide if she was telling the truth. She didn't give him time to think it through, but started out briskly. He fell into step.

"They sighted a tiger," he said after a while, "coming down the mountainside yesterday."

"I hadn't heard."

"They say Mount Merapi will erupt because of it. Tigers coming down is a sign."

"You mean, if tigers come down the mountainside the volcano will erupt?"

"Always."

She glanced down at him. His lips were straight, firm as rock. Perhaps he believed it. No, he did not believe it.

"This dalang we see now will not be as good as Ki-Dalang Gito-suwoko," the little man said after a long silence.

"Yes, I know."

"Who told you?" He halted to squint up at her.

"The Sakirman servants."

Mas Slamat scoffed and twirled his umbrella. "You must not listen to them. The cook is from Sumatra."

To tease him she wanted to say, "Who told you?" Instead she admitted the cook was indeed from Sumatra.

"I know Sumatra," he declared. "Rough people, no civilization." He pronounced "civilization" in six distinct syllables.

Suddenly Maggie recalled the afternoon in Palembang when she tripped while returning the insolent stare of three men who swaggered toward her along the sidewalk, tripped on a buckled square of cement and fell, exposing both legs to mid-thigh and twisting an ankle. The men stared. No one helped her get up. She had been a little crazy in Palembang. That was certainly true from her saner perspective now. Crazy in that town with its chicken guts spilled in the market mud, its one-legged men, its aphrodisiacs made of fermented crocodile, its angry people eking out existence upriver on some of the hottest swampland in the world. But she remembered the scarlet chilies too, piled in brilliant pyramids, and the spicy food. She had that good memory of Palembang.

So Maggie was surprised when Mas Slamat began to talk about Sumatran chilies, as if he had read her mind. He told a story about a Sumatran who died of apoplexy after eating a dozen Padang chilies on a dare. "Simply too much for him. Choked, turned blue. Hottest chilies anywhere. It is a brutal place, Nonya."

He walked slowly, in silence, head bowed, perhaps to emphasize what he would say next. "You must listen only to me," he declared. "I know what I know. I have many languages at my disposal. If you listen to me, don't worry. In this way you will find success in Yogya."

As they walked, Maggie found herself reciting under her breath, "*Akal apal sumpel mipil rewel nusul pol.*" She thought she was pronouncing the words almost silently, but her little companion cleared his throat and told her that her *l* sound was very bad. If that man couldn't correct her *l* sound, he was obviously good for nothing.

Maggie smiled and the muscles in her face had no sooner changed than she realized that her smile had insulted him.

Mas Slamat's toothless gums worked awhile as if rehearsing a speech. "Do not think, Nonya, I am looking for money," he said. "Money is not actively sought. We Javanese with Mas or Raden before our names are not businessmen. We do not hunt money. Money will flow to a person because he has power. So don't worry. I am not seeking money from you, only companionship and dignity. If you insist on taking lessons from this fellow, it is no business of mine."

With that, he doffed his hat and led the way into the theater.

———————

The Agastya Art Institute was a rather fancy name for a small cement theater in a compound far down a residential lane. The theater seated hardly fifty people, and this evening half the seats were empty for a performance of wayang golek, a play using three-dimensional puppets. According to Mas Slamat, wayang golek was less popular and less magical than wayang kulit. There was no lit shadow screen, and the dolls were more human-looking, therefore more worldly. "I do not like wayang golek," he announced grandly.

A small gamelan orchestra faced the stage, which was a wooden frame supported horizontally by massive twin trunks of bamboo. There were more puppets lined up along the trunks (stuck into the soft bamboo by central rods) than there were people in the theater. So displayed, the puppets made a bright row of personages in ornate costumes, court headdresses, banded fezzes, their faces elegantly handsome or grotesquely hideous.

The dalang sat below and slightly behind the stage, near a large box from which he took other puppets when needed. He manipulated them by the head-controlling central rod and by separate sticks for

223

the arms. Much of the action depended on his flicking a puppet's long sash. To add excitement he banged a piece of metal against the wooden box with his right foot.

Mas Slamat explained the plot of this Islamic drama—something about the adventures of Muhammad's uncle, the Arabian prince Amir Hamzah—but the whole thing seemed interminable to Maggie aside from sudden bursts of energy when the dalang whipped the puppets through the air, making them fly or shake from fright. The dalang seemed bored, often reciting lines while gazing at the open window of the hall, as if hoping something might come through it to break the monotony.

Members of the orchestra smoked, even while playing—tapping the bronze gongs with woolen hammers or plucking the strings of a zither or hitting a two-sided drum. A little girl wandered among the seated players or threatened to smack a gong with a mallet she'd picked up or stretched out and put her head in a player's lap while he struck the ironwood keys of a gambang with padded sticks.

Frequently Mas Slamat breathed a mixed odor of tobacco and milk into Maggie's face as he explained things. The kayon, for example. It was a leaf-shaped leather figure stuck stage center before the play began. Thereafter it was moved around, jammed into the bamboo at a tilt or waved or fluttered. It could mean a forest, a palace gate, a mountain, a crypt, a river, a fire, a storm. Swelling at its base and tapering to a flamelike point, the shape of the kayon was that of the Islamic Tree of Life. During a performance, the kayon was always visible somewhere; at the conclusion the dalang stuck it back in the center. Then people could resume the course of their lives. The kayon was the symbol of wayang. The kayon was the visual heart of Java.

His explanations were to Maggie better than the performance, although she tried to like things in it. She admired the way the dalang could make his puppets cross the stage; they reminded her of Mas Slamat's swaying walk. But she was disappointed. Leaving the theater, she felt depressed.

As if divining that, Mas Slamat said, "Don't worry. You will see better. I will make sure of it."

"I would like to see Ki-Dalang Gitosuwoko."

Mas Slamat swung his umbrella grandiosely. "Ah, that would be good."

224

"I think right now his mind is on Borobudur, not on performing."

"Sometimes he gives performances to raise money. Officials take it from him to use for Borobudur and"—Mas Slamat snapped his fingers—"money gone. The dalang has given much, got nothing done." Mas Slamat chuckled, as if pleased by an idealist's failure.

"Perhaps he needs help."

He caught the implication immediately. "Do you know how to help him? Can you get money?"

"No, no," Maggie said, alarmed by his thinking she could. "But I believe he's right about saving Borobudur. There must be more than one way to go about it. I think people could help."

"Then you must help."

"You think so?"

"You have friends at the embassy. Your husband has American friends in business. Of course you can help."

"I told you—" Maggie began to deny what she seemed to have denied every time they met: that she had the means to supply Mas Slamat with whatever he needed.

He did now what he always did when she failed to admit her power and affluence—pulled his hat down squarely over his ears as if to shut out her denials. "Come to my house," he said, leading the way briskly.

After they had walked a few blocks, Mas Slamat slowed down, grew restive, and slapped his thigh rhythmically with the rolled umbrella. Thought had overtaken him. They slowed further. The lane was lit intermittently by light from houses along the way. "It must be done!" he said abruptly with a harder thump against his thigh for emphasis. "You must meet the holy man Raden Harjanta Prijohoetomo. Yesterday I went to him and he made prediction. He quoted Malay proverb: '*Anjing gelak, babi berani*: The dogs are fierce, the pigs daring.'" Mas Slamat paused and smiled expectantly, as if sure Maggie would understand. When she merely stood there, he frowned and thumped his thigh again with the umbrella. "The Reds and the sons of Islam are spoiled for a fight."

"I think you mean spoiling for a fight."

"He predicted they would fight."

"Some people would agree with him."

Mas Slamat ignored the possibility that anyone might have a similar revelation. Striking a pose, thrusting the umbrella out in a swift gesture somewhat like a riposte, he said, "The holy man saw them fighting in a dream and we won!"

"The Muslims?"

Mas Slamat gave her a sharp look. "Of course we won. We slaughtered them all, the streets ran blood, and none escaped. Every Communist lay slaughtered, and Allah was praised by all mankind. So said R. Harjanta Prijohoetomo, and he is not even Muslim."

"I thought he was."

"He calls himself Muslim, Buddhist, Hindu, Christian." Mas Slamat grinned as if he had just told a joke. "A great man but strange. He is holy, we all know he is holy, yet I will not believe everything he says. Of course, I believe his last prediction. We will win; we will leave them bloody and dying in the street!" After they had walked a little way, Mas Slamat began fidgeting again. Finally he halted. "Nonya," he said, "I cannot take you to my house. I have other business. The electricity is not working. Good night."

Leaving her there, Mas Slamat rushed into the night. When his short swaying figure had vanished in the darkness, Maggie turned and made her way home alone.

Twenty-four

When the plane from Jakarta landed at Yogya Airport, Maggie was waiting with Mas Slamat. By stretching skyward his little arm that held the umbrella he was able to shade them both from a sun whose scalding heat had turned the surface of tarmac into a caldron of hot black soup. He had pestered Maggie for a chance to meet her husband. As Mas Slamat grandly put it, "Your business husband, Nonya, deserves to know who in Yogya can help him. Permit me kindly to accompany you."

Vern was surprised by the presence of the little Yogyanese. By lapsing into sullen silence on the ride into town Vern showed how surprise can quickly become displeasure, while Maggie brooded over the mistake of bringing Mas Slamat along. She had brought him as much from a sense of celebration as from a desire to satisfy his curiosity. Maggie's hope for a festive greeting (paltry though it was, with the welcoming committee consisting only of herself and Mas Slamat) had nonetheless blinded her to Vern's predictable desire for a reunion untainted by a third person.

While husband and wife brooded, Mas Slamat did most of the

talking. He warned Tuan Gardner of Communist activity, as if the business husband had arrived in this country from the moon. As his response to the little man's patronizing tone, Vern glanced balefully at his wife beside him. Seated next to the driver, turning to emphasize certain points, Mas Slamat assured the American couple that with proper caution and good advice there was nothing to fear. The good advice should come from Mas Slamat, Mas Slamat maintained, while handing Vern a calling card. Maggie figured he probably didn't trust her to show her husband the card she already had. Vern studied his closely until Mas Slamat, realizing it was in the wrong language, leaned over, snatched the German card away, and substituted one in English. He spoke of the need of foreign support for the restoration of Borobudur, a famous place nearby, while shifting his urgent gaze from husband to wife, wife to husband, like a famished man studying hot entrées on a steam table.

"What is in there?" he asked suddenly, and when Vern didn't respond, pointed to the gift-wrapped package lying in the business husband's lap. "Don't worry," Mas Slamat declared and pursed his lips as if assessing the true danger he was hiding from a fool. "While visiting Yogya, you must put yourself in my hands. I know everything. I have languages and a commitment to the welfare of Nonya Gardner."

"He really has been helpful," Maggie confirmed, smiling hopefully at her husband, who did not smile back.

As the car approached Ngasem, the bird market, Mas Slamat suddenly asked to be let out. He had forgotten to finish a letter that must be sent immediately to a very dear friend in France. Speaking rapid Javanese to the driver—too rapid for Maggie to catch it—he scarcely waited for the car to halt before opening the door and scrambling into the street. Turning, he lifted his porkpie hat high in a grandiose but hurried salute and strode off, umbrella swaying from his crooked arm.

"Who in the hell was *that*?" Vern asked when the car continued toward the Sakirman residence.

"Just someone I met. He has—I don't know—something special about him. I think Mas Slamat tries to get into people's good graces, and when he feels he's failing, he runs away to save his honor."

"I see. How does he make a living?"

"Frankly, I don't know."

"I see. Why in hell do you put up with him?"

"Because I like him." Maggie nearly added, "And because I think he needs me."

Vern shoved the gift-wrapped package at her. "I think he wanted me to give this to you in front of him. Anyway, sweetheart, here."

She excitedly stripped off the paper and withdrew a splendidly crafted handbag, the kind produced in the Batak country of northern Sumatra.

"Remember I told you in Palembang? You could probably find the best Batak bags in Jakarta."

Naturally she remembered. What delighted her was Vern remembering too. She kissed him, then passed her hand lightly over the soft leather of the rust-colored bag. Her obvious pleasure in the gift had its effect on Vern. He thanked her for her letter, the one with the lipstick signature, as he called it, and at first she didn't comprehend the appeal it had for him, because the garish lip print she had made on the paper in a moment of defiant whimsy had seemed ugly to her, like a grimy bear paw in snow. She kissed him again, surprised by her temporary forgetfulness of sexual power.

He began talking about Project Palm Tree; it was still becalmed. Nothing would happen until the army brass decided when to diversify the investment portfolio of OPSUS by going ahead with the hotel on Bali. They wanted him back in four days, primarily because he would be missed at government parties where people liked to gawk at a live American in Sukarno's anti-American Indonesia. For the next few days, Larry Foard was in charge and, of course, Larry was "on pins." If there was anything the little Cornish shipbuilder hated, it was authority, his own as much as anyone else's, even if it was authority to do nothing.

"Larry went with me to the airport. Know what he said before I boarded?" Vern chuckled at the memory. " 'It's a sod of a thing to ask,' he said, 'but how about giving me that jacket of yours, the linen one you got in Hong Kong? I understand there's a bloody lot of crashes between Jakarta and Yogya.' That's what goes for humor with Larry Foard," he said genially. "And I said to him, I said I wouldn't give him an old pair of dirty socks."

Maggie said nothing, but gripped her husband's hand and held it against her thigh, until the warmth gathered there like water bubbling from a spring and communicated to them both a first stirring of passion, a hint of what was awaiting them in the silence and solitude of a bedroom only five minutes away.

She was riding him like a horse. She felt he was trying to reach a destination hidden so far within her that it continued beyond her body, as if he were traveling a long black tube into infinite space. Maggie liked to mount and ride him this way, like a bucking bronco, her hands circling and crushing her breasts, her head flung back the way a bird drinks, her pelvis moving in rippling tides, the brown patch between her legs now meeting and now parting from and now meeting again the dark musky field of his groin, until leaning over him she clenched his shoulders for better purchase, her breasts gyrating madly now, back arching like a bow, and thrust thrust thrust thrust at him as he did at her until they both came.

Later, as they lay side by side, each returning home, Vern swung himself up on one elbow and looked down on her. Sweat dripped from his chin onto her shoulder; with forefinger and thumb he gently manipulated the nipple of her right breast. She stared down at that forefinger; it had been slashed by a saw during construction work, leaving a whitish indentation from knuckle to fingernail, a troughlike scar that seemed to brutalize his entire hand. For a few moments she wanted to free herself from such a hand, but the moments passed into acceptance and pleasure, even though the image of his scarred finger remained with Maggie when she got up and went into the bathroom. She couldn't remember when anything disagreeable about him before had stayed in memory this way, a bothersome image, almost a willed desire to make something of very little.

Later, having bathed and dressed, she was combing her hair in front of the mirror. The door was open, so she could hear the jaunty strains of "Black Bottom Stomp," played by Jelly Roll Morton's Red Hot Peppers. Abruptly the music stopped, and she could hear the ugly scrape of the player arm being slid clumsily across the record's surface. The sound made her teeth clench, and then in the mirror she saw Vern coming into view behind her. She felt his hands on her hips, felt their big flat warmth, a proprietorial gesture, because then he withdrew them so he could lean against the doorway.

"Sweetheart," she said with a faint smile, "please be careful with the records. They're pretty worn already and I can't get replacements out here."

"I'm sorry." He was frowning. His hair looked ragged from his efforts at drying it. His shirt, not yet buttoned, exposed dark curly hair on a broad chest. "I was sitting there, looking at the garden, and thinking how much I love you, sweetheart. And I was wondering why you do some of the things you do."

"For example?" She ran the comb vigorously through her hair.

"For example, you're studying Javanese as if your life depends on it."

"I don't think my life depends on it."

"Well, you're at it six hours a day."

"Maybe more."

"But pretty soon we'll be in Bali, where they don't speak Javanese."

"I know."

"Then why? You won't have time to gain fluency."

Maggie shrugged instead of saying, "I just want to learn the language, sweetheart, so what's wrong with that?" She would not defend herself. Resistance rolled through her like a sluggish swell of oil.

There was something urgent, almost desperate, in Vern's sudden demand for an explanation of her behavior. This had never happened before. Perhaps inherent in separation was the growth of personal caprice and self-doubt. Perhaps she ought to go back to Jakarta with him. But that was a possibility she left unsaid. Maggie pulled the comb once more through her hair, as if the gesture itself could shift their conversation elsewhere. She said, "Did you really meet Sukarno?"

Vern smiled as if happy to end an unwise attack. "I really did meet him."

"What was he like?"

"Going to fat, conceited, charming, tired, tireless."

"I can't tell from that if you liked him."

"I liked the guts, the ambition, the daring. I liked him because he studied architecture, though I don't share his love for Le Corbusier."

Extending her arms, Maggie grasped him around the neck the way children grip a post to swing around it. She looked into his weathered face, into his dark eyes where, during their first days on Samosir Island, she had discovered a steady river of deep feeling, and Maggie felt guilty for having sidestepped an argument with Vern Gardner as she might have done with a man she didn't love. She leaned against him, her lips against his ear, and whispered, "I'll give up Javanese and you give up the hotel and we'll go back to Lake Toba."

Vern drew back slightly to study her.

"We can find a secret place on Samosir and stay there," Maggie claimed. "We'll never come back. We can learn to fish."

"Sure, I'm for it." He pecked her cheek. Such a patronizing gesture, avuncular and dismissive, turned Maggie cold. Vern had refused to acknowledge there was something in her that could believe in fantasy. She let go of him and eased past his body into the bedroom.

"You're not really for it," she said. "Or for anything like it."

"I always like a trip."

"You do. But I mean you're not for going to a place and staying there." Maggie saw Inam passing the window, the girl's slim hips undulating through the swampy heat of the courtyard. "You need new things to build, sweetheart. You need change. In two months you wouldn't be able to stand Lake Toba."

"Could you?"

"I think I could. I'd probably just be settling in when you felt the urge to go. You'd adapt fast and then get bored. I'd fret and slog along but go deeper into the life until it was mine. And you'd be gone. And there we'd be."

When he said nothing, Maggie turned to look at his stricken expression. Laughing uneasily, she said, "Come on, there are other places to go. Let's go to Borobudur. If we stay here much longer, I'll want another rodeo ride."

Before driving out to the temple, they stopped at the train station where troops were loading for Jakarta. This was Achmad Bachtiar's battalion, which would be temporarily assigned to the First Honorary Palace Guard of the Cakrabirawa Regiment during the festivities on Armed Forces Day. Half of Yogya, it seemed, had come to the station to give their honored boys a send-off. Maggie had promised Ali she would come, although as a local representative of the PKI he could not be seen here among army troops. So with Vern beside her, she searched through the crowd for Sergeant Bachtiar.

"There he is," she told her husband.

232

As they moved through the crowd toward Achmad, he kissed a child held out to him by a tiny woman in a sarong. Seeing the foreigners, he lowered his eyes as if ashamed of a display of affection in front of them. He was sullen while thanking Maggie for coming to the station. He eyed Vern with suspicion.

"Congratulations to your unit. My wife tells me it's the 454th." Vern was speaking Bahasa Indonesia.

Achmad brightened at the American's knowledge of the battalion. "Yes, it is."

"Do you know Jakarta?"

"It will be my first time."

Maggie was watching the small woman hurrying away with the child in her arms. "Is that your family, Achmad?"

He mumbled it was, looking from one foreigner to another, lips tight.

"You have a lovely wife and child."

Achmad stared at Maggie.

"Do you think the Reds will cause trouble on Armed Forces Day?" Vern asked him.

"They better not."

"Where is Pak Bambang?" Maggie asked.

"In the village, working."

"And Ali?"

"He's causing trouble."

"I don't understand."

Achmad repeated it slowly, in both Ngoko and Krama.

"He is your friend," Maggie answered in uncertain Krama. "And you are his friend. You let him use your bike."

On their way back to the car, which was parked on a side street, Maggie expected Vern to say something about the conversation in Javanese. She awaited it like a blow, but he said nothing, which she interpreted as his acceptance of her language study and which proved, if proof were needed, that she was becoming too defensive. Maggie had always disdained the sort of paranoid sensitivity that some people felt was an obligatory part of love. In college she had walked away bored from bull sessions devoted to and-he-said-that-which-made-me-think-so-I-said-that-which-made-him-wonder. Either you loved or you did not love had always been her philosophy, learned too from a mother whose knowledge of love came from romance magazines. Regardless of the source of her ideal, Maggie had been loyal to it. She let feeling think for her, and if she cared for a man, that was enough. The whys and wherefores, Maggie believed, would fall into place as naturally as a plant grows.

She and Vern were silently crossing the street to the car when Maggie noticed a figure standing beneath a warung awning some distance away. It was a man in shadows. Then he was gone, like someone glimpsed in a Hitchcock movie, a presence that would haunt the characters through the entire filmed nightmare. But this was no ominous image. This was Ali. Had he come for a last glimpse of his old village friend on the way to Jakarta? Or had he come to see the American husband? From the outset of her friendship with Ali Gitosuwoko, she had felt on his part a romantic interest, though probably so deeply buried that he was not fully aware of it. That had not worried her. She had always had the gift of making friends among men who with more encouragement might have wanted more. But his improvident appearance today was unsettling. His furtiveness implied an intensity of emotion that might force her to break off their friendship.

———————

Then they were at Borobudur. Maggie was her husband's guide and led the way up the precipitous stairs of the temple. She was aware of chattering like a girl, but then she felt at home among these ruins, as if they belonged to her—or she belonged to them. She told Vern a story heard from the housemaid Inam. A high-school student once wrote a school essay on the subject of winning one million rupiah in a lottery. What would you do with such a sum? was the idea. This girl decided to travel to any place on earth that had snow. She wanted to see the snow falling, lying on the ground. She wanted to feel it melting on her fingers.

"It's a wonderful story," Maggie said when they reached the first terrace.

"Stands to reason the kid would want that," Vern said. "We all want what we don't have."

After they had walked around two terraces, Maggie asked him his opinion of Borobudur. She felt her lips parting expectantly.

Vern looked around for a few thoughtful moments. "They must

have built the temple here," he said, "because the area was full of peasants. I can't think of another reason. That way they'd have a ready supply of slave labor. The fields must have been neglected while the thing was built. Probably had famines."

"They did." She felt an unreasonable sense of guilt, as if she herself had oppressed those people a thousand years ago. Was he conscious of making her feel bad? "What do you think of the architecture?"

"Unimaginative. And what a mistake, building it on a hilltop in this climate. Moisture goes straight into the stone, buckles and splits it."

"That's what the dalang says."

"The dalang," Vern repeated. "You've mentioned him before."

"Have I?"

"In a letter you said you'd met one. And you mentioned him earlier today."

"I forgot."

"What's this dalang like?"

She caught the similarity of his question and hers earlier about Sukarno. "Arrogant," she said. "Educated, strange." She did not add, "Attractive, unpredictable."

"Strange." It was the part of her description that Vern chose to comment on. "Maybe his strangeness is genetic. I hear these dalang families intermarry." When she laughed, Vern said defensively, "That's what I hear."

"He's strange because of his profession, I think. People around here worship dalangs. It makes him something like a religious leader."

"Like one of those TV showmen who make a fortune selling Christ? He's your friend too?"

Maggie shrugged as she had shrugged when questioned about her reasons for studying Javanese. It could become a habit, she thought bleakly. When they reached the highest point of the stupa, Maggie began talking about the need to restore Borobudur. "What do you think?" she asked as they started down.

"I think restoring this place would take some doing. For one thing, it would cost a fortune. You'd have to disassemble the temple, take down the stones one by one—I don't know, maybe a million of them—and wash and treat each one chemically and then get them all back in the right order. Did I say a fortune? Two fortunes."

"But can it be done?"

Vern pursed his lips without saying anything.

"You're not interested."

"You should see yourself," Vern said with a smile. "You're shading your eyes from the glare. I can see your wedding band and your blue eyes, angry as hell. What's wrong, sweetheart?"

"I'm not angry. I just thought Borobudur would interest you."

"Not especially."

"But you're an architect."

"I'm a builder."

"Can't a builder be interested in a place like Borobudur?"

"Not this builder." He led the way down and they were silent until reaching the bottom. He turned there and said in a low voice thick from his own anger, "I am definitely not interested. No. Because this temple has nothing to do with me." He took a short, furious breath. "Or with you or with any of us. With anyone alive. It's the difference between a stuffed dog and a real one."

"Vern."

"I've seen the cathedrals, I've read the books, but when I left school I left all that hocus-pocus behind and became a builder."

"But, Vern—"

"I build things for the present."

Maggie fell into step with him. Her own voice sounded small to her compared to his, but firm. "I think it's possible to have both—things of the past and things of the present."

"Not if you have limited funds. I wouldn't give a dime for Borobudur until people who lived near it had what they wanted."

"Which is?"

"What we have. TVs, cars, supermarkets."

"Vern."

"I mean it."

"You'd make a trash heap of Java. Why not leave a part of the world free of our mess? Their banana peels rot, but our tin cans and plastics don't. Our kind of garbage just stays and piles up."

"Plastics hold what people want to carry. Much of what they eat is in tin cans. Engines get them around. TV takes your mind off problems. Since when have you become a do-gooder?"

"Preserving the past is holding on to history."

236

"It's like the peace marches. People in them mean well, but they just get in the way of what has to be done." The car was ahead. When they were inside, Vern said, "I'll be happy when people here have what we have. Then preserve the past. Why not?"

When he tried to take her hand, Maggie withdrew it. "You talk about what we have. What we have hasn't brought much happiness to a lot of people."

"Happiness isn't the point."

"What is?"

Vern searched for the word. Then he said, "Stimulation. It's what people want. They want arousal. They figure it's what we have in the West and they want it too. I just want them to have it fast."

"What's the rush?"

Again he tried to take her hand; this time she let him. "Maybe so the old folks can have fun too," he said, "before they're gone. I don't even care how these people are going to deal with cars and television and everything. That's their business. I'm in the supply business. I build what they want and let them take it from there."

"You wash your hands of it."

"Progress never came with a moral. Not in the history of this species it didn't."

After this exchange, they were silent on the way back to Yogya, though they held hands. Sometimes he squeezed her hand, sometimes she his, and they kept their hands together until reaching the Sakirman residence.

In Maggie's room they stood apart, regarding each other warily.

"You're angry," he said.

"So are you."

"Come back to Jakarta with me."

"What does that have to do with my being angry? It doesn't change the way I feel about your indifference to a temple crumbling out there. Indifference from someone who could do something about it. Going back to Jakarta won't change that."

"Jakarta is safer than they say. When push comes to shove, I don't think these people will fight. And anyway, you're running around with cultists—"

"What?"

"This puppeteer. You said yourself he was strange. And what about the odd little guy this morning? With Sakirman's wife gone, you're alone. It's no place for you anymore."

"You forget I did three months of fieldwork in Sumatra. I'm not too far from a doctorate in anthropology, for God's sake. I can take care of myself."

"What I'm trying to say is this separation isn't doing us any good."

"I know that, Vern." The truth of it took the edge of anger from her voice. "But Jakarta is still dangerous, isn't it? Going back there now would put me in a cage. I want to stay here awhile."

"So be it." His arms hung limp at his sides.

Her own arms encircled his waist. "We're fools to argue."

"Yes. I'm too damn stubborn."

"I'm too damn stubborn too." She put both hands to his face, framing it. "My husband won't be back for a while. If you're interested, we have time." She felt herself going into his embrace as if into a whirlpool of warm water. They were going to play the old game of infidelity again. But suddenly against her cheek he declared sharply, "I don't want to play that anymore."

She pulled back and looked at him.

"The idea is twisted," he said. "After all, I *am* your husband."

"Then we won't play it. Just love me."

"I do. I did from the moment I saw you at Lake Toba. I always will."

"I mean, now. Love me now, right here and right now."

Twenty-five

Achmad Bachtiar had known Jakarta was big, but not this big or this dirty. He had imagined it clean and sparkling, all tall buildings and boulevards and public gardens. His wife had been here, so she ought to know something, but she hadn't prepared him for the squalor, for the noise and heat and dust, so much worse than Yogya. But of course women always said yes when they meant no and held back unpleasant truth for fear you'd get angry. Every man knew that much. Every man had been taught that by his mother in the village—with a laugh, with a warning too that if he didn't listen to her he'd end up listening to a more faithless woman.

Even so, Achmad intended to lecture his wife when he got home. Tell the truth, he'd yell. If that didn't frighten her enough, he'd shake her by the shoulders. And he'd say, tell your husband the truth no matter what it is.

Satisfied with this imagined confrontation, Achmad walked through a slum in western Jakarta. He held a rumpled piece of paper with his sister's address on it. He was in uniform and proudly wore the insignia of the 454th Battalion, Diponegoro Division, although

239

he detested the progressive men in his company. They were going Red. Maybe a fourth of them were sympathizers, perhaps a fifth were members of the PKI. He would never understand them, let alone someone from his own village like Ali Gitosuwoko, who had gone off to Jakarta as a student and returned as a Red organizer. They were atheists and rioters and anarchists. So how could someone like Ali, whose family had been close to the Bachtiars for generations, be hoodwinked by such rascals? It was a mystery. Even Bambang didn't understand his brother. At the mention of Ali, Bambang would stare at his feet and shake his head slowly from side to side, like an old half-blind elephant.

The Reds were worse here, more powerful and dangerous. At the Halim Air Base, where his battalion bivouacked, the Air Force Staff and Command School was teaching Marxism. Teaching it. And PKI volunteers received weapons training right on the base from experienced commandos, men who had fought honorably in West Irian and Malaysia. What must such heroes feel, sharing their hard-earned knowledge with atheists and rioters?

But if that made Achmad uneasy, so did most things in Jakarta. Everywhere he went he heard of army corruption, of scandals, of cheating and smuggling. Very little of it could be true. Achmad was convinced of that. The army had been his refuge, his bastion; his reputation as a man depended on it. When his wife looked up at him in his uniform, Achmad felt like a sultan. Yesterday, while looking at bracelets for her in a shop, he'd overheard a customer tell the owner how soldiers were terrorizing his neighborhood, demanding money for protection, threatening girls. Achmad had walked up to him. Quietly he asked the man to apologize for telling such lies. The man did, instantly.

Achmad recalled the incident now, as he made his way along the stinking canals of the kampong. He read the acronyms painted on walls. NASAKOM was everywhere. It was a slogan he could not wholly agree with, even if it did come from the Great Leader of the Revolution. He agreed with nationalism and religion as pillars of the country's strength. But not communism, never communism. How could this upstart idea, based upon the political ambitions of alien Russians and Chinese, ever take hold in the ancient soil of Java?

He'd have changed the slogan to NASA, a fitting call to national pride. But KOM tacked onto it—never. That was an affront to his Muslim ancestry, to his village that had labored for centuries under gotong royong, the time-honored policy of mutual help. So he was alarmed that many men in his battalion would raise their fists and call out "NASAKOM!" when greeting one another. Of course, when this happened he said nothing; he willed his expression to reveal nothing. No one must know how he felt, except foreigners like that couple a few days ago at the train station. Because they didn't count, you could tell such people things. He had told them, for example, the Reds had better not cause trouble in Jakarta. He had voiced the threat. Otherwise, you never told anyone what you thought, not if you were a good soldier. You kept things to yourself. You did your duty.

Few people, he noticed, smiled at him as they did in Yogya. Many frowned at the sight of his uniform. But they were poor, ignorant, living with rats in a stench of urine and garbage. He glanced at the rickety shops with their cheap hardware, their flyblown food. Many huts were made of cartons, bailing wire, sheets of galvanized zinc. Squatters were stirring kettles along the narrow walkways. Some of them halfheartedly lifted their hands. "*Kasi uang,*" they begged with voices scarcely audible.

First thing Achmad would tell his wife when he got back: "There are places you wouldn't believe existed in our country. Praise Allah. In His wisdom He has chosen Yogya for us."

He felt sad in this kampong, knowing his sister lived in it. But after the death of her husband, she had refused to come home. She decided to remain in Jakarta where she had lived with her husband. Admirable decision for a widow: to live close to her memories of him. But to live here? Achmad felt sorry for her.

When he showed the paper with Endang's address on it to enough people and finally located her house, Achmad was somewhat heartened. Hers was a neat little house on a block of shacks, with a shiny tin roof and flowerpots on the windowsill. Knocking on the door, he heard a dog bark from the rear, so she probably had a garden.

First thing Achmad did upon seeing her pallid little face in the doorway crack was to thrust out the gift he'd brought from Yogya. His wife had selected it: a piece of machine-tooled batik; not expensive, but of a traditional pattern. Neither he nor his wife had been sure that traditional batik was still available in the modern city of Jakarta.

After a sembah, Endang took the package into her hands as if it were a newborn baby. For a while she looked at it before stepping aside so he could come in.

She had bought durian for him. Even though it was the season, durian was still expensive. As his fingers dipped into the split fruit and scooped out creamy gobs of pungent meat, Achmad wondered how she could afford durian, or, for that matter, the house itself. She had shown him the garden—surprisingly big for the house, and planted with a tall kenari tree, some caliandra bushes, bougain-villea, hibiscus, jasmine. It could have been the garden of rich priyayi people.

And the furniture, though sparse, was new. And in a closet he noticed sarongs neatly piled on a shelf—a lot of them, some of silk and fine linen. Did she really buy such things by taking in laundry? There had been none drying on the spotless roof.

And another thing: she was getting fat.

"Are you feeling well?" he asked guardedly.

"Yes, aside from having bad dreams." She sat on the couch, very pale, very small except for her belly.

"Wash your feet before going to bed. It will stop the bad dreams."

She nodded. "Yes, I think I knew that. But I forgot."

Again he asked. "Sister, are you all right?" He noticed she was wearing a spot of green paste on her forehead to scare off the Evil Eye.

"Things are happening around here," she said after a while.

"What things?"

"They caught a Communist and held his head under water till he drowned."

Achmad had a flashing image of shit and a severed rooster's comb floating in one of the canals on his way here. But he said, "That's not so bad, a Communist."

She leaned forward, grasping her hands as if in despair. "But you said Ali is home, working for the Communists. Won't that happen to him?"

242

"He's safe. It's his own village." Achmad believed that; although what Ali was doing annoyed everybody, no one would touch him. He was a Gitosuwoko.

Achmad asked once again. "What's wrong? Are you all right?"

There was a knock at the door. Endang jumped up as if terrified and rushed to it. Opening it a crack, she whispered frantically. Just as Achmad was getting up to see what was happening, a short, thin man carrying a tattered briefcase came into the room. He had thin lips that smiled without showing teeth. His ears, flat to his head, and slicked-down hair gave him the appearance of a small burrowing animal. He sembahed, then stretched out his hand for a Western handshake, introducing himself as Kamarusaman bin Ahmed Mubaidah.

Achmad did not like Western handshakes, yet touched the man's hand cursorily.

Endang, looking distressed, explained that Tuan Kamarusaman was an old friend who had helped her with business after her husband's death. Tuan Kamarusaman was in foreign trade.

Obviously she hadn't expected this man to come. Achmad felt she must have told him not to come while her brother was here, but he had come anyway.

They all sat down.

Sjam continued to smile from his thin lips. "I did my service during the struggle for independence. Her poor husband—caught in a tree. I understand a dog got him up there, and the Malayan police shot him. Confrontation has not been a success." He offered a pack of cigarettes—Achmad put up his hand in refusal—then lit one for himself.

"I find smoking helps in the heat," Sjam said, blowing a perfect circle into the air. "I don't do well in the heat. I get sore throats from it."

Achmad watched his sister rise to go brew some tea.

"I'm curious about men in service today. It's so much harder than it was in my time. Your unit?" Sjam asked.

Achmad told him.

The skinny little man slapped his knee. It seemed like a Western gesture to Achmad; this man Kamarusaman must do business with foreigners, eat with them, laugh with them.

243

"What an honor!" Sjam declared. "You've been brought from Yogya for Armed Forces Day."

"Every year a new unit's brought here for it," Achmad said deprecatingly.

"But this year is your year."

Achmad kept his face hard, devoid of response.

For a while the little man puffed thoughtfully on the cigarette, which he held as if it were delicate, between thumb and forefinger. Then he began talking about the plight of Jakarta. There was so much hypocrisy, deceit, and laziness in the government offices. Principles of the revolution were neglected, forgotten, in the public frenzy for success and money. "Perhaps you have heard of the Waringin Finance Company Limited of Singapore." Sjam didn't wait for a response, but went on. "It's run by cukongs from Jakarta. It provides capital for smuggling rubber and tin. Some of it goes to a smelting refinery in West Germany. They produce seltine earth. That's used in the color TV industry."

Achmad said nothing.

"So we'll have color TV here too someday," Sjam added. "Army men should know what's going on. After all, even in the army there's corruption, intrigue, all sorts of things going on."

Achmad didn't acknowledge the comment.

"Have you heard the latest scandal?"

"I hear rumors," Achmad said coolly.

Endang came with a pot of tea, a glass for Tuan Kamarusaman and a fresh one for Achmad.

"How do you people in the Diponegoro Division view things?" Sjam asked, blowing on the surface of his cup.

"I don't understand you."

"About corruption."

"No good army man likes corruption."

"Of course. And rumors of a coup—If this thing with the generals flares up or the PKI causes trouble—"

Achmad said nothing.

"I wonder if the Diponegoro Division will act."

"The division obeys orders."

Sjam blinked at him, sipped tea, took a puff of the cigarette. "You don't eat rice while it's hot, do you?"

"I do not."

Sjam shrugged. "I only ask these questions as an interested citizen. I'm concerned about the nation. I'm concerned about the army, if it will do its duty in an emergency."

"The Diponegoro Division obeys orders."

"You'd be surprised how many people in Jakarta are interested in the opinion of fighting men like yourself." Sjam leaned forward as if readying himself for something important. "They want to know what you think. In fact, I know people who would pay to know. Pay for your opinion. But it's not strange when you think about it, is it? Because these are strange times. Knowledge is worth money, isn't that so?"

Achmad's eyes met those of Kamarusaman. His own remained steady, while the other eyes wavered, looked away.

Sjam cleared his throat impatiently. Then getting to his feet, he glanced hard at Endang, who jumped up. "I have work to do," he announced. "I'm going to the docks now. If only you knew, Sergeant, what went on there—the customs officials, the army supply officers. But"—Sjam threw up his hands dismissively—"you believe it's only rumor. Peace be with you. Praise Allah." He gave Achmad a parting sembah, picked up his briefcase, and went to the door, with Endang at his heels. They went outside and spoke in low voices. Achmad had finished his tea before Endang came back, looking even paler, her face almost white, though the room, protected from afternoon sun by the roof's overhang, was quite dark.

"Is he keeping you?" Achmad asked sharply.

His sister hung her head.

Achmad felt anger working in him, but another emotion overpowered it. He struggled with himself, wanting to reprimand or even revile her, perhaps get to his feet and beat her. Others in the Bachtiar family would have done that. But he was away from home, this was a slum in Jakarta, and his little sister had food, clothing, a house, and a garden.

Rising, Achmad stared a moment at her—she did not look up—and rushed from the room. Outside, the sunlight was blinding. He lunged forward, almost knocking down an old woman carrying a ten-gallon can on her back. He went through the kampong so rapidly that people stepped fearfully out of his way. Sweat burst through the pores of his skin, but he never slowed down. He continued on until finding himself in downtown Jakarta. A man passing by smiled at him. Achmad knew it was because of the uniform. He swept his forehead with the back of his hand and slowed down, conscious of his sweaty shirt. A soldier, a petty officer, should not wear a sweaty shirt among civilians. He entered a warung more for the shade than for a soda. Later, cooled off, he walked aimlessly through the streets, thinking only of heroes, their names silently in his mouth, a roll call of the great: Haji Agus Salim, Husni Thamrin, Diponegoro, Hayam Wuruk, Gajah Mada, Fatahillah, Airlangga. He felt strange then, perhaps from too much heat and sun, but it seemed to Achmad Bachtiar that the spirits of those brave men were hovering nearby. It was as the dukuns profess: spirits come when a man is in need; they give him succor; they guide him.

So he would tell no one in the village about his sister. But he would never see her again.

Twenty-six

Project Palm Tree was still dead in the water. When Vern returned to Jakarta he had hoped for some movement, but everything was the same. The way OPSUS worked was a compendium of inefficient business practices. Profound deference to superiors was matched by utter disdain for inferiors and cowardly avoidance of conflict among equals; there was no low-level consultation, no self-correcting feedback among officers and clerks. The name Project Palm Tree was tossed around until it achieved a kind of symbolic life of its own. It existed as language. The name was like the acronyms that substituted for progress and accomplishment in Indonesia. Realizing a goal was equated with putting up a slogan. You made an announcement, gave a party, worked up current statistics based on future projections, held conferences, another press meeting, gave another party, and what had been done? Nothing. Vern was getting sick of it.

He understood, moreover, that OPSUS was basically a thick web of contractual agreements, a complex network of dummy companies. He couldn't sort them out any more than he could trace the winding course by which Susanto Sakirman ended up getting a rake-off from the Army Veterans Retirement Fund—he'd learned of that recently. God knows how many people in the web were manipulating accounts and projects for self-aggrandizement.

Never a patient man when it came to getting a project under way, Vern Gardner was edging toward a break with OPSUS. He had already written letters of inquiry to construction firms in Singapore and Delhi.

So it was in a gloomy mood that he accepted an invitation to meet with someone new, someone who represented another link in the intricate chain of Indonesian business. General Sakirman had said, beaming, "Now you'll get started," which could mean almost anything. It was the kind of cryptic remark that Vern had grown accustomed to, not only from Sakirman but from desk clerks, becak drivers, from anyone you had to deal with in Jakarta.

This sort of pessimistic thinking accompanied him into the Glodok District, the heart of Chinatown.

His years in Asia had prepared Vern for Chinatowns anywhere. They came from the same mold: two- or three-story buildings with shop-lined arcades along gridiron streets. Fruits sold in the markets might differ; otherwise, the products for sale were identical: the canned goods, the hardware, the paper money for funerals, the mahjongg counters.

His driver pulled up in front of a temple. Vern, along with Hashim, got out. Behind an ironwork fence was the marble courtyard of the temple, always a familiar haven within the blare and rush of Chinatown streets. Even so, this temple was a colorful one: the ivory-and-red building with its moon windows and curving roof lined by winged metal dragons glittered in sunlight, glittered and seemed to waver like something that had skin.

General Sakirman had instructed Vern to wait here at the temple. No sense asking why. Sakirman's method of doing things, be it running his office or meeting a girlfriend, carried the stamp of paranoiac circumspection.

Vern, with Hashim a few steps behind him, strolled through the two-tiered pagoda. The roof was topped by a pink-tipped white lotus and under it was a huge bronze bowl filled with sand. Pungent smoke from a hundred joss sticks floated over the sand and spiraled upward.

Impatient, Vern went into the main temple, where countless red candles were burning, some larger around than a man could circle with outstretched arms. Crimson, shiny, a surging flame of orange trembling out of their wicks. Always the same candles. In Hong Kong, Saigon, Bangkok. Vern began pacing. He walked over to a glass-topped counter that displayed plaster buddhas in garish color and calendars for sale. While he was peering down restlessly at them, someone spoke his name.

Vern turned to face a tall, brawny Chinese.

"You come," the Chinese said in Bahasa. Gesturing toward the courtyard with a stubby hand, he added, "Alone."

Vern nodded it was all right, so Hashim, suddenly alert like a guard dog, relaxed his shoulders and leaned against a temple pillar.

Having a bodyguard had provided Vern with jokes at the hotel bar, but now he missed Hashim when the big Chinese guided him into a narrow winding lane. They went a long way before stopping in front of a shabby teahouse. The Chinese pointed brusquely, then took up a position at the entrance, folding his arms.

The teahouse was dimly lit, deserted save for one man at a far table. Vern got the feeling that the place had been cleared for this meeting. The man was a tiny Chinese in a Western sports jacket and open-collared shirt, and when he got to his feet he looked like someone ready for a game of golf.

When Vern approached, the Chinese extended his hand—Vern saw on it the liver spots of age—and introduced himself as Sutopo Salim. The name was Indonesian, but clearly he was Chinese.

"Excuse the secrecy," he said in British English, "but these are difficult times. Is your bodyguard satisfactory?"

"Yes, very." Vern sat down at the table, wondering how the man knew about Hashim. A waiter instantly brought tea.

"I think Americans need a bodyguard in Jakarta as matters stand now," Sutopo Salim said. "I believe your wife stays in Yogya. That is a fine idea. Yogya is old, safe. Did you hear the American naval attaché has been deprived of electricity by a Communist labor union?"

"I haven't read the paper today."

"It hasn't been reported in the paper. Would you care for rice cakes?"

In the next hour Vern learned a lot about Project Palm Tree that he hadn't known before. The project was actually being financed through The East India Finance Limited of Singapore as a pilot program for expanded tourism in the area, in spite of, as Sutopo Salim called it, "difficult times." As soon as the situation stabilized, tourism would become a major industry. At least that was how the Chinese community in Jakarta saw things. They were prepared to invest heavily in such enterprises as a measure of faith in Sukarno's hold on the Indonesian conscience. When the present crisis passed, the cukongs wanted no delay in expanding their financial control through the Indies. That's the way Sutopo Salim put it. He added that he and his colleagues were happy to have an American builder on Project Palm Tree; American know-how was still respected if American politics were not.

From a briefcase he took out a sheaf of Vern's sketches and proceeded to analyze them. Estimates of space should include an arcade, one large enough to accommodate a score of shops. Although Bali had few automobiles at present, a vast parking lot should be figured in.

Vern agreed. He liked this Chinese moneyman, who identified himself officially as director of PT Seragam Technical Supply, which Vern knew was the name used by the chief financial agent for the army. Sutopo Salim was a Hokkien, his family originally from the Amoy region of Fukien. Recently he'd been in Hong Kong on business, so he hadn't had the pleasure of meeting the American builder until now.

Vern put two and two together. This Hokkien cukong was in full control of the money supply available to OPSUS. Nothing went on without his approval and participation, so his absence from Jakarta had brought Project Palm Tree to a halt. Standing in shadows behind the uniformed officials of OPSUS was the real boss: Sutopo Salim.

He suggested that Vern go to Bali for a look at sites. With General Sakirman's permission, of course.

Vern stared at him.

"Yes," said Sutopo Salim. "You must ask his permission, certainly not mine. You will get accustomed to asking permission of the right

250

people. Three generations of my family have lived here. We are Peranakan Chinese, Indonesian-born. We are legal citizens. Yet we are also foreigners, like you. And as foreigners we must often ask permission."

"I understand."

"Do you like the army?"

"I served in one."

"Then you have a feeling for it. After all, where would we be without the army? No permits, no licenses, no authorizations." Sutopo Salim spread his hands out, as if proving a point rather than satirizing it. "And no hotel." He studied Vern openly. "May I ask what you think of Jakarta?"

Vern did not hold back. He said the northern half of the city, dominated by the waterfront and Chinatown, was terribly congested. The other, less crowded half, spreading southward like a stain, was in danger of becoming so loosely planned that the traffic there would soon be even worse.

"Is that what you think of when you think of Jakarta, Mr. Gardner? Traffic?"

"Traffic's what comes to mind."

The cukong rubbed his cheek thoughtfully. "I suppose it might to a foreigner. We are so used to it we never think of the time it takes to cross the city."

"I once lived in Chicago, a very cold and windy place. I couldn't understand why visitors shivered. You see, I had grown used to it."

Sutopo Salim offered a cigarette from a silver case; perhaps it was a gesture of appreciation—Vern's analogy had been artfully courteous. "Very well then. When you think of Jakarta you think of traffic. Permit me to ask, Mr. Gardner, what do you see as Indonesia's greatest problem in the future?" When Vern hesitated, the cukong said, "Have I asked an embarrassing question?"

"Not embarrassing." Again Vern paused.

"But I think you feel your answer might offend me."

"Someone asked that question a few weeks ago and my answer annoyed him. He said what I thought was a problem was not important. The greatest problem of Indonesia, he said, had always been entanglement with the West."

The cukong covered a smile with two fingers.

"He also claimed," Vern said, "you fared much better with the Japanese."

Sutopo Salim, a Chinese, frowned.

"He claimed the Japanese encouraged a new spirit. They laid the groundwork for Indonesian independence and showed Asia it could live without the West. They spread a new philosophy—that a man's skill was worth more than his birth. He said other things, but I've forgotten them."

"I must say, he was quite rude for an Indonesian. And to praise the Japanese was an unusual way of criticizing the West. So your answer to his question was—"

"Repair. I told him the country's future would probably depend on repair. The big problem wouldn't be money or desire for progress or technical know-how, but the ability in the long run to repair things. If you can't repair what you buy, you waste your money. Without mechanics and service personnel who know what to do with parts, without an army of people who can install and maintain machines, the purchase of equipment soon comes to nothing."

"You attacked our potential for development."

"Yes, I was as blunt as he was rude."

"Blunt but in my opinion you were also correct," the little cukong said quietly.

Returning to the temple for Hashim, Vern told himself the project seemed to have a real chance at last.

And he was right. The project was off dead center now that the boss was back in town. Half the accountants on the staff were assigned elsewhere, and in their place draftsmen and engineers suddenly appeared. Sakirman showed up every day for consultation, however minimal that was. The project team accumulated design sketches, contacted supply companies, estimated costs realistically, and evinced signs of working toward a perceived goal.

In this busy and hopeful atmosphere Vern found it hard to think of Jakarta as embattled, dangerous, on the verge of catastrophe. Every day he had half a mind to write his wife as a husband should and demand that she return to Jakarta. But what surprised him each day was his indecisiveness, a problem he'd never had in previous relationships with women. He had always known what he wanted, and they had known too, which had made his liaisons concise and effective, in a sense like good business deals. But love had insinuated into his character a new and alarming timidity. He seemed to know better what Maggie wanted for herself than what he wanted for himself.

So Vern was thinking as he shaved. Looking in the mirror he saw a strong but not handsome face. A Eurasian woman he had known in Singapore, bedded, and almost married, had told him at the breakup, "Since we've come to this, I have a confession to make. I never liked your looks. You look like one of those American—Do you call them boxers? Like a boxer."

Vern stuck out his tongue at the mirror. His first serious act of the day. He wasn't used to self-scrutiny; he found it embarrassing. While dressing, he told himself that Maggie shouldn't come back here. Jakarta was still dangerous. Love made people selfish, he thought. And reckless.

Just as he zipped up his pants, there was a knock on his hotel-room door. Opening it, he stared down at a young Chinese girl who was smiling fiercely.

In good English she said, "I am pleased to meet you, Mr. Gardner. You don't know me but I know you." She giggled, clapping one hand over her mouth. "My father speaks of you, so I must meet you. So here I am. Thank you."

Vern studied her: petite, dressed in a white blouse and a Western skirt of dull brown cotton. Her face, narrow for a Chinese, hinted of some native blood.

"Who is your father?" he asked.

"Mr. Sutopo Salim. Or you know him by Yap Swie Kie? But he would not use Chinese name, I think."

"Did he send you?"

Shaking her head, the girl seemed ready to giggle again as if they were sharing a joke.

"Does he know you've come here?"

"My name is Yanti." She brushed past him into the room. She talked. She told him she was a student of architecture, she loved America, she wanted to speak with him because he knew about both. She had told him all that before crossing the room to the couch, where she flung herself down proprietorally.

How old? Vern wondered. Eighteen?

As if he had asked out loud, the girl Yanti said, "I am nineteen, second-year student at university. I can identify European cathedrals from photographs. Test me if you wish. How is my English?"

Smiling, Vern sat in a chair opposite the couch. "Your English is good."

"Father had us speak English when we started to talk. I love America. I will go there someday. But last year the government stopped the granting visas, so I must wait. But I will go. I will appreciate learning about America from you, Mr. Gardner."

"Well, that's a tall order, Yanti—It's Yanti?"

The girl cocked her head to study him. "You don't understand my name. My family is Peranakan Tionghoa. We are Chinese children of the Indies, so our names are Indonesian. Totok Chinese refuse such names. They keep close to China." And added, as if responding to a question, "No, I am not Communist. I walk in demonstrations against them. PKI are traitors and henchmen of Mao Tse-tung." Having stared into space during this rather mechanical announcement, she looked sharply at Vern. "Are you going somewhere, Mr. Gardner?"

"As a matter of fact, I am." Vern got to his feet. "I have an appointment."

"Can I go with you?"

"Go with me?"

"I am happy to talk to architect from America. Thank you."

He couldn't help smiling. "I have a degree in architecture, but I'm only a builder."

"So can I go with you?"

"You can go downstairs with me. We can talk on the way." Vern frowned deliberately, hoping it would persuade the girl to get off the couch. But she remained there a few moments as if considering the chances of staying until he came back. Then, reluctantly, she got up and followed him to the door.

Her long, straight hair kept falling into her eyes, so she had to brush it back as they went down the stairs, and she moved in little jerky bursts of energy. Vern smiled.

"There is Chinese problem in this country," Yanti said, halting midway down the stairs. "It is not easy being Chinese in this country. Many Indonesians don't understand. They think we are all Totoks, who follow what Communist mainland says. The Totok have own clubs, they send children to schools that teach Chinese, they send money home to mainland. They don't think Indonesia is their home. I am clear, Mr. Gardner?"

"You are clear, Yanti." Two Dutchmen whom he'd met last night in the bar came down the stairway. Passing him with the young girl, they smiled faintly—knowingly, it occurred to Vern.

"I can't speak good Chinese," she said, unwilling to continue down the stairs. "I never went to Chinese school. I don't want to go to China. All these things are known by native Indonesians who are my friends. They never accuse me of being Chinese. You must understand things here."

"I am trying, Yanti."

"My father chose Indonesian citizenship in 1950. He believed in this country." At last she took a step downward and Vern kept pace with her. "So he rarely use Chinese name. Neither do I. We are Indonesians. If I am architect someday, I build things for Indonesians."

"Good for you."

She giggled, once again clapping a hand over her mouth. They had reached the lobby. "I am glad we are talking one architect to other. Not yet, of course. But someday. Maybe." She giggled again as they started toward the hotel entrance. "Tell me about America," she said. "Have you seen houses of Frank Lloyd Wright? I have in books." She had difficulty with Lloyd: it came out Royd.

As Vern was about to answer, Hashim appeared from behind a pillar, glaring at them both.

"Is the car here, Hashim?"

The bodyguard nodded, attempting not to look again at the girl.

"Is that bodyguard?" she asked airily. "Father has four. Last year was riots against the Chinese. We must be careful. Communists hate us for being loyal to government."

"You seem to like politics."

"Thank you, I do."

Outside, when the car pulled up, Vern said, "I'm glad we met, Yanti. Give your father my respects."

"No, no, no!" She bent forward, giggling. "He would not want me here. He is old-fashion. I am modern girl."

"Yes, I believe you are."

Getting into the car, he looked out at her. "I understand how your father feels."

"You are not modern, Mr. Gardner?"

"Not about young women visiting men in their hotel rooms."

"But you are American. You must be modern!" She waved gaily as the car pulled away, and Vern waved back. He found himself still waving through the rear window until the hotel vanished around a curve.

Later in the day, recalling Yanti, he thought differently about her than he had when they met. Then she had merely seemed girlish and brash. Now he recalled a woman who masked serious ambition behind a giggle. Some men might even consider her dangerous, a woman of vaguely defined but genuine power that was yoked to a reckless spirit and good looks. Odd thought. But he kept it in mind. The idea of Yanti being dangerous gave him a little thrill.

Twenty-seven

Death to atheists
DEATH TO REDS
DEATH TO AIDIT
DOWN WITH PKI

These words were scrawled in black on the walls and door of PKI headquarters in Yogya. As Ali came up the street, he saw a party member applying whitewash to the huge painted letters.

Hatred of the party was far more obvious in the city than it was in the villages. Nevertheless, since coming out here from Jakarta, he had met resistance everywhere, even in the village where he had lived as a boy. People looked upon him as a stranger from the big city. Compounding his problem was the nature of village life, the reality of it that he had forgotten during his years in Jakarta. The classic demography for Communist success was missing here in Central Java—there just weren't enough poor peasants to recruit, not nearly enough field workers who had grievances or who had at least considered the possibility that they might be victims of injustice. Most of the poor didn't know they were or they knew it and accepted their poverty as Allah's will. So the young organizer was hard put to find someone to organize.

Moreover, in Ali's own village the resident Communist, a bland little fellow named Narto, was untrustworthy and ineffectual. Narto knew nothing, did nothing, could offer no guidance or advice, but simply collected a small monthly stipend from PKI headquarters in Yogya.

These grim thoughts preoccupied Ali as he entered that headquarters and waited for the district leader, Comrade Pramu, to see him. He disliked Pramu. In Jakarta you could ask for a transfer out of a job that wasn't going well and you would probably get it. But in Yogya there was no choice; you were stuck with Comrade Pramu. Out here your belief in communism was put to the test. That's what Ali liked about it, the challenge, but sometimes he just felt down.

After a long time Comrade Pramu came to the office door and motioned with a little flick of the wrist for Ali to come in. Sitting down in the dark little room, Ali felt his buttocks tilt because half the cane was torn from the bottom of the chair. He didn't mind. He enjoyed the idea of Comrade Pramu having a shabby office.

The comrade sat at a desk devoid of paper; there was an inkstand, a framed photo of his fat wife, a telephone—the appearance of a desk readied for use but not yet used. Pramu was a broad, thick man, the sort you might find in West Java but rarely here, where people ate sparingly and disliked the look of self-indulgence. To emphasize his importance, Pramu opened a drawer, took out a sheaf of papers, and turned them over awhile before looking up at Ali.

"I called you in for something important," he said. "You must say nothing to anyone."

This warning infuriated Ali, a cadre himself now for two years. Even so, he relaxed the muscles of his face: Pramu mustn't know how offended he was.

Pramu mentioned a communiqué from Jakarta that hinted of an important event. Something might happen soon. Everyone must be prepared to take advantage of it.

"It is now the twenty-eighth," Pramu said. "Perhaps we can expect something within a few days."

Ali said nothing.

Pramu toyed with the edge of the inkstand, letting the suspense build. He had a flair for the dramatic, Ali had to admit. He might have become an inferior dalang in a town unaccustomed to good performances.

"If something happens," Pramu finally continued, "a revolutionary council will manage the country." He waited for the enormity of that idea to sink in. "We will support this council in every possible way. Banners, posters, speeches, meetings, demonstrations. I will give you instructions when the time comes. But if you hear something on the radio—let's say, this council has come into existence—by all means instruct the villagers to support it."

Instruct the villagers. It was a phrase that Ali repeated ruefully to himself. He had tried to organize a meeting about land reform last week; only a score of PKI sympathizers, Narto, and five "dedicated" Communists attended. Two of the committed Reds spent most of the time complaining that counterrevolutionaries had stolen their land. It turned out that these Reds were well-to-do landowners who wanted to use the party to regain their property.

And afterward Narto wrung his hands at the thought of establishing a revolutionary training session in the village. Ali was going to explain how demonstrations took place, how you made Molotov cocktails, how you set up roadblocks that forced travelers to understand the plight of landless men, and how you overturned trucks hauling produce to emphasize the fact that while food was stacked within the wooden panels, there were women and children within walking distance who didn't have enough to eat. They have enough to eat, argued Narto. Anyway, he thought such training was premature (and in his heart of hearts, so did Ali). Narto added that farmers would be frightened of the idea of violence. This, of course, was something Ali would never believe. Having come from the region, he knew better. He had seen farmers go at each other with harvest knives because one of them, during an argument, had inadvertently crushed the other's rice shoots with his heel.

Instruct them? A Red worker had tried that a few years ago. He had stayed with the headman for three days in the village, telling people the Russians and Chinese were coming and would torture anyone who wasn't Communist. By joining the PKI you could save your life and never pay taxes again. He also talked of Communist angels in Islamic heaven and Judgment Day when all non-Commu-

259

nists would be consigned to hell. Even among the ignorant peasants who flocked in to hear the stories, there was grave skepticism and finally anger, because some of them wondered if he was amusing himself (probably, Ali thought) by insulting them.

That clever man had made Ali's task harder. Getting the subdistrict head and the village head together for a courteous discussion of mutual problems, Ali felt them studying him closely, searching for the slightest sign of condescension or arrogance. Yet here was Comrade Pramu telling him to give people messages from on high. It was a measure of Pramu's stupidity and laziness; had he traveled to the outlying villages and seen for himself, he would have known better than to order people "instructed." He might have at least said "tell" them. He was no better than that traveling Red organizer who had either tried to play on their primitive fears or out of some private frustration had made fun of them.

Ali was so angry that he'd left PKI headquarters and started down the road before considering what had really been said in there. Intentionally vague, Comrade Pramu had still managed to say enough. He'd been talking about a coup, an overthrow. That's what the Revolutionary Council meant. Would Aidit be the new ruler of Indonesia? Better such a dedicated man than what they had now—a womanizer living in palaces. Sukarno had been a leader of the independence movement. Good, praise him. Sukarno was now behaving like a sultan. Bad, depose him. Communism taught that society must change for the welfare of people. Such change was coming now, and he, Ali Gitosuwoko, was going to help bring it about. He felt the palms of his hands sweating.

Ali was staying in Bambang's house, which embarrassed his anti-Communist brother. Of course, it would embarrass Bambang more if he didn't: any relative, let alone a brother, must be granted hospitality. But they kept clear of each other. At night Ali was always seeing local officials, farmers, shopkeepers, peasants from outlying fields, so he and Bambang rarely met. Luckily Ali stayed in a little garden hut, ordinarily used for storage. He had insisted on this. It gave him time to think, when he lay on an old mattress within a muzzy circle of smells—those of gunnysacks, machine oil, flowers—

while twenty feet away, from his brother's house, came the radio wail of gamelan.

Only after Bambang went to the foundry did Ali take breakfast. He sat on the veranda where Bambang's wife, Melani, served him coffee and a plate of nasi goreng. She was pregnant with her third child. It gave her skin a breathtaking softness that Ali tried not to look at. He kept mixing up the sight of her with an image of tall Maggie. Terrified, he felt his loins stirring, while Melani poured more coffee, relayed some idle village gossip, turned unfortunately so he could see the curve of her breast.

And in the midst of Ali's discomfort, Bambang came into view, his big shaggy head thrust forward between broad shoulders like a bull.

He tramped onto the veranda and stood looking down at Ali. "What have you been doing?" he roared.

Startled, Melani rushed into the house.

"Brother," Ali said coolly, "do you want everyone to hear? Please sit down." Looking at his fierce brother, Ali wondered if Bambang somehow knew of the forbidden desire that was still receding in him. Had Bambang come for that? To protect Melani from unwanted advances? To punish the intruder who shared his blood? Ali was afraid but somehow strangely relaxed, as if the angry man he faced was easier to deal with than with his feelings a few minutes earlier.

"You've been talking revolution at the foundry," Bambang said.

"I have not been near the foundry."

"Jangkung has listened to your stupid talk."

"Jangkung came to a meeting, yes."

"And he says things in the foundry, things he doesn't understand, and even when we laugh at him, he keeps on saying them. As if you bewitched him. Let him alone, brother."

"I won't encourage him to come to meetings. But if he comes, he comes."

Bambang was drumming his thick soiled fingers on the table. And for a moment Ali remembered their childhood days together: how Bambang, big and passionate, would get into trouble; how he, smarter but in his own way just as bold, would try to get him out of it.

"Brother," said the gong maker, "if you stay here you'll only cause trouble. I think you know that."

"I'm trying to help the people of my village."

"They don't want communism. Narto and his little Red bunch are enough. People have a good life in my village. Maybe in some of the neighboring places they have trouble, but not here. People help one another. You know that, don't you? Don't you remember how it's always been? There's nothing for you here. Go away, brother."

Ali met the gong maker's angry stare. "I have work to do. Land reform hasn't begun here, although in many parts of the country—"

"You Reds have people fighting in the fields. I know all about it. We aren't stupid here. Why don't you let things be?"

"You sound like Uncle," Ali said bitterly. "Those are his aristocratic sentiments: let things be, don't look around, think only of old temples and puppets."

"If I sound like Ki-Dalang Budi, I'm content." Bambang always called their uncle by his formal name. Ali never did.

"I can't understand," Ali said, bringing up old matters, "why you choose to honor him."

"Because Father made him head of our family."

"He flattered and tricked Father into it."

"Never. He's a true dalang, a great one. Father knew he would be."

Ali wanted to say, "You defend Uncle because he buys gongs from you," but realized suddenly how wrong the argument was. An old shadow flickered across his reasoning. Was it right for a Communist to worry about the dispensation of an inheritance? Principle is the issue, Ali told himself. Family pride. Uncle had wormed his way into Father's good graces. The house should have gone to either son. That was the proper choice. The issue was family pride and principle and nothing more. Yet sometimes he wondered if jealousy wasn't behind his hatred of Uncle. He felt uneasy with the argument. He wanted out of it. Suddenly he wanted out of all conflict with his brother. Something seemed to be hovering nearby: their past together, his memory of it.

He said, "Brother." He paused. He said it again, "Brother," in a gentler tone. "I'll move out of your house. You've done your duty. The family won't be disgraced if I move now. I'll stay with Narto."

"If you stay in the village at all, stay here. This is your home as well as mine."

262

Ali shook his head; reaching out shyly, he touched his brother's hand. "It's better I go." He nearly added, "Especially now, when I'm performing in a wayang drama that will shake your world." And he thought something further, something he never would have said: Especially since this morning, when I looked at your wife with longing.

———————

That afternoon he moved into Narto's house. There was a flurry when he came in—children, Narto's wife gawking at him—and little Narto at his heels, a fawning man who told Ali how welcome he was, how privileged they were to have him here in their modest house (modest it was), especially because they were newcomers to the village and not accustomed to such honor, but of course they were admirers of the Gitosuwoko family, who were not heartless bourgeois landowners like some other important people in the area, but an honorable family that had given someone like him to the Communist party to work for the common good and socialist glory, admirable admirable, and so they were privileged beyond their worth to have him here and they extended a limitless invitation for him to remain, and of course soon, someday soon, a revolutionary training session might be just the thing for village youth, but maybe without the roadblock and bombing instructions, and when he returned to Jakarta would he tell the powers of the PKI of the good work being done here?

Ali looked at him, a man old before his time, with squinty eyes, a limp, a cough. He worked in a brick factory. One child had TB, another was deaf. His wife coughed often, and Ali suspected she sometimes hacked up blood. It was the saddest household he'd ever seen. He looked at Narto in a new light. And that first evening, as he lay in his room listening to sporadic coughing from the two other rooms into which six people were crowded—for he had run into sudden surprising resistance from Narto at the suggestion that he might share a whole room allotted him—Ali understood why Narto had so little to offer the Communist party; the fellow was too busy surviving.

At that moment Ali felt a surge of emotion, a fresh tide of commitment, flow through his veins. How simple life was. No theory was needed once you saw your goal distinctly. You were like cattle that finds the way home. At the outset of Ali's life in the party, it was to people like Narto and his family that he had dedicated himself. How easy it was to forget such commitment. But as long as he kept his commitment in mind, nothing could stop him. He felt stronger than at any time in his life.

Later, having fallen into a dreamless sleep, he awakened and sat bolt upright, sweating profusely. Had he started to dream? He couldn't remember. But filling his vision in the blackness of the silent room was Maggie's face, her brown hair framing it. What would happen to her in the event of a coup? Then Ali realized he was tumescent. He lay on his back and breathed heavily into the darkness. He must not think of her, of Melani, of any woman. There was plenty for him to do on this earth aside from loving women. Things were going to happen soon. That alone must occupy his thoughts.

But it was a long time before he could sleep. She was in his mind, the tall, broad-shouldered woman from another world: her blue eyes grave, her blue eyes oceanlike, possessing thoughts he couldn't enter, that must always be alien to him.

Twenty-eight

Maggie was walking through the gloomy Sono Budoyo museum. From worn and moldering cards, either tacked or glued next to exhibits, nearly all of which needed repair, she absorbed facts facts facts.

Men had lived in Java earlier than in most places on this planet. Solo man, named after a fossil discovered near the town of Surakarta, had walked across the Sunda Strait from Asia a half million years ago, before the ocean swallowed up the natural bridge. A cannibal, he lived among elephants and hippos. Pygmies, the first wave of migrants, appeared in Java thirty thousand years ago, followed by Wayak man, the true ancestor of Indonesians.

In 1512 the Portuguese set up trading posts in Indonesia.

In 1812 the English looted Yogya.

In 1942 the Japanese occupied Yogya.

In 1948 the Dutch bombed Yogya.

This dusty town of puppets and music? Maggie was hot, sweaty; she dabbed a handkerchief at forehead, neck, throat. Sono Budoyo museum could use air-conditioning, at least a ceiling fan, and a better labeling system and better lights. She felt as though Vern were standing beside her, her criticism his, a remorseless condemnation of what was old in favor of what was new. In their early days together, when Maggie was still under the shadow of illness, his opinions, delivered like nails driven into wood, had appealed to her because they represented the accumulated vigor of a healthy man. Now they seemed to represent indifference and shortsightedness. His attitude toward Borobudur was distressing—callous. Borobudur was a prodigious reminder of man's spirit; it must be saved, it must, and her husband was wrong.

Turning into another dim room and discovering a bench, Maggie sat down wearily. After finishing her language lesson, she had biked to the main market. Unlike the Palembang market, it wasn't sinister, just busy: displays of clothing, fruit, dishes, old Dutch-style chests with dangling locks, pie tins, books, shoe polish, tennis balls (where in hell had they got tennis balls and for what reason in a town that had no courts?), bolts of cloth, bras (lacy) laid out on bamboo mats, pink cakes fuzzy from coconut coating, kitchen spoons, garden hose, screws in bins, used thermoses, silver-plated candlesticks doubtlessly from the Netherlands, weight scales, wire in coils, saws, batteries, stacked bricks.

She had come out of there dizzy. Dogs were scooting underfoot, as skinny as the people who aimed kicks at them, because the Javanese were no kinder to dogs than the Sumatrans had been. As she headed for the museum, wheeling her bike to it only a few blocks away, she studied faces as openly as passersby studied hers. These were a spare, neat, ascetic people, as remote now as they had seemed to Maggie on the day of her arrival. They either contained their emotion or resisted it; she had not decided which. Surely their appearance matched their spirit: lean, slight, almost spindly—living signatures of leather puppets, the elongated silhouettes of which hung from almost every shop wall. Which came first, she wondered: the look of the Yogyanese or the look of their puppets? Would Dalang Budi know? Would he care?

She had a sudden image of him: the high cheekbones, like an Indian's, the wide-set eyes with the pristine gaze of a child who hasn't learned yet to hide behind a mask of humility. She was thinking about him when a slim young man swung around the corner of the room; in his haste he nearly collided with the bench.

"Ali! What are you doing here?"

He was panting, his dark eyes aglow. "Looking for you."

She could have asked how he had tracked her down, but of course that must have been easy. Aside from some East German engineers who were building a sugar mill, a few Dutch businessmen on trips of nostalgia, a couple of French journalists passing through, there weren't any foreigners in Yogya whom she knew of. Certainly not tall Western women. Ali must have started from the language guru's house and simply asked anyone for the *orang asing perempuan*; people would have guided him unerringly here.

He sat beside her on the bench, but at the edge of it.

"Is something wrong?" she asked.

Ali did not seem to hear, so absorbed was he in his own thoughts. There was a long silence. Then he looked up, his narrow face scowling, as if in response to something they'd been discussing.

"How long you be in Yogya?" he asked sharply.

"I really don't know."

"Where is husband?"

"You know where he is, Ali. Is anything wrong?"

"Much happening." Again silence. Again Maggie respected his mood by saying nothing. Then suddenly he began. "Your president send more army to Vietnam. More bombing. Fighting at place call Danang. Your president is war criminal."

Maggie said nothing.

"President Johnson, the Premier Rusk—I know their names—and Saigon puppet, Nguyen Cao Ky, they should be tried in court of world for crime against humanity."

"Ali, I am your friend, but I am not a Communist," she said quietly. "I don't see a lot of things the way you do."

"Bombing is right?"

"No. But the problems facing America aren't those facing your government. I don't say we're right. But I don't say the Communist countries are right either."

"And CIA undermake—undermine our government. Pay our generals to be spies and traitor." He fell again into brooding silence.

Maggie wiped her neck with the damp handkerchief. He hadn't sought her out just to villify America. But from batik, from using the canting and pouring the melted wax, from the study of Javanese with its bewildering social contexts, from the example of austere people she met daily, from the massive heat and blanketing sunlight, from the quiet march of diurnal events hour by hour into nighttime at a pace so gradual it seemed hardly to have happened at all, from the idea of Java itself, this ancient and steady land, she was learning patience, and so instead of questioning him further, Maggie sat in the gloomy museum and waited and waited.

"Tell me about Beatles," he said suddenly.

Maggie studied his face for a message, for a guidepost to the direction of their conversation. But he was being Javanese right now—implacably stone-faced. These people controlled emotion like turning a faucet. "Well," she said, "the Beatles are very, very popular musicians."

"Is *Hard Day's Night* political film? It was seen in Hong Kong."

"It's a funny and joyful movie. It's not political."

"And *Help!*" he persisted. "New one. Is political?"

"I haven't seen it, Ali."

"Is political?"

"I should think not."

"It could. It could mean help against bourgeois corruption. Is possible?"

"Yes, possible."

"I think is political."

Maggie was staring at a collection of wayang kulit puppets suspended by strings on the opposite wall. It was too dark really to see their features well. Some were monsters; some, the slim elegant figures of aristocratic warriors. Dalang Budi lived in their world. She noticed a large hard-shelled insect walking along one string like a tightrope performer. Silence thickened the way heat thickened in this room, both like heavy gas being pumped into the museum from huge generators. It was a grim thought, but helped her to wait and to wait and to wait. She wouldn't insult him by looking at her watch—this young man was suffering through something—but they must have sat now in silence for nearly half an hour.

"Things happening," he finally began. "You stay some time, Nonya?"

His formal use of "Nonya" could mean he was distancing himself from her, and it put her on guard. She felt it was somehow an act of friendship. "Yes," she told him. "I think so, Ali."

"Be prepared."

"For what?"

"If something happen, Nonya Maggie, look to me." He got up from the bench, lips trembling. Then they edged into a smile, widening into what seemed to Maggie like a boastful smile. "Yes. Look to me if something happen here." He had drawn himself up grandly. "Husband, he stays in Jakarta, but *I* am here. I protect you." He emphasized "protect" in a way that suggested it had been looked up in a dictionary, savored, practiced. "Is what I found you to say. I protect you, Nonya Maggie!" Not waiting for a reply, Ali turned and walked briskly from the room.

She might ask Mas Slamat what was happening, because that evening she was meeting him. She had his note in hand—the scrawl enormous and childlike—with his address and a plea (or command) to come visit him at his house. So she was walking down a dusty lane at sunset, halting passersby and asking the way. It was surely harder for her to find Mas Slamat than for him to find her. She went up the wrong street twice, and was beginning to despair, when he hobbled out of the shadows. Maggie got the distinct impression that he had been watching her for some time.

Doffing his hat, he apologized immediately for having left her after the performance of wayang golek. "I had letter to mail to Europe," he explained. "Come now to my house." He touched her elbow as if to guide her. It really was an elegant gesture. "I live in santri Muslim neighborhood. You must be known to live here."

"What if a non-Muslim moved in?"

He shook his head. "No."

"But if one did," she persisted.

Mas Slamat halted and looked up at her in the last light. "He would be warned, then slaughtered."

They turned a corner, and in an area far from those in which she

269

had searched for his house, Mas Slamat stopped. He stopped so precipitously that Maggie went on a few paces before checking herself. She watched him pull an enormous key from his baggy trousers and insert it into the lock of a small rickety-looking door that might have been pushed in, she figured, with one good kick.

When the door was opened, he stepped back courteously and let her go in first.

It was too dark inside to see much, but Maggie got the impression of a very large house with a high ceiling, and when his little figure preceded her into a room, she felt as though they had entered a warehouse. The air seemed to recede, as it appears to do in enormous rooms, while she discerned objects coming out of the dimness: boxes, crates, huge old armoires rising like sentinels along the walls. He took her on a quick inspection of the place, and it was hard for Maggie to know where to concentrate—whether on this houseful of ancient and modern trash or on his reaction to showing it to her. He seemed at once proud and embarrassed, claiming it was his ancestral house but needed much repair.

"Watch out," he warned her, going from the main room into another, where a clothesline was strung above a trio of linoleum-topped tables piled with newspapers and dirty dishes. A refrigerator was barricaded behind other tables cluttered with junk; its door could not have been opened for a long time, perhaps for years, perhaps, Maggie thought as she peered at a coating of dust across the front of the refrigerator, since she had been a child.

"Needs much repair," he muttered, guiding her around some cardboard boxes filled with paper and a rusty bicycle surely as old as she was, perhaps as old as Mas Slamat.

Back in the main room he lit a kerosene lamp—"Lights out, broken"—and placed it on a small round table, after one imperious hand had swept off a number of books which clattered to the floor. Then he was gone, shuffling away into another part of the cavernous wreck.

Lamplight illuminated the main room in all its chaos: tall bookcases, the glass either removed or broken, loaded with books stacked in unsteady pyramids; and overstuffed chairs draped with old clothing; and more boxes overflowing with paper metal plastic wood. Is he a junk dealer? she wondered.

He returned with a small lacquered box, which he opened carefully.

She watched him remove things from it, identifying them as areca seeds, slaked lime, and betel leaf. He rolled two betel leaves with the seeds and lime and added wads of tobacco. He handed one quid to her.

She hesitated.

"Welcome to my house," he said proudly and slipped a quid of sirih under his lower lip.

"If you have gas on stomach," Mas Slamat told her, "this will take away. Also good for teeth. In old days people painted their teeth black because they liked black color on teeth rather than red color from betel." The quid gave him the look of someone who'd just been hit in the mouth. "Betel won't stain you for long time. Look at me. I have chewed betel for years, but my teeth did not turn red."

Maggie wondered if he remembered that he had no teeth. Or if he thought she didn't know he had none.

Mas Slamat leaned to one side of his chair and squirted red liquid onto the floor. "Is all right," he said. "Don't worry, Nonya. You can spit. I have my servant clean up."

Indeed, she felt the need to spit, as the bitter red seeds inside the leaf were causing her mouth to fill with saliva. She'd rather just swallow it, but that might offend him, so Maggie leaned over and spit her own stream of red juice, spattering the torn cover of a book lying there.

Mas Slamat smiled. "Indians put aniseed and cardamom in their sirih, but we do not. We like as it is."

Next he showed her letters and postcards from all over the world. He had big ragged folders of them. Apparently Mas Slamat had met everyone who passed through Yogya. He was immensely proud of these messages from abroad, although many of them were torn, faded, falling into ruin like his other possessions.

"My wife does not live here anymore," he said.

"I didn't know you were married."

Raising his outsized hand, Mas Slamat put up four fingers. "My sons."

"Are any of them in Yogya?"

He shook his head, not a trace of regret in his expression. "My house is very big," he boasted.

"Indeed it is."

"I have big garden too."

She smiled, acknowledging the vastness of his home.

"Is your house in States as big?"

"Definitely not."

"I did not think so."

There was an arrogance in his tone that startled Maggie, but then she was talking to an aristocrat. Or at least he called himself one. He probably was. And that's why the place was such a mess. This revelation came to her while Mas Slamat rolled two more quids of sirih. He refused to work like other people. He spent his time searching for foreigners with whom he could share a heritage of superiority. And so the ancestral home had simply fallen into ruin. There was a kind of grotesque splendor to the way he lived. Or so she felt because she was high—the sirih was a narcotic. The sirih made his house somehow romantic and grand. She was high all right. Back in high school they had smoked reefers sometimes (for her it was in special homage to jazz musicians), and the feeling was not altogether different from what she felt now. Rolling the bitter quid around in her salivating mouth, Maggie let the high it gave her take control.

She looked past the flickering lamp at Mas Slamat's austere, wrinkled face. Old devil.

"Thank you," she said, "for inviting me."

With dignity he sat up straighter. "I consider myself your friend. If something happened, Nonya, permit me to offer my services."

That reminded her of the peculiar scene with Ali. Leaning forward, she said in a tone made confidential by the sirih, "Tell me, Mas Slamat. Is something going to happen?"

"Nonya?"

"Is anything wrong?"

Thoughtfully he placed a large thumb on the mole. "Two houses away, last afternoon," he said, "some crows were over them in the sky. That means death. There will soon be death in the neighborhood."

"I mean anything wrong in the city, in Java."

"Price of rice is high."

"Yes. I mean something else. Of course I know the Reds and the army are at each other's throats. Reds and Muslims too. But that's been the state of affairs as long as I'm over here. Something is about to happen—is that it? Something worse than public accusations and a bit of rioting. Am I right?"

He sat even straighter. "Muslims will slaughter them if they come to our neighborhoods."

"What I mean is, is this a possibility based on fact or on feeling? Are people simply nervous, Mas Slamat, or are there signs of new trouble?" Maggie smiled. "Don't be afraid of telling me the truth. I'm not afraid of it."

Ignoring her question, Mas Slamat said, "When Communists come into my neighborhood, they will be slaughtered."

"That's what I'm asking. Are they supposed to be coming?"

Mas Slamat opened his hands in a gesture of indifference. "If they come, they will be slaughtered."

"And if they don't come? If they don't start up? Will it blow over? Will the situation remain the same?"

He sat back, chomping his toothless gums. "R. Harjanta Prijohoetomo says something will happen. I told you."

"Yes, the holy man. He predicts a catastrophe."

In the light flickering across Mas Slamat's face the mole had taken on the look of a smudge. "They should not try," he said, his voice small and cold and furious. "We will slaughter them."

Having insisted on walking home in defiance of the holy man's prediction of imminent disaster, Maggie heard along the evening lane a distant sound of struck gongs. That was behind her. Another set of gongs was struck ahead of her. The nighttime street was awash in the sound of gamelan.

It reminded her of yesterday when the dalang, at her invitation, paid a visit to hear her jazz records.

They sat on a veranda in front of the Sakirman courtyard while Chicago jazz filled the air and curious servants peered around corners, mouths agape.

Neither she nor the dalang had mentioned the crisis that today so absorbed Ali and Mas Slamat.

Within the blue shade of the veranda, they had drunk tea while the warped discs spun on the turntable, sending into the heavy air a syncopated blast of "Cake Walkin' Babies from Home" by the Red Onion Jazz Babies, featuring Louis Armstrong and Sidney Bechet.

In this sort of early jazz, Maggie explained, there were fewer solos, more ensemble work, and several melodies were improvised at the same time, perhaps something like gamelan with its many layers of overlapping melody, and when the dalang agreed that such a practice might resemble gamelan, she felt vindicated in having read everything she could find about Javanese music during the last few days.

In turn he explained the two tuning scales of gamelan, each of which had its own quality (he preferred the five-toned scale of slendro, because it lent itself to deep feeling, whereas the seven-toned scale of pelog was identified with majestic detachment). He described the change in instrumentation for soft and loud compositions, the different phrase lengths, the concept of iklas, whereby the musician strove not to compete with other players but to recede into the ensemble and thereby achieve a state of isolated exaltation. The difference between Chicago and New Orleans music was the lack in Chicago of a trombone or at least of traditional trombone playing; there was less economy of phrase and more cascading runs than in New Orleans jazz, she told him, and he told her that the balungun, or skeleton melody, was played by the sarons and the slentem, the only instruments limited in performance to what was written down. He showed by diagram the difference in musical notation as practiced in Yogya and Solo. She compared the cornet playing of Louis and Bix: Louis, more dramatic, his range wider; Bix, more reflective, his tone cooler.

And so through the afternoon, refreshed by pots of Javanese tea, they exchanged ideas about music. In Singapore, the dalang said, he had studied Western classics with an English cellist who had retired out there and had brought along a large record collection. The dalang's favorite composers? Mozart, Debussy.

"Bix liked Debussy."

"Where did you study music?" the dalang asked.

"In my town the local music store was where you studied. You could study drums because the clerk played them. The owner's wife taught piano. The owner could give you horn lessons. I took trumpet, because it was the glory of early jazz. I wanted to know the technical side."

"You did not study to play?"

"I never had creative ambitions. My pleasure comes from the things others do. But someone like you can't understand that."

"No. I must do it myself."

"I suppose for you it's a need."

"It is."

"Art for you is not self-effacing."

"I'm sorry, I don't understand."

"Can I be frank? You're not modest. You don't live for other people. You want more than anything to express yourself."

The dalang, teacup halfway to his lips, put it down, as if this gesture would convey surprise. Even before he spoke, Maggie realized that in his mind she had just stated the obvious. "Of course I want that," Dalang Budi said. "I am not modest at all."

"But you tell me gamelan musicians are. They don't want to stand out."

"No, they do not."

"So their pleasure comes from losing themselves in the group."

"And from mastering all the instruments. That way they can go from playing a saron to a barong to a ketuk. If a musician doesn't change instruments, even playing those he doesn't like to play, he is considered impolite or even worse—selfish. You are a beautiful woman," he said. "Self-expression is maybe a third or fourth thing, not too important for gamelan. So in Western sense gamelan is not very creative."

Maggie stared hard at him before replying. "No, I suppose gamelan is not creative in a Western sense. But you are."

"Yes," he said matter-of-factly, "I am."

"And you don't try to hide it. You're not interested in communal spirit."

"No. I am a dalang."

It was only after she had watched him cross the sun-drenched courtyard, the hilt of his kris flashing at the small of his back, that Maggie let herself think of what he had inserted, almost surreptitiously, into their conversation. "You are a beautiful woman"—said without a change of intonation, as if it were one more technical comment about music.

She had better not see him anymore.

That was what Maggie had thought yesterday, when his flattering words haunted her long after he left, the phrase coming into her conscious mind as it had come into their conversation—without warning. But tonight, walking home from her visit with Mas Slamat, she decided that such caution was unnecessary. After all, they had talked for hours without saying anything especially personal, much less intimate. Formality had been marred only by his sudden "You are a beautiful woman," which he had delivered so swiftly, so casually, that it surfaced into memory like a phrase half remembered from a dream. And though the words continued to resonate through her consciousness with the staying power of a struck gong, there was nothing to fear. She was her own boss. That's what her father had always admonished her to be, while shoving his face close to hers, his bloodshot eyes bulging, his breath smelling of whiskey. "Girl," he said with the harsh intensity of a drunk, "you damn well *better* be your own boss."

And she was. She had accepted the dalang's invitation to attend a wayang performance tomorrow evening, and that's exactly what she would do.

Twenty-nine

She received a letter from Vern. It began with endearments, somewhat stiffly expressed and banal, but that was fine with Maggie; her husband wasn't the sort of lover who talked of feelings instead of having them.

"We are now making progress on the project," he wrote, "because the guy who runs the show, a Chinese financier, is back in town. I'll be making a trip to Bali soon. I could pick you up or meet you there. Maybe you'll find Bali more interesting than Java (I'm sorry for bullying you about the language thing—learn a dozen of them, sweetheart, if you want to). At any rate, Bali is in the cards.

"Jakarta is hot as blazes. Bakes the spit in your mouth. And every day there are incidents—demonstrations either by the PKI or the Muslims and spontaneous riots and minor violence caused by gangs of unemployed kids who need something to do. Posters everywhere. Slapped on next to each other, one says Islam is terrific and the other says communism is terrific. It's like a good old American campaign for the presidency. The army is out in force, marching up and down, carrying rifles at the ready, looking forward to trouble on Armed

Forces Day. As Larry says, it gets you a bit nervy. I'm glad you're out of here, sweetheart. I asked you to come back only because I wanted you with me so much. All right, I was selfish. But I do feel the crisis is going to blow over and Jakarta will soon be safe again— or at least relatively safe. When push comes to shove, these people will back down. Sweetheart, after the hotel is built, you and I should have a honeymoon. Ever since our week together at Lake Toba, I've been hard at work on something or other. That's no way to run a marriage! We need time together. You made sense when you said we ought to go back to Samosir. Sometimes I feel we don't quite know each other, I mean, in the sense of the day-to-day kind of relationship I remember my parents having. I don't know how to write about it, so I'll say what I have to say when we're together again. Well, that's about it. I'll let you know when plans firm up. Love you, sweetheart. I miss you, beautiful, I miss you a lot, and that's the truth. Vern."

He'll say what he has to say when we're together again. Maggie wondered what that could be. The day-to-day relationship of his parents was something he would have to explain, because surely the day-to-day relationship of her own parents had been nothing to shout about.

After getting his letter, Maggie had written him one of her own in which she never mentioned Samosir or Bali or the Javanese language. She had sworn to put a lot of love into the letter, but once again it came out chatty: food, sight-seeing in Yogya, intrigues among the servants, a letter from Susanto Sakirman, who had found gambling companions in Malang.

If Vern's endearments sounded banal, it wasn't because he didn't mean them. His feelings reached beyond the words that carried them. But to Maggie's dismay her own letters not only sounded banal, they signaled up a banal attitude, the result of haste and just plain superficiality, and she damn well knew it, as the words leapt from the surface of her mind like minnows from a languid pond. Her fast little letters came from a lassitude of feeling, as if weariness and duty combined to get them done with a small expenditure of energy. Maggie wasn't proud of them, in fact she was ashamed of them, and she blamed her coldness on what was happening these days in Java.

A sense of crisis was engulfing the land. People hung back, postponed and suspended their lives while potential events gathered somewhere in the distance. It was like waiting for a storm to rumble through and restore noise in a world that had suddenly become hushed. Yet the Javanese would not cancel a wayang kulit performance, such as tonight's, even if the entire country stood on the verge of what Mas Slamat, quoting the holy man, called "a terrible disaster." All day long the servants had been discussing the wayang play scheduled for this evening. Their intensity—it resembled religious fervor—reminded Maggie of a college campus on the day of a big game.

That evening the dalang picked her up in a horse-drawn dokar. Again the Sakirman servants clustered at windows and peeked around corners to see their tall guest escorted toward the waiting carriage, their eyes shifting from her to the great man in his dalang's sarong, blouse, and headdress.

Recently she had learned from Inam a few more things about the Gitosuwoko family. The dalang's older brother had been the greatest performer of his time. Some years ago he was giving a wayang play in Sasono Hinggil, the great hall south of the kraton. They had put up loudspeakers to carry his voice to hundreds of people who couldn't get inside the building. Precisely at the moment that the hero died, Central Java was rocked by an earthquake. People inside Sasono Hinggil started to panic, but the dalang never faltered, never lost concentration, and so the audience calmed down enough to watch the rest of his performance, though the lamp over his head swayed back and forth and the cloth of the screen rippled wildly. Later there were people who accused him of bringing on the earthquake to make the hero's death more dramatic.

Maggie was incredulous. "They thought he could cause an earthquake?"

"But he could," Inam declared. "A great dalang has the knowledge of shadows. There are maybe three great dalangs alive today. Ki-Dalang Gitosuwoko is one of them." Inam was speaking Bahasa Indonesia, but shifted into Krama Javanese when she spoke directly of Ki-Dalang Gitosuwoko.

And now Maggie sat next to Ki-Dalang Gitosuwoko. He was, as usual, quiet, if not remote. But he was never really remote; his presence was too vivid for that. Words could hardly have made him more palpably there. But Maggie wondered if she was merely succumbing to the Javanese mystique that equated puppeteers and sorcerers. She felt defensive, ready to resist the pull of superstition, as they drove along in the dokar. And she felt shy after their last meeting. The phrase continued to ambush Maggie: "You are a beautiful woman," his declaration leaping out of a forest of words like a small but dangerous beast. They rode in silence.

The dokar swayed into the square on one side of which stood the Sasono Hinggil. Dozens of becaks were parked near the Dutch-columned entrance. Coconut-cake hawkers were going through the crowd. When people saw Ki-Dalang Gitosuwoko get out of a dokar, they backed off instinctively and made a path for him into the hall. That they concentrated on him and not on a tall female foreigner, Maggie knew, was a measure of his charisma. She was accustomed to curious stares, yet with him she was nothing more than a shadow. She felt a strange elation, as if electrical current passed from him through her to him again, engulfing them in shared energy.

Entering the great hall, she saw past the rows of auditorium seats a red-bordered screen set on the wide base of two huge bamboo logs. On either side of the screen, thrust into the bamboo by their horn sticks, were two rows of puppets, a fantastic army of nearly a hundred: some with wings, some with long, weasellike noses, with spidery arms and ornate headdresses, some with bulbous heads and monstrous expressions—all of these attenuated figures facing the blank white screen. At least a score of gamelan musicians were already seated behind the dalang's cushion, smoking and chatting among their bronze instruments.

Dalang Budi took her to the front row, near the bonang kettle gongs. A bonang player who was puffing on a cigarette saw the dalang and made a deep sembah.

Two men in traditional sarongs came up and spoke to the dalang in Javanese. Maggie could make out some of the Krama they were using. Whole phrases came from her lessons with the guru. For example, Dalang Budi responded elegantly to an inquiry about his health: *"Wilujeng, pangestunipun"* ("I am well, thanks to your good wishes"). And one of the men apologized humbly for any errors he might make during their conversation, using a highly stylized phrase learned by Maggie that very day, because the language guru said it was often employed at wayang performances (he loftily refused to explain why): *Kula nyuwun samudra gunging pangapunten*. The word "samudra" was a literary word for "ocean," but damn it, she had forgotten the exact translation.

After the two men left—Maggie guessed from their effusive manner they were local officials—the dalang turned to face her, his shoulders squared. Such an alert bearing probably came from meditation, she thought—he looked as sturdy as a tree trunk. So for a time he was going to give her his full attention. It was like being handed a little gift, and Maggie didn't like that. Yet the next moment she felt ashamed of her pettiness. Her emotions seemed to be careening around as if shaken in a centrifuge.

While the orchestra was tuning up, he explained certain symbols (Maggie didn't tell him she already knew their meanings): the screen was heaven, the logs supporting it were earth, and of course the puppets were men. And the dalang was god. He said the last casually, without emphasis. Not from modesty, Maggie decided—from the indifference felt by someone certain of the truth.

He explained the plot for tonight's lakon—something about the Great War between two warrior clans, the Pandavas and the Kauravas. The Pandavas were essentially good, the Kauravas bad, but often their virtues and vices merged, and what the puppets ultimately enacted was conflict within the human heart.

She listened, and although Maggie concentrated, she understood that part of her mind was taking in something other than his words. They were communicating only a portion of what he meant. It was as if he were holding two conversations with her at once: one through words and the other through a kind of presence inaccessible to words, something akin to her old fantasy: the voice speaking from behind a door, urging her to listen listen listen. He was not hypnotizing her, though at times she wondered if he might be doing just that, because sometimes when he looked at her, Maggie felt confused, in a sense frightened, like someone searching for a place to hide.

By then the auditorium had begun filling up. Hundreds were already seated, dozens more squatted on the wide windowsills, when the evening's dalang made his entrance. Bronze percussion in the gamelan orchestra began striking the lingering notes of a prelude. There was polite, subdued clapping as a short, stocky man made his way to the dalang's cushion. An ornately hilted kris was shoved in his belt at the back. Above his head a lamp was burning coconut oil, the six-inch wick sending up a flickering light against the screen.

He sat a few moments with head bent forward as if in prayer, then checked the large wooden box to his left where puppets were piled in sequential order for use in tonight's performance.

He rapped sharply five times with a large wooden tapper against the puppet chest, and the tempo and melody of the introductory music changed instantly.

Dalang Budi leaned toward her to whisper. She felt his closeness; it was like a touch. "Gamelan now plays 'Ajak-ajakan Nem,' the first song. Dalang is now saying, 'The hills and mountains are where I live, so I take the strength of their storms for my own.' "

The seated dalang reached above his head to the bronze lamp and adjusted its flaming wick. Then carefully pulling the Tree of Life out of the bamboo trunk, he held it across his lap. With his left hand, he bent the kayon's leather tip and spoke another prayer, this time silently.

Dalang Budi, again leaning toward her, translated the silent prayer. " 'Let my body be as large and strong as a mountain. Let the people here show pity and love in the presence of the God of Light.' "

Then placing the kayon against the screen's upper-right corner, the puppeteer twirled it three times and thrust its buffalo-horn stick into the bamboo at the screen's lower-right edge.

The play began.

Three hours later the first of three acts had ended. Those initial hours featured elaborate scenes at court, youth's time of instruction in the arts of refinement. The second act, which she was watching now, would last another three hours; it represented adulthood, a search for identity and values, and as such incorporated some major battles. The final act, which would conclude at dawn, brought in the wisdom of old age, when good finally triumphed over evil, and the nine-hour play ended with a dance of victory.

There was no real intermission, but an interlude of gamelan at the end of *Patet Nem,* the first part.

Dalang Budi said abruptly, "You don't like it."

This was in fact true. For Maggie the wayang play represented an aristocratic world of lofty sentiments but vicious intrigue, grand speeches but tumultuous warfare, and greed and lust, a world in which men acted like gods, gods like clowns. Even a leap of the imagination left her at a considerable distance from such a world. Should she tell him? Between men and women there was always a choice between heartless honesty and timid deceit. But the choice applied only when love was at issue. She had no reason to be anything but quietly frank. She would tell Dalang Budi she did not like the play. But instead she heard herself say, "Perhaps if I saw a different performance—" and hated the compromise it implied.

His uncompromising answer came back instantly. "The performance is not great. But I do not think it is why you dislike wayang. What you have been seeing, though not great, is good enough if you like wayang. You don't like wayang because it is a world you don't like. It will take time to like it, if you ever do."

In the middle of *Patet Sanga,* the second part, he took her to the other side of the screen, where only shadows of the puppets were visible. Just as the reality of performance had controlled the view from the dalang's side, so here illusion took charge: what had been gold, red, and green puppets now became black images highlighted by tiny holes. Nothing seemed anchored. Shapes melted into one another, broke apart, and somehow created new spaces of their own in which objects occupied the same space at the same time. The distance of puppets to the screen was always changing, so that their silhouettes went from sharp to indistinct to sharp again, giving them the odd quality of coming into existence and fading out of it and returning again at the command of divine but perverse whimsy. What happened on this side of the screen might have been a deliberate illustration of the theory that we live in a chaotic universe. The images floated through a vaporous landscape, filling Maggie's mind with a strange new appreciation of them. This was a world of savage beauty and cosmic mystery as well as human greed and lust; what happened here was governed by different laws of time and space, offering a wayward morality and possibilities that multiplied through a logic of their own making.

"Which side do you like better?" Dalang Budi asked, when they had returned to their seats in the auditorium.

"The shadow side."

He nodded. "It is not as popular. But it is the side I like too. You have a feeling for the hidden."

She regarded him closely. Was that meant as a compliment? Probably. A more subtle approach than "You are a beautiful woman." It was better not to ask him what he meant.

And so Maggie sat back to enjoy the rest of the performance. By two o'clock in the morning, not one seat in the auditorium was empty. People crouched on windowsills, leaned against walls, crowded into doorways. The later the hour the more intense became the audience. Smoke from kretek cigarettes lent to the nighttime air a pungency of cloves. The Flower Battle scene had just been completed. Arjuna, the dashing Pandava hero, had just dispatched three ogres.

And Maggie was feeling sick. It came over her in a rush: headache, nausea. A fever?

Maggie didn't want to ruin this remarkable evening, but she felt rotten. Today on the street she had eaten a bowlful of bakmee, a concoction of noodles and vegetables. So she must have a touch of food poisoning. Or could it be a recurrence of the bad thing? No. Not malaria. It was food poisoning.

At last, unable to cope any longer, she turned to the dalang. "I'm not feeling well. I have to go home. I'm so sorry, but I can't stay."

Reaching out, he touched her hand with his. His touch of concern lasted a moment yet she knew she would carry the feeling of it with her from the auditorium and into the night.

He did not offer to take her home. For him to leave now would insult the dalang giving the performance.

"It cannot be done," Dalang Budi said. "But I will arrange for you—"

"No," Maggie told him sharply. Then in a softer voice she said, "No thank you. You stay here. I'm well enough to get home by myself."

In another man she would have found his attitude disrespectful. *Disrespectful.* During her high-school and college days if a date had failed to take her home, right to her *door,* for whatever reason, Maggie would have refused to see him again. She had always demanded respect, had never hidden her desperate need for it from herself or from other people, who used to laugh and say, "Maggie, you live by an old-fashioned code of honor." And she would laugh back, while imagining a scene where she could deliver this unsaid speech: "I have a drunk for a father, a drudge for a mother, my sister sleeps around, and I haven't got one cent in the bank, but you had better treat me right, fella, you had better give me some respect, or you will never see me again." She hadn't wanted gallantry, just a show of the consideration given to girls from "good families." Nevertheless, from this Javanese aristocrat she wanted nothing, not even a hint of the civility she had always demanded. It was not necessary for him to get out of his seat and take her outside to the waiting becaks. A man manipulating puppets and singing and cueing an orchestra expected him to be sitting there in the first row until dawn, and he must do exactly that, even if Central Java had another earthquake or if she dropped stone-cold dead at his feet. Dalang Budi was abiding by a code of honor and she was determined to acknowledge her respect for it.

"You must stay here," she said again. "I understand." So with a crisp good-bye she got to her feet and wove up the aisle, feeling giddy but pleased with herself.

Outside, hailing a becak, Maggie took the first of a whole armada that rushed toward her. She slumped into the seat and gave her address. There was a full moon overhead. The ragged little man pumped the bike slowly, moving away from the great hall. His sinewy calves gleamed in moonlight as his becak crossed the alun-alun and reached the shadows of narrow lanes.

He spoke Bahasa, so she could understand everything he said while pedaling along. He knew a lot about wayang. He brought to a judgment of tonight's play the precise enthusiasm of a connoisseur. "This play," he said, "is best seen when Bapak"—he was using the politest form of address—"Ki-Dalang Gitosuwoko does it. He does it even better than his brother did. You must see him."

"I would like to." By talking to the becak driver Maggie hoped to get her mind off how she felt. If she thought about it, she might vomit.

"But he does not do wayang often anymore. When the sultan is in Yogya, then Bapak Ki-Dalang Gitosuwoko performs. If you see him, you will know the difference from what you saw tonight."

A wave of nausea rippled through her. She bent forward. "Tell me," she said, folding both arms across her stomach, "why is he so good?"

285

"Because he is master of magic and close to the gods."

"Does he practice magic?"

"All of the good dalangs do," the becak driver claimed.

Maggie took deep breaths, hoping she'd get home before vomiting. Then they were in front of the Sakirman residence. She asked the driver to go get someone, and while he went up the front walk, Maggie gritted her teeth and hung on.

Inam came and helped her out of the becak. Maggie clung to the supporting arm, whispering, "I'm all right. It's food poisoning. The bakmee—" But she felt sicker. Putting one hand to her forehead, Maggie tried to calculate the fever. At least 101 or 102.

Then they were inside and Inam was undressing her. No, Maggie thought, it couldn't be the bad thing again. Not malaria. It was food poisoning. She drank thirstily when Inam brought water.

"I will stay outside the room, Nonya."

"I'll be fine. Go back to sleep."

"I will stay outside the room, Nonya. Right outside."

Maggie reached for the girl's hand, gripped it hard. "A feeling for what's hidden. What does that mean?"

"Nonya? You just please rest now."

Hardly had Inam left the room than Maggie fell into a fitful sleep. Images flashed during sudden waking moments. She couldn't get into a comfortable position. Her forehead and cheeks burned, her eyes on fire under the lids. Then she plummeted into profound sleep from which objects in a dream began to emerge slowly, dimly, as if from the sea. Gray water at dusk. It was not the sea, but a mountain-ringed lake. She was watching a fisherman who stood waist-deep in Lake Toba. Shoving his dugout lengthwise, rather than side to side, he emptied it of water and climbed in. Sliding on a half-moon of silver at dusk. She was on the shore watching as he hunkered in the boat, knees to chest, feathering the paddle with short rhythmic strokes. And then, while standing on Samosir Island, she was somehow able to view him up close, so close she could see downy hair on his slow, tireless hands. He turned them politely for her to see. They appeared huge, then small again, as he returned to the lake. With two fingers he moved the paddle in a circular motion. Rag around the neck, dirty cap on his head, his legs cinched up torturously, with a single stroke the fisherman made his dugout glide over the lake as on ice, until

286

Maggie realized that he was not a fisherman at all but a wayang puppet and the boat was made of leather too and they were moving across a white screen toward her, where she stood on the shore of Samosir.

And then hands were swimming past her eyes like fish, hands holding paddles, hard long poles that menaced her, poking at her groin until she protected it with both hands, and then Maggie was sitting upright in bed, arms hugging her breasts. She was shaking violently. Opening her mouth to call Inam, she couldn't get a sound past her chattering teeth. Lying down and doubling up, Maggie breathed spasmodically into the pillow, seeking warmth from it. He had touched her with one of those magic hands tonight. He said she had a feeling for what was hidden. What was hidden was her feeling was what he meant. She didn't trust him. She must not trust him. She would keep away from the man. She would leave for Jakarta in the morning. The pillow was soaked with sweat and felt icy. Her body began to flutter and whip around, and it felt as if her bones were loosening one from another like a tangle of strings coming apart—a familiar, terrifying sensation. At last she got a word out: "Inam." And again: "Inam!"

The bad thing had come back.

Patet Sanga

Midnight to Three A.M.

Thirty

Infantry sergeant Achmad Bachtiar was aroused from a nightmare shortly before midnight on 30 September 1965.

A soldier poked his head into the tent at the Halim Air Base outside of Jakarta and yelled, "Alert! Alert! Combat ready! Aerial Survey! Fifteen minutes! Aerial Survey! Fifteen minutes!"

Achmad and two other noncoms shared the tent. Standing at the open flap, they rubbed their eyes and stared at people running through moonlight. A lieutenant came along.

"What unit, sergeants?"

"First Honorary Guard, sir. Diponegoro 454th," Achmad told him.

"Aerial Survey. On the double."

Ten minutes later, armed and dressed in battle fatigues, Achmad and his companions joined about thirty other noncoms and officers in Aerial Survey's auditorium.

Lieutenant Colonel Untung stood at a podium, gripping it, looking grave. He wore three rows of combat ribbons, a pair of thick glasses.

"We have a mission tonight," he said and waited for everyone to get seated.

A mission. Tonight. Led by Colonel Untung.

This surprising announcement excited Achmad, whose battalion had served under Colonel Untung in the West Irian campaign. Achmad had parachuted with him into the jungle on a commando raid. Around his neck Achmad wore a charm that Colonel Untung had presented to him. A famous dukun had blessed a number of these charms to commemorate the raid, and his blessing made them magical. Along with others so honored, Achmad believed the wearer of such a charm was invulnerable to bullets.

He recalled that earlier mission now: the plane door sliding back and their leap into the void, hearing their chutes boom, ripple, balloon out into white bowls above their heads while hot air funneled up from the New Guinean earth at the dropping men, a blast of wind spiraling out of a furnace of jungle, hitting their chins before hitting their cheeks. Far below had been a vast green sheet of rain forest that rapidly became a misshapen network of voluted and ragged trees, ferns, leaves, a ghostly haven of shadows approaching faster and faster until it consumed the paratroopers. He remembered vividly the Papuan guides with their hair dyed orange, their potbellies and penis sheaths, their knobby fingers clutching bunches of tiny poisoned arrows as they led the way on trails visible only to them through a graveyard of rotting vegetation into a spiderweb silkiness of jungle that left Achmad both exalted and terrified.

Images of that mission flashed through his mind while he listened to his old commander, Colonel Untung, explain the need for a new and even more dangerous mission.

Gripping the podium, his knuckles white from tension, the colonel accused the American CIA of bringing on the immediate crisis. They wanted to overthrow Bung Karno, because, along with other Western colonialists, they felt that by destroying the Great Revolution they could regain control of Indonesia. These lackeys from the West had managed recently to conspire with the worst of traitors—with high-ranking army officers who had taken the easy road, the path of dishonor; who were rich, corrupt, addicted to European vices; who had forgotten the principles of revolution; who had learned to think wrong; who believed only in self-aggrandizement; who threatened the existence of the state, of the Beloved Leader himself; who were traitors, a council of traitors, a council of traitorous generals.

292

Colonel Untung's voice rose to a crescendo.

Achmad's blood was racing, heat was in his cheeks. The nation embattled. Traitors in their midst.

Then the colonel read a roll call of them:

Lieutenant General A. Yani, Army Chief of Staff

Major General Suprapto, Second Deputy Chief of Staff

Major General M. Harjono, Third Deputy Chief of Staff

Major General S. Parman, Chief of Intelligence

Brigadier General D. Pandjaitan, Chief of Logistics

Brigadier General Sutojo, Inspector of Justice

General A. Nasution, Defense Minister

Achmad was stunned: the army chief of staff and the defense minister—news of their treachery was like a house buckling, its timbers crashing down. It could mean the end of Indonesia as a country. Traitors. In control of national security.

The colonel went on. A revolutionary council, composed of loyal members of the armed forces and other patriots, had been created to deal with this emergency. Its object: to prevent the generals from attempting a coup. "Our mission," continued the colonel, "has been named by the council: GETAPS, the Thirtieth of September Movement."

Achmad nervously absorbed the following instructions: GETAPS units would depart for Jakarta at 0130 in seven squads. Each squad was to arrest a general at his home and return him to the air base. A sergeant passed out combat orders to the squad commanders. There were tactical parameters to observe, but they allowed for more individual judgment than Achmad had known in previous operations. Each commander rose and read off the composition of his force. Achmad heard his name, his assigned duty: to enter the house and arrest General Yani, whose code name was Jonson. That was all. No precise instructions for conducting the raid, no extended orders.

A young lieutenant from the 530th asked if there were restrictions on the use of force.

Untung stared at him a long time before replying. "None," the colonel said. "No restrictions. Think of what we do tonight as a wayang performance, a lakon," Untung said, still gripping the podium. "This lakon is called *Getaps*. We need the courage of Bima, the daring of Gatutkaca, the wisdom of Kresna. Play your parts skillfully.

There is no rehearsal for *Getaps*. I have seen Ki-Dalang Gitosuwoko perform *The Birth of Kala* to cleanse and purify a village. Before morning comes, as dalang of *Getaps* I swear to equal him." Untung warned that arresting the generals could prove difficult. "We don't know the extent of their home defenses. So be masters of action, like Arjuna." Whipping off his glasses, Colonel Untung cried out, "The fate of our country is in our hands!"

As they filed out of the auditorium, Achmad Bachtiar wondered if his life had ever possessed as much meaning as it did now. The colonel's reference to wayang had burned into his heart like a brand of fire. He saw himself as a black sinewy figure against a white screen, a Pandava warrior caught up in the turmoil of a battle that would end with a dance of victory.

———

At the entrance of the Aerial Survey Building three men were standing in the shadowed light of a Quonset hut. Achmad recognized two of them: the tall uniformed man was Air Marshal Dhani; the skinny little civilian was the trader in foreign goods whom he had met at his sister's house.

Someone near Achmad was saying, "That's Aidit over there."

The third man: round face, bulging eyes. Chairman of the Communist party.

What, Achmad wondered, was Kamarusaman bin Ahmed Mubaidah doing with such men? Standing next to the air marshal? That made him somehow important. And with the head man of PKI? For a paralyzing moment Achmad entertained the idea that his sister had joined the PKI and was working with her lover for Aidit. Without realizing it, he had slowed down and his eyes met those of Kamarusaman. The little man stepped forward, smiling. Achmad froze. The other commandos had rushed on, so that when the two met, no one else was there, the air marshal and the Communist chairman having gone too.

"There you are!" Sjam did a quick sembah and thrust out his hand.

Achmad fingered the butt of his holstered pistol, as if avoiding the proffered hand.

Sjam shrugged. He would not acknowledge the insult.

"So you are in GETAPS," he said airily. "You will make history." Getting no response, he added, "Don't let any of them escape."

"Why? Do you think a few generals can ruin our country?"

Sjam pursed his lips as if considering that possibility. "After this is over," he said, "come see me. I can help you."

"Are you a Red?"

Sjam grinned. "A patriot."

"Are you good to my sister?"

Sjam stared at the pistol butt that Achmad's hand still covered.

"If you hurt my sister, I will kill you."

"Why would I hurt your sister? Don't worry about that," Sjam told him. "When this is over, come see me and we'll talk about the future. A lot of army people do very well. I can help you as I've helped them."

"That's the reason for tonight's raid. To end the sort of corruption you're talking about."

"Granted there's corruption. Everyone knows it," Sjam admitted with a broad smile. "But what you'd do for me has nothing to do with corruption. It's all a matter of information. That's the modern world." He reached out to pat Achmad's shoulder reassuringly, then pulled back his hand. "You'll see. I'll explain it."

Achmad let his hand fall away from the pistol butt. Energy had drained from his fingers, though they still trembled. Achmad turned to walk away, then turned back. "Never," he told Sjam evenly, "hurt my sister."

He broke into a trot, heading for the airstrip where, clustered on the tarmac, the GETAPS squads would go over their combat instructions before climbing into the waiting lorries.

Achmad's squad of thirty was bound for a fashionable outer district of Jakarta, where the army chief of staff lived. As his lorry rumbled through the warm night, Achmad listened to some of his men chattering the way troops do before an operation. They were still complaining that their rations had been cut by Supply and Logistics; after all, free rice and sugar had been an inducement to join the army. But here they were, past midnight, speeding through the streets of Jakarta on a dangerous mission, and without free rice.

Men chattering, grumbling. Achmad was accustomed to it. He could have stopped them, but let them go on. Spurts of self-righteous anger gave them confidence before action.

A soldier kneeling against the lorry slats was saying breathlessly, "He better not give us trouble."

Someone asked, "Who?"

"Didn't you hear the lieutenant? We're arresting the chief of staff."

"Praise Allah."

"It's nothing to fear. It's our duty."

Someone else said, "No one will give *me* trouble."

"You don't call him the chief of staff. You call him by the code name, Jonson."

"If it's the chief of staff, it's the chief of staff."

"Jonson. That's an English word."

"All right, Jonson."

"Sutojo is Toyota, the Japanese car."

"I forgot the password."

"*Ampera.*"

"And after we say the 'People's Burden,' what is the reply?"

"*Takari.* I hope you haven't forgotten Bung Karno's speech: 'A Year of Self-reliance.'"

"So it's *Ampera* and *Takari.*"

"You're not going to forget again, are you?"

"No, but I forgot the squad's code name."

"*Pasopati.* We are *Pasopati.*"

"I thought we were *Bimasaki.*"

"That's the 454th at Merdeka Square. Don't you listen?"

"Of course I listen."

Soldiers listened, Achmad thought, but nerves made them forget.

"How can we arrest the chief of staff?" someone said. "Isn't that treason?"

"Quiet," Achmad told his men sternly. He stood forward in the lorry, his hands spread on top of the hot cab. Headlights shone on high gates and the steel fences of grand estates whose facades were too far beyond the rolling lawns to be seen.

Now the lead lorry, just in front of his own, was slowing down. It stopped in front of a locked gate with a sweeping brick fence on both sides.

Achmad, assuming command, sent half a dozen men out to cut telephone lines. The gate padlock was surprisingly flimsy. A big wire cutter chewed through it in seconds. Then men were fanning out across the dark lawn, heading in zigzag patterns toward two dim lights shining at opposite ends of a rambling villa. While troops ringed the entire house—their assault rifles trained on windows—Achmad and another sergeant, leading a dozen men, rushed to the front door.

It wasn't locked.

That irritated Achmad. You could walk right into this mansion. The arrogance of it, he thought.

Achmad pulled back the bolt on his Kalashnikov. Stepping out of moonlight into the cooler interior of the dark house, he heard floorboards creak under his paratroop boots, under the boots of his entering men.

A slit of light appeared ahead. Then a wide yellow shaft of it spread across the foyer as a door opened fully, revealing a small figure.

"Who is there?" asked a childish voice.

Achmad waved for his men to spread out. "Soldiers," he said.

"Ah, you want my father?" The boy in shorts walked forward, one hand tentatively at his mouth, as if the comfort of sucking his thumb might become necessary.

Achmad figured he was six or seven. This was an unpleasant surprise. "Yes," he said. "We want to see your father. President Sukarno wants to see him now, so we've come for him."

"What?" The boy slipped the thumb into his mouth.

Stepping cautiously toward him, Achmad said, "We're the escort." Close to the boy, he bent down. "Where is your father?"

The boy pointed toward a door on the left, but as he did so, the door swung open and a light went on, dim but bright enough to illuminate the foyer. A man in white pajamas was standing in the doorway's rectangle of yellow. Achmad recognized him from news photos. Despite his rumpled hair and sleep-bloated face, the man was clearly General Yani, army chief of staff.

"General, we have come for you," Achmad said, appalled by the tremor in his voice.

"Come for me?" Yani lunged forward, flailing his arms angrily. "How dare you enter my house at this hour!"

Another sergeant leapt in front of Achmad and bobbed his head deferentially; he would have sembahed had he not been holding a Kalashnikov. "Sir, General, we've come to take you to the palace."

Yani narrowed his eyes; his paunch stood out pale and rounded from his partially buttoned pajamas. "To the palace? Why to the palace?"

"The president wants to see you," the sergeant said. "We're sorry about the late hour," he added.

The general shook his head. "I don't like this. Coming armed into my house. Why didn't you phone? What's wrong here?"

"Emergency," put in Achmad. His voice sounded stronger to him now. "There wasn't time."

"Well," Yani paused, looking from one sergeant to the other, "I'll take a bath and be with you."

As the general turned away, Achmad stepped forward and grabbed his arm. "No. There isn't time, sir. Come now."

"Insolent—" Yani broke free, giving Achmad a stinging blow across the face with the back of his hand. It nearly sent Achmad reeling.

Grunting with satisfaction, Yani started back to his glass-doored bedroom. "I'll bathe and come when I'm ready."

"You must come now!" Achmad shouted at the swaggering general who had reached the glass door. "Sir! General! Come now!" Achmad's cheek seemed to be on fire; his breath came heavily, as if he'd been running. Achmad felt as though his chute had just opened with a sudden jerk of tension, a rush of air, and the jungle below him was looming up like a huge mouth. "General!" he heard himself yell in a fury.

Yani opened the door and entered his bedroom without a backward glance.

Achmad had crossed the foyer. A few feet from the milky glass, he saw General Yani receding behind it like something wavy beneath water. Holding the forehand grip of his Kalashnikov tightly with one hand and the box magazine with the other, Achmad squeezed off five or six 7.62-mm rounds. Glass tumbled like an avalanche on a frozen mountain; when it had stopped crashing down, he saw through the shattered door the fallen body of General Yani, his riddled pajama back soaked in blood, his legs askew, twitching.

Achmad turned the doorknob, and just as he was entering the bedroom, something hurtled past him toward the man lying near the bed.

It was a boy. Older than the other one, screaming.

In dismay Achmad rushed over, reached down, and yanked at the boy's arm. "Don't do that," Achmad told him, as if admonishing a village kid for some prank.

298

But the boy pulled free and turned the general's face upward. Yani's eyes blinked drowsily. His lips were moving.

"Get up," Achmad told the boy, who burrowed his face against his father's neck. Achmad slung the Kalashnikov across his back, feeling tubular warmth along his right shoulder blade. If it weren't for the boy, he'd feel good, because what he had done had been right.

Other raiders had come into the room.

The other sergeant smiled and patted Achmad's arm.

Two raiders started to pry the boy loose from his father, who was breathing in a slow, labored way. As if in troubled meditation, thought Achmad. As if in prayer.

But Yani wasn't praying, he was trying to call out. When finally he murmured "Udik," the boy screamed again, kicking to get free.

Other raiders took hold of Yani, getting purchase under his armpits. "Udik, Udik," the wounded man called weakly. The boy, breaking loose, gripped the general's left thigh when they started to drag him away, his bare heels skidding across the floor.

Achmad got Udik by both shoulders and pulled hard. The child possessed a strength of desperation that shocked Achmad, who yanked furiously and at last detached son from father. He held Udik off the floor, kicking and screaming, until the general had been hauled through the foyer and out of the house, leaving a trail of blood behind.

Then Achmad released the boy, who bolted through the foyer into back rooms, leaving his own sort of trail, a loud spiraling agony of sound.

Slowly Achmad followed the other raiders back to their lorries.

Thirty-one

Achmad was standing forward in the lorry, hands on the warm cab again, as night air rushed past his face.

Someone whistled in awe. "I think he's dead." Then: "Yes, he is. Jonson is dead."

By intervals of light slanting in from passing streets, Achmad saw a couple of men bending over General Yani, who lay between the seated rows of raiders.

"Sergeant," one of them called out. "He's dead. Jonson's dead."

Achmad said nothing.

The soldiers went on talking. "He deserved what he got," someone said.

"What did he do?"

"Enough to get what he got."

"Were we supposed to arrest him?"

"I don't know. I wasn't there. I was outside on the lawn."

"I know. I was there."

"So what happened?"

There was silence, a silence that Achmad knew would be broken as soon as he was out of earshot. Then they'd discuss how he had been insulted, slapped, and how, when the general disobeyed the order to come along, Sergeant Bachtiar, to defend his honor, had shot him in the back through a glass door.

None of the men seated here had been on the New Guinea jump. They had never experienced the terror and exaltation of combat, so now in the lorry they tried to bolster their courage by chattering like monkeys. Most of them had no idea of what soldiering really was.

But in other lorries there were veterans who knew. A few of them had already let him know he had done his duty. They had given him a pat on the arm, a smile of comradeship, whereas these silly boys, hardly more than recruits, eyed him warily, judgmentally.

When the lorries reached Halim, they were routed through the base to an unused area on the swampy perimeter called Lubang Buaya, Crocodile Hole, where there was an old well and a dilapidated hut with an atap roof.

Arriving there, the lorries were parked in a little clearing. This was the first squad back from the mission. Out of the hut emerged a young lieutenant who was in charge of securing the arrested generals. Lieutenant Dul Arief, tall and morose-looking, stuck a thumb inside his gun belt as if to steady himself. While Achmad's lorry began unloading, the lieutenant paced up and down anxiously. Seeing a couple of men pull a body out of the rear, Dul Arief rushed forward with a cry. "What's this? What? General Yani?" He stared openmouthed at the corpse. "What happened? What happened?"

Stepping up, Achmad saluted the lieutenant. "Sergeant Achmad Bachtiar, sir. The general resisted arrest, sir."

"Who shot him?"

"I did, sir."

"In the back?"

"I told him to come along. I warned him, but he kept walking." Achmad added in a burst of anger, "He slapped me in the face."

The lieutenant studied him in the glare of lorry headlights. "You weren't told to kill him."

"We were told to bring him back."

"Not like this."

"We were told no restrictions on the use of force, sir."

"Yes. Well—yes." Shaking his head, the lieutenant walked away.

At this moment other lorries appeared on the wooded path leading to the hut. Men of this second squad were soon telling their own story. They had cornered General Harjono in his bedroom. When he refused to come out, they had shot the door down and captured him. While taking him through the garden, he got free and ran, so they shot him for fear he'd escape.

Achmad looked down at Harjono's body. It wore pajama bottoms. It was terribly mangled; Harjono had been opened wide below his left nipple to his right hipbone, so that a large rippling coil of intestine lay exposed.

As if answering a question—How could gunshots make such a wound?—a raider said, "We bayoneted him too. Big shot from Jakarta. What was he?"

Someone said, "A deputy chief of staff."

"Big shot from Jakarta."

Someone else said, "That makes two big shots. The chief of staff and his deputy."

"You aren't supposed to say that. You're supposed to use their code names. Jonson and— What is this one's code name?"

Kneeling beside Harjono's body, Lieutenant Dul Arief scowled up at the men. "You were supposed to get him here alive."

A third squad appeared through the wooded swampland. They brought someone in alive—Major General Suprapto, second deputy chief of staff. His hands were tied behind him, his mouth bled. When they pulled him out of the lorry, he yelled, "I demand to know your authority for this! Who's in charge?"

They had stuck torches on poles near the hut; in the flickering light Lieutenant Dul Arief regarded the muscular general warily. "I am in charge, General."

"Then untie me, Lieutenant. I demand—"

"I won't listen to your demands, General."

"I—"

"No, General!" Dul Arief turned to a corporal. "Take him into the hut."

Coming through the darkness was the sound of another motor. A jeep rumbled into the circle of torchlight, giving the vehicular password—headlights flashed three times. A young lieutenant leapt out. He had important news for Dul Arief. Units of the 454th Diponegoro and the 530th Brawidyaya battalions (he forgot to use their code name, *Bimasaki*), now under Colonel Untung's direct command, had taken up positions in downtown Jakarta at Merdeka Square.

Raiders who overheard the report cheered; even Lieutenant Dul Arief began to smile.

Bimasaki controlled access to the radio station and the Telecommunications Building. Once the GETAPS rebels had taken KOSTRAD headquarters, the city would be theirs.

"Who's in charge at KOSTRAD?" Dul Arief asked the young lieutenant.

"General Suharto."

Dul Arief shrugged as if that were unimportant, but Achmad, standing nearby, felt it was very important. He had served with Suharto, a tough campaigner who knew the jungle. Achmad nearly said, "He won't surrender easily."

The young lieutenant had other news that could prove decisive. Tanks and armored cars, perhaps fifty altogether, were on their way from Bandung in support of GETAPS.

"We're winning," a sergeant said to Achmad.

"I don't like Suharto being at KOSTRAD. He's a good soldier."

"We've got downtown Jakarta. And with tanks from Bandung, we'll have reinforcements enough to secure the whole city." After a pause the sergeant said, "Are you the one who killed Yani?"

"Yes." Achmad expected a word of reassurance, but none came.

Instead the sergeant said, "It's a strange night. Who ordered him killed?"

"You were at the briefing," Achmad told him. "You heard the colonel say no restrictions on the use of force."

"Yes, I heard . . ." The sergeant's voice trailed off. He left unfinished the idea that freedom to use force and the actual use of it represented an ethical gap.

Achmad was about to argue that force was needed when traitors attempted to escape, but just then more lorries arrived.

Another dead man was unloaded: General Pandjaitan, chief of army logistics. He had given the GETAPS rebels a lot of trouble. From his bedroom he had fired off a Sten gun until finally they persuaded him to come out by threatening to massacre his entire family. Actually, they had already killed a nephew and severely wounded another.

General Pandjaitan had come from his bedroom in full-dress uniform with a chestful of medals. They grabbed him and hustled him from the house. General Pandjaitan yelled obscenities at a young soldier who gripped his arm while they crossed the courtyard. Then he tried to struggle free, giving the soldier reason to knock him down. Someone hit him in the face with a rifle butt. Someone else kicked him in the groin. And then somehow a submachine gun went off a dozen times or so and Pandjaitan was dead.

The squads that returned from their raids began to stray into the undergrowth, looking for a place to nap, or they headed for the main base by a dirt road that meandered through swampland. Some stayed at Lubang Buaya, dozing beneath torchlight with their backs against the hut.

Achmad remained awake. He would see the mission through to its end. He squatted inside the hut in a small room where three corpses lay, side by side, and General Suprapto sat cross-legged, arms bound, staring straight ahead.

Achmad didn't look at the dead men, but at the living general's face, which looked cadaverous in the murky light of a dangling low-wattage bulb. He wanted to say something to the general. He wanted to explain his own idea of military life. Honor guards of ancient Yogyanese sultans had been fearless, committed, abstemious men who considered their honor more valuable than life. By dint of loyalty and purity of spirit they had earned the right to wear the special kris of palace service. Instead of chasing women, they meditated. They ate sparingly. No fancy vehicles for them; they walked. They honed their bodies through disciplined exercise into weapons capable of defending their royal master. Achmad wanted to say, "Corruption brought you to this, and arrogance and rudeness. I killed the chief of staff tonight for slapping me." But he said nothing and was half nodding over his imagined speech when yet another squad was heard arriving.

He rushed out in time to see General Sutojo, inspector of justice, helped out of a lorry. His cheek looked crushed; one eye was swollen closed; his breath came in thready gusts.

"What happened?" Achmad asked a corporal from that squad.

"Somebody hit him. I don't know."

A jeep was pulling into the torchlight. When it stopped, a major leapt out and yelled for Lieutenant Dul Arief, who came running.

"I hear there are dead," the major said loudly. He was not a man accustomed to modulating his voice. Heavyset, thickly bearded—rare for a Javanese—he bellowed when Lieutenant Dul Arief told him: "Three! Who gave the order for that?"

"I never gave such an order, Major Gatot."

"Who did? Why were they killed?"

The lieutenant threw up his hands in a show of helplessness. "It happened."

"Happened? Killings don't just *happen*."

"Tonight they have. I think the men feared someone might escape."

Major Gatot spit disdainfully between his feet. "I thought these were crack troops."

Achmad stepped forward. "Major, at the briefing we were told no restrictions on the use of force."

"*Killing* force, sergeant?" Major Gatot looked down at his muddy boots, as if wondering how to clean them. When he looked up again, his face had lost its expression of outrage. He seemed thoughtful and turned from Achmad to the lieutenant. "What about those still alive?" he asked in a low voice.

"What about them, Major?"

"At a trial they'd be asked what happened here. Do you understand, Lieutenant?"

"Yes, Major."

Gatot shook his head, spitting again. "You don't understand." Drawing Dul Arief aside, he began to talk, but loudly enough for Achmad to overhear. The major was saying that the damage was done, that there was nothing to do but keep the mistake within proper limits. That is, evidence of the mistake must be minimal. And the way you kept evidence to a minimum was to remove it. "There is a great difference," he told the lieutenant, "between evidence that talks and evidence that has no voice. My blessed father told me that. Praise Allah."

"I understand, Major."

"Do you, Lieutenant? I hope so, for everyone's sake. What we don't need is evidence that talks." Major Gatot seemed to be weighing Dul Arief's ability to handle the situation. Then with a sigh he said, "You should return to headquarters."

"I've been assigned here, Major."

"I am ordering you to headquarters. Leave noncoms in charge here."

"Their orders, sir?"

"To stay here."

"And what else, sir?"

"Nothing more."

"What about that talking evidence?"

Major Gatot drew himself up, as if on the verge of confiding. But he checked himself. "Come to headquarters, Lieutenant."

The major turned and saw Achmad. "Sergeant," he said, gesturing, "we're going to headquarters. Put any other prisoners in the hut and await orders." He paused, then added, "Do nothing without orders. Your orders are to do nothing without orders."

"Yes, sir, Major."

"Stand back if you have to. You will not interfere with anything."

"I don't understand, sir."

"You don't need to understand. Do as you're told."

"I will await orders, sir." Achmad saluted and watched the lieutenant and the major drive off.

Now there was no commissioned officer at Crocodile Hole.

Evidence that can talk and evidence that has no voice. Did the major want the remaining generals killed? Officers had their reasons for doing what they did; that's why they were officers—it was their burden. If the prisoners were killed, Achmad told himself, it was no concern of his. He obeyed whatever orders were given to him. He had just been given orders to do nothing, and that's what he would do. He had done what was right so far and would continue to do what was right. Achmad leaned against a tree to smoke a cigarette. He inhaled slowly, deeply, as if the smoke was his reward for being a good soldier.

Half an hour passed; soon it would be dawn, but for a while longer darkness would stand like a wall at the border of torchlight. Achmad, having returned to the hut, was called out by a soldier who reported someone coming down the road.

When Achmad went outside, he saw a procession of young people strolling through the ground mist. "Who are they?" he asked a soldier.

"Reds from the base."

They were the young Reds training in guerrilla warfare at Halim in case of further confrontations with Malaysia. Sukarno in his pro-Communist phase had agreed to it. Air Marshal Dhani, a vociferous sympathizer, had implemented it.

So down the road they came: members of Pemuda Rakyat, the Popular Youth Front; and Gerwani, the Indonesian Women's Movement; and SOBSI, the Communist labor union. Some had flashlights and swung yellow arcs along their path. Talking, giggling, at least fifty of them were coming out of the darkness. Even before they got to the hut, Achmad could smell on the advancing wind the pungent woody odor of hashish.

"Comrades!" a girl called out.

Seated soldiers, smiling at the sight of women, began to rise. "Do you know the password, girls? If you don't, you'll have to pay a penalty."

"I bet I know what kind of penalty that is," a girl said, laughing.

A boy shouted defiantly, "Let us see the traitors! We heard about them! Where are the traitors?"

How had they heard? Achmad wondered. Had Major Gatot turned them loose? Ordinarily Achmad would have ordered them out of the area, but his orders were to do nothing, so he stepped aside and let the young Reds swagger into the circle of torchlight.

Another boy yelled out, "We want to see them! Those already asleep, those still awake!"

So they knew of the killings. Major Gatot had deliberately set them loose, that was certain. Their sullen eager faces reminded Achmad of a pack of dogs. Hashish had brutalized them. Achmad trembled from anger, but stood aside, allowing them to join the soldiers. Soon the morning air was filled with the smell of the drug.

Furious! But he would do nothing. The order was plain: do nothing. So the major was letting events unroll like the plot of a wayang play. Achmad walked out of the torchlit area into undergrowth from which he could see an ivory slice of moon just over some prickly swamp trees. He heard yelling behind him.

"We want those traitors! They slandered us! Slandered Aidit! Slandered the labor union, the dirty fuckers! Let them pay for it! Right, comrades? Soldiers? Aren't we all comrades?"

"Let's go see the scum!"

"Comrade soldiers, we love you!"

"How much, sweetheart? Show us!"

Laughter, noise—the sound of scuffling. The men were already fighting over a girl. But Achmad wouldn't look. He meant to carry out his orders to the letter.

Hearing the sound of motors, he walked back into the circle of light. There were girls smoking with soldiers who turned to stare at him challengingly a moment. From the hut came angry shouts and laughter. Lorries pulled up and stopped. They had brought back General Parman, chief of intelligence. He hopped unfettered from the rear of a lorry. He wore pressed khakis, a billed cap, and carried a swagger stick.

"Where is the officer in charge?" he asked with a lugubrious glance at a soldier who was hurrying a girl into the shadows.

Achmad stepped forward without saluting.

"You're in charge, Sergeant?"

"Yes, General."

"Do you have a field phone?"

"No, General."

Parman looked around, his eyebrows arching in astonishment. "Who are these people? What is this?" He was staring at a soldier embracing a girl against the hut. "I was supposed to meet the president here, but obviously *that's* not going to happen." He slapped his thigh with the swagger stick for emphasis.

"No, General."

"For what purpose have I been tricked and brought here, Sergeant? Answer me!" When Achmad said nothing, General Parman cut at the air impatiently with his stick. "Answer me!"

"You've been arrested, General."

Parman cocked his head as if he'd just heard something amusing. Throwing his head back, he laughed. Then he grimaced. "Now get on your field phone, Sergeant, and find me someone I can talk to."

Once again he cut the air with his stick, a swift curve of assertiveness from the hand of someone accustomed to giving orders. A weary, frightened soldier who had been at Crocodile Hole all evening saw this gesture as an attack on his sergeant. Rushing forward he swung his rifle, the barrel connecting with shattering impact on the general's jaw. Bone gave way, the whole left side of Parman's face seemed to ease downward, like earth collapsing in a quake. Groaning, he slid to his knees, thrusting his arms out to support himself. He hunched slightly as if ready to vomit, but there wasn't time for that, because two more soldiers were at him, lifting their rifles and bringing the barrels down across his back, thighs. Someone fired twice.

At last, out of military instinct, Achmad gave an order. "Stop firing!" he yelled, but from a score of circling soldiers another shot rang out. General Parman lay still, while young Reds poured out of the hut to see what was going on. A boy clapped. So did another. Others began shouting slogans. A girl stepped up and spit on the wounded man. Soldiers stood by, clutching fat cheroots filled with hashish and tobacco.

Another prisoner quietly climbed out of the lorry and disappeared into the shadows. He was a policeman who'd been riding his bike in the Parman neighborhood; they brought him along because he had witnessed the general's capture.

Achmad saw him slip away, but said nothing. He had already disobeyed his orders by commanding the men to cease firing. Suddenly he felt exhausted. Achmad sat against a tree beyond the torchlight and watched as Reds and soldiers dragged the wounded general into the hut. Achmad did not want to think; he wanted to sleep. The most delicious thing in the world would be a long, dreamless sleep. Sometimes in the village he went to bed shortly after sundown and wouldn't stir until late the next morning when grunting pigs and crowing roosters drew him from the black void back into the world. He wished for such peace now, the peace of a black void. They were in there, laughing and yelling. Well, let them do what they wanted. He had his orders. He would not disobey again.

The last squad was arriving. They shouted out their failure before the lorries could halt.

Defense Minister Nasution had escaped!

A sergeant whom Achmad knew from the 530th Battalion came over and slumped down wearily beside him. "Not good," the sergeant said, lighting up a cigarette. "What are these Red kids doing here?"

"They came to see the traitors."

"You people are letting them?"

"Yes. We're letting them do what they want."

"Who's in charge here?" the sergeant asked incredulously.

"I am. All the commissioned officers have gone to headquarters."

"We were stopped at the gate. Our lieutenant went directly there too. What's the idea?"

"If anything happens here, the officers won't be responsible."

The sergeant, a longtime veteran, laughed scornfully.

"My orders," Achmad said, "are to do nothing."

"What does that mean?"

"I'm not supposed to do anything without a specific order."

"What about taking a piss?"

Achmad grinned. "I'll have to hold it."

"It's a strange night," the sergeant murmured.

They fell silent, hearing muffled sounds, laughter, yells from the hut.

"I already disobeyed orders," Achmad said. "I told the men to stop shooting one of the prisoners."

"I've been an army man since independence, but I've never seen anything like this. We got to Nasution's house about 0315 and cordoned it off. A guard next door got nosy, then nasty, so we shot him and that woke up Nasution's household. We forced ourselves in. You won't believe what happened. We saw Nasution peeking around a bedroom door. Someone shot at him—without orders—but missed anyway. When we got to the bedroom door, his wife kept it closed from the other side. I mean she held it shut. One woman against three strong men, and she won for nearly a minute. She must have loved him, right? By the time we got in there, Nasution had ducked into a side room with a back door. He reached the courtyard, scaled a wall, and dropped into the property of the Iraqi ambassador." The sergeant laughed ruefully.

So one got away, Achmad was thinking. He remembered what Kamarusaman had said: Don't let any of them escape.

"We paid Nasution back for getting away," the sergeant continued. "First of all, we stole everything we could carry. In that lorry over there we even have the kitchen cutlery. And look what else we brought along—one of his aides. Lieutenant Tendean." An officer with tape over his mouth was being led into the hut. His taped wrists were crossed over his buttocks. "Tendean pulled an old Chinese pistol on us. One of those square-nosed heavy things, one of those old .38-caliber ones. You know the kind I mean?" The sergeant puffed briskly on his cigarette. "What I'm not proud of, though, is what happened to the kids. We shot a couple of them."

Achmad leaned forward. "What? Nasution's kids?"

"Two of his little girls. I think the littler one is hurt bad." The sergeant stared at two soldiers who were staggering out of the hut with one of the Gerwani girls between them. "I think the kid was shot in the back."

Achmad groaned.

"Well, I can't say I'm proud of it. Look at that." The sergeant jabbed his cigarette at people sprawled around the perimeter of the hut. They were either stunned from hashish or groping at one another. From within the hut came shouted slogans, voices raised in anger and song.

"Since when," grumbled the sergeant, "does the army fraternize with Reds? I can find myself a nice girl without going for a Red whore and her lectures on Marxism. Reds are whores and pimps."

"It isn't good," Achmad said, feeling a wave of fatigue surge through him like sludge. He wondered if there was strength enough left in his legs for him to stand up.

"It's a strange night," murmured the sergeant.

———————

A thin band of blue light was appearing in the east, dimly outlining the flat, broad leaves of nipa palms, when Achmad, half dozing, heard the first scream.

It came from the hut. Then there was another. His orders were to do— But then he was on his feet, drawn by a series of agonizing cries. He was running past the parked lorries into a small clearing in front of the hut from which a Red youngster was lurching, vomit trickling down his chin. Achmad bumped into a girl in the doorway; she was sobbing, hands flat against her cheekbones. When he turned into the first room, what Achmad saw brought him to a halt.

Soldiers together with Reds—male and female—were bringing rifle butts down against the fallen generals. Other were shooting point-blank with pistols or thrusting with bayonets. Perhaps a score of them were in there, ranged screaming around the dead and dying.

Getting farther into the room, pushing people aside, Achmad stood in a swirl of acrid smoke and saw what he would never forget for the rest of his life: a boy had pulled the pajamas of a dead general down to his ankles; wielding a harvest knife, a girl lifted the dead man's penis and with a slow stroke of the blade began slicing through the flesh as through a sausage, severing it from his body. A gush of dark blood welled out of the hole like a fountain, spattering her own groin as she knelt beside the corpse. She laughed hysterically, stumbled to her feet, still absently holding the limp bloody flesh.

Then Achmad heard himself shouting. He was giving orders. Slipping the Kalashnikov off his back, Achmad waved it around and ordered them out of there out out out out out! He squeezed off a few warning rounds into the atap roof, and the room instantly cleared.

Achmad was left with corpses. He stared in horror at faces with eyes gouged out, at ripped bellies and hacked limbs, at gratuitous slaughter—men killed many times over. He sat down on the floor, feeling wetness against his legs. It was blood. Worse than so much blood and death was his sense of spirits hovering nearby. Demons, they were demons; they were demons with immense tongues and bulging eyes who had come down from mountains, up from the dark crocodile well, trooping out of one world into another on a malicious orgy of destruction. This was their fault. It had to be theirs. Humans could have done none of this without direction from elsewhere, from the demon hole, from the blackness of mountains, from a world of other reasons.

So he had given orders, but only to save the young Reds and the soldiers from harm and only after the generals were dead or dying. He had known that to let them die was his duty all along. A professional soldier does what he is told. Achmad felt unable to rise. With the Kalashnikov lying across his lap, he sat on the wet floor, breathing the stale hashish smoke, the stench of cordite.

Someone was yelling outside.

Finding the strength to get up, Achmad went to the door and stood there. Men were lying around weeping, staring blankly into the soft blue light. A corporal sat in a jeep, too astonished by what he saw to get out of it.

"Corporal," Achmad called.

"Who's in charge, Sergeant?"

"I am."

"News from Bandung. The tanks and armored cars never left. The units there decided not to join us." The corporal shrugged behind the wheel, looking shyly at Achmad for reassurance. "Too bad, right?"

"Yes, too bad."

"What's going on here, Sergeant?" He stared at weeping men, at girls too stunned for tears. They clustered in groups like cattle weathering a storm.

"Never mind, Corporal. Go back to headquarters." Achmad watched the jeep drive off, then turned to listen to a field radio cradled in a soldier's arm.

A voice from Radio Republik Indonesia was saying, "Early today a newly formed organization of patriots called GETAPS, the Thirtieth of September Movement, arrested a council of seven generals who had been plotting to overthrow the government."

Seven generals? Nasution got away. Six generals and one junior officer. The broadcast must have been written earlier, Achmad decided.

"Those captured," the voice continued, "had planned to launch a coup on Armed Forces Day with the help of the United States Central Intelligence Agency and lackeys from Malaysia financed by the British. Colonel Untung, who masterminded the arrest of those traitors, has secured the safety of our Beloved Leader, Bung Karno. Long live Bung Karno! Long live Freedom! Long live the Revolutionary Forces! Long live the Revolution! Long live Indonesia!"

Achmad looked around at the disheveled weeping revelers and felt the need to walk away, to distance himself from this place. He started down the road, following tire treads in the mud.

Achmad shuffled along, watching the dawn light lift heavily from the earth—a curtain of blue iron. He stopped often to listen for voices among the swamp trees. If he could hear them, they would surely be happy voices, their sound the terrible sound of demonic happiness, because tonight the spirits had done a full measure of mischief.

Achmad slogged forward, watching colors descend from the sky into blue-black objects along the path, giving the swamp things definition, the outline and texture and hue of familiarity. Everything was as it should be. Had nothing really changed? He walked into a mangrove swamp, feeling the keen sting of branches against his face. It was good to be alive. He had a wife and a little son quite safe in a village far away. But then a terrible sadness overtook Achmad Bachtiar and he sat down in the mud. Crossing his legs, he stared at some ants trekking through the swamp grass near his muddy boots. What had he done? Had he been a good soldier? Had he put his soul in jeopardy?

Achmad let his body stretch itself out on the swampy ground. There had been enough killing for a while. He was tired of it. He was tired. Fatigue was flowing through his veins like slag, beating in a slow, steady pulse between his eyes. He wanted to sleep a long time. Kamarusaman had corrupted his sister. She might well have been one of those murderous kids tonight, delirious on drugs, unbounded by human feeling, doing the dirty work of an officer who wished to escape blame. What blame? The generals deserved what they got. Well, they deserved arrest, but their arrogance had brought them even more than that. Endang might have been with the Reds tonight. After all, her lover had been with the chairman of the PKI tonight. Endang could have sucked up hashish smoke herself, his little sister Endang, betrayed by her filthy lover, impregnated by him. Kamarusaman must die.

Orders to do nothing. Do nothing without orders.

Swampy dampness was seeping through his clothes as he lay on the ground. Sleep was what he wanted more than anything, a blessed void removed from evil. Evil had come down from mountains and had joined with evil creeping from a dry well and together they had hovered above swampland until almost dawn, at which time, coalescing into a swollen monster unseen by human eyes, such evil had swept down on the hut, had gripped the plaster walls in rotting arms and rocked the foundation and into human mouths inside the smoky rooms had breathed the terrible stench of madness.

Sunshine fell abruptly across Achmad's face. He closed his eyes, a golden haze roiling against the lids. It was going to be day, but for him it was still night. Exhaustion was sloshing through his body like water thickened with mud—back and forth and back and forth and back and forth until the heavy rhythm lulled him. He eased slowly into sleep.

Thirty-two

She remembered a hand holding hers. And someone urging her to swallow something: medicine, bitter tasting. And then Inam—she saw the girl's narrow solemn face swirling out of hot images—bathing her forehead with a wet towel. She remembered the hand again, holding tight; it was like a ship's anchor in a stormy sea. And then coming through a malarial hallucination was his face: dark, square, the eyes set wide, and she tried to ask him if she was hypnotized once more, had he done it to her again and if so the joke had gone far enough and if he didn't stop using magic on her she wouldn't let him hold her hand, but she wasn't sure that the words came out.

There were many bouts of sleep, which she dreaded, because they drained whatever energy she had and left her with a recollection of nightmares that crept through her fever remorselessly, leaving a residue of faintly remembered horror like the slime left by snails.

At last, after a paroxysm of chills and fever and its long, dull legacy of prostration, Maggie lay on the sweat-soaked bed and listened during blessed moments of clarity to a fierce storm breaking over Yogya. The metallic sound of raindrops hitting against the galvanized roof reminded her of Padang, in Sumatra, where every afternoon without fail a phalanx of cumulonimbus clouds had marched seaward from the mountains to dump thick, brutal showers on the port city. The rain fell so hard it pulled leaves off the trees and shook out small lizards from their hiding places to cling upside down on the hotel ceiling. From up there they stared at her as if hypnotized by the tumult, until the storm swung away like an iron gate, letting the blue back in, and they skittered off.

Mas Slamat, she believed, had sat awhile beside her bed, maybe yesterday. Who else had been to see her? People had loomed out of the fever for a few moments and merged again with images drifting through her mind. The dalang had come here, though, and held her hand. Of that she was certain—her hand in his. At Lake Toba she and Vern had stood on Samosir's dinosaur-backed hill and watched the island fishermen in their boats, the small, dark taciturn men laying nets, their hands in quick economical motion like a musician fingering keys. Hands ceaseless, bewitching.

There was sleep again and in it she dreamed of a fisherman landing a boat. Never in actuality had she seen a Samosir fisherman bring his boat in; it was as if they left and returned to harbor by magical transfer between lake and shore. But in the dream this fisherman beached his boat and came toward her, went past her, and entered a fishing hut nearby. She followed him inside and let him run his fishy sun-blackened hands along her flanks, but he didn't go further, and she wanted him so badly that the dream turned into a nightmare of unsatisfied desire from which she awakened with a cry of dismay.

After that the chills and fever subsided. She slept less and listened to the doctor's reassurance that malarial attacks diminished in intensity each time they returned. Chlorguanide would have her up in a few days. Maggie learned from Inam that the dalang had come to the house shortly after dawn that first morning (having paid his respects to the performing dalang) to see how she was. He had gone himself for the doctor—not a witch doctor, a shaman, a dukun, but a physician with degrees from Amsterdam. The dalang's reliance on Western medicine did not square with his reputation among the people for practicing magic. She wanted to know more about him; there was a growing need in Maggie to understand him and it exasperated her. Confinement to a sickbed forced her to acknowledge what was happening: she was infatuated, just like a teenage girl. It would pass, of course, but for the moment Maggie Gardner felt herself gripped by lovesickness as intensely as she had been racked and shaken by malaria.

On impulse she started to pester Inam for information about the dalang. She was shamelessly frank about it, speaking up in a whisper from the sickbed: asking, seeking, probing insistently. If shocked and confused by such blatant requests from a married woman about a man not her husband, Inam didn't show it, but put aside her cultural reticence and proved equal to Maggie in frankness, as if they were old friends whose feelings for each other overrode timidity and common sense. What Inam didn't know, she discovered by sounding out people in the neighborhood for much of the afternoon. Then sitting beside the bed, fixing the haggard woman with a steady gaze, Inam made her report.

The dalang's wife had died five years ago after six years of marriage and two miscarriages. She had been carrying a third child when a cholera epidemic broke out suddenly, like a violent summer storm, and as suddenly disappeared, lasting less than a month but taking with it the dalang's hopes for a family.

Maggie was not satisfied. She had to know more.

"Inam, was she pretty?"

"I don't know, Nonya."

"I want to know if she was pretty."

And the answer came back an hour later: "Not pretty in the West, I think. She was little." Inam measured the height from the floor, her palm held chin high. Less than five feet.

"Was she pretty," Maggie asked, "in a Javanese way?"

Inam hesitated.

Pretty, Maggie decided.

"Perhaps a little pretty," Inam said.

Damn pretty: dark, petite, doubtlessly with large, clear eyes, her hair pulled back into a shining rope that curled at the hollow of her throat.

Maggie had to know more. And Inam went out and got the facts. The wife had been the daughter of a rich priyayi from Solo, and in her youth had danced the serimpi in the sultan's court. Grimly Maggie envisioned a slender girl regally flicking a batik sash alongside other elegant dancers in the music pavilion of the kraton.

"Nonya, she liked many things. She liked clothes and jewelry and was always asking for them. She always wanted things, always asking and always taking. This is what people say about her."

Maggie hated the satisfaction she felt upon learning that the otherwise perfect wife had been greedy—hated the feeling but indulged it—and the remainder of that afternoon Maggie dwelled on this imperfection until she felt sorry for the husband of such a woman and concluded that although the wife's death by cholera must have been horrible, in the scheme of things the dalang was better off the way he was now.

———————

That conviction seemed to increase the rate of Maggie's recovery. She asked for a radio, but Inam was evasive—the two radios in the household were broken. No, she didn't know offhand where she could get another. Perhaps tomorrow somewhere. Her odd behavior frightened Maggie. Had something happened to the dalang? Had it been reported in a news broadcast? It was a wild surmise but in this state of mind Maggie could not help but think that the gods had looked down disapprovingly on her mad infatuation and had chosen this way to punish such a fool.

"We have not told you—" Inam began.

Maggie felt her chest constrict.

"Because you were sick. But Nonya, something bad has happened."

"Who was hurt?"

"Some generals plotted to overthrow the government and they were killed, and now the Communists are blamed for it and no one knows what will happen."

"Generals," Maggie repeated, sinking back against the pillow. "Communists killed them."

"I don't believe the Communists did it," Inam declared. She had once told Maggie that her brother was a Communist. "But they are blamed."

"Is your brother all right?"

"I don't know where he is."

"And my friend Ali?"

"He came two days ago, but you were asleep. I asked him what would happen to him and my brother. He just said the Communists didn't do it."

318

The satisfaction that Maggie had felt because of the dalang's well-deserved freedom began to drain away and was replaced by concern for a friend who had offered to protect her if anything happened. Perhaps it was Ali who needed protection.

"Inam, bring me a radio," Maggie said firmly. And she added, "Send someone to the village to find out about Ali."

"I can go myself, Nonya. Unless you want me for something else."

"Yes, go yourself. That would be better."

A crisis affecting an entire country was returning her to the real world. She was glad to send Inam on a different and far worthier mission than those concerning the dalang. Maggie sighed with relief.

Thirty-three

Within a few days everyone in Jakarta had sorted out the events that took place on the Night of the Generals and the subsequent hours that led to the collapse of the 30th of September Movement. What Vern didn't know outright he learned at the hotel bar where he drank soda water and listened to diplomats and businessmen unravel the intricacies of the GETAPS escapade. General Suharto had swiftly taken military command, breaking the rebel resistance both in Jakarta and at Halim Air Base within a day. The rebel leaders, including Chairman Aidit and chief plotter Sjam and the great patriot Colonel Untung, had scattered throughout Java.

The corpses of the six slain generals and the aide were found at Crocodile Hole, stuffed down the well. While army photographers and television cameramen stood nearby, frogmen were lowered into it and after a while, over the rim of the muddy hole, appeared the mutilated bodies, roped together like linked sausages. The army newspapers blamed the Communist party for the murders and the attempted coup and what was described as a plot to kidnap the Beloved

Leader—perhaps the most inflammatory charge of all, according to Western observers at the hotel bar.

Discovery of the mangled bodies had swift repercussions. For one thing, the hotel bar temporarily closed, so that Vern and other foreigners had nowhere to go in the evening. For another, the army declared a sundown-to-sunup curfew in Jakarta, cut telephone communications with the outside world, and canceled all flights into Indonesia. Photos of the seven victims were telexed to army units throughout the country, and commanders were warned that the rebels might attack outposts and other installations in the attempt to destroy the entire officers' corps.

All employees of OPSUS were expected to attend the funeral for these national heroes. To make sure of foreign participation, General Sakirman pestered his American architect a half-dozen times for confirmation that he would be prominently there when "the seven were carried to rest," as the general called it.

In spite of the turmoil, Vern was in good spirits, having worried initially that the crisis might bring Project Palm Tree to a halt. Then after a day had passed without national collapse, he resumed thinking the way he always thought: that these little flurries of harebrained politics were part of life in the Third World. You lived with them, dealt with them, and kept your own eye on the ball. In a few days GETAPS would be forgotten.

Going down to the lobby that morning, he felt relaxed—until Yanti leapt up from a chair and rushed forward. The Chinese girl was gripping a newspaper and even before reaching him seemed to be thrusting it into his hand.

"Read, Mr. Gardner, read!"

She slammed the Red newspaper, *Harian Rakyat,* against his chest and giggled so loudly that people turned to stare at them.

A front-page editorial accused the murdered generals of having plotted a coup. To eliminate such traitors was "correct." Colonel Untung was called the savior of his country. Through his commitment to progressive ideas he had brought to a safe and honorable conclusion the "internal army affair" and expressed the will of the people.

The Communist party had obviously compromised itself by running this editorial and backing a political movement that no longer existed.

"See, Mr. Gardner?"

He looked from the paper to the girl, whose face glistened from the sweat of excitement.

"Yes, I see. The Reds made a stupid mistake," he said. "They should have kept their mouths shut."

"There is demonstration today against them."

"Listen, young lady, stay clear of that kind of thing."

"I will demonstrate."

"I don't think your father would like that."

Yanti smiled up at him. "And you, Mr. Gardner? Would you like it?"

He tried to look severe, yet so irresistible was the girl's good humor, he felt himself smiling too. "Just let the thing blow over. Stay out of it."

"Already there is fighting in streets."

"I told you, Yanti." He really did feel severe. "Stay out of it."

"I will fight for my country."

"Yes, I know. You're Indonesian." He watched the effect of his sarcasm register on the girl's face: surprise, then disappointment. So he tried to placate her. "The patriotic thing right now would be to stand aside and let the authorities restore order. That's their job."

"Mr. Gardner, would you fight for your country?"

"I fought for my country." When she began to smile the triumphant smile of a debater, he added, "As a soldier. Demonstrating is not soldiering."

"Communists kidnapped our generals."

"You don't know that."

"I will demonstrate."

Vern looked hard at her. The girl's eyes were brilliant from determination. He couldn't help but admire her spunk while fearing for her safety. It occurred to him with a shock that her safety was truly important to him. "At least don't get out in front, for God's sake," he said irritably. "Stay at the back and to the side. If your people break for cover, you're better off there. Will you promise me that?"

"Well, I promise."

"I have to make a phone call now."

322

"To your wife?"

He noticed her eyes narrow. Did it matter to her? "Yes, to my wife."

"You won't get through."

Minutes later, after she had left the hotel and he tried to call, Vern discovered that Yanti was right: all lines were down to Central Java as they had been down since the crisis began. But in the immediate aftermath of such an emergency that was par for the course. After all, the crisis was limited to Jakarta. He felt himself relaxing again.

Even so, the trouble might spread. While waiting in the lobby for Larry Foard to show up, Vern heard a new rumor: the Red newspaper editorial was stirring up more hatred than anyone could have expected; months of tension seemed to have found their focus.

So along with Larry Foard he was prominently there when thousands of Jakartans assembled at Merdeka Square not to witness the Armed Forces Day parade, scheduled for this Monday, October 4, but to pay last respects to murdered men who had overnight become national heroes.

Having elbowed through the crowds and presented their credentials to a fancily dressed cordon of policemen, Vern and Larry shuffled into the long line waiting to pass by the closed coffins within a humid hall at Army Headquarters. Aside from Indonesian officials, there were many foreign diplomats, their handkerchiefs out and conspicuous in the heat, who were preparing to gaze down respectfully at the sealed boxes. Huge containers of incense clouded the sweltering air and lent to the smell of sweat a cloyingly sweet perfume. Vern heard sobbing as the line moved forward. Seated in an alcove were the families of the dead men, comforted by military aides and relatives.

"Who's the one pacing?" Larry whispered with a nudge and nodded toward a husky general stamping around behind the line of coffins in scruffy battle fatigues.

"Suharto, I think," Vern said. He had seen a rather blurred photo in the newspaper. But whoever the pacing officer was, he made no effort to hide his anger. His rather plump face, which must have been normally placid, was twisted into an expression of extravagant emotion: impatience, outrage, fury. Vern figured the general wanted everyone who filed past the corpses to appreciate the extent of his disapproval of what had happened. Yes, indeed. A day of happy spectacle had been transferred into a day of sorrow and mourning—and doubtlessly into an occasion for public commitment to revenge. That was clear to Vern. That had not been clear to him until the pacing general behind the coffins made it clear. Indonesia was in for real trouble. These army boys, Vern realized, weren't going to let this opportunity go by. The enemy was going to get it.

General Nasution made his appearance just as Vern and Larry were coming to the coffins. A murmur filled the hall when Nasution hobbled in on crutches, surrounded by a heavily armed guard. The angry general rushed forward to take the bemused defense minister's arm.

"A sod of a thing," Larry whispered. "His daughter's dying in hospital."

"And a lot of people are going to pay," Vern said, staring down at the tinted photograph of General Yani, which lay on top of his flag-draped coffin. Yani. He remembered Yani chasing a young dolly through a midnight garden. A flagrantly public cocksman. Looking up he saw General Sakirman standing among staff officers beyond the last coffin. When their eyes met, Sakirman smiled. He was pleased that his American architect had come; in fact, he was already whispering his little triumph to fellow officers. Vern gave him a solemn nod of appropriate recognition, wondering how many crooked deals Sakirman had been in on with Yani and with some of the other brave heroes resting in their wooden boxes.

Vern felt depressed when he and Larry got out of the close hall into the hot sunlight. It was just too damn stagy. This funeral ceremony was the means to an end that might very well rip the country apart. He wasn't sure what he meant—of course, the Reds would be blamed, but he couldn't envision what was as yet only a shadow at the edge of his mind—and still couldn't explain his foreboding to Larry when they pushed through the crowd struggling to see the limousines pulling up to Army Headquarters.

Even after they were seated in their car and had begun the long drive southward to Kalibata Cemetery, he had this feeling of impending doom, so he was surprised—and confirmed in his fear—when Larry launched into his favorite story about the anteater, as if he had never told it in countless bars whenever he felt sick to death of his life. It was always the same. He had been in Bengkulu, Sumatra, lolling on the beach when a boy came along with an anteater to sell. Larry bought it: the cord holding the animal had rubbed its neck raw and blood was dripping into the sand. Once it belonged to him, Larry put the anteater against a tree, figuring it would climb out of harm's way. But the creature just clung there. Three men came along and tried to pry it off. They couldn't. Larry said in the car, as he had said many times in his cups, "Hell of a beast. Did you know it shits and pisses out of the same hole?" He got into an agument with the three men because one wanted to kill the anteater with a knife. Why? Perhaps because it was stronger than three men combined. Larry ended by paying off those fellows too. Damn anteater had cost him a bundle, and look what it did, it just held on to the damn tree. It was still clinging there the last time he looked back while heading down the beach. What ever happened to it? Did the thing climb up or climb down or get a knife in its gizzard or did the enterprising boy come along and retake it for another sale?

These were proper questions for midnight boozing in a bar, but not now, not on the way to a cemetery. That's what Vern thought and that's what he told Larry. "There's something about that damn story I don't like."

"Damned if you aren't right, mate," Larry admitted grimly.

All the way out there through streets lined with thousands of sobbing women and somber men who watched the coffins (strapped to the top of armored cars) head for heroic burial, Vern Gardner tried to get his mind off the impending calamity. After all, it might not occur. His fear of it was based only on the public look of a general's face.

Vern tried to fix on something else—his recent idea for converting primitive latrines into an integrated sewage system. You could outfit sedimentation tanks to produce methane gas and generate a petrochemical industry; the methane would be the starting point for a large number of compounds with end products drastically needed here: plastics and detergents, for example. He'd talked at the Hotel Indonesia bar about it with a rubber exporter from Sweden. The Swede had thought the idea was feasible. Over a few more drinks than the Swede needed (still on the wagon, Vern had soda water), they decided that implementation was simple: a small team of chemists and some Indonesian rupiah siphoned off the government's hugely profitable system of graft and corruption.

But Vern kept seeing that general's angry face—the public fury of General Suharto, who now controlled Jakarta, while the president of the country was pacing through a palace in Bogor, stunned by the vulnerability he had suspected only Allah knew was his.

"Larry."

"Yes?"

"Why did you tell that story about the anteater?"

"I don't know. It came to me." After a moment's thought he added, "Everything's a bit dodgy, isn't it?"

"I don't want to hear that story anymore."

"Very well. I thought you already told me that."

"Pitiful animal clinging to a tree. For God's sake, Larry."

"Awfully sorry, old chap."

"Because there's something fatalistic and helpless about it. A real Asian story, for God's sake."

"All right, mate. I won't tell it again." Larry said after a long silence, "Are you getting on pins about her?"

"Yes."

"You mustn't worry. She's safe in Yogya."

Vern stared from the slow-moving car at flagpoles rising out of little residential gardens to fly the red-and-white flag of Indonesia at half-staff. Up ahead, between the pressing lines of spectators, were rows of tanks (Vern recognized the Soviet medium T-44s; a bunch of them had been given to Sukarno during the good old days) with their three-inch guns arched over the road in salute at a forty-five-degree angle. "I think we're almost there," Vern said.

It was his good fortune to meet an acquaintance at the Kalibata Cemetery—Jack Rutledge, American diplomat. Jack Rutledge often came to the bar of the Hotel Indonesia and had a few drinks with expatriates like Vern. A few too many drinks for a diplomat, because after enough gin and bitters Jack Rutledge would hold forth on topics best kept to himself. Vern gave him a year at most before the embassy understood how poor a security risk he was. Even so, when the funeral finally drew to a close, Vern sought him out among the sweating dignitaries and suggested that they get together, say, at a nice little Chinese restaurant in Pentu Kecil for lunch. The idea was to enlist Jack's help over Peking duck (asking outright would elicit an official no) in getting a message to Maggie through diplomatic channels.

Vern was waiting impatiently at a back table of Liong Liong when Rutledge finally appeared—a tall, shambling blond with the slightly bloated features of someone who had once been a trim athlete and had then given up exercise. From the lopsided way that Rutledge was smiling, Vern figured he'd already been at the gin. And indeed, before he even sat down, Rutledge admitted to "hoisting a few" with one of the French military attachés who had also been near collapse at that damn funeral today, what heat, what infernal heat, and in formal dress too, and all those generals lined up there acting hurt and angry and insulted as if Jesus Christ had just been crucified again.

Looking at the florid face, the glazed blue eyes, Vern decided that giving Jack Rutledge an additional year in the Foreign Service was more than he deserved—than he would probably get.

But Vern chuckled in expedient appreciation of what Jack Rutledge obviously felt was a witticism—the allusion to Jesus Christ crucified—and ordered drinks from a passing waiter.

"Well, what did you think?" Rutledge asked vaguely. "I've eaten here. The food's not bad, though I prefer that place down the street—"

"Cahaya Kota."

"That's the one. Well, what did you think? We all thought Sukarno would arrive by helicopter at the last moment, but no-show on a day like this? I can't believe it. No one can believe it." Rutledge blew out his cheeks in wonder. "I mean, he promoted them all posthumously, but the army was livid about him not coming. It was an insult. There was, of course, the matter of his personal security at a time of crisis, but what the hell, it was a chance he should have taken. And look at the Chinese—absent too. That's a horse of a different color, though. I mean— Ah!" The drinks arrived and Rutledge, grasping his gin and bitters, sipped noisily, his soft lips trembling like those of a horse at a watering trough. "Good good good. A day like this sure dries you out. Infernal heat, unbelievable. Funeral had to be held, didn't it, on one of the hottest damnedest days of the year. Did you know it was one of the hottest days of the year? Of course, Peking hasn't commented on the coup attempt."

"I suppose they think it's unfair to blame it on the Reds," Vern got in while Rutledge was drinking—nearly draining the glass, so that Vern waved to the waiter for a refill.

"Sure they think it's unfair," Rutledge agreed. "We expect Peking to send a few sharply worded messages to the Indonesian government. And from a Chinese perspective, no wonder Peking is pissed. After all, the Indo Army has already searched the office of the Chinese commercial counselor and the living quarters of the Chinese Embassy staff, if you can believe *that*, and in Medan the police stood aside and let some hooligans tear down the Chinese Consulate's national emblem and flag. Any Red, foreign or domestic, is a dirty murderer to official Indonesia right now. I'm not talking about Sukarno, though. He's out there all by himself. I'm talking about the rest of government."

"Yes," Vern said.

Sighing, Rutledge folded his hands over a paunch; the gesture seemed oddly aged for such a young man. "Peking and Jakarta sure aren't bedfellows anymore. But that's the drill in this part of the world. *Comme ci, comme ça.* Not a fucking moment of stability wherever you look. Sometimes when I get up in the morning, I say to myself, 'Well, it's going to be a nice day,' but within minutes of stepping into the heat and noise and craziness and deceit and wheeling and dealing of this place, I'm wondering how I'll last until noon. I sure as hell look forward to a new posting. I'd take Saudi Arabia, Peru, any damn place. Shall we have one for the road?"

"We haven't had lunch yet, Jack."

"You order," Rutledge said without interest. "And another gin and bitters for me. By the way, what's that you're having?"

"Soda."

"No gin?" Rutledge snorted. "I suppose you've got this all figured out."

"You mean the coup? No. Not at all. Who did it?"

"You don't sound very interested."

Vern shrugged.

328

"The Reds." Rutledge leaned forward conspiratorially. He seemed more determined than ever to impress this American who drank soda water. He claimed that the PKI had engineered the plot. Their motives were obvious. Fearing Sukarno's health would worsen and leave them out in the cold, they had taken the calculated but desperate risk of wiping out the army's high command. Aidit was at Halim on the Night of the Generals, directing the entire operation. Young Red volunteers had been positioned at the airfield to support the 30th of September Movement—and look how they supported it! Then the Reds had the unbridled arrogance to endorse the rebel raid in their newspaper even before they knew what its outcome might be. They were too damn cocky, Rutledge declared, his words thickening. They counted too much on Sukarno's help, while suffering from poor communications and lack of planning. But then the PKI leaders had always deluded themselves. Fearing spies, they had always restricted knowledge of their plans to the Politburo and a few members of the Central Committee. They had never won over to their side a mass proletariat. This brand of communism was nothing more than a sad blend of religious and mystical influences coupled to a vague desire for social change.

Vern recognized in Rutledge's phrasing as well as his attitude the official stance of the United States government in Jakarta.

Dismissively waving his hand, Rutledge said, "The PKI is show biz, but this fellow Suharto is one tough customer. Smiles, doesn't say much, can mash you like a cockroach. It won't take him long to take charge of the whole country." He grinned fatuously and added, "But don't quote me."

"Whoever takes charge," Vern said, "I hope they do it soon and get back to work."

That stark pragmatism startled Rutledge. "Let's hope they do better than *that*, Vern. For example, they could do better with the U.S. of A. They sure have given us hell this year. Seizing our libraries, to say nothing of American property." He hunched forward and held out a big pudgy hand as if ready to count its fingers. "Just in Sumatra alone they've taken over U.S. rubber acreage worth eighty million bucks, if you can believe it."

Vern shook his head slowly, as if the thought had never occurred to him that such a thing could have happened during his decade out here in Asia.

"Add palm-oil plantations and petroleum fields to that, and these greedy little folks have seized three hundred million dollars in American assets."

"That's a lot," Vern noted blandly.

Rutledge laughed. "You could say that's a lot, you really could, and you could say more if you knew the full extent of it. And what was Sukarno's excuse for butchering us economically? He linked us with Britain in the creation of Malaysia. Another of his self-serving arguments. Who in hell does he think he's fooling?"

"I don't think our support of Belgium in the Congo affair has endeared us to Third World countries like Indonesia. That sort of thing has given us a bad name. So when we support something, the Third World gets suspicious. Not that we're necessarily wrong. We're just looking out for Number One like everyone else." Vern felt he might be going too far in his teasing of the attaché, but sometimes he got carried away in the presence of so much vanity.

Rutledge acted as if he hadn't heard. "All that nonsense about the CIA. If the CIA did everything it was accused of doing, it would be a major world power in itself. What a joke."

Vern laughed in discreet concurrence. But he really believed that the CIA was probably a major power out here. Subversion was the sort of thing that made Asia tick. Of course, power politics in the Western sense was still somewhat untried in the area, press coverage of any value was still fragmentary, political motivation was often baffling and obscure, official justice and punishment were swiftly lost in the man-swarming daily life of Asia, so that covert action offered a practical and often most effective way of promoting change. Anyway, Vern told himself, what would happen would happen. That much of Asia had rubbed off on him: the cool-eyed fatalistic view of human events. It was why he hated Larry's anteater story; that image of a slow-witted creature pathetically holding on for dear life in a way that jeopardized further life was too close to the kind of thinking that sometimes kept him awake at night. Vern Gardner worked hard every day not to give in to such negativism.

Right now he was growing tired of Rutledge and politics. What had brought him here in the first place? He loved someone. He carried

330

Maggie's image around with him like his own skin. In his impatience Vern just came out with it, suddenly, apropos of nothing.

"Jack, I wonder. My wife's in Yogya right now—"

Rutledge smiled complacently. "Well, don't worry. Not one foreigner has had trouble. She's better off there than here."

"Yes, I understand that, Jack. But I can't get through to her, you see."

"Don't you work for something in the army?" He sat up as if becoming wary. And he knew and they both knew he knew that Vern worked for OPSUS.

"They won't do it. Not right now. My boss says the phone lines are open only for military business. No exceptions. They're on war alert. If he can't do it, then I don't know an Indonesian who can."

Pursing his lips, Rutledge nodded. "Sure. They've all got religion right now. They're all saints—spit and polish. It'll last maybe a week."

Vern went on patiently in a low voice. "You see, Jack, I'd just like to get a little message through, something reassuring. No big deal."

Rutledge nodded, his plump face abruptly impassive, professional.

Vern, panicky, then asked flat out if by diplomatic pouch or telex Jack could reach Yogya, informing Mrs. Gardner (Vern shoved a slip of paper across the table) that everything was all right here. Vern paused. "Jack, what I'm asking is, can you do this for me?"

With a grumpy sigh, Rutledge picked up the piece of paper.

"How about another drink, some food? Anything you want. I'm buying." Vern was too relieved at the moment to realize his offer sounded like a petty bribe.

"No thanks," Rutledge said coldly. "I have an appointment." Getting to his feet, he was prepared to turn and leave when a parting shot occurred to him. "I told you, Gardner." It was now "Gardner" instead of "Vern." He said, "Not a single instance of violence against a foreigner. I'm sure your wife must know that. I'm sure she can hang on. You once told me she's something of an Asian hand, didn't you?" The edge of his mouth lifted disdainfully. "But if you insist, I'll send a telex to the consulate there. She'll get it."

"You sons of bitches," Vern said.

"What did you say?"

"I said you're sons of bitches, Rutledge. You particularly. You are a son of a bitch."

Shaking his head slowly in measured reproach, as if subjected to the tantrum of a child, Rutledge turned unsteadily on his heel and lurched out of the restaurant.

Vern knew, of course, that he had gone too far. Chances were that Rutledge wouldn't send the telex now. But Maggie understood what was going on; she could deal with it; she'd act like the Asia hand she'd become. Fuck Rutledge.

He waved off a waiter carrying a menu.

Love makes you overprotective, he thought gloomily. Love makes you foolish. But at least it doesn't make you a son of a bitch.

———————

Leaving the restaurant, Vern walked into the crowded streets of a steamy Jakartan afternoon. Hashim, waiting at the entrance, fell in behind him, for at the bodyguard's insistence they no longer walked together—staying apart could give Hashim an advantage in case of sudden attack. Jack Rutledge might scoff at the idea of violence against foreigners in Jakarta, but General Sakirman didn't want to take chances with his precious American architect.

They had gone only a block when a wide boulevard afforded them a hectic vista: arcs of sunlight colliding against rooftops; lorries and buses pressed together, pouring thick clouds of exhaust into the white air. Also approaching the boulevard, as Vern reached it, was a solid phalanx of marchers who brought the dense traffic to a halt. Carrying banners and brandishing their fists, the demonstrators went around stalled vehicles like a river around rocks.

Turning, Vern said to Hashim, "Who are they?"

"KAP-GESTAPU."

Vern had heard of it only this morning—one of those organizations formed as often happened in Indonesia on the spur of the moment, a desperate cure-all for national crisis. The Action Front to Crush the 30th of September Movement was led by Subchan, an organizer of Muslim youth groups, who had rallied young anti-Red leaders within hours of the coup attempt and within a couple of days had become an ominous power in Jakartan politics. So here they were, a horde of youngsters carrying banners that spelled out in bold letters their threats to the PKI and its leaders: DISSOLVE THE PKI! KILL AIDIT! CRUSH THE REDS! And a slogan that stunned Vern until he thought more about it: LONG LIVE AMERICA! A one-hundred-

332

eighty-degree shift in Indonesian allegiance from the Chinese to the imperialistic government that the Chinese hated most.

He was absorbing this proof of Indonesian volatility when something caught his eye in the midst of the procession: a short, slim, pretty girl with long hair, a jerky gait, a narrow face for a Chinese. He yelled out, "Yanti! Yanti!"

Within seconds she came running, her mouth drawn open into a rollicky smile.

She was carrying a sheaf of stickers that read CRUSH PKI!— probably for defacing windshields. Holding them out proudly, as if they were a gift or a badge of courage, Yanti reached him and with her free hand gripped his arm. Vern was shocked by this simple, nonchalant, yet intimate gesture; so much so, that he drew back a little.

"You, Yanti," he said, "you weren't at the back and to the side as I told you."

She shook her head happily.

"You promised me if you got into one of these silly demonstrations, you'd at least position yourself sensibly—back and to the side."

"I broke promise."

"What are you doing with the Muslims?"

"Yes, I am one like themselves."

Even though she had an Indonesian name and called herself Peranakan Tionghoa, Vern had kept the stereotypic idea of her being either a Buddhist or a Christian if her heritage was Chinese—surely not a Muslim. Doubtlessly, her father had become a Muslim for business reasons in this Islamic country, but perhaps Yanti took it all seriously. "Are you a santri Muslim?"

Yanti laughed. "No. I pray sometimes Friday noon. But politically I am good Muslim and Muslim is against Reds."

At least she is traditionally Chinese in her pragmatism, Vern thought. "Yanti, go home," he told her with the severity of a father.

"No."

"Your father wouldn't like this. There could be violence. Believe me, Yanti. I've seen it. Crowds get out of hand."

"I go where brothers and sisters go."

He stared hard at her, then at the street churning with exuberant young people like herself. "All right," he said with a sigh of defeat.

"But position yourself better. To the side and rear of the march."

"You care for me, Mr. Gardner." Her voice carried in its tone not a question but a statement, as if she had thought a long time about him before they'd met here in the dusky street of crisis.

"Sure I care."

"You like me much."

"Well, sure I like you. I don't want you to get hurt."

"Can I come see you? We talk about architecture."

"No."

"I will come see you. What time tomorrow?"

"Yanti."

"At five in evening. Is five okay for you?"

He nodded but she was gone before he could add something cautionary, something avuncular and neutral to establish certain parameters for the visit. He watched her run back to the line of marchers—directly into their midst, not to the side and rear—and join without hesitation in the loud chanting that grew as resonant and irresistible as a pounding succession of ocean waves: "CRUSH THE PKI! CRUSH THE PKI! CRUSH THE PKI! CRUSH THE PKI!"

Thirty-four

After hearing a radio account of the funeral services, Maggie got out of bed and with Inam's assistance walked a little for the first time. She insisted on sitting outside under the roofing overhang while a steady drizzle tattooed the galvanized tin above her head. She had with her one of her favorite books—Malinowski's study of the Trobriand Islanders, a classic analysis of society and a groundbreaking attack on the evolutionary approach to kinship behavior. Maggie read awhile, taking comfort from the pattering rain as well as from the slow, heavy, systematic anthropology of Malinowski. It was like being back home in the Midwest, a student among the college library stacks, catching a glimpse of afternoon rain through the window.

But not quite. It was not all that cozy here with a shadow of uncertainty lying across each moment of recent time. During her recuperation, Maggie had felt walled off emotionally from what was happening beyond the courtyard. People came to see her, all right, but employed their Javanese deviousness to the obvious goal of sparing Nonya Maggie details of the crisis. Which only made her more nervous. A few of Susanto Sakirman's gambling buddies had showed up, but they seemed indifferent to anything other than dice and cards. People came from the batik factory and retained their reserve. Mas Slamat had proved the most willing if not the most reliable source of information.

The dalang had never come again after the first morning, having gone to Solo on business. He had not yet returned (Inam checked to make sure). Ali had not yet reappeared in Yogya either.

Her language teacher came every day, but refused to discuss anything except the meaning of words in at least two forms—for example, *abot* (Ngoko) and *awrat* (Krama) for "difficult"—and a series of sentences that she must memorize without fail, whatever her state of health.

During pauses in her reading, Maggie repeated one of them: *"Layange wis tekan, durung?"* ("Did the letter get here yet or not?"). It was a question she often asked Inam, even though no mail was coming from Jakarta. Another sentence she meant to use often was *Isa apa ora?* (Can it be done or not?). If the crisis continued, that would be a basic question.

Maggie laid the book in her lap and stared at the intensely green garden, wet and drooping beneath the roiling sky. Inam had put beside her chair a small table with the record player on it; a long, snaky black extension cord led into the pavilion. There were half a dozen discs beside her. She put one on and grimaced at the scratchy sound. She needed replacements for the records brought out here, but there was no chance of getting them now.

While she carefully lowered the arm onto the Johnny Dodds Washboard Band's rendition of "Bucktown Stomp," Maggie thought grimly of the difference, anywhere in Asia, between the priorities of a native and a foreigner. The native looked at things from a life-and-death perspective; the foreigner through habit focused on comfort. She was annoyed by the crisis, because phonograph records would be even harder to get; Ali saw in it a potential for losing everything, even his life. Well, she wasn't that callous; no need to take upon yourself the guilt of his nation and your own, Maggie thought. Even so, while the jaunty rhythms of "Bucktown Stomp" filled the drizzly air, she wished for commitment such as many Indonesians must have to their beliefs during this crisis; and the idea of commitment brought Bix Beiderbecke to mind. He had thought only of his music; that's what everyone who knew him said. He lived for something beyond his own needs, like the artist he was, as a patriot must or as a mother does or great scholars and actors do or like anyone who sees beyond the immediate horizon into another world and sets out for it. As she had never done. As the voice behind the door had always told her to do. As she would do someday?

Roused from this reverie when the record came to the end, Maggie lifted the phono arm and shut off the machine. Fatigued, she nearly fell asleep and would have done so had not Inam appeared to announce in a brisk manner that someone was here to see her. It had to be Mas Slamat; when he came for a visit, the girl's voice took on this particular tone of brisk impatience, as if she were attempting to hide her disapproval while warning Nonya Maggie to be careful. Maggie knew what the Sakirman household thought of Mas Slamat.

He came onto the veranda with his porkpie hat in one hand, his rolled umbrella in the other. His toothless gums were chomping, as if he were putting the finishing touches on a speech. But when he came up to Maggie's chair and took the one opposite, Mas Slamat said nothing, just turned his face slightly toward the garden so that his gaze came at her sideways and enhanced the impression he gave of guile, cunning, evasiveness.

Maggie smiled at him. Mas Slamat had visited her faithfully every day. "Do you think I'm better?" she asked.

He studied her imperiously, mouth pursed. "You will be better if you listen to me." He took a small amulet from his shirt pocket. Opening it—an oval of plated tin with a cheap tin chain—Mas Slamat removed a piece of paper and handed it to Maggie.

She unfolded it.

"Notice," said Mas Slamat, "the numbers add up in all directions to fifteen. Fifteen is magical."

This is what Maggie saw:

		FIRE		
	8	3	4	
AIR	1	5	9	EARTH
	6	7	2	
		WATER		

"R. Harjanta Prijohoetomo, director of the World Peace Radiating Center, made this magic square. Kindly please notice the powerful five in the middle," urged Mas Slamat. "To cure your fever the holy man wrote numbers up, down, to the side, crossways, starting with squares from the south where water is. He gives it to you with his blessing. You must wear it in amulet, and if you do this, your fever"— he raised his hands and swept them out to the sides—"vanish. It is certain."

Taking the amulet from him, she refolded the magic square and placed it inside the tin oval, saying, "Thank you, my good friend, and thank the holy man."

"You needn't pay R. Harjanta Prijohoetomo for it. It is a gift."

After wondering if the holy man expected payment, Maggie figured it was too late to offer it now—that would be an insult—so she said, "I am honored," and held the amulet up high. "Thank him for it. It's very special and I realize how special it is."

"When will you see him?" It sounded more like a command than a question.

"When I'm better. After the magic square does its work." She fastened the chain behind her neck; the amulet hung at the hollow of her throat.

"You will need R. Harjanta Prijohoetomo to help you through difficult times," Mas Slamat declared. Hunching forward, the little man began a gloomy analysis of the political crisis. It was surely the fault of the Communists. All newspapers in Jakarta were now banned, except the army-sponsored *Angkatan Bersenjata* and *Berita Yudha;* the Red paper, *Harian Rakyat,* had supported the coup and revealed the Communists to be in league with the devil. That's what Mas Slamat said—*in league with the devil*. And he reported that here in Central Java some army men sympathetic to the Reds had kidnapped and strangled top-ranking officers of a local division. Now the chief of intelligence, a known Communist, had taken charge of the 7th Diponegoro Division, giving the PKI tremendous advantage in the struggle for control of military forces in the region. Mas Slamat spoke as if, after memorizing the facts, he had rehearsed telling them to Maggie. She knew he wanted praise; so she praised him for his knowledge of the situation.

In response, Mas Slamat sat back with an empty-mouthed smile and fingered his mole. "There is little of value I don't know. Some people may know languages, but they haven't experience of human nature and access to information that I do. I am unique, Nonya."

"Yes," Maggie agreed, "you are."

"The acting governor of Central Java is Sujono Atmo, also a Communist," Mas Slamat added, as if to confirm his unique access to information. "But you must not worry. We will not let those people take over."

"We?" she asked, but there wasn't time for him to reply, because Inam appeared on the veranda again. She bent and whispered into Maggie's ear. "It is your friend from the village. Should he wait?"

Before Maggie could decide, Ali came rushing across the courtyard. After a quick glance at Mas Slamat he came forward and shook Maggie's hand vigorously, the way he might shake the hand of a Western man. "How are you?" he asked breathlessly in Bahasa. "I have been organizing in the fields, so I couldn't come, but you seem—" He struggled for an appropriate word. "You look proper," he said in English.

She introduced the two men. For a while they floundered with language. Maggie knew enough Javanese now to realize they were attempting to establish status (even Ali, the Communist) by using Krama, then Ngoko, settling after a few stumbling sentences on the more formal Krama, which meant they had decided to behave warily but as respectful equals for the time being. After Ali had taken a chair at his side, Mas Slamat leaned forward, slipped a cigarette from a pack for himself, then thrust it at Ali. Ali took one from the pack and leaned forward quickly to offer Mas Slamat a light.

To Maggie their actions, so stylized, seemed choreographed. Their conversation followed a similar pattern as they located each other's relatives geographically and probed to uncover relationships that might bring understanding. Maggie had never seen Ali operate as a priyayi until now. It helped her to understand the conflict in him: the Communist worker who was the son of an aristocrat.

Finally, the two men sat back with faint smiles that told her they were satisfied; and it occurred to Maggie that although they had arrived at such equanimity through a complex ritual, perhaps it enabled them to establish contact more effectively than Western men, coming from disparate interests, could have managed in such a short time.

She wondered if, in front of Mas Slamat, it would be indiscreet to ask Ali about the present crisis. She was beginning to know some things about the Javanese, and this knowledge made her cautious, especially since it was unsystematic and often more baffling than helpful. She knew, for example, that people usually thought in Ngoko, though they spoke more often in Krama. The tendency in Ngoko was to abbreviate, in Krama to expand. To call a person by name rather than by kinship or occupational name was to be familiar, almost intimate. Physical orientation in space was a vital part of Javanese well-being; to convey a feeling of confusion, therefore, you described it in terms of direction, of losing your way. But from the trivia she had picked up so far, Maggie couldn't figure out the conversational ethics of a situation like the one in which the three of them now found themselves: the country stood on the verge of civil war; Muslim and Red were acknowledged enemies; and representatives of those factions were sitting here on opposite sides of a sick, rawboned gal from Iowa.

But she ought to have known that unpredictable Java would provide a ready solution.

Ali began talking openly about the crisis. Just like that. As if discussing the weather. In English he gave his listeners what he called an up-to-date report. It was perfectly clear at last, Ali told them, that the 30th of September Movement was an internal problem for the army. The PKI had not been involved; that, too, was perfectly clear. The Politburo, only yesterday, had released a statement calling on all party members to cooperate fully with authorities and to support without fail the president's appeal for unity and calm.

"To support Bung Karno's appeal for unity, the calm, and the peace," he said.

Having rephrased this vital point to include peace, Ali continued. Just this morning (his voice was slow and measured, suggesting recitation from a prepared text), the Regional Committee in Yogya had denied any Communist involvement in the attempted coup.

"The governor of Central Java"—Ali turned to look directly at Mas Slamat—"is member of the party."

340

"Sujono Atmo. *Acting* governor," the little man corrected.

That did not deter Ali, who went on in the same low patient tone, as if speaking to bright but misinformed children. "The governor call on local officials to help armed forces." Ali tapped one fisted hand against the other palm. "What more can PKI do to prove faith?" He smiled shyly at Mas Slamat: it was an appeal for approval, Maggie felt.

The little man regarded Ali thoughtfully, and then, as if reaching a decision, let his toothless mouth curl into an answering smile. "Good faith is good faith whoever shows it. I saw you in the streets demonstrating after the coup."

"Yes, I carried banner. Our local PKI supported purge."

"Purge?"

"Of generals who plotted against government."

"Quite right to do so," Mas Slamat agreed.

Maggie was surprised by his complacency. She had previously understood Mas Slamat to be an aggressive Muslim, ready to slaughter the Reds at a moment's notice, but here he was agreeing with Ali's explanation, which she recognized (and surely so did cunning little Mas Slamat) as the PKI's hasty cover-up of a political goof.

She might have been pleased by this newfound show of tolerance—might have if she hadn't known how devious Mas Slamat could be. Then suddenly she wondered what he meant. Quite right to demonstrate? Or quite right to kill the generals? Mas Slamat had left his opinion floating in air. It disturbed her then and continued to make her feel uneasy after Mas Slamat rose and cut short his visit.

"What did you think of him?" Maggie asked Ali as they watched Mas Slamat amble away at his curious gait, a sailor maneuvering along a rolling deck.

"He seemed to prove, I mean approve, to approve PKI policy," Ali said in English.

"Do you think so? Do you think he was sympathetic?" Ali's lack of skepticism alarmed her; it made him seem vulnerable.

"Nation will starting to be sympathetic."

"There have been arrests of party members in Jakarta, Ali. Burning and looting of PKI buildings. They looted Aidit's house. I heard it on the radio. I'm sure you know that."

"I go on with land reform. That is assignment and I still do it."

"I'm worried about you."

"Worried?" Ali chortled contemptuously.

"This is a volatile situation."

"Volatile?"

"Changeable. You could be in great danger. All it would take is for people to suddenly blame everything wrong in this country on the Communists. It could happen. And where would you be, Ali?"

He assured her that he was safe in the village. As a respected maker of gamelan instruments, his brother, Bambang, had considerable influence among the villagers. Moreover, the Gitosuwoko family had lived in the region for generations.

Of course that was true—and Ali's insouciance was aristocratic. Perhaps this Communist thing is a passing phase, Maggie thought, and Ali will ultimately return to his priyayi roots, take up the responsibilities of noblesse oblige, and defend the family honor into a ripe old age. That made more sense than his blind acceptance of rebellion. She just hoped that Ali would get through this present crisis without incident. Maggie was three or four years older than Ali, yet she felt much older. In spite of the dangerous course he had set himself on, Ali seemed to lack any real sense of that danger—a sure sign of immaturity. His family history had put an embroidered veil between him and the real world. He was like a normally wild animal that has been raised as a pet and is now thrown back into the jungle. She feared for him, but could say nothing. Even so, when he rose to leave, she thrust her hand out eagerly for him to take. Ali held it longer than propriety would dictate—they both knew it—so she gave him a reassuring smile, as if to say, "Everything is all right. We are friends and can feel this way."

Alone again, Maggie noticed the clouds pulling asunder in the west; a slice of lustrous blue appeared in the gap, followed by iridescent sunlight pouring down on the dripping garden. Maggie had always loved the beauty of late afternoon when gray skies opened up and let the sunlight in, a soft golden glow spreading across the greenery like butter. In spite of fever, which left her forehead dry and prickly, Maggie felt as though her veins were suffused with light too, bathed in it, refreshed by it. She had always liked the poetry of Keats. Fragments came to mind now and then, just as one did now: "Rich in the simple worship of a day." Keats meant passionate life to her; his doomed love for Fanny Brawne had seemed the essence of heartbreak and romantic tragedy.

Funny thing, but Vern liked the romantic poets too, perhaps because in college he'd had to take a humanities elective and so during registration had chosen at random Romantic Poetry I. Naturally, so Maggie thought, his favorite among the romantics was Blake, the toughest of them—someone who could write (and Vern quoted this line often in defense of his blunt philosophy of progress): "Drive your cart and your plow over the bones of the dead." Good old Vern. She welcomed his presence in her mind, especially during this lovely sunset. He was, of course, the man she really wanted.

That certitude lasted an hour. Once again Inam came across the courtyard with an announcement; this time, in awe, she stammered it out. The dalang was here.

So there was another ambush lying in wait for Maggie. She wasn't prepared for her reaction to the sight of that man striding across the courtyard in his batik sarong and blouse and Javanese headgear that fit snugly against his skull, with handkerchief-like ends poking behind each ear. She watched in a kind of stunned wonder: his big, broad feet in their sandals coming across the muddy ground, his mouth set in determination, one square hand gripping a package, his eyes fixed utterly on her—that was plain before she could even see the whites— the steady gaze of someone accustomed to meditating on a single bead of thought.

Ambushed by her feelings.

By the time Dalang Budi had crossed the courtyard, Maggie had worked herself into a shy, defensive mood. Even so, she smiled as he approached and she could feel her mouth tighten in a conscious effort to smile even more. When she spoke to him, it was not shyly at all but in a surprisingly bold tone of annoyance. "I missed you in the last few days. Where have you been?"

He didn't seem to comprehend her mood—at least he didn't react to it—but sat down in the chair that Mas Slamat had recently occupied. He answered with casual directness that he had been in Solo making funeral arrangements for an old dalang who had been a close friend of the family. "I am so glad to see you looking so well. So much better." Accompanied by a warm smile his words seemed to mean more; he might have been saying, "You look beautiful." Maggie felt the heat suffusing her face and hated the lack of control it represented. In an effort to regain control, she moved their conversation to neutral ground. "What do you think of the crisis?" When he looked at her in a puzzled way, Maggie wondered if he understood what she was talking about. If not, he was the only person in Indonesia who wouldn't react today to the word "crisis." There was no telling what he did know.

"I wonder," she began again, "if the crisis is widespread or if it's chiefly in Jakarta."

"Jakarta affects the villages. We're a nation dominated politically by one city, and that's a problem. If there's violence in Jakarta, people in villages think they should have violence, too." His comments, although reasonable, seemed curiously detached, as if he were a historian commenting on events of a millennium ago.

"So you expect violence in the Yogya area?"

"Nothing has happened that I know of. But I told Ali he should leave our village for a while."

"You told him? When?"

"Today. This morning."

"He never told me you met today. He never said you'd returned to Yogya. He was here just a while ago."

"My nephew won't listen to me; perhaps he will to you if you explain the danger."

"I have. He seems to believe the family name can protect him."

"So it will if things go as they should. Of course, that's not always possible."

"Not here or anywhere."

"Especially not here." The dalang reached out and gave her the wrapped package. "To help you recuperate."

So he was gone and what he had left behind was circling on the turntable: Benny Goodman's Carnegie Hall Concert of 16 January 1938.

Somehow the dalang had found a copy of the Goodman concert and one of Miles Davis and John Coltrane recorded in 1958. Astonished, she had told him he really was a magician to have found American jazz records in Surakarta, Indonesia. With that blend of humility and arrogance she was learning to expect of him, Budi explained that he had found them through luck *and* intuition gathering dust on the cluttered back table of a sundries store. Obviously he had combed Solo for them.

Dalang Budi. Sweet man. He accomplished this miracle in Surakarta, Indonesia, in the midst of a national crisis.

Yet she felt different about him now. There was no problem there, she decided. It had only seemed so when she had had that initial look at him today. She was less vulnerable than yesterday and felt a renewed self-confidence that coincided with a sweaty forehead: her fever had broken. Had the magic square from the World Peace Radiating Center really worked? She touched the amulet dangling at her throat.

So she was herself again. And there was no reason why she couldn't remain right here a while longer, crisis or no crisis, near the sultan's kraton and the bird market and the narrow winding streets of Yogya where there were people like Mas Slamat and she could study Javanese and learn the secrets of a great if strange civilization and somehow work for the restoration of Borobudur, because that had occurred to her often during the long hours in bed, and somehow she could remain steadfastly committed to the restoration of Borobudur; yes, the rescue of a great monument to the human spirit that she truly believed it was; it would be a commitment, and she could have further conversations with Dalang Budi, whom she no longer feared, but with whom she might share thoughts about music and wayang and commitment to principles among other things and . . . and . . . find whatever it was the voice behind the door was urging her to find before going back to the man she really loved.

Thirty-five

Ali was sure that the Communist party would survive the Night of the Generals, yet each day brought more bad news, a deepening of the crisis, even out here in the villages of Central Java.

Rumors grew more outrageous as they moved along the rural roads: Bung Karno had been murdered; an advance guard of invading Malaysian troops was already on the outskirts of Yogya; the CIA had bombed all the airports. As yet, however, Ali hadn't heard of violence in the surrounding villages. He continued to plan for agrarian reform, explaining to skeptical farmers the necessity of strengthening peasant groups for the implementation of land-grant law, holding seminars on bank loans and the establishment of courts that would bring greedy landlords to justice, tacking up PKI posters on trees leading to the fields, becoming a daily presence in the lives of villagers. But often, as Ali hurried along dusty lanes, he felt eyes on him.

This uneasy feeling augmented a sense of failure in Ali Gitosuwoko. He had come back to the ancestral village with a vision: class struggle in the countryside would bring higher wages, lower rents and interest rates, the transfer of land to peasants who worked it, and finally a

346

return, under patronage of the PKI, to the old concept of spontaneous cooperation, gotong royong, by which Javanese farmers had helped one another for centuries. He had believed in the PKI's rural offensive, in the political realization of the Six Goods: social and economic programs that would benefit the illiterate poor. But landlords had statistically transferred acreage marked for peasant distribution to their sycophant stooges, the kakitangan, and to distant relatives whom they had never met and to business associates who resided in the graveyard, thereby circumventing the agrarian law through bogus registry of excess land. Peasants who had never received their legal minimum of five acres because of this deception were unwilling to confront their oppressors. Indeed, when Ali talked to them they preferred to defend the local landowners rather than support someone who had come from Jakarta.

And Ali discovered in himself a dismaying tendency (typical, he was painfully aware, of the urban priyayi class) to look upon wong desa—the village peasant—as an ignorant dolt who couldn't be helped. Ali began to understand (or rather to remember from childhood) how ambition and ingenuity often ruined a peasant. If, say, a village farmer got hold of a new fertilizer that yielded better crops, he went against traditional community practices, and his independent success effectively ostracized him from the only life he knew. On the other hand, one way to establish superiority over his fellows was to live without doing manual labor. Having nothing to do was ultimately a positive value.

The village offered other irritants to a young utopian. There was the old woman who decades ago had been the mistress of a Dutch official. A title of nobility was still used by people when addressing her. This had always been the honor conferred by villagers on someone who had climbed so high. And then there was nightly gambling in smoky huts of plaited bamboo, sometimes resulting in massive wins and losses that were responsible for blood feuds carried on from generation to generation—alliances, intrigues, brooding jealousies that hamstrung officials who sought cooperation for public projects. Somehow politicized in the back lanes of remote villages, gambling debts prevented the building of dams needed for irrigation and of bridges over local rivers otherwise forded after as much as a half day's journey up or downstream.

Ali struggled with his impatience, his dismay, his growing pessimism until a larger reality confronted him at last: Comrade Pramu called a meeting at Yogya headquarters.

Or rather at a side-street warung, not headquarters—and with the messenger's admonition to maintain absolute secrecy. This prepared Ali for something unusual. Suddenly the world beyond his village loomed large again in his mind. He was ready for anything.

Even so, Ali was stunned when he drew a bamboo curtain aside and walked into the back room of the warung. Sitting at a table with Comrade Pramu, the district chief, was a bespectacled mild-looking man whom he had heard speak many times but from afar, Chairman D. N. Aidit of the PKI.

At university Ali had come under the paternal tutelage of a professor who espoused communism and whose influence had brought the young student from Yogya into the party. When the professor died, in a private pantheon of heroes Ali had replaced him with Chairman Aidit. Here, in Ali's estimation, was a messianic ruler, the legendary Ratu Adil, come at last to create the utopia that Ali's father had traditionally described in the prelude to wayang dramas: the *Panjang punjung pasir wukir loh jinawi gemah ripah karta tur raharja,* a land of power and fertility, peace and justice, bound together by the will of a virtuous king. That had been Chairman Aidit, speaking from podiums in Jakarta about the new day of Communist rule. Ali had heard in these impassioned words a description of the ideal world of wayang, with himself as part of it, contributing in a small way to its creation.

Here he was, having just touched the hand of such a visionary who could—would—bring the new world about. Aidit, on meeting him (they were coolly introduced by Comrade Pramu), had congratulated Ali for leading a PKI demonstration through Yogya on the day after the coup attempt. Congratulated him. And he was sitting in the chairman's presence almost as an equal. Ali was so overwhelmed by his good fortune that he scarcely noticed the arrival of someone else. This was M. H. Lukman, first deputy chairman of the PKI, a minister of state in Sukarno's cabinet.

Lukman swept back unruly hair from a sallow forehead. He seemed breathless, a state accentuated by his gaunt appearance. Lukman had just arrived in Yogya and had come to this meeting with news of an emergency cabinet session held at the palace in Bogor.

Ali realized with astonishment that he was going to hear Lukman's report at the same time that the chairman heard it. It was like becoming important within an instant.

Lukman, sipping a cup of hot tea, began to talk. "At the meeting I read our official statement. I disassociated us from the arrest of the generals. As we agreed," he said to Aidit, "I called it an internal affair of the army."

"How was the statement received?" Aidit asked, his glance momentarily on Ali, which gave him a thrill.

"Politely," replied Lukman after a thoughtful pause. "But suspiciously, I think. Then as chairman of the provisionary parliament, I read a statement prepared by Vice Marshal Dhani."

"Is Dhani still free?"

"He turned his plane around and flew back to Halim. I don't know the details," said Lukman, smiling for the first time, "but somehow he got to the palace. He's there now under Sukarno's protection."

"What did Dhani's statement say?"

"That he's ordered the arrest of air force officers responsible for training Communists at Halim."

Aidit laughed sourly. "Officers *he* ordered to do the training." The chairman quoted an old proverb. "When a dead tree falls, the woodpeckers share in its death."

"You think Dhani will fall?"

"Of course. He's a dead man. How did Sukarno behave at the session?"

"Frightened."

"Frightened? I'm surprised. I can imagine him being many things, but not frightened."

"Frightened, conciliatory. And devious."

Aidit laughed ruefully. "Of course."

"He let the foreign minister do most of the talking. Speaking for him, Subandrio called the murders barbarous. He claimed through Subandrio he never condoned the formation of a revolutionary council."

Aidit shrugged and murmured, "Well," as if all this were obvious.

"Subandrio urged a political solution to the crisis. No retaliation against the rebels. No bloodbaths."

Aidit smiled uncertainly. "That would be nice. The question we all must ask is this: Does Sukarno still have any influence?"

"Yes, that's the question."

They fell silent. Comrade Pramu, sitting next to Ali on chairs distanced from the table, whispered to him, "Have more tea brought in."

He treats me like a servant, Ali thought bitterly, yet got up and went into the warung to order tea in a brisk tone of command. The three men in the back room were from the Generation of 45, and therefore no matter how hard he tried, they would never accept him. They had been raised during the turbulence of Japanese occupation and had emerged from World War Two mentally tough, prepared to fight for independence. Instead of formal education they had been given military training by their conquerors; instead of theory they possessed the practical knowledge of survivors. He envied them that. Turning to reenter the back room, Ali felt inadequate, so much so that he wanted to run out of the warung and go straight back to his village.

When he returned and sat down silently next to Comrade Pramu, Lukman was droning on in his dispassionate way. He was describing to Chairman Aidit what had happened in Jakarta on the day that Nasution's five-year-old daughter, dead of gunshot wounds, was buried in the Heroes' Cemetery. Admiral Eddy Martadinata, a determined foe of communism, had whispered to young Muslim leaders present at the funeral, *"Sikat"* ("Sweep"). Lukman reported that Muslim students had done just that against Communist strongholds in Jakarta: swept through, looted, and burned official buildings as well as the private residences of PKI officers—his own and Aidit's included. PKI and SOBSI headquarters were now ashes, and so were Pemuda Rakyat and Gerwani dormitories. Fourteen colleges with avowed Reds on their faculties had been closed. Demonstrators marched daily through the streets calling for the ouster of Reds from national politics. Lukman paused. "And calling for your execution. Mine as well."

Taking off his glasses, Aidit cleaned them carefully with the corner of a handkerchief. "Go on," he said quietly.

"Northern Sumatra is bad."

"Well." Aidit waved his hand through the air as if in casual comment about the weather. "Muslim country."

"Aceh is very bad. There are reports of a massacre up there."

Aidit turned to him with a startled look.

"Yes. A General Djuarsa says—" Lukman took out a piece of paper and read from it. " 'Due to the quick and appropriate action of the people of Aceh the region is already cleared of counterrevolutionary G 30 S elements.' " Lukman pursed his lips thoughtfully. "From the sketchy reports we're getting from there, the general has massacred almost all the Communists in Aceh." Again Lukman paused. "I estimate fifteen hundred. Of course, we've never been strong there, but fifteen hundred—" He let the estimate hang in the close air like a dirty rag.

Ali caught Chairman Aidit smiling at him. At first Ali was surprised, then understood that the smile was impersonal, an involuntary expression of nerves.

"Now," said Lukman, running a hand through his black hair, "we have to worry about the army here in Yogya." He nodded to Comrade Pramu, who was so proud to be called on that he jumped up at attention.

"According to my information, the army is getting stronger," Pramu admitted. What happened yesterday was proof of that, he told the chairman. Three officers who had supported the 30th of September Movement returned to divisional headquarters and confessed their error. "They begged forgiveness on their knees."

"Go on," said Aidit when Pramu hesitated.

"The local commander is trying to persuade other rebels to do the same. He promises if they surrender, they'll be welcomed with open arms."

"You believe that?"

"No. But he has a reputation for cleverness."

"You think he'll succeed?"

"I do, comrade."

Aidit sighed. To Ali he seemed abruptly old and tired, almost detached from what was happening. And yet within moments another change came over the chairman. He sat up straight and said in a loud, clear voice, "So we must back off and wait. Our people here must cooperate with the army." It was the decision of a resolute man, and Ali felt again that he was in the presence of a hero.

"Avoid actions that make you look rebellious or in any way seem to approve of rebellion," Aidit said.

"That may not be easy," Comrade Pramu told him with a tight little smile. "Some of our villages south of here are panicky."

"What does that mean?"

"I hear rumors."

"Yes, go on," Aidit said impatiently.

"Some of these villages, *our* villages, are threatening a day of naked terror."

"A day of naked terror?"

"That's what they call it. If either the army or the Muslims cause them trouble, they will fight."

"No," Aidit said, shaking his head. "We can't have that."

Pramu was a man who smiled while giving bad news. "If they aren't calmed down, these villagers will definitely fight. They will murder people in the name of the PKI." Leaning forward, Pramu nodded perfunctorily in Ali's direction. "Comrade Gitosuwoko knows these people. I think if he went into their villages and explained our official policy, he might calm them down."

Chairman Aidit turned to the young man. "Can you do that?"

Aware that Pramu had recommended him for the mission because it was risky indeed, Ali met the appraising eyes of his hero and said in a voice so confident it sounded boastful, "Yes, I can do that!"

Thirty-six

Having come into Yogya, Ali wanted to stop off and see Nonya Maggie before returning to the countryside. But there wasn't time, since the Sakirman residence was across town. Only a block from the warung, however, was the home of Mas Slamat, whose address Nonya Maggie had given him. So he hurried there to get the latest word about her recuperation.

Knocking on the door, he waited impatiently for a minute, then turned to leave and was a few steps away when at his back he heard, "I'm here!"

Mas Slamat, his porkpie hat cocked at a jaunty angle, was standing in the doorway, munching his toothless gums and holding an umbrella. "I would ask you in, but I'm on my way to the post office. I'm expecting a letter from America."

Ali thought that was strange, because not a scrap of mail had moved through Java since the crisis had begun. But he said nothing and waited until the little man had joined him before walking in the direction of a becak stand. He asked about Maggie's health. The little man touched his arm reassuringly. "Much better," Mas Slamat said.

"She's a young woman and recovers fast. But where is her husband? That's what I ask myself."

"No one can travel now." For a moment Ali wondered how Lukman had reached Yogya from Jakarta. But of course the party must have underground means of transportation known only to the Politburo. Surely not known to him. Once again Ali felt left out.

"Just the same," Mas Slamat said, "I think her husband stays away too long. She is a young woman."

Ali glanced at him.

"Your uncle brings her music." Mas Slamat looked straight ahead as he waddled along. "That American music. It is terrible music."

"My uncle told me he likes it."

Mas Slamat snorted. "I saw your father perform often. And his father. My father, when he went to court, would allow me to stand under the fig trees near the performing pendopo and watch your grandfather rehearse. You know, of course, where I mean."

Ali knew. There were a few ancient fig trees facing the pendopo where his father and his father's father used to perform wayang for the sultan. Ali had never seen his uncle perform there, not there or anywhere else.

"Permit me this blunt observation," Mas Slamat said. "Your father was a greater dalang than your uncle."

They walked in silence, and it occurred to Ali that he was closer to this strange little man than to anyone in the village. Ali felt saddened by his emotional dependence on ancestry, yet this was the truth: he was comfortable in the company of Mas Slamat with whom he had nothing more in common really than their mutual friendship with an American woman—that and their priyayi background.

When they reached the becak stand, Ali stopped to say good-bye. "Tell Nonya Maggie I will see her when I can."

Mas Slamat nodded, then looked at him sideways with a faint smile. "How are you treated now in the villages?"

"With respect."

"I am glad to hear it."

"People realize we Communists had nothing to do with the murders."

"Then you are safe?"

"Yes, I think I am."

"*La ilaha illa 'llah.* I have seen enough of life to know that chanting the shahadah five times a day is all that really matters. It is true. The Confession of Faith is more powerful than Marx." Mas Slamat detained him further by again touching his arm. "One thing more. The doctrine of Marxism is created by the human mind. So it breeds confusion. Whereas Islam is created by God. It cannot be laid low by the theories of all the theorists in the world."

"That is a matter of opinion," Ali said coolly and met the little man's stare.

"I admired your father. I wish you well."

"And I wish you well."

"God is *Al Ghaib*. So we can't know what our destiny will be."

"*Al Ghaib,*" Ali repeated. "The Mysterious and Unapproachable."

"Then you remember the teachings."

"They were part of my childhood."

Once again Mas Slamat touched his arm; there was a comfortable familiarity about this touch that gave Ali the odd but strong feeling they were like brothers.

"The Prophet taught that all men are equal before God," Mas Slamat said. "Do you believe that?"

"I believe all men are equal before the law."

"If we are equal, God has made us equal. *La ilaha illa 'llah.*" His gums munched silently a few moments. "If you recited the shahadah every day, you would give up Marxism."

"I think not," Ali said, but kept his tone soft, polite.

"I respected your father." Mas Slamat paused, as if struggling with an idea he did not yet understand. Then he repeated himself. "I wish you well. I want you to be safe. We belong in the same world. Nonya Maggie is a nice young foreign woman, but she can never be in our world. I have found her a holy man who will keep her safe until the husband comes."

"Safe?"

"Safe from evil."

"From harm during the crisis?"

"There is more than one kind of crisis. Do you know the old Malay saying? '*Ada laut, ada-lah perompak laut:* Where there is sea, there are

355

pirates.' " Turning slightly, his smile sidelong, Mas Slamat looked like someone engaging in a conspiracy. "But I don't worry about her, because she has friends like us. I worry about you."

Ali smiled.

"No, it is true, I worry about a young inexperienced man like you at a time of such confusion. It is not easy to see the path clearly at such times. And yet I know the remedy for everything. Say the sha-hadah and it will keep you safe. Without it?" He shook his head dramatically.

"Thank you, but I am already safe. What I believe in is right. And my father said if you believe in what is right you are safe from harm. Your soul is."

"Without the shahadah no one is safe. I am making it my business to help you understand that."

The little man was speaking too boldly for a priyayi gentleman; they both knew that members of their class would think he was very rude. Yet Ali, who based his life on the efficacy of conviction, was charmed by Mas Slamat's doggedness, so in High Krama he said politely, "I am grateful for your concern."

After climbing into a becak, Ali waved at the little Muslim who stood in the noon glare, umbrella thrust under his arm, eyes squinting from beneath the felt brim of his hat. Ali smiled in open comradeship as the becak drove away.

Left by the becak at a river crossing, Ali took a ferry, then a bus, and prepared for a five-hour journey southward, more than fifty kilo-meters beyond his own village, to a remote area where, according to Comrade Pramu, a trio of villages, known for their Communist al-legiance, were threatening violence against "running dogs" who had accused the party unfairly of plotting the Night of the Generals. When Ali thought about it on the bus, the mission undertaken so confidently was unlike anything he had attempted in his life: he must persuade men not to seek vengeance against their enemies.

On the hot rattling trip southward he had the time and desire for reflection. His encounter with Mas Slamat had deepened in him a sense of his failure at winning over the peasantry. He had moved too far away from them for too long. He had lost his feeling for their

356

religion, even though intellectually he could trace and understand the appeal of Islam in his homeland.

Five hundred years ago it had freed the common man from bondage to feudal Hindu elitism. All men, according to Islam, were made of the same clay—even the Great Prophet. A fine strong vision, one that had appealed wonderfully to Ali in his youth. It was a religion that honored trade and hard work and cleanliness of body. All such positive aspects of Islam he recognized.

Yet he also knew that it protected landowners more than peasants; it frowned on innovation; it wished to create a state—a Negara Islam—ruled according to outdated principles under an autocratic leadership that willfully neglected contemporary problems. The outcome of such thinking was often a penchant for recklessness and violence. At university he had been appalled by the hotheaded impetuosity of students who followed the Himpunan Mahasiswa Islam into rashly conceived demonstrations against anything that caught their fancy. Now in the villages their less educated counterparts followed the Nahdatul Ulama, a traditional Islamic party that branded everyone who didn't accept its principles—including other Muslims—kafir: nonbelievers, against whom they were ready to fight a Holy War anytime, anywhere. All they lacked was a leader, a slogan, a battle cry.

Ali saw in them what he saw in capitalists: the seeds of discord that bring inequality, bondage, and suffering to a nation. If only he could persuade them that he had the answer. It was that simple. Because he did, he had the answer. It was the certainty of his life. Ali didn't know the extent of his hatred for his uncle. He didn't know the extent of his interest in the foreign woman or, much worse, of his lust for his brother's wife. He didn't know his own potential or recognize fully his own fears and hopes. This alone he knew: that communism was the answer to the problems of his country.

It was late afternoon when Ali's bus drove into the village square. On the outskirts, he had seen a few crows circling a rooftop; that would mean an omen of death to the villagers. In such remote places they bathed their krises with the ritualistic solemnity used to bathe a king; they wore amulets to protect themselves from evil spirits; and they were convinced that some people could change shape into that of animals. On the way in, he noticed that flowers had been scattered at a crossroads to appease genies or ghosts or other monsters of their imagination. His poor country. Its history had been known and symbolized only by what kings did. The splendor of a few fat dissolute tyrants was Java's splendor. He hated that. The people of his villages had been left a legacy of patience by their ancestors but only as grim compensation for lack of human rights and dignity. They had never counted. That's why they had no sense of time, no need to complete actions they had begun. Often he had seen them start something and then blithely walk away. In their faces was a blank stoicism, a turning off of sensation, an escape into dark fields of a dreamland they created from years under a hot flat sky.

Getting off the bus, he noticed two men standing in the shade of a wall; they both held carbines of World War Two vintage, the sort of weapon Ali had often seen in villages. One smoked a cigarette in a bamboo pipe. The other came forward, waiting until the bus drove on before coming up to Ali and harshly demanding to know who he was.

Minutes later Ali sat in a hot, dim room, its door barred with an iron rod. The two men sat opposite him on a bench. An old woman came in with a pot of tea, three glasses.

Then an old man, the village lurah, hobbled in. He took a chair opposite Ali at a small table and, leaning forward, squinted hard. "I see him in you," the chieftain said with a smile. "I saw your father perform many times. Once right here in this village. He did a wayang purwa lakon, *Anuman Duta*. It was for the circumcision ceremony of my third son, the wragil."

The old woman, pouring tea, shook her head. "The panggulu."

"My second son." The old man shrugged, as if indifferent to the correction. "But it was *Anuman Duta*. No one could do *Anuman* like your venerable father. No one ever will. But it cost me to bring him here, let me tell you. Great artists aren't cheap."

"He sold four good cows to pay for that wayang," the old woman said, pausing at the room's back doorway.

A heavyset man shouldered past her and entered. Briskly he identified himself as the local PKI leader. The armed men cleared out at a look from him; so did the old lurah.

Ali understood immediately that the Red leader was self-important, crude, impulsive. What he represented was what Chairman Aidit had always warned against: arrogant independence of cadres in the distant villages. Until there was a sense of unity throughout the nation, the party would suffer. Ali thought about it while the man bragged about his utter domination of this village. It was 90 percent Communist. What other villages could boast of percentages like that? There were only a few followers of the PNI and NU living here. Everyone else supported the PKI.

"That was until yesterday," he added with a satisfied guffaw. "Now we are solid PKI here. Show me another village that can say that." He mentioned the two nearby villages that also backed the Communist party. "We were always closer to a hundred percent than they were. Now we are a hundred percent. What can they say? Only that we are better."

"You are now one hundred percent PKI?" Ali asked slowly, absorbing the idea.

"We are," the leader said proudly.

"What happened?"

"Come along, let me show you."

The leader unbarred the door and led the way through back lanes of the village. Slipped through his belt was a long steel ani, a curved harvesting knife. He talked as they strolled along, while nodding pleasantly to villagers who passed by. "I am tired of rumors. They say troops are coming into the country. If it's war, let it be war. We had a kiyai here. He was always chanting Arabic prayers and wishing for a Holy War. He ran a Quranic school. My own son went to the pesantren awhile because it was the best place to learn reading. But when I heard what the old devil was teaching there, telling the students how evil communism was, I pulled the boy out. We won't have any Holy War here—or troops either. We take care of ourselves like good Marxists. There. There they are."

He had stopped at the edge of a clearing on the village outskirts. Ali followed the leader's gaze to some thickly branched banyan trees. There were dark bundles among the leaves of a tree that assumed the shape of human bodies when Ali stepped closer for a better look. They were naked men hanging from branches, with their hands tied behind their backs, their feet lashed together.

"That one"—the leader pointed—"is the kiyai."

Ali stared aghast at the corpse, which was blackened and swollen, with flies swarming around a multitude of dried gashes on the torso. A bamboo stick protruded from the Muslim teacher's anus.

Ali turned to the PKI leader. Speaking, Ali felt his voice tremble. "What happened here?"

Quietly the leader explained, while they stood beneath the banyan tree, that people had heard enough rumors. If troops were on the way, they had to be met with force. If it was war, then traitors and spies must be done away with, because that was the rule of war. So they had rounded up the six men prominent in village politics who did not belong to the PKI. "Those two"—he pointed upward, squinting as he sought out the right bodies—"were members of Nahdatul Ulama, along with the kiyai, of course. All fanatics. All ready for Holy War. The other three belonged to the national party. We took them into the square and questioned them."

"How did you question them?"

The leader opened his hands out as if explaining something obvious. "Tied them up, beat them a little to get them talking, because the assholes wouldn't talk at first."

"What did you want to learn from them?"

"What they'd tell the troops if any came to the village. Finally we got them all to admit the truth." The leader smiled.

"Which was?"

"They would tell the army anything they were asked."

Ali figured all they could do was identify the other villagers as Reds, something known throughout the region. But from the abrupt hardening of the leader's jawline Ali understood that the PKI supporters in this village were close to panic. Fear gave them the imaginations they ordinarily didn't have. They must have been thinking up all sorts of plots and dangers, culminating in the gratuitous violence that had taken place yesterday in the square and at the banyan tree.

Nevertheless, he almost asked why they had taken the final step—obscenely violating the teacher's body with a bamboo stick. Almost, but did not. Because he understood that the leader would answer only with a shrug, a pursed mouth, a vague explanation. It must have happened suddenly, Ali thought. Someone wildly aroused by blood and pain must have simply broken off a piece of bamboo and rammed it into the dying man without the slightest idea of what he was doing, with nothing more perhaps than a mixed outcry of fear and triumph.

Ali walked away. He stayed the night with the PKI leader and journeyed the next day to the other two villages. Nothing had happened in them yet. He urged the PKI leadership to be cautious, to set an example for the more impulsive Muslims elsewhere in the region, so that people would say, "The Communists are reasonable." But the leadership had already heard of the "Banyan Tree Executions" and seemed eager to emulate that village's boldness. Ali had the sinking feeling that when he left these villages the mayhem would begin.

When he finally arrived home, Ali could not find Narto. His wife said the PKI organizer had gone to the fields early that morning and would not likely return until night. Ali sembahed and left the house. He went to see his brother, although they had scarcely spoken lately.

Bambang was at the foundry, and upon seeing Ali, he began to scowl. Nevertheless, he came out of the hot smoky room and squatted with Ali along a shaded wall, near the courtyard where workmen were chasing some finished gongs. Ali had not intended to say anything about the murders at the banyan tree, but within seconds he blurted it out, hearing in his voice the disgraceful trembling that revealed the depth of his horror, anguish, despair.

Bambang listened in silence, staring down at his charcoal-blackened hands. When Ali paused, Bambang turned and said softly, "There is nothing you can do. Nothing anyone can do now. It will come."

"You mean, violence?"

"I feel it coming. Everyone feels it."

"I don't understand what's happening."

"Of course it's hard for you, brother. You believed in something, but now you don't know what to believe in."

"I believe in Marxism," Ali said defiantly, but even he could hear the forced confidence in his voice.

"The battalions have returned from Jakarta," Bambang said. "But Achmad didn't come home."

"What happened to him?"

"Achmad deserted." Bambang intertwined his big knobby fingers and looked hard at them, as if at something he had never seen before. "He was there at the Night of the Generals. Then he disappeared. If they catch him, they will execute him."

"I don't understand."

They sat awhile in silence. Ali felt closer to his brother than he had in a long time, perhaps because they shared an ignorance of why such things were happening in their world. Achmad was a soldier if he was anything, yet at a time of crisis he had deserted his unit. The Communist party represented sanity, progress, a chance for the future, yet its followers had brutally and senselessly murdered their fellow villagers. And violence hovered in the air like those nameless plagues in ancient Java that threatened the known world if saints did not preach them away in the nick of time. Ali understood nothing, but at least he sat beside his brother against the sun-heated wall and they felt each other's confusion, sadness, fear.

As they were sitting there, a farmer hurried up, his mouth working excitedly before he reached them. "Narto!" he shouted at Ali. The farmer was a Red sympathizer who sometimes attended Ali's little gatherings to talk about the land grants that hadn't been made. "Narto! We found him in a ditch, his throat cut with an ani." The farmer waved his own ani through the air as if acting out the murder.

Ali got to his feet. "Who did it?"

The farmer shook his head. "Narto was working in the northern fields this morning. We found him in a drainage ditch west of there. They really cut deep. His head's only held on by some skin. You should see it."

"They? Who are they?"

"I don't know. But they almost cut his head right off."

Beyond the farmer's shoulder Ali could see a man standing under a tree. He was a short, thin man whose face had a bluish tint under the shading branches. He was a tukang-idjon, a moneylender who journeyed from village to village, buying future crops from local farmers at dirt-cheap prices. This particular moneylender worked for an army organization. Ali had put a major effort into warning the villagers of the man's machinations. They had never met. Now they stared at each other across the courtyard. The tukang-idjon was smiling; he must have heard that a Red had been murdered in the fields today.

362

"Be careful."

Ali looked at his brother's square, brooding face.

Bambang repeated the warning, this time in a surprisingly gentle voice. "Be careful, brother. It has begun."

Ali nodded, turning to stare again at the blue man beneath the tree. "Yes, it's come here now."

Thirty-seven

"**P**lease, madam, be so kind as to wait here," said the small, immaculate, austere woman, "and I will see if it is possible." Taking the letter from Maggie, she left the room. Had the language been Dutch or French or German instead of English, the words coming out of that elegant Javanese mouth, Maggie guessed, would have been just as formal, just as correct.

Maggie sat in the waiting room of a brick mansion called the Pangeranan, the Prince's House, near the Pura Mangunegaran, the palace of the junior line of the royal family of Surakarta. The Pangeranan was a complex of buildings connected by open corridors: a larger, grander, older, and far seedier place than the Sakirman manor. Maggie understood that in prewar days, when the Dutch still employed royalty as governmental figureheads, this dalem had sustained a staff of fifty people; now it was the residence of one old woman, Ibu Pangeran, or Madam Prince, whose deceased husband, a prince, had once been a high official in Solo.

Wiping her forehead, Maggie fought the possibility that she was still too weak to undertake this kind of thing. After all, she had been out of bed less than a week. The doctor had cautioned her to go slow, though recovery from malarial relapse was usually swift.

Maggie felt there wasn't time to lose; if she was going to accomplish anything, she must do it now. Vern might send for her any day; his message via the U.S. Consulate had said all was well in Jakarta. The local newspaper in Yogya had claimed yesterday that "a solution to the crisis was imminent." Of course, this contradicted Inam's reports of clubbings and stranglings on the road, midnight raids in kampongs, slaughter with curved harvest knives in the fields. Having listened politely to the wide-eyed girl, Maggie chose to believe the newspapers.

On the third day out of bed, she had accompanied Mas Slamat to the holy man's house. It was on a side street with life-sized cement statues of the bird-god Garuda and the clown-god Semar at the entrance.

There was a frightful clutter inside, rivaling that of Mas Slamat's house. The tiny front room was dominated by the holy man's desk on which sat an empty aquarium. Dry rocks inside it were covered with dust, and as Maggie sat on a bench beside Mas Slamat awaiting the holy man, she wondered if the empty aquarium and dusty rocks and great piles of smudged paper and half-filled tea glasses—five or six of them—and ashtrays overflowing with cigarette butts constituted some kind of cosmic statement. She was not prepared to believe in anything the holy man said. And while waiting for him, Maggie wondered why she had come in the first place. Curiosity, of course. And Borobudur. Otherwise, there was no point in the visit. She was not a gullible American ready to sign up for a course in Enlightenment. She had no illusions; she had never yearned for immersion in some kind of oceanic unity with the divine. She didn't believe in salvation. She believed in surrendering to an idea that had a goal, because that made life worth living—the zest, the energy, the Bix-like concentration that come from commitment to something on this earth.

So when the holy man finally appeared, wearing a peaked wool cap in the stifling heat, and a filthy checked shirt and baggy Western corduroy pants, Maggie was ready for everything but belief.

He offered her a cigarette, and Maggie took it because Mas Slamat had solemnly warned her that to refuse a cigarette from the holy man was to lose any chance of getting his help. Obediently she lit up. But the tea brought by a little boy was daunting; it contained so much sugar that some separated out like sand.

While the room filled with thick smoke, she listened to the holy man's monologue—for that's what conversation was to him—punctuated often by grunting chortles of satisfaction. He did not waste time on a prelude to his philosophy, but launched into his primary belief, which was that Java was the spiritual hope of the world. Salvation depended on Java because it and it alone was the source of every major religion. How could this be true if you considered Buddhism and Hinduism and Islam and Christianity? the holy man asked rhetorically and chuckled. This was true because once upon a time a great continent had contained Africa, the Middle East, South India, Ceylon, Malaya, Sumatra, Java, Tahiti, Hawaii, and Los Angeles. When divine Providence decided to split up the continent by teleological explosion, Java assumed the position of sacred ascendancy. In short, they were now sitting at the hallowed center of the world.

Having delivered himself of this dogma, R. Harjanta Prijohoetomo blew a huge cloud of smoke into the air and said with far more directness than most Indonesians, "What do you want?"

"I want to save Borobudur."

The holy man laughed.

"I mean it, Pak Guru."

"Oh, I can see you do. And why not? I have great respect for Buddhism. Wait a moment." He grabbed a bunch of soiled papers and riffled through them so brusquely that a few got loose and floated down like dirty feathers to the floor. "I have a pamphlet somewhere. It is one of my finest works. 'Generation of World Peace and Prosperity Through the Avatar of Buddha.' I sent it to a conference in Japan, last year I think it was, but they didn't reply. Too unsettling for traditionalists. My ideas contained too much radiating energy. It must have radiated right through them and made them feel as if they were in an earthquake." He guffawed. "Where is that pamphlet?"

While he kept digging through the forest of paper, Maggie said, "My friend Mas Slamat tells me you would be interested in saving Borobudur."

"Me?" The holy man blinked, startled. "I have no money."

"But you know people who do."

And so it was through the World Peace Radiating Center that Maggie got a short letter of introduction to the princess in Surakarta. It was not quite what she wanted, but according to both Mas Slamat and the holy man it would get her an interview, because the princess had such admiration for the work of the center. After a flowery salutation the letter was curt, almost dismissive, surely guarded: "This is to introduce a woman from Los Angeles"—apparently the holy man had a fixation on that city—"who wants money to save Borobudur. In my opinion she seems honest."

With it in hand Maggie resolved to go on her own. She sensed that Mas Slamat, as a traveling companion, might be more trouble than help. She set out the next morning.

Because of the crisis, it was impossible to get a private car to go beyond the city limits, where politics might provide an excuse for hijacking. So Maggie took the local bus early in the morning from a station near the alun-alun. Although hers was only the second stop within town, the bus was nearly full. Passengers grasped their luggage—rope-tied satchels, burlap bags, wicker baskets—the type that was lugged eternally from place to place throughout Asia. This too was Asia, Maggie knew: in the midst of war and revolution and natural disaster, local buses still ran, carrying livestock and people, sacks of rice and bits of cloth.

The bus roared off, and a few kilometers out of Yogya, Maggie saw a massive tower of golden brick rising from the roadside greenery—the ancient Hindu temple of Prambanan—and beyond it, in the far distance, the blue volcano of Loro Jonggrang, like a ghosty double exposure of Prambanan: what man had made and what God had put here merging into one cone-shaped image of serenity.

After confinement to a sickbed, Maggie welcomed the sixty-kilometer ride. She stared through the open window at tobacco fields, where counterbalanced irrigation buckets stood like giant grasshoppers, and at little towns famous for wood carving and at one town famed throughout Java for its tukang gigi shops with their grotesque signs—gaping mouths displaying huge molars and cuspids—advertising the manufacture and installation of wooden false teeth.

After three hours on the bumpy road, the bus rattled into Surakarta. According to the people of this proud city, its sultan remained rightful heir to the ancient kingdom of Central Java, and they resented a like claim from Yogyakarta. During the fight for independence, Solo had remained aloof; indeed, had been suspected of favoring the Dutch, who deeply admired Solonese culture.

To Maggie, as they entered its outskirts, Solo looked like a dreary town, spread out like slabs of gray macadam under the shimmering glare. Squads of becaks patrolled the hot streets, and people under shop roofs of galvanized zinc squinted motionlessly into sunlight as bleak as snow. There were panting dogs, and lathered oxen drawing along gerobak carts. Beauty in Solo, she decided, must be hidden.

Her hotel was large and shabby, the old residence of a prince who used to install his concubines in cottages while he lived in an opposite wing. A set of gamelan instruments was placed along one side of the high open veranda that served as a lobby. In her cottage she found a basket of fruit wrapped in crinkly transparent paper with compliments of the manager written in Bahasa Indonesia. The furniture was heavy, in the Dutch style: big shadowy hulks placed side by side, so that the room appeared much smaller than it was. Electrical wattage was typically low, but sufficient for her to read a notice tacked to her door.

REGULATION THREE: *Be advised it is against State Law 61/ 53 to fetch into this hotel premises a prustitute or prustitutes under any and all circumstanse.*

Maggie wondered if this was one of the cottages in which the prince had installed his women and the notice was a sardonic reminder of that time. Or, more probably, had it been put here in dubious English as an expression of Solonese contempt for the mundane vices of foreigners?

The bed was already turned down, a triangle of spotless white sheet lying against a brown batik coverlet. She stared at the bed, letting her mind thrash around without finding an idea to hold on to. Then she sat on the edge of the bed and stared into the gloom. She was thinking of him. Only he was not Vern, not her husband. And why not Vern? They were sexually compatible; she admired the easy way he embraced a life of adventure; she appreciated his tolerance of her own interests; they shared a liking for Asia. So what the hell was wrong? Nothing. Nothing and nothing and nothing. And yet sitting here in an old Javanese city, she kept thinking of another man. After some college escapades with a number of young men, Maggie had looked forward to steadiness, to a clear road and one man to travel it with, and yet here she sat in this gloomy room in a strange city thinking about a man who made puppets move and who lived the life of a nobleman.

Maggie shook her head, felt her mouth lift into a wry smile. She was letting herself be drawn into the oldest spell of all. Even as she behaved like a fool, she coolly sat back and watched herself do it. Was that what other silly women did too? Was that why men called women silly? And what, then, were men? Even the questions seemed timeless, hackneyed, foolish.

For a while she lay back on the bed and rested, even though she didn't feel tired. She ought to feel tired after the trip, yet she felt only a renewed surge of excitement. Rising, Maggie unpacked her little suitcase and dressed for the hot streets in a white cotton skirt, khaki blouse, sandals, a wide-brimmed straw hat. As she applied lipstick in the murky bathroom, she remembered Mas Salamat saying that Yogyanese men liked to marry snobbish girls from Solo, all of whom were expert in the use of cosmetics. He added, "It is also known that the girls of Solo walk like hungry tigers." And he had given Maggie one of his sly tight smiles.

Looking around for her handbag, Maggie realized she had left the Batak at home—the bag Vern had brought her from Jakarta as a gift, the bag rarely out of her hand since he'd put it there. But this morning, Maggie remembered, she had removed things from the Batak bag and put them into the old frayed one. She had taken it along instead.

———

Having sat almost an hour in the waiting room of the Prince's House, Maggie began fidgeting with the frayed piping of the handbag. Perhaps this was a feckless adventure, worthy of pretentious classmates she had despised in college for their dedication to "good works" at the service of a neurotic need for recognition. She was on the verge of leaving when Ibu Poedjosoedarmo, secretary to Madam Prince, reappeared, wearing a dour smile on thin unpainted lips. From the look of the woman, Maggie was prepared to say, "Thank Ibu Pangeran anyway."

"If you would be so kind as to follow me, Ibu Pangeran will see you now. This way please."

Through the corridors to a pavilion and beyond it to a courtyard and beyond that to a small enclosed garden, Maggie saw a tiny woman in dull batik sarong, blouse, and shawl sitting on a bulky Dutch chair under a frangipani tree. Ibu Poedjosoedarmo made the introductions and manuevered Maggie to a low-lying bench in front of the princess.

From this position Maggie was looking up at the wasted old woman whose beady eyes fixed her with an iron gaze.

Maggie returned that gaze steadily.

The secretary interpreted for them. The princess spoke in a high reedy voice. "Ibu Pangeran hopes you speak Dutch," said Ibu Poedjosoedarmo.

"I'm sorry."

"Ibu Pangeran would have enjoyed the opportunity to speak that distinguished language with someone who knew it as well as she does. Her father had been a regent of Central Java." Ibu Poedjosoedarmo paused to let the fact sink in. Maggie smiled to acknowledge that it had. "In the opinion of Ibu Pangeran the new republic is doomed. I think I speak for her when I say that the destruction of the old system of government and civility spelled the downfall of our Javanese way of life." When the secretary paused, Maggie smiled again. Then the little old woman, who had been staring grimly at Maggie, said something.

"Ibu Pangeran wonders why a foreign woman is interested in the preservation of Borobudur. Are you Buddhist?"

"No, I am not Buddhist. I simply think the temple is one of the great wonders of the world and should be preserved."

The secretary's translation of this sentiment brought nothing to the masklike face of the old woman, whose next words Maggie partially understood. ". . . she . . . knows anything."

"Ibu Pangeran would like to know—"

"I know what she would like to know. If I know anything."

When the secretary translated, the old woman's mouth opened slightly and then she smiled. The secretary smiled too. So they appreciated the foreigner's knowledge of their language. The old woman said something, this time so rapidly that Maggie could not follow.

"Ibu Pangeran would like to know which you prefer, Solonese or Yogyanese dance."

"I have never seen Solonese dance."

370

For the next half hour Maggie listened to the two women explain differences between the dance styles of the two cities. They seemed eager to make sure she understood. The greatest difference of style occurred in the male dances. The men of Yogya turned their feet out so they could utilize a sideways jump step, whereas the dancers of Solo only slid their feet along. No one with good sense ever questioned the supremacy of Solo.

"Ibu Pangeran wants you to know that in her day ceremonial dances were prohibited outside the kraton. She danced there herself as a girl. Her specialty was the putri. Grace and timidity were valued. The leg was never raised above knee level, the elbow never higher than the shoulder. None of this flirting with the eyes that the Balinese do. Ibu Pangeran wants you to know that she and her companions always fixed their eyes downward as befits modest women, descendants of the court of ancient Mataram. They practiced ngenceng, absolute restraint. Ibu Pangeran says her expression during the dance was as tight as a drumhead." When the secretary demonstrated by daintily tapping an invisible drum, from her big Dutch chair the old woman smiled broadly. "Control," Ibu Poedjosoedarmo continued, "was everything. Today people of the republic are degenerates who dance for money and debase the art of Mataram." Almost in the same breath the secretary added, "Ibu Pangeran does not know R. Harjanta Prijohoetomo, and suggests that if you undertake the restoration of Borobudur, you must choose well your companions and advisers."

During a short silence, Maggie attempted to smile in a controlled way at the old woman who was nearly lost in the big Dutch chair. It is all over, Maggie thought. They thought she was a fool, a typical busybody from overseas who wanted to change the world to fit a Western concept of it.

So it was with great surprise that Maggie heard the secretary declare, after a short exchange with Madam Prince, "You will be pleased to know that Ibu Pangeran says the idea of saving Borobudur is a noble one. She also says that you are a determined young woman. If you go forward with such a project wisely, you can rely on Ibu Pangeran for support. You must appreciate, Bu Gardner, that here sits the principal wife of a prince who served as patih to the last regent of Central Java. He had sixteen children by four wives, but Ibu Pangeran was the padmi, and so when you have her support, you have the support of someone beyond reproach, unequaled today in this land. In all modesty this is true."

"Yes, I understand that, I—" Maggie was flustered by the unpredictable woman, at once critical and generous, arrogant and eager for recognition. "I appreciate the honor and I think—"

The secretary waved off further gratitude. "Please do not embarrass Ibu Pangeran with your praises. She is nearing the end of a long life and wishes to go to Allah in a spirit of humility. As for the details of her participation, you may keep in touch with me."

"Then, Ibu Poedjosoedarmo, I can count on this?"

The secretary stiffened, as if the question was insulting. "Ibu Pangeran has said what she means."

"Yes, of course. I understand. And—I will count on her support."

In spite of her state of health—theoretically she was in the midst of recuperation—Maggie had never felt better. So pleased was she with her achievement that upon leaving the Pangeranan she headed out to see the city.

At the kraton museum (still open in spite of the crisis) she looked at Hindu bronzes, Chinese porcelains, jeweled krises, and a deep-bodied carriage given to a sultan by the Dutch East India Company a few centuries ago. At the other palace, the Mangunegaran, she heard gamelan playing from a green-columned pendopo (the orchestra was called Drifting in Smiles) and casually inspected a collection of bric-a-brac that included wayang topeng masks and three silver chastity belts.

She strolled around Pasar Trewindu, a market featuring antique oil lamps with opaque white glass shades and counterweights ornamented with lion-and-palm motifs. And while looking at a brass sirih set (bought for Mas Slamat, who would probably hide it away among the junk of his house and continue to chew betel from the battered old set he kept near his cluttered table), Maggie admitted to herself that she felt lonely and that in her loneliness she was thinking not of Vern but of the other one.

She went to the toy market and entered Mickey Morse, a big store that sold children's books and wooden pull animals. She idled there, yanking a red chicken along by a string, getting it to clank and clatter. There were tiny metal tea sets and miniature xylophones with silver-colored keys between wooden struts. Instead of cops and robbers, these kids played at gamelan. Would she ever have kids of her own? Once she had mentioned it casually to Vern, who had smiled without comment. Well, there was time for that.

Back in the street, she glanced at colored posters laid out on the ground. They were sold by young men whose studiedly bored and leanly handsome faces suggested they had another occupation when the sun went down over a nearby district, an area well known in Solo for "carnal irregularities." Now the dark young men were selling posters of Jesus Christ and Bung Karno and a medieval fairy in diaphanous gown stepping through a European forest.

In Pasar Klewer, under the west gate of the kraton, she walked among countless batik stalls. Loudspeakers were blaring gamelan music, making the liquid sounds of moonlight come out tinny and harsh. For Vern she bought a brightly patterned batik shirt (the colors of Central Java were too muted for his taste) from the northern district of Pekalongan. On impulse she bought her husband a second shirt, aware as she paid for the two that she was thinking of another man. Then she considered a wide salmon-pink sash (it would hold a sheathed kris against the small of a man's back), but put it down. Then she bought yet another shirt for Vern, this one in traditional brown and indigo.

Weary of the crowded bazaars, Maggie wandered into residential areas, down lanes from which, on either side at this hour, she could hear the voices of women and children reciting Islamic prayers. Dokars were clumping along the hot lanes, stirring dust as similar vehicles must have done on these same lanes for centuries. She glanced into swept courtyards that stood in front of vast, dark, low-slung buildings set at a distance from the lane, from the noise, from the twentieth century, Maggie thought. On the main streets today she had witnessed signs of the current crisis: soldiers peering over the canvas sides of lorries, policemen carrying unslung rifles in the backs of open jeeps. But here in the drowsy lanes of Solo she had retreated into the past of Java itself.

She understood why the Dutch loved Java. It was not only the wealth they could take from this country. Those big, clumsy fair-skinned people (like myself, she thought) had come from a cool, damp place into this sunny land of a thousand islands where the small, graceful inhabitants had skin the soft color of creamed coffee, and in the midst of such greenery and perfumed breezes, the weary Dutchmen must have felt they had reached paradise.

The crisis would not last, she thought. It would vanish into the timeless sunlight. The anthropologist in Maggie told her, "No, you must look at facts," but she was under the spell of the Spice Islands and of Surakarta, and remained solidly fixed in the web of fantasy until she returned to the hotel and walked down the cobbled path to the little cottage where a prince's woman might have roomed a half century ago. Before unlocking the door, she looked up at the gibbous moon in a sunset sky. It was like a white boat sailing in the dark-blue distance, and nothing that happened on this earth could halt its journey. A sense of exaltation, not unlike that induced by the deepest fever, followed Maggie into the room, where she flung herself down on the bed and fell instantly into a dreamless nap that was interrupted finally by the sound of gentle but rapid knocking at the door.

Sleepily opening it, Maggie looked out at the small bellboy dressed in the uniform of a sultan's attendant, its ornate gold trimming threadbare and ratty. He had carried her bag from the lobby today. Now he had a bouquet of flowers in his hand and on his moonlit face a broad smile. "Nonya, the dalang is here," he said breathlessly in Bahasa Indonesia. "He is in the lobby waiting. Ki-Dalang Gitosuwoko is here. Here!" The boy thrust the bouquet at her.

Thirty-eight

They sat in a Chinese restaurant at a table cordoned off, as were the others, by lattice screens. Maggie faced the cashier's desk behind which sat the wizened proprietor, glasses low on his nose, his mottled hand holding a pen that scratched endlessly on a ledger. The dim, spare room had yellowish walls that were water-stained in places to a rust color. While thunder rolled against those walls, the dalang explained that the Sakirman staff had told him where she was staying.

He had come to Surakarta for nyekar—further graveside rituals to honor the old dalang who had recently died. After nyekar there had been a ceremonial meal offered by the family. Cones of rice nearly two feet high were served at the slametan; afterward a modin recited prayers from the Quran.

"I would like to see that someday," Maggie said.

"I'm afraid it's restricted to men."

"Afraid? You don't like it restricted to men?"

"I was using 'afraid' as English use it. Wasn't I correct?"

"You were. 'Afraid' can be used as a polite way of saying sorry when you don't mean it." Maggie smiled. "You really mean you don't mind restricting slametan to men."

"I accept the tradition."

And why shouldn't he? Maggie thought. He was, after all, a product of his culture, just as she was a product of hers. Yet she had hoped for a sign from him, a sudden sharing of new ideas, an impulse toward change, something unpredictable, perhaps even outrageous, that would commemorate for Maggie what she had been feeling ever since she had first seen him tonight in the lobby of the hotel. Maggie had nearly turned and fled when he smiled at her approach; she had felt the proverbial weakness in her legs, the light-headedness, the foolish symptoms suffered by an infatuated dope.

She told Budi about her successful interview with Ibu Pangeran and could not help feeling a sense of triumph when he reacted with surprise.

"I would never have thought of asking her," Budi admitted.

"I suppose it would be embarrassing for you both."

"You understand the Javanese mind."

"I think not."

"But you already sense the truth—that the Javanese mind is a jungle. You can't see through or cut through it. You must know the little paths and sometimes they lead nowhere. I would not have gone to Ibu Pangeran, even for Borobudur. I'd have thought she would be shocked by a dalang asking money from a princess. She'd have thought she was being rude to discuss money with a dalang. And that is only the beginning of the twists and turns."

"She told me the dances of Solo were superior of those of Yogya. The male dancing is especially good here."

"She did not tell you, though, that Yogya males can learn Solo dancing but Solo males cannot learn Yogya. The training for our men is much harder and their legs develop in a more athletic way. What made you think of seeing Ibu Pangeran?"

She told him about the holy man and the letter of introduction. When he withheld comment, Maggie felt sure he did not approve of the director of the World Peace Radiating Center. "The princess told me she had never heard of R. Harjanta Prijohoetomo."

"It's common for Javanese to make more of a relationship than is there. He probably met her once and afterward claimed they were old friends." Budi paused while a wave of thunder boomed around the sides of the restaurant. "I can see it as you, a foreigner, do—as something vain and pretentious and even deceitful. But I also see it as natural in a country where social contacts mean so much, perhaps a great deal more than in the West. As a boy I saw things only through Javanese eyes. But after going abroad, everything I saw changed. I returned with double vision. It took away innocence."

"Do you regret that?"

"I regret the loss of absolute beliefs. They help you when you do what I do."

"I have never seen you do what you do. I've wondered when you'll perform again."

"I have not performed in a long time," he said quickly. "Here come the shrimp."

While they ate, she asked him about his nephew and the crisis. So far as he knew, there was no organized violence in the Gitosuwoko area. "Ali is a rather timid young man. I can't see him getting into trouble."

"Neither can I. But he's a dedicated Communist."

"He is at the moment."

"But this is a moment when he could get into trouble."

"I am glad he has you for a friend."

"I don't think he likes my friendship with you," Maggie observed bluntly.

"No, my nephew has never forgiven me for becoming a dalang at his own father's insistence."

"I worry about him."

"So do I."

She believed he meant it. "Will the crisis last long? Will there really be violence?"

"I can't see that happening. Even during the fight for independence there was not much bloodshed. It is something I admire in my people—their reasonableness at time of war. In a moment of panic or fury, they might run amok, but they regain control quickly. We don't have a history of violence. We believe strongly in accommodation. I think the crisis will end soon."

"That's what my husband thinks too." She noticed that his eyes widened slightly when she mentioned her husband, and in fact Maggie was disconcerted by her own sudden reluctance to say the words "my husband." So, in defiance of that reluctance, Maggie said them again, but in a context she hadn't thought through—the words just came out. "You never ask me about my husband."

"I expect you to tell me what I should know."

"What do you want to know?"

Budi shrugged. "You've been married a year and he is a builder. Does he believe in what he builds?"

"He believes in progress."

"And you, do you believe in progress?"

"Not at any cost."

"But he does? At any cost?"

"He's dedicated."

"Like your musician Bix Beiderbecke."

"I don't think Vern would see it that way. He's not a dreamer; he's got too much common sense to die for something he can't change. Bix didn't care about common sense. He died for a dream, for something he wanted but couldn't have, for music he wasn't equipped to write."

"I thought you told me he died of alcohol."

"Someone once said of Bix he died of everything. I think he died because he couldn't go farther with his music, so he drank himself to death. His dream killed him. He couldn't go farther at the thing that meant life to him so he lost the will to live. That's my theory. You see, I'm a romantic."

"I think you are. But to gain your admiration is it necessary to die for a dream?"

"You're laughing at me." When he smiled without denying it, Maggie said, "I have never had a strong commitment, but I admire people who do."

"Like your husband."

"I admire him, yes, but I can't share his belief in progress at the expense of other things—"

"Like Borobudur."

"Yes, like Borobudur."

"So now I know as much about your husband as I should know."

This remark upset Maggie, as if his obvious dismissal of Vern was the result of her leading him to it. "Vern is a good man," she declared.

"I am sure he is."

"You must meet him."

"Perhaps when the crisis is over, he'll come here and we can meet."

It was a prospect that Maggie disliked—feared—and from the tense expression on the dalang's face she knew that he also disliked the idea. But he did not fear it. The man fears nothing, she thought.

While they ate, Maggie glanced sidelong at him. His face seemed leaner and darker today, the jawline more pronounced. And his ears were slightly pointed, reminding her of a fox. His appearance seemed to have changed to conform to a new alertness. Sometimes when he looked up from his plate or glanced across the room and his eyes came back to meet hers, he had the taut, wary expression of an animal.

He was talking about Borobudur while she watched him. He admitted that support from a Solonese princess could renew public interest in the restoration. He had dedicated the proceeds of two wayang performances a few years ago to the project, but the money vanished somehow when local officials got hold of it. Budi opened his hands as if gold were pouring out of them, heaps of swag through the fingers of an impractical idealist.

"You are giving new life to Borobudur," he said to Maggie. On the tabletop he traced the geometrical design of Borobudur from a bird's-eye view. It was his theory that the temple had been constructed like a tantric yantra, a meditative pattern used for centuries by followers of Left-Handed Tantra in the quest for salvation.

That was it, Maggie thought: the look of an animal caught in a sudden glare. She had seen this on country roads in Iowa. Once, driving home late from college, she had almost hit a fox with a bird in its jaws rushing across the macadam, its yellow eyes flaring up astonished and brilliant in the headlights.

Perhaps it was the accompaniment of thunder that gave the dalang such a primal look. She found herself studying his hand when he lifted a teacup, his throat as he swallowed, his eyes when they shifted abruptly to meet hers. He was indeed handsome. And powerful. But it would not happen.

When they left the restaurant, the rainstorm had swept on through, leaving the air pungent from smells of wet vegetation. They walked back to the hotel, and just as they approached it, more rain pelted down. They ran to the east wing where the row of cottages stood beside an arbored promenade. She would not let him in. Working her key into the lock of her cabin, Maggie opened the door and flicked the light switch. The room remained dark. Then stepping back into what was now a steady drizzle, she noticed the other cottages were also dark, save for one from whose window a light flickered, suggesting a candle—Asian hotels supplied their rooms with candles because of frequent outages.

I will not let him in, Maggie swore. But she told him to step out of the rain. There was no phone in the cabin, so she couldn't call the desk. While she stumbled around, rummaging blindly through armoire drawers and the bathroom cabinet, he remained dutifully at the door, just out of the rain. When she told him there were no candles, he offered to get some from the main desk, turned, and left.

Maggie found her way through the darkness to the bed. Sitting gingerly on its edge, she watched the open door and listened to the patter of rain. There were two chairs and a coffee table in the sitting area beyond the bed. He could sit in one of those chairs until the rain ended. Then he must leave.

Maggie felt her hands trembling, as if she were expecting something terrible to come out of the rain. But only the dalang would come out of it, a patrician who would never press a woman unless she offered herself. And I have not offered myself, Maggie thought. Neither of them had stepped out of line this evening, not by word or gesture. Nothing had happened; nothing would happen.

But he had showed up, hadn't he, with a bouquet of flowers, and he had looked at her in a way every woman recognizes. It was the look from a man across the room or at a train station or on the street, a look of sexual appetite, a burning look, both dangerous and exciting. She had seen it plenty of times, but rarely in Indonesia, and surely not from a famous puppeteer fifteen years her senior, and she a married woman whose husband awaited her anxiously in an embattled city. What was she thinking? Was a look, a common glance of casual desire, was that how aristocratic Javanese artists seduced a woman—by the look in their eyes? Stupidly romantic notion, she knew. She was sure she knew. But she had no idea what he was thinking. Did he in fact have any idea what she feared, hoped for, had already decided to reject? Perhaps he was utterly innocent. Perhaps he had no sense of what a Western woman might feel under the circumstances. Perhaps everything was in her mind. And that's certainly where it would remain, in her mind, a foolish thought such as she might have had in her high-school days, when an attractive boy smiled at her in geometry class.

Then there was a black shape in the open doorway, hunched over as it came out of the rain. Abruptly a plume of orange light illuminated the room. Dalang Budi held a candle, its light emphasizing his high cheekbones. Quickly he looked around for something to place the candle in. Maggie jumped up, glancing back at the bedside table. Rushing to it she picked up the ashtray there, but he had already found another and set the candle in it, placing it on the coffee table. Holding her own ashtray, Maggie sat down and invited him to sit there—there. She pointed across the table at a chair opposite her own. He sat down. Maggie felt they were acting out a series of memorized movements—a choreographed skirmish on a candlelit battleground. Now the rain was heavy again, beating on the cabin's tiled roof.

They looked at each other across the wavering light. She wanted to say something amusing, but could think of nothing. She wanted to break the tension, to make something harmless out of what was happening, so in this spirit she almost described those trashy old romances when there's a storm and the honorable hero rushes to the chaste heroine's room to reassure her that it will soon pass and just as he gets there the lights go out, exactly like tonight, and she falls into his arms, frightened of the thunder, and he holds her close and, if it's a movie, there's a fade-out and you know what happens. But of course the dalang wouldn't think of such Western trash; probably he was thinking of romantic trash familiar to his own culture.

"I liked the restaurant," she said blandly.

Just then a stormy gust of wind swept through the door that they had left discreetly open and gutted the candle, leaving the room in darkness.

She heard him fumbling for matches.

"Let it go," she heard herself say.

"Did you say let it go?"

"We don't need the candle. It's—pleasant in the darkness with the wind blowing." But she added quickly, "Well, maybe we do need some light."

But instead of lighting the candle, Dalang Budi rose and closed the door, then found his chair again in the darkness. "It is Solo's best restaurant," he said.

"It really is good."

"There are a few other good restaurants, but Solonese say it is the best."

Rain was now battering the tiled roof. Maggie waited for something. Not far away, not much farther than arms' length away, a man was sitting in the pitch-black room listening to the rain, just as she was, and thinking the same thoughts. He must be. He must be frightened too. No, not that man. But uncertain. No. Then what, what must he be thinking and feeling? Again she thought of his predatory look, his fearless eyes caught in the sudden glare of headlights. "What do you think of me?" she heard herself asking.

He said nothing for so long that Maggie was sure he meant to ignore her question; it must have sounded incredibly bold to his Javanese ear. The rain stopped then, as if the elemental force of it had rammed into a wall. Through the abrupt silence his voice came at last. "My English is not good enough to tell you. I think you are a beautiful woman. I like your music. I like your belief in a man who lives and dies for music, because I have known three such men in my life who lived only for gamelan and gave their lives to it. I like your belief in Borobudur and what it means and why it must be saved and what you did today. There is something else about you I can't find words for. Not even in Javanese. In wayang it is sometimes that way— that I hold a character in my hand and he must say something that carries great meaning and I feel the need to find words for this moment, but I can't find them and so I move him around the screen as a substitute for what he should say, and the audience doesn't know what he could have said. They accept what I give them, the movement, the action, but I know there is more to say for the full meaning and the moment is lost. I cannot do it, and this is how I feel now in trying to say what it is I feel about you. But when I look at you I feel it through my body. It is a powerful desire for you, more than I have felt for any woman, even for my wife when she was with me." He stopped.

Maggie heard the sound of raindrops dripping from leaf to leaf.

"The rain has stopped," he said. "Yes, it has really stopped this time."

Suddenly through the damp air there came a chorus of brittle, insistent chirping from a myriad of unseen insects.

"I must go," he said dully, as if acknowledging that something had been decided. "The rain has stopped."

It was time for her to say something. At first she was sure her voice wouldn't carry across the few feet that separated them. But when she spoke, her voice was surprisingly confident—in it a pure note of command. "Don't go. I don't want you to go."

They were silent in the darkness, while out there an army of frogs began croaking. The frogs and insects were putting up a wall of sound around the cottage.

When Maggie spoke again, she felt her words go sharply into the night, and their clarity thrilled her as if someone else, far braver than she, had said them. "Don't go. Come here. Please find your way over here to me."

Ears filled with birdsong, eyelids shut against the soft early light, Maggie remembered.

Last night, once over their initial nervousness, she and the dalang had made love with gentle intimacy; the memory of their slow loving warmed her. The second time she had got on top and rode. Enough moonlight, in the aftermath of rain, had come through the open window for her to see his eyes below her, his carnal eyes wide open, intent, hungry, as he held her hunted body in the grip of a hunter.

Then later, as they lay side by side, he had talked in a strange new way. Budi (for that's what she had called him in her passion) spoke of what she had never suspected—what he felt was his failure as a dalang. After his wife's death he had gone to Sumatra—yes, the Lake Toba region—where for a few months he meditated, but the effort gained him nothing, and he came back with his grief intact but his commitment to performing gone. For three years he kept performing, but it became more and more mechanical, until he stopped last year—not because people recognized his loss of desire, but because he could no longer sleep. He had terrible insomnia; sometimes for weeks at a time he slept only an hour or two a night.

"It's strange," Budi told her, lips against her cheek, "how you can come apart and people don't see it."

The idea of such a man "coming apart" struck Maggie as very strange; indeed, so incongruous that for a while she wouldn't believe it. But as they lay together, he finally convinced her: Ki-Dalang Budi Gitosuwoko had lost the will to perform, a fact unknown to anyone save himself and now Maggie Gardner of Iowa.

"You loved her that much," Maggie whispered.

But he denied that his wife's death was the only reason for his failure. This claim seemed too pat to Maggie who, after giving herself, was prepared to regret it. "You loved her that much," she insisted.

"I loved her, but I also loved wayang. I lost faith in what I could do as a dalang."

"But if you loved what you did—"

"I wanted to do more than I could—like your Bix. I understand him." Budi caressed her shoulder—it was like punctuation to what he was saying—while he explained the horror of his craving, the desire to do colossal and terrifying things in the world of wayang. And with this growth in desire came the burgeoning conviction that he had reached the utmost border of his talent, and that beyond it lay appalling tracks of mediocrity, obscured in mists of despair, beckoning to him through the last dark decades of his life. The desperation and sadness in his voice gripped Maggie as nothing had ever done. A vise of sorrow clamped her heart so that she knew she really loved him. It was not infatuation. She loved this man, and in an instant understood that for her there was only one thing worthwhile in life now—to help him regain faith in himself.

Still, perhaps his confession was too pat, too convenient. Perhaps he thought it would appeal to her romantic nature if he shared something with her tragic hero. She could understand a man trying that, a man of intellect and sensitivity who was unbound by conventional morality. Perhaps he had merely used her. Was she that blind? Women could be that blind, they could, and she had known a few. Did he think a little fling with a foreign woman would be diverting? Panicky, she nearly leapt out of bed. Instead she took a deep breath and held it, attempting to control herself by a ball of air clenched in her throat. When finally she exhaled, Maggie felt calmer and knew that she would stay where she was, that she had already decided to stay and would stay and stay and stay as long as he wanted her, and so Maggie shut her eyes, feeling on her naked body the sweep of a breeze coming through the open window.

He was stirring beside her—behind her—and she opened her eyes to stare at the window whose square was filled with churning blue space. Maggie didn't turn toward him, but remained as she was, on her side. She felt his hand touch her hip tentatively, then move against it in little circles, and with fingers barely grazing her flesh explore further: her stomach, her navel (probed slightly by a fingertip); after delicious hesitation brushing against her pubic hair; her sex—his forefinger gently rubbing the dry lips of it; and then with palm flat against her skin his hand ascended past her stomach, her rib cage, to cup each breast; fingers pressed, released, pressed again, drawing on the soft flesh as if it were tensile, something to be spun out like silk. He was transforming her body, making it feel strange, giving it a new shape. Again she held her breath, this time in anticipation. The hand that gave life to puppets now seemed to give separate life to each part of her body it touched. Then his hand was on her cheek, lightly touching her closed eyelids, her cheek once more—sliding across it like cloth against glass, her chin, and down the same path again: each breast, her stomach, her pubic hair, and this time when his hand reached her sex, after another moment of hesitation, one finger touched the entrance, eased into her wetness, and she gasped. Between her buttocks now his cock, slippery from its juices, moved slowly up and down as in a trough, and at last went under them to replace his finger, to enter her. Already her hips were moving in rhythm to strokes that had not yet begun. Aware of this, Maggie stilled herself, waiting, while he soaked in her awhile. One hand gripped her neck, a suggestion of possible brutality, surely an act of control, while the other alternately caressed each breast, pulling each nipple gently. Move, she wanted to tell him, biting her lip, attempting to still the rhythm awakening again in her hips. Yet he waited, soaking, caressing. His breath came steadily like warm little gusts of wind against her jawbone.

His chest warmed her back, the hair of his groin lightly scratched her buttocks as he curved below them, between them, his flesh warming the center of her. She had nearly been lulled into accepting such quiescent lovemaking as what he wanted now when abruptly he began to move, slowly at first, with long, smooth strokes, then with rapid, piercing jabs. She had never felt so penetrated, not even when Vern had slammed into her with his powerful hips. Never so pierced as now when Budi's cock jerked to a rhythm so breakneck and relentless it was like a motor gone wild. She held for a few moments the image of a stake turned rapidly against a piece of wood to build a fire, smoke rising from the churning point, and then the image was replaced by sensation only, the feeling of heat between her legs, the friction against the walls of her cunt, the involuntary pumping of her own hips.

He had been so gentle last night; this savagely headlong motion of wayward joy took her by surprise. Sure that he could go no faster, that the velocity of his thrusts could not increase, Maggie was amazed, for an instant fearful, when she felt him accelerating inside her, making her come almost before she knew it was going to happen. Her hips were still gyrating spasmodically when, with a loud groan, he emptied himself into her.

She felt her heart pounding and then the sense of her rapid heartbeat was supplanted by awareness of their pulsing loins; she felt them throbbing together in quick little contractions. "Ah, it's so good," she murmured.

"Nothing beyond . . ." he began to say, then pulled her earlobe into his mouth, sucking it like a small berry.

"Good, that's good," she said.

"Nothing beyond . . ."

"Yes," she said, not knowing exactly what he meant. She was not facing him but speaking into the sweaty pillow. His voice, coming from behind her, was gusty, unattached, it seemed, to the flesh hot against her back, buttocks, flanks.

"I forgot what you were."

"I felt it." She understood the meaning of "what." And now she understood what he meant by "Nothing beyond."

She felt him leaving her, and when they were separate, Maggie turned to look at him. Passion had not yet receded from his face; it was in the glazed eyes, the trembling mouth. She licked sweat from his upper lip, drawing into her nostrils the musky odor of his body. Over them hovered the pungent smell of their excretions.

"So good," she murmured again, kissing his wet cheeks and forehead. Last night they had not allowed themselves what she had once heard was a special Asian intimacy . . . a kiss with tongues touching. Now she opened his lips with her tongue, plunging possessively into his warm mouth, and gave herself fully to the pleasure of it.

Thirty-nine

A copy of a U.S. Embassy telex, received from the consulate in Yogya, awaited Vern when he arrived for work at OPSUS: telescoped into a few words was the good news that Maggie was all right and knew he was all right too.

With his wife safe, Vern had only to weather the storm here in Jakarta. Thus far it hadn't been bad, aside from an annoying curfew and squads of army vehicles rumbling through the streets with soldiers glaring at the sidewalks, hoping for trouble, and the frighteningly persistent rumors of potential carnage in the back lanes.

There was still no chance of traveling outside of Jakarta except by local bus to military checkpoints, where, of course, he'd be turned around and sent back. General Sakirman refused to help. Just as Jack Rutledge had cynically predicted of army officers, "They'll get religion and hold on to it for a few weeks." Sakirman had indeed taken on a sanctimonious tone when turning down Vern's plea for some kind of official pass to Yogya.

"I can't see my own wife," Sakirman announced grandly, "so during the crisis you and I must sacrifice equally," without adding what Vern knew: Susanto Sakirman was ensconced in a guarded villa somewhere outside of Malang, in West Java, while her long-suffering husband continued his philandering in blacked-out mansions where officers still partied the whole night long.

In spite of army insistence upon strict observance of the rules of martial law, OPSUS officers did business on their own behalf as usual. Vern observed what might appear innocuous to visitors at headquarters: whispering in the corridors accompanied by tense nods of agreement or disagreement; the shuttling of unfamiliar civilians into unused offices for unscheduled meetings; and the passing of documents from briefcase to briefcase, all of which to the trained eye meant deals, rake-offs, illegal investments.

With a similar regard for practical results, General Sakirman kept Project Palm Tree going forward on a sluggish if rational schedule: architectural drawings were accumulated, cost estimates compared, specifications analyzed, with the first of December still designated as groundbreaking day at a site on Sanur Beach, the island of Bali. Not that Sakirman would allow Vern to travel there yet for a look-see. But because of the apparent determination of the general and his OPSUS aides to meet that goal whatever else happened in the country, Vern believed they would all be there on 1 December, watching a local bigwig scoop up the first shovelful of dirt, inaugurating construction of the Garuda Hotel.

To match the spirit of the project Vern worked consistently if not strenuously. Each day, with bodyguard Hashim at his side, Vern went to work and returned each evening to the hotel, where he ate and had a few soft drinks at the bar and went to bed. That was his drab routine during the crisis, broken only by visits from Yanti, who came with endless questions about the general practice of architecture, about the specific project he was working on, about American customs, about his wife.

"What's the drill, mate?" Larry Foard asked one morning on the way to work. "Is a little bird getting into your nest?"

Vern laughed. "Nothing doing."

"Platonic is it?"

"Well, why not? What else is there to do in a curfewed city but shoot the breeze with people? The kid's funny, she's interesting, she knows something about architecture."

Larry threw up his hands in mock alarm. "Don't get me wrong, mate! You know me. I wouldn't imply anything. I figured that was it—she's a funny little bird and smart and all of that and you're as pure as the driven snow."

"You come by your suspicions honestly," Vern said. "I never knew you to like a woman for anything except a fuck."

"That's right."

What Vern could not explain to the little boatbuilder from Cornwall was his genuine liking for the girl, but liking that went no further than liking. Not that he didn't find her attractive. She was not so much pretty as vivacious and witty and somehow amusingly bold. Between them there was, so Vern assured himself, mutual admiration softened by levity into a nice friendship. That's all: a relationship that could only puzzle someone like Larry Foard. There was no sense explaining, Vern decided, how every morning he opened the door and Yanti marched into his hotel room, and how they had coffee together, the event rigorously staged, with him sitting in a straight-backed chair, her on the couch, and a table between them, and how, from this little scene, a man and a woman could derive satisfaction. Larry would just grin cynically.

Vern Gardner had made love to enough women in his lifetime for sexual prowess not to count as a way of defining himself. He had developed the simplest of moral codes over the years: if a woman wants you, she'll let you know, and then you make your move; and if she doesn't want you, give her a smile and go your merry way. Nothing subtle about that. The philosophy was good enough for a man like himself out here in the middle of Asia. That's how he had got along before meeting Maggie. Now he was taken. He was as straight as a goddamn die. He was committed to his marriage.

Even so, the last time he met with Sutopo Salim (who seemed to prefer progress reports from the American rather than from OPSUS generals), Vern had felt somewhat uneasy about his relationship with the cukong's daughter.

Where and how he met the cukong had become an established practice: in a Chinatown teahouse, emptied out beforehand by body-guards. The Hokkien businessman sipped tea and spoke with a kind of weary calm about the crisis. What it would do to business, of course, worried him. And do to the Chinese, even loyalists like himself, who had surrendered their heritage for the chance to be Indonesian citizens. There had been a recent increase in anti-Chinese feeling throughout the capital. People were again using the old Javanese term *"caping"*—pointed hat—as a contemptuous epithet for Chinese. Yesterday there had been a fight with bottles and clubs between Muslim and Chinese students at Republika University.

The little man leaned forward and began to explain, as he might explain an investment, what it had been like to be Chinese under the Dutch before World War Two. Although the restriction was not always observed, by law no Chinese could live outside the boundaries of Chinatown in Jakarta. "You needed a pass to travel anywhere." Sutopo Salim rubbed his liver-spotted hands together in slow ruminative circles. "You had to show the pass to police, or, for that matter, to anyone who asked to see it. Anyone. Even to a Javanese dog if it barked for it." He liked his own witticism; smiled in appreciation of it; continued kneading his mottled hands. "Then you were restricted to certain areas within any town you visited. You paid twice the taxes that a European did who was living here. To become a citizen you had to be fluent in Dutch; the qualification was waived for non-Chinese. You couldn't buy a single acre of farmland." Throwing up both hands, he said, "Well, there is much more."

So the cukong had responded to the crisis by remembering his past, as if memory behaved like an old wound in damp weather. He never asked Vern anything about Yanti. Perhaps he didn't even know his daughter was seeing the American. Had he felt the slightest suspicion, of course, his men could have discovered the truth in an hour. One of these days that just might happen, and Vern would then have to deal with the consequences. There shouldn't be any, given the nature of his relationship with Yanti, yet he understood that Sutopo Salim was capable of matching revenge to insult in a perfect equation of moral justice, Chinese style.

At present the cukong was out of the country. He was shoring up his financial empire in Singapore, readying himself for any eventuality back home.

Vern was therefore safe, and that fact—he thought of his position in terms of safe and dangerous—disturbed him, because, after all, he had nothing to hide from the cukong. Yanti came each morning for a talk and sat across the table from him. Being a healthy and experienced man, Vern understood, accepted, and disregarded fleeting stabs of desire during their conversations when he allowed his eyes to take her in: the lustrous black hair, the soft clear skin, her trim figure, her legs—a bit of thigh flashing as she crossed them in the pleated skirt. But these sexual tremors proved nothing to him except that he missed his wife.

Larry and Vern sat in the hotel bar having a drink (Larry a tot of gin, Vern a glass of soda water) when Jack Rutledge shuffled in.

"In his cups as usual," Larry muttered. He despised a man who couldn't hold his liquor at least until midnight.

But Vern went over to the consul and invited him for a drink.

"You're inviting a son of a bitch for a drink?" asked Rutledge sourly.

"Look, Jack, don't hold that against me. I was worried stiff about my wife."

"I wouldn't have sent the telexes for you if I hadn't understood that."

"Come on, let me buy you a drink. You gave me back my sanity."

Rutledge's bright, boozy smile was a testament to his love of approval. "Anything I can do, let me know," he said expansively. "We got to pull together at a time like this. Damn madhouse, isn't it? The army was turned loose today."

"Turned loose?"

Rutledge lit a cigarette and squinted through the smoke. "House-to-house searches for Reds. People squealing on their neighbors—some of them just getting even for old scores, nothing about communism in it."

"Of course. That's to be expected."

With a laugh Rutledge reached out and cuffed Vern's arm. "You old cynic. You old lecher."

"What's that?" Vern asked with a tight smile.

"Oh, come on. How many foreigners are running around Jakarta these days? It's a fishbowl life, Vern. You're banging a little Chinese chick."

"That's news to me."

"Look, nothing intended. What you do is your business. Live and let live is the way I go." He paused for confirmation.

"Sure it is."

"I just wish you'd go back to drinking something besides dishwater." Finishing his gin and waving at the boy for another, Rutledge said, "Let me tell you I wouldn't want to be Chinese in Jakarta these days. Between China and Indonesia the honeymoon is definitely over, I mean over. Could you do me a favor, my British friend," he said to Larry. "I'm wedged in here. Could you go get that boy and tell him I want another?" To Vern he said, "After waiting table here for a year or two or three they still don't know what you mean when you point to an empty glass. I was saying?"

"About China." Vern watched Larry rise with a scowl and walk toward the bar.

"China? What I was saying is about these Muslim organizations. They're shouting for the government to break diplomatic relations with China. Damn Chinese have handled things badly. Not only failed to send a representative to the generals' funeral, last week they again refused to fly the embassy flag at half-staff in honor of two colonels. The ones murdered by Reds near Yogya."

"Near Yogya?"

Rutledge clapped Vern on the back. "You're worrying about your wife. Well, don't. It was somewhere near Yogya that these army guys went through a Red village in a jeep and they stopped for something and these two officers got skewered by knives or something. It's between the army and the Reds. It doesn't have to do with us. What was I saying? All kinds of things are going on. Hey, thanks, Brit," he said to Larry who came back to the table bearing a gin and bitters. "Anything I can do you for, let me know. I was saying?"

"About China," Vern told him.

"Yeah, well, the Indo diplomats are going around Embassy Row telling everybody the Chinese are trying to impose their will on a faithful ally. Poor-little-put-upon-me kind of stuff." Rutledge chuckled. "But we might suffer."

"We?"

Rutledge gave him a contemptuous glance. "For God's sake, Gardner, when I say 'we,' don't you remember you're an *American*? Just yesterday something happened back home. Indonesia's ambassador protested to the State Department. The *Washington Post* had published a report linking Sukarno to the coup."

"Any truth in it?"

"Nah. But the ambassador insists the phony report came from the CIA."

"Did it?"

"Jesus Christ, everything including bad weather's blamed on the CIA. Here I am illegally relaying messages for you and you start acting like a knee-jerk liberal. It's the stuff you're drinking, Vern. What I'm really wondering is how these people are going to come out of this thing without catastrophe. There could be a massacre, at least in Jakarta."

Vern shrugged.

"You don't find that upsetting, a massacre? You find that boring?"

"I was just thinking, maybe these people need to clean house. It's what William Blake said—"

"Blake? The poet? You read poetry, Vern?" That struck him as funny, and he laughed.

"I had to read some in college. You won't believe this, but on honeymoon in Medan my wife and I read Blake from a book she has. Lay in bed reading Blake."

Both Larry Foard and Jack Rutledge guffawed.

"Don't worry. I'm still the uneducated ditchdigger you think I am. But Blake said: 'The tygers of wrath are better than the horses of instruction—' Better or wiser, I forget which. He spelled tiger with a *y*."

Rutledge seemed for a moment sober; at least he was studying Vern carefully. "What in hell does that mean? Tigers of wrath, horses of instruction?"

"Maybe it means you learn more by doing something than by thinking about it. Or nobody can tell you what to do, you have to find out for yourself. Or it's best to get rid of anger than keep it in. Something like that."

"Something like that." Rutledge turned to Larry. "What can you do with him, huh? Now he's quoting William Blake."

"Blake also said," Vern continued, " 'Drive your plow over the bones of the dead.' "

"I like that," Larry said.

"You two." Rutledge shook his head in amusement.

"Two what? I'd very much like to know what you mean by 'you

two.' " Larry's voice was low but so tense that both men stared at him.

Vern got to his feet and told Larry to come along; they had an appointment.

Outside the hotel, gripping Larry's arm, Vern said, "No sense getting into a fight. And don't tell me it wasn't coming. I saw it coming."

"Right, mate. It was coming."

"I don't like him either, but he's government and right now it helps to know some government."

"Funny chap that. Just don't put me in the way of him again."

"Let's go eat."

They went back into the hotel, tiptoed past the doorway to the bar, where Jack was slouched over a new drink, and headed for the dining room.

Vern had let go of Larry's arm, and as they reached the dining room, Larry said, "I liked the bit of Blake. 'Tygers of wrath'—well, we might be seeing some of those, mightn't we, in coming days."

But Vern wasn't listening. He was thinking of Rutledge accusing him of having an affair with Yanti. No sense, though, in getting riled about it. After all, looked at from a certain viewpoint it must seem plausible.

Forty

A lmost five thousand of them (in a Muslim newspaper the estimate would be doubled or even tripled) filed past the white-columned building that housed the office of Foreign Minister Subandrio.

Waving their banners, they shouted, "Crush the PKI! Death to Aidit! Death to the Reds! Death to Subandrio!" The army, having cooperated during all the demonstrations thus far, controlled traffic and allowed the marchers plenty of time to make their protest felt.

In Yanti's opinion it was successful, although the foreign minister failed to make an appearance on the balcony and address the demonstrators. Yanti's best friend, Utami, agreed that the protest had had an impact, but she was more restrained in her enthusiasm (she would check first with her boyfriend Siregar, an intellectual who had convinced her he knew everything).

The marchers stayed in recognizable formation until out of sight of Subandrio's building. That was by plan, and although a few students were unruly, most of them managed to hold ranks until then, after which there was a letting go: posters lowered, armbands put away, a lot of talk. Their faces were flushed, their eyes shining, their voices hoarse from yelling slogans. This was the best part of politics for Yanti. She felt that something important was happening. All of these people raising their arms in unison gave her a thrilling sense of unity, and at such moments she forgot her heritage and felt wholly Indonesian, a child of a great new nation. She was walking through the crowd of relaxing marchers when someone caught her eye.

He was a small ragged man standing at the edge of the milling crowd with his hand stretched out. Often beggars followed a march so that when it ended they could rush forward and get a few rupiah from excited young students. Because the sight of beggars was so familiar, Yanti was surprised at her sudden interest in this shabby fellow who stood rocklike, as if stunned, as if oblivious not only of the crowd but of his own hand outstretched in the attitude of begging. Abruptly she felt his eyes meeting hers. She would never forget those eyes: deep in their sockets, the black irises burning with unnatural light, as if it came from within, from a terrible place in his mind. She felt herself walking toward the shabby figure who seemed lost, woebegone, in a torn shirt and trousers too big for him.

What was odd was the way he suddenly pulled himself up, as if to attention, when she got closer. Maybe he wants to look proud, Yanti thought, while opening her money pouch and taking out a rupiah. He needed only a shave and pressed clothes to look like a soldier.

Because of this proudly rigid stance of his, Yanti held out the money timidly. For a moment he hesitated, then his hand shot out and grabbed the bill. Yanti opened her mouth as if to speak, but she had nothing to say and just stood there while he gave her a last furious glance and turned, lurched forward, groped through the crowd, fiercely trying to get away from her as fast as possible.

Yanti felt someone jerk her elbow roughly. She glanced around at Utami, who had come up alongside and was now squinting at the retreating beggar.

"We meet the others," Utami told her briskly, staring at the bent back vanishing into the crowd, "at the warung on Jalan Malaka. Siregar chose it. We have to criticize one another and learn from experience, he says. We need better discipline next time, and I agree with him. He says we should get the army more involved in Muslim activities. We could start by asking to use their bullhorns, he says. I think it's a good idea. Well? Yanti?"

"Yes, a very good idea," Yanti acknowledged eagerly.

"I wasn't sure you heard me. I thought you were still thinking about that beggar." Utami, taller and darker, had a broad, flat nose and close-set eyes. Until recently she had ignored Yanti's Chinese heritage when students gathered to discuss politics. But in the last few days, after accusing Peking of masterminding the Night of the Generals, she would turn to ask Yanti her opinion, because it was good, she would say with a smile for their companions, "to know what Chinese think about Chinese." Of course Yanti attacked Peking with more vehemence than any of them, but she had the feeling that Utami was suspicious of her.

"I saw you give that beggar money," Utami declared. "I never give anything to someone healthy. It's against Allah if you give to someone who can work."

"You're right." Yanti's cheeks felt suddenly hot. "Allah wants us to work. But the beggar looked sick to me."

Utami continued in a singsong voice, as if reciting. "In the *Hadiths* it says the Great Prophet commanded his people to keep themselves clean and to work hard. Men like that beggar are a disgrace in the eyes of Allah. He's probably kafir. You probably gave money to a disbeliever and a thief."

Yanti said nothing more, but hung her head and followed Utami into the crowd. The truth was her own father was kafir, although he professed the faith for business reasons. As for herself, she believed in God during prayers and then forgot about Him afterward. Unlike her friend Utami, she lacked spiritual discipline and was not a real Indonesian. Everything about her seemed fake except the desire to belong, the desire to believe, the desire, yes, to be loved.

As they headed for the meeting at Siregar's warung, Yanti let a fantasy worm its way into her consciousness. This had happened often lately, and after initial resistance, she succumbed to it each time. She stands in front of huge plate-glass windows overlooking the ocean; two children, both having the Western eyes of Mister Vernon and

398

her own mouth, are playing in the sand while the surf booms, and she, their mother, watches them contentedly from the house.

So it had come to begging, and not only that but begging from women and not only that but begging from Chinese women. This did Achmad Bachtiar, sergeant in the famed 454th Diponegoro Battalion, mutter to himself while rushing into a warung where he wolfed down a plateful of rice and vegetables, his first food in two days.

Feeling better, he wondered if now he would go to see his sister. Every day since his desertion a fortnight ago, Achmad had asked himself, Will you go today, learn where the seducer is, find and kill him? But every day he had put it off. Every day since bribing a lorry driver to smuggle him out of Halim Air Base, he had roamed the kampongs of Jakarta in search of the strength to exact revenge. Although he prayed to Allah for such strength, he felt in himself a black emptiness like the well at Crocodile Hole where he had finished his military career.

So he had wandered through Jakarta, living initially on money he had brought from the base and then on his begging. Achmad Bachtiar was not interested in making a new start. His whole life had been given to public service; now that was over. What counted now was something very personal. The importance of familial honor had always been spelled out by his grandfather, who often warned the Bachtiar men in old Malay, *"Hilang bini, boleh mengganti, hilang budi, badan mencelakakan"* ("A lost wife can be replaced, but the loss of character spells ruin"). That's why he accepted the idea of begging. It took from him everything honorable except the concentration he needed to succeed at the only thing that still mattered: to find Kamarusaman bin Ahmed Mubaidah, the corrupter of his sister, and by killing this seducer to regain the reputation of the Bachtiar family. Not even a last look at his wife and child could matter now, even though they were in his waking thoughts each morning in the back lanes where he slept alongside other men who existed too among mangy dogs that snapped at their heels and who picked through tin cans along Ciliwang Canal for scraps of food and who begged as he did from anyone—even Chinese women.

Sometimes the heat and clutter of these slums led him northward to the harbor for a breath of air. He squatted in the shade of buckling shacks and watched the bumboats gliding from dock to dock in onshore breezes coming out of the haze. Other men also stared at the measureless distance as if it were an approaching ship. Some were stevedores, waiting for a job loading cargo on a steamer or prahu.

One afternoon, sitting with such dockworkers in silence, Achmad watched them get up as a group and head for a man calling to them from dockside. That left Achmad and a weathered old man who sat with a broad-brimmed hat hiding his face.

Aside from grunting out a phrase now and then, Achmad had said nothing in days. Now he said, "You, old man, will you talk to me?"

The old man nodded from under the conical hat but said nothing.

So Achmad did the talking. He talked and talked. In a rambling way he spoke of duty and corruption and honor and dishonor. "Allah is great," he told the man under the conical hat. "He will punish me. But I hope for a little time before He does. As a man of honor I ask for permission to take revenge. Understand this. This is important. I have no regrets for killing a man who insulted me by slapping my face. That was unforgivable of him. I feel pure joy at the memory of killing that man. But the massacre is another thing. It occurred while I stood there and did nothing. General Harjono was mangled. I saw his guts hanging out. There was a girl with a knife bending over, well, she was drugged and so she didn't know what she did, but she did it. And for that and for all of that I feel ashamed. I can't let go of it. The shadow crosses my path even at noon. It comes at night when I'm dreaming." Achmad paused, glancing again at the conical hat. "And another man has also insulted me, my sister, my family. Before I pay God the debt owed to Him, let me satisfy myself on that score too. That's my prayer. *Inshallah,* I will have revenge first. *Al-hamdu lillah.*"

Achmad got to his feet and hitched up his torn trousers, which were sagging around his thin waist. It was time. The strength was in him, surging through his veins like monsoon rain coursing down the side of Mount Merapi. He was going to his sister.

He slapped her hard after taking a single step inside the little house. Endang reeled back, gasping, and covered her face with both hands.

400

"Don't worry," Achmad told her, breathing heavily. "I won't do it again. That's for carrying his child." It was clearly showing under the faded sarong. Achmad sat down and stared disconsolately at his sister, remembering how she had been as a girl—sweet and quiet and good. Endang had always said, "I like it less" rather than "I don't like it," the way a bolder tidak woman expressed disapproval. Endang reminded him of his wife, also a kurang woman, and such a reminder saddened him, because surely he would never see his wife again. While Endang wept from the pain and humiliation of his blow, Achmad waited, kneading his fingers and fidgeting, although slapping her was what his father would have done to a woman who brought disgrace to the household.

Achmad began to feel better, because he knew that he had located the strength within, that it was his forever now, that he would do what he had to do, that there was still a chance for him to regain a sense of honor. He cleared his throat and asked his sister where Kamarusaman bin Ahmed Mubaidah was. Never mind that the man had shamed her; that was in the past; now the mistake could be rectified. There were matters to discuss—a dowry, for example.

Endang stopped sobbing when he mentioned this possibility. She opened her fingers slightly and peered between them at her brother.

So the deception was working. Encouraged, he went further, his voice calm and low and soothing. He felt certain that under the circumstances, once they understood the mutual benefit of cooperation, he and Kamarusaman bin Ahmed Mubaidah could reach an agreement. Surely marriage would come of it, if only they had a chance to meet and discuss everything. Achmad smiled brightly and opened his hands out. "A talk will solve our problem. When and where can we meet?"

He was bitterly disappointed when his sister, who seemed convinced of his sincerity, claimed to have no idea when such a meeting might take place. She had not seen Kamarusaman bin Ahmed Mubaidah since the day before the Night of the Generals. He might have gone away for a while, she suggested, because of the crisis—to protect his business.

Achmad tried to assess what was happening here. Was his sister stupid? Was she deceiving him? Was she capable of lying to her own brother about something as important as the whereabouts of her seducer? Before Achmad could decide, a knock at the door startled him.

"I have deserted from the army," he whispered rapidly. "They may be looking for me. I'll hide in there." He rushed into a small bedroom, drew the door almost shut—almost, because if he closed it, someone might think there was someone in there. Glancing around, he saw an unshuttered window. He could leap through it and run if necessary.

There were voices outside, his sister's low one and a male voice of sufficient courtesy for Achmad to relax a little. Police and armed soldiers were far more brusque.

He heard Endang let the man in. From her respectful tone he figured the man must have the appearance of someone of standing. Then, with the door ajar, he could see part of a man's body sitting on the couch. Trunk and thin arm in white shirt, left thigh in batik sarong, and across the lap a briefcase. But the man was leaning forward, obviously eager for the interview, so Achmad could not see his face.

The man introduced himself as a business partner of Kamarusaman bin Ahmed Mubaidah. Since the crisis they had lost communication. He added, "It is common these days, Nonya." When Endang did not reply, he continued. "I am anxious to find him. We have an important business deal, so I must contact him right away. It's urgent, Nonya. Our business depends on it. Do you understand?"

"Yes."

"Good. If you would be so kind as to help me locate him, I would be most grateful." When there was no reply, he added tensely, "Can you tell me where he is?"

"No, Tuan, I am sorry."

There was a long pause. Through the crack, Achmad could see the knuckles of one hand whiten as it gripped the briefcase.

"I can understand your reluctance, Nonya. These are difficult times. But our business depends on my finding him as soon as possible."

"I am sorry, Tuan. Forgive me."

There was yet another long pause. "If I don't find him soon, we could lose everything."

"I have not seen him, Tuan. I am sorry. Please forgive me."

The man moved, got up, and walked out of Achmad's visual range.

"Please do what you can, Nonya, to find him. It is for his own benefit, believe me."

"I believe you, Tuan. I am sorry, please forgive me, but I don't know where he is."

"Try, Nonya. Here."

"No thank you, Tuan. I can't take that."

"It will help with expenses. Take it."

"Thank you, Tuan."

"There will be more if you locate him. Much more, believe me."

"Yes, Tuan."

Achmad waited, holding his breath until he heard the front door close with a dry little click. Then he rushed out, flying past his sister without a word. On the street, he glanced around wildly and saw a thin, rather tall man hurrying away with a briefcase under his arm. The man wore a Western fedora.

At the corner he hailed a becak. After the man got in, Achmad hailed another and followed. He had a little money left from what the Chinese girl had given him at the demonstration. But it wouldn't take him far in the becak. As the driver pedaled through the kampong, Achmad heard the loud fierce strains of "Indonesia Raja Merdeka," the national anthem, coming from a warung radio. He nearly lifted his hand in salute. Along the street some boys were pasting up posters on a wall: HANG AIDIT! DOWN WITH REDS! PKI IS LACKEY OF CIA! CIA IS CHINESE INTELLIGENCE AGENCY—THE REAL ENEMY!

Fortunately for Achmad the ride was not long. He let the tall businessman get out of the leading becak before he left his own. Achmad paid and stood back from the street at the entrance of a grocery stall. He watched the man enter a two-story house that had an iron gate. Two men in plain khaki stood at the entrance, both wearing sunglasses.

"Interested in him?"

Achmad whirled and looked around, not seeing at first the wizened little man sitting hunched against a box of coconuts inside the stall.

The little man grinned. "Are you interested in him, the one who went in there?"

Achmad almost denied it, but with another look at the little man—

obviously the stall sweeper—naked from the waist up, wearing only a pair of torn shorts and ripped sandals, he said, "Do you know who the man is?"

"What?"

Achmad thrust his last rupiah note into the stall sweeper's hand. "Do you know who that man is?"

"I do," the sweeper said, nodding vigorously. "Hartono. Big shot in the PKI."

"He's a Red? Is that a Red hideout?" Achmad squinted at the house where the two men in dark glasses seemed to be guarding the entrance.

"No. They're army," the sweeper explained.

"Is he under arrest?" When the sweeper hesitated, Achmad said, "Will you tell me what's happening? I have no more money. I mean it. You have my last rupiah."

After studying him a few moments, the sweeper sighed. "I believe you. The army has him under arrest. A kind of arrest."

"I don't understand."

"It's a time when most people don't understand much."

"The guards let him come and go?"

"That's what you don't understand. Everybody around here knows he's working for the army." The sweeper snapped his fingers. "Yesterday the PKI, today the army—who knows tomorrow? That's why he dines on ikan lele and I eat shit off the street." The little man grinned cheerfully. "You have to know what you're doing in this life. You have to understand things."

"Hartono," Achmad said, "so that's who he is. A Red."

"He finds out where his comrades are and tells the army," explained the sweeper. "That's right. He's an informer. At a time like this he'll do just fine." The little man suddenly frowned. "But you, you don't understand anything. If you're a Red, better stay clear of Hartono. That's a snake who bites."

"Thank you, friend."

"People like us should stick together," the little man said. "I don't care about your politics, but I know one thing—you live off the street like I do." He laughed, showing toothless gums.

Achmad, hurrying away, was shaken by his thoughts. He wasn't thinking about his sister's corrupter or about the Red informer but about fish. Ikan lele, black fish topped with green chilies, was a specialty from Sumatra—Achmad's favorite dish—and that's what he was thinking about. But the strength within asserted itself and brought him back to the only thing that mattered: killing Sjam.

So a Red informer was hunting him too.

Achmad shuddered. Would the army, with the help of Hartono, get to Sjam before he did? He was sweating profusely. It had been like that when his chute crumpled, flinging him to the damp earth, and with his comrades he had rushed into the jungle of New Guinea, wild for combat.

Forty-one

She loved him. There was no denying it. Part of every day, one way or another, she was with him, and every moment away from him was filled with longing. Maggie had never felt anything like it before. It was the stuff of storybook romance; she was living all the clichés. Either in her quarters at the Sakirman residence or in the Gitosuwoko compound they went to bed together, openly, without regard for the astonished servants who hovered just out of sight, as stunned by such flaunting of convention as by the political crisis that had gripped Yogya.

Maggie couldn't help herself. She had never wanted any man so much. Each time they made love she let the romance of it—for what else was this but romance?—wash over her like a warm tide. Whatever they did together, she found in it the same warmth after rapture, the same feeling of oceanic protection, and soon afterward the same feeling of emptiness to be filled again by love.

Budi was unpredictable in his passion, guided solely, Maggie knew, by whatever the moment brought to his mind, his heart, his body. He moved around her unresisting flesh like a panting wolf or lay calmly beside her like a puppy, licking the nipples of her breasts for what seemed hours. At times he was gentle, his hands adept at memorizing her body, as if she were a pakem padalangan—performance guide for one of his wayang plays. At other times he roughly parted her legs and flicked his tongue so rapidly across the hard bead between them that she wondered, in her ecstasy, if some kind of mythic serpent, a god transformed, was thrashing at her center. When he took her she never knew what to expect: a lover who made her feel that her own sensations deeply mattered to him or a satyr bent upon satisfying his own appetite as swiftly and brutally as he could. She wanted him either way, having no desire or will to choose which man he presented to her, and sometimes he gave her both Budis within minutes of each other, catching her off guard, pushing her beyond accumulated sexual habits into a world of unknown pleasure, and thereby ridding her of the last vestige of independence from the power of love. She listened to herself moan—no, not moan like a lady, but scream so shrilly that the whole compound must have heard the animalistic sound and then, good God, they must have also heard her accompany such an outcry with obscenities yelled in English, which fortunately they would not have understood, gathered as they probably were, under a shaded pavilion, rapt, hands at their throats in astonishment, their eyes straining to see what was hidden from sight but not from imagination.

Maggie was surprised that he never tried to maintain secrecy. It occurred to her in a spasm of distrust that perhaps he was behaving like a boastful male, like college boys who describe to frat brothers the details of their sexual adventures. But that idea passed. Maggie knew he was neither a braggart nor a coward. He would not be moved by pettiness, but would act without regard for consequences other than those he imposed on himself. He would not back away from his feelings—not Ki-Dalang Budi Gitosuwoko.

When they talked of love, Maggie found in his perception of it something bordering upon fate, coming close to lending their passion the sanctity of the inevitable, which was how she herself felt about it: what had happened to them was beyond moral judgment because it was beyond choice.

On the other hand, Maggie could not find in herself more intellectual justification than this weak appeal to destiny. For her what was happening was a continual torment. That, however, was a demand on herself that Maggie welcomed. She understood the temptation to rationalize, to disregard, to falsify, and by such means to come out of adultery smelling like a rose. Maggie was determined to look at everything head-on, including her sense of guilt, as if peering into an auto wreck at someone she loved. This was betrayal, this was wrong, this was selfish, and yet this was overwhelming, an irresistible tide of emotion she could not hold back.

She felt, however, that the dalang viewed their love as something merely essential and transparent as crystal, and although he was fully involved in it, Budi could step aside and look at their love with detachment before plunging back into the midst of it. He would not weigh the right and wrong, not that man, but withdraw himself emotionally a little while only to prepare for a new onslaught of passion—his emotions like the sexual act itself: amoral, insistent, joyous. If someone (perhaps one of her old friends from Iowa with whom she no longer shared anything but memories of mutual loyalty) had asked Maggie, "Do you trust this man, do you trust what is happening?" she would have replied without hesitation, "I trust his emotions, but I trust nothing that is happening."

She felt herself moving through fog, a mist that obscured everything aside from passion, so that day went into day like water into water. She let herself dream through each moment of her love for him.

Then the private dream turned into public reality when an officer from OPSUS came to see her.

This officer, on military business, had arrived in Yogya to assess the damage done to an OPSUS-owned kretek cigarette factory. A roving youth gang—it was not known whether Muslim or Red— had used the national crisis as an excuse to break in, furiously to dismantle machines, and to haul away as much loot as they could carry. The financial loss had prompted the army (otherwise so cautious and frugal and inconspicuous these days in the conduct of business) to send an investigator on a special flight to Yogya.

The officer had been instructed by General Sakirman (at Vern's insistence) to drop by the compound and see how the architect's wife was.

He was a small mustachioed man who obviously felt his superior had imposed upon him by sending him to see a foreign woman at a time like this. He didn't stay long enough for a cup of tea, but merely reported that Tuan Gardner was in good health and sent greetings to Nonya Gardner. Maggie fully understood that whatever she might say the officer would tell Vern exactly what he had just conveyed to her: good health and greetings.

Of course, she could scribble a note, but that would never do: "Darling, I have something to tell you. Somehow, I don't know how, I've fallen in love with someone else. Must close now since this officer is in a hurry. Love. Your wife."

Maggie stared at the man; he was tapping his thigh with an index finger, so self-important that, unlike Javanese, who practice courtesy at the expense of communication, he let his impatience glitter through. I must tell Vern, she said to herself in panic, as if until this moment her husband had been waiting in the fog, out of sight.

"Tell my husband," she heard herself say in a trembling voice, "we'll have a lot to discuss when we get together again."

The officer nodded, saluted briskly, and turned.

"Wait," Maggie said. "Have you got that? Would you tell me what I want my husband to hear?"

He repeated it badly and had to endure three more repetitions before the foreign woman was satisfied and let him get back to his important mission.

Watching him rush across the sunlit courtyard, Maggie felt something gripping her stomach, tightening into a knot. Was it the bad thing again? she wondered, but then clearly understood: her body was merely telling her that what was happening had only just begun.

She knew every note of every number on the Benny Goodman record by now; and when Krupa and Goodman were working on the last measures of their duet, Maggie turned from the letter she was writing and waited a few moments, ready for Jess Stacy's piano solo at the end of "Sing Sing Sing."

When it was over, she continued writing to the owner of a batik factory in Yogya.

"That is why the Committee for Safeguarding Borobudur is being created. What better time to think of saving the heritage of Java than when politics are thrusting the country into turmoil? The crisis will pass, but the largest stupa in the world will continue to stand right here."

Maggie paused, wondering how to broach the matter of the factory owner's financial contribution. With the dalang she had already worked out the general pitch to be used for all requests: helping restore Borobudur would be an act of goodwill and acts of goodwill added spiritual merit to life, good health to a family (a Javanese touch), and more business to a business.

Maggie's problem was to lead discreetly into a discussion of money. Each request had to be shaped to the individual's status in the community. Once the letters were written, Budi would translate them into high Javanese.

"Bu."

It was Inam who had come around the veranda. The girl never called her Nonya anymore, but the Javanese Ibu, for married woman, and lately the more familiar Bu.

"This has come from Pak Candra." Inam held out a sealed letter, which she opened, read, and translated at Maggie's request. There were a few lines of flowery salutation and obsequious good wishes, after which Pak Candra, who owned three concessions in the covered market of Pasar Beringharjo, expressed a desire to cooperate in any way he could, although at present that might be curtailed because of certain commitments and hardships of a temporary but pressing nature.

"Is he saying no?" Maggie asked.

"I think," said Inam after a thoughtful pause, "he is saying yes, but only if you go and talk to him and buy a little something."

"You mean flatter him."

Inam still had difficulty with her mistress's bluntness, and they both smiled, acknowledging it.

"You mean go to him in the role of a foreigner who looks as if she might be Dutch and bring back the good old days?" Maggie laughed outright. "Flatter him with my important presence?"

"I think he will give money if you pay attention to him, if you—coax him." The girl covered her embarrassed smile with both hands. "Yes," she said. "Tell him he is important and you need his help, something no one else but he can give, or the project will fail."

410

"You'd make a fine businesswoman, Inam."

"No, no," the girl said in alarm. "I never reach so high."

"I will go to him tomorrow." Noting the grim line of the girl's mouth, Maggie asked, "Is there anything wrong with my going tomorrow?"

"No, Bu. Except—someone has stolen your bicycle."

"I see. Can I borrow yours?"

"I don't think you can, Bu. They also stole mine. It is happening in the neighborhood. Boys are taking advantage of the crisis."

"I see. Have you heard anything?" Maggie was asking, as she did every morning, about Inam's missing brother.

"No, Bu, nothing."

"We have a saying in America: no news is good news." But Maggie had heard on the radio that members of Red youth groups were being rounded up in certain areas (never designated in the news reports) for questioning about activities that could threaten the peace of the country. When the girl stood there as if summoning courage to say more, Maggie asked her what was wrong.

"Another person, Bu, is also missing."

"I see. I think you must mean a young man." When Inam said nothing, Maggie declared, "I think it is a young man."

"Yes, Bu."

"He's also a Communist?"

The girl nodded.

"Inam, are you mixed up in politics?"

"Only my brother and—he, they are."

"You never mention your parents. Haven't they heard anything from your brother?"

"They are santri Muslim, not abangan like me. They have not spoken to my brother in months because he is a member of PKI."

"Maybe the crisis won't last long. People say it won't." She wanted to add, "That's the opinion of the man I love," but of course she could not. In fact, none of the Sakirman staff ever mentioned the dalang to her, not even Inam, who discreetly neglected to announce his arrival these days at the residence. He came into the compound at evening and left at dawn like a Javanese ghost.

Maggie told the girl that they were going out now to buy two bicycles and two locks, which the stolen ones never had, and they would keep the locked bikes inside her pavilion where neighborhood boys would never enter. (Whenever they saw her on the street they scattered, giggling in fear, because a foreign woman gathered spirits around her body as she walked, like scraps of cloud, and these spirits could attack anyone who annoyed her.)

After getting a new bike, Maggie would ride out to the university this afternoon and talk to people in the Archaeological Department. She understood there were two professors at UGM who were familiar with Borobudur. There were things she must know about climatic conditions and the structure of soils and local earthquakes and what she had learned through her reading to call "petrography." She must accumulate facts if she was going to convince the Javanese that they must restore the thousand-year-old temple.

Every day she worked on her promotional pitch, hoping it was eloquent without being patronizing, hoping that the influential and the rich would listen and believe, because only twelve miles out of town was something that would be there tomorrow and next week and for decades to come if cared for, a witness of centuries, a glorious monument that held secrets of the human heart and would stand for many centuries more at the foot of twin volcanoes, only twelve miles away, just twelve miles from where the present inheritors of Javanese history and tradition were now eating and sleeping, who had it in their power to preserve the stones of Borobudur that had commanded a hill for one thousand years, that could speak to untold future generations throughout the world about the yearning of mankind for God.

Yesterday Maggie had gone to see another old widow, this one not a princess but exceedingly rich, a priyayi woman whose husband had defied the Dutch after working for them a half century. When Maggie got up to leave, having received a rather vague promise of possible support, the old woman had said thoughtfully, almost reluctantly, and perhaps even a shade disapprovingly, "You are becoming Javanese."

"Oh, no."

"But you are. I have seen it happen a few times. I have seen someone come into this country and look around and say this is where I belong."

"Well, perhaps in a way that's how I feel."

"I know it is, Ibu Gardner. But you must practice your Krama very hard."

"Do I speak it that badly?" Maggie asked with a smile, having tried out a number of phrases during the interview.

"No, your Krama is good for as long as you have worked on it. But it takes years to master."

"Can foreigners really master it?"

"They can. Some have." Finally the stern old woman smiled. "You could."

Forty-two

Where was Achmad Bachtiar? To Ali it was not an important question (or at least far less important than others), but to his brother, Bambang, it was as important as if a Gitosuwoko had been the deserter. Because Achmad Bachtiar and Bambang had been like brothers since boyhood, and had only stopped being inseparable when Achmad took another path by deciding that life in the army was better than life in a gong factory; his apprenticeship there had been less promising than that of Bambang, who was bigger and stronger and who came from a family of dalangs and gamelan musicians.

It was now common knowledge in the village that Achmad had deserted. He had been a member of the raiding party that kidnapped and murdered the generals. Although only the ranking officers of the operation had been arrested or were sought, Achmad had chosen to flee anyway.

So went the story brought back to Yogya by men of the 454th Battalion. It was a story that Bambang refused to believe, and few within earshot of the foundry were brave enough to disagree with him. But in the back lanes they whispered about Achmad Bachtiar,

searching through the past for incidents that might have foreshad-
owed his treachery.

Bambang had his own version of what could have happened. Achmad Bachtiar must have undertaken the raid as a disciplined, obedient
sergeant. A noncommissioned officer would not have been responsible
for planning such an important raid and was therefore not answerable
for its terrible result. Surely Achmad Bachtiar never expected punishment, not even a reprimand, for carrying out orders. He had done
nothing but his duty. Wasn't that so? Bambang would demand of
anyone bold enough to stand firm and argue.

So Achmad had deserted for another reason, Bambang explained
at the foundry entrance to anyone who would listen. Such an honorable man—had he ever been otherwise in a lifetime of living in this
village?—would always behave honorably. So why had he abruptly
vanished, letting the world call him a traitor? Something of vital
importance must have put him on such a desperate course. What
could it have been? It could not have been his wife and child. They
were safe in the village, where everyone was safe except that worthless
Communist, Narto, who had never belonged here anyway. But what
about Achmad's sister? She was in Jakarta, where there was a curfew
and daily rioting and murder in the streets and martial law. His poor
widowed sister, defenseless in a big ugly, violent city. What might
have happened to her during the crisis? Who could know? But if her
brother received word that she was in trouble, a poor defenseless
widow, what might he do, Achmad Bachtiar, a man of undoubted
honor? To protect his sister he would do anything. "Anything!" Bambang would smack one hard flat palm with his ironlike fist.

After this explanation, if anyone had displayed the temerity (no
one did) to point out the dishonor that Achmad brought to the village
by deserting his post during a crisis, Bambang would have argued
(after delivering a blow with that ironlike fist) that Achmad Bachtiar
was on the contrary a man who brought honor to the village by
adhering to tradition. He believed in adat, the old ways, and adat
demanded that a man provide first for his sister if she was unmarried
or widowed before thinking of himself or even of his wife and child.
An honorable man like Achmad Bachtiar would observe adat to the
death.

So what had happened? Bambang would open his hands out as if they were pages of a book in a gesture emphasizing the simplicity of his explanation. Why, Endang had needed her brother, but unable to get leave during the crisis, Achmad had been forced to make a choice between his ancient familial obligation and service to his country. He had gone to his sister straightaway, without a thought of the public consequences.

No one disagreed with Bambang, although a few whispered in the back lanes that his version of adat was not everyone's idea of tradition. Some people argued that a man should think of wife and child before sister. Others argued that Bambang was right. But the argument took place out of his earshot. And not a voice was raised against him when he took Achmad's wife and child into his own household until arrangements could be made for their return to her own family in a village some thirty kilometers away.

Also staying in Bambang's house was Ali, who had returned there after the Narto murder. He had not been threatened, not at all, but eyes were on his back wherever he walked, and rumors of pitched battles in the surrounding countryside between Muslim farmers and Reds were coming into the village every day. Ali continued to lecture on land reform to anyone who would pause a few moments before escaping from his presence, because no one wanted to be near a Red organizer, not even one whose family had been in the village for generations.

Narto's family, however, had no such ties to the village; scared witless, they fled during the night before he was even buried. The few other acknowledged Reds in the village kept silent and when not working holed up behind shuttered windows in their houses.

Ali helped the Achmad Bachtiar family get ready to leave; he watched them climb into the back of an old cart drawn by an ox. Bambang had paid for the gerobak, a way of travel much slower but also more expensive than local buses, which were unreliable during the crisis (sometimes, in the face of ominous rumors, the drivers parked them on the side of the road and simply waited for better news).

As Ali stood next to his brother and watched the gerobak rattle away, Bambang turned suddenly to exclaim, "Achmad is a man of honor, whatever you think. He lives by adat."

"Yes, he does live by adat. And adat is merely feudalism," Ali

416

declared. "Because sultans made the rules centuries ago, should we follow them like slaves? If Achmad deserted for adat, how silly."

"Watch what you say, brother. One Red is already dead here. Do you think people will stand for your ideas after what the Reds have done to this country? Do you know why you're still alive? The Gitosuwoko name."

"Brother"—Ali was smiling—"you're as blunt as Bima. You too were born to speak Ngoko to everyone. Father used to say that: 'I've got a Bima in the house—not a word of Krama comes out of his mouth.' Remember him saying that?"

But his brother had already set out in the direction of loud sound— metal clanging against metal. Watching him walk away so briskly, Ali was aware of how close they had become in the last few days. It was true. They had somehow found brotherhood again. In their brusqueness with each other there was an old familiarity such as they had known as boys. Ali felt himself closing ranks with his brother against the whole village, because ultimately what mattered was not the village but the Gitosuwoko family. That was true, even when he tried to deny in himself the power and tenacity of a past that clung to him like a leech in a flooded padi.

He was going into Yogya. That had been his habit since the crisis began: every other day a trip through the surrounding fields and across the river by footbridge where he hired a becak to take him into the city. The countryside here was safe, at least now, although there were rumors of violence farther south, particularly around the village where Ali had seen men hanging in a tree. Like other people who came into Yogya, he got most of his information at the bus station. Travelers drank tea at a warung there and spread the news. It was from them that he heard of truckloads of paratroopers swooping down on the Red village some days ago, and afterward vultures were seen hovering over the roofs and a stench blew out of its paths when the wind was right. No one entered or left there. Soldiers wearing berets stopped people from going in; the village was off limits to everyone but military personnel.

Ali would listen to such stories and quietly go his way. Had people at the bus station known of his affiliation with the PKI, they might have given him trouble. They might have pushed, even beaten him.

Hard to say. At the moment emotions were as erratic as the flight of sparrows. But he continued to come and go without incident. Arriving in Yogya he would first visit Mas Slamat, who led him into the dim cluttered old house and served him a watery tea. They sat in the stale twilight air of the cavernous central room while the little man described a past he deeply yearned for: a time when priyayi gentlemen gave their waking hours wholly to the court, the plays and festivals and processions that marked the grandeur of sultanic rule.

In spite of himself Ali listened in a kind of rapture to the little man who had given up ordinary work for the pursuit of memory. Mas Slamat captured the essence of a glorious time gone by, of an era when their ancestors had followed the tortuous but exacting path of adat, which Ali publicly ridiculed, as a good Communist should, but which, since coming home, he had privately begun to admire again.

Today, he didn't find Mas Slamat at home when he knocked at the warped old door, so Ali set out for the Sakirman compound, ordinarily his second stop in Yogya. He no longer lusted after Nonya Maggie (that phase of his interest in her having mercifully passed), but he had come to admire the tall foreigner who studied Javanese and wanted to restore Borobudur. Not that she would succeed at either task, in his opinion. But such persistence was something that most of his own people lacked. They were too easily defeated by obstacles, and so his admiration for Nonya Maggie was mixed with envy.

This morning, as Ali sat with her on the veranda, having noticed a Javanese grammar lying on a table, he brought up the subject of cultures and her dedication to his. "In your place," he said, "I would not care so much for Java."

"Why not?"

"I would have interest only in my own culture."

"You are sure of that?"

"I am sure."

Nonya Maggie frowned thoughtfully. "Perhaps some people always know where they belong. I still don't know."

"Someday you will," Ali assured her—but without adding what he really believed, that she did not belong here. To change the subject he pointed to a small portable typewriter sitting on the table and asked where she had found something like that in Yogya.

"I dragged it all the way from America."

418

"You write stories with it?"

"Only letters." She explained they were written to UNESCO and to government agencies in Holland that might want to help in the preservation of a temple they'd admired during colonial days. She had also written to archaeological departments in every European university she could find the address of. Then of course there were letters to her own alma mater and a host of other American colleges and foundations.

Listening to her eager espousal of the silly project, Ali marveled at her ability to blot out what was happening around her. Were all foreigners so blind? Perhaps they were; ultimately they would leave here, and such a comforting prospect allowed them to be foolish, like children at play. Nonya Maggie was writing all these letters when not a scrap of mail was moving in or out of Indonesia.

Feeling a sudden need to protect this admirable but muddled woman, he said, "Be careful where you go. Something can happen anytime, anyplace."

She was staring at him, but in a way that let him understand she had heard his words without paying attention to them. Her mind was occupied elsewhere.

So he waited patiently for her to come back. Birds fluttered in a nearby tree and the girl Inam walked across the glare of the swept courtyard. He knew that her brother was a member of the local PKI, that the boy was missing. A lot of Reds were missing these days; perhaps like Comrade Pramu they had simply bolted and looked for a place to hide until the tension eased. Watching the girl's lithe body in its progress across the sunny yard, Ali supplanted her image with that of his brother's wife, Melani. He couldn't help himself, although it was a terrible thing to do. Lately he couldn't get Melani out of his thoughts. He was a man walking into destiny, a dedicated man who must be prepared to fight for principle, yet his mind was boiling with images of a round smooth face and large limpid eyes and breasts moving liquidly beneath a sarong and slim brown calves promising more treasure a few hand lengths upward. . . . It was bad enough to let desire for a woman weaken you when you needed strength for a crisis. It was even worse to covet your brother's wife. To rid himself of the despicable imagining, Ali blinked rapidly, as if blinded by sunlight.

Nonya Maggie said abruptly, "I'm sorry. Did you ask me something?"

Had he? He too had been lost in thought. Then he remembered. "I told you be careful."

"Oh, I will be. Don't worry. Ali, there's a favor I must ask you."

Without hesitation—he did like this woman—Ali said eagerly, "Please ask. I will do."

Nonya Maggie laughed. "First hear what it is. You see, I believe your uncle wants to see you."

Ali was too stunned to reply.

"I believe," she continued, "he's afraid for you because of the crisis."

"He told you to tell me?"

"He did not. I am interfering, I know. But maybe it's time you got together."

Ali could feel her eyes as if they were hands touching him.

"I think," she went on, "people should forget their differences at a time like this. When the world's collapsing, we need each other." She lifted her hands and wrung them in helpless embarrassment. "I shouldn't preach. Forgive me."

"You want me to see Uncle?"

"Yes."

"Then I will see him." Ali felt a sudden lift of emotion, a kind of joy, as if the promise he was making had already been there, held secretly in his mind, waiting to be called forth. In truth he did want to see his uncle. Nonya Maggie had given him the excuse.

But noticing a look of satisfaction on her face, Ali felt a new emotion, a rush of anger. Who was this foreign woman to interfere in the affairs of the Gitosuwokos? But he knew the answer almost before asking himself the question. She had the right of someone deeply involved in their lives, maybe more in the life of Dalang Budi Gitosuwoko than in his own.

"You like my uncle much?" he asked sharply.

"I do. Very much."

"Does husband know?"

Uncensored by the fear of consequence, his impulsive remark had an impact. Nonya Maggie's lips parted, her eyes widened, as if she had been struck physically. But he didn't want to hurt this woman, not Nonya Maggie, who had a reckless love for his country. To cancel

420

the effect of a jealousy he hadn't known he could feel, Ali added, "What I mean, does husband know how famous dalang my uncle is?"

"He knows," Nonya Maggie said with an uncertain smile.

"Good," Ali declared briskly, as if everything were fine. "Maybe they meet someday. I go now."

Moments later, as they parted at the courtyard doorway, Nonya Maggie seemed at ease again. She spoke of Mas Slamat. "I'm glad you're friends. He loves your visits."

Ali looked up at her (coming only to her shoulder was no longer a source of shame for him) and saw in her face something quite new. She was both more confident and more detached, as if part of her consciousness were here and another part elsewhere. It was like dreaming and waking at the same time, a common enough phenomenon among his own people, who yearned for privacy in the midst of an intense communal life. But he had never seen such an expression of dreaming on a Western face until now. It was a peculiar observation, and he carried it with him into the noonday light.

Forty-three

In the midday glare it took Ali a few moments to locate his uncle under the shaded roof of the pendopo, although he heard the dalang long before seeing him, for from within the blue interior of the open pavilion a soft but high-pitched chant drifted into the blazing light of the courtyard. Uncle was practicing a suluk; he rhythmically tapped the large puppet box that had been set beside him with a wooden tapper held between the large and second toes of his right foot as he sat cross-legged. Of course, Ali knew this without seeing it. How often, during his childhood, had Ali known his father to rehearse for a play by singing a mood song while striking the kotak with a chempala!

Wayang, the shadow world: at noonday it was nothing more than a puppeteer's exercise. Hands of a dalang moved invisible objects through blank air against an imaginary screen as he spoke dialogue or sang songs, creating the rhythm of unseen events. But at nighttime a world of passion and splendor and violence took shape in air trembling within the glow of an oil lamp. Ali had seen his father make such a world of shadows. Crossing the courtyard to the pavilion, he admitted to himself that his uncle could do the same.

Approaching, he saw his uncle peering out into the sunlight, surprised by such a visitor. Dalang Budi Gitosuwoko was wearing traditional dress today. Ali noted it: a blangkon squared on his head, a sarong pelekat scrupulously pressed, a kejama open at his throat—all in the muted batiks of the sultan's court.

Dalang Budi had stopped singing when he saw his nephew. Politely Ali urged him to continue, while climbing onto the platform of the pendopo. After a moment's hesitation, he saluted his uncle with a sembah, then crept on his knees halfway to the puppet box. Halting there he waited for his uncle to nod. When the nod came, he sat down cross-legged and faced the older man.

Suddenly Ali felt it had been a mistake for him to come here, to confront in a pliant almost humble mood someone he had hated for so long. He had come on nothing more than an impulsive promise given to a woman whom, admittedly, he would have trouble refusing anything. But here he was and he had shown proper respect for an older, honored relative. What happened next would be up to his uncle.

So Ali was relieved to see his overture reciprocated. Dalang Budi expressed concern for his safety during the crisis. Expressed it with obvious feeling, although Ali wondered how much the man really understood of what was happening beyond the compound walls. Did his uncle know, for example, that the regional PKI office was closed? And not only closed but burned to the ground by Muslim hooligans? That no party leadership existed in the region? That Comrade Pramu had simply vanished—had either fled or been killed? Did his uncle know of the chaos out there, the seething possibilities of violence on any lane in Central Java?

From his uncle's questions then, Ali felt sure that just as he had suspected the dalang knew very little indeed. His questions were those a child might ask. Are you safe? Has anyone threatened you? What is happening to the PKI? Questions a knowledgeable man would not even care to ask at a time of such uncertainty.

"Will you stay in the village?" his uncle asked.

"I will until told otherwise."

"Who will tell you?"

"The Regional Office of the PKI."

"But you just told me the Regional Office doesn't exist any longer. It was burned down."

"Then I'll wait until it's built again. I have no choice. I'm a cadre of the PKI." He added without thinking, "If only we had guns." When his uncle chose not to comment, he went on. "We should have armed long ago. But we counted too much on Sukarno. We believed he'd do more than simply encourage us. We leaned on his leadership. That was our great mistake. Our Confucian mistake."

The dalang leaned forward as if this remark especially interested him. "Confucian?"

"I despise Confucianism." Seeing his uncle smile, he said coldly, "Perhaps to you I sound like a foolish student. But I mean what I say. I despise Confucianism. Everywhere the Chinese go they spread it like a disease. Have you any idea how destructive it is? *If a ruler is wise and benevolent his people will be wise and benevolent:* that's a philosophy of tyranny."

"Some people call it a philosophy of faith in man."

"Propaganda of tyrants. You want to save that old temple out there. Do you know what it represents? The misery of thousands forced to build it and other thousands who starved to death when they couldn't grow crops because every bit of labor went into raising those stones to the glory of tyrants. Why are you smiling? Why are you looking at me that way?"

"Because I know your father would be proud of you."

"Proud? He'd be furious at the things I'm saying!"

"Proud because you think."

To that compliment, which seemed honestly given, Ali had nothing to say; he struggled with embarrassment in a gathering silence. Yet he also knew that the dalang might appreciate his logic without understanding its application. What could his uncle know of power in the real world? Ali had fled to Jakarta to escape the misshapen world of Javanese aristocrats.

Life in the capital had forced Ali to think of power in a different way than men like his father and his uncle had been taught to believe. To them power was a fixed thing, an unchanging amount of psychic strength coming from a divine source. A concentration of power in one place meant a lack of it in another. It was therefore something

424

to be managed and conserved, as you would care for the limited acreage of a rice field.

Thanks to Communist doctrine he knew that the old way of understanding power was wrong and harmful. It was symbolic rather than utilitarian, and consequently the design of a plan meant more than its effectiveness. Such priyayi ideas led to stagnation. Communism had ripped such fantasies from his mind, torn them out like weeds from a garden.

In Jakarta he had learned the truth. The newly found nation had been built upon ancient dreams, superstitions, games of status, a guileful heritage of passivity. What, for example, did people admire in a politician? His ability to outflank opponents by creating new symbols was what they looked for. His enforcement of policy was less important. Sukarno had survived for decades this way. The nation took mystic radiance for law. It was terrible.

As if coming out of one of those fabled trances that captivate the Javanese imagination, Ali realized that he had actually been saying such things, here, in the family compound. He had been lecturing an older relative. He had been able to do it only by deliberately forgetting that fact, and by letting the present crisis unleash him from the restraint of tradition. And his uncle? Dalang Budi Gitosuwoko had sat quietly, neither disagreeing with a shake of his head nor agreeing with a nod. He had simply listened.

Ali stopped talking, suddenly, and his uncle said, "Yes, your father would have been very proud of you."

"How can that be, Uncle? Neither of you could agree with anything I have said."

"I paid little attention to what you said."

"You gave the appearance of listening."

"I was listening to the past. To things your father used to say and I heard him in you—his voice at least, his intensity."

"I don't want to discuss my father with you."

"Perhaps it's time to do just that. You must understand what happened."

"I don't want to discuss it."

"Your father was a sick man for years. It was miraculous he survived such a long time. When he understood that he couldn't wait for you to become old enough for training, he decided to train me. There was no question of letting the Gitosuwoko tradition go. I came back from Singapore at his request. I gave up the idea of going to the West for study."

"You wanted to leave Java?"

"I did not want to be a dalang. I came back for the family."

"I never knew that."

"But you know now. Does it make any difference?"

"I have no right to judge you, Uncle."

"But you do judge me. Does it make any difference?"

"No. Because I never wanted what you have." This was a lie. Ali had often told himself that he had never wanted to be a dalang, but at this moment he felt deeply what a lie it really was. Had he been old enough to train—and good enough to train, because his uncle had not mentioned the fatal element of talent—he would probably have turned his back on communism and become a dalang.

So his uncle was making him face up to a lie that had dominated his life for years. It made Ali shake inwardly with rage, and so in this mood, maliciously, he said the words, "Nonya Maggie."

"Yes?" His uncle looked like an animal aroused by a sound of danger.

"She asked me to come here."

"She worries about you too."

"You know a lot about what she thinks and feels." When he got no reply, Ali went on at breakneck speed. "I asked her if she liked you, and she said yes, and if her husband knew how much she liked you, and she—Well, I didn't really ask this, because I didn't have to. I knew the answer, and I didn't want to embarrass her, although she doesn't deserve my sympathy, because what she feels is wrong, a married woman, and . . . and . . ." Ali stopped, knowing that to speak further would lead to the question of his uncle's feelings.

There was a long silence, which his uncle finally broke. "I love the woman."

Ali heard his own voice but scarcely recognized the high, thin trembling sound of it. "Do you mean love or like, Uncle?"

"Love. I love her."

"I think maybe I have known that." So now anything could be said. "You love her in the way a man loves a woman."

"Of course. Just that."

426

There was a kind of matter-of-fact quality to the dalang's voice that encouraged Ali to speak as directly. "You can see I'm surprised," Ali said, his voice stronger. "I am very surprised. I am shocked—and disappointed. Even though I am your nephew I think of you as other people do, as a dalang, which makes you different from other men."

"I am like any other."

"You are not like any other." Ali heard anger in his voice. "Another man could love such a woman, a foreigner, the wife of someone else, but not you. My father, your father, they would die of shame."

The dalang's face was calm; that expression of absolute composure convinced Ali there was nothing more to say. It was like a personal defeat. All his ruminations about the dalang's unworldly views and naive isolation from the centers of reality were nothing compared to the calm conviction on that square, dark face. If the dalang knew nothing about the uses of power, at least he wielded it intuitively, utterly. No one else could do what he was doing, Ali felt. No other priyayi in Java would declare love for a foreign woman, let alone a married foreign woman, and would—Was he sleeping with her? He must be. That accounted for her faraway look and his look of granite. They had walled themselves off from the world and the power of that idea awed Ali. He found himself rising and sembahing respectfully to his uncle.

"So be it," he said in the resigned tone of a santri Muslim who has handed over his fate to Allah. Now he could even change the subject without self-consciousness. "I have not heard you sing for a long time. Are you practicing for a performance?"

"I am only making contact again with wayang. Nephew, there is something more to say. You must learn to touch the world lightly and not often. You don't want to use yourself up."

"I want to use myself up in the service of my people."

"Very well, but try not to worry."

"Of course I worry."

"Worry gives you to the world. Worry makes you hold fast to things and tires you out."

"Don't you worry, Uncle?"

The dalang laughed. "Yes, I worry. I worry about Borobudur. That's why I'll perform again someday, to raise money for the restoration."

"You've done that before and corrupt officials saw to it the money never got to Borobudur. You don't understand how things work. You live in a dream, Uncle." Ali was astonished at his boldness. Such out-and-out criticism of a family elder—containing no modulation, without an accompanying smile or gesture of deference—was beyond his own experience and surely beyond that of his uncle too. What was happening now was raw, unmediated between them—startling in this compound, within this pavilion where Ali's father had ruled with a glance.

Even so, the dalang never changed expression. "Each of us," he said, "chooses his own attachments—the things that will use us up. I would say ultimately it's foolish to attach yourself to anything but love."

"Love of your country is love. Love between a man and a woman is not everything. Other love's as important."

"I think not."

Ali sembahed once again and carried into the courtyard the awe that he had felt in his uncle's presence. It was useless to hate such a man. It was like hating the ocean or a storm.

As he crossed the courtyard, Ali heard behind him his uncle singing the suluk again. He felt himself transported by the exuberant sound into the past when he had sat on the edge of the pendopo, this same pendopo, and idly listened to his teacher-father patiently explain to his student-uncle the subtleties of wayang singing.

Those forgotten explanations now drifted back into Ali's consciousness as a breeze might drift into this courtyard, the very one which he had walked across countless times as a boy, often at the call of his stern father seated within the blue shade of this same pendopo.

Hurrying down the lane, Ali could not sort out the emotions he felt. He barely registered the sight of a dozen boys carrying signs on the way to a demonstration: HOLY WAR! KILL REDS! KILL AIDIT! KILL OUR ENEMIES AND WORSHIP ALLAH!

Ali brushed past them. His mind was broodingly filled with images of Nonya Maggie, the tall *orang asing,* with her long legs and broad shoulders and full breasts and blue eyes. It was not her fault that such a terrible thing had happened. She was, after all, a foreigner who could be easily tempted by a man like his uncle. Ali felt a blind rage because his uncle, through a reckless choice, was bringing dishonor

428

to the family name. I am a Gitosuwoko, Ali told himself. But a Communist too. I won't ever let them forget that.

Somewhat calmer, he slowed his pace and looked for a shady warung where he could drink some tea and collect his thoughts, because there was work to be done, organizing to carry out. Until he received official orders, he, Ali Gitosuwoko, would stay where he was and do his duty. Whatever the crisis brought, he had his own road to follow.

That settled, he felt better, but while approaching a warung shed at a crossroads, Ali saw in his mind the solemn but pretty face of his brother's wife, her rounded figure moving liquidly in a sarong as she worked in the kitchen. He couldn't help himself. It was, as the dalang had said, an attachment, but one he would have never chosen, one that horrified him. He tried to rid his mind of her image by daydreaming of another woman, any woman (except the tall foreigner), by imagining his own wife, a shadowy unknown woman right now, but she would be calm and modest, and someday, like Melani, she would cook her husband's food, give him children, and care for him in his old age.

Forty-four

They left the dalang's warm bed before dawn and climbed into the old car, really a Japanese Army scout car (the old driver proudly identified it as a Kurogane-designed Type 95) that had been converted shortly after the war. The old man would not have ventured outside of Yogya had it not been for the dalang. But driving such an honored person anywhere was a boast worth risking his life for. So he often drove the dalang and the foreign woman to Borobudur.

Today, however, they were heading for the Hindu temple at Prambanan, ten miles out of town. As they rode, Maggie reached out and touched the dalang's hand, a hand practiced not only in puppetry but in love, as he had demonstrated in the blackness of early morning by running it lightly across each breast until her nipples tingled and she begged him to enter her.

In a tinge of blue light coming through the car window she could see his profile, the strong nose, prominent chin, high forehead, and for a moment Maggie found herself comparing this profile to that of Vern Gardner—comparing them and finding them somehow disturbingly similar. But the moment passed, and she gripped Budi's

430

hand more tightly, as if their clasped hands could turn away the current of guilt that surged through her veins at sudden unexpected moments.

She never mentioned her husband for fear Budi might say, "If you feel such guilt, you must not be happy, and if you're not happy, you should not be with me." He was capable of something cool and logical, something straightforward like that, something wise but lacking a Western kind of compassion. She no longer doubted his love, yet too much in their upbringing separated them from the sort of mundane safe understanding she could develop with a man of her own culture. Maggie wondered if she could ever say the simple things to him: I love that tie. Have you got the tickets? Let me tell you what that awful woman did today.

Blazing, dramatic—that was Budi Gitosuwoko as a lover, but as a man he was often remote, if not cold, stark in his opinions, so intrepid and restrained that ordinary dangers and problems did not seem to exist for him. He had told Ali about their love affair and then had told her that he had told his nephew, but without needing a reaction from her, as if the admission were too commonplace for discussion.

Initially she had been upset. She would have preferred telling Ali herself, and on a few occasions had almost blurted it out, especially that time when he had suddenly and rather cryptically asked if her husband knew about the famous dalang here in Yogya. She had been on the verge of telling him then, because he seemed to be right on the edge, waiting for her to do so. But perhaps it had been better for Budi to tell him. Budi must have done it in an artless, forthright, almost diffident manner—disarming the sensitive young man. She hoped for the day when uncle and nephew would be close again.

As they rode along, Budi was explaining the plot of a wayang play. In *Irawan's Wedding* an intended bride is kidnapped by an ogre and eventually rescued. It takes place in the fantasy land of Amarta, where heroes never age, damsels remain beautiful, and evil is thwarted. His older brother had performed it during the struggle for independence. Perhaps the lighthearted mood, which had been so different from the mood of embattled Indonesia, coupled to the obvious symbolism of justice prevailing over wickedness, accounted for the lakon being immensely successful.

Maggie listened, but she was really thinking of Borobudur and of

Budi's relationship to it. He talked often of restoring the temple, yet his enthusiasm seemed to be tinged with naïveté. The truth was he had no head for business. He could spin worlds from his talent the way a spider spins webs from its body: handle puppets, sing, tell jokes, keep a story going for nine long hours. But to deal with government bureaucrats and organizations at whose mercy he would be while restoring Borobudur, the dalang needed more practical experience than his temperament would ever let him acquire. He would never quite understand how to jockey for patronage, plead for money, scheme, and persist in the face of ignorance, greed, jealousy.

That, Maggie decided, was where she came in. Whatever else happened, she felt it was her destiny to help Budi restore the great temple. She had learned in grad school how to write grant proposals, how to maneuver among the rocks and shoals of academe. That knowledge and experience she could apply here. And she also had in her favor a blind love for this man and a brassy American ingenuity. Indeed, she had never felt more blatantly, joyously American than while planning the restoration of Borobudur.

A few days ago, during a spasmodic turn of luck in this unpredictable country, the mail had started running again, so that Inam had come to her with a stack of letters.

There was one from Vern. He must have received one from her, their letters passing in mail trains after having lain in depots for days. Hers would sound chatty and empty and innocent enough, having been written during the time when she believed her feeling for the dalang was only infatuation that would soon pass. She opened Vern's letter.

It contained an old report about Jakarta, but recent news broadcasts confirmed that it was still valid. He wrote that there was rioting, but so far no extensive violence. Some street beatings, some arson, some looting—that kind of thing. He missed her. He missed her terribly. It was painful for Maggie to read. And yet a third time this man who was ordinarily reticent about love wrote it down: "I miss you, sweetheart, more than you can imagine, and I'm not kidding." But he felt it was better for her to stay clear of Jakarta. He hadn't yet found a way of getting out to Yogya: transportation was controlled by army combat units. Reading this part of the letter, Maggie trembled. What if tomorrow or the next day he came knocking at the pavilion door while she lay in another man's arms?

There was a letter from her mother in reply to one Maggie had sent during her first days in Yogya. Her mother complained about the manager at the department store, long hours, low pay. Complained about two corns on her right foot. Complained about the neighbor across the way who had divorced her husband and in plain sight of everyone was bringing in men at all hours, right up the front steps and into the house, and they left anytime they pleased, with her leaning out the window waving gaily good night or good morning, whatever it happened to be.

There was no letter from her father.

There had been no reply to her letter to the Archaeological Service in Jakarta, but Budi assured her it was because of the crisis. She wasn't so sure. But she did receive an encouraging letter from the Museum of Antiquities in Leiden along with an 1873 monograph on Borobudur by C. Leemans translated into good English. She figured that all the scholars associated with Borobudur would soon be known to her, and their names—Oldenberg, Pleyte, Kaern, Foucher, Brandes, Krom, Slutterheim, Bosch, Kempers—would become as familiar as the names of leading experts in her own field of study.

Biking these days down the troop-laden streets of Yogya, she often went to the American Consulate and glared at the red-faced marine guards at the sentry box, wanting to say, "You look so high and mighty, well, fuck you, boys, I am going in there!" while she cooled her heels and waited for entry as she did every time, because they all acted as if they had never seen her before. Allowed into the consulate, she pored through its library, sifting through materials for grant proposals and bilateral aid programs and foundation applications and international funding schemes, searching for ways to squeeze out a few bucks and a little world attention. She had found her destiny here. It was as inevitable as the sun coming up.

And the sun did come up. They saw the central spire of Prambanan catch against its bricks a flood of sunshine when the old scout car rumbled off the main road onto a dirt path. It was Maggie's first close view of the thousand-year-old Hindu temple. Prambanan had been built about the same time as Borobudur; she had the facts, of course. At first sight people usually felt, so Maggie had read, that it was more impressive than the Buddhist temple, and now she could see why. Unlike Borobudur, which was squat on its hillside until you climbed the ramparts and oversaw the entire valley, Prambanan thrust dramatically upward, its three peaks representing the main Hindu gods. For Maggie, in this early light, the central tower possessed a rocketlike potency in its illusionary lunge upward, upward, upward toward Mount Meru, abode of divinity.

When they got out of the car and strolled past the outer ruins to the central courtyard, Budi explained that villagers hereabouts called this place the Valley of the Dead. Apparently the temple had been built to house the ashes of Hindu princes.

Maggie stared at the tallest of the three spires, the central one, dedicated to Shiva the Destroyer. Inside it were statues of a number of gods, and the goddess Durga, who by popular account was actually a figure from Javanese legend, Loro Jonggrang, the Slender Virgin, who had been turned to stone by her rejected lover. Through the heat and glare as she looked upward, Maggie felt a comparison coming like something wriggling on the end of a line: she and Vern, Loro Jonggrang and the rejected lover—a weird, disturbing comparison leaping with lightning quickness across the centuries.

When they climbed up the steep stairway and peered inside the chamber, Maggie saw the goddess-virgin. Her nose was missing and her stone breasts had been worn smooth over the centuries by the pressure of many hands placed on them for good luck. The hallucinatory moment had passed. Maggie felt good, almost professional, almost scholarly, as she studied Prambanan.

Coming down from the internal chambers of the temple, Maggie stopped for a look at the lively sculptural reliefs on the balustrades that illustrated events from the *Ramayana*. On other walls there were tiny lions in niches and a menagerie of imaginary creatures. Maggie was so absorbed by the wealth of sculptural detail that she didn't notice Budi leave her side. When finally she looked around, she saw him below, at ground level, down on one knee, inspecting something.

When she reached him, Maggie let out a cry of horror. Sticking out of the mud was a human hand, swollen but with the skin intact, its fingers clenching the empty air.

It had rained the night before. That's all the dalang said, while moving gingerly along the lower wall of the temple. But she understood him: rain had washed away the muddy earth and exposed the shallowly buried corpses. Budi stopped now and then, studying a piece of clothing, a visible ear, a foot, even a bare chest thrust up as if from the sea, its skin with the bruised look of an overripe pear.

Maggie said nothing, but stood silently by and waited. She was watching him. His face, as he moved calmly, almost sluggishly through this garden of death, took on an expression she had never seen there before. Despite the growing intensity of this look, Maggie could not tell what it meant. Pity? Anger? Surprise? Perhaps none of them, perhaps all.

When abruptly he turned from the dozen or more visible corpses and walked out of the courtyard, Maggie followed, just as if they had discussed what to do and were simply doing it. They crossed northward, past the third of the main towers, the one dedicated to Vishnu, and walked beyond scores of battered minor shrines. Then she knew where he was going.

A farmer wearing a conical hat was stooping in a rice padi, yanking out weeds. Budi, stopping on the edge of the padi, called out a polite good morning.

The man, looking up, straightened his back and regarded Budi a long time from under the shade of his hat.

"I have seen you before," the man said.

Budi identified himself.

The farmer sembahed, but without the enthusiasm Maggie had usually seen people show when meeting the dalang.

"There are bodies in the temple," Budi said calmly—carefully, it seemed to Maggie, as if there mustn't be too much made of this discovery.

"Yes." The farmer removed his hat and wiped his forehead with the back of his hand. "They had a fight two days ago right there."

"They did? Friend, who were they?"

"Reds and Muslims." He turned and pointed with the hat into the eastern distance, where sunlight had thrown a ring of gold around a

435

blue mountain. "Reds have a village over there. And over there"—
he pointed northward—"the Muslims have one. Santris. Very strict.
I don't have any trouble myself." Grinning, he put his hat back on.
"I am Katolik. Only family in my village that is. My politics are
Christian. I belong to Partai Katolik, and I alone around here belong
to it. So we aren't bothered by what's going on. Who cares about
Christians at a time like this?" He chuckled as if revealing something
he had done that was very cunning. "I thank God for my grandfather
who became Christian in Sembalang one summer. People used to
laugh at us, but now they don't. They don't care about us at all. We're
forgotten, thanks to Jesus Christ Our Savior."

"There was a fight?" Budi asked when the farmer paused.

"Reds came over here and said to the Muslim boys, 'Let's have it
out,' and so they came over here to the Valley of the Dead, because
that would seem the right place for a fight. I think so too. I stood
right over there." He pointed past his field to a clump of guava trees.
"I watched them go at one another with bamboo spears and ani like
this one." He took the curved knife at his belt out of its scabbard
and waved it briefly, grinning, before putting it away. "Muslims got
the worst of it, but then they were only boys. The Reds were men.
When the boys asked for mercy, the Reds said, 'All right, throw down
your weapons and we'll let you go.' Then when the boys did that,
the Reds butchered them." The man shrugged his thin shoulders.
"You never know. They say wash your face to forget a death, but I
have washed mine a dozen times and I still see them dying."

Maggie was still listening to the mournful voice of the farmer when
Budi began walking away. Again she followed, wondering if he had
forgotten her. Walking back into the courtyard of the temple, he
climbed the stairs of a small shrine east of Shiva's; here was a free-
standing sculpture of the great god's mount, the bull Nandi.

Maggie followed and halted when she came within sight of the
dalang; he was squatting out of the sunshine against a shrine wall,
near the buttocks of the stone bull. A ray of light flowed across the
top of Budi's head, giving his black hair a sheen. For an instant she
thought of her fingers rippling through it, because he was alive and
beautiful and they were hideous down there. Then she knelt down
and waited.

436

Maggie was not accustomed to being with anyone who could remain so silent, so utterly motionless. Usually, when people were quiet around her, Maggie felt at least they were aware of her presence. She did not feel Budi was aware of hers, although only a few feet separated them where they crouched under the wall.

Just as Maggie was accepting the condition, forgetting his presence in the contemplation of her own silence, Budi muttered, "I see."

She did not feel he wanted her to reply, so Maggie said nothing.

Then he turned his head fully to stare at her. "It's an old custom to ask dalangs what they see. I remember once I asked my brother this question: 'What do you see?' And he told me, 'I see what you see, neither more nor less. But we see differently. What you see is what's in front of you at the moment. Sometimes you put what you see at the moment with things you have seen before. But not always. Whereas what I see I carry with me and put with everything else I've seen until it makes a pattern, as you might make a pattern of batik.' My brother said to me, 'I always make a pattern from what I see, but you do or maybe you don't. It depends. What you see now and what you saw yesterday and what you will see tomorrow sometimes remain apart from one another. They dance in front of your eyes like something strange and unconnected. For me, however, seeing is confirming the world as I already know it. It's as far from mysticism as anything can be. What I see is the real world and what you see is only part real because it's all broken up in pieces. Make it all real someday, Budi, or you will never understand what it means to see.'"

Budi fell silent, and again Maggie waited. Then he said, "I tried to do what he did, and sometimes I succeeded. That is, I put things together as though on a string—time past, present, and in a way time future. I could see them hanging there, all in a row, in a pattern. I thought I had been seeing in his way, but now I know I failed."

"Failed how?"

"I never put the world outside of mine inside of mine. The string of things mattered only to me, although if I had actually looked, I would have seen the other things as well. I misunderstood what my brother said. He confirmed not only his own but other worlds. I confirmed only mine."

Of course, she knew that. Anyone who knew the dalang must know that. He lived in his own world, unrepentingly outside the world of others. Yet until this moment he had never known about himself what was obvious to everyone else. He had just made a philosophical statement out of something as obvious as the sun rising. Was that the way of great men? Maggie wondered. At times they lacked the sense of the smallest child, of the biggest fool. But his eyes were opened now; that was clear. The corpses awash in mud, with their bodies adrift in the shame of violence, had brought Ki-Dalang Budi Gitosuwoko into a world he had never before entered.

Rising, she went to him and took his hand. She tried to calm her trembling fingers as they held his. And so Maggie sat there, holding on to destiny, because nothing, not even the Valley of the Dead, could take from her grasp this man and Borobudur.

―――――――

On her return home that afternoon from Prambanan, she was thinking of the evening to come. He would stay here tonight and be with her while the moon sailed across the compound roofs. That's how Maggie thought of the moon—sailing in an ocean of sky. She felt her mind fill with cheap poetry, but that was all right. Nothing must be held back now. He had begun to suffer, that was certain. For Maggie it was like watching leaves turn color in autumn or a caterpillar turn into a butterfly: something absolute, irrevocable. She had seen him visibly change as his world opened outward into the troubled land of Indonesia.

If her husband found a way to get here and if he came to her pavilion in the night and found her with her lover, what would she do? She would face it if it happened. But she would not let herself live in the fear of it. There wasn't time for private fears now. What she and Budi had seen today at the Hindu temple had changed everything, as if they had walked through a mirror and like adult Alices had entered another world. Because not only Budi but she herself as well had been taken by the scruff of the neck and shaken.

And so it was with difficulty that Maggie focused on the old servant who abruptly appeared, lips trembling, hands clasped at her breast.

"Yes?" Maggie began reacting to the alarm shown by the old woman. She half rose from the chair. "What's wrong? What's happened?"

438

"Inam is gone, Nonya."

"Where is she?"

"Soldiers came and took her away."

Maggie was on her feet. "What for? Why?"

"Soldiers did not say." The old woman waved her hands ineffectually in the air. "Inam is gone."

Forty-five

The small mustachioed officer who came to see Vern at OPSUS stood impatiently in the doorway while delivering his message brought from Yogya: Nonya Gardner was in good health and sent greetings. With that he turned and would have set out at a brisk military pace had not Vern called him back loudly to demand more information.

The officer, tapping his thigh impatiently—for he had important work to do—insisted there was nothing to report except health and wishes, so Vern let him go. It was like letting a dog go that had been chained to a post. Vern watched his thin shoulders bobbing rhythmically down the row of offices, then dipping out of sight. So Maggie was in good health; if that was not much information, at least it was vital.

How he missed her.

And then when mail arrived with the suddenness of blue sky after a storm, he had received a letter from his wife. It was full of enthusiasm for the Javanese language and her impossible dream of restoring that

Buddhist temple, but at least the words were written by her in her slanted girlish script.

He missed her. And he was getting horny.

Not that he couldn't deal with it. Throughout his life Vern's easygoing acceptance of sexuality had enabled him to separate it from his true feelings. He loved Maggie; he had sex with her. They were not mutually exclusive, but neither did one depend on the other. Vern believed that.

But he also believed that morality was a matter of not hurting other people if you could avoid it. Which was why he kept himself under strict control around Yanti. Each day he felt more drawn to her. Well, the truth was she flirted with him, and they both knew that if he made a pass, she would go for it. They both knew it, although surely the girl had no real understanding of what "going for it" would mean. If not a virgin, surely Yanti had little experience. He would only cause her a lot of trouble if they had a fling. Here is where his bare bones of a philosophy came in: if he could—*and* he could—he must avoid hurting her.

But his wife was out there some hundreds of miles away in Central Java. Making love to her would be just right—legally, morally, anyway you looked at it, hallelujah. And so Vern set about trying to get to Yogya in spite of the moratorium on flights other than those strictly tied to the present crisis.

He knew enough not to ask General Sakirman, whose demeanor these days was solemnly pious, his ethics those of a holy man. If Vern asked the general for help and got a refusal, anything further he might do would be tantamount to disobedience, and though a foreign civilian, he still operated under the rules and regulations of OPSUS. He could lose the contract just when theoretical plans were edging close to implementation of Project Palm Tree.

So Vern went to a junior officer in OPSUS. This lieutenant in supply had a reputation for masterminding more deals than the rest of the staff put together. He was fat, smiling, bespectacled, and in a low-echelon post that gave him access to people without the limelight that can bring a con man down. Over some mint tea in Vern's office they had a little talk; money in a plain envelope lay on the desk; the officer, after some conversation, took up the envelope; and the next day Vern found himself at, of all places, Halim Air Base awaiting a military flight to Yogya. He kept congratulating himself on his knowledge of Indonesian corruption, while warming a bench in the waiting shed.

Half an hour before flight time an air force colonel came in and studied Vern briefly. The officer then left and minutes later a captain appeared, holding a slip of paper. Looking at Vern, he read from it crisply in Bahasa Indonesia. Vern had no trouble following the words, which informed him that because of the present crisis no foreigner, including personnel attached to the Indonesian military, could be granted transportation until further notice. Vern regarded the officer closely, and from that stern expression he understood there was no sense in arguing, no possibility of dragging out another bulging unaddressed envelope that could make things right.

So back to Jakarta he went, and the next day received an irate note on U.S. Embassy stationery from Jack Rutledge. "If, Mr. Gardner," the message read, "you persist in disobeying explicit regulations issued by the Indonesian government during the present emergency, your own government will be forced to intervene. What I'm saying, Vern, is we'll throw you the hell out of the country if you can't behave. And no more telexes for a while. See you for drinks one of these days, maybe."

That afternoon Sakirman called him in, furious too. Vern took the dressing-down (obviously Sakirman enjoyed this official occasion to castigate an American) with calm equanimity coupled to a humble apology, although he refused to cooperate when Sakirman demanded that he reveal his method of getting flight clearance. Sakirman asked for the information but with a diffidence that made Vern wonder if indeed the general would rather not know who in his organization was arranging such things. Corruption breeds fear among the corrupted; let sleeping dogs lie. Those had been guiding principles since Vern had joined OPSUS. The top brass seemed ready to let the whole thing drop, if only the foreigner didn't provide disclosures through his own ignorance. Vern emerged from the abortive scheme with respect intact for the supply lieutenant who had covered his tracks well enough to connive again another day.

And so Vern must wait awhile longer for his Maggie. When Sakirman called him in later that afternoon, Vern figured he would get another lecture on duty and sacrifice, a pious reminder of their mutual deprivation—"if your Maggie is not with you, my Sus is not with me either"—so Vern was surprised by the general's friendly smile when he stepped into the office.

"Bung Karno wishes to see American architect once again more," Sakirman announced, beaming.

When Vern climbed out of the copter on the lawn of the presidential palace in Bogor, he had no illusions about this visit. Sukarno, sick and embattled, perhaps in his own arrogant way courageous, must be looking for diversion other than the countless dollies who paraded through his bedroom surely more for reputation than pleasure during these long, weary days following the Night of the Generals. Like other men under the gun, Sukarno must have looked back longingly at his carefree student days—for him, at the Bandung Technical Institute as an architectural engineering student. The president's fit of nostalgia must have conjured up an American who was going to build a hotel no taller than a palm tree.

And after Vern had clicked his way through the marble-floored reception halls of the palace to the Beloved Leader's private study, he soon learned that his guess was correct. Sukarno greeted him effusively, reaching across a glass-topped desk to shake his hand and remind him that they were in a sense brothers by virtue of their education and their mutual love of eighteenth-century French architecture.

When seated across the desk from Sukarno, Vern had a few quick moments to study the Beloved Leader before they began talking. Sukarno looked far wearier than at their first meeting. His cheeks seemed more deeply pitted by smallpox scars, perhaps because a pasty yellow complexion emphasized them. Even so, his movements were still surprisingly rapid, and he steepled his fingers in a gesture that suggested quick but efficient thinking, although at times during their conversation, his speech thickened and a pall came over his eyes, as if his mental acuity had suddenly left him like something falling from a cliff.

At first they discussed Project Palm Tree, which the president insisted on calling Project Mango Tree. Called it Mango Tree so often that Vern wouldn't have been surprised if the next day Bung Karno phoned OPSUS and ordered the name changed. Father of his country, Sukarno could still do that. Whimsical yes, but not the buffoon that Western journalists sometimes made him out to be. Vern had the respect for Sukarno that he would have had back home for a congressman who made silly speeches and pinched girls in the corridors but who got legislation through. Sukarno had certainly proved himself wonderfully adept at political games. For years in public forums he had shuffled the principles of Islam and nationalism and Marxism like a deck of cards. He had cajoled and bullied the Indonesian islanders, suspicious of one another for centuries, into accepting the idea of unity. Whatever his excesses, Bung Karno was still worshiped by millions across the mountains and fields of a vast nation. This was true, even though recent events had forced him to compromise in a way he would not have dreamed possible a few months ago.

Vern had watched along with the entire nation how daily the Beloved Leader's absolute power had been chipped away. Sukarno had formally acceded to the army's demand for Suharto's appointment as commander of the army, which in today's political climate made Sukarno's chief rival the second most powerful man in the country. And he had bowed to Suharto's request to remove Foreign Minister Subandrio from KOTI, the supreme governing body, and then to dismiss Vice Marshal Dhani as head of the air force, and finally Sukarno had been forced by advisers both loyal and hostile to give Suharto full authority to establish special military courts for the trial of Reds. Vern had heard that Suharto even had the power to appoint the judges of such courts and himself determine who should be tried. Clearly, Sukarno was hard-pressed, yet just as clearly, if he so desired, the Beloved Leader could change the project's name from Palm Tree to Mango Tree in an instant.

During a pause in their conversation, Sukarno scratched the top of his left hand with his right. Vern noticed that both hands were raw from such scratching. Moreover, the president's lips often twitched, as if his facial muscles were out of control.

Suddenly he exclaimed, "I am shocked by the killings, I am amazed and distressed by them! How can it be?" He didn't wait for Vern's response but added, "Of course, the coup thing was a minor incident. It was blown out of proportion by people who've tried for years to shit on me."

Vern wasn't surprised by the vulgarity. Sukarno often used such words in speeches as an appeal to the Marhaen, the common people whose unqualified support had always been the bulwark of his policies. But he was surprised by Sukarno's open defensiveness with a foreigner. Steepling his hands, his slack jaws moving in choppy little waves of vigor, he maintained (using the same phrase that Vern had heard on the radio) that the attempted coup was nothing more than "a ripple on the ocean of the Indonesian Revolution"—a statement that had drawn public outcries from high-ranking army officers, who pointed dramatically southward in the direction of the murdered generals' graves.

Sukarno seemed momentarily to have forgotten his listener as he launched into a diatribe against divisive elements in society. Then he praised the Communist party, as he'd been doing lately in speeches. No other political party had stood up against the Dutch the way the PKI had done. Of course, as recent events indicated, the Communists had behaved stupidly; they were like rats that had eaten a big slice of the cake and had then tried to eat the foundation of the house as well.

"In catching the rats," he declared, "we should not burn the house." And he went on. And on and on, until Vern noticed tiny silvery beads appearing on his forehead, as if sweat had crystallized. And then Vern recalled someone at the hotel bar talking about Sukarno's kidney insufficiency and "uremic frost" appearing on the skin of someone suffering from it.

Sukarno mentioned, without logical introduction to the subject, that he feared nothing. His courage did not come from a magic kris given to him by a woman who meditated in a cave—a stupid rumor spread by spies from Malaysia and journalists from the West who were all salesmen of hate, excuse me, American, but you know it is true, you won't admit it but you know it, and so I just laugh at such rumors and go my way as I have always done, for the good of the people, of this great nation, until by spiritual struggle we will have arrived at a symphony of victory, and then all their rumors will come crashing down, crashing down crashing down, and they'll stop saying my six wives and other women have fucked away my energy because they will realize then that nothing can destroy the sort of energy I have, it comes from God Himself, given to me (and here he brandished both clenched fists and brought them down heavily on the glass-topped desk) for the sole purpose of leading my people into the Golden Age, leading them leading them leading them into the Golden Age!

He paused, breathing rapidly, running his tongue across his lips. When he got his breath back, Sukarno asked almost timidly, "Do you ever have a bad taste in your mouth?"

Discreetly Vern answered, "Sometimes."

"Yes, so do I." Sukarno, relieved, sat back with a smile. "I take sodium bicarbonate. They've put me on a low-protein diet, but I can eat as much salt as I want. What do you think, American?"

"Of what, Bung Karno?"

The president hesitated, as if he'd forgotten his question. Then he said, leaning over in the hunched manner of sharing a confidence, "What do they say about me at OPSUS? I ask merely from curiosity. I'm interested in the observations of informed and sympathetic foreigners like yourself. How they perceive things."

"I understand, sir." Vern was not sure what to say. He could not tell the truth: that he had heard young army officers (made progressively bold because of their superiors' public disdain for the president) laugh outright at Sukarno's old-fashioned Javanese morality, an amalgam of wayang and superstition, featuring rhetoric rather than substance, ritual rather than action, acronyms rather than programs; that he had overheard a captain mimicking one of the president's more cryptic and ill-considered phrases: "Revolution is a dynamically dialectical process or a dialectically dynamic process"; that often lately he had listened to personnel express contempt for a man who talked unity but was so afraid of criticism that he was forever sizing up who was for and who against him; that even corporals and sergeants were outspoken enough these days to accuse the Beloved Leader of being so drugged by women and blinded by Reds that he couldn't even retool himself (which brought a brave titter of laughter from a knot of listeners who a month earlier would have blanched had they heard such traitorous remarks spoken).

Vern said to the president, "Because I'm a foreigner, the people at OPSUS don't confide in me."

Sukarno tightened his lips; for a moment his eyes narrowed in shrewd assessment. "You overhear nothing?"

"They stop talking when I come along."

"I see. Then they are discussing something of importance."

Vern cleared his throat, as Sukarno himself often did, to buy time for a reply. "During the crisis I suppose much of what they discuss is important."

"At least in front of you they remain discreet."

Vern watched the president relax and sit back. So that was what he'd been looking for—a sign, a clue to attitude. He wanted to know how officers were behaving. He had not expected Vern to reveal any secrets and surely he would not have bothered with a foreigner's interpretation of events. Sukarno merely wanted to know if opposition to him had become bold enough for a public display in front of a foreigner. Vern had not been candid. He felt bad about it. After all, Sukarno had revealed for a moment the sort of psychological acuity that had brought him to the pinnacle of power. Had he been given a true picture—or even a partially true one—of the way things stood at OPSUS he might have acted upon it swiftly, effectively, for his own sake. But a shake-up of OPSUS would not be in Vern's interests. Charity begins at home, his father used to say. Vern smiled, folded his hands, and gave away nothing.

The interview was running down as Sukarno shifted to a few bland denunciations of Malaysia, a mechanically delivered declaration of faith in the anti-imperialistic axis formed by Jakarta, Phnom Penh, Hanoi, and Peking—all of which suggested that the president of the republic did not trust his architect-brother to keep silent about their meeting and so was ending it on a public note of conventional politics.

Sure of no better opportunity, Vern spoke of his wife in Yogya and his difficulty in getting permission from the military to fly there.

Sukarno shrugged his shoulders. "One lover of eighteenth-century French architecture must help another. I'll see to it."

Vern already had the information written down on a piece of paper. He slipped it across the desk for Sukarno to glance at before those large, limpid, weary but intelligent eyes turned toward him again.

"What do you think, American?"

"Of what, Bung Karno?"

"Of the slaughter. Of the incredible killing."

Sukarno's face slackened into contemplation. It was like a death mask—skin the color of yellowed parchment, tiny crystals of urea

447

beading the forehead—except that the frown accompanying Sukarno's reverie was so terribly that of a living man in anguish. Vern started. It was as if for this instant Bung Karno were naked. Surely his emotions were. Surely the man was suffering. This was no performance in front of a microphone, no fist waving, no pompous rhetoric. Sukarno seemed to be looking inward but then somehow through himself and outward into the breadth of his land, where perhaps at this moment someone was being murdered in the name of God or country.

Vern said, "Let's hope the crisis doesn't last long." It was a weak reply, but could a strong one have followed on the heels of the president's obvious distress? Sukarno was, for this moment, alone with catastrophe.

Vern carried that image of the isolated president with him from the private study through the long corridors and the high-ceilinged reception halls with their elephant tusks mounted on teak platforms and their mirrors and marble floors and their European chandeliers.

Later that evening, when he met Larry for a drink at the hotel bar, Vern would mention it. "I never saw anyone so alone. As if he was in mourning."

"Maybe he was just bloody knackered."

"No, not just tired. He felt like hell."

"I wouldn't have expected the bloke to worry about anything except his own skin."

"I think he did today. I looked it up, Larry. 'The tygers of wrath are wiser'—I think I used to say 'better,' but I was wrong—'are *wiser* than the horses of instruction.' That's what Blake said."

Larry rubbed his big horsey jaw while studying Vern. "Looked it up where, mate?"

"At the American Embassy. They salvaged a few books from the USIS Library. I looked it up."

"Why, mate?" Larry was smiling faintly, still rubbing his chin.

"Because . . . because I read that stuff in college. It's the only poetry I know. And because it applies." He did not add, "And because it was something Maggie and I did together, read some of the stuff now and then while we lay in bed."

"It applies here, mate?"

"Sure. It applies to what's happening." Vern meant it. He had thought it through. "Sukarno today, he was thinking about what was happening. The massacres have sobered him up. It's like a cold shower sobering up a drunk. Here is a guy who's manipulative. These people don't like to make political decisions, so for years he's exploited their weakness. He feeds their need for symbols. We know that. He calls on Allah and Thomas Jefferson and Lenin and anybody else he can think of and he shakes his fist and yells into a mike and gets what he wants. But out there his people are killing one another and he's finally thinking about it."

"Maybe too late."

"Probably too late. But he's damn smart and what's happening might earn him some common sense."

"What will he do with it?"

"That's the point. He'll just pour it into a bottle and throw the bottle into the ocean."

"What in hell are you talking about, mate?"

"He won't be able to use his good sense. Except in some act of desperation."

Larry guffawed. "Living in this country where you never get a direct answer is affecting the way you talk, old boy. What in bloody hell is this, pouring good sense into a bottle?"

"What he's learning will be like a message in a bottle. SOS. Help me. Thrown into the great big ocean to float around forever."

"So?"

"So it'll be useless. It's like everything they do. They live on hopes and believe in miracles. On miracles, on the remotest possibilities, on messages in a bottle that hopefully get ashore. Sukarno has always had fantastic gifts but used them foolishly. Now, if he gets an inkling of what to do to stop this thing, they won't let him. I know they won't let him. He'll know what to do, he'll finally have the common sense to do it, but he'll just have to bottle it and throw it away."

Larry reached over and touched Vern's wrist. "Never saw you like this, mate. You're a bit off. It's more like me with the Sumatran anteater. Remember the poor bloke holding on to the tree?"

"I remember."

After a long silence, when Larry spoke again his voice was light,

449

casual. Obviously he wanted to change the mood. "Say, where's the Chinese bird gone? Has she flown the coop? She didn't come this morning."

"How do you know?" Vern asked in surprise.

"You always mention it when she comes to see you."

"Do I?"

Larry laughed and motioned for the waiter to bring another soda water and another gin. "You're proud of the bird coming to see you each morning."

"I'm not."

"You are."

Now it was Vern's turn to laugh. "She didn't come to see me this morning because there was a demonstration."

"I thought you put your foot down on those things."

"I did."

"Well, I'll say this for her—she's a restive sort. A bit of independent."

They finished their drinks in silence and only spoke again when the waiter came with another round. During that silence, Vern knew, they were both thinking the same thing: when would this harmless friendship between an aging American builder and a young Chinese student take an abrupt turn into something else, something unmanageable?

That would never happen, Vern told himself, warily regarding his English friend and wondering what tomorrow would bring.

"Sukarno promised to get me a flight to Yogya," he said in a hopeful voice.

"That won't happen."

"Why not? We got along. He seemed to mean it."

"I heard Sukarno makes a hundred promises a day and maybe keeps one."

Vern nodded. It was, of course, what he had heard too.

———————

In the dream he was standing in a long line of men. It led from a veranda through a narrow doorway down a corridor to the door of a closed room. The men were laughing and talking while they waited. Now and then a man would come out of the room, buttoning his pants or buckling his belt, so that Vern realized he was standing in

450

a line to get into a brothel. When he got to the front and it was his turn to go inside, he opened the door and saw Yanti lying naked on a bed, one hand gripping a bundle of rupiah, the other waving him on in. As he approached the bed, his hands eagerly fumbling at his belt, he noticed there was another bed in the room. On it lay Maggie with a heavyset man pumping her furiously. She was looking past his hairy back and grinning. Vern leapt at the man, tearing him away from her, the hard long penis wobbling in the air as it came out, and suddenly there were people clutching Vern, hitting him, screaming, dragging him away. Then he was propped against the corridor wall, crying, while the line of men waited and hooted at him derisively and continued to enter and leave the room.

When he awoke, sitting bolt upright, his heart pounding violently, Vern could hear the last strands of a loud anguishing moan—his own—fading into the morning light.

Forty-six

Kamarusaman bin Ahmed Mubaidah came along the familiar lane of the dirty kampong holding a cigarette in his hand. He was coughing and had a sore throat; the heat gave him sore throats. Here he was hunted like a rat and had to suffer from a sore throat as well.

Plastered on shop walls were torn old posters exhorting vigilance against Malaysian spies, against NEKOLIM—neocolonialism, colonialism, imperialism—and supporting Sukarno's idea of unity through NASAKOM—nationalism, religion, communism—but today most of these posters had been overlaid with anti-Red propaganda. Slapped against Sukarno's smiling face with lumpy glue were curved scimitars held over the necks of captured Communists. That sort of thing. Sjam could not help but be amused by this turn of events, even though his life was now at stake.

That morning he had left a Red safe house, one of the few remaining in Jakarta (he paid through the nose to get a mat to sleep on in there and still didn't trust the little rodent who was getting rich off fugitives), sneaked into his home, and said good-bye to his wife and kids.

The two girls cried, but the boy, only three, hadn't been sure it was necessary until seeing his sisters do it; then he'd joined in with a high-pitched, enthusiastic wail that outdid them both. Sjam expected great things of him. That boy, given the chance, would outstrip anything he himself had done in life.

Not that that would be so difficult, he thought gloomily while passing a hardware shop. Looking into its interior, he saw a jar of gelasen, reminding him suddenly, achingly, of his boyhood when he used to dip kite strings into this sort of glass paste to give them a cutting edge in battles over the skies of Jakarta, when the city of Jakarta had still been called Batavia, when the Dutch, whom he had fought valiantly in the streets of Yogya during the struggle for independence, had ruled this land from pillared colonial offices on the town square of Taman Fatahillah.

So taken was Sjam with the memory that he bumped headlong into a passing becak, which sent him sprawling. Both the driver and a passenger, leaning out of the carriage, accused him of causing the accident, and Sjam, getting to his feet, agreed with them and apologized profusely and sembahed. He hurried off while the driver still yelled abuse. Sjam was disgusted by this misadventure; the last thing he needed was to call attention to himself.

Turning into a narrow lane, he stood beside a wall and waited until feeling calmer. He patted his oiled hair, slicking it down again, lit another cigarette, and drew so deeply that he brought on a coughing fit. If they threw him into one of those jungle prisons in the outer islands, he wouldn't last a month, Sjam knew. Across the lane he noticed a little shop that sold birds. Well, why not. Quickly selecting a young parrot, he bought it, a bamboo cage too, and set out through the kampong.

Maintaining a casual, inconspicuous pace, he tried also to maintain his spirits at a high level, but they began to sink like a landslide of mud. He had no idea what had happened to the beach house near Carita. There was no sense going there and having someone recognize him. Probably one of the workmen who had robbed him blind all these years would hurry off to the police and turn him in for a reward. If only his wife could have gone to her rich santri family and enlisted their help, but no, she refused out of shame. Anyway, they would have done nothing except, perhaps, like a Carita workman, also turned him in, not for reward but to prove their political loyalty and perpetuate their illegal business practices.

In frustration Sjam kicked at some refuse littering the dirt lane of the kampong. With a little luck his life could have been different. But look where he had come from—this filthy place. It was a wonder he had risen from it at all. He had been an editor of a labor magazine, an official of the dockworkers' union, and, most important, a freedom fighter in the struggle for independence.

Moreover, in the planning of GETAPS, he had been at the forefront of decisions. He carried with him these days a troubled but exhilarating memory of the plotters at work: Colonel Untung, pompous and inordinately greedy for recognition; Major Sujono, logical and deliberate; Sigit, a quarrelsome fellow who was also a coward and had pulled out at the last moment; Wahjudi, who commanded an air defense unit in the Jakarta Military Command; and then, of course, Colonel Latief, whose pretty wife was suckling a child that evening when they'd all met in his house. Latief had been taken; a news broadcast had reported that. Sujono and Untung as well. And according to reports heard on the street, Njoto was still holed up in the presidential palace in Bogor under Sukarno's shaky protection. Sjam wouldn't mind hearing of Njoto's capture. Whenever he thought of the bearish, shambling drunk with his intellectual arrogance and Western ways, Sjam recalled how contemptuous Njoto had been of him simply because he'd come out of the impoverished warrens of Jakarta. A great Communist, Njoto. Let him rot.

Sjam, as he walked, contented himself with those last exciting hours of GETAPS—before it collapsed through the stupidity of bland theoreticians like Aidit and blustering fools like Air Marshal Dhani. At Halim, shortly before and shortly after the coup, Sjam had practically been in charge of the whole operation. Actually he shared leadership with none other than Brigadier General Supardjo, commander of Combat Command in Kalimantan. He and Supardjo shared. On the morning of 1 October, when Supardjo conducted negotiations with a frightened Sukarno at the airfield, from whom had the general asked advice upon returning to the plotters? From whom? He had gone straightaway to Kamarusaman bin Ahmed Mubaidah. And who had

454

suggested that General Pranoto succeed the missing Yani as chief of staff? Kamarusaman bin Ahmed Mubaidah. And why had everyone listened to the suggestion of Kamarusaman bin Ahmed Mubaidah? Because he had pointed out to them that Pranoto was a simple, incorruptible, dull-witted man who would do what he was told. The Reds had Kamarusaman bin Ahmed Mubaidah to thank for that. If they had placed full trust in Kamarusaman bin Ahmed Mubaidah, things might be different today.

The memory of those few moments of power was nearly enough to blind Sjam to his present danger. In the midst of all those plotters he had emerged as the most decisive, the most inventive. It was true. For a few hours he had put his finger on the pulse of a nation's heart, felt its complex rhythm throb in his own veins. For a little while he had know the orgasmic thrill of holding the destiny of other men in his hand, as if they were fledgling birds breathing there, vulnerable, dependent on his mercy, trusting him not to clench his fist and crush the life from their frail bodies.

Had he not been so bewitched by this sense of power, he might have slipped from notice and fled before his name and activities had found their way into the little black book of every intelligence officer and policeman in Indonesia.

Men spoke of the lust for power. They were right. No woman had ever given Sjam a rush of ecstasy such as the exercise of power had given him on the Night of the Generals.

He thrust the parrot cage out to her when Endang opened the door. As she took it with a happy little gasp, Sjam noticed that her belly had swelled considerably since he'd seen her a fortnight ago. Was that possible? Perhaps pride gave him an exaggerated idea of her pregnancy, as if the swiftness of her enlargement was a function of his potency. He had done the same thing with his wife; each time she'd become pregnant, Sjam had inspected her every day for signs of increased distension. He, a man capable of self-scrutiny, was amused by his own masculine arrogance.

Even so, he told Endang that she was much bigger now. She responded with a shy smile, as if he'd complimented her. Then gently she admonished him for spending money on such luxuries, but all the while she was pursing her lips at the bird, clucking at it, her large dark eyes intent upon the variegated colors shifting along the wooden bar.

The sight of her so quietly and innocently absorbed by his gift made Sjam, for a moment, sorrowful. He would probably be else-where when she had the baby. With luck, he'd have made final ar-rangements for Malacca or Singapore, though it was extremely difficult these days to slip out of the country. Without luck, he'd be imprisoned or dead. The sad thought struck him, therefore, as Endang cooed at the parrot, that he might never see their child. He loved this woman. The realization, as sudden and unexpected as a midnight blow in an alley, sent him to the couch, where he sat down heavily and said it to himself again, painfully, sorrowfully: I love this woman.

When she called his name, Sjam looked up and saw her with both hands held at the tied sash of her sarong. It was their signal for love. Her eyebrows raised questioningly when he hesitated.

"No," he said, shaking his head. "Not now. Not yet. There are things to get straight. First, has anyone come looking for me?"

"You are safe with me."

Sjam laughed. "That's a pleasant thought, being safe somewhere. You haven't said anything? Have the neighbors asked about me?"

"No, not a word."

And in fact Sjam had approached the neighborhood warily, glanc-ing from side to side, getting a feel for the place. Had he sensed people were watching him closely, had he felt something was wrong, Sjam would have turned instantly and hurried away.

Now he sat back with a sigh and explained as much as he felt the woman should know. These were dangerous times. People had ac-cused him of certain political activities, none of which had involved him, but then such false accusations were common today when people let their jealousies overrule their good sense. But given the way things were right now, he had to get away for a while—exactly where he didn't know. She must not worry, however, because he would send money and always take care of her, always.

During this explanation Endang sat in a chair opposite him, hands clasped in her lap, eyes filling with tears. It occurred to Sjam, again with the visceral force of revelation, that the woman actually cared for him. That, of course, could be one of those delusions similiar to

456

his conviction that her belly grew perceptively larger every day. But there was a look in her eyes that seemed true, and the sight of her anguished face drew from him a feeling akin to deep sorrow, such as he had felt at the death of his father, and for a few incredible moments Kamarusaman bin Ahmed Mubaidah fought back his own tears.

He was telling her to be patient about the money until the mail service began again. He had just slipped a large roll of rupiah bills onto the little table between them when the door was flung open and a slim, ragged-looking young man lunged into the room.

Sjam, leaning forward and preparing to flee, recognized Endang's brother. He remained as he was, therefore, and tried to smile. "No need to break the door down," Sjam said in the jocular tone he'd assumed in the past with the sergeant. "Come in, please. Your sister and I were discussing business. Would you bolt the door?"

Achmad stood in the middle of the room, breathing heavily. A growth of dark beard, sun-reddened eyes, unruly hair, the dusty rags he wore, all gave him the appearance of a Jakartan beggar. Sjam understood that something was terribly wrong, but said nothing. He was aware that the young man was teetering on the edge; a wrong word might send him over it and bring trouble. That, at least, was clear. Sjam waited.

It was Endang who got up, walked behind her motionless brother, and quietly bolted the door.

Finally, Sjam said, "Nonya, some tea."

When she left the room, Sjam motioned to a chair, but Achmad remained where he stood, arms rigidly at his sides, eyes staring.

"You look tired," Sjam noted cautiously.

"I deserted. Didn't you know that?"

"I didn't know that."

"Didn't my sister tell you?"

"She told me nothing."

"Didn't she tell you I've been looking for you?"

"No, she did not. You've been looking for me?"

Achmad suddenly smiled, as if he felt in control of the situation. "Yes, we must talk about GETAPS."

Sjam looked past him where the woman had gone; the kitchen was a shedlike room a few paces beyond the main house itself. "Wait a minute," he said. "Don't talk too loudly. Does she know?"

"All she needs to know is when the baby's coming."

Sjam said nothing.

"I killed Yani," Achmad said, his smile broadening.

"Keep your voice down. Please don't say such things."

"I saw them killed and tortured at Crocodile Hole." Achmad threw up in his hands. "Well, it doesn't matter." Then he sat down.

At this lowering of tension, Sjam felt relaxed enough to sit back on the couch. The young Javanese sergeant from the sticks couldn't handle the big city, politics, convulsions of a great nation. Sjam, the veteran, felt the same contempt for him that he'd felt for Endang's husband, who had been treed by dogs and shot down like a monkey.

"What are you doing now?" Sjam asked lazily. "Begging in the streets?"

"No, as I said, I've been looking for you."

"I still don't know why. Certainly not to discuss GETAPS. That's over. And dangerous to discuss, young man."

"I've been looking for you for a better reason. To kill you."

It was said in such a low casual voice that at first Sjam wasn't sure he understood the words. Then he remembered the last time they'd met, on the base at Halim before the raiding operation had begun. There, almost in earshot of Aidit and Vice Marshal Dhani, when the fate of a nation hung in the balance, this young soldier had taken the time to threaten him—something about treating his sister right or else. But that had been the histrionics expected of a young military man newly emerged from Javanese village life with all of its rituals and customs and boasts and hotheaded defense of ancestry. He had thought nothing of it. He didn't think much of it now. And Sjam would have sat back rather contentedly, awaiting tea while the young fool calmed down, had not Achmad Bachtiar then pulled a service revolver from beneath his voluminous dirty shirt and pointed it squarely, without the slightest trembling, at Sjam's head.

"You might tell me," Sjam said, trying to keep the trembling out of his voice, "what that is for."

"I am going to kill you."

"What have I done? Is it because of the Movement? I'm not a Communist. What I did was the act of a patriot." He felt his voice getting thin and high as he looked at the unwavering barrel of a gun.

458

"My sister—"

"I respect your sister. I have always respected her."

"She's carrying your child."

"Did she tell you that? I can see by your face, she didn't. You can't accuse me of things like that. Put the gun down and let's talk."

At that moment Endang came into the room, carrying a tray with a teapot and cups, which she promptly dropped at the sight of the gun.

And before anything else happened, a sound boomed in from the side of the house, impelled across the room as though from a cannon. Sjam leapt to his feet, having forgotten the gun. Achmad jumped up too, and Endang gripped her throat with both hands as a metallic voice followed the first tinny blast of sound.

"House surrounded! Come out with hands over heads! You have ten seconds!"

Achmad burst out with a wild laugh, lowering the gun, as if he too had forgotten its existence. "They have found you," he said to Sjam, grinning.

"What are you talking about?"

"Hartono led them to you. Hartono betrayed you."

"Hartono?" Hartono. For a moment Sjam groped through memory for a man to go with the name Hartono. Then he remembered: a taut, arrogant face, a briefcase clasped in both hands. Hartono, one of the ambitious young Reds who followed Aidit like dogs following a bitch.

"Time's up! Come out or we come in firing!"

"Let's get out of here," shouted Sjam, making for the front door, already with one hand over his head. Slipping the bolt, he motioned for the stunned woman to come along, and when for a moment she hesitated, as if paralyzed by fear, he gestured furiously. "Get out get out get out!"

After she had gone through the doorway, he followed, hands over his head, and from behind him Sjam heard the floorboard creak as Achmad crossed the threshold too.

In front of them was a line of men holding revolvers and rifles, all in civilian clothes.

So Hartono betrayed me, Sjam thought bitterly. He didn't even know Hartono.

But Hartono had not betrayed him. That was clear within minutes of the interrogation conducted behind the house in the tidy little garden Endang worked in daily. These men, army intelligence officers, weren't even looking for him. They had come for Achmad, a deserter who had been spotted recently in downtown Jakarta by an air force noncom with whom he'd been friendly during his stay at Halim.

As one of the men roughly tied Achmad's hands behind his back and cinched the rope tightly, Sjam felt a surge of relief. He might get out of this after all. They let Endang go, ordering her back into the house. She went without a single backward glance, and Sjam liked that; it showed that the quiet woman, somewhere within her timid mind, had the instinct of a survivor. Good. That was a good omen for their child, who would need a resourceful mother in this mean world.

Then they examined his papers—in order—and questioned him about his activities. He told them that he had cared for Nonya Endang's business affairs since her husband had died heroically in the clash with Malaya. The intelligence men whispered together. Then one of them asked him about his connection with the deserter.

Sjam looked over the officer's shoulder at the slim hunched figure of the deserter. "I just arrived and he was here. He identified himself as Nonya Endang's brother. From the way she was acting, I think he'd been threatening her. Demanding money, something like that." Sjam paused, assessing the effect of this account on the officer. Heartened, he continued. "So I told the man he'd better treat his sister right or he'd have to deal with me. I have friends in the army, old acquaintances. You see, I fought against the Dutch in '46, '48. I fought against their paratroopers in the streets of Yogya. Anyway—"

The officer reached out and touched Sjam's arm. "We came for him, not you. Take it easy."

For a moment Sjam hesitated. Seeing that he'd actually been released, he turned and walked slowly toward the back door of the house. The corrugated tin roof flashed in sunlight. That was a good thing about her, he thought. She never put laundry on the roof. A clean flashing roof was something to be proud of in a neighborhood.

"You!" he heard behind him. Turning, he felt his heart sink. Another of the officers, yanking Achmad along by the rope as he would an animal, was coming toward him. "Let's see those papers again," the officer said.

Achmad was smiling. So he'd told them about GETAPS.

Trying to be casual, Sjam watched his hands tremble as he pulled out his papers. From the corner of his eye he saw one of the officers thumbing through a small black notebook, alerted now to the possibility of finding the name Kamarusaman bin Ahmed Mubaidah.

———————

Seated on benches opposite each other in the bemo van that had been converted since the crisis into a pickup for prisoners, the two men held themselves erect, because it put less pressure on hands secured tightly behind their backs.

Achmad was smiling contentedly.

Sjam smiled back. "You're happy now."

"Yes, I am. Though I'd be happier if I'd put a bullet in your brain."

"Look at it this way. I'll suffer longer now. Your revenge will last longer. But I don't suppose you think that far ahead, do you?"

And Sjam knew he would indeed suffer longer. He wanted a smoke, even though his throat felt sorer than ever. Well, maybe he'd see Pono in prison somewhere. They had picked up that fool Pono within a week of GETAPS. If he knew Pono, the man would tell anything they wanted to know without realizing he was telling them a thing. Stupidity had its reward. Walujo, that fervent Communist with the sallow face and the heavy-lidded eyes, had performed exactly as people expected he would: with utmost violence. It had made the newspaper. He had pulled a gun and shot three policemen dead before going down himself.

That sort of melodrama did not appeal to Sjam. As the bemo rattled along, he entertained the old image of himself as a rat sniffing each corner of a dark room. Rats were survivors, and so was he.

And so was Endang. Good girl. She would live to bear their child and teach it how to survive.

Good girl.

Yet she was responsible for his downfall. For one thing, she had failed to tell him about Hartono. Of course she knew that with knowledge of someone on his trail he would never venture back to this neighborhood—he would not have seen her again. She had wanted

461

to make sure the father of her unborn child kept coming around.

And she had failed to tell her crazy brother an intelligent lie—perhaps "Kamarusaman bin Ahmed Mubaidah has fled to Singapore," or something equally unimaginative but effective—so that the hothead would have gone away. But without Endang saying anything, her brother had patiently waited for his enemy to show up. Like a typical Javanese woman she had refused to lie to an older brother.

Her actions had been determined long ago, probably when she was hardly big enough to totter around a village hut and listen to women talk of family obedience, of love and the shame that can come with it—mixing the ideas like a thick soup in her little head.

Sjam sighed. She may have brought down the two men she loved most, but Endang was a fine woman.

Abruptly he said to the deserter who sat opposite him in the van, "I love your sister. She is a good girl."

Staring dully ahead, Achmad did not look at him.

"Perhaps that means nothing to an honorable soldier like you," Sjam continued. "But if you hadn't turned me in like the fool you are, I'd have seen to it she always had money for herself and the child. Always. Because I know how to make money and I love the woman." He waited for a response, but then gave up. He could see in the young man's eyes the blank look of utter contentment. Whatever happened to Achmad Bachtiar now, he had carried out his final responsible act and could look upon the rest of his life, however long it lasted, with perfect equanimity. Somehow in his Javanese mind he had paid his debt to God, country, and family. So be it. Sjam forgot about him.

He thought about himself while the van moved inexorably closer to the place he would never leave alive. Yet oddly he began to think of the future with anticipation. His love of challenge at this grim moment surprised even Sjam. If they didn't execute him right away, if they interrogated him or even brought him to trial, he'd give them a show they would never forget. He would name names, names he had never heard of as well, and throw them off balance with deliberate misunderstanding of their questions and contradict himself about facts (but not so blatantly that they'd torture him out of malice; he could not stand pain, he would not stand it), and in various ways spill his guts so enthusiastically, so cunningly, that those hypocritical army officers, in a display of manly disgust, would turn away from him while secretly admiring his ability to survive another day, to eke out a few more moments of life by using his wits.

On the other hand, perhaps he would be more fortunate. His sore throat could get worse; he could become feverish and mortally ill; he could deprive them of their fun and do it without needing the courage to take his own life. That would be more luck than he'd probably have.

If only they gave him a smoke where he was going.

Forty-seven

When Ali came in from a walk through the fields (there was little for him to do these days but walk and think and hope for change), Bambang was waiting for him on the little veranda, pacing like a caged tiger. Again Ali had the strange feeling that they were closer now than they had been since childhood. Perhaps his older brother felt protective of him during the crisis. Ali had come to recognize surely that his safety in the village was in full measure due to Bambang, a man both respected and feared by his neighbors.

Now Bambang was scowling, and when Ali reached him, the burly founder clenched his fists. "You have a visitor," he said in a low, tense voice. "He's in your room." When Ali nodded and started past him, Bambang added, "I don't want him here tonight."

Ali regarded his brother closely. In recent days there had been a new tension, almost bordering on fear, in Bambang's expression, in the dark eyes, in the tight dusty lips.

"I would not have asked him to stay, whoever he is."

"I want him out of here, brother, because he is a man in trouble.

I owe him nothing. He's not a member of our family. I have no reason to give him protection."

"That's probably not why he came."

When Ali walked into his tiny room, however, he understood Bambang's anxiety. The tall, thin man awaiting Ali surely looked troublesome. The nervous sunken eyes, the hard set of the jaw, the animalistic wariness of each gesture, marked this man as either dangerous or running from danger.

His name was Satir. He wasted no words, as if there wasn't time for amenities. He had got Ali's name and village from Chairman Aidit a few days ago.

Ali's hopes soared; if Aidit was still alive, there was a chance to regroup, to fight back. He learned from Satir that Chairman Aidit was operating out of Solo, moving each day from village to village in the company of a small force from Pemuda Rakyat, which had since dispersed, because traveling together as a group made them too conspicuous, especially since RPKAD and elements of the strategic corps of KOSTRAD were operating in the vicinity. These days Chairman Aidit got around on a motor scooter.

Ali smiled at the thought of the great man, the Ratu Adil of their time, gripping the handlebars of a put-put, his thick spectacles flashing in sunlight. It made Aidit all the greater.

He said to Satir, in fact, "What a great man."

Satir shrugged off the remark. He seemed to be running, already in midflight, although he sat on a rickety chair, his legs splayed out in the way an exhausted man sits. "What are you going to do, comrade?" he asked Ali bluntly.

"What am I going to do?"

"Are you going to sit in this dead village while the world falls apart?"

That's exactly what Ali had been doing. Minutes ago, coming from the fields, he had asked himself a similar question: Is there anything you can do?

"Listen to me," Satir began, but immediately paused when Melani cleared her throat, waited for permission, and entered the room with a tea tray, pot, and cups.

Ali regarded her with open admiration as she bent and with the slow ritualized movements of a Javanese woman poured tea for them.

When she left, Satir spoke with the ardor of someone possessed by a vision. Leaning forward in his chair, ignoring the tea, he told Ali of going to North Vietnam a year ago with a dozen other PKI cadres to study guerrilla tactics. They had learned how to construct networks of underground tunnels that connected covert encampments and bunkers. They had learned how a small force of guerrillas can keep much larger forces in check, infiltrate and take over villages, control through terror entire rural neighborhoods, demoralize local government until the people turn to new leadership. "That's how Mao succeeded," he claimed. "That's how we can do it here."

"Yes," Ali said. Here was a man who talked the way Ali had been thinking in recent days: it was time for action. "We've relied too much on Bung Karno."

Satir shrugged that remark off too, as if it were either obvious or irrelevant.

"I'm heading for East Java. We'll be setting up an underground training camp there. We'll fight back."

"Yes," Ali said. Without another thought he added, "Take me with you."

Satir raised his eyebrows. "You'd go?"

"I agree we have to fight back. I understand that now. If we had trained earlier, this wouldn't be happening. We have to show them we're serious men."

For a few moments Satir seemed to assess him. Ali had the distinct feeling that the guerrilla fighter didn't want to be burdened with him. "It's better I go alone. Better you join up with people here."

"But who's ready to fight?"

"South of here some Communist villages are fighting. Chairman Aidit told me."

Ali remembered the men hanging in the tree. The Reds had been confident in that village all right. At least for a day. "One village I know of has been taken by paratroopers. Vultures circle overhead."

"But other villages haven't been taken." The guerrilla fighter studied Ali, as if annoyed by his hesitancy. "If you want to fight, fight."

An hour later, after the man had eaten and bathed and left by foot on an eastward-leading path through the fields, Ali gathered his own few possessions, packed them in his suitcase, fastened it with some loops of rope, and went to find Melani. He told her he was leaving for a while. When she frowned painfully, he felt a stab of joy—she would miss him! Somberly he told her not to worry. "And tell my brother I thank him for everything he has done, for all he has tried to do. For"—he paused—"protecting me."

Minutes later Ali was on the road leading southward, peering into the distance for a trail of ballooning dust that would signal the approach of a local bus.

A day later, as darkness set in, Ali Gitosuwoko was living in a different world.

He crouched alongside an open window, clutching a rifle, awaiting the first sign of troops, hearing other men in the room coughing, shifting their weight, knocking their weapons against the walls to make a metallic sound.

Yesterday by bus he had crossed the Ova River, then by wagon he had gone farther south, and then by foot he had reached the town of Wonosari and slogged west of it a dozen kilometers to a village. The village was almost in shouting distance of the one whose PKI sympathizers had murdered the anti-Communists and then succumbed to an attack by RPKAD paracommandos. When Ali saw it in the distance, there were no vultures circling overhead. Maybe there hadn't been any at all. A passing farmer maintained that the RPKAD units had left the area for points southward. When Ali reached one of the other villages he was seeking, he was halted by armed men who demanded his papers and questioned him closely and only when assured of his PKI affiliation allowed him into the square.

He was told that the village, solidly Communist, awaited the return of RPKAD troops. They would make a stand in the lanes and houses of their village. A wrinkled old headman, gripping an ani knife, squatted in the shade of a guava tree and swore to Ali (they were eager to impress someone who had been a cadre in Jakarta and had met Chairman Aidit) they would all fight, every one of them, to the death. A pale young woman was brought forward to tell Ali that she had escaped what was now called the Village of Vultures. The troops had come in and searched every house. They killed anyone who was more than twelve years old—or seemed that old. A few women were kept in a house, to be raped. She had been raped, well, how many times she couldn't remember, but they kept coming in, grinning, coming in and dropping their pants and the hut was steaming in the noon heat and smelled powerfully of their sexual leavings in her and she lay there swimming in what they left until at last tired they went away with the promise of coming back after a nap in the afternoon and that's when she had managed to get away, leaving four other women too frightened to move from where they lay in a puddle of male fluids and so she had got out of there and in the glare and heat of high afternoon she had run and run and run through the padis run and run until a fire leapt into her throat and she fainted away and then roused herself and got to her feet in the muddy water and set out again, running and running and running until she had come here where these good Communist people, these comrades, these men and women of a new day, had brought her in, welcomed her, given—

She was pulled back, having had her say. Ali looked around at the men circling him, waiting for him to respond, while holding bamboo staves and ani knives. It seemed to Ali then as if his whole life had narrowed to this moment, like a wide uncertainly swirling river funneling into a narrow channel to bring all its force at last into a white rapids. He had believed in communism. He had worked for it. And coming back to his village he had also renewed his faith in the Javanese way of life, in the honor that infused it, in the traditions followed by his ancestors. Everything made sense now: the principles of his youth had joined with the principles of his manhood—the wayang world of his ancestors coupled to the social consciousness of Karl Marx. Somehow it had happened, somehow, and as he looked up into the expectant faces of these peasants, whose understanding of communism must have scarcely gone past the desire for more land and clearer justice, Ali Gitosuwoko knew exactly what he must do.

"I am staying here," he told them.

A man came forward holding an old Dutch rifle across his forearms. "You will have this," the man said.

"No, no, I'll use what the rest use. Give me an ani."

But they insisted that he should have one of the few guns available. He was, after all, a cadre from Jakarta and therefore an important representative of an organization in the service of which they were preparing to die. They were honored that he had come to them. The least they could do was offer him the best weapon in the village.

Ali nodded, reached out, and took it.

Back in the Dutch days the villages used a chain of tong-tongs—long wooden drums in the shape of a cylinder, suspended on poles and struck by clubs—to signal across padis and rivers and warn one another of enemy patrols. Tong-tongs were being used again. Ali heard the dull yet resonant sound throbbing through the lazy night air, sending everyone in the village to hidden posts from which to meet the attack.

So it has come to this, Ali thought. He had taken seriously his dedication to the cause of communism, yet not until recently had he envisioned it leading him to actual violence. Not even when he'd seen the murders committed in the name of Marxism in that other village, not even when he'd seen the men hanging from the tree. Because those things happened to others. The truth was he'd continued to live the hermetic life of his ancestors even in the midst of Jakarta, even now in the swirl of national catastrophe. Now, at least, he had stepped from the soft airless world of his past into a harsher but livelier world. Gripping the gun, he waited.

What happened next would be beyond Ali Gitosuwoko's ability to remember precisely as it had happened, much less to comprehend how it had happened. There was movement outside the house, then flashes of light accompanied by nasty little popping sounds, and people moving and himself moving into the frame of the open window, pulling the small curved piece of metal with his finger, pulling it, pulling it, and then bringing the gun down, reloading, and feeling the movement around him, hearing the terrible piercing cry of someone in pain, and sensing more movement, running, falling, and himself—how had it happened?—bolting through the open back door of the house, his legs churning and carrying him through the darkness until he crashed into something, into a tree, finding himself sprawled alongside it, the gun gone and forgotten when he staggered up and kept moving kept running running just like the young woman had run from her village until he too felt the fire spreading from his throat into his chest and in his eyes little lights seemed to be exploding and he knew he had fallen again, this time in water, into a padi smelling powerfully of vegetation, of decay, of sprouting plants, of dead frogs, of the scum of algae, and he was up again, up on his feet lunging forward and he was gone, out of there, running down a rutted path blindly until he fell again, this time with his eyes staring upward at a moonless but star-filled sky, and for a few moments he felt at peace, for his mind seemed to empty itself of everything but its recognition of a pattern of lights above him, and then he was up again up on his feet plunging mindlessly through the dark night, alone, as he had been that time in his boyhood when on inexplicable impulse he had risen from sleep and soundlessly left the house and walked out into the fields under such a sky as this one, feeling himself alone with the sky, feeling himself isolated with millions and millions of stars in a universe that swallowed him up soundlessly as it did now, this moment, outside a village south of Yogya and a few kilometers away from the town of Wonosari.

Forty-eight

She saw the low-slung building ahead with the flag of Indonesia flying from a white metal pole in front of the circular drive where several jeeps were parked and two soldiers, rifles held diagonally at their chests, stood at the entrance. Maggie entered the drive and parked her bike to one side, aware that both guards were eyeing her curiously.

Pulling the brim of her straw hat low, Maggie passed by them and entered the local army headquarters. A clerk at a desk glanced up from some papers with the startled look of a small animal.

"I want to speak to an officer," Maggie said in Bahasa Indonesia.

Without replying, the clerk got up and scurried into an office along a corridor. Uniformed men, passing by with rifles slung on their backs or sheaves of paper in their hands, stared at her. Maggie stared back until they looked away.

The clerk returned almost immediately and beckoned to her from a distance, as if fearful of getting too close to a foreigner. But Maggie was heartened by his quick return. Perhaps they were efficient here at Diponegoro Divisional Headquarters.

Following him, she came to a closed door along the corridor. He knocked rapidly and hurried away, leaving her standing there, while men went up and down the hall, a couple of them brushing unnecessarily against her—getting a free feel. Finally the door opened and another clerk led her into a large room filled with desks where other clerks were shuffling stacks of paper or pecking at old typewriters whose keys sounded like stones falling into a pond. Eyes lifted, regarded her for a tense furtive instant, then returned to work. The clerk took her to a bench where she sat for a long time, long enough to see a shadow lengthen across a man's shoulder, fall to his desk, and slither toward her like a dark snake.

If there was one thing Maggie Gardner had vowed to do, it was to remain calm and patient; without that, among these people who believed composure under stress was an essential virtue, she would be lost. She gripped her Batak bag in both hands and repeated to herself, Patience . . . patience . . . patience.

Finally a sergeant came along and motioned—quite rudely for a Javanese—with a crooked finger, so she was prepared for bad treatment when he took her to the open door of a tiny office. A lieutenant sat waiting for her, ramrod straight and obviously determined to make an impression of military severity on this foreigner. He nodded slightly. She took it for permission to enter the room and stepped inside. There was a chair beside his desk, but he didn't offer it to her.

Though she did not know the word for his rank, Maggie spoke in Krama Javanese, politely hoping that he was well. Hearing the "*Ngaturaken sugeng*, Pak Lieutenant," he raised his eyebrows slightly but that was all. He did not reply, "*Inggih, wilujeng*," but said, "*Kabar baik*"—he was quite well—in Bahasa Indonesia. That was best, Maggie figured, since she didn't have enough Javanese yet to do more than handle the amenities.

At least she had made an effort—and made yet another: she gave him what she felt was a winning smile. But again he refused to take the bait. His eyes were set closer together than usual in a Malay face and his jaw was weak and his teeth prominent. He was about her age. Obviously he was not going to help her with the interview, so Maggie took over. She tried to be indirect and expansive; she said obvious things, following the Javanese way: the weather was very hot and her immense and profound admiration for Yogya continued to

472

grow in spite of the heat (exaggeration was no sin in a Javanese exchange) and she fervently hoped that the lieutenant and his family were safe and healthy during the crisis, which of course would soon be terminated through the good offices of the president and the government and the army of Indonesia.

He still hadn't invited her to sit down. Maggie figured she had not impressed him. There was not even a hint of masculine interest in her in his eyes.

Finally, as she was taking a breath to describe her immense and profound admiration for Yogyanese culture, the lieutenant asked curtly, "What do you want?"

If you're doing it Western style, Maggie thought, then here we go. "What I want, Lieutenant, is information about a missing person."

"That is a police matter."

"No, Lieutenant, because this missing person was last seen in the company of soldiers."

"Arrested?"

"At least taken away."

"The sergeant at the desk to your left as you go out will talk to you. You can file a report."

"Lieutenant, I am a guest in General Sakirman's house. Lieutenant General Pranot Sakirman, Operasi Khusus." She added in English to scare him with a foreign language, "The Army Strategic Reserve Command, Jakarta."

"Please sit down."

Of course. How simple. She ought to have mentioned the Sakirman name at the outset. Maggie sat down and felt a rush of optimism, perhaps too much of it, because instantly she launched into a description of Inam, a trusted Sakirman servant, who had mysteriously been whisked away by soldiers. Surely it must have been a mistake. General and Nonya Sakirman would be glad to know that their loyal servant had been freed and had returned to the family compound. Suddenly Maggie stopped talking. She had been running on without keeping a close eye on the face of this lieutenant. It had assumed a masklike rigidity, a cold displeasure. Perhaps she had counted too much on the Sakirman name.

After a brief silence, he asked what she was doing in Yogya, and when she told him that she was on a visit while her husband worked on a project for OPSUS in Jakarta, his expression didn't change. "You will wait outside," he told her imperiously.

———————

Hours later, it was three and a half hours later, having watched clerks and helmeted soldiers and other officers troop in and out of the lieutenant's office, Maggie was finally called in again. This time he kept her standing throughout the interview. He wanted to know her own politics in America, and when she explained that she was an Independent, neither Republican nor Democrat, the lieutenant nodded but clearly without understanding what she meant.

"What are your politics here in Java?"

"I have no politics in Java."

"A known organizer of the PKI has been seen with you at the compound."

So they had gone out there and investigated while she sat in this office. They must have terrified the Sakirman staff. But Maggie also knew that if they had spilled the beans about Ali, they had also mentioned the dalang. That could be in her favor, because obviously she was now undergoing a serious interrogation herself.

"I have many friends in Yogya," she replied.

"Yes, I believe you do. What did the Red tell you?"

"About what?"

"The coup. The PKI organization."

"Absolutely nothing. All he ever told me about communism—" She paused, watching the officer lean forward. "He was organizing the peasants to protect their fields. Something like that," she said. She said, "Lieutenant, I came here to find out what you did with the girl. The Sakirmans will be anxious about her."

The lieutenant waved his hand. "No need for that. If she's a patriot, the general will be pleased. If not, the general will be equally pleased by her arrest."

"Then she's actually been arrested?"

"Detained."

"Inam has done nothing. I know she has a brother— But she's just a girl. And she's liked by Nonya Sakirman, I can tell you that. She can be vouched for."

It occurred to Maggie, when he met these words without a flicker of emotion, that the lieutenant was reflecting a new mood within the

474

army—insolent, domineering, unafraid of old guard officers like Sakirman, who, after all, was only in supply. Those who counted right now must be field officers carrying weapons. She noticed on the lieutenant's belt a holstered revolver.

He seemed to be deciding what to do with her. Finally he picked up a pencil and tapped it on a pile of papers, once. He told her that he would personally keep track of the case, that she ought not to worry herself about the girl, who would be treated fairly, that if there was any change in the situation she would be notified so that she could also assure General and Nonya Sakirman of the appropriate disposition of what was now a military matter.

This long explanation, accompanied by little gestures with both hands, was almost like backing down on his part. He was afraid of going too far. He was trying to keep a host of balls in the air—the Sakirmans, the famous dalang, the foreign woman, himself. Aware that his position was not therefore solid, Maggie took a deep breath and said, "Lieutenant, I want to see the girl now."

"You cannot, Nonya, I am sorry."

"Where is she?"

"I don't know."

"Don't know?" Maggie felt her control slipping away—it was like a car skidding across an icy road back in Iowa. "Somebody here must know where she is. I want to see her! Why can't I see her? I'm not a dukun. I won't use black magic to spirit her away." Out of control, she knew—that was a bit of useless sarcasm. "Is there any reason I can't see and talk to her a few moments?" Her voice was now cajoling, "To see how she is? If I can bring her something to eat or clothes or something—before you understand the mistake you're making?"

"You cannot see her, Nonya, I am sorry. I don't know where she is. She has been taken somewhere."

"Where?"

"If there is anything to report, we will contact you." He held the pencil poised over documents on his desk in the gesture of a somewhat compassionate but exceptionally busy man. "We will let you know."

"Let me know now, Lieutenant," Maggie pleaded. "She hasn't done anything. Why are you doing this? What's the point? You can't blame her for what her brother does!" Maggie had taken a couple of steps forward and found herself leaning over the desk, looking down at him, one of her hands gripping the desktop, the other holding the Batak bag against her breasts. She had been shouting. She knew she had because abruptly there were people behind her. Turning, she saw three clerks at the door, peering in like a row of awakened puppies. "Lieutenant," she said to him and stopped in confusion. "Lieutenant," she said again, "I will come back tomorrow."

"Inquire if you wish," he told her coldly and leaned forward, having edged back from her while she was making the aggressive move over his desk, her bag a potential weapon.

Maggie stepped back. "I do wish, sir. I will be back tomorrow. I am—" She paused then wildly said it. "I am representing Lieutenant General Pranot Sakirman!"

Somehow she got out of the building and onto her bike. Pedaling along at a feverish pace, Maggie felt tears in her eyes.

That evening she did not tell Budi for fear that she would involve him unpleasantly with the authorities, because although they would respect him for what he was, in these patriotic times, when even a general had no power to stem the fervor of arrests, not even Ki-Dalang Gitosuwoko was safe. She said nothing about Inam. They slept in his compound, and the next day at dawn she pedaled back to her own where she remained just long enough to put in an appearance among the wondering servants, not one of whom mentioned the interrogation that must have taken place here yesterday afternoon. Then she was back at army headquarters, undergoing the same process but ending up in the office of another lieutenant, this one less stern than the other but more devious, so that she left once again in tears and frustration, unable to discover even if Inam was still alive.

Forty-nine

After days—he was not sure how many, because they merged into one another like water—Ali found himself near his own village. He hid in a small clump of bushes near a padi until a boy came along the path. Crawling out of the bushes, Ali stood up straight and called out familiarly to the boy, who, at the sudden appearance of a man, had turned, ready to bolt.

"Listen, boy," Ali said, smiling, "you know me. Here." He motioned; after a short hesitation the boy approached. Ali held out a pencil (one of the few things he still had with him; everything else was back in that village). "Yes, it's yours," he told the boy, encouraging him to take it.

The boy, wearing a loincloth, took the pencil as if it were hot and, once assured it would do nothing to him, turned it slowly.

"Do you know what that can do?"

"Yes," the boy said uncertainly.

"It can write on paper."

"I know that," the boy claimed.

"You can have it if you will bring Charangwaspa here to me." He used Bambang's foundry name; everyone in the village knew the gong maker by it.

The boy turned the pencil, slipped it between his chocolate-colored belly and the gray loincloth. "Here?"

"Yes, here. I'll wait under that tree." He pointed to a nipa palm off the path a little.

"I know you. You are the Red."

"I am Charangwaspa's brother." Ali frowned severely. "If you don't bring him right away, what I gave you will turn into a snake. But if you bring him right away, it will be the best magic you can have."

Thoughtfully, the boy studied Ali, closing his upper teeth over his lower lip tightly. Then he relaxed. "I will bring him."

Ali watched the boy trot off, then sat down under the nipa palm. Inspecting his shirt and sarong, wet, muddy, torn, he realized the boy had shown considerable courage not to flee instantly upon seeing such a ragged man appear on the path. Ali felt himself trembling. He couldn't tell if it was from fatigue and hunger or from the fear that had been following him while he stumbled through padis and across village trails, heading north, trying to get here. All the way he had felt something just behind him, although looking over his shoulder he saw nothing. Then at sundown yesterday, when he crept into a thicket of bamboo to rest, Ali realized that the only thing following him was fear and the memory of fear as it had propelled him out of the besieged village into the nighttime fields.

"Brother."

He started, then looked down the path to see Bambang coming along with a palu in his hand. The beaklike head of the hammer swung rhythmically alongside his black pants, a powdery sheen to them from foundry dust.

Ali stood up. "Brother."

Bambang halted on the path, waited for a sudden spasm of coughing to subside, then motioned for Ali to follow him deeper into the undergrowth. They sat side by side, hidden from view by vines and weeds and leafy banana trees. Insects buzzed around them. Bambang swatted at them with his battered felt foundry hat. Then he told Ali that the entire countryside had heard of the battle near Wonosari.

478

Studying his brother with obvious displeasure, he added, "I think you were there."

"Yes. I got away."

"Others didn't. The soldiers brought them into Wonosari by the truckload for interrogation. We heard it by radio."

"Were many killed?"

Bambang shook his head. He gave Ali a glance of disdain. "After a few shots, they quit fighting. Maybe two or three were killed. But you can be sure of one thing. The ones who surrendered have named you. They had your name, didn't they?"

Ali nodded sheepishly. He felt as though they were boys again, and his older brother was admonishing him for doing something wrong—something stupid. So the Red villagers had put up only token resistance. That was a kind of relief. If they had fought bravely with many casualties, he would never forgive himself. As if he would ever forgive himself anyway.

Bambang, brushing flies from his charcoal-darkened face, reported that the moneylender had returned today to the village and was warning everyone to stay clear of Communists, who, as he had predicted, were rampaging through the countryside, killing and looting. "People have talked to me about you," Bambang said, turning to look at Ali directly. "Men I work with are talking about you. Panji told me they had a meeting last night. They decided he should tell me I couldn't keep you in my house anymore."

"Panji was with them?"

Bambang kept batting at the whirling flies. His silence meant that Panji had joined the others who were against him. Panji, head of the foundry, had always backed Bambang, second-in-command there, until now.

"You can't fight the entire village, brother. I will not go back there," Ali declared.

"Where will you go?"

Ali knew. He had thought about it while staggering through the rice fields yesterday. He was going to find the guerrilla fighter Satir in East Java. He would go to the underground training camp and learn what he'd been ignorant of when he had tried to fight, so that when he fought again he would know what to do.

479

"I'll be going east."

Bambang nodded and stopped hitting at the flies. He stared at his bare feet, black from foundry dirt. He was struggling to say something, but said nothing.

"I know what you want to say," Ali told him. "You are sorry you can't help me anymore."

"Yes, that's what I want to say." He looked up suddenly. "I'll get you clothes and money."

"Thank you."

Relieved at being able to act, Bambang jumped to his feet. "I'll have Melani collect some things for you and bring them."

"No," Ali said. "Don't have her bring them."

Bambang cocked his head in surprise. "Why not?"

"Because, well, it might already be dangerous. You better bring them yourself."

"Yes, you're right."

While Ali watched his broad-shouldered brother hurry down the path toward the village, he wanted to call him back and tell him to send Melani after all—so he could say good-bye for the last time, so he could tell her he loved her, so he could make a desperate attempt to persuade her to go away with him or at the very least to plead with her for love right now in the bushes with flies swirling around their naked bodies.

He had done the right thing, dissuading Bambang from sending her out here.

He came to Yogya where he could catch a bus eastward if they were still running. At the station he learned a bus might leave in midafternoon for Wonogiri and Ponorogo. With time on his hands Ali decided to take a becak out to the Sakirman residence. This decision carried with it a realization: his early attraction to the foreign woman, beginning in curiosity and physical desire, had grown into a steady liking for her. He felt a kind of strange kinship with Nonya Maggie Gardner even though he knew her now for an adulteress.

Ali was convinced he had come to the brink of a great adventure. Standing at the edge of such change, he felt a strong need to say his good-byes to the past. Nonya Maggie was a recent but important part of that past, and saying good-bye to her, given the circumstances,

480

was almost like saying good-bye to his uncle, which could not happen without him doing something stupid, like apologizing or in some traditional way exposing to view the priyayi aristocrat that was still in him.

When he got to the Sakirman compound, the resonating notes of a struck gender greeted him on the path to the courtyard. The instrument was being played very badly. The player was failing to dampen the bronze keys, so that the sound vibrating through the courtyard as he reached it was chaotic, almost brutal, bearing no resemblance to the sweet melodies associated with this instrument, perhaps the chief glory of gamelan.

So he was not surprised to see Maggie sitting inside the central pendopo, cross-legged in front of a gender. Its boxlike frame, containing bars suspended over bamboo resonating chambers, had been brought into the pavilion for her to play. Or practice on. Or abuse. She was banging away at the bronze keys with two slentem-type padded mallets, while a thin little man, dressed in the subdued batiks of a court musician, sat grimly beside her, smoking a cigarette and giving instructions.

Ali laughed. His own laughter surprised him, as if he had quite forgotten why people made such a sound or how.

Maggie waved and got to her feet awkwardly, as befitted a big-boned foreign woman. Ali felt, as he went toward her, that every Indonesian must take secret comfort in the way these tall white foreigners could never make a graceful gesture.

"Why a gender?" he called out to her. "It's the hardest thing of all to play!" He was speaking Bahasa Indonesia, having no interest in English anymore. He was leaving it behind with his priyayi heritage of isolation and beautiful music and advantages.

Maggie stood at the edge of the pendopo, waiting for him. She wore Western slacks and a pullover blouse with her brown hair pulled back into a little tail held by a rubber band. Desire pulsed a moment through Ali as he came closer. No wonder his uncle—

"Did it sound that terrible?" she asked, smiling.

"Worse!" Such banter pleased him. There was, after all, hope. Though he was a man in danger, poised for flight, most likely soon to be hunted, he could still joke with this American woman at her expense and have both of them enjoy it.

They sat on the edge of the pendopo, dangling their feet and looking past the blue shade of the overhang to the blazing sweep of the courtyard. After a few more witticisms about her musicianship, they fell silent.

Then Maggie spoke first. "They have taken Inam away. I've tried everything to find out where she is, but I can't learn anything from the army."

"You won't either."

"What will they do to her?"

Ali shrugged. He wouldn't tell Nonya Maggie that the girl had sometimes acted as a courier between an outlying Communist cell and PKI headquarters in Yogya. Surely by now she had been hauled off to a detention center. If she were lucky. "They'll hold her for a while, then let her go."

"You don't believe that."

Ali said nothing, but stared into the hard light.

"I think you've come to tell me good-bye."

He turned and looked at her sunburned face, her blue eyes. They looked childish to him, bright and empty, and for a dismaying instant he wanted to tell her so and hurt her for being here safe and having a lover whom he hated. But staring hard at the tall woman, he understood that she was far from a fool; even though a foreigner, she was worthy of a dalang. In the next instant he felt the anger wash over him again. "Don't think you are superior to us."

"Ali?"

"We were exploited by the Portuguese, the Spanish, the Chinese, the Dutch, the Japanese, and the entire West, including the British, including you. If we're hurting ourselves, we have earned the right."

"Yes. I agree."

Softened by her claim, which seemed too quickly made to be false, he said, "I think you do. Something good will come of this for my people. We'll learn caution and gain strength and then we'll proclaim ourselves a Communist nation." He smiled at her. "You don't agree with that."

"I have no idea who'll come out on top."

He chuckled grimly. "You are detached from the outcome."

"Army generals or Communists or Muslims or Sukarno—they

aren't what I care about, so yes, I'm detached from their success or failure."

"Yet you stay here. You learn our language. You work on batik. You play our musical instruments. You have already made a life here."

"You know about us—about your uncle and me. He told me you know."

Unaccustomed to such frankness from a woman, Ali could think of nothing to say.

"We both worry about you."

"That won't be necessary," he said crisply, wanting distance from her emotions. "I'm leaving. I'm going to the east." He could not help adding boastfully, "I'm going to train for combat."

"Ali."

"We must let the world know our lives are committed to the future."

"Forgive me, good friend, but that sounds like something you read in a book." She paused. "I didn't mean that."

"But you did mean it. You want to discourage me because you like me." He heard the tenderness in his voice, wanted to check it but could not. "I can never judge you, Nonya Maggie. Not you." He found a hard tone again. "I have no right to judge anyone until I've proved myself. Do you love him?"

"Yes," she said without hesitation. "Very much."

At the brink of adventure he felt anything was possible. He must say whatever was on his mind. "And your husband?"

"I wanted to tell him face-to-face, but it's no good waiting any longer. I've written him."

"You intend staying here?"

"Yes."

"In spite of what is happening—this—" He swept his hand at the courtyard as if to encompass Indonesia's turmoil.

"I will stay here."

"Your love is that great?" He was incredulous, in awe, as if witness to a passion unimagined by him before.

"Yes. That great."

He got off the pendopo. Standing in front of the foreign woman with her brown hair tied back, her blue eyes regarding him, Ali wanted to say something breathtaking. Instead, he said rather stiffly, reverting to the formal courtesy of his boyhood, "I will always remember you, Nonya Maggie. And I thank you."

Halfway down the lane from the Sakirman residence, Ali saw a familiar figure coming along, a small, frail-looking man who swayed from side to side as if accommodating himself to the rolling motion of a ship.

When they got closer, Mas Slamat removed his porkpie hat and doffed it courteously. "You have been to see her?" He didn't wait for the answer, knowing it. "I wonder why General Sakirman lets her stay. It is said in Malay, *'Pipit itu sama pipit juga, dan yang enggang sama enggang.'*"

As a boy, Ali had heard the old saying in the village—"Sparrows must mate with sparrows, hornbills with hornbills"—to criticize a man and a woman from different classes for falling in love. But Mas Slamat meant race, not class. He was talking about a Javanese dalang and a woman from America.

Clearly the little man was prepared to speak openly, so Ali responded, trying to appear casual, as if they were discussing something quite common. After all, once the violence ended, Indonesia would be part of a new world and they would all look at life in a different way. Ali felt a surge of optimism while maintaining that General Sakirman did not know what was happening between his houseguest and Ki-Dalang Budi Gitosuwoko, but even if he did, there would be no cause for trouble. "He would let her stay in his house. He would understand."

"Not possible."

"They are hurting no one. And my uncle is still a famous dalang, a respected man."

Mas Slamat tightened his toothless gums. "Famous, yes, but not respected much longer."

"She has written her American husband," Ali said. "She will stay here in Yogya."

"That remains to be seen."

"I believe her."

"How can we take the word of someone who never prays to Allah?" This was the santri in Mas Slamat. There was no sense arguing with him. Ali liked the man—at least felt with him the bond of tradition.

"You heard of good Muslims murdered?" Mas Slamat asked, chewing his gums.

"There are good men murdered everywhere these days."

"Good Muslims in a village near Wonosari."

"Yes, I heard. And Communists fought army units in another village near there because the army attacked them."

"Because they murdered good Muslims."

A flashing image of men hanging from a tree. Ali said nothing.

"Where are you going?" Mas Slamat pointed to the small bundle of clothing that Bambang had given Ali.

Ali hesitated. But, after all, they were priyayis together, raised by the same adat, though no longer committed to the same principles. "I'm leaving Yogya for a while."

"You would do better to pray in a mosque. But leaving is better than staying now. That is, if you remain a Communist."

"I am a Communist."

Mas Slamat chewed his gums vigorously, as if working toward a decision. Then he said, "I know ulamas and kiyais, important leaders who can help you back to Islam. *Allahu Akbar*. I can take you to them now."

Smiling, Ali reached out and touched the man's thin little arm. "Thank you, but not now. I'm going east today. Hopefully the buses are running."

"I know the buses. In an hour or so a bus should be leaving for the east—through Wonogiri to Ponorogo and you can get to Madiun or Blitar from there. I know the route. By going that way you cut off a long journey through the south. I know these things. How long will you be gone?"

"Who knows? Good-bye, friend. Do what you can to help her."

Mas Slamat lifted his hat slightly and held it there, over his head. "I will do that. *Bismillah*."

"We will surely meet again."

"*Inshallah*."

Ali turned and walked briskly away. At his back he heard the quavering voice of the little man pleading with him. "Give up the murdering! Stay with good Muslims!"

But Ali kept going.

The bus was at least as old as he was. Ali sat toward the front with a good view of the tiny driver and the huge steering wheel he turned with difficulty but enthusiasm. The split leather cushion on which Ali sat was held together by swathes of tape, and the broken springs under it rammed his buttocks with each jolt of the bus. The window wouldn't open, so Ali had to look through its smudged glass at the suburbs of Yogya passing by. Women wearing shawls around their heads were washing clothes on a riverbank. It was already hot in the bus; a small fan attached to the dashboard wasn't working. A man sitting just behind the driver was talking loudly and waving a cigarette. The driver turned every few moments to grunt his assent or dissent, the wheel in his inattentive grasp stretching his short arms to their limit. Exposed wires like animal guts lay in profusion between his legs—legs that could barely reach the pedals. As Ali was looking at this, the man behind the driver suddenly turned and gave him a long, bold stare.

Such un-Javanese rudeness was common these days. People were suspicious of one another, and the best way to protect yourself was to be arrogantly confident and stare down anyone who stared at you. So Ali stared back until the man turned away.

Schoolgirls were marching along the road in white blouses, gray skirts, heavy leather shoes, their heads hidden in white Islamic hoods. In and around the city were they attending school during the crisis? That possibility pleased Ali. Life did go on. Passing them the driver used his loud hooter liberally, then halted a few kilometers farther on to pick up half a dozen women at a roadside station. An old couple were selling eggs and cigarettes and bananas there. From the window Ali could see a flooded ditch; a dead pig, grossly bloated, lay in it and a huge turd nudged one of its legs.

After the women were on, struggling with their bundles and wicker baskets, the driver waited until his conductor, standing at the back, yelled "Go!" and then set out in a fury of exhaust. Ali felt happy as he watched some ducks feeding in a harvested padi. Life did go on. The ducks fed in fields that had been cropped within the last week, and as the bus continued down the road, he saw rice drying on cloth spread on the ground, and in the distance a gray buffalo was pulling its plow through the meaty soil of a shorn field in preparation for new planting. A broad coolie hat obscured the face of a farmer guiding it from behind. Life went on. This was a brave and beautiful country.

Ali sat back, closed his eyes, and let the swaying motion of the bus lull him into needed sleep.

He awakened suddenly when the bus, lurching, threw him forward. The driver, yelling and turning the wheel violently, had jammed the brake down with the full force of his skinny leg.

Ali sat up and looked through the windshield, its view obscured by huge wipers, and saw an army truck coming to a halt obliquely across the road just ahead. Soldiers were pouring out. A captain and a sergeant, pistols drawn, were approaching the bus.

For me, Ali thought. But perhaps not. They couldn't know he was on the bus.

He didn't turn around when the rear door opened with a metallic creak. The women were wailing already, and a man's authoritative voice boomed out to silence them. Ali did not turn, even when he heard boots clomping down the aisle. The boots halted at Ali's row.

Ali looked up and knew he was lost.

"You are Ali Gitosuwoko," the captain stated, not asked. "Come along." He didn't even demand papers.

Ali got up and without a word followed the captain and sergeant from the bus, while the seated women, glancing at him, began to sputter in the aftermath of fear and relief.

Off the bus, Ali stood quietly while someone lashed his hands together behind his back, cinching the knot up until a flash of pain brought from him a little grunt.

"Don't worry," said the soldier who tied the knot. "You'll be feeling a lot more than that before we're through."

"How did you find me?" Ali asked. But by the time they had shoved him roughly into the lorry, he no longer needed to ask. Mas Slamat, that good Muslim, must have gone to police headquarters with the news that an important Communist leader (his flair for the dramatic would make it seem as though Chairman Aidit himself was less important than such a man) had just headed out of Yogya on the eastbound bus. Mas Slamat. Of course. So I have been stupid again, Ali thought. "Immense though the world is, I always miss when I strike at it." He had never realized until now how clearly the sad old proverb applied to himself.

As the lorry jiggled away, he could see the bus setting out again in the opposite direction, its tires spinning and sending up flurries of dust, bound for freedom. Well, perhaps he had never really wanted freedom. Perhaps he had really wanted to end his life where he had spent his childhood, because he was from Central Java, from the family Gitosuwoko, known in the area.

I will never see her again, Ali told himself as the image of Melani, bent over work in the kitchen, filled his vision until he saw nothing else, not even the soldiers grinning at him from the opposite bench.

Fifty

The new rumors passing among Jakartans, as quickly as small change, possessed a nightmarish quality, as if people sat upright in their sleep to yell out the details of their dreams before forgetting them.

One thing was certain: thousands of people were being slaughtered across the length and breadth of Java. Precise figures were unavailable, would have been unavailable even if they had been known. Vern had lived in Asia long enough to know that catastrophes were always understated; a thousand drowned in a flood would appear on the back page of a Delhi or Bangkok or Rangoon newspaper as a hundred. But reports that Vern heard now at the hotel bar or in the offices of OPSUS were assuming the monotonous regularity of truth.

The purge of Reds and their sympathizers had gone beyond a punishing retaliation into the murky horror of wholesale butchery. If entire villages were considered Red, everyone died in them aside from infants. Sometimes the army went into anti-Red villages to deliver fiery speeches, after which they passed out rifles and bayonets and pointed the villagers in the direction of Red villages a few kilometers away. Black-shirted Muslim boys often marched at the fore-front. They were primed for "a Holy War" by kiyais and ulama leaders. When they arrived in predominately Red villages, they checked off names against a PKI membership list or simply listened to locals who identified the guilty—the guilty according to their own lights, since it was reported that many were not Reds at all but victims of clan animosities and land disputes that at last found a solution through murder.

Sometimes the victims were taken by lorry to an execution site outside of town. Often they dug their own graves. The method of execution varied. If the army did the work itself, usually the slaughter was accomplished by firing squad, a merciful way compared to what happened if youth groups were given the honor of doing it. They wielded harvest knives and sickles with enthusiasm but alas without skill. Kneeling with thumbs tied behind their backs so tightly that the swollen appendages looked like plums, heads bowed over the edges of their hastily dug graves, the victims were decapitated by one, two, or sometimes by three or even more hacking blows.

Others were hauled down to riverbanks, where their throats were cut and their corpses rolled into the current. When enough of them effectively blocked further passage downstream, bodies were washed ashore or wedged against the banks, where dogs stood in muddy water and tore at exposed flesh and squawking vultures fought over what remained.

There were no trials. Usually Red activists were summarily killed. Village authorities, cowed by local military commanders, stood aside and let victims be chosen and executed, frequently by garroting with a hemp rope twisted at each end around stubby blocks of wood. Sometimes passive followers of communism were sent off to detention camps, which quickly filled up so that schools and military compounds had to be used as makeshift prisons.

There were stories. Often to protect themselves, families turned in the names of cousins and nephews who lived in nearby villages, hoping that such a show of anti-Red sentiment would prevent their own massacre. Once a column of armored cars was coming down a road, when ahead of it a dozen women were blocking the way. When the first car rumbled up, the women turned and pulled down their sarongs, baring their asses in extreme insult. Infuriated, the commander ordered his machine gunner to open fire on them. After the women had been shot, villagers rushed out of the fields to pick up the bodies. Mistaking their intention, the commander ordered his gunner to kill them too. Which he promptly did.

In Cirebon they set up a guillotine for efficiency and speed.

Severed heads were skewered on bamboo stakes that were then driven into the ground at village crossroads to promote a grisly civic pride.

Sometimes the demoralized Reds fought back. To secure weapons, the lack of which had led to their quick and utter defeat, a few die-hard Reds attacked police stations and military outposts. Once armed, these furious and frustrated men turned on civilians or took soldiers prisoner, torturing them by inserting slivers of bamboo into their ears, their penises.

One afternoon at OPSUS, while Vern sat in a corner and listened quietly, a group of young officers exchanged such rumors, outdoing one another with accounts of the horror. Suddenly a lieutenant, who had been looking impatiently at Vern, walked over to him. "Do you understand what we're saying?" the officer asked in Bahasa.

Vern told him he understood some of it; actually, he understood all of it.

"So what do you think?"

"I think it is sad."

The young officer sat down on the bench beside Vern. "You think there is no justice in my country. You judge us." Without waiting for a reply, he said angrily, "These Reds are out to make trouble. We have trouble enough feeding people without Reds giving us still more trouble. So we must kill them. We have no time for your idea of justice. Reds must go. Today or tomorrow at the latest."

"You see it as a fight for survival then," said Vern carefully.

"We save ourselves first, then look to justice. Justice is for people who have time to spend on it."

Vern did not argue that people could survive and have justice too.

The young officer, getting to his feet, convinced of victory in the argument, added before walking away, "The world is going fast, so we must catch up. If people get in our way, like the Reds, we push them aside."

Vern nodded, having no stomach for debate. He had watched

Asians struggling for years to get a foothold in the sort of world he himself had been born into. He lacked the conviction, much less the impertinence to say, "If you succeed by setting justice aside, when you reach your goal you'll have twisted it out of all recognition." Because he wasn't sure he believed that. They had fought against odds for centuries. Now they had their own flag, and if they dealt with a political party in such a violent way, well, he just couldn't tell them they were wrong. A fat cat can't do that. Even so, he thought they were wrong. What was happening here in Indonesia worked its way through him, eating into a sensibility, an ethics, a place of moral outrage that he hadn't known existed in the tough, unsentimental skeptic he thought he was.

So he was grateful, relieved, almost joyful when General Sakirman called him in one morning and ordered him to leave within a week for Bali to choose a construction site. The urgency in Sakirman's voice suggested that OPSUS was ready, either from design or desperation, to plumb a new source of income. The generals had decided that crisis or no crisis it was time for Project Palm Tree to provide them with a new financial world to conquer.

Sakirman's order coincided with a renewal of the on-again, off-again postal service in Java, so Vern wrote his wife, telling her the good news: at least he'd get some respite from hot, violent Jakarta. The bad news was that Sakirman absolutely refused a stopover in Yogya. Vern concluded the letter, "And so, Maggie dearest, it will be awhile longer before we're together again. You know me. I'm not one for fancy talk. But the truth is I love you and miss you and can't wait to hold you in my arms."

Vern, accompanied by Larry Foard and bodyguard Hashim, stayed at a guesthouse in Denpasar, the little city that served as capital of Bali, an island of three million. The first morning after their arrival Vern awoke to hear an odd little sound outside his window. Looking out, he saw two Balinese girls walking along a path. Coral grinding under their bare feet was the gently crunching sound he had heard. The girls carried baskets of red hibiscus and white frangipani flowers. The courtyard was filled with stone sculptures of Hindu gods. Stopping at each one—green from moss, wet from dew—the girls placed a blossom behind each stone ear.

492

It was a storybook scene, and Vern had been an Asian hand long enough to distrust the cute, the pretty, the exotic out here. He suspended judgment on a place until, as he put it, "I've had a look at the outhouse." Even so, that first morning in Bali he was swept up by a sense of being somewhere unique on earth. Perhaps it was simply the mildew that gave this little island such an odd atmosphere. Everything took on a diaphanous green coat in the warm, wet fecund climate. A mossy look softened the outline of every object, and gave him an uneasy feeling of having been transported back into an antediluvian age of dripping ferns and swampy fogs. He couldn't get over it. Bali had worked some kind of magic on him before he'd spent twenty-four hours on its shores. He felt like a tourist in Asia for the first time in years, and it gave him a little jolt of pleasure.

But there wasn't time to enjoy the leisure of a tourist. General Sakirman, a man who did little himself, expected a lot from those who worked under him, especially now at a time when efficiency and honesty were fashionable. Possible construction sites on the coast were a few miles from Denpasar. Sudjani, hired to translate for the two Western builders, rented a car. Boyish-looking, he was always slicking his hair down with a purple comb embedded with rhinestones. He had once been the houseboy for a French artist from whom he had learned both French and English. Bright and snappy, his large eyes often narrowing in humor, Sudjani had declared himself willing to help with anything—bluntly, yet somehow not coarsely, he'd asked if Tuan would like a girl or a boy to sleep with. "I can arrange," he claimed eagerly. No doubt, so Vern and Larry agreed, the young man's ability to arrange such matters was a chief reason for OPSUS hiring him to meet their officers who came to Bali on business.

At the district of Sanur, along the seacoast, Vern found the site he wanted. Farther north the Japanese were still building their own hotel, the Bali Beach, the sort of ugly ten-story structure that Vern was glad the government no longer allowed to go up on these silver beaches.

In following days he let the island come at him like a soft breath, like one of its onshore breezes. He strolled in a Sanur market, past oiled paper umbrellas, joss sticks, pots and pans. Everywhere there was food: garlic, herbs, yellow sugar, maize, rice, bottles of chili sauce, dried fish, fish paste. Market women wore brassieres or nothing above their sarongs, as they sold rice cakes, grilled chicken, sweets wrapped in banana leaves. Sudjani, at his side, would say something in Balinese about a particularly attractive girl and then merrily clap his hand over his mouth, giving Vern a shrewd glance, as if hoping this salacious remark spoken in a language unknown to the red-faced foreigner would have the desired effect. Clearly Sudjani would consider himself humiliated if he failed to get this Tuan in bed with a pretty Balinese boy or girl before the week had ended.

It was not enough to select the site. It had to be OK'd by the gods before any self-respecting Balinese workman would labor on it, and so without hesitation Vern went along with the ceremony arranged for by Sudjani. A local priest, wearing a red-and-gold miter, came to the site, which at present was a sandy bit of jungle near the ocean. The priest made a rectangle with four sticks. Into it he flung holy water from a siwamba bowl and prayed with flowers held between his outstretched palms. Of all the gods, Sudjani explained to Vern, the priest had chiefly to appease Batara Guru, Supreme Teacher of Brahman priests, a god with four hands: two clasped forever in prayer, a third holding a Hindu rosary, and the fourth a bamboo switch for swatting flies. The priest scooped up some earth from within the staked-out rectangle, wrapped it in a white cloth, and dragged it through the scented smoke of a little fire. Sudjani claimed that the priest would take this earth home and sleep with his head on it. If his dream tonight was good, this was a good site; if not, they must look elsewhere. Sudjani paused expectantly. In the ensuing silence Vern became aware that both Sudjani and the priest were waiting for something. Of course. Vern reached into his pocket and came out with two ringgits, then added another to insure a good dream.

As they left the area, Vern noticed some children huddled under a rickety wooden table that had been set for no discernible reason in a nearby rice field. Under the table, chattering like monkeys, the children kept out of the sun.

And for no discernible reason the sight of them created in Vern a strong desire for this site to be the right one.

Next morning Sudjani reported that the siwa priest had dreamed a good dream. They had their site.

But there was still something to be done before the site could be used. A center post, purely ceremonial, must be erected in the middle of the construction area. First, the hole was dug by workmen who moved carefully around it; under no circumstances must their shadows fall upon it or sickness and trouble would inevitably be the fate of anyone who lived in a house erected around this center post. Next, an offering was made. Into the hole were laid some pieces of brazil-wood, ebony wood, a candlenut, a broken axhead, a Chinese coin with a square hole stamped out of it, and a short length of scrap iron. A chicken was beheaded over the hole so that blood spilled down into it. Then the body was dumped in to serve as a kind of symbolic cushion for the post to rest on. Batara Guru was summoned by the priest, His blessing requested, after which the ritual ended—that is, once Vern had donated a few more ringgits to the god.

Next day shipping arrangements for construction materials from Jakarta were made in Denpasar. That night Vern and Larry paid a visit to the site in moonlight. Waves came rolling sluggishly in, like soft lumpy pillows. The scent of flowers blew across their faces. At their backs stood coconut palms and breadfruit trees with foot-long serrated leaves and white mango with pink blossoms and huge banyans strewn with shaggy moss.

"When a good man dies," Larry was saying, "they build a hundred-foot tower of bamboo and work for weeks, months, decorating it, so on cremation day they can put the corpse inside. Then they burn up the whole bloody thing. All that work gone in a few seconds. I like that."

Vern turned to look at him.

"I do," Larry maintained. "I like the way they feel about the value of things. Because they love what doesn't last: flowers and huge towers they burn up and the grace of dancers who retire at thirteen. I like it. Ephemeral things. That's what they worship. Bloody good."

But Vern wasn't listening. He was thinking of Maggie standing beside him on this beach. He'd say, "We'll eat saté lembat, Maggie. I thought of you when I first had it here, because the stuff's really spicy. It's turtle meat and spices and coconut cream all mixed together in a dough and roasted over coals on a bamboo stick." He wouldn't tell her what Sudjani had explained: that a sea turtle takes hours to die, even after its head and limbs are severed from the body. The guts keep pulsating and the jaws snap and the claws contract long after the shell has been removed and the separate parts are lying in the sand.

They'd eat saté lembat, breadfruit, salak, and mangosteen. Then they'd stroll down the beach, and in the warm onshore breezes they'd hold hands, and if they wanted to—and he'd want to—they could slip into the undergrowth and make love under the scented Balinese sky.

"What did you say?" he asked Larry, who nevertheless didn't repeat what he had said, aware that Vern was really somewhere else.

———

When they got back to Jakarta, a letter from Yogya was waiting for Vern.

He went upstairs to his room before opening it.

Dear Vern:

This is the hardest letter I have ever had to write. Surely what I have to say should be said directly to you, not by the easily misunderstood medium of a letter. But no one can tell when the crisis will end or travel return to normal. I can't let this go on. I have to write it down in words that can't possibly tell you what I feel. Vern, I will put it down without the sort of embellishments I know you equate with dishonesty. The thing is, my dear Vern— and I mean that, my dear, dear Vern—I have somehow—it is very strange to put this down on paper, as if what I am describing has happened to someone else—I have fallen in love with another man. Here in Yogya. A dalang fifteen years older than I am—a man I hardly know, perhaps can never know, a man who lives in another world than mine, than most of his own people live in. What I am saying is it is all wrong and crazy and yet at the same time inevitable, the sanest thing in my life.

Vern, I'm saying I am deeply in love with someone else. It is no passing flirtation, please don't think it is, no little fling created by the mystery of this land and the tensions of the crisis. It is— I don't know why or how—but it is real and deep and lasting. There is nothing I can do about it or, frankly, that I want to do about it. I never thought in my wildest dreams I would hurt any- one this way, much less you, Vern Gardner, who has never done me the slightest harm, who has only given me comfort and love.

496

But there is no way out for me, dear man. I never really believed in wild romance, yet suddenly it has stepped up and wrapped me in its black cloak and spirited me away to a world I never knew existed, and so here I am and here I will stay.

Please don't try to change my mind. Please don't get here by hook or crook merely to slap my face and tell me what a fool I am. You'd be capable of that, I know, and you'd be justified. But you are also capable of understanding what has happened, of thinking about it thoroughly and slowly before acting. Then you'll know what to do and that is nothing. You'll let me go my way, as I must no matter what anyone says, and you will therefore keep the love I once gave you and I will keep yours, cherish it always in my heart as something rare and beautiful that happened between us.

Maggie

Patet Manjura
Three A.M. *to Dawn*

Fifty-one

While the island of Java seemed to be whirling around Maggie Gardner like storm-tossed wreckage, her own life had taken on a strict daily pattern. It was a life with the sort of clockwork precision that she had known in graduate school. Up at dawn in the dalang's compound, she washed and kissed him good-bye and pedaled back to the Sakirman compound for public breakfast and afterward a music lesson. Then there was a morning trip to the Diponegoro Divisional Headquarters, where she waited patiently for an officer, any officer, to see her so she could hear him claim they had no new information about "the missing girl." After declaring her intention to return the next day for another inquiry, Maggie rode her bike all over Yogya to promote the restoration of Borobudur. She visited priyayi homes shrouded in greenery and tin-roofed shops in the noisy markets; headed for outlying batik factories; tracked down court officials in the kraton; tramped through the university, hunting for staff and faculty; prowled through dance and gamelan academies; showed up without invitation at government agencies for logistics, for cultural affairs, for transportation, for agriculture, for banking, for anything that had an office door and a name on it—traveling down kilometers of corridor and sitting on countless benches and forcing upon her sweaty face interminable useless smiles. Maggie went anywhere that she might meet people who would listen to the needs of Borobudur.

Usually she told them more than they had ever known about the thousand-year-old temple that was as familiar to them as the old oak tree on the corner had been to Maggie when she never looked at it on her way to school. To skeptical batik merchants, and indifferent bureaucrats, and haughty old ladies of the para bandara—noble remnants of the ancient state of Mataram—she explained patiently and with all the humility she could muster how the temple was first noticed in modern times by Thomas Raffles, lieutenant governor of Java during the British days in the early nineteenth century, and how the first restoration was undertaken a few decades later by a Dutch photographer, who filled in hollows of the paving with sand, and how in 1886 a Dutch archaeologist excavated hidden reliefs, and how the Dutch from 1907 through 1911 did another restoration and used concrete instead of sand to rid the foundation of rainwater, and how it was now the rightful pleasure and privilege of the great new nation of Indonesia to go beyond the old restorations and ultimately rebuild Borobudur into a monument of the spirit that the entire world could again admire and envy.

Such speeches were exhausting to give in this seething town of heat and rumor, especially when they were often met with scorn or disbelief. She knew what people were thinking: how could this crazy foreigner be interested in a pile of old stones that had been out there for centuries and without anyone's help would be out there for centuries more?

After her efforts for Borobudur, she took two hours of language lessons, then returned to the dalang's compound where she watched him practice with the puppets or sing—not with any goal in view, according to him, but simply to renew his feeling for lakon plays. There was dinner and afterward, perhaps, an intimate and impromptu gamelan recital if some of his friends dropped by (and wonderfully they did drop by, the crisis notwithstanding; Maggie had the feeling they would drop by even if an earthquake ripped through Yogya, forcing them to leap over gaping crevices to get there). On these occasions, to spare him as much discomfort as possible without actually hiding, she merely sembahed and remained apart, a shadowy presence, as Javanese women had been for centuries, although never once did he ask for her discretion, much less display the slightest embarrassment from her being with him. He even hinted that when she felt more comfortable with his friends, they would benefit from her knowledge of American jazz.

The best part of the evening was when she was alone with him. They sat under the moon and watched the big flat sheets of palm leaf rattling in island breezes. Sometimes she knew that he was thinking of the bodies at Prambanan; since that grisly discovery he had been a different man. Not that he did or said anything that signaled the difference. She just felt it as a sudden wall rising up invisibly between them, a terrible isolating image that set them apart. Yet when they went inside to make love, it was as if nothing beyond the compound could ever affect them.

In their room together they created a world as unpredictable as the one outside the compound. There might be between them quick and casual sex. Or she might put on a sarong, knowing full well that a Western woman, much less a tall and rawboned one, could never really look good in it, and parade around while he pretended that she was as graceful and elegant as a princess at the sultan's court, until they both burst into laughter. Or he would keep her out of the bedroom for a long time and then shyly lead her inside, where she found, strewed enticingly on the bed, a lush design of hibiscus and orchids and frangipani, with a subtle incense hovering above the white sheet down to which he would draw her gently into the enchanted glen of a long lost fantasy of hers from girlhood. Or he would grumble about his own immoderate desire, blaming it on the need to perform while he could and calling himself Arjuna past the prime of love, but not, it seemed, meaning any of it or only part of it and thereby keeping her on edge as much through his self-mockery as through his erotic skill.

Sometimes he gave their passion the odd sense of being endlessly protracted but inevitable, like an action in nature, a flower unfolding at daybreak, so that sometimes she nearly fell asleep (or was it into a trance she fell?), from which suddenly she emerged and he along with her, their mutual arousal manifest and irrepressible, having been nurtured by unhurried touching. This was strange exploratory lovemaking, which, at any moment, could transform itself into a great but simple fuck.

Whatever happened, there always followed a closeness that Maggie began to visualize as a single consciousness. Their sharing was like a pulsing heart at the end of her mind, a tiny heart beating and beating and beating until her eyes closed and she edged into a space between sleeping and waking where she remained snugly, secretly, for long intervals of time.

One morning he asked her to leave the Sakirman house permanently and move into his own. So he was prepared to throw aside the reputation of generations like an old rag. It occurred to Maggie that the only other man she had ever known who possessed that sort of willful independence was her husband.

She did not give Budi her answer that morning.

———————

When she arrived at the Sakirman compound shortly after dawn, the oldest of the servants, Utami, came forward with mail clutched in her mottled hand.

So the mail was running again.

Maggie shuffled through it for a letter from Vern, but there was none. He must be receiving hers today or perhaps tomorrow. He would know everything then. Her awareness of this left her with a mixed feeling of fear and relief.

There was a letter from Susanto in Malang. She opened that one. "Mrs. Gardner. Not easy to write English but I try. Forget servant Inam, she is Communist and brother to. Stay safe in house please. My husband lets your husband go in Yogya when possibel but not now. Please stay calm in house and say notning. Your friend, Susanto Sakirman."

Maggie looked up quickly to see old Utami squinting curiously at the letter that was out of her reach and beyond her understanding. The old woman, whenever she inquired about Inam, grinned and called her "Yu," contemptuous Ngoko for a young woman of the lower class. Utami had shown no interest in Inam's fate. The truth was, Maggie figured, Utami felt relieved that a clever young woman who threatened her position was out of the compound.

So the Diponegoro headquarters had contacted General Sakirman in Jakarta and he in turn had got word to his wife in Malang about the Communist traitor working as a servant in their Yogyanese household. Susanto had made it very clear: Maggie, girl, keep your mouth shut and your hands clean.

While she stood there, holding the letter, Maggie saw a man crossing the courtyard toward her. He wore a white shirt, baggy pants, a Western fedora, and sunglasses. Obviously he hadn't bothered to wait at the main entrance to be admitted. This ain't no gentleman, Maggie told herself, and noticed the old woman scurrying away. Maggie waited for him alone.

He touched the brim of his hat. Perhaps the Dutch had taught his father to do that—he was too young to have learned it from them himself. He did not bother with introductions but simply began questioning her.

"Nonya," he said, looking not at her but at the mail she held in her hand, "do you know Chinaman Chong?"

"I know Pak Chong, yes. I know his batik shop."

"Do you know Pak Sadli?"

"Yes, I know him too." She had also shopped in his booth and knew him better than Chong, who used to be called "Pak Chong," but in the present atmosphere was referred to as "Chinaman Chong." Pak Sadli was santri; he had told her so proudly and often. His narrow head had distinctly Mongolian eyes, which suggested that perhaps there was some Chinese in him too. He had lips that pursed up and wriggled like worms when he conjured up a special price, which meant an outrageous markup for the foreign woman. Once he sold her a bad piece of goods; when she returned it, he admitted it was bad but explained it away by saying he had a lot of mouths to feed.

"Have you ever heard Chinaman Chong make a speech?"

"No."

"A speech praising Mao and the Chinese Reds?"

"No. I never knew he made speeches."

"Pak Sadli says he made many speeches."

"Well, they compete for business, don't they? Across the street from each other, selling the same kind of goods."

The man studied her openly, and his cool boldness frightened Maggie. She suspected that he was BPI, an agent of the Central Intelligence

Board, an autonomous investigatory unit with dubious loyalty to Sukarno or maybe to other officials of government or perhaps now to the army. "Have you seen the Chinaman's library?"

"No. I never knew him well enough to be invited to see it."

Stepping forward, the man thrust a page from a book at her; from its jagged edge it must have been ripped out. "Look," he demanded.

Maggie saw that the page was covered with Chinese characters.

"Do you know what this says?" the man asked.

"I can't read Chinese."

"What do you think it says?"

"I haven't any idea."

"What if I told you it says Bung Karno must be overthrown?"

"All I know is that Pak Chong always talks about Taoism and long life. Do you read Chinese? Maybe it's a treatise on long life." Maggie tried to smile after noting his expression turn from confusion to disapproval to anger.

"You have many Red friends," he declared.

"I do not."

"What are you doing in Yogya?"

"You can ask at Diponegoro Divisional Headquarters. I think they know all about me." She added, without thinking it through, "I have many friends here, among them Ki-Dalang Budi Gitosuwoko. Perhaps you can ask him if I'm a Communist."

That caught him off guard and he blinked rapidly. Either he was surprised by her friendship with a famous dalang or by her shameless acknowledgment of their adultery. She couldn't decide which, but took fleeting pleasure from the agent's confusion and his hasty retreat.

That was a round she had won, but Maggie no longer felt safe in this compound. Crossing the courtyard to the main house, she noticed two servants leaning into shadows and watching her.

Clearly the Sakirmans would not protect her much longer, especially if she made daily visits to army headquarters in search of information about a missing girl who had been arrested for Communist activities. She couldn't ask Vern for help, not after he received her letter. There was a good chance of being deported unless she found someone to defend her. That would have to be her lover, who also happened to be a famous and respected man.

506

That evening she arrived at his compound with her bags in the back of a gerobak. She no longer kept from him her attempts to discover what had happened to Inam. She described today's interview with a man who was most certainly BPI. She told him the truth: that she had written her husband, telling him about them; that she could no longer expect protection from the Sakirmans; that she never wanted to leave this country; that her best chance of staying in Indonesia was to stay here with him.

"And will you also stay for me?" he asked, his smile strangely wistful. "Will you stay with me in spite of the terrible things happening in my country?"

That night there was no music, little talk, and they lay apart, each thoughtful. Finally he said, "My nephew is dead."

She rose up on one elbow and peered through moonlight at him. "Bambang?"

"My nephew Ali."

"Ali? No, it's not possible. Only a few days ago—"

"He was taken off a bus. Later they put him and some other Communists into a truck and drove them down to a river and slit their throats and threw them in."

"Can you be sure? Ali? Only a few days ago—"

"Someone I know knows someone who was there and saw it happen." After a pause he added, "And I think helped it happen."

Sinking back on the bed, Maggie said nothing. They turned away from each other, and there was no lovemaking that night.

Next day during her rounds of the city, Maggie learned that Pak Sadli had gone to the local police station, where he accused Chinaman Chong of treason to the Republic of Indonesia. On the basis of this accusation justice had been swift, uncomplicated. Chinaman Chong had been executed against the latrine shed behind the station. So were his two older sons. A boy of seven and a girl of ten, along with his wife, had been generously spared. A shop owner told Maggie that Pak Sadli had expressed sorrow for the death of a fellow merchant, although he also felt proud of his patriotic action in the service of the country.

507

Maggie was brooding about the murder when she rode up to the Gitosuwoko compound. To her surprise Mas Slamat was standing there under a shade tree, his toothless mouth working even before she got off the bike.

"How did you know I would be here?" She wondered if he shadowed her like a private eye and kept a little black book, noting down where she went and the times.

He did not answer. She knew he would not answer.

Mas Slamat chewed his gums a few moments. "The holy man," he finally said, "would like to see you."

"I'd like to see him too. I want his help on Borobudur."

Mas Slamat narrowed his eyes into a squint. He was chewing furiously, as if something special was on his mind. "What does Dalang Gitosuwoko think of you seeing the holy man?"

She felt he was probably being rude in Javanese terms by asking such a thing. So she decided to tease him. "Why would Dalang Gitosuwoko wonder about me seeing anyone?"

Mas Slamat chewed.

"As a matter of fact, I suppose he wouldn't care one way or another if I see the holy man." With satisfaction she watched Mas Slamat chomp faster. "Or maybe Dalang Gitosuwoko would like it."

"Does he believe in things the holy man believes in?" Mas Slamat's whole face was held in an expression of suspense, ready to become a look of astonishment if she answered wrong.

"Shouldn't he believe in such things?"

"Good Muslims should believe only in Muslim holy men."

"You talk a lot about good Muslims these days, Mas Slamat."

He reached up and fingered the ugly mole thoughtfully.

"Did you know," Maggie said to him, "the army sends a company of men out to Prambanan every night? They use the temple walls for executions. They execute Communists."

"Reds killed good Muslims there a few weeks ago."

"But every night now the army is executing sixty, seventy, a hundred people against those walls. None of them has been accused in court or tried."

"Yes," he said.

"What does the holy man think about that?"

"The holy man hasn't time for politics. He prays for wealth."

508

"Then I guess we're praying for the same thing." When he gave her a puzzled look, she added, "I need money for Borobudur. What does he want it for?"

"For the World Peace Radiating Center. He is looking for tuyul. That is child ghost who will help you get rich if you gain its favor. He prays to Chinese gods for that. They are liked by tuyuls."

"Maybe I won't see the holy man tomorrow."

"Something wrong, Nonya?"

"Ali has been killed."

For a few moments Mas Slamat stood there without moving; even his ceaseless lips were still. Then he started to work them again. "He would not listen to me."

"What did you tell him?"

"I told him to come back to Islam. Now he has been punished. When he got on that bus he was escaping from God."

"You knew he took a bus?"

"Of course. I am sorry for him, but I am not sorry for telling them."

"Telling who?"

"The police. Which bus he was on."

"Let me understand," she said in a low voice, trying hard for control. "Because Ali wouldn't become a Muslim again, you turned him in?"

"I did."

"You horrible little son of a bitch," Maggie gasped, staggering past him and leaving him there, umbrella held in the crook of his arm, his cool eyes regarding her steadily from within the shade of his porkpie hat.

Fifty-two

Not far from the ancestral village of the Gitosuwokos, in an atap hut under a steady rain, sat the chairman of the Communist party of Indonesia, a man worshiped by Ali Gitosuwoko as the Ratu Adil, messiah of his people. He had been caught by paratroopers a few days ago. Blindfolded, ordered to keep both hands flat on his head, he had sat for hours cross-legged in the mud until they brought him to this isolated hut. An officer had given him a small desk, a chair, a pen, and a few sheets of paper. He had been ordered to write a detailed account of how the PKI had planned the murder of the generals, the kidnapping of the president, the takeover of Indonesia. When he refused, the officer shrugged and told him, "I suppose then we will have to write it ourselves. That can be done, you know." When Aidit still refused, the officer went away.

From him, a rather kind man who came back now and then to see if anything had been written, the chairman learned of Air Marshal Dhani's arrest in the presidential palace in Bogor. That meant the end of Sukarno's power—he could no longer protect anyone. Inquiring about members of the Politburo, Aidit learned that most of them had been taken—Lukman and Njoto among them—and that a few were already dead. When he asked about his closest aides, Aidit was assured that they too were under arrest. "Hartono too?" Somehow he felt that the young man would outsmart his pursuers.

The officer, shaking his head, laughed grimly. "Hartono is quite safe," he said. "How do you think we found you?"

A week ago Hartono had been in the area, along with others who were resolved to plan a comeback for the party. Obviously Hartono had come out here for another reason—to locate his comrades (especially the chairman) and turn them in.

Now, as Aidit sat listening to the falling rain, that same officer came into the hut. He stood silently for a while, staring at the seated prisoner.

Aidit felt as though the officer's eyes were draining him of energy. So this was what it was like when they came for you.

"We're going now," the officer said quietly.

Aidit got to his feet, then looked at the blank paper on the table. Sitting down again, he picked up the pen and said with an apologetic smile, "I think I will make a little statement."

"A confession?"

"A statement of principle."

"There isn't time for that."

"I am a member of the president's cabinet. What I have to say is important."

"Only a confession is important." Waiting for a response, the officer beckoned when none came. "We're going now."

As they left the hut, Aidit glanced at the gray roiling clouds overhead. A raindrop hit his left eye, and the feel of it—cool, silvery— reminded him of his childhood when he played in the rain.

Abruptly his attention shifted to a squad of waiting soldiers toward whom the officer was leading him. With men in front and behind, he started down a narrow muddy path on either side of which was jungle. He smelled the greenery in the rain, while he thought of his wife and her cataracts. She wouldn't get an operation now. She'd go blind, but she was a brave, uncomplaining woman, who would give them plenty of trouble when they finally caught her.

511

The path seemed to widen slightly, and that frightened him. As long as they walked along this narrow muddy path, nothing would happen. Everything depended upon it. If the path widened or changed shape in any way, something might happen. Dipa Nusantara Aidit, chairman of the Partai Komunis Indonesia, third-largest Communist party in the world, he told himself, was going to die. In his mid-forties. That fact, his comparatively young age, gave him a sudden wrenching pang of grief. The loss of so many additional years was the most terrible thing of all to contemplate in the few minutes he had left. Surely every man facing premature death felt the same. His reaction was quite ordinary. He was certainly not a hero, although many of the young cadres had worshiped him. But perhaps in the last minutes before execution there were never any heroes. A man could make a noble speech at the last, but surely in his mind he felt a common panic, an appalling sense of waste, the numbing realization that soon he would not be able to mourn himself.

The officer gripped his elbow as they walked side by side with the squad of soldiers in front and at the rear. Aidit asked him if they had much farther to go, but received no answer. The officer's face seemed drawn, tired, consumed by private thoughts.

Along the left side of the path there was a ditch, and the heavy persistent rainfall had nearly filled it. In a few hours the water would be washing over into the path. But how did he know that? He would not be here to verify it.

Now the path widened into a small clearing at the far end of which was a gnarled banyan tree. He pulled free from the officer's grip and asked sharply, "What will you do with me?" When the officer seemed puzzled, he added in a softer voice, "After I'm dead."

He wasn't sure if the officer answered, because two of the soldiers came alongside and each took him roughly by an arm. He looked at the banyan tree toward which they were moving him. The sensation of moving was a little like floating or gliding, because he seemed to have lost sensation in his legs. After he was dead, they would fling his body into a ditch where the rain would soak through his bloody clothing and spatter against his face, his hands, his legs, and after a while everything that he was would settle into the mud, sink down, pull apart, seep away.

I was right, he said to himself. I had the answer for my country.

Taking a deep breath, D. N. Aidit tried to relax so that the soldiers could do cleanly and quickly what they had to do.

What he loved most in this world was swinging the long-headed hammer, the palu, against red-hot metal, hearing the loud demonic clamor, then feeling the metallic resistance, like a live thing, go snaking up his arms at each stroke. He, in the role of Charangwaspa, chief half brother to Panji Sepuh, always hit first to establish the correct place for the blows, after which the three other half brothers, each by rank, brought their own palus down upon the glowing gong: Handaga, Wirun, Kartala, in strict order, as if the stability of the universe depended upon this unchanging sequence of hammering.

Someday Bambang would assume the role of Panji Sepuh, which meant, as chief gongsmith, he would pour the molten bronze into its mold and manipulate the supit tongs to hold the job during forging. Until then he was in charge of the anvil. Today he had noticed that Panji Sepuh was coughing furiously, his haggard face more drawn than usual, his pallor worse, his eyes squinting and glazed. And he had scarcely spoken to Bambang while they worked.

But then few people were speaking to Bambang these days. Because of his Communist brother, he was being ostracized, a fearsome thing in an outlying village where everyone depended on neighbors for entertainment, work, sustenance, ultimately for survival.

This morning at the forge, lifting the palu above a large gong ageng, he had noticed Handaga eyeing him steadily. In itself this was not unusual. Everyone knew how jealous Handaga was of him, especially because he was younger and less experienced than the narrow-chested Handaga, third at the forge only because his wife was Panji Sepuh's older sister's third daughter. Bambang had been feeling lately that the two of them must have it out, yet open confrontation was frowned upon in the village. Time worked things out, although nowadays it was violence, not Javanese courtesy and patience, that got things done. Ali, for example, had been taken off a bus and trucked away to a detention camp, if rumors were correct. Poor foolish Ali wouldn't be given time for working things out. And then there was Achmad. An intelligence officer had come to the village a few days ago inquiring about Sergeant Bachtiar, who had deserted his post and was being held for trial on charges of treason. Bambang had spoken to him, but the officer's reluctance to exchange information suggested to the gong founder that villagers had talked to him first, making him suspicious of the sergeant's old friend.

Such distrust pervaded the air, it seemed to Bambang. His brother and his best friend were victims of the crisis; that was clear. He didn't care what they had done; they were both fine men. What they did was merely a consequence of bad judgment, not bad hearts. Ali possessed the silly ideas of a young man who had not yet assimilated his education. Achmad, well—perhaps his intense patriotism had led him to do something that might seem treasonable to others, especially at a time of capricious suspicion. There was an old Javanese saying: If emotions go out of control you go with them, flying through the air together into the mouth of a demon. Achmad was blinded by flights of fantasy, just like Ali. Their fault was very Javanese: a desire to escape reality through dreams of perfection and heroism. Bambang was not like that. He had always understood control, just the way his uncle did. He had always aligned himself with his uncle because he felt the two of them were wiser than most men. Such arrogance he kept a secret, of course, saving a show of pride for where it rightly belonged—in the foundry when he brought down a palu so expertly that even Panji Sepuh hissed in appreciation while kneeling with tongs at the rim of heated metal.

Now, leaving the dark foundry for the soft yellow light of late afternoon, Bambang saw a small man hesitating under a tree before stepping out toward him. It was the tukang-idjon, who had been buying up rice futures in the village the last few days. He bobbed courteously and sembahed while approaching Bambang.

"Tuan Charangwaspa, I have not had a chance to pay my respects recently." Grimacing, he said, "I have heard of your bad luck."

"What bad luck?"

"Your brother's bad luck, I mean. No one would accuse you of being a Communist." He laughed, his eyes steady and cold. "I have told people, 'Let him alone.' "

"Let who alone?"

"I have told them, don't blame Tuan Charangwaspa for what his brother did. When they say, 'If Tuan Charangwaspa disliked what his brother did, why did he take the fellow into his house and feed and protect him?' I tell them, 'Never mind. It is over now. Let him alone.' "

Bambang said nothing, but brushed past the moneylender and headed home, seeing Melani whisking the front veranda of their house with a bamboo broom.

They had made love and now she slept, but Bambang lay awake. Even while holding her in his arms, he had been assailed by strange images that flashed through his mind with the power and speed of palus at the forge. One image remained: the thoughtful face of Handaga. The expression had been one of measuring, as if Handaga, instead of Panji Sepuh, must reckon the correct amounts of tin and copper that make a gong. Lips compressed, eyes burning steadily: an outward show of calculation, of bitter regard. And it came suddenly to Bambang that a decision had been made. Otherwise the moneylender would not have been so bold on the village path today. Handaga would not have dared to stare so insolently. And no one ever came anymore to the house, not even Melani's women friends. Today they had not. She had told him with a little look of bewilderment and pain that they had not. Someone always came to see her, to exchange a word, every day. But not today.

He turned to look at her sleeping face in the moonlight. He had loved this woman since childhood, when along with other children they had teased the buffalo soaking in ponds. Lately she had been especially tender to him, and on this very night it had been Melani who initiated their lovemaking.

Perhaps because she also knew. But if she knew, could she sleep this way? Melani could. She had deep control of herself, a control rivaling Uncle's.

Bambang got up silently from their mattress and slipped out of the room.

Standing at the front door leading to the veranda, he peered into the moonlit night. They were out there; he felt their presence among the foliage, along the path. There must have been a meeting of the council this evening. They would have talked of many things—prices for tools, the coming festival, a neighborhood footpath needing repair—before someone mentioned the danger of harboring godless men in the village. Something like that. And someone would have asked innocently, Had such a thing been done? And someone would have replied, The gong maker Bambang had harbored his brother in his own house long after protecting Reds was seen as an act of treason. There would have been gasps of wonder, as if until that minute no one in the village had known about it. And then someone would have inquired, What must be done? The pause would have been long, thoughtful, as if infinite possibilities must be taken into account until a wise and judicious decision could be made. In fact, they had already known. Just as he knew now, standing in the open doorway with moonlight streaming over his feet.

But maybe not tonight. And if not tonight, he could gather up Melani and the children and escape. But escape where? Uncle would take them in. Uncle would protect them. Of course, and he, Bambang Gitosuwoko, master gongsmith, would cower inside the compound like a frightened girl, hoping that a ulama's prayers, paid for by Uncle, would bring him better luck.

Bambang went inside and took a harvest knife from a wall hook. He used this ani in the fields when a neighbor, fearful of losing his padi to bad weather, needed help in harvesting. A Gitosuwoko kris would be better, Bambang thought, but the two of them were in the possession of Uncle, as they should be. For a moment he thought of writing a note to Uncle, paying his last respects to the upholder of the family name. But there probably wasn't time. Bambang did not want to wait until they called him out with a whisper. He wanted to go out there and call them loudly. "Here! Here I am! Bambang Gitosuwoko!"

Gripping the wooden handle of the ani, he went again to the open doorway. For a moment he hesitated, wondering if there was time for him to look once more at Melani, then at the children. But that would only weaken him. He needed all his strength to meet them out there, to wield the knife this last time, to show them who he really was.

Taking a deep breath, regripping the ani handle, Bambang Gitosuwoko strolled onto the veranda as if it were bright noontime. Once again he hesitated, struck by another vision so distant and tender that for a few more moments he fell into a reverie. He and Ali were boys again. Ali, full of mischief, had slipped a chili into his brother's mound of rice, and when Bambang bit into it the sensation was like putting his tongue against a red-hot gong. He had chased and caught Ali under the big jackfruit tree. He was going to hit his smaller brother, but for some reason he just turned and walked away. Ali yelled insults at his back as if he were a coward. And as he slouched homeward, feeling confused by his action, he noticed his uncle, a grown man then, standing beside a banana palm, smiling at him. Uncle must have seen what happened. Bambang felt ashamed. They said nothing as Bambang passed by, but their heads both turned so they could watch each other, and Uncle kept smiling, smiling. Bambang had picked up his pace then, and by the time he reached home, he was running happily. He remembered that now, and the memory somehow gave him strength.

On the veranda Bambang held his breath, listening. But all that came to him was a silence through which he heard from long ago his father say the old saying, "We all die but have different graves." He couldn't remember now the circumstances that had provoked this from his father. But the saying was not altogether true, because when he died he would be buried in the village of his ancestors and they would all be together in the earth. People wouldn't deny him that. They would kill him but let him have his rightful place here.

He heard nothing but the silence and turned to go back inside until they worked up enough courage to come get him.

Then he heard something—a rustling from the clump of trees in a compound across the lane.

Leaving the veranda, he walked down the front path to his gate, unlatched and swung it back, and relatched it carefully once he was through. He strolled into the middle of the lane and waited. Something moved into his vision, then leftward out of it. Something else was moving to the right. Perhaps they had already surrounded him. Founders like himself, accustomed to the noise of hammers, didn't move so quietly. Out there were farmers who could move barefoot through padis with the softness of herons.

Gripping the handle of his knife as tightly as if it were a smithy's hammer, Bambang took a deep breath and yelled loudly enough to awaken his ancestors, "Here I am! Here! Right here! Bambang Gitosuwoko!"

Fifty-three

Although he was entering the village on a tragic mission, his thoughts veered away from it to his love for a woman he should have nothing to do with. She had moved into the compound, now lived with him openly. Had it not been a time of tumultuous events, the whole city of Yogya would not only be aware of it but would fear the consequences, because it represented a great rupture of normal order. People would be desperate to stop it, and surely by now—within a week of this foreign woman entering into "concubinage" in the home of a dalang—there would have been a delegation of leaders, mostly religious, solemnly requesting an audience with Kyahi Dalang Budi Gitosuwoko. Not that he would have granted it. Perhaps he would have gone to the front veranda and with a crisp bow informed them that the only thing he would discuss was wayang.

Nothing could change his feeling for her, not even a change in her feeling for him. As he rode by oxcart into the village, bound for his dead nephew's house, Budi had a flashing image of Maggie under him as he straddled her at dawn today, his purplish hardness working along the slippery channel that she made for him between her cupped white breasts, her eyes, glazed but steady, watching him above her until, closing his own, he came. He had not expected such frank passion in a Western woman. But then he had never met anyone like his Maggie: it was what he called her in English, "My Maggie."

There was about her a yearning to get past what was obviously there and go straight to the hidden heart of things. He felt a similar desire, a need to draw back the veil and enter worlds unimagined. And she was brave enough, driven enough, to go with him. The love of adventuring beyond limits—not merely a superficial interest in novelty—had drawn them together. What had started with Borobudur, their mutual desire to save the old temple, had become a pervasive curiosity about each other, which he knew was one way of describing love.

The oxcart having stopped, he got down in the village square. He had halted here deliberately to let everyone have a chance to see his arrival. A poor impression on these villagers would make his task harder. He must be every inch a dalang. Before he reached Bambang's house, not a half kilometer away, the lurah, the village headman, should be at his side, panting and sembahing and smiling.

And so he was.

Dalang Budi assumed a stern, unyielding expression when asking for an explanation of what had happened here, though he didn't expect a satisfactory reply. He didn't get one either. All he could find out was that unfortunately his nephew had been set upon by wandering bandits and killed. Next day his nephew's wife had taken the children and left without saying where she was going. The lurah shrugged, pursing his lips in finality.

"And where is my other nephew?" Budi was certain that by now the lurah knew of Ali's death too.

The lurah professed to know nothing of the dalang's other nephew except that the young man hadn't been seen in the village for some time.

Budi understood that he was being treated as an outsider, an extraordinary occurrence for a Gitosuwoko, especially for a Gitosuwoko who was also a dalang. Power, he believed, was a fixed substance; it resided in a particular man from whom it could fly elsewhere without warning, charmed into flight by someone who wanted it more than he did. These days all power seemed to have flown into the khaki uniforms of the Indonesian Army.

"Where is my nephew Bambang buried?"

The lurah took him beyond the village to a small cemetery. There were five freshly dug graves; on four of the mounds bright flowers were strewed. Without having to ask, Budi went up to the undecorated grave, knelt, and prayed. His prayer was not directed to Allah or to any god; his prayer was directed toward a light that for years had appeared upon the dark screen of his closed eyes when he meditated. His prayer was without words. He merely observed the light, which began pulsing and changing colors. The pulsing expanded to include the entire space within the screen of his closed eyes; there were spidery filaments to the light that hooked and twisted around, and their lazy, undirected motions produced in him sudden calm, as if the world had dropped away—mountain, plain, ocean—leaving him suspended, bodiless, in light.

Rising finally, Budi studied the other, decorated graves. "So my nephew managed to take four of them with him."

"Kyahi?"

"Those bandits," Budi said. "He killed four of them before they killed him. I see you buried them here too."

The lurah stared at the graves wordlessly.

"An act of generosity," Budi said, "to bury those bandits. And then to give them flowers as well."

"Ah."

Walking back to the village, Budi halted suddenly and turned to the lurah. "Tell me about the funeral rites." When the lurah said nothing, Budi waited, and when there was still no reply, he said, "My nephew is a Gitosuwoko. We have had rites in this village for centuries. Here is what you will do. You will remove the corpse from the ground and bathe my nephew after laying him across seven stems of banana tree. Arrange to have a modin come and powder his body and cover his sex with banana leaves and fill every cavity of him with cotton and put red paint on his lips. Wrap him in white cotton," Budi said, knowing full well that the lurah was thoroughly versed in what to do, "and tie the ends of it over his head and at his feet. I want

520

him placed on a bamboo litter in his house, head to the north. I want the modin to read from the Quran. Tomorrow I'll come back to lead the procession to the grave. Afterward I'll give a sedekah ngesur siti for the entire village. I want apem cooked and the tumpeng rice piled two feet high and every man in this village to come. Spare no expense in giving a great feast, do you understand? Every day for forty days I want you, Pak Lurah, to place an offering under the bed of my nephew. Let no one move into his house. It is a house of the dead until I say it is not. I'll have another sedekah feast then and another on the hundredth day."

Budi took out his money purse and handed over a fistful of rupiah to the village headman, commanding him as well to see that flowers were placed on the grave every morning. The lurah was given a bonus for overlooking the administration of these tasks.

"If you do as I say, you'll get another bonus. Otherwise I'll go to the subdistrict head and complain about you." It occurred to Budi that he was strong when giving people money to do something, but weak when asking them to give him money. He turned and walked back to the square. Approaching the oxcart, he wanted suddenly to grip the lurah's thin shoulders (the little man stayed at his side, hands raised in a perpetual sembah of respect) and demand to know why the village had murdered a man whose only sin had been to protect his own brother. But from the faces of villagers ringing the oxcart in expectation of a famous dalang doing something peculiar, something they could gleefully and maliciously describe to their grandchildren in years hence, Budi understood that they had closed ranks against him and that he must exhibit absolute control of himself.

Getting into the oxcart, he glanced around expressionlessly and said nothing except to the driver. As the cart rattled away, he experienced an emotion that he had been taught since childhood to fight against, to overcome or be defeated by—the tempting but dangerous emotion of anger. Anger burned in him like a coal in his dead nephew's foundry, when the bellows, blowing on it, brought to its surface a terrific heat. He had seen the bellows transform such a coal into a golden uncoiling snake. His anger felt like that now, something alive and writhing in the pit of his stomach. While his driver whipped the ox into a loping, swaying gait, Budi Gitosuwoko understood that he

521

could not live with such anger; it would burn him up if he didn't find a way of changing it into something else—just as his nephew used to change a lump of hot copper into a resonate gong.

Returning to Yogya, he went straight to the local branch of Radio Republik Indonesia. Broadcasting had returned to a normal schedule again, although most of the programs, aside from gamelan recitals, were of a religious nature, featuring interpretations of the Quran and government-sponsored exhortations for people to remain calm and do their duty. The local manager was overjoyed by Dalang Gitosuwoko's proposal, and a call to the main office in Jakarta brought an equally enthusiastic response. The manager said, beaming, "People want a relief from crisis. Nothing could be better than wayang."

Budi had been taught by his brother that the more he locked within himself the psychic power developed by meditation and rehearsal, the more capable he would be of using it in performance. To give yourself outside of wayang was to lose your mastery of the puppets. Because they knew if you were in complete control of them or not; they felt the power of your hands, and when you lost it, they felt that too.

So he had nurtured his power prudently, sharing the secrets of wayang only with his guru brother and other performers whom he trusted. Now, however, he felt it was false, even destructive, to slink off by himself and leave the woman he loved out of his most intimate creative moments. He resolved to share all of his preparations with her. So he began by telling her what he had in mind. He was going to perform again, but this would be unlike any performance he had ever given. Until now he had worked within the tradition to create a world of eternal illusion. Now he wanted to tell the people of Indonesia what they did not want to hear.

Instead of a private courtyard or a pavilion in the sultan's palace, he had chosen a very public site for the performance—beneath the walls of Prambanan, within a short walking distance of hastily dug graves. And to reach the largest audience possible, he had arranged for the performance to be broadcast on national radio.

From two hundred wayang kulit plays written over a millennium, Budi selected for this performance one of the most celebrated in the repertoire, *The Death of Karna,* a wayang purwa derived from the Indian epic poem *Mahabharata.* He realized that for a foreigner to understand what he was doing, he must begin at the beginning and explain each step to Maggie.

As they sat within the courtyard's shaded pavilion, he gave her a brief idea of the plot. *Karna* was one of many plays that described the Great War between the rival Pandava and Kaurava clans. It begins on the seventh day of battle. Of the Kauravan king's ninety-eight brothers, only four have survived. On the Pandava side, the sons of two great leaders, Bima and Arjuna, have been killed. The main conflict is between Arjuna and the Kauravan warrior Karna, who unknown to Arjuna is his half brother. The play asks should a man be faithful to his comrades while knowing their cause is wrong. The ironies emerging from such an ethical question give *Karna* its sublime pathos.

"Now the play will ask something different," he told her. "How should we live in the midst of catastrophe? Can we ignore it if it doesn't touch us directly, knowing if we don't ignore it we might go mad? The inhabitants of wayang would take the answer for granted: it would not be possible for them to turn away from disaster, because the world is interconnected, every bit of it, from water in the ocean to the gods above—all of a piece, like a wave moving through itself."

To begin, he reacquainted himself with the formal structure of *Karna.* Although he had a complete dramatic guide, a pakem padalangan, in which musical cues and narrative were written down precisely, he preferred to use what dalangs called "a bone guide," which described the standard action in general terms. This skeletal script, given to him by his brother, had been written by their father and provided the sort of freedom for improvisation that he would need.

Countless questions arose immediately. Would there be a long and complicated gara-gara, a clown scene in Part Two? What standard scenes could be dropped, what others inserted? Which suluks would he sing and for which of them would he need to write new lyrics? How long would each battle last? Of one aspect of performance he was sure, however: he would work in the Yogya style, which featured vigorous action, instead of the Solo style, which emphasized subtle emotion. His father, he told Maggie, had been adept at both styles.

"There will be nothing subtle in what I have to say," Budi promised.

After workmen had set up a screen on two huge bamboo logs inside the courtyard pavilion, Budi made sure that the upper log of this debog touched the lower edge of the screen's frame and that the lower log projected outward eight inches—in that way the puppet sticks could be jammed into its gleaming green pulp. Next to him, when he sat down, was his kotak, the large wooden box that held the puppets. He recalled for Maggie how his brother always began a lesson with the same observation: that the removal of puppets from the kotak was like a birth, a new beginning. The kotak was also the graveyard where puppets were laid to rest when their tale was told; everything must have an end, and all must go to God at last. Only after restating that philosophy would his brother begin the lesson.

In performance Budi always listened to the kendang drum player, who cued the orchestra for changes in rhythm and dynamics. But for rehearsal the dalang needed only Pak Seno, an old musician who had played gender during the time of his father. With a cigarette dangling from thin lips in a haggard face, Pak Seno sat behind Budi at the xylophone, his two padded hammers moving tirelessly over the bronze keys. Next to him sat the dalang's favorite student, Basuki, a boy whose bright dark eyes fixed steadfastly on his master, as if hypnotized by a cobra.

And then there was Maggie.

She was there behind him every moment of rehearsal, and when he entered the world of wayang, no longer did he go alone, but felt, burning at his shoulder, the woman's eyes traveling with him into the heart of Astina, Land of the Elephants, where great warriors and their brave women rejoiced, despaired, fought, and died forever, their wickedness and goodness merging finally through divine words, divine music, divine action into life beyond life, so that the gods themselves gasped in wonder.

She was there behind him, watching and listening, and he took her on such journeys. He had never taken anyone before, not even old Pak Seno. His flight of imagination had been solitary, but now Budi Gitosuwoko carried her along. He felt it powerfully and knew it was real.

After rehearsal, when they had eaten and made love and lay together, he would speak further of wayang. How it had begun centuries ago, when people sought help from the spirits of the dead by praying to shadows. Then for a long while it had become a plaything of the sultans and their courtiers, a rarefied art enjoyed in the palaces. But today he was fashioning a drama not to propitiate the dead or to please the mighty but to unsettle a nation.

He had been careful not to rehearse the gara-gara scenes in front of Pak Seno and his student Basuki; those scenes went far beyond the gentle criticism of rice prices and mild corruption, which dalangs sometimes featured in their clown scenes. He especially feared Basuki, who was a fine sensitive student, but whose devotion might not be sublimely immutable like that of Karna, the wayang embodiment of fidelity. The rehearsal of these insertions was held after his assistants' departure, when he sat alone with Maggie in the pendopo.

They lay now together with moonlight glowing along their entwined legs. Budi spoke softly. He told her what he thought he would never tell anyone. Each night and each morning during his preparation for a wayang lakon, he got out a family kris, went into the prayer room, lay the dagger before him on the prayer rug, and worshiped it. For twelve generations this one had been in the Gitosuwoko family. The kris was eleven-waved in the Nogososro style; both its blade and hilt had been fashioned by the great empu Ki Supo. Down the center of the blade the damascene design was that of a snake instead of the usual elephant's trunk. The scabbard had been made in the understated Gayaman style with embossed tendril ornamentation. The name of this family kris was Pasopati, in honor of the magical arrow created by Lord Shiva. Bright as the sun, equal to the fire of death, burning all it touched, it was first used by Shiva to destroy three demon cities. When Arjuna was given Pasopati as a reward for undergoing spiritual austerities, in the Great War he defeated Karna with it.

Budi's prayers to Kris Pasopati often brought him sudden visions of long ago—centuries ago: turbaned men in silk robes riding gilded elephants, golden spires gleaming on mosques in lands he had never seen, iron-backed rivers and vast forests and drifting images of sparkling rings, of damask pillows, of veiled faces, of sunlight gleaming on marble floors he had never walked. Only flashes. Unconnected. Out of a past he had never known.

"The past of your family," Maggie said. "It's that vivid to you."

"Is it possible I see things that happened centuries ago?"

"You ask me?" She laughed softly. "A woman of the West?"

"A romantic woman from the West."

"Yes. A romantic woman from the West in love."

He drew her closer until her breath grazed his throat. This must never end, he thought, never never end. And the thought stayed with him until it ended in their mutual sleep.

Fifty-four

She had been afraid for him the moment he declared his intention to perform a wayang lakon in order to tell people what they didn't want to hear. In that instant Maggie understood that he had become "political," as her college classmates used to call it. The bodies surfacing in the Prambanan mud like flotsam from the sea, the death of his nephews, his abrupt awakening into a world devoid of art as he had known it had all converged and were now pulling him to the brink of recklessness.

Yet she never tried to dissuade him from performing the play. For one thing, her knowledge of wayang was not subtle enough for her to judge accurately how far he was deviating from tradition. Nor could she assess the impact of such a departure on his audience. To understand radicalism you have to know something about conservatism, she realized.

But that wasn't the main reason for her silence. Maggie understood that she had fallen in love with a man who could give only part of himself. There were unexplored regions of Ki-Dalang Budi Gitosuwoko that no one would ever reach, perhaps not even Budi, certainly not herself. She had sacrificed her girlish American dream of knowing someone completely, of sharing everything in life with a man she loved. She had never expected such a thing with Vern either, though she had hoped with time that it might be possible. Such intimacy could never be possible with Budi.

She backed off therefore from the demons of anger and frustration and grief and moral outrage that were thrusting him into the national crisis, forcing him to act in a new way, urging him into discoveries and commitments only he himself could make or understand. She could neither help nor stop him. She might as well try to hold back a flood.

Meanwhile she learned about the world that had sustained him so many years. When she was not at army headquarters or listening to radio reports from Jakarta about rioting, or lecturing the rich on why they should give money to Borobudur, while troops marching by made her shout to a potential donor *"Tha inggih?"* ("So how about it?") over the noise of their boots, Maggie sat on the edge of the pendopo watching Budi rehearse.

Sometimes, during a lull, he taught her things that only dalangs knew. While sirens wailed in the distance (more frequently each day), he showed her how to hold puppets. He held the gapit, or central stick, higher on its stem for the larger puppets, some of which weighed a couple of pounds. He rarely held more than two at a time, although in *Karna* he would hold three when the clowns Gareng and Petruk carried off the corpse of slain Sanjaya.

He explained the positioning of characters in front of the screen, their gapits stuck in the pulpy debog. The major character was placed to the dalang's right with, say, only one or two retainers behind him, while the enemy were ranged on the left, often as many as half a dozen. For this reason Budi sat somewhat left of center to bring his hands closer to the larger number of puppets that had to be moved.

He showed her secrets of technique. His brother, who had learned the secrets from their father, had taught Budi how to enliven the first appearance of new characters. You had them do some business before ramming them into the debog. You had a character fix his headgear, cough, stroke his mustache, rearrange his dotot—a large rectangular cloth draped around the hips—shove his armlets up higher, brandish his weapon. Budi taught her how to do a sembah with puppets. You moved the arm sticks with only the thumb of the hand holding the gapit. Then he illustrated the various gaits of puppets as they moved across the screen. A refined character like Arjuna walked smoothly, without vertical motion, his arms hanging straight down. A rough character like Bima bounded forward in great leaps, his rear arm cocked behind his head, his forearm raised and ready for attack.

The angle at which Budi held a puppet was often vital in creating an emotion. Angles distorted the shadows cast against the screen, making for constant interplay between sharp and blurred, black and gray, aggressiveness and timidity. But he never showed Maggie how he did it during rehearsal, because he practiced in daytime, when no oil lamp dangled above the screen. Actually for him the creation of shadows required no rehearsal—he had practiced the technique too often. And he would rather improvise the angle during performance. It was one of the major freedoms of wayang, using shadows to bring forth a mood, an emotion, a feeling.

He explained the rudiments of battle to her. A perang was a linked series of motions: meeting, attacking, fleeing, pursuing, in a continuous choreography of fleeting shadows, while the gamelan played "Sampak Sanga" at a terrific tempo. He showed her how he cued the orchestra (he continued to rehearse only with Pak Seno's gender accompaniment), either by verbal commands within the spoken narrative or by smacking the wooden tapper against the kotak or by singing a musical phrase.

From her recent lessons she understood enough about the gender to appreciate Pak Seno's mastery of it. Yet every day when he came to accompany Budi, she exchanged only perfunctory greetings with the old man. He hadn't bothered to learn the official language—Bahasa Indonesia—and her Javanese wasn't good enough for extended conversations. He certainly didn't approve of her. Wearing his blangkon and dark courtly batiks and his kris wedged under a wide cloth belt at the small of his back, the old man either ignored her or glared scornfully just past her shoulder. Perhaps Budi's father would have done the same; perhaps even his brother, almost twenty years his senior, also would have been outraged by such a woman living in the compound of Gitosuwoko dalangs.

But Maggie could talk to Basuki, the young student who spoke excellent Indonesia and even some phrases of English, which matched her Javanese. He seemed to worship the dalang. Once he told her, "I pray to Allah every day for him." Ordinarily that would have pleased her, but she remembered the treacherous Mas Slamat, whose piety had led to a good man's death.

She felt herself living in a world of tilting perspectives. Part of the day she listened to the gender and watched puppets crossing the white screen. Another part of the day she suffered the humiliations of a cruel bureaucracy that would not even let her know if a young girl was still alive. Then she was writing letters, begging for money, or waiting in anterooms for emaciated solitaries from another era to grant her an audience for a few minutes so she could beg face-to-face. Then at night there was lovemaking that utterly detached her from everything that had happened during the day. And then of course there was the continuous past that stayed with Maggie throughout her waking moments, clinging to her memory as a smell clings to the skin—sometimes the smell of a pine forest, a musty attic, a back alley—so that they were all there with her, her parents and friends from Iowa and college and her husband Vernon Gardner, while she pedaled along the tense streets of Yogya.

Mail had been irregular, but one morning she received a rumpled letter from Jakarta.

Dear Maggie:
   I have your letter. I can't figure out what's going on. I am trying not to judge you, not to come to any conclusion. Maybe when we see each other, we can get it straightened out. I think it will have to wait until then, whenever that is.

                                                                    Vern

She was surprised by the mildness of her reaction to a letter that she had dreaded reading. Perhaps his restraint made it easier. But something less appealing was also present in the way she could read and set it aside. Time had already started its thuddingly dull and efficient reconstruction work. Vern's face was becoming shadowy. Her affection for him was merging with guilt into a homogeneous presence that drifted lumpy and gray across her mind until suddenly, at odd moments, it collapsed down on her to cover her thoughts like damp wool.

She too hoped that someday they would meet again, though not to get back together. All along she had wanted to see Vern and explain as well as she could what had happened. If Vern showed up here in Yogya, she would simply take a deep breath and face him. But it was unlikely he would get here for quite a while. General Sakirman would see to that. This was no time for domestic histrionics involving a foreign employee of OPSUS and his adulterous wife, who had been a Sakirman houseguest. If Gardner should get to Yogya and stir up trouble, it would look bad for the general at a time when he had to look good. Vern wouldn't get close to Yogya as long as the winner of the national struggle—army or PKI—was in doubt, as long as military necessity made saints of the generals. She had learned that much about the Javanese mind.

Even so, Maggie often rehearsed an imaginary scene in which Vern crossed the courtyard to the pendopo while Budi was singing a suluk and she was listening. She would intercept Vern before the two men met. "This is between us," she'd tell Vern and thereby avoid any violence. Then Maggie would draw him aside and they would walk to the center of the courtyard, where, under a blazing sun, they would stand facing each other. She pictured the white air, felt the heat, as they talked in the muffled way of a dream in which there is feeling to words without sound to them until Vern said distinctly, "Then it is really over," and walked out of her life.

They had eaten dinner, but instead of strolling in the garden or sitting on the veranda, Budi went to his desk for more work. Maggie sat on the veranda alone and at a low volume played "That Da Da Strain" by the New Orleans Rhythm Kings, the jaunty pulse of which she loved even though record wear had reduced some of the sound to scratchings on a blackboard.

Someone was crossing the moonlit courtyard, so Maggie leaned over and picked up the phono arm, feeling a prick of fear.

But it was Basuki, a frail boy of sixteen who looked more like eleven or twelve.

"Did the master want you to come back tonight?" Maggie asked.

"No, Bu, excuse me, Bu, but I just thought he might be working some more and I wanted to watch."

This was not how Budi worked. Either he asked you to attend a rehearsal or you did not come. It was known. Surely his pupil Basuki knew it better than anyone.

"I'll tell him you came," Maggie said coolly. "But I think he wants privacy."

The boy turned, ready to rush off.

"Basuki," she said, causing him to halt. "Very well," she added with a sigh, "I won't tell him you came."

"Thank you, Bu."

"But I'm curious. Why did you do such a thing? Come here to watch without his permission?"

He shrugged, and for an instant Maggie was reminded of her own teenage days when on impulse she did precisely what she knew was wrong.

"I won't tell him you came," she repeated with a smile.

His dark face was slashed by moonlight, so that his nose looked large, almost like that of a wayang ogre. "I came because I thought he would be rehearsing the clown scenes. He never rehearses them during the day."

That was true, of course—they contained much of the political material he was inserting secretly.

"He is very funny," Basuki said. "I think he is funnier than any dalang now alive."

"Perhaps you're prejudiced."

"No, no. Everyone says how funny he is. That's why I want to be here when he does the clown scenes."

"I think, Basuki, you must ask his permission."

When the boy had scooted off, surely relieved that the master had not discovered his recklessness, Maggie got up and went into the main part of the house. Budi had his desk here.

She saw him bent over it, head resting on his arms. Budi, exhausted, had fallen asleep. It occurred to her that he was under terrific pressure, perhaps even more than she realized. Not only was he harassed by the normal preparation for a performance, but tormented as well by the new demand he had placed on himself to tell people what they didn't want to hear.

Approaching, she saw his left profile: slack lips, closed eyes, the soft look of cheeks that ordinarily seemed tightly stretched over the prominent cheekbones. He was like a child, and she remembered something long forgotten that her mother, in a nostalgic mood, had once told her about her father. "That man, he was so nice when we first got married, let me tell you, and I loved to watch him sleep, he was like a little boy, so innocent and good and needing caring for, and— Well, of course, that was a long time ago."

Mother was right: innocent, good, vulnerable.

Someday she would tell Budi what she had known ever since their first night together: he was the person behind the door back in Iowa who had whispered to her, telling her to go, to find whatever it was she was looking for. What she had been looking for all along without knowing it, Maggie knew now, was the person who had been whispering behind the door, beckoning her onward and onward and onward until she found what she was looking for, right here in this place and at this moment of time, a man sleeping like a boy bent over his schoolbooks, this man, her love.

Fifty-five

S hortly after Mister Vernon's return from Bali, he told her something astonishing, something longed for but so remote that she had never believed it would come true: his wife had left him. She had given him up for another man. Yanti had sat on the couch of his hotel room, her knees touching tightly, and listened to his stumbling revelation. He didn't look at her once while saying that his wife had written him. In the letter she had been very direct. Another man had come into her life suddenly and she could not give him up. She would stay in Yogya. The man was an Indonesian. That, too, amazed Yanti, who could not imagine the tall American giving her Western heart to a Javanese who was surely a dark little man.

So knees together Yanti had waited, had hoped that after this admission Mister Vernon would do something—move toward her in some way (which way she had not yet envisioned clearly). But something had held him back then and in following weeks. His new freedom had not brought him closer to her but rather the opposite, so that he had discouraged her visits until she went to see him only a couple of times a week; and then usually his bodyguard was sitting glumly in the other room, the door open so she could see his square impassive face. Mister Vernon was holding back for a reason other than his interest in her (Yanti was sure of his interest in her! Sure of it!), and she suspected the reason was his wayward wife. Perhaps he was waiting to see if she would change her mind.

This was almost as surprising as the initial news of the wife's declared adultery. A Chinese man would turn instantly away from such a wife and take solace from his concubines (her own father had two, had always had at least two, even when her mother had lived).

And so Yanti waited and hoped, while the rest of her life was consumed by the crisis, by the daily demonstrations, by the burgeoning intensity of them.

In the streets there were many rumors about President Sukarno. It was said, for example, that Sukarno had raped a fourteen-year-old girl when abroad on a trip. Where this had happened was not clear; rumors varied from Tokyo to Colombo to Lahore. When she had repeated the rumor to Mister Vernon, he had frowned and cautioned her against easy assessments of such a man as Sukarno, who, after all, was a chief architect of Indonesian independence. Mister Vernon even accused her of lacking a sense of history, of her entire generation lacking it, because most of them hadn't been born during Sukarno's finest hour.

To his sour appraisal of her political activities Yanti turned a deaf ear. After all, he was so much older than her classmates at the university. Mister Vernon could have no idea of their dedication to justice and a new world. And, of course, he was a foreigner.

Yanti had recently helped prepare a student statement for the press (it would appear in an army-sponsored newspaper) asking President Sukarno to explain how the GESTAPU incident could have taken place. In an answering speech, furious and obviously embattled, Sukarno had claimed that it had come as a complete surprise to him; that the whole affair must have resulted from "inappropriate judgment" on the part of PKI leadership; that Western subversives, led by the American CIA, surely had encouraged the coup attempt; and that those who had participated in the strange little adventure were (reverting to the slang used in an appeal to the Marhaens of the street) plain nuts. Why, Sukarno had asked rhetorically, must he alone be questioned? What about Nasution? He had been minister of defense at the time.

This provocative speech (students were outraged at his attack on Nasution, who had lost a little daughter in the coup) had provided the occasion for another demonstration. In the attempt to shore up his weakened position, Sukarno had reshuffled his cabinet, firing not only Nasution but other anti-Reds and in the process keeping members who, if not pro-Red or sympathetic to the Communists, were loyalists who rubber-stamped his every wish. This infuriated both the army and the students, bringing them together in close cooperation and leading to a special demonstration today against the installation of Sukarno's new cabinet.

Yanti walked with comrades toward the rallying area. Everywhere they saw students funneling toward it, waving posters and banners and the national flag, its plain red stripe above a white stripe the reverse of Poland's, the same as Monaco's (a fact solemnly noted and debated by students who, among other changes, wished to redesign the flag). Boys on motor scooters were weaving through gathering traffic, and a few blocks from the marshaling area, other students had shoved parked cars across the main thoroughfare, letting air out of tires and bringing downtown Jakarta to a standstill. Yanti viewed the traffic jam with satisfaction. The student Standing Committee on Demonstrations, of which Yanti was a member, had lit upon this method of preventing cabinet ministers from getting to the palace for the ceremony.

In a recent scuffle with Cakrabirawa guards, students had been beaten with rifle butts. The bloody shirt of one of those injured students was now displayed on a pole, as if a flag itself.

"Chinese go home!" a man yelled from the sidewalk at Yanti, who walked beside a boy and two girls, all from the School of Architecture.

"She's as much Indonesian as you are!" the boy yelled back, and the two girls, along with Yanti, glared wrathfully at him.

Yanti was accustomed to this sort of abuse, especially these days when it was fashionable on the streets of Jakarta to put down Red China by taunting anyone who looked Chinese. Even so, each time it happened Yanti felt betrayed by her own country. She fought back

536

self-pity. She tried not to think of her heritage. Long ago her great-uncle had brought to Java a Chinese girl from Bali to have children by her. She had been a slave in Bali; she was a slave in Jakarta; she was uneducated, nothing more than breeding soil for a man who wished to maintain racial purity in his family. At least her father had broken with that tradition and married a native woman—one who could read and write. Yanti thanked her father for bringing her into the mainstream of a country she was now fighting for.

As they got closer to the marshaling area, Yanti's mind wandered from the impending demonstration, going into another, secret world, where images loomed out of nowhere and reminded her of the inchoate yearnings she had felt as a young girl but had described to no one save her best friend.

But the images Yanti entertained now were too secret and dangerous for any sharing. She would have withheld them even from her best friend. Because these images were of physical love. Physical love. Physical. Love. With Mister Vernon.

They are in his hotel room talking and then somehow—somehow because he has become strangely quiet and so has she—her hands have unaccountably started to remove her blouse, her skirt. She sees his eyes fixed on the motion of her hands as they undo buttons, slip things off, until . . . And here the images blur, fall away, and next she is lying in bed beside him, his face hovering tenderly above hers, and though she can't see beyond his face, because she's concentrating on the look of it, she knows they are both naked, yet somehow bodiless. There is no sensation coming from their touch. It's as if they are floating, cloudlike, against each other through an indeterminate atmosphere. But then, but then (Yanti's face grew hot, her legs weak as she walked alongside her companions toward the marshaling area), without actually seeing him do it, she feels him enter her. Sometimes when this imagined sensation occurs, he feels small, like a finger wriggling inside her body, but more often he feels immense, a frightening thing expanding like a balloon until she feels ready to explode from being so filled by him, and in the imagining she lets out a silent scream and he holds her holds her holds her.

Now, as always, Yanti felt the juices seeping along her thighs. She understood this was the delicious torment of unsatisfied desire, and from the unmistakable message of her loins, Yanti Salim knew without doubt that if ever Mister Vernon touched her, she would give herself to him then and there, unhesitatingly, completely.

Now she was in the thick of it. Thousands were milling around Merdeka Square in front of the palace. There had already been fiery speeches, among them one by Brigadier General Sarwo Edhie, the commander of the RPKAD paracommandos who had retaken Halim Air Base from the rebels on 2 October, and who later had swept through Central Java with his troops, destroying Red strongholds. Today he demanded that Sukarno's new cabinet be "retooled" before it was even sworn in. Another speaker yelled until he was hoarse about the need to dissolve the Communist party without delay and brand every member of it a traitor to the state and execute every one of them immediately. A student got up and complained of bus fares that had risen fivefold in recent months. When that student got down from the makeshift speakers' platform, another took his place and wondered rhetorically why the president had included in his new cabinet a boss of the underworld, Iman Sjafe'l, who as chief of Special Security Affairs would have the power to use gangs of ruffians against anyone lawfully opposing Sukarno—a speech so raw and bold that even the student radicals listening to it stared at the bespectacled kid in stunned bewilderment.

Student after student climbed onto the bamboo platform and shouted about politics, economics, the glory of Indonesia, and the threat from abroad. While speeches multiplied, the traffic did too, until police motorcycles with their outriders in polished white helmets were unable to navigate among the motionless cars. They failed to clear the way for limousines carrying new ministers to the installation ceremony. Dignitaries in cutaways and top hats, afraid to be late, got out of their cars before reaching the palace grounds and flailed with the help of policemen through crowds of screaming protesters.

Suddenly a deafening new noise competed with the speakers in the square. Helicopters were coming over the palace roof to swoop down on the crowd; the commotion was aimed at dispersing the demonstrators, but most of them, including Yanti, raised their fists defiantly. Younger students, many no more than twelve or thirteen years old,

538

marched forward in a giggling group and thrust their placards upward as if trying to spear the copters.

Someone on the platform was reading a message sent by General Suharto—"I regard these actions as manifestations of social control"—but the students were too excited to comprehend his support of their demonstration. They were milling, chanting, and pressing toward the gate where rows of Cakrabirawa guards awaited them, helmets glittering, Sten guns at the ready position diagonally across their chests. One of their jeeps, nosing through the dense throng, could go no farther, and its occupants, leaning out, demanded to be let through. A stone bounced off the hood. Another stone smashed the windshield. A third bloodied a guard's head; he bent forward, the blood running down his face.

The sight of blood seemed to energize the crowd, which surged forward with renewed energy toward the waiting guards. An officer shouted through a bullhorn, warning the students to back away, but not many heard him through the overhead din that the copters were making and their own rhythmic yelling of "Retool the cabinet! Hang Subandrio! Retool the cabinet! Hang Subandrio!"

Street vendors selling souvenir pictures of Nasution and his grieving wife were being shoved around, and they couldn't get through the pushing students who kept coming forward, waving their banners and placards, screaming slogans into the noonday brightness. And Yanti came with them, front and center, not to the side and rear as Vern had made her promise, a promise she had laughingly never kept.

She felt her lungs fill with the joy of shouting "Hang Subandrio! Retool the cabinet!" when the first popping sounds began. Ahead, not more than twenty yards ahead, the palace guards were firing their guns into the air. "Hang Subandrio! Retool the cabinet!" On either side of Yanti the arms of her companions touched hers; students were moving together; they were moving in a tide as one person, and the exhilaration Yanti felt at that moment was unlike anything she had ever known. "Hang Subandrio! Retool the cabinet!" Her mouth was so filled with sound and energy that her eyes scarcely beheld what was presented to them: the sudden lowering of the gun barrels to chest level, the sudden widening of the guards' eyes as a new command was given, the steady pullback of finger against trigger.

But she felt the impact; it sent her backward, her legs clear off the ground, her body left sprawling. Her ears were filled with a new sound, a horrified screaming from all sides, and then turning, she noticed a boy lying quite near. He had no face. But she was alive, wasn't she, only knocked down, except that turning her eyes toward herself, what she saw was not possible: her stomach had burst open like a gate kicked through. Blood rushed out unbelievably, so much of it, so much through a hole ragged like crushed paper, and she heard herself yelling at the sight of her own life running out of her body. Then she was jerking, her legs were, but she couldn't stop the spasmodic motion of her dying, and yet there was no pain, there was none, there was no pain, there was none, there was no pain, there was none, there was none.

Fifty-six

He heard on the radio that today at the palace there had been an unruly demonstration with the result that palace guards opened fire and killed two students, wounding numerous others. The dead were Arief Rahman Hakim, a medical student at the university, and Yanti Salim, a high-school student.

Yanti Salim.

But it couldn't be his Yanti. The dead girl was a high-school student. Or had the news report been mistaken? It took Vern half a day to sort out the true facts within the swirling chaos of Jakarta. An OPSUS officer owed Vern a favor (Vern had written a few letters for him in English to stateside cousins). Through another cousin who worked at an army-sponsored newspaper the OPSUS officer had obtained the only information available. Yanti Salim, a student whose affiliation was unknown, had been shot dead in front of the palace gate, and her father, an Indo-Chinese businessman, had signed for the body and removed it from the city morgue.

Indo-Chinese businessman. Vern tried to locate Sutopo Salim, but he was not at his office and no one there would give out the home address. Back at OPSUS Vern had to bribe a clerk with a dozen packs of kretek cigarettes before getting it.

And when he went out to the western suburb where Sutopo Salim lived, Vern (and Hashim) confronted a familiar figure pacing in front of the high whitewashed wall and padlocked iron gate: the thickset scowling bodyguard whom they had first met at a Chinese temple. Wearing the kind of soft battered fedora that Vern used to see among the Hong Kong Chinese, the Salim bodyguard would not initially even admit that this was Salim property. He and Hashim stared balefully at each other. Finally he said, "No one at home." When Vern handed him a note asking Tuan Salim to contact him immediately at the Hotel Indonesia, reluctantly the guard put it in his pocket, shifting his gaze between Vern and Hashim, as if he'd never seen them before.

Not his Yanti. But it was. That night Vern sat in the bar of the hotel, listening to a crackling radio provide details of the day's tragedy. While the broadcaster rattled on, often contradicting himself when a new report came along, Vern drank soda with a silent Larry Foard at his side. Not his Yanti, but it was. The smiling, happy, yet aggressive girl who brought her architectural drawings for him to see, who sat on his couch and denounced the government's alliance with a Communist country filled with a billion people who shared her genes—sat there smiling and holding her knees together and letting him savor how easy it would be for them to part slowly and let her slim brown legs welcome him in.

Vernon Gardner was not one to turn down a piece of ass (the way he would ordinarily express it), but he never thought of this vivacious, inexperienced girl as that. In retrospect he didn't know what to think of their relationship. Perhaps they should have become lovers; he would have had that to remember. Or perhaps he might have held her tenderly and kissed her lips just once and told her how much he cared but how impossible the situation really was. That would not have happened, of course. They would have gone past such a sweet idealistic interlude almost immediately. In retrospect, when he allowed himself to think beyond the horror of her death, Vern knew that he had resisted his desire to touch Yanti not because of any romantic notion or some arcane sense of honor, but simply because he wanted to avoid the complications it would have caused. Had he seduced her,

Vern felt, the inexperienced girl would have followed him around like a puppy, trusting, full of hope. And the fact remained, he couldn't deny it—he still loved Maggie.

Not his Yanti, but it was. And so in spite of his vow never to drink alcohol again, he changed from soda to gin and got drunk enough for Larry to help him upstairs to bed. Next morning, hung over, he heard the latest news reports. The medical student, Arief Rahman Hakim, was receiving a hero's burial. His body was transported through the streets in an army personnel carrier draped with flowers. Bouquets had been sent (this was carefully noted) by Generals Suharto and Nasution, the latter still in mourning for his young daughter; huge wreaths had come from specific army units such as KOSTRAD, RPKAD, and the Siliwangi Division. The widows of murdered Generals Pandjaitan and Yani were attending the funeral. (Hearing the name Yani, Vern recalled again the satyric Yani stumbling through the bushes after a giggling night butterfly.) Shops were closed along the line of procession and flags everywhere were flown at half-staff, even from government buildings. The student movement had its martyr at last—one to match the army's six generals.

But there was no further mention of the other fatality: the "high-school" girl, Yanti Salim. That there wasn't any gave Vern momentary hope; at a time of such turbulence and confusion a mistake was easy to make. It hadn't been Yanti, his Yanti. But while he was shaving, a message came for him from her father: "Come to my office tomorrow. I assume you wish to see me about third daughter's death. Salim."

Third daughter: the Chinese way of identifying children. Vern had never heard the man call Yanti "third daughter." It was as if tragedy had stripped from Sutopo Salim the veneer of an Indonesian businessman and revealed a Chinese father.

In the hotel lobby Vern got an army-sponsored newspaper, the only one available this morning. On the front page was a large photograph of Arief Rahman Hakim, a rather handsome young Javanese. Almost every column in the paper dealt with the story of his murder by palace guards (enemies of the regular army because of their loyalty to Sukarno). Yanti's death was mentioned in one sentence on page three.

At last Vern understood the Javanese reasoning behind the report of her death. Neither the student organizations nor the army backing them wished to have someone with Chinese blood as their martyr— let alone a girl, let alone a Chinese girl who had been studying architecture at the best Indonesian university. They had the perfect martyr in Arief Rahman Hakim, a boy of pure blood with a good Muslim background who had been training to help the nation's sick.

Vern absorbed the grim irony of Yanti's tragic end. She had harbored romantic notions about her role in the country's history, but not even in death could she realize them.

On his way by becak (few cars would dare the frenzied streets) into a Chinese quarter of the city, Vern read the newspaper. Sukarno had banned all student organizations and closed the university. When Vern mentioned these facts to the becak driver, the man laughed gaily. He had been out by the university today and had seen the army tents pitched on lawns there. Armored cars were lined up in rows at the main gate, their guns pointing toward the buildings inside which students were still assembling, whatever Bung Karno said, and yelling their slogans and making their speeches.

A voluble and eager man, the becak driver began to mimic one of the student speakers. " 'Our comrade, Arief Rahman Hakim, didn't ride in fancy cars. He was never protected from the people. Only people who live in palaces need protection from the people.' That's what the boy said while those guns were pointing from the main gate at him."

"Did the soldiers give him trouble?"

"They just stood around smoking, and when their officers weren't looking they winked at the girls and nodded in agreement to what the students were saying. What do they care so long as they get rice and a place to sleep? I have a brother in the army and I know."

The martyr's name was heard everywhere, not only on the beleaguered campus. This morning on the radio Vern had heard Arief Rahman Hakim conjured righteously in a speech delivered by a university student—a performance condoned by the army since the Jakarta Command under Suharto's control had sponsored the program: "Arief Rahman Hakim did not die in vain. Every drop of his blood will be avenged. We demand that the new Red cabinet be dissolved and those self-satisfied new ministers, plotting the downfall of our beloved country, be sent to jail where they belong!"

On the next news broadcast Vern heard that a furious Sukarno had just outlawed the public assembly of more than five people. There was also a new curfew, this one beginning as early as ten in the evening and lasting until 6:30 A.M.—patently unmanageable, since half the business of this heat-dominated city would be under way long before curfew ended in the morning.

Subandrio's name surfaced ceaselessly throughout the broadcast. Criticism of his foreign policy, especially that which dealt with Red China, was so minutely detailed that an outsider listening to Indonesian news for the first time might have thought nothing else mattered save the country's relationship with the Chinese.

Subandrio was becoming a scapegoat for the president. In every political downfall that Vern knew about there was always one smart, energetic character who knowingly allowed himself to be sacrificed to a dying cause. Subandrio was taking the blame for domestic policy as well as foreign affairs. He was responsible for rising prices; for governmental corruption; for the failure to control the disruptive PKI; for letting chaos get a grip on the whole country. Subandrio was called a Communist, a diabolical leftist, a traitor, an evil counselor, a vicious plotter, a series of wayang terms associated with ogres and demons and wicked court ministers. The list of pejorative names grew longer as the radio broadcasts continued to attack Sukarno by attacking his right-hand man, until Vern, thoroughly bored and incapable of separating fact from fiction within such a deluge of charges, could listen no longer.

Now in the becak he listened to the driver savaging the government, the Communists, the army—everyone in the land except becak drivers. To look at something other than posters glued over posters on every passing wall, he continued to stare at the newspaper. Before reaching the Office of PT Seragam Technical Supply, he read a short article about the missing chairman of the Communist party, D. N. Aidit. Aidit had been seen throughout Central and East Java, planning subversive activities. Could he be in both areas at the same time? For that matter, Vern wondered, was the article merely a smoke screen? Was Aidit still alive? Vern had heard rumors of captured Red leaders being summarily executed. Thinking of the Communist leader turned Vern to sad recollections of Yanti.

Once he'd asked her if she had ever seen Chairman Aidit.

"From a distance once," she said. "He had fat eyes like a frog."

When Vern laughed, she added hastily, "I shouldn't say that."

"Well, isn't it true?"

"It's true, but— Do women in America say things only because they're true?"

"Sometimes. Men, women—and children do."

She nodded solemnly. "I should know that. Americans are free."

"In some ways." His qualification brought a look of disappointment to the girl's face. So he added with good cheer, "But that's about the best the world has to offer."

And she had smiled again.

The offices of PT Seragam Technical Supply (a firm with financial tentacles throughout the East and a major source of funds for the entire military establishment) were shabby little boxes above a Chinese hardware store. But having spent time in Hong Kong and Singapore, Vern was accustomed to a neurotic show of modesty among Chinese businessmen. If you had money, you mustn't flaunt it but hide who you were under one of those ubiquitous gray fedoras and do business out of an airless room with peeling walls. Back home, once past a plain exterior, you could have a room deep within the house where you could enjoy in utmost privacy something priceless, like a Ming porcelain or a Sung painting.

Last night in the bar Vern had heard about new troubles for Indo-Chinese. In Semarang they had been ordered to display signs outside their houses: citizen Chinese painted their names in white on black boards; noncitizen, in white on red boards. There were already thousands of Sumatran Chinese waiting in a deportation camp outside of Medan. They were not allowed to sell or transfer property left behind.

The director of PT Seragam Technical Supply had his office off to the side. It contained a plain desk, three chairs, and a small table on which a tea set could be placed. When Vern entered, he noticed some writing under a glass-covered frame on one wall—it looked like Arabic calligraphy to him—and behind the desk a Muslim prayer rug was hanging.

546

Vern had time to look around because the director was not there at the moment. On the desk Vern saw a framed family photograph that must have been taken years ago. There was Sutopo in a Western suit gazing stiffly out of the picture and next to him an equally formal woman in a plain black dress, her high collar buttoned under her chin, her eyes intelligent and cold. Ranged on either side of the seated couple were three boys and three girls. The smallest girl, her hair cut straight across her forehead, must be Yanti, though little in the compressed lips and the frightened expression of this severely posed youngster reminded him of the vivacious woman she would become. Vern was studying the photo when Sutopo entered, shook his hand briskly, and sat behind the desk.

They regarded each other the way old friends might do who have seen a lot of water go over the dam since last they met.

"Thank you for coming," Sutopo finally said.

"I am very sorry—"

"Yes. The Malays say, '*Gajah sama gajah berjuang, pelanduk mati di-tengah-tengah*. When elephants fight, the mouse deer between them is killed.' "

This use of a proverb to describe the murder of a child would have been in another sort of man unfeeling and detached, but Vern understood Sutopo Salim. Restraint was so habitual in the cukong that he could express himself no other way. "I liked your daughter," Vern said. "I respected her. She was a fine young woman." He added, knowing he must, "We met, you know. Perhaps she told you."

"No, she did not. But I knew."

That, of course, did not surprise Vern, who had sometimes wondered if the entire hotel staff was in Sutopo Salim's employ, watching like duennas each time the girl came to the hotel.

"She came to discuss architecture and America."

The cukong now smiled faintly. "Third daughter loved the idea of America."

"Yes, actually that was it—the idea of America, all noble and shining." Vern felt he must also say more about their relationship. "I saw her because she seemed genuinely interested in my country and in architecture. I felt somewhat like a teacher."

"Yes," the financier said, "I know."

Vern was sure now of Sutopo Salim's investigatory power. Perhaps even Hashim, yawning in the other room, might have been making reports. Surely the maids must have studied the bedroom sheets for any telltale signs. The waiter who brought morning tea for them must have kept a close eye on her demeanor, on her skirt, on the seating arrangement. Had Vern laid one hand on the girl, it was clear to him now, Sutopo would have had him thrown out of the country within twenty-four hours.

"About the funeral—" Vern began.

"No funeral. Thank you for your consideration, but there will be no funeral except within the family."

"I understand. Of course."

"You are thinking of Arief Rahman Hakim's national funeral."

Vern shrugged.

"Well, it is sensible policy. They have an appropriate martyr. I am glad they didn't choose third daughter for a similar fate." An aide came into the office and Sutopo excused himself a few moments to bend over a document, read, and sign it. "Perhaps you must think me unfeeling, but work goes on, even today. I have the responsibility of many lives in my hands."

"I understand that."

Sutopo studied Vern. "Yes, I think you do. I think you will stay here and do your work. You are not a man to run."

"No, I am not."

"I must apologize for your misfortune."

At first Vern thought the old rascal even knew about Maggie leaving him, but then Sutopo mentioned the difficulty of traveling today in Java. "I could have arranged for you to fly to Yogya, but under the circumstances—my position at present—I could not take the chance."

"Thank you. I understand." Vern did not mention Sukarno's offer, which had come to nothing.

"But the work on Project Palm Tree goes well?"

"Yes, very well. The site at Sanur is extraordinary. We're in the process of shipping materials to Bali."

"And so life goes on."

When Vern got up to leave, the little Chinese businessman, having somehow divined Vern's interest in the art on the walls (perhaps one of Sutopo's minions had observed him looking at the calligraphy and the rug while waiting for the interview to begin), explained that the

548

calligraphy spelled out *"Bism Allah al-Rahman al-Rahim"* ("In the name of God, the merciful, the compassionate") and was done in the style of Thuluth, a classical script popular among the Arabians; the Turkish-made prayer rug with its representation of a mihrab was a rather good example of Ghiordes knotting: fifty-nine to sixty-two knots per square centimeter.

A nice touch. This Chinese Indonesian for business purposes had become an expert in the Islamic arts. Vern could imagine him sitting in the restaurants of Singapore and Hong Kong, drinking tea with Middle Eastern oilmen and mesmerizing them with his knowledge of their culture. So life goes on.

In the hotel bar that night Vern was drinking alone when Larry Foard came in, sat down, and sighed dramatically. He rubbed his grizzled jaw with thick workingman's fingers. "A blooming rough day on the docks," he said. "We loaded the two forward holds with our pneumatic equipment and those foundation rods we can't get in Bali. Vern?"

"Good."

"Ship ought to get under way, if there's no hitch, in a week. Actually, it's going smoothly. You wouldn't know by these balmy people that their government is collapsing. Dock crane operators were singing as usual, that Muslim gibberish they love. And the stevedores, everyone—what funny chaps, when you think about it. Vern?"

"Yes, good."

Larry studied him. "I hear they're going to name streets all over the country in honor of Yani. They've already started here in Jakarta. Sukarno ordered it. Jenderal A. Yani Jalan. That's one army bloke who won't be forgotten. Vern?"

"Yes."

"Even so, I think Sukarno is going down. They're going to get him through Subandrio. Typical. If you want to finish someone off in this country, you shoot his brother. Vern, are you all right?"

"Sure."

"You're hitting the sauce a bit hard, aren't you, old chap? I mean after that long layoff. I met a correspondent from Radio Prague at the dock today. He told me how some kids had chased him through a kampong. Wanted to kill him, but he got away. The interesting thing is he never sorted out if they knew who he was—a reporter for the West or for the Soviet bloc. We had a laugh about that. Vern? What are you thinking?"

Vern turned to look at him. "I think William Blake was a tough old buzzard: 'Drive your plows and your carts over the bones of the dead.' It's good advice but hard to follow."

Larry touched his arm. "No, mate, it isn't hard to follow. Except for you it is at the moment. Come on, a gin on me."

Fifty-seven

Under the wall of Prambanan the red-bordered white screen had been set up and a lamp hung by wire above it. People were sitting on the ground on both sides of the screen, while the twenty-man gamelan orchestra occupied the side against the wall, the dalang's side. That's where Maggie sat too, just as she had sat behind him in the pendopo during countless hours of rehearsal. She had come to Prambanan with him at dusk when he inspected the preparation for the lakon: that the screen had been fastened tightly to the debog; that the two bamboo logs forming the debog were properly installed; that the garuda-shaped bronze lantern had been hung exactly sixteen inches away from the screen and six above his head when he was seated; that the puppets in use for the evening had been placed in easy reach and in sequence of use; that the remaining puppets had been lined up properly on either side of the screen, stuck in the debog to seem like two approaching processions, or else stowed away in the wooden chest; that the kayon, or Tree of Life, had been fixed squarely in front of the screen, to remain there until its removal marked the beginning of the play. When he had adjusted the wick of the coconut-oil-burning lantern, Dalang Budi was ready.

Usually the majority of people sat behind the dalang to watch a puppet show; fewer sat on the other side of the screen to see the shadow play that was projected there. Tonight, however, given the configuration of space at the temple, fewer people would have the chance to watch Dalang Budi Gitosuwoko at work. At least a thousand would see the shadow-play side of the screen. Perhaps only a couple of hundred would be able to crowd together and study the way this great dalang handled Arjuna, Karna, the Princess Srikandi.

A pity, Maggie thought, that more people wouldn't see him work. He looked handsome tonight in his traditional batik sarong, blouse, and headdress. The kris he wore was not Kris Pasopati, but his personal one (Kris Pasopati never left the compound). She had watched from a discreet distance earlier this evening as he had bowed and prayed to the old heirloom, and then had intoned the traditional prayer of dalangs: "Om, Om, Om, O God of Light and Soul, may the flame in tonight's lamp burn brightly and give me insight into the lives of my characters, so that the people who watch will suffer and laugh and learn from what is done until dawn."

From the moment when Budi removed the kayon from the debog, twirled it three times, and placed it to the right of the screen, *The Death of Karna* had gripped the audience. Even Maggie, who had heard the narrative countless times, was transfixed by his description of the Kauravan Kingdom of Astina, its natural beauties and utopian way of life before tumultuous war brought sorrow to its people. Budi assumed for the rendition of such loveliness and happiness a voice deep, buttery, resonant—a voice that Maggie had heard at midnight in the soft glowing time after love.

So he began on this note of sweet nostalgia. But he had cautioned her. The audience assembled at the temple and listening across the land would be unprepared for what was going to happen. She must expect the first reaction when he described the Kauravan king, Duryudana: "This great king we all know has merit as a warrior and orator and leader of his people. We call him affectionately 'bung.' Yet this 'brother' can't curb his own desires much less those of others who are supposed to help him lead. He listens to bad counsel. Out of willfulness he puts his trust in the wrong men. Such a brother is dangerous, no matter how sweetly he talks. His slogans bring confusion, his promises delay."

What astonished Maggie was the immediate response from both sides of the screen—wild shouting that would not abate sufficiently for him to continue. "Bung Karno, Bung Karno!" "Who? Shut up!" "What's going on?" "Keep quiet!" "Shut up!" "Who?" "Bung Karno!" "Disgrace!" Maggie felt a thrill of fear. The reaction surpassed anything she had imagined. In the wild yelling she heard the stinging note of total fury. Were they angry at Budi or at Sukarno or at one another? For minutes afterward, the audience kept up the sound of an anger deep and unremitting to the extent that Budi could scarcely be heard as he moved into the Audience Scene, singing "Patet Nam Ageng," a song describing the king's sorrow at the loss of ninety-four of his ninety-eight brothers.

Only when complications of plot took over their full attention did the spectators regain their Javanese calm.

Nothing disturbed the course of events that ended Part One. Karna, having killed Gatutkaca, the son of Pandava leader Bima, was made supreme commander of the Kauravan forces. Troops prepared for battle, and Karna went home to say good-bye to his wife. In the Pandava camp there was profound grief—the mother of Gatutkaca had thrown herself on her son's funeral pyre. Bima, bereft of wife and son, and Arjuna, who had also lost a son in the war, swore revenge. Meanwhile, Karna faced a dilemma: he had promised his mother not to shed the blood of his half brother Arjuna. In order to kill the Pandava hero, Karna gave the task to another Kauravan nobleman. Tents of the opposing forces were pitched at the battlefield, and so ended Patet Nem.

When, to begin the second part, Budi began singing "Patet Sanga Wantauh"—"The scent of flowers mixes with the prayers of gurus that sound like the murmuring of bees"—Maggie felt her hands balling into sweaty fists.

He began the narration with continuous rappings. "One two three four five six seven eight nine ten! One the land. Two the sea encircling the land. Three the mountain holding the land in place. Four the rice planted in the land. Five the plain with its flocks and herds. Six the

553

forest covering what the rice and herds do not. Seven the holy men who pray for us all. Eight the sky hovering over the earth. Nine the Gods. Ten the King who shines above all men.

"But none of these things can escape the cataclysmic upheaval that now shakes the world."

He then spoke of oceans boiling, volcanoes erupting, animals dying, pestilence sweeping the land, panic and darkness and the roar of dragons. This description usually opened the second act of *Karna*. But to it Budi had appended references of his own. He added to the mythic plagues the modern ones of imprisonment and execution without trial, guilt by association, forces led blindly into confrontations that had nothing to do with honor, with rightful inheritance, with courage, and everything to do with opportunism, with jealousy, with bids for raw power.

The audience was silent, while the speech went on, delivered in a low, tense, hypnotic tone.

And at this point, rapping the box five times, the dalang signaled the orchestra to play "Sampak Sanga" at medium tempo, while he fluttered the kayon to represent the world in convulsion. When he plunged the stick of the kayon down on the left side of the screen, the clown scene began with Petruk dancing into view, his tall skeletal figure jerking to the rhythmic pulses of the gamelan.

From the opposite side of the screen came his squat, cross-eyed, pigeon-toed brother Gareng. Seeing his tall younger brother, Gareng lifted one of his misshapen arms and tried vainly to give a smart military salute.

Leaning forward, his long nose like the beak of a stork, his mouth cavernous and smiling, Petruk yelled, "Hey, you, why the salute?"

GARENG: Sorry. I thought you were a member of the general staff.

PETRUK: I'm a Communist. Did you generals cause all the trouble?

His own voice flat and low, Gareng said, "What trouble?"

PETRUK: Look around you, you fool.

GARENG: I'm not a fool, I'm a general.

PETRUK: Same thing.

GARENG: What's a Communist?

PETRUK: A Communist is someone who knows the truth. Have you got a cigarette? I need a cigarette.

554

GARENG: If I had a cigarette, I'd smoke it myself. What's the truth?

PETRUK: What a Communist says it is.

Scratching his head, Gareng said, "Then maybe I ought to give up the army and become a Communist. I like the idea of the truth being what I say it is."

PETRUK: You see why I'm a Communist? Here, give me your lance.

GARENG: Why should I do that?

PETRUK: Because I say so and I am a Communist, and didn't I tell you a Communist knows what is best? If I say give it to me, you must do so.

GARENG: You still haven't told me what the truth is.

PETRUK: We own everything equally. Therefore, you must give me your lance. If it is yours, it is also mine.

GARENG: Ah, I see. So that's the truth: we own equally. Well, here's my lance then.

The lance carried by Gareng was transferred by the dalang to Petruk. Gareng scratched his head again.

GARENG: Now you have both lances. But aren't we supposed to share equally?

PETRUK: We do. Right now I'm taking care of both our shares. That's my contribution. I'm public-spirited. I care. I'm working for us both.

GARENG: But what am I supposed to do?

PETRUK: Work for us both too. Didn't you say you're a general? Well then, protect us.

GARENG: How can I be a general without my lance? Give it back to me!

PETRUK: Why should I? Wouldn't I be a fool to give it back so you could stick me in the belly with it?

GARENG: That's what I'm going to do when I get it back!

A tussle for possession of the lances began. Five quick raps from the dalang cued the orchestra to play "Sampak Sanga" at up tempo. The brothers kicked, butted, pulled each other's twisted topknots of hair. Suddenly they stopped fighting and listened to someone approaching, singing a song. Getting up, they rushed off to the left, while Semar entered from the right.

The dalang sang "Patet Sanga Cugag," which described the turmoil in nature subsiding to coincide with the entrance of the fat clown, who was also a god. Semar had a turned-up nose, a potbelly, a huge behind, feminine breasts. He came on mumbling, "Where are my darling handsome sons? When they hear me coming, they always run away. Ah, well, I'll lure them with a song the way leaders lure people with a speech."

The dalang sang "Sendon Kagok Ketanan," a risqué ballad about a bridegroom desperately trying to remove his clothes while his impatient bride waited.

The audience laughed. Maggie looked around with relief. When the brothers had been making fun of Communists and the army there had been complete silence.

Gareng rushed in from the left, complaining about his younger brother to their father, Semar, who tried to placate him. Then Petruk appeared, defending his right to have both lances. "That fool," he said, pointing at his older brother, "will only hurt himself with a lance. I took it only to protect him from it."

Another scuffle began. Semar watched benignly for a while. Then he yelled loud enough for them to stop. "My charming sons," he began, "to what purpose are you fighting? Tell me that!"

GARENG: He cheated me of my lance!

PETRUK: He gave it to me of his own free will!

SEMAR: There are two lances, right?

GARENG AND PETRUK: Right, wise and just father.

SEMAR: So there is one for you and one for you.

The brothers looked at each other. "No," they said in unison.

SEMAR: There is another solution. Each of you will have half of what your brother has. Do you agree?

GARENG AND PETRUK: Yes!

SEMAR: Give me the lances.

Petruk gave them to him, and Semar cracked them in two (a difficult feat with the dalang's thumb and forefinger) and handed half of Petruk's lance to Gareng, half of Gareng's to Petruk. Then Semar gave each brother the other half of each lance.

SEMAR: Well, that's settled. see how easy everything is when you think clearly?

GARENG: Think what clearly?

556

PETRUK: Of where your self-interest lies. Now I have half of yours as well as half of my own. I am content.

GARENG: Am I content too? I have only the halves of two broken lances.

SEMAR: Of course you're content. Self-interest doesn't lie in hurting each other. But then who knows anything? There was a man who got on a bus with the name LUCKY sprawled across its side. But it only brought him *untung malang*.

Murmuring rippled through the crowd. They got the pun all right. Colonel Untung, one of the conspirators, had been captured on a bus that bore this name—Untung: Lucky. What had surprised Maggie throughout Budi's preparation for the play had been his grasp of politics. There were other remarks, detailed observations and puns that involved the Communists, the army, the student rioters (Petruk declared himself one in the skit), and Muslim extremists (Gareng functioned as a santri during a heated exchange), that proved he had been more aware of the current scene than she had realized.

Semar finally ended the long gara-gara with the god-clown's admonition to his "darling boys" that they had work to do. They must all three rush to the assistance of their master Arjuna, who needed their help to prevent another catastrophe in nature, "Because without vigilance, sweet boys, the ocean boils, the rain turns to rock, and our bowels explode. Because the touch of a butterfly's wing can stop a king's heart. Run! Run! There's no time to waste!" The boys stopped quarreling and the trio danced wildly off stage while the dalang sang "Patet Sanga Cugag," so well known by many spectators that they hummed along with him. Three raps, the gamelan played "Lara-lara," and the next scene began.

Maggie felt the audience relax—felt it as if a great slouching beast in her presence had suddenly vanished, leaving in its place harmless creatures like herself. The impassioned silence had suggested that people understood thoroughly what was happening. Shoulder to shoulder they had sat waiting through the gara-gara, not a word spoken among them, rapt, motionless, perhaps stunned. Maggie wondered if they expected the dalang to break the terrible tension and recapture the familiar spirit of ancient wayang. The merry dancing that ended the gara-gara and his singing of the popular "Patet Sanga

Cugag" might have suggested to them that he would no longer depart from tradition, that he would now give them what they had come to see and hear. For the moment, at least, they were sitting back as audiences must have done for hundreds of years, calmly awaiting the inevitable battle, the final victory. But however they behaved, Maggie knew this in her heart: they would not stop Dalang Budi Gitosuwoko from performing his own special version of *The Death of Karna*.

Fifty-eight

To Maggie's relief the ensuing drama went smoothly right through the second part into the third, with battles taking place that led to a confrontation between two great warriors. Caught up by Dalang Budi's skill, the audience seemed to forget his political comments. Maggie understood how cleverly he had paced himself. Had he gone farther all at once, hammering the point home, the audience might have halted the play, bringing the national broadcast to a close. But at the edge of Javanese patience he had drawn back, returned to the ancient story, its battles of courage, its profound sorrow, its commitment to shining ideals, its shimmering patterns of action, its immense themes of loyalty and love.

Maggie went around the screen at times, as other people did, to view the drama from the other side. She marveled at the combat of shadows, for until tonight she had never seen them projected by Budi on a screen. The shadows of the angled puppets danced, twisted, vanished, and returned in an instant, a whirl of black and gray motion, while the dalang's noises of battle shook the night air of Prambanan. Once, when he hissed like a cat, the audience as one person drew in breath fearfully, astonished, as if a magical feline had abruptly leapt into their faces. She could fully appreciate tonight what a great artist he was, and when Arjuna's arrow Pasopati finally pierced Karna's neck, ending the battle, and Budi sang the tragic melody "Sendon Tlutur," his voice was so filled with grief that she felt tears in her eyes. Looking around, she saw other people weeping too.

Then came the general melee to the percussive tune of "Sampak Manjura." Having led the Pandavas to victory, Bima did an exuberant dance. People clapped in time to the huge puppet's fanciful swaying and leaping. They were happy in this victory of good over evil. They had forgotten the earlier censorious manner of the great dalang.

Maggie again balled her fists. There was a glow in the east; dawn was only minutes away. Nine hours ago Budi had begun; now he was finishing exactly when the effect would be greatest.

After the dance, Kresna went to their chief ally, bowed, and reported. "Noble Arjuna slew Karna. Our powerful Bima hurled back the Kauravan army with great losses to them. Victory is ours!"

The dalang rapped three times sharply, cueing the orchestra to begin the final vigorous gending, "Gangsaran." But just as the thumping sounds of gong and xylophone filled the bowl of the sky—its edges defined now, its color a churning orange and blue—Semar pranced into the center of the screen. Budi rapped vigorously for silence. Surprised by this unexpected cue, the orchestra halted in mid-phrase, a bonang still resonating after the sound from other instruments had trembled away in the dawn air.

Semar was laughing. Budi's voice boomed out, startling the audience, some of whom had already started to rise. "Sit down, sit down!" yelled the clown-god sharply.

As if responding to authority, everyone plummeted down.

"Have you liked our play? How did you like my darling sons, one the general and the other the Red? How did you like their squabbling? Did it seem familiar? Do you really believe good won over evil? Are you the Pandavas and your enemies, whoever they are, the Kauravas? You believe such things?" Semar laughed uproariously, his bulbous body jerking up and down. "How did you like the world of wayang? Didn't you enter it and curl up like a weary dog? Because that's what we do in this land—behave like dogs and look the other way when something bad happens. Like dogs! Yes! For example—"

Semar waddled swiftly to the left side of the screen, planting his bare feet down, pointing with a long, crooked finger off the stage. "Over there, within hearing distance, honorable guests, you can find hundreds of bodies. Oh, yes, I mean what I say. Hundreds of them. More corpses than people in this audience. Just under the surface of the ground. A good monsoon rain will uncover them all right, the torn and tortured bodies, the eviscerated guts, the gouged-out eyes, the hacked-off limbs. But you will be gone before they rise out of the mud like things from the sea. You will go home happy, satisfied, your minds filled with art like bellies filled with food. You'll forget the dead lying not a hundred steps away from your feet. Even though they are the dead of your shame. Muslim and Communist and soldier, the innocent along with the guilty, the good and the bad, the bad and the good, they have all found such sad and foolish deaths. While you, good people of Java, go about your business day after day. Right here, within earshot of my voice, the army has lined up their victims and shot them against the stone walls, finishing them off like chickens, while the great king sits in his palaces with his women and the pretenders to his throne plot among themselves and the youngsters give up their books to carry signs, to push, to loot, to burn, to shout mindlessly while the tanks rumble and the politicians glance warily from side to side and the people die ignominiously throughout the land as they have done right here, here on the site of an ancient temple honored by time and by meaning and by the beauty of art, and so here we are at last, all of us, as though we too were great warriors, the Pandavas and Kauravas, and so all of us are here, you good people of Java and the corpses of your brethren, and so we are all here, all of us, the foolish and tainted of this earth, the hypocrites, the torturers, the indifferent, all gathered here on this ancient site where our ancestors built a huge temple a thousand years ago and so it has come to this, so we have all arrived here at this hour when the sun rises on another day and we must greet it like this, indifferent witnesses to murder and profound folly. Oh, it is that, it is folly! Folly! Folly!"

Semar jabbed his finger rapidly at the audience, a gesture of contempt and fury, then began a jaunty dance, humming loudly, springing up into the air like a huge misshapen ball, with the early light strong enough now to make him finally disappear against the screen, a faint shade of gray against white, while the audience sprang to its feet, yelling, waving fists at the screen, at the vanishing Semar, at the dalang.

There was no lively "Rucak Ceruk" to end the performance and send the audience on its way. In the midst of Budi's speech the orchestra had fled from its instruments, and when he ceremoniously, calmly, returned the kayon to the center of the debog, officially bringing this evening to a close, only a few musicians were left to gather up their hammers, their flutes, the instruments that could be carried away.

The dalang sat hunched in front of the screen. People surged near, but kept at a certain distance, as if an invisible circle had been drawn around him, beyond which they could not go, as if fear and reverence had drawn such a protective circle against their entry. They were screaming at him, insulting him, calling him a traitor, a Communist, a man of the CIA, but not one of them crossed the hallowed line. He never moved, but closing his eyes appeared to be meditating. The crowd didn't stay. Having galvanized them into fury, his words also scattered them, sending them into the new morning with a burden of horror or guilt or denial, so that within minutes the Prambanan setting for *The Death of Karna* was almost deserted.

The crew of Radio Republik Indonesia, stunned and confused, hastily packed away their equipment (but not before Maggie learned from them that they had not stopped the broadcast—after all, no one had ordered them to), slung it all into their van and rattled swiftly away in the growing light. Remaining there with the dalang and Maggie were a few workmen who were anxious to load the screen, the chestful of puppets, and the assembly of bronze instruments back into the lorry and return all of these things to his house so they could get paid. Basuki, who was supposed to help his master stow away the puppets, had vanished. Maggie put them back into the kotak while Budi continued to sit cross-legged in front of the debog, eyes closed. The lantern above his head cast a pallid spurt of flame into the blue air. The sun, appearing molten across the tops of trees, flung a deeper red across the screen, where for hours the puppets and their shadows had cavorted and fought, creating against the white rectangle a world of violent splendor.

When everything was packed, Maggie went up to Budi, knelt beside him, and whispered in his ear, "We are ready. You are the finest man I have ever known."

That day the dalang slept. Everyone knew that he would sleep, so Maggie expected no one would visit him. She got the army-dominated local paper and found a brief notice about the wayang lakon on the back page. It merely stated the facts: who, what, when, where. Nothing more. Maggie went to the local radio station and after much difficulty got someone there to admit that the broadcast had gone out to the nation, that probably millions had heard it. Radio Republik Indonesia's spokesman did not comment on the performance. It was a Javanese way of showing disapproval.

Maggie could understand such disapproval. A wayang performance given by someone of Dalang Gitosuwoko's reputation was like a World Series game back in the States. Everyone had expected so much from him. Throughout Java they must have leaned toward their radio sets, eager for the words that would transport them out of present misery into a world of wayang, into fantasy, into the ripe, surging, but harmless emotions of ancient kings and warriors. Instead, he had taken on the entire nation, the violence and shame of the crisis, without aligning himself with any group, so that his words bit deeply into every conscience in a way nothing else could. No politician, no religious leader, no government official, would have an audience as vast and responsive as the one that he had held in the palm of his hand last night. Looking back on it, Maggie realized that he had added phrases in the heat of his final speech. Never in rehearsal had his voice boomed out so brutally, so fiercely, with such devastating effect. That he had come out of it alive was perhaps a miracle. They had ringed him, vilifying him for uprooting their deepest shame and fear. Tradition had saved him. He was a great dalang. They could not touch him.

All that day while he slept the sleep of exhaustion, Maggie went over the events of last night. She wanted a better understanding of the audience. They had yelled at his criticism of Sukarno, yet for the ensuing clown scene they had sat very still. Even when Semar came on for the final speech, no one tried to yell him down. Only afterward had perhaps fifty people circled like a pack of wolves around Budi to

563

scream insults. It occurred to her that the original outburst from the audience, when he attacked Sukarno, had been spontaneous. Caught unaware, they had reacted. Later, steeled for more commentary, they withdrew into Javanese impassiveness. After the performance, shoulder to shoulder, they felt enough shared courage to shout at him but not enough to rush him. People so afraid of their emotions, capable of acting only in concert, had the perfect temperament for mass slaughter. This judgment did not, however, provoke in her a righteous hatred of them. She was thankful for that. She loved them differently now, perhaps as Budi loved them: for their unabashed enjoyment of wayang and in spite of their indifference to its ideals.

In the late afternoon, she went into his room and lay down beside him.

All the next day Budi waited for visitors. After his performances people always came to pay their respects—often there were dozens at his door—so in anticipation Budi had the usual tea and sweet cakes set on a table in the courtyard. He waved off Maggie's quiet warning that perhaps no one would come. He put aside good sense and acted on hope. She loved him for it. Only a truly wise man would let the faintest of hopes govern his actions at a time of despair. It meant he understood the unpredictability of life. And yet despair was paramount right now.

Surely someday he would be able to set it aside and see clearly what he had done. Millions had been out there listening to the radio broadcast. Thousands would learn by word of mouth what it had been like to sit among the privileged few that evening at Prambanan. He had rebuked an entire nation. Where else in the world could an artist try such a thing—and succeed? But, of course, for the privilege of speaking his mind on a single night, he had given up his career.

And if she had a chance to change things? Maggie would not have it otherwise. Somehow they would manage, because they had each other. That old cliché used to amuse her; now it moved in her blood like an ancient truth.

The following night after dinner, they sat on the veranda of their pavilion. Stars seemed to crowd one another for room on the black panoply.

She got up and put on a record: the Wolverines Band, featuring

Bix. While it played, she said, "I was thinking today if you were a jazz musician you'd sound more like Louis Armstrong than Bix. Back in the twenties Louis had a big, brassy warm tone and a wide range of ideas and more technique than anyone who ever played the instrument, and he was always thinking ahead, so his solos built to great climaxes. When he improvised, his lines were never sloppy or commonplace. There was no one like Louis." She reached over and touched his hand. "Or like you. But then I decided no, you were finally more like Bix. Not in what you do but in what you think of it. He was never satisfied. I know you aren't either. His work never gave him comfort once it was done. I don't think yours does either. And no one had his dedication. He lived for music. You're like that with wayang."

"You're too romantic. It was you who gave me back the dedication."

"You'd have found it again on your own. I understood that at Prambanan. It was like putting a fish back in water." She felt talkative, but wanted to match his reflective mood. Perhaps he was still exhausted by the performance. Or still despairing. She said reassuringly, "I think what you did will mean something. People will never forget it. You spoke out without taking sides. You made them look at the waste, the tragedy. You've changed things."

"No," he said, "I don't think so."

Maggie leaned forward. His face was in shadows behind a pillar that stood between him and the moonlight. "You don't think *Karna* will make a difference?"

"No."

"Did you feel that way? I mean, from the beginning when you decided to do it—that it wouldn't matter?"

"Wayang was a means of making fun of the Dutch, so it's been used politically before. But no, I never felt the other night would make a difference."

"But the intensity, the hard work—"

"I did it for myself even while telling myself I was doing it for my country. I did it to be part of the reckless present."

"You're belittling what you did. I don't like it when you put yourself down."

"Put myself down?" He didn't understand the idiom.

"I like you arrogant," she said with a laugh. "When you don't give a damn what anyone thinks. But I know you gave a damn about that performance. I know that."

"Oh, I did. I was angry and full of virtue and I solved some technical problems and extended what I can do in certain scenes. But when the performance was over, I was drained of everything that led to it."

"You always surprise me. I thought you would hold on to the feeling."

"Are you disappointed?"

"I'm not sure. I think you made a difference, though. But whether you did or didn't, what you did was great, and even that doesn't matter, because what really matters to me is loving you." After a silence so long and deep that it seemed strange, Maggie said, "Where are you?" And then she said, "I make you smile."

"I'm smiling because a Javanese woman would never ask such a question."

"If I become a Javanese woman, it will be with an American need to ask such questions. A moment ago you seemed very far away."

"I was thinking of Kris Pasopati. Of everything in this house it's the most enduring—it and the other family kris. They stand for the Gitosuwokos. It has always been so. But now Pasopati is missing."

"You mean—stolen?"

"It was kept behind a secret panel in the wall. Only two of the servants knew its whereabouts."

"What do they say?"

"They are gone."

Maggie said nothing more. Obviously people now felt the dalang was sufficiently disgraced for them to steal from him. The future had begun. Reaching out, she took one of his hands in both of hers and turned it slowly, as if she were inspecting a finely crafted piece of jewelry. "I love this hand," she told him and looked up with a smile.

———————

Going inside, they lay down and held each other gently, too exhausted for love. Does he understand better than I do, Maggie wondered, what is in store for us? *Karna* had been a grand gesture, but tomorrow not a soul in Java would dare to hire him for a wayang performance. The play had made a difference all right—to their own lives. Maggie spooned herself against him from behind, her breasts and belly and thighs wedged securely against his back and buttocks.

She was already planning their future. He could teach; surely there were students who would come to him as long as he remained out of the limelight. And she could teach English. Already on her travels around Yogya people had shyly asked if she would ever give English lessons.

He had asked if she were disappointed because his righteous anger had ended with the end of the play. Her answer had been equivocal. Now, feeling her body against his, Maggie knew the real answer. She would not want this man to remain in a world that wasn't his. Her lover had left his own world to speak to another. Now he had returned. Whether he performed or not, Budi had gone back to living in the world of wayang. He was the man she had first met, the man she had fallen in love with. And that, really, was what she wanted. In the morning, she would waken him by whispering in his ear, "I am not disappointed."

As she fell asleep, Maggie had a soft indistinct vision of their sitting together in a little garden, the moon hovering above the serrated leaves of a banana palm, Budi reaching out for her hand, their hands touching, the night deepening and the moon rising and rising and rising until it stood directly overhead, a moon of Asia, its warm light coming down upon them. . . .

There was a sound, a faraway murmur like Bix playing from across the river, his cornet muted, the melody faint. Her eyes opened suddenly and her body jerked in the effort to marshal itself. Budi was already sitting up, looking toward the door beyond which someone was calling his name softly, tauntingly. "Gitosuwoko, come out here. Pasopati is waiting. You, Gitosuwoko, come out here."

Hardly before she knew what was happening, Budi had leapt to his feet, moved to the door, and flung it open.

"Don't go out there!" Maggie cried.

Ignoring her warning, he rushed into the courtyard.

Before she could call out again, she heard a scream, the sound cut short by a rattling cough. By the time she reached the door, three figures, casting shadows under brilliant moonlight, had raced across the courtyard and into the darkness between buildings.

He was stretched out, a dagger in his naked chest. They had driven it in deep, at least half of its eleven waves within his body. The kris was Pasopati. And skewered on the blade up to the hilt was a piece

567

of paper. Bending low over him, she saw the large crude letters: "*MATA-MATA DENGAN CIA.*" Sitting down beside him, she cradled his head in her arms and waited for something to happen, for the horror to come slouching finally from the darkness, a great shambling shadow that engulfed and held her a long time, it seemed, before she found her voice, before she filled the night with the first wailing notes of a grief that wouldn't end.

Fifty-nine

He received a letter from Maggie. Mail delivery had been regular for a while, although once again it had come to a halt, so this was one of the last letters to slip through.

Vern wouldn't expect another from her anyway, not for some time. She described the death of her lover to whom the assassins had pinned "AGENT FOR THE CIA." Had he been? From the tone of her letter Maggie thought of him as some kind of martyr. Vern considered that a grim prospect—to compete with a martyr. Although he hadn't given up—would he ever lose hope that they would be together again?— he felt it was altogether sensible for him to let time do its inevitable work before asking his wife to reconsider her decision. She was grieving; the letter made that clear. So he would be patient, never an easy thing for him.

On 6 March, when he was preparing for an OPSUS trip to Bali, the Laskar Arief Rahman Hakim—a new militant university group named after the martyred medical student—attacked the Foreign Ministry, ransacked it while troops sympathetic to the students stood idly by. Ripping out furniture, scattering documents and flinging them from windows, the students threw rocks at the police riot squad that finally arrived. When tear-gas canisters were lobbed into the building, the coughing students at last capitulated.

Next day the American Embassy became a target. Jack Rutledge talked about it at the hotel bar (now that Vern was back on the sauce, they were friends again). Three hundred kids had climbed over the grill fence, torched embassy cars, tossed rocks through the ambassador's windows, pulled down the American flag, and replaced it with the red-and-white colors of Indonesia. "So you're running to Bali tomorrow," Jack said, punching Vern lightly on the arm. "Leaving poor guys like me to hold down the fort."

Before leaving for the airport the next day, Vern went to the office for a last meeting with General Sakirman, who liked to feel he was in charge.

When he walked into the general's office, Sakirman was not there. A fat woman in kebaya and sarong was sitting there instead, not in front of the desk, but to one side, as if occupying part of the general's authority. She regarded Vern with a long, hard look, the way a schoolmarm might study a wayward boy. She was the Wife, and she had the haughty assertive look of a major stockholder in a large organization, which of course she was: 40 percent of PROPELAD, the holding company that had loaned OPSUS the money to finance Project Palm Tree, belonged to Susanto Sakirman.

Vern gave her a respectful nod and turned to leave, but she called him imperiously back. It occurred to him that she had arranged for her husband to be absent so she could conduct a little interview of her own. She asked if he had heard from his wife. Without awaiting his reply, Susanto told him, "I have not." Then she declared, "Ki-Dalang Gitosuwoko was not regular in his life at last."

"I am aware of that."

Her broad face was twisted by an expression of contempt, as if she wondered why he hadn't walked or crawled all the way to Yogya and dug up his wife's dead lover and plunged a kris into the rotting corpse. "You are aware. How long you been aware?"

"That's hard to say. I wasn't able to get out to Yogya, as you probably know. So what happened there is not clear to me." Vern controlled himself. If he wanted to build his hotel, he'd have to go through with this interview.

The fat woman got to her feet. "We in army must show moral path in time of troubles. We could not give transportation to you. We could not help you to Yogya. We in army must show the moral examples to others." She waited.

"Yes," Vern said noncommittally.

"After Bali, when you have done work, you get plane to Yogya."

So that's what she wanted to tell him—she personally had made the decision, not her husband. It was Vern's guess that she wanted him to show up in Yogya and thrash the adulteress to an inch of her life, thereby saving the world for virtuous women like herself.

"Army control now. So you go," she said and waited.

"Thank you," Vern said coolly.

Susanto Sakirman frowned, turned, and left the room. Watching her waddle through the doorway, her buttocks swinging like unlatched parts of a gate, Vern felt a twinge of compassion for his boss, whose natural gift for deceit had surely been augmented by a long association with his Sus.

But there was no time for such reflections. Something was up. A young officer was stopping at each desk, excitedly whispering the news. Within minutes the Army Radio station broadcast it: At his Bogor palace today President Sukarno had met with representatives of General Suharto. After a fruitful discussion about the country's welfare he had written a letter "ordering" General Suharto "to take all measures considered necessary to guarantee the security, calm, and stability of the government and the revolution."

So control had passed from Sukarno to Suharto. It was all over except for the shouting. Except for the shouting and perhaps, Vern thought, for a little more killing.

———

Larry met him with a car at the airport. Riding northward on the road to Denpasar, the little Englishman kept up a constant chatter, as if afraid any silence might bring them to the subject of Maggie.

"What about this, mate. I was on the beach yesterday, inspecting equipment at the site, when two boys came along with an anteater. Remember my anteater in Bengkulu?"

"How can I forget?"

"I was bloody sure the boys would try to sell it to me. Give me a peek at the raw neck so I'd take it off their hands for a few rupiah. But they walked past without a glance. That was a relief. Around Sanur, I understand, there's a lot of black magic and things going bump in the night. I don't care for tricks being played on me— illusions and hallucinations and that sort of bloody thing. Look."

From the car window Larry pointed at a skinny dog trotting along a ditch, its pink tongue lolling. "That's the Balinese variety of anjing," Larry explained, shaking his head. "He's the mangiest, dirtiest, laziest, sickest, most incredibly stupid animal that God ever put on this earth, aside from us, and I shudder to think if I don't come back in the next life as something rather topping, something fearless like an eagle or a shark, I jolly well might return as one of these Balinese dogs. Bugger all. Nothing could be worse."

"Have you seen the dogs of Benares?" Vern asked. "They're worse."

"No."

"Believe me. These Balinese dogs are living in paradise compared to them."

"No." Larry blew his breath out in awe.

For a moment Vern indulged in the memory of Benares and the dogs there, running in frantic packs, snapping at one another in their frenzy, eyes glazed from pain and fear, their lean suppurating bodies atremble. "What's the situation here?"

"Reports of violence in outlying villages, but they've missed the slaughter. At least so far."

"So far?"

"Well, Sudjani has been giving me a rundown on the Reds in Bali. Seems they're an arrogant lot. Their leader has made millions. They ridicule Hindu beliefs. They brag about their power and threaten to take over the country like the Dutch did."

"They're doing that *now?*" Vern asked incredulously.

"They've toned down, I understand. But Sudjani thinks it's too late. They'll pay for being like the Japs and the Dutch. That's the connection he makes."

"You mean we got here in time for another massacre?"

"Wouldn't that be our bloody luck."

They rode in silence.

"I feel sorry for the Dutch," Vern said finally. "They always get the blame. Anything the Indos do wrong, they point to the Dutch—the Dutchmen did it. A few days ago I met a Dutchman at the bar, and he went on about the universities and museums. He was here for a museum himself. In the midst of this fuckup he's here cataloging and buying stuff. What the Indos turn their backs on, the Dutch pay attention to."

"But the Dutch treated these blokes like slaves."

"No denying it. The West can't live down colonialism. It's what we're stuck with. People have what's theirs, their own country, and that's that."

"But look at this mess. There's got to be a better way."

"We could do something about it. Is that what you mean?"

"We could, mate."

"It's their country no matter what they do with it. It's theirs to wreck if they want to. I wonder if we have that straight yet."

"You're the one who's always insisting on bringing them progress."

"Sure, I am. That's because I've got a colonial mind. We all have. We've been saddled with it for centuries." After a pause he said, "Larry, the guy she was with got killed."

"Jesus."

"Maybe after we're finished here, I'll stop and see her in Yogya."

"Ah, I'm glad."

"She's staying there. She won't ever leave."

"Don't be too sure, old boy. She might change her mind someday."

"Maggie? I don't think so. But then maybe I never did understand her."

"While there's life there's hope."

Looking straight ahead, Vern was silent. As the car rattled along, he saw youngsters sitting in yards or under pavilions practicing gamelan. Their older brothers were playing badminton on dirt courts. In the fields stood bamboo rods bent over the padis with colored rags fluttering at the ends. Not stolid scarecrows but elongated wisps like the shadow puppets or the spidery sculptures of Bali. It was all of a piece, this land—the art, the music, the rice fields. Through gaps in woodland he could see the ocean with outriggers on it, the prows shaped like the gaping mouths of swordfish and eyes painted on hulls so the boats could see at night.

573

"Well," he began, feeling Larry turn to listen. But that's all he said, and once again they rode in silence.

———————

In Bali he awakened to the sound of roosters crowing. There was never that incessant raucous blare he'd been accustomed to in India—the sound of crows cawing in your final dream before you came into consciousness. Everywhere in Bali you saw chickens and roosters. The roosters seemed proud but dumb. Maybe they showed sense only as chicks, when they cut on a dime and followed their mother as closely as her own breath, surging around, pecking at the earth but with one eye on her slightest movement so they could remain precisely in her wake, huddling under her as safely as coconuts clustered on a tree. He wished for Maggie, to share his feelings about stupid roosters with her; but his mind filled slowly with the image of a pretty young Chinese face, the narrowed eyes sparkling with humor.

Dogs of Benares. It had been years since he'd thought of them, their fearful lives, their scrounging and suffering and vicious little deaths.

That day he worked hard. Sudjani followed him around explaining things. The translator laughed heartily at crowds of Balinese lined up alongside the construction site, watching the ground being turned, the single bulldozer rocking to and fro over the muddy field. "Balinese don't like water," he said happily, as if he weren't one of them. "They fish but don't go into the ocean. They can't understand why you build a hotel on the beach. A beach is the road that leads into hell. Why don't you build on the mountains? That's closer to the gods, they say."

Sudjani also regaled him with stories about the Reds, whom he feared and hated. Turned out a group of Reds had bought his uncle out of a piece of land and failed to pay him his rightful share.

Isn't the world the same everywhere? Vern wondered grimly. In recent days, he had felt a strange new feeling, as if he were experiencing the sensation of emptiness, and it was ballooning within him, pushing aside what was really there, leaving only its own self, its hollowness, its void, its lack of anything as the reality of Vernon Gardner. Somehow he had always managed, whatever happened, to see in life a challenge, an expectation, a potential that someone, perhaps himself,

574

could seize and develop and add to the general sum of possibilities in the world. But now he was just going through the motions. He was rattled by peculiar thoughts. He found himself picturing those elongated Indonesian puppets with the narrow waists and ungainly arms and long, sharp noses. How could she have fallen in love with a man who tried to make creatures looking like insects perform like kings?

And he remembered inconsequential moments with Maggie. For example, the time in a Medan hotel when they wanted ice at a bar, but the barmaid along with three of her friends, all *behind* the bar, continued a conversation. Maggie had walked up and yelled loudly, *"Es! Es! Es!"* But they had merely smiled, while from the kitchen behind them issued a terrible complexity of noise—things stirring and banging and falling—until he and Maggie were in stitches, wondering, for God's sake, what mayhem their request had caused in there. Finally, after a long, long time, two gin and tonics (the order was one gin and tonic, one lime and soda), *without* ice, came not from the bar but from the kitchen, brought by a tiny boy whom the barmaid and her companions ignored while continuing their conversation, grouped around the array of barside bottles. How he and Maggie had laughed. Maggie had a meat-and-potatoes laugh. No holding back. He had never met a woman who laughed so openly.

Every night in Denpasar he and Larry drank. They took their tots of gin into the night air and stood under the stars, looking up at the Southern Cross, which glittered like a huge diamond opposite the half-submerged Big Dipper.

Every day Sudjani brought in ominous news. Because the price of rice had increased by 700 percent in the last six months, people in the villages were starving. They were eating bark off the trees. They blamed their plight on the Reds, who had come like Dutchmen to usurp land belonging to the gods. Only two years ago, because of their anger at farmers who were disrespectful to the land, the gods had caused the sacred mountain of Gunung Agung to erupt. Thousands of Balinese had been punished by death. According to Sudjani, the gods would exact still more suffering if the Reds weren't destroyed.

There was a kind of awestruck conviction in Sudjani's voice (at odd moments the translator gave up his acquired cynicism and reverted to the beliefs of his childhood) that reminded Vern of speakers in the streets of Jakarta whose use of prophecy and the supernatural to explain politics had whipped crowds into a frenzy.

To Larry he said, "I hope we finish before the real trouble starts."

"You've been saying that since our first day in Jakarta."

"You think I'm a worrywart?"

"No, mate, I wish you were. Until we slap the last bit of plaster on the last wall, I'll be on pins."

"It'll be good to get out of here."

"On another job."

"Of course on another job."

"I'm glad to hear that, mate. You sound a bit more like your own sweet self."

"I feel more like myself," Vern claimed, but the truth was he had lost the old feeling of impatience for new adventure. He feared that an emptiness was growing in him like a sort of cancer. Every morning he tried to work himself into renewed enthusiasm, but every morning he failed. Until losing Maggie, he had never failed. He wanted to regret having fallen in love with her, but he couldn't do that either.

Sixty

After great pain a formal feeling comes." She remembered that from college days and was pretty sure Emily Dickinson had written it. At any rate, it was true—true for her. In days following Budi's death, she managed to hang on, to do what was necessary. She went through the aftermath without faltering, with a feeling of ice in her veins as she talked and thought and adjusted.

The penghulu of a mosque that Budi used to attend now and then had assumed control of the estate according to the Syafi'itic school of Muslim law. He had come to the compound within hours of the news of the dalang's murder. He had known about Maggie, apparently from the dalang himself. For someone in his eighties the Muslim functionary had a lecherous eye and liked her immediately.

He established that the dalang's sole heir was Melani Gitosuwoko, wife of the dead nephew. According to law, she would get the house and everything in it, including the pusaka, or heirlooms. Maggie, who moved out of the compound the next day into a local hotel, would have liked to keep Kris Pasopati, to guard it for the family. That was a foolish aim for a foreign woman, and she knew it, yet expressed her desire to the old man, who seemed stunned for a moment by such boldness. That didn't deter Maggie from suggesting to the penghulu that Ki-Dalang Gitosuwoko be buried at Borobudur, a place that had meant so much to him. At first the penghulu argued that generations of Gitosuwokos were buried in a nearby village, but when she pointed out that the villagers there had turned their backs on one of his nephews and murdered another, the old man acquiesced and saw to it that the ground was purchased without delay near Borobudur.

Few people attended the funeral. Basuki, who had disappeared the night of the performance, never showed up, although Pak Seno arrived with half a dozen other gamelan musicians. Melani traveled in from her parents' village, a wan little woman afraid to speak to the foreign mistress of her dead husband's dead uncle, yet they stood side by side at the freshly dug grave while the old penghulu recited from the Quran. Wrapped in white cotton cloth, Budi was carried by bamboo litter to the grave and lowered in. The penghulu was helped down beside him. Loosening the bandages surrounding the dalang's head, he exposed a cheek and ear into which he shouted the Muslim Confession of Faith a dozen times. After the gravediggers helped him out, he intoned another prayer from the Quran. The grave was covered, flowers strewed across it. Maggie felt that her jaws were wired, the skin of her face frozen, her eyelids pinned open, as she watched Melani deposit a little gift on the fresh clay: a rice cone, some coconut cookies, a bouquet of frangipani, and an old Dutch coin.

Two days later Maggie moved from the local hotel into a small house with bamboo walls and a tiny garden of breadfruit trees and banana palms. It was located near Taman Sari, once the pleasure garden of sultans and now a ruined assembly of brick watercourses. She put her suitcases down and stared at the old high-backed Dutch chair and the moth-eaten sofa that constituted the furniture in the first of three tiny rooms. What was going to happen now? She didn't know, but Maggie Gardner was not someone to mope and go around "hanging crepe," as her father used to say of her mother.

Then she fell apart.

An old woman came in every morning and every evening to prepare food (the penghulu had arranged for it), but otherwise Maggie saw no one. She sat on the sofa or lay on the mat in her bedroom. She had never known it was possible to feel such pain. "My heart is broken" had always seemed to her one of those romantic notions that had nothing to do with the real world. But the raw physical presence of grief was now apparent to Maggie. It felt sometimes as if her insides were being pulled asunder, like dough in a baker's hand, an organic counterpart to what was happening in her mind: the horror, the disbelief, the sudden illogical hope of awakening out of this nightmare, the panic, the repetitive reliving of moments both wonderful and terrible until life itself assumed the dull monotony of obsessive remembering. She had brought from Medan a book on the Vedanta philosophy of India, and during the hot endless hours in the aftermath of his funeral, she searched wildly through its pages for a hope of reincarnation that would assure them life together in another go-around.

She never found that solace, but in the place of comfort she began to develop a belief in God. It was as if like a phoenix He appeared in the ashes of her grief. What God was or meant, His properties and His demands on her, were at this early stage of belief as yet unknown to Maggie Gardner, but she felt the presence of something hitherto lacking in her life. Back in Iowa she had sometimes envied her friends who had faith, even while scorning the rituals they went through to guarantee and augment it. Now she felt stirring in her, like a fetus, the substance of Another and she had no better word for it than God. It gave her no joy or satisfaction, however, but was simply there, a thing she could not rid herself of, a thing wondrous and strange that might someday, somehow, assert itself and overwhelm her life.

Or she would shake it off. That too was possible. Because there were all sorts of possibilities, and it was this realization, coming over a period of a few weeks, that finally took Maggie Gardner out of the tiny bedroom and into the garden and from the garden into the lane and from there into the bewildering labyrinth of paths that characterized the Taman Sari district of Yogyakarta.

She wanted desperately to talk to someone about him. Walking through the back lanes on the shaded side, Maggie worked through scenarios that described her dead lover to a shadowy listener. She unburdened herself of lost dreams. She had carried the secret hope, after his murder, that she was pregnant. Susanto had once lectured her about making babies. A Javanese woman without children was no better than a ghost on the mountain. It was a mark of Allah's favor to have as many as possible. But two days after the funeral Maggie had her period.

She carried on discussions about jazz and wayang and Borobudur with her imagined companion. "You see," she said, the words soundless as she strolled down crowded lanes, "my husband's commitment isn't to people but to a process, to things always in the process of changing. My lover's commitment wasn't to people either but also to a process. Yet that process never brought about change; it handled the same things again and again, the materials of permanence, the dramas created over centuries, so that whatever happens they will last in themselves, they will be experienced by men and women passing through life, and they'll survive each generation. That was his commitment—to wayang and Borobudur, things that last—and it will be mine now."

Buoyed by these monologues, Maggie started to write letters again. And letters began arriving at the little house, for with a cessation of rioting in Java, the mail service was almost normal. She got a reply from a former Indonesian minister of education and culture who agreed to work actively for the project. And finally the director general of the Archaeological Service sent off a little note that at least recognized the existence of the Committee for Safeguarding Borobudur. A lesser functionary also responded, showing cautious interest in the program if sufficient funds could be located and if the political situation remained stable.

Then a representative of Netherlands Engineering Consultants wrote a letter of inquiry to Maggie. It contained a questionnaire that they would like answered prior to finalization of the project so that they might bid on contracts. "Prior to finalization"—the phrase was in English and fired Maggie's imagination. She saw herself among a crowd of workers approaching the gray lichen-infested foundation of Borobudur, notebooks in hand, concrete mixers and bulldozers and cranes all lined up behind them in preparation for launching an immediate attack on the problems of her beloved temple, for that's what it was now, her beloved Borobudur.

In her loneliness Maggie went now and then to the local hotel, had a club soda in the bar, a terrible meal in the dining room, simply in the hope of finding someone from the West to talk to. Obviously, she had to balance the desire for company with the probability of a few nasty encounters—traveling men on the lookout for women like herself. For Maggie it was worth the risk at this time in her life. And her assessment was correct: a Dutchman, two Frenchmen, an Indian who could not stop talking about his Oxford education, they saw in her a compliant woman if not a whore and treated her with sufficient disdain to send her out of the bar tearful and furious. But she met others, because Westerners were starting to come back to Java. They told her things about Indonesia that she would not have learned from within. Observers abroad were now estimating that in the aftermath of the coup attempt many thousands had been murdered—perhaps half a million, even a million. Tens of thousands had been sent to jungle prison camps. Maggie thought of Inam. Was the girl out there in the sweltering rain forest, dying a little each day from disease and malnutrition? Maggie's trips to army headquarters began again.

In spite of a loneliness that drove her to sit for hours in the shabby hotel, Maggie was determined to stay in Yogya. She realized soon after the funeral that the army had decided to ignore her. In fact, they might even view her continued stay in Yogya as beneficial, reminding people as it did of the dalang's final descent into madness—taking on a foreign mistress, speaking treason through a wayang lakon. It was not farfetched, she decided, for the Javanese mind to come up with such a convoluted analysis. After all, the army's suppression of political dissent must be justified by the use of symbols. One of them might as well be a foreign woman who walked freely through Yogya as living proof that the dalang had been crazy, his criticism reckless, his judgment clouded by lust.

One afternoon, while Maggie was typing a letter on her portable, from the front gate came a shouted *"Kula nuwun!"* This was happening lately—people were using the Javanese formula for announcing their approach when they came to her house. Rising from the little desk, she called out, *"Mangga!"* And the voice got closer, *"Kula nuwun."* From the front door Maggie saw a thin little man, quite elderly, struggle up the short narrow path to the house. *"Mangga,"* she said, inviting him in. With a sembah he entered and at the threshold said once again, *"Nuwun."*

Maggie led him into the small front room and had him sit in the old Dutch chair at the south, near the door—the proper place for a guest—and took her position as the hostess at the northern end of the sofa. When they were both seated, Maggie said, *"Ngaturaken sugeng."*

"Pangestunipun." He introduced himself as Pak Cerma, the uncle of Melani Gitosuwoko.

"My Javanese is not very good yet. Can we speak Bahasa Indonesia?"

He nodded somberly. Pak Cerma had a long nose, bloodless lips, and beady eyes set close together in a narrow, bony face. He wore subdued batiks, a traditional skullcap, and a brown scarf around his chicken-scrawny neck although the heat was stifling. He sat with his knees together, his feet parallel, while on his lap lay two packages wrapped in bright splashes of flowered paper.

Maggie offered him tea, but he declined and instead spoke of the weather, which hadn't changed in weeks. He managed, however, to describe it for ten minutes before getting to the point: his niece wanted Ibu Maggie to have two little gifts and begged her humbly to accept them as mementos from the family. The little man got up with the slow ceremonial grace endemic to the Javanese and handed Maggie the two packages.

"Please," he said, "open them."

The first package contained a book. He explained that it was an old copy of Mpu Kanwa's great Kakawin poem of the eleventh century, *Arjunawiwaha,* written in a language few people could read today. "But the dalang read it," Pak Cerma said, his face without expression. "My niece hopes you will accept this little gift."

"It's not a little gift. It's very wonderful. She is very generous and I thank her for it."

He was looking at the other package, so Maggie unwrapped it and drew in her breath sharply. Lying in a rough wooden box was a scabbard and a dagger—Kris Pasopati, its eleven-waved blade smelling of lime and of the arsenic that had been rubbed in to clean away the dalang's blood. Also in the box was his folded kamus, the waistband Budi had always worn to hold his kris during a performance.

"I think you know," Maggie said, her voice trembling, "I will not accept it for myself. I will keep Pasopati for a dalang who will come along someday. As long as I live here in Java, I will hold it for him, whoever he is. If I should leave Java or die here before a dalang who deserves it comes along, I will see that it returns to the Gitosuwoko family through Melani."

Pak Cerma nodded.

"Melani and her children are always welcome in this house."

He nodded.

"Pak Cerma, you will tell her how I feel?"

He nodded.

Minutes later, watching the elderly man sway down the path, Maggie no longer knew how she felt. Stunned, grateful, bewildered; the emotions surged as Maggie wondered if she would ever understand the Javanese. Who had made the decisions about the book and the dagger? Perhaps the old penghulu or Pak Cerma or someone else hovering in the background. Surely not Melani, yet Maggie felt that the girl must have wanted her to have these things. Why? Maggie didn't know. She simply remembered the young widow standing beside her at the grave, the solemn delicate face like a flower not yet fully opened.

———

Next morning she took the book to her language teacher.

"It is in ancient Javanese," he told her, turning the leather-bound volume slowly in both hands. "The script is Palawa."

"The dalang put a marker here," she said, "and he wrote on it a nine and a five."

The guru looked at the page. "It is Sarga five, bait nine—the ninth stanza of the fifth book. *Ri Tatwanyan Maya Sahana,*" he read. "*Hananing Bhawa Siluman.* 'The world is just a game, a thing of no value.' "

Back home, Maggie sat in the garden under a breadfruit tree and watched the sunrays filter down upon the swept clay at her feet. She had the book opened in her lap to that page. She would never have understood him. But she would have always loved him.

Sixty-one

When the massacre began on Bali, erupting violently as if in emulation of Gunung Agung, to protect his investment in American know-how General Sakirman sent Hashim to the island as Vern Gardner's bodyguard again. The thickset Sumatran presented Vern with a .38-caliber revolver in case they somehow got separated—or "I get killed," Hashim stated matter-of-factly.

When it finally began, the massacre on Bali was far more ferocious than it had been on Java. To purge the island of demonic evil, civilians outdid the army in carrying out executions. Most of the work was done by black-shirted youngsters, members of the Partai Nasional Indonesia, who called themselves Tamins. They went by truck from village to village, checking off names against hastily collected lists of Reds, of Red sympathizers, of leftists, or of villagers suspected of one thing or another—hoarding rice, being rich, practicing black magic. Most of the PKI were nominally Communist, ignorant of the philosophy. At least that's what Vern gathered. They knew only that they liked the political party with the hammer and sickle because it stood for land reform and more money.

584

Sometimes the army captured Reds who had escaped a village dragnet and returned them with orders for the village itself to carry out the execution. There was no torture. Heads were cut off, throats slit. Usually it was done in an orderly, quiet fashion, with speeches beforehand. The Tamins hoped that the Reds, by dying for their mistakes in this life, would be reincarnated happily in the next. Now and then the Reds fought, but usually they cooperated with the purification rites by submitting meekly. They put on white burial robes and marched calmly to the site of execution. There were, however, reports of murderous orgies as entire villages, including the children, turned out to chase and stone their victims. There was no time for Hindu cremations. Bodies were cleared away by carting them to the evil sea or dumping them into mass graves. Old feuds were settled. People got the names of their enemies put on the lists. Protest was considered bad form. The word was suddenly out: Bali was harboring evil spirits who wanted to destroy the Hindu gods; if these malignant forces were not removed immediately, new catastrophes lay in wait for the island—perhaps another volcanic eruption. The leader of the PKI on Bali was murdered, his fabulous mansion sacked. So was the palace of the pro-Red governor's father. The lust for revenge deepened. Chinese and Javanese merchants were stoned, clubbed, hacked to death. The Balinese night was streaked by flame as shops and even entire villages were burned to the ground.

Every day Vern Gardner went to work, methodically constructing the beach hotel. He was using alternating masses of red brick and gray sandstone for the walls. Every day he watched the laborers on scaffolds roofed by woven coconut-palm leaves. The coolies were women; he noticed that the biggest loads were given to the older women, who accepted their lot without complaint.

In the interiors Vern was using hard woods such as teak, jackfruit, and the compact blood-red sawo, which was smoothed with pumice and given a high sheen by rubbing it with bamboo.

As he said to Larry one night, "The only way people like us can survive over here is to act like horses with blinders on."

They were having dinner in a dirty little Chinese restaurant, one of half a dozen down a narrow street in Denpasar. There were many rickety shops in the district, run by Cantonese in undershirts and bearded Indians from Bombay who wore European vests over long-tailed cotton blouses. The shops were laden with joss sticks, paper umbrellas, baskets of yellow sugar, tin pots, plastic bowls, over which hovered the acrid smell of fermented fish paste and the gentle scent of cempaka flowers.

"In Java you can get away with wearing blinders," Larry said while staring at a cockroach as it was licked up by the snakelike tongue of a gecko that had been stalking it on the opposite wall. "But you can't wear blinders here is my opinion. You have to watch where you're going because everything's so bloody public. You can't go it alone, you know what I mean? I wish we were building the hotel somewhere else. Not here in Sanur."

"Why?"

"It's spooky, it's weird, it's full of black magic. They say people go into trances and leave their bodies for a while and go about like bloody demons doing bad things."

"You believe that?"

"You know I don't. Except I'm uncomfortable around it. A workman came around today trying to sell me an amulet. The thing had a piece of broken mirror embedded in it. He said if I wore it it would ward off evil."

"Then they better all wear them. They're dying like flies on this island," Vern said.

"As if they welcome it."

"You think that too? Why do they die that way? What is it? Bravery? Faith? Stupidity? Indifference?" He was thinking of a story that Sudjani had told him. In 1906, when the Dutch marched toward Denpasar, the local sultan and his retinue stood their ground, dressed in ceremonial white with flowers in their hair. When the Dutch soldiers were less than a hundred feet away, the sultan gave a signal and his priest plunged a jeweled kris into his royal heart. His wives jostled one another in the effort to commit suicide over his body so their own would touch his. Holding spears, courtiers rushed the Dutch troops, who had no alternative but to open fire. Contemptuously, ladies flung their jewels at the soldiers in payment for killing them. Appalled, the troops nevertheless continued to fire into the huddled mass of white-clad aristocrats. One of the courtiers went among the wounded stabbing them with a kris until he himself fell, after which another one took up the task. When they were all dead, another group

586

of Balinese appeared, this time led by the sultan's twelve-year-old brother. Neglecting the Dutch appeal to back off, they flung themselves forward in a wild rage that ended in complete massacre. That's what the Balinese were capable of. "Yes," Vern said. "It's as if they welcome it."

He noticed Larry staring at him curiously. "What's wrong?"

"That's what I want to know, old chap." Pointing with one of his large scarred fingers, Larry said, "Your hand, it's trembling."

So it was. "Maybe I've been drinking too much." Vern felt embarrassed. He had the odd feeling that for the moment his hand didn't belong to him. It was responding to the inner command of someone else.

"You haven't been drinking too much," Larry said. And in one of his characteristic moments of blunt comment, he added, "All of it is getting to you, old boy."

Vern didn't have to ask what was getting to him. He knew. But he said, "Nothing's getting to me. I better cut down on the gin."

***

He had driven the jeep down to Kuta Beach for the sunset. Most of the day it had rained; workmen hunched under their banana-leaf umbrellas, while the raindrops came down upon the slick surface like tiny bullets. Vern had sat in the truck with Sudjani, waiting out the rain. The green color of the surrounding jungle softened in the downpour and the grounds surrounding the brick-and-sandstone walls of the hotel seemed to liquefy into coffee thickened by cream. Sudjani kept up a running commentary on the weaknesses of his people. He sat drawing on a cigarette and staring through the blurred windshield of the truck, as if expecting a calamity to take place before his eyes. He said farmers buried knives in their padis, handles hidden, blades at a slant, so that people who came to steal rice would have their feet sliced open. He said villages were polluted by the birth of twins.

As clouds lumbered in, releasing torrents like an avalanche of silvery veils, Sudjani puffed vigorously, happily, on a new cigarette. He said that among upper castes a child's actual name was kept a secret. Why was it kept a secret? He asked the question of himself. For fear enemies would get hold of it and through its sacredness perform black magic against the child.

When Vern asked him if he believed that, Sudjani blithely ignored the question, saying that Balinese often poison one another. To make sure something was safe to eat, you gave it first to a dog. Poison was a bad way to die. He saw a pretty girl who had aroused jealousy among some women at weekend markets eat something one day and walk about twenty steps and fall slowly to her knees and begin to cough up a black liquid and then vomit blood and writhe around for at least an hour before her face turned green and she got stiff as a board and made a sound like low thunder and died. A dog that licked up her vomit also died.

Vern looked at Sudjani, who had a bulging forehead and squinty eyes and an empty space where three or four teeth had once been.

Mercifully, the rain stopped and everyone went back to work. Vern had forgotten that during the storm, when he'd been sitting in the truck with Sudjani, his bodyguard, Hashim, had been sitting behind them. But that was the way it was: Hashim was so quiet you hardly knew he existed. And therefore, toward the end of the workday, when Hashim suddenly appeared at his side and said, "Tuan," Vern was mildly surprised.

Having been around foreigners in the capacity of a bodyguard for some years now, Hashim could speak some English. Usually he and Vern spoke a terse Bahasa Indonesia, but now, drawing himself up as if ready to deliver a speech, Hashim said "Tuan" again. He repeated it, "Tuan," and finally went on. "My country not yet twenty year," he said, looking Vern in the eye. "We don't know sometimes what to do. One thing go bad, all go bad. Saving Indonesia"—he turned and made the popping sounds children make when pretending to shoot a gun—"seven army men killed. We think so kill one hundred thousands time seven. Saving Indonesia. One thing go bad in your country, you think other things don't go bad. Because you are two hundred, three hundred, four hundred year old, not twenty."

Standing on Kuta Beach now, awaiting the sunset, Vern remembered Hashim's words. Perhaps the sanest man he'd met in this country had been at his side all this time, Vern thought, but he hadn't known it.

That idea was interrupted by a feeling—he felt eyes watching him and turned. A Balinese boy in shorts and a smaller girl were behind him, staring. When he met their stare, their eyes never wavered.

"Hello," he said. When they didn't respond, he said in Bahasa, *"Slamat malam. Apa kabar?"*

The boy, who was about fourteen, answered, and so a conversation began. Rami and his little sister Aju lived in a village north of Kuta Beach.

"Do you come to swim?" Vern asked.

The boy backed away a step, horrified at the suggestion, which Vern had thoughtlessly made—no Balinese children went into the ocean, that evil place! The boy explained that they had come to see the foreigner who was building a hotel near the water. It was true that Vern often came here to watch the spectacular sunsets at Kuta, but until now he had never noticed the children. "You have seen me here before?"

"Many times," the boy declared gravely.

Neither of them wore a breast cloth. Aju's nipples were enlarged; soon she would have breasts. She held tightly to her brother's hand, while he explained proudly that he took care of the family ducks and did a lot of weeding and his sister carried loads and cooked. Rami had a cigarette wedged between his head and left ear. He reached for it. "We will smoke together," the boy said.

Vern didn't want to complicate things by saying he hated smoking, so when the lit cigarette was offered, he took a cursory puff; the boy smoked away as they squatted on the beach and the sun rolled heavily toward the ocean. Vern studied the two children, their almond eyes and sleek hair. When the cigarette was finished, he rose to go, but Rami asked him if they could meet again tomorrow at the same time.

It was settled. And the next evening they met and the next. Vern Gardner learned from the clever, talkative boy. He learned that Balinese didn't think much of foreigners—the sharp noses, the big chins, the blue eyes. And red-haired foreigners were considered ugly; after all, witches and demons had red hair. And of course the Balinese despised the big, uneven teeth of foreigners.

"Why don't you file them?" Rami asked. He ordered his sister to open her mouth, which she did instantly. "See how short and even her teeth are? How will you get into the spirit world if you don't have your teeth filed properly? Or do you wait until you die and then the priest does it before you're burned?" Rami reached out and touched Vern's arm reassuringly. "Have it done soon. Don't worry about the pain. It lasts only half an hour and feels like a shiver. Doesn't it?" For confirmation he asked his sister, who nodded vigorously and smiled.

"Our teeth filings," Rami said, "are buried behind the family shrine."

They were such happy children that Vern was startled on their third meeting when Rami said, "We are having a Barong dance tomorrow, because our village is polluted by evil and we have to get rid of it. Yesterday they killed Cimol. Cimol was a friend of my father, a Communist too."

"Your father is a Communist?"

Rami shrugged, to seem casual, but a deep, anguished frown crossed his face.

"Is your father all right?"

Rami shrugged again.

After a long silence Vern said, "Will the Barong dance do anything to help your father?"

"It could. It must," Rami said with sudden decisiveness.

As he was leaving, Vern turned thoughtfully and said, "Would you mind if I watched the dance?"

The children smiled broadly. It was as if their luck had changed. And Vern wondered if perhaps they had made contact with him for this purpose.

He asked Larry to come with him, but the shipbuilder from Cornwall had found himself a girl in Denpasar. To help him locate the village, Vern took Sudjani along. In the car driving out there, Sudjani said, "Balinese are selfish people. They never help their neighbors. If a neighbor's child gets lost, they just sit and watch it wander around. If livestock gets loose, they don't inform the unlucky owner. Each household protects itself, prays only for itself, donates nothing unless there's a gain in return. During the eruption of Gunung Agung, people stole from the refugees who took shelter in their homes." Sudjani laughed, as if his renditions of greed and deceit and selfishness helped to put a distance between himself and such iniquity.

Vern switched off, giving his attention to the Bali that was passing the car window. A knobby-kneed boy came along the road. On his

590

head he was carrying a tattered black plastic suitcase overflowing with laundry. He was a dirty, skinny boy who, from the evidence of his smiling face, would be supremely happy if only he had a bit, only a bit more money in his life.

Vern turned sharply back to Sudjani, who had just said something disturbing. There was a rumor of another eruption. For a week there had been heavy rain, and some people on the mountain claimed to have heard rumbling from the belly of Gunung Agung. That could mean an increase in the killings, according to Sudjani.

"You mean, villagers will connect the volcano with the Reds?"

"Of course," Sudjani said gaily. "Bad things are always connected."

The jeep could go no farther down the narrow muddy lane, so Vern and Sudjani got out and walked the last couple of meters through a late morning in which clouds were breaking up like sections of creamy cake and sunlight came lancing through, washing out the color of breadfruit trees and coconut palms, white mangoes, intricately limbed banyans. Black-rice terraces came into view, their surfaces shimmering with reflected wisps of cloud. Ducks stayed close to the bamboo pole from which a white rag fluttered. Sudjani explained that they were trained to live out their lives around such poles. They never strayed far, never. "That is Balinese," he claimed. "Even the ducks stay close to home."

They slogged through the mud of a morning that was heating up. Pale pink-skinned buffalo and long-necked cattle stood in deep valleys; Vern could see thatched huts tucked away in the greenery and rice warehouses and temples all connected by brown footpaths. It was very beautiful, but he didn't tell Sudjani that. The interpreter would have snorted in derision.

On the outskirts of the village Rami and his sister came rushing suddenly from a cluster of breadfruit trees. They had been waiting since dawn. "That is Balinese," Sudjani noted with a disapproving sigh. Vern nearly reached out and tousled the little girl's hair, but at the last instant pulled his hand back and saved them both the embarrassment of his touching her head, the most sacred part of the Balinese body. He had learned this the hard way—tousling the hair of his construction boss's boy. The man had nearly quit; only Vern's earnest and abject apology had saved the day.

591

As they entered the village, they passed women who had smeared a green paste on their foreheads to ward off the Evil Eye.

"How is your father?" Vern asked the boy.

Rami shrugged.

Sudjani then questioned him in Balinese. With a faint smile the interpreter explained that both the boy's uncle and his father had left the village last night.

"You mean, escaped," said Vern.

"Tuan," said Sudjani, "you must be careful."

"Ask him who he's living with."

Sudjani asked. The children were living with their mother and aunt.

"That sounds OK. What do you think, Sudjani?"

"Think?"

"How serious is it?"

The interpreter for the first time in Vern's memory seemed to have nothing to say, no opinion to express, no information to impart.

They walked into the village, where a couple of boys Rami's age were leading a half dozen pigs. They were huge pigs with stomachs like stuffed gunnysacks that bumped along the ground as they waddled forward on stiff, bony legs. The boys eyed Rami and the foreigner, whispered between themselves, giggled. Rami pretended not to notice, but Aju stuck her finger in her mouth.

They went past the central square, the town temple, and the bale agung, an assembling hall where old men were hunched under the thatched roof, chewing sirih and spitting blood-red streams of saliva onto the packed earth. Two men in white robes were standing nearby. Sudjani explained they were priests, and within an hour the Barong would take place right here.

At the children's family compound two women were setting out little packets of banana leaf that contained a few grains of rice, a flower, salt, and a dash of chili pepper. Sudjani explained it was food for the spirits of the house. No one could eat until they were fed, that is, no one except the dogs that trailed after the women and fought over spilled grains. No matter how brutally they were kicked away, they came back, snapping at one another and competing with the spirits for a pinch of salt, a swallow of rice.

The women who set out the ritual offering were the children's

592

mother and aunt. They bowed to Vern from a respectful distance, but otherwise showed no interest in him.

"You are too high for them," observed Sudjani. Then he amended the remark. "They are djaba, the outsiders. We are much too high for them."

The children took their foreigner and Sudjani into the small main house, its only light coming from open doorways, front and rear. Food was laid out on banana leaves—rice and spicy vegetables. Vern followed Sudjani's practice of holding the banana leaf in his left hand, using his right to shovel the food in. He tried, unsuccessfully, to drink from a bamboo bottle by holding it, as Sudjani did, at arm's length and letting the tuak, or palm liquor, fall into his mouth. The children tittered from the doorway, where they sat side by side, intently watching.

Sudjani was at his entertaining best. When a volcano erupted two years ago, a priest ordered everyone into the Pura Dalem, the Temple of Death, near the cemetery of their village. Everyone put on his best clothes and jewelry, while the priest conducted rites for the dead. Then they all lay down in family groups—father alongside eldest son, children together, mother with infant pressed to her breast—and pulled white sheets over their bodies. When the lava came, they must have heard the sizzling its huge red wall was making through the undergrowth. A boy saw it all; he had strayed out of the temple and lived. He saw the immense wall of flame advance and crash like an ocean wave against the temple, collapsing it like a banana leaf. He claimed there wasn't a single cry. Not even from a baby. The lava flattened the temple and everyone in it within seconds, leaving behind it an iron-gray slab of stone and not another sign that the Pura Dalem or the villagers had ever been there.

Sudjani belched loudly. Vern could see through the open back door the two women nod approvingly. So Vern forced a belch of his own; they began smiling.

"You see," Sudjani said to Vern, "many people refused to fight for their lives when the volcano erupted."

"I don't understand."

"If they ran, they must go to a new place. They didn't like that. Better to die where they were." He belched again. The two women were now smiling broadly. "Whole villages went down like that. People just squatted and waited and died. Their neighbors wouldn't bury them or their ashes though. Burying them might defile the other villages that weren't touched. Anyway, the police were paid to do such things. So let them do it. That is Balinese."

Vern turned to the front doorway where Rami and Aju sat watching. "What will your father do? Will he try to get away?"

Rami shrugged.

"Look," Vern said to Sudjani, "the kids here are all right, aren't they? They're safe?"

"They are not Communists," Sudjani replied evasively.

"But they are children of a Communist."

"That is true. It is time for Barong," he said, raising his finger. There was a low resonating sound coming from the distance. "That is the kulkul drum. Barong will start soon."

When Vern got to his feet, the children rushed into the room. Aju took his hand. The feeling of her fingers in his caught Vern unawares. Such a delicate small thing, each of her fingers. He looked down at them lost in his hand.

As they left the house, Rami talked excitedly. He had spoken to the priest this morning. "He said don't worry because you are Christian. Buddha is younger brother of Shiva. Sanghyang Widi is first cousin of Shiva and Buddha."

Vern looked across at Sudjani. "Sanghyang Widi?"

"Your Jesus Christ."

"And so," continued the boy happily, "Sanghyang Widi can also find a good place to rest when he comes to Bali. The priest says he will be welcome in our temple."

Sudjani was hanging back.

"What's wrong?" Vern asked.

"I have a friend in that house." He pointed to a compound. "I'll take a rest of my own. I beg your permission—"

So Vern, a child on each hand, went to the Barong.

People crowding into the central square had changed into finery. Both men and women wore skirts of batik and the men turbans. Each of these udeng had been tied differently, so that the corners and crests of intricately bunched cotton never looked the same. Some people wore Malay sarongs with two overlapping pleats in front. About half the women had draped brilliantly colored seledangs over their breasts. People had brought offerings to the dance—rice cakes and floral arrangements of calendula, frangipani, scented cempaka flowers, white moon orchids, canna lilies, and salak fruit with its dark-brown rinds having the texture of snakeskin.

When the Barong appeared suddenly out of undergrowth behind the town temple, everyone screamed. It was a big creature, manipulated by two men fore and aft within its decorated body, which bore resemblance to a lion. The mythical beast had a coat of black crow's feathers, a broad ruff of tooled leather, a harness hung with mirrors and bells, eyes black and staring, its red face enclosed in a headdress of gold with hanging pompons. Most spectacular was its huge beard of human hair. When not used, Rami said, this most sacred part of the Barong was wrapped in magic cloth and kept in the Temple of the Dead.

The Barong fought for people, Rami declared. Without the Barong they had no hope against the witch Rangda.

Another scream; from the opposite side of the surrounding jungle came a smaller but far more grotesque creature. Around her neck hung a rope necklace signifying human entrails. Her long, red-flannel tongue meant fire and death, Rami explained. Her pendulous breasts were big bags of sawdust that swayed as she danced forward, scattering small children who had come up close. As she moaned and gurgled and swung her shaggy head, she waved a white cloth. That was powerful magic, Rami said.

Barong and Rangda fought. They fought to determine the fate of humanity. When Barong seemed on the verge of losing, he was joined by a dozen young villagers holding krises. Rangda waved her magic cloth at them; enchanted, they turned the daggers upon themselves, but in deep trance (Vern would have sworn to it), they never broke the skin of their chests, although repeatedly they seemed to jab themselves without restraint.

"Is it going well now?" Vern asked the boy, as they stood with the crowd circling the dancers.

Rami grinned. "Very well now."

But suddenly, while Barong was switching his tail and smacking his jaws, his front legs collapsed. Men rushed forward, hoping to keep the mask from touching the ground (that would have polluted the village beyond redemption). A priest and assistants helped the front performer out of the costume. His eyes rolled back, his limbs jerked; he had fallen into a trance during the performance.

Vern looked around. People were gripping their fists to their chests, moaning and crying, in profound distress. Another man slipped into the front part of the costume, allowing the dance to continue. But Vern could see from the terrified spectators that this had been a catastrophic omen.

Even though the Barong finally chased the witch away—Rangda cannot die—the villagers remained shaken, depressed, fearful.

Rami with Aju's hand firmly in his own led the way back toward the compound where Sudjani had gone.

"I am sorry," Vern said, not sure what he meant.

The boy said nothing, but stared at the ground as they walked. Aju had thrust her forefinger back into her mouth.

"Listen to me," said Vern, meeting the frightened and suspicious eyes of a passing woman who had a green dot on her forehead, "what happened doesn't matter. Your father got away."

Rami said nothing, but wouldn't meet Vern's eyes. Clearly the boy was disappointed in him. With dismay Vern realized that the children had counted on him to bring the Barong good luck—to bring their fugitive father good luck.

"He did get away, didn't he?" Vern asked, wanting assurance himself.

At this point Sudjani appeared, swaying, red-eyed, at the compound gate, a very drunk translator. He had been drinking tuak with his friends, who, like himself, were of the Gusti caste, and therefore, according to Sudjani, people of influence and education. They knew how to behave with foreigners. Sudjani invited him to join them.

Vern knew enough now about Bali to take Sudjani's claim for what it really was, an empty boast. Sudjani had once been a houseboy, something a Gusti would never do, not even if he were starving. Sudjani had learned English and French from a French artist who preferred boys to girls. That was fine with Vern, but the translator was becoming tiresome. He was savaging his own people to make himself look good. He was lying about his caste. He wanted to align

596

himself with foreigners. His was the universal folly of appearing to be what he was not to someone who didn't care what he was.

"We're going back to the hotel," Vern said, watching the crestfallen children shuffle away. He might as well go back, because there was nothing more for him to do here. Any good luck he might have brought the kids had surely been canceled by the guy going into a trance inside the Barong. These feckless, capricious people. Handsome, artistic, silly people who had in them the capacity for the improbable. Watching the two kids vanish around a corner, Vern felt a tremor of fear and nearly went after them. But Sudjani had taken his arm familiarly with the grip of a drunk.

"Then back we go, back we go," muttered the translator. "Don't you worry about what happened today."

"Do I look worried?"

Sudjani giggled. "People go into trances easily in these villages. You'd be surprised what they do." With his free hand he fanned his face rapidly. "Ah, it is getting hot. It will be a hot day. So you want to go back, we go back. At your service, Tuan."

"What will happen now?"

"Happen now, Tuan?"

"In this village. What might happen?"

Sudjani grinned and tightened his grip on Vern's arm until Vern pulled free. "What will happen I don't know. Anything might happen. It always does, Barong or no Barong. If the dance goes well or doesn't go well, something always comes out of it. This is Bali."

Sixty-two

Rain was coming over the hills, making the lanes misty, the interior of their house dark and soft. Then the clouds lifted, the coolness fading with them, and a stifling heat rumbled in to envelop everything. The murderous sun appeared, stalking bones and eyes, its heat turning into a cataract of steam that he was trying to move through to get to her, and she was saying, "I love Samosir Island. We must never leave it." But she was in a boat leaving the island. She called to him halfway across the lake, "We must never leave it!"

"Tuan."

He felt a pressure against his arm, his eyes opened, drawing him out of the dream, and he looked into Hashim's flat, square face. The bodyguard told him that Sudjani had come to the hotel this morning with bad news.

Someone had come into market with chickens to sell and had spread the word among the stalls that in one of the villages people had run amok. "He was talking about the village where you saw the Barong," Hashim said.

"Running amok?"

"That's what Sudjani said the man said."

"Where is Sudjani?" Vern asked, getting out of bed.

"In the courtyard."

"Running amok? They've been running amok?" Dressing rapidly, Vern wished that he had followed his fleeting impulse two days ago— gathered the kids up and got them out of there. He took the holstered .38 from the dresser and stuck a box of shells into his pants pocket. Since the war he hadn't fired a shot, hadn't even felt a bullet. He had forgotten how concentrated in weight they were. Heavy, compact little things. Going down the hall, he knocked hard and long at Larry's door.

Finally the Englishman appeared, holding a towel around his waist. Over his hairy shoulder Vern could see the girl in bed, naked, staring back without bothering to pull the sheet up.

Vern explained what was happening in the village.

Scratching his dark shaggy head, Larry mumbled sleepily, "Balmy bastards."

"I'm going out there."

"You're going where, mate?"

"I'm sick of it."

Larry smiled and rubbed his chin. "So am I."

"I'm sick of watching. I'm going out there."

"Because of the nippers?" Larry shook his head. "Don't interfere, mate. There's nothing you can do. It's a sod of a thing to say, but the blooming bastards must have already done them in."

"I'm going out there."

They stared at each other.

Larry's eyes wavered; he made a slight movement, as if to turn and authenticate the presence of a naked girl.

"I'm going," Vern said.

"Don't make a bloody fool of yourself." To dull the sting of this remark, Larry tried to smile. "Mate, we've been together a long time. We've seen it all out here—enough to know what we can and can't do. We're here to build something. I shouldn't like to think of you going political."

"I'm not going political. But I'm going out there." For a moment longer he hesitated. Then he touched Larry's arm. "I'm going out there," he said gently, almost as if in apology. "When I come back, we'll have a drink." Turning, he walked briskly away, hearing behind him Larry's admonishment, "All right, mate, but don't forget to come back! You better come back, damn you!"

Vern could not find Sudjani anywhere. The hotel people shook their heads, as if they had never seen the Balinese interpreter who came each morning to collect his two foreigners. Good old Sudjani, quintessential complainer—he knows the right time to disappear, Vern thought. So did the jeep driver.

Vern got the keys from the hotel manager and climbed into the driver's seat. Before he could switch on, Hashim appeared, strapping on his own .38.

"Are you coming as my bodyguard," Vern asked sharply, "or because you want to?"

"Both."

"You're sure you want to do this? I'm going out there. I've had enough."

For an answer Hashim got in and stared straight ahead. Vern started the jeep.

It was a gray morning, but without rain. As they drove northward on the narrow dirt road, they saw people going as usual to work or market. Strapped to the side of a motor scooter, in two woven satchels of coconut leaves, were a pair of fighting cocks. Their long tail feathers stuck out behind to keep them from getting damaged. Perhaps Sudjani is wrong, thought Vern. How could people be running amok only miles away from people going to work or market or a cockfight?

When they came to the village road, yesterday afternoon's sunshine had dried the mud sufficiently for them to proceed almost to the village outskirts. When Vern pulled the jeep alongside some tangled vanilla vines, he offered the keys to Hashim. "Wait here," he said.

"No, Tuan."

"If we leave the jeep unprotected, they might strip the damn thing. You better stay here."

"No."

They got out in time to meet a pack of dogs with their wiry tails curved stiffly like half-moons over bony flanks. Panting, slit-eyed, the dogs were judging the chances of getting something somehow. For a moment Vern remembered the dogs of Benares. It put him in the right mood. Yes, people could be going to work or market or a cockfight while other people were murdering one another. Because he had seen the whining, snapping, festering dogs of Benares clustered in hungry packs in front of temples where priests and devotees were piously invoking the gods of the Ganges. He kicked out. The dogs scattered with some of them whimpering from habit, as if imagining the familiar pain of a foot hitting them in the side, the chest, the eye.

"Look," Vern said. Over the tips of breadfruit trees covered with white orchids, he saw ahead a wispy curl of gray smoke mixing with gray clouds.

Around the bend of the road came two women carrying earthen pots on their heads. They wore dots of green paste on their foreheads, but only their eyes slewed around to follow the passage of the white man and his companion. Then half a dozen children, about Aju's age, appeared. They were in rags, but each wore a tiny silver box on a string around the neck. "As protection from evil?" Vern asked. The heavyset Minangkabau nodded. So evil was everywhere. How many Reds and leftists and unpopular villagers had been slaughtered around here? Was it really possible in idyllic Bali? He thought of the dogs.

"Where are Rami and Aju?" Vern asked the children, but they scattered from his voice as the dogs had scattered from his feet.

Outskirts of the village. Waxy white gardenias, shrubs with pink blossoms, windowless clay walls, high-pitched atap roofs, brick gateways flanked by stone shrines, a Hindu god draped in a white robe, a waringen tree with a profusion of roots like tangled rope—what he saw came at Vern in quick fragments. He remembered now. It was how things had come at him during the war—speeding pieces of the world taken in and discarded instantly to leave room for the next and the next and the next until something important happened.

Then there were women sweeping the yards, and old men in T-shirts and sarongs sitting beside the road, where they had placed their fighting cocks in bell-shaped cages to enjoy the morning air. Overhead, although he never shifted his gaze to see them, he could hear the trained pigeons at their morning exercise, flying across the village, belled with brass whistles that made a humming sound. The villagers did nothing more than stare briefly, then look away. And once again Vern began hoping.

But the smoke was thicker after they had passed the central square and the bale bandjar where more old men were sitting, chewing sirih. The smoke came from ahead and smelled bad—not scented like burning pine or cendana.

"Their kuren," Vern said, walking faster. Within a few minutes they had reached the house, its walls collapsed inward against the smoldering thatch. The other pavilions in the compound were also destroyed. "Look for them," Vern said, trembling. But they didn't find the children in the rubble. They did find the mother. She was lying next to the smashed clay walls of the kitchen, her throat slit wide enough for a mangy dog to get its tongue inside and lick as if in a trough.

"They must be around here," Vern said. Standing outside the compound, he noticed across the way, on the veranda of a house, two women delousing each other. One stopped briefly to eye him, then went back with her quick expert hands to roam through the long hair of her companion.

"The river," Hashim said.

Although the Sumatran had never seen it, apparently he had a feel for its direction as he set off eastward. Vern followed. They passed a row of three shops on the verandas of which sat three wood-carvers, old men working at ornate sculptures of banana trees and orchids; their gouges moved slowly, methodically against the hard wood of jackfruit trunks. They did not look up when the two strangers passed.

"Did you notice?" Vern asked as they hurried out of the village. Drawing his .38 he said, "Only women and children and old men."

Before they reached the river, perhaps a kilometer from the village, it began to rain, a dull, steady thud on the atap roofing of rice warehouses and on palm leaves and shrines tucked within the undergrowth. The light was changing, ebbing and flowing through the greenery. The light came in flat glistening sheets with the intensity of tin in sunshine. The green was deep, succulent, as if the color itself were edible. Flower stems, wet and heavy, lay over in the posture of exhaustion. All this he saw while moving along the path—saw it all in the quick visual bursts of a man hunting. He was not thinking, only taking in sensations, watching the disparate bits of time and space come at him, fly in, fly out, let him go on to the next and the next and the next.

"There," Hashim said, pointing through a tangle of greenery beyond a curve in the path.

Vern saw the long, brown rope of river, the bank strewed with vegetation, with breadfruit and clusters of bamboo and the aerial filaments of waringens draped in fern. Then he saw the men.

"Hashim," he said. They looked at each other. "I want those children if they're still alive."

They moved forward slowly, together, coming to a clearing near the riverbank. There were at least a score of young men ringing the area. They wore black shirts, ceremonial udengs on their heads. They carried bamboo stakes, curved harvest knives. One of them had a pistol. Vern recognized the model, because he'd once sold one to a navy officer on Guam—8-mm Taisho 04 Nambu, a semiautomatic notorious for having a weak striker spring. After all this time, it probably didn't work, but when the young Tamin saw him approaching, the old pistol came up like a snake's head and followed him.

But Vern was looking elsewhere. As he and Hashim approached, he could see between the legs of the black-shirted Tamins a pile of bodies. Coming along slowly, he began counting, got to a dozen, lost count. So the boys had been out all night scouring the countryside, rounding up and slaughtering anyone who had managed to escape. It was a more effective exorcism than practiced by Barong, he figured grimly, even as he heard himself call out in Bahasa, *"Apa kabar, sahabat-sahabat! Damai!"* His expression of friendship and peaceful intention had no effect on the young men, who continued to glower at him, their weapons held chest high.

"Maybe you should try," he said to Hashim.

But before the Sumatran could try his own Bahasa on the sullen young men, from undergrowth to the left came a half dozen more of them, roughly pushing a group of people with their hands tied behind their backs.

Among the captives were Rami and Aju.

"What in hell," Vern said under his breath. "They're going to murder them." He did not wait longer, but stepped toward the riverbank. The captors halted with their prisoners; the other Tamins moved closer together. Vern felt the gun trembling in his hand as he held it close to his thigh. It could be a Mexican standoff, he thought. There were more of them, but he and Hashim had the firepower. He would stand there. He would goddamn not back down.

And then Hashim did something remarkable. The chunky Sumatran took a few brisk and decisive steps forward, halting within a few feet of a young man who carried a bamboo lance. Slowly raising his pistol, Hashim took deliberate aim and fired. The young man's head thundered backward, broke; some of its contents blew out behind, raining blood and brains on his companions.

Vern was so startled he didn't move. That might have been the best possible thing—to do nothing. Because when the tremendous explosion had reverberated among the glistening palm trees and vanished in them, and a few birds, hiding in their wet leaves, had flapped away into the roiling sky, no one else moved either. The young man with the Nambu held it out, pointing the muzzle at Hashim, but that's all. The others stood there staring at their dead companion.

Hashim said calmly, "We want those two children over there." He pointed with his free hand toward the group of captives.

Having regained his composure, Vern stepped forward, his own pistol slewing back and forth over the black-shirted Tamins at the riverbank. "Rami," he said. "Aju."

When they failed to move, he repeated their names sharply, like a scolding parent.

Hands behind their backs, they shuffled toward him. Vern watched the Nambu turn from Hashim to himself. He looked directly at the young man holding it. "You," he said. Vern had never felt more decisive, more sure of himself. "Put it down or I will shoot you."

The Tamin didn't move. The muzzle didn't waver.

"I am going to shoot you." Vern cocked his pistol. In the silence on that riverbank he heard the soft plopping sound of raindrops against leaves. One, two, he counted slowly to himself. I will fire on three.

The young man dropped the Nambu.

To Rami, who stood against his right leg, Vern said quietly, "Where is your father?" When the boy didn't answer, he asked, "Is he over there?" Vern was looking at the pile of bodies along the riverbank.

"Yes, Tuan."

"Then we're going." He glanced at Hashim. "I'll start out with them. Cover us."

Until this moment he had not considered their chances logically. Emotion had governed everything. But now he wanted desperately to bring them all out of it. Holding the gun with one hand, he withdrew his pocketknife with the other, flipped the blade out, and cut the thong around Rami's wrists. "Take care of your sister," Vern said, and bending down to the boy's ear, he whispered, "If anything happens, take her and run—run as fast as you can."

So they got through the village, almost every step of the way glancing back to see if they were being followed. But apparently Hashim had spooked the Tamins with that single terrible action.

Fortunately, the jeep was untouched.

The rain tapered off and ended as they drove away with the two children huddled together in the backseat. As he struggled through the muddy ruts of the narrow road, Vern was thinking wildly. He'd get the kids out of here, maybe on a Bugis schooner for Sarawak or Australia or Singapore. And maybe, to make sure they got there, he'd go along and see to it, go the whole damn way, arrange life for them, get them ensconced, safe somewhere. Because he had to see someone get out of this damn thing alive, intact, able to enjoy. He'd get them out by plane or ship or rowboat if he had to. He would do that much.

Looking over at Hashim, who stared impassively ahead, Vern started to laugh. He couldn't help it. He laughed into the wind that was breaking up clouds over the ocean. He said, "Is it going to be all right, Hashim? Is it going to be all right?"

And the question swirled back through the jeep in a current of damp air. Vern's laughter followed; his relief and fear and hope were sweeping back over the exhausted children, their heads lolling, their faces slack in deep and dreamless sleep.

Sixty-three

S he was giving English lessons now. Every day, when her teaching schedule permitted, Maggie went out to Borobudur. A man who owned a car in Yogya, a loyal old patron of the dalang, had his driver take her there free of charge.

There was no longer danger on the road. Having eliminated the PKI from the political scene by murdering many of them and jailing the others, the army had spent the last few weeks curtailing the fervor of young Muslims who felt the excitement of a Holy War and hoped to continue the bloodbath unabated. Finally the exhausted boys had stepped aside and obeyed the military commanders. Violence in Central Java had nearly ceased.

It had rained heavily today in the remorseless manner of Southeast Asian monsoons. As the car approached the temple site, ditches overflowed into the road, carrying palm leaves, strips of bamboo, drowned chickens, great buffalo turds that had floated over the restraining mud rims of padis and were sailing alongside the car tires as they skidded back and forth in the ruts. When the immense but squat pyramid came into view, suddenly the rain stopped, and a streak of blue appeared in the parting seam of a black cloud. The driver exclaimed "Ahhh!" Perhaps he found magical significance in this abrupt change of the weather, although the next moment the seam closed and left a thick blanket of clouds again.

Getting out of the car, Maggie walked along the cobbled temple approach, then slipping her sandals off and carrying them, she sloshed through the muddy ground toward a grove of bamboo perhaps a hundred yards from the path. At the edge of the grove was a mound of earth, the flowers decorating it sodden and limp. Tomorrow the village modin, a minor priest she had hired, would come around and replace the flowers, burn incense, and sweep the grave clean of debris that had fallen during the rainstorm. Wooden markers were stuck at either end. Only after three years, by local tradition, could stone markers be put up at the grave. She would see to it then. She would be here.

In the evenings lately, after a walk in the scented air of Java, she sat awhile beside a kerosene lamp under one of the breadfruit trees in the garden and read Shelley. She hadn't much cared for him in college—the skeptic who mistrusted his own idealizations. Now she read him with interest and struggled along with him in his hope for immortality and for the everlastingness of beauty and in his despair of believing either were actually true. Last night a phrase from "Alastor" held her in its grip until she wept. She remembered it now, looking down at the wood-marked grave:

> Thou art fled
> Like some frail exhalation.

Today she remained only a short time, looking at the bunches of spongy flowers, some rotten bananas, and the overripe halves of a coconut piled at one end. The modin had told her yesterday that many people were coming to pay their respects. They drifted in singly or in twos and threes, silently presenting flowers or laying down an offering of fruit. Some of them recited incantations—nyekar for the dead. The modin, a crafty little man, had smiled and winked. She couldn't be sure if he had told her such things to please her or if overcoming their shame and fear some people had actually been to the grave.

Retracing her way to the path, Maggie began climbing the steps of Borobudur, whose pitted gray surfaces were slick from rain. Recently she had written letters to UNESCO; to the Royal Institute of Linguistics and Anthropology in Holland; to Buddhist organizations in Japan that might be interested in the restoration. Her correspondence was carried on now by hand, because the typewriter ribbon had worn out and there were none to buy in a city that had been lacking supplies from abroad for months. As she walked upward, Maggie imagined the stones newly polished, the cracks cinched up, the sagging galleries stiffened—microscopes and cameras and winches all coming into play in the process of analyzing and numbering and dismantling and cleaning and reassembling the great temple.

How ironic that Vernon Gardner, who loved architecture, who possessed a proved ability to build things, who had acquired more experience than he could ever call on, this man who might save Borobudur, was wholly indifferent to it, contemptuous of these old stones because they wouldn't be used to house tourists or create electricity.

But that was mean-spirited of her, Maggie knew. She remembered him saying, "I'd like them all to be haji, I'd like them to have money enough to get to Mecca and win their white hat." That had touched her. Because Vernon Gardner did have his own brand of faith; he just mixed progress with religion, gadgets with happiness.

Climbing to the fifth open terrace with a sweeping view of the countryside, Maggie stared at a mist that swirled above the trees, sending ghostly tendrils down among the leaves and branches, as if seeking within the greenery the heart of it. She had first come here with Budi. Now she found on the windswept terrace a kind of peace.

Sometimes, while standing here, she returned in memory to Sumatra, to her time with Vern on the island of Samosir, where she had watched the slow, tireless hands of fishermen in motion, not a wasted gesture in the way they feathered a canoe paddle, and she thought of the hands of men that had caressed her body, and her memory narrowed then to the hands of Budi, hands that could bring puppets to life, that could bring her to life as well, and she wished for those hands, wished for them wished for them until only a brisk walk around the terrace could steady her.

This morning she had given a private English lesson to the son of a wealthy priyayi family. Bent over an English grammar in her tiny

608

living room, Dahlan had attempted to sort out tenses. The boy wasn't allowed to speak Javanese outside the home; by his father's express command he had to speak either English or Bahasa, because both were languages of commerce. So he struggled with English tenses, definite articles, pronouns of gender—difficult for someone learning Bahasa as well, a language that didn't have them.

In shorts and a starched white shirt he had hunched forward in the high-backed chair. Maggie had sat opposite him with a view of flowers in a vase, her laundry laid across the arm of the sofa for her old servant to pick up later.

"I see," the boy said, looking up from eyes glazed by the effort of thought. "I saw. I seen."

"Have seen."

"I have seen. I"—again the boy paused—"had seen."

"Good."

"I shall seen."

"Shall see."

Dahlan was sweating from the mental exercise. His father had ordered him not to make mistakes. Maggie got him a plate of kueh lapis, multicolored cakes that she knew he liked. While he ate, Maggie studied him, her mouth set in a faint smile, as if in longing. His father was a government official of sufficient nobility to warrant the title of Raden. Like many Javanese fathers, he stayed aloof from his son, but in this case the aloofness was greatly pronounced and coupled to the jealousy of a man whose young son made him feel old. Raden Suryowinoto never spoke to Maggie of Dahlan except with amused disdain and accepted good reports about the boy with exaggerated skepticism.

Maggie asked suddenly, "Dahlan, what do you do after school?"

The boy shrugged. It was typical priyayi wariness—as the Javanese say, "The crocodile is quick to go under, slow to come up." Would the boy ever surface for her, let her into his life?

"Do you climb trees? Play riddle games? Do you catch fish?"

After a long pause, he said in a low confidential voice, "Fly kites with my cousin. We do it behind the garden."

How familiar this sounded to Maggie. Flying kites had been Budi's chief pleasure as a boy. He hadn't had much fun from what she gathered. The household he had grown up in had been serious, a group of people functioning within a dominant aesthetic. How different from her own childhood, the chaos and desperation of it, with the drunk and the martyr and the bad girl and—What had she herself been? The one who wanted out, who had frantically sought escape, who had gnawed her way to freedom like a trapped and desperate rat.

Working with Dahlan, she superimposed his young image on that of her dead lover as she imagined him at twelve. Budi must have been something like this boy: shy, diffident, earnest, wonderfully appealing. If only she'd had a child with Budi, a baby who in a decade would be growing into a boy like Dahlan. It saddened her terribly to think that it had not happened. Even worse was the knowledge that this great Javanese artist had left no one behind. His only heir was a sweet but ignorant girl locked into village life forever. When Budi had finally opened the windows and flung back the door and stepped into the world, the world struck him down.

She was thinking such dismal thoughts when out of the corner of her eye, as she stood on the fifth terrace of Borobudur, Maggie saw something moving across the wet stones, something slipping behind a granite buddha in its beehive stupa. Whoever was behind there had an umbrella—its black tip and part of its rolled length projected past the dagoba. Squinting, Maggie leaned forward to see if one of the diamond-shaped holes would reveal who was hiding behind the dagoba, but from this distance she saw only the weathered shoulder of a stone buddha.

Finally, summoning the nerve—her heart was pounding from fear—Maggie called out in a loud but trembling voice, "Who is there? Who is behind the dagoba?"

She waited, but nothing happened, and her fear deepened. Once again she called out, her voice losing its firmness.

This time the whole length of the umbrella appeared with the hand holding it—the hand of Mas Slamat, whose face appeared next: solemn, sunken from lack of teeth, the eyes hidden by the brim of his porkpie hat. Had she ever seen him without a cigarette dangling from his pursed lips? And the jaunty feather in his hat was now drooping from dampness. She could not help but smile at the peculiar look of him, even while scolding him for frightening her.

Mas Slamat swayed a few steps toward her, then halted to doff his hat with a tentative motion he had obviously meant to be graceful. "*Bismillah*. I was afraid you would be angry."

"Why are you here?" But the question was unnecessary. He had obviously come to Borobudur to meet her and beg forgiveness. Maggie felt her jaw tighten.

"Everyone knows about you," he said calmly and walked a few steps closer, as if somehow confident.

She felt her whole body stiffen.

"They all know about the grave, how you take care of it. They are pleased even if they don't say so."

Maggie would not give him the satisfaction of asking who they were.

"Holy man says you will stay here and work to save Borobudur." When she failed to respond, he doffed his hat again, this time more decisively. "They are all going to help you. Holy man wants to see you, Nonya."

"Why did you do it?"

"Nonya?" He had managed to sidle up to her. His parted mouth displayed a few yellow stumps.

"Ali never did anything to you."

"Has his body been found?" His lips moved into an anxious smile. "Are all the bodies found?"

"I told him come back to Islam, but he went on with foolishness. He would make a world we couldn't live in." He drew himself up proudly. "I am santri Muslim."

The way he drew up his emaciated little body in the shabby Western pants and food-stained shirt told Maggie what she needed to know: he felt his betrayal of Ali had been justified—more than that, had been his spiritual duty. Nothing she might say would change that.

Staring at him, noticing his lips tremble in anticipation of her decision about him, Maggie forgot Mas Slamat for a moment, and it seemed as if the sweet little servant girl Inam passed before her eyes, and Ali, his gaze level and serious and his jaw set purposefully, and the Chinese batik dealer and her own lover, all of them speeding past her vision in an instant, alive in memory, alive in a world that Mas Slamat knew far better than she did.

Maggie leaned against a dagoba, feeling its wet, cool surface against her bare arm. Mas Slamat squatted while waiting. He was absolutely motionless in the middle of the terrace, like a caricature of the buddhas surrounding him.

Maggie straightened up. There was no sense trying to change things. If she remained here, she must learn to live with everything that happened. She was not in charge; they were. "Come along," she said.

"Nonya?"

"I'll give you a ride back to Yogya. Did you get here by bus? Come along." She added, "My friend."

As they descended the steep stairway, it began to rain again, softly now. He opened his umbrella and insisted on holding it over her head, though it took the full extension of his arm to do so.

"Don't worry," he was saying. "A man like me with eight languages can be invaluable to you. We'll work together. That's what the holy man says, though sometimes I don't believe in his ideas. No need to find another assistant now that I am here again. I am the one. I know everything you need. Do you understand that, Nonya?"

"Yes," she said. "I understand."

"*Bismillah*. Then we begin together again. I know so many people, you see. You must be careful about dealing with them. Restoring this place is a difficult job, and I will help, though I cannot see why you would put such effort into the place, this old temple. But then you come from another land. Nonya?"

"Yes," she said. "Perhaps that is why. But I am going to do it, Mas Slamat."

"Oh, they all know that, and they will help you. Believe me, this is true: Ki-Dalang Gitosuwoko, until he went mad, was the greatest dalang in the land. That is, Yogya style. And they are all respectful of you, because they know you are becoming one of us. You are staying and tending his grave and they know you now. Do you understand, Nonya?"

"Yes," she said, "I understand."

Sixty-four

The ailing president of Indonesia was holed up in his palaces, while acting officially in his name the new leader, General Suharto, was purging leftist elements in every ministry, among them Subandrio, who had been arrested for treason.

In Bali the uncoordinated mayhem had come to an end. RPKAD units went into the villages and carried out executions thenceforth in an orderly fashion by firing squad. True to his word, Vern managed to get the children out of Bali by bribing a freighter captain to smuggle them into Hong Kong. Sutopo Salim helped by arranging for them to be received there and placed in an orphanage until Vern could decide what to do with them.

After the initial phase of hotel construction had been completed, Vern returned to Jakarta. There was a rumor that he would soon be offered another contract, but Vern felt a familiar restlessness, and the prospect of building more hotels no higher than a palm tree had lost some of its charm. Sensing the moodiness of his prize architect, General Sakirman gave him a short holiday—insisted on sending him to Yogya, just as Susanto Sakirman had promised. The irony was that commercial flights had just resumed—erratically scheduled, true—but he might have got to Yogya without military assistance.

He took a taxi from the airport straight to the Taman Sari area. He had been corresponding with Maggie, their letters aloof and curt, but at least he knew where she was living. Hashim, no longer needed as a bodyguard, was with him for the last time. Back in the capital Hashim would be reassigned. As they started up the bewildering maze of lanes, kids followed them, screaming at their heels. One labyrinthine path led into another so that they often got lost and had to ask their way. House numbers meant little. They asked for the foreign woman. When finally they located the little house, Vern told his bodyguard to wait outside.

"I won't be long," he said. Was that true? He hoped not; he hoped that he would go inside that little house and find her and stay until they both left it together.

Unlatching the wooden gate, Vern entered the tiny compound. Underfoot was a pebble path now being crisscrossed by trails of red ants. There were palms along the twenty-foot way and they obscured part of the bamboo walls ahead, but he saw enough to know that his wife was living in a shack. Approaching the open doorway he heard from within the darkness the scratchy notes of old-time jazz. She was still at it, and for a moment he thought of supplying her with new needles and fresh discs.

"Maggie!" he called, halting at the two-step stairway to the veranda that was slightly tilted, as if one side of the house were heavier than the other.

He heard her voice call something out. It must have been Javanese, but sounded like "Mango." Then she appeared in the doorway. Maggie wore a kebaya and jeans and a kerchief around her brown hair, giving her the look of someone busy cleaning.

She came forward with her shoulders hunched, collapsing inward with arms close to her sides, in the way a big, tall woman has of making herself look smaller. This habit of hers was more pronounced than ever, now that she lived among the little Javanese.

They met on the veranda. He had intended to shake hands or embrace her gently or do nothing at all or—or something like that; whenever he had tried on the plane trip to imagine their meeting, he never got past looking at her. He didn't now. He stared at those clear wide-set eyes whose color he always forgot—were they blue or gray?—but whose effect never failed to surprise him, as he was surprised now. Stunned by her presence, he stood there and let her reach out and touch both of his elbows lightly with the tips of her fingers. When she leaned slightly forward, so did he. Their lips met dryly, then she asked him inside.

"I'm glad you came," she said with feeling. "We needed to meet."

It was dim inside, as Javanese houses generally are. The house, as she had described it in a letter, was small, and indeed, it was very small. She had a couch, a chair, and nothing else in the front room. From where Vern sat on the couch, he could see through a doorway another tiny room—a woven mat on the floor was probably her bed.

He said, without criticism but as a statement of fact, "I see you've gone native."

"Would you like some tea?"

"I'd like some gin."

"Sorry." Maggie sat in the chair opposite him, her hands clasped as she leaned forward, legs widely apart in the jeans. She looked beautiful to him.

"I thought you went on the wagon," she said after a long silence.

Here was a chance to say, "I went on the wagon because of you," but then he'd have to add, "I went off because of another woman." To explain that would be uselessly complicated, and right now his emotions were complicated enough. So he shrugged. "I went off, that's all."

"How's Project Palm Tree?" Maggie asked with the ease of someone accustomed to small talk. She was picking up the habit from these excessively polite Javanese, and it angered him.

But he merely said, "On the way. Getting there."

"And Larry?"

"Larry's Larry."

"I believe that. Did you have any trouble on Bali?"

"No."

"How are the Sakirmans?"

"Your friend Susanto—"

"She's not my friend."

"She's back in Jakarta. During the crisis the general got religion, but now he's his old self. Rake-offs, bribes, the whole thing."

"The whole thing," she repeated. "I think they let you come here once they were certain I wouldn't embarrass them further."

Beautiful woman. Crestfallen, he realized that Maggie was more beautiful than he had even remembered. "Jakarta's getting back to normal. Everything's the same."

"Maybe that's the worst of it."

"I know what you mean," Vern said. "But you know what Blake said. 'Drive your cart and your plow over the bones of the dead.' And that's what they're doing. Thousands of throats cut, thousands of heads bashed in, thousands of guts spilled, and what they do now in Jakarta is exchange rumors about Sukarno. Can a man as sick as Bung Karno still make it with women? Meanwhile, Suharto's turning the country into a military state. Maggie, you can't change anything."

"What do you mean?"

"You and me, people like us from the West, we can come out here and live awhile and make a living, help out, learn a few things, but essentially we don't belong. Look what happened. These people slaughtered one another while we just stood around watching. We were spectators."

"Is that what we were?" Maggie shook her head as if denying it. "You can't interfere in the destiny of other people. I agree with that. But you can join them."

"It's not what I want."

"I know that. You want to go to the next thing."

"Don't make it sound criminal."

"I don't mean it that way. I really don't. I think I'm learning tolerance. When so many people you know . . . and love . . . are murdered around you, you feel anger and helplessness and finally a kind of understanding that this is what life is."

"You don't want to save the Indonesians from themselves?" he asked with a smile.

"I only want to save an old temple."

"Have you got a job?"

She explained that the local university had just reopened and for want of foreign instructors had hired her to teach English. "Once qualified people come back, I'll probably lose the job. For now it's perfect."

"So you really are staying."

"I'm staying."

"Goddamn it, Maggie." He gripped his hands and stared at them as he hunched over.

"Do you realize, Vern, this is probably the best conversation we ever had?"

He didn't want to hear that. Somehow it made this a definitive, a final conversation. People who stayed together endured one bland exchange after another into a glorious old age.

"Do you remember who started the game?" Maggie asked suddenly.

Looking up, he found to his surprise that she was smiling broadly.

"You'd come in pretending you were my lover when my husband was gone?"

"Oh, that. I don't remember who started it."

"You did, Vern. I'm sure you did."

"I don't remember."

"Wasn't it odd?"

"No more so, I suppose, than the games most couples play."

"But that particular idea— Do you think we understood something was wrong? On some level? I've thought about it lately."

"Nothing was wrong," Vern declared. "At least not from my side." In the spirit of hopefulness, he had forgotten the realization of a few moments earlier that they had lived with an abyss gaping between them.

They sat in silence again. Vern broke it finally by saying, "I think of Lake Toba."

"So do I." She added shyly, "We had wonderful times there. I often dream of it."

"You do?"

"Of our Batak house on Samosir Island. Remember it?"

"Of course."

"I dream of the fishermen in their boats. Did you know we never saw one of them come back to shore? We saw them go out and we saw them anchor in the cove, but we never saw them come back in."

"I didn't know."

"Perhaps the game we played, perhaps it meant something about love and loyalty between us, Vern. Or maybe what happened had nothing to do with the people we really are. Indonesia probably had a lot to do with it."

"Yes, a lot."

"Obviously the crisis did. I think maybe we might have been all right under other circumstances. But that's hindsight. And there's nothing worse than postmortems. And there's this other thing, this fact I can't change. You see, Vern, you must understand and believe this: I loved him. I have to tell you that. I really loved him."

Vern had been waiting for her to say something about the lover. Even in Bali they had heard about the crazy puppeteer. He had raved against Sukarno, the government, and the Muslims during a nation-wide broadcast of a puppet play. He had been a member of the PKI; soon after the performance, soldiers killed him while he was resisting arrest for treason. Vern had intended to ask Maggie had the guy really been a Red. How had he been killed? Why had she got herself mixed up with someone like that?

Getting up, Vern went briskly to the door. "I don't like to go over this thing," he declared angrily. "I'm really amazed at myself, I'm ashamed."

"Ashamed?" She was following behind him.

"For being so damned civilized. Maybe we'd be better off if I beat hell out of you for being unfaithful. You'd get rid of guilt, I'd get rid of frustration." He went outside and stood blinking at the sunlight beyond the shade of the veranda. Past the gate he could see Hashim waiting under a tree. "I love you, Maggie. I always will. And I'll always want you back." He turned to look at her where she stood, within the shadows of the room, her white face there a blue oblong. "Just let me know. Just keep in touch."

"You really don't think I'll stay here."

"What can you do here anyway, for Christ's sake? So you get the language down and raise a little money for that temple, what's left? What's in it for you?"

Her hands went to her hips. For an instant Vern wondered if this was what she had done as a defiant child—slapped her hands against her hips and looked up at the adults, screwing her face into a rebellious frown.

"What's in it for me?" She repeated his question rhetorically. Her lips, full but unpainted, were trembling. "The trees, Vern. I like them. And the taste of the fruit and the dust under my feet, Vern."

He felt himself smiling rigidly, a measure of his inability to match this sort of ambiguous drama. Was it sarcasm or proof of her feck-lessness? "Good-bye," he said. "For now."

He started to turn away, but taking a few steps forward, she reached his side and stood in his path, looking at him, their eyes level.

"Listen, Vern. The temple will rest on five slabs of reinforced concrete. At least that's the way we see it now. Of course, someone like you would be more specific. Right, Vern?"

Edging away from her, off the veranda, he took a step forward.

"The walls," she said behind him in a voice rising higher each moment, "they'll be protected by screens of araldite and a lead sheet at the base. To stop the capillary action of rainwater. Isn't that right, Vern? Do I have it right? And surrounding the fill is a filter. To keep earth from being carried away by flooding. We've got to maintain the internal stability. That's what they tell me. Are they right, Vern?" she asked shrilly. "Are we on the right track? If anyone knows, you do, damn it!"

As he walked past the banana palms to the gate, a huge leaf slid along his arm, raking it like a rough finger; and he heard at his back her voice lifting into a shriek. "Guilt? I don't feel any! I never felt guilty about this! You don't understand! There's nothing I should feel guilty about! It wasn't that way!"

And when he turned into the lane, seeing Hashim waiting for him under the shady palm, Vern heard her last words hurled high and frantically into the afternoon heat: "I have lots of letters to write! Can you send me some typewriter ribbons, Vern? For an Underwood Portable!"

———————

Later, seated in the plane rising from Yogya Airport, he gazed down at the checkerboard of padis spreading out from the red-tiled roofs of the city. So he had lost her. All his life he would regret it. Yet he understood his capacity for making the most of what life offered him. What he had now was a job to do and he would do it. If Maggie came to mind often—she did now, she would in the future, for God's sake, perhaps she always would—the sorrow and the sense of failure would not bring him down. He was not the kind to go down. Sometimes he rather wished he were, because that would signal a depth of feeling, and in his darkest moments—those of midnight dread— Vern Gardner wondered if there was in him very much feeling, the kind that people write and sing about, or at least enough feeling for him to bring forth and use when the going got rough. Maybe it would all be different now if he had flung himself at her feet or taken her roughly in his arms and sworn his love or if he had done something equally dramatic, something irresistible and overwhelming, that would have pried her loose from her grand schemes and let him draw her back into his life.

But such hypothetical questions never clung to Vernon Gardner for long. He dug into his briefcase and pulled out a folder thick with architectural plans. Glancing at his bodyguard, Vern was surprised by the expression on Hashim's big square face before it resumed a masklike imperturbability. The fleeting look had been one of curiosity; Hashim had been studying the foreigner with a kind of awed puzzlement. And Vern suddenly remembered Hashim waiting beneath the shade tree in Taman Sari. The husky Sumatran, peering back at the lovely woman whom they were leaving behind, must have wondered how Tuan Gardner could possibly resist taking her along.